# THE WILDSIDE PRESS
# TREASURY OF GREAT SCIENCE
# FICTION SHORT NOVELS

# THE WILDSIDE PRESS TREASURY OF GREAT SCIENCE FICTION SHORT NOVELS

COMPILED BY
## ROBERT SILVERBERG
## & MARTIN H. GREENBERG

WILDSIDE PRESS

*The following page constitutes an extension of the copyright page. The authors gratefully acknowledge permission to include material from the following:*

# ACKNOWLEDGMENTS

"Beyond Bedlam," by Wyman Guin. Copyright © 1951 by Galaxy Publishing Corporation. Reprinted by permission of Larry Sternig Literary Agency.

"Equinoctial," by John Varley. Copyright © 1977 by David Gerrold. Reprinted by permission of Kirby McCauley Ltd.

"By His Bootstraps," by Robert A. Heinlein. Copyright © 1941 by Street & Smith. Copyright © 1968 by Robert A. Heinlein. Reprinted by permission of Robert A. Heinlein.

"The Golden Helix," by Theodore Sturgeon. Copyright © 1954 by Standard Magazines, Inc. Reprinted by permission of Kirby McCauley Ltd.

"Born With the Dead," by Robert Silverberg. Copyright © 1974 by Robert Silverberg. Reprinted by permission of the author.

"Second Game," by Charles V. De Vet and Katherine MacLean. Copyright © 1958 by Street & Smith Publications, Inc. Reprinted by permission of the authors and of Virginia Kidd, Literary Agent.

"The Dead Past," by Isaac Asimov. Copyright © 1956 by Street & Smith Publications, Inc. Reprinted by permission of the author.

"The Road to the Sea," by Arthur C. Clarke. Copyright © 1950 by Wings Publishing Company, Inc. Reprinted by permission of the author and the author's agents, Scott Meredith Literary Agency, Inc., 845 Third Ave., N.Y., N.Y. 10022

"The Star Pit," by Samuel R. Delany. Copyright © 1966 by Galaxy Publishing Corporation. Reprinted by permission of the author and Henry Morrison, Inc., his agents.

"Giant Killer," by A. Bertram Chandler. Copyright © 1945 by Street & Smith Publications, Inc. Reprinted by permission of the author and the author's agents, Scott Meredith Literary Agency, Inc., 845 Third Ave., N.Y., N.Y. 10022

"A Case of Conscience," by James Blish. Copyright © 1953 by Quinn Publishing Company, Inc. Reprinted by permission of Richard Curtis Associates, agents for the author's estate.

"Dio," by Damon Knight. Copyright © 1957 by Royal Publications, Inc. Reprinted by permission of the author.

"Houston, Houston, Do You Read?" by James Tiptree, Jr. Copyright © 1976 by Fawcett Publications, Inc. Reprinted by permission of the author's agent, Robert P. Mills, Ltd.

"On the Storm Planet," by Cordwainer Smith. Copyright © 1965 by Galaxy Publishing Corporation. Reprinted by permission of Scott Meredith Literary Agency, Inc., 845 Third Ave., N.Y., N.Y. 10022, agents for the author's estate.

"The Miracle Workers," by Jack Vance. Copyright © 1958 by Jack Vance. Reprinted by permission of Kirby McCauley Ltd.

# Contents

*Introduction* ix

*Beyond Bedlam* Wyman Guin 3

*Equinoctial* John Varley 55

*By His Bootstraps* Robert A. Heinlein 100

*The Golden Helix* Theodore Sturgeon 149

*Born With the Dead* Robert Silverberg 200

*Second Game* Charles V. De Vet and Katherine MacLean 263

*The Dead Past* Isaac Asimov 302

*The Road to the Sea* Arthur C. Clarke 346

*The Star Pit* Samuel R. Delany 391

*Giant Killer* A. Bertram Chandler 448

*A Case of Conscience* James Blish 493

*Dio* Damon Knight 549

*Houston, Houston, Do You Read?* James Tiptree, Jr. 583

*On the Storm Planet* Cordwainer Smith 634

*The Miracle Workers* Jack Vance 706

# Introduction

The short novel—or "novella," as some prefer to call it—is one of the richest and most rewarding of literary forms. Spanning twenty to thirty thousand words, usually, it allows for more extended development of theme and character than does the short story, without making the elaborate structural demands of the full-length book. Thus it provides an intense, detailed exploration of its subject, partaking to some degree both of the concentrated focus of the short story and of the broad scope of the novel.

Some of the greatest works of modern literature fall into the class of novellas. Consider Mann's "Death in Venice," Joyce's "The Dead," Melville's "Billy Budd," and Conrad's "Heart of Darkness"—or Faulkner's "The Bear," Tolstoi's "The Death of Ivan Ilych," Carson McCullers's "Ballad of the Sad Cafe." Yet for all its triumphs, the novella has proven to be an awkward item in the world of commercial publishing, generally too short to stand alone as an independent book, too long to fit into the conventional collection of short pieces. Only through special efforts are even the finest of short novels kept before the reading public.

That problem has been particularly acute in science fiction, a field that lends itself with unusual grace to the novella form. Since a prime task of the science fiction writer is to create carefully detailed worlds of the imagination, room for invention is a necessity. The short story can give only a single vivid glimpse of the invented world; the full-length novel frequently becomes so enmeshed in the obligations of plot and counterplot that the background recedes to a secondary position. But the short novel, leisurely without being discursive, is ideal for the sort of world-creation that is science fiction's specialty, and since the days of H.G. Wells and his classic novella "The Time Machine" it has exerted a powerful attraction for science fiction writers. Because science fiction magazines, for many years the dominant vehicle for publication of imaginative stories, were generally receptive to stories of the middle lengths, an abundant literature of science fiction novellas has accrued.

But in the transfer from magazine to book the usual problems of publishing conventions have intervened. Some writers have resorted to expanding classic twenty-five thousand–word stories into novels of the traditional sixty thousand to seventy-five thousand words, not always with happy results; others have included their novellas in collections of their short stories, and such collections rarely get the attention that novels do; and although anthologies of short science fiction stories abound, few of them have the space to include more than one or two novellas. Even in our own 754-page *Arbor House Treasury of Modern Science Fiction* there was room for only three or four stories that could be considered short novels.

To demonstrate the extraordinary potential of the science fiction novella, then, we have compiled a companion volume of equal size, containing fifteen major works in this odd but highly satisfying intermediate length. They include stories written between 1941 and 1977. Nearly all these novellas were warmly acclaimed when they first were published—there are a good many Hugo and Nebula award winners among them—but because of the inconveniences their length can cause, many of them now are difficult to find in current editions. It gives us great pleasure to return them to print in a book big enough to accommodate so many of them, and thus able to show by example after example how superbly fitted the novella form is for the creation of the unique "pocket universes" of science fiction.

—Robert Silverberg
—Martin Harry Greenberg

# THE WILDSIDE PRESS TREASURY OF GREAT SCIENCE FICTION SHORT NOVELS

# Beyond Bedlam

*Travel to the moon, to the planets of our solar system, and to the stars used to be considered the essence of science fiction. However, in the last three decades some of the most imaginative and remarkable works in this field have focused on the flights that take place in "inner space," examining the nature of normality and reality.*

*In the magnificent and pioneering "Beyond Bedlam," Wyman Guin writes of what it means to be "normal" in a world of universal schizophrenia.*

The opening afternoon class for Mary Walden's ego-shift was almost over, and Mary was practically certain the teacher would not call on her to recite her assignment, when Carl Blair got it into his mind to try to pass her a dirty note. Mary knew it would be a screamingly funny ego-shifting room limerick and was about to reach for the note when Mrs. Harris's voice crackled through the room.

"Carl Blair! I believe you have an important message. Surely you will want the whole class to hear it. Come forward, please."

As he made his way before the class, the boy's blush-covered freckles reappeared against his growing pallor. Haltingly and in an agonized monotone, he recited from the note:

> *"There was a young hyper named Phil,*
> *Who kept a third head for a thrill.*
> *Said he, 'It's all right,*
> *I enjoy my plight.*
> *I shift my third out when it's chill.'"*

The class didn't dare laugh. Their eyes burned down at their laps in shame. Mary managed to throw Carl Blair a compassionate glance as he returned to his seat, but she instantly regretted ever having been kind to him.

"Mary Walden, you seemed uncommonly interested in reading something just now. Perhaps you wouldn't mind reading your assignment to the class."

There it was, and just when the class was almost over. Mary could have scratched Carl Blair. She clutched her paper grimly and strode to the front.

"Today's assignment in pharmacy history is, 'Schizophrenia Since the Ancient Prepharmacy Days.'" Mary took enough breath to get into the first paragraph.

"Schizophrenia is where two or more personalities live in the same brain. The ancients of the twentieth century actually looked upon schizophrenia as a disease! Everyone felt it was very shameful to have a schizophrenic person in the family, and, since children lived right with the same parents who had borne them, it was very bad. If you were a schizophrenic child in the twentieth century, you would be locked up behind bars and people would call you—"

Mary blushed and stumbled over the daring word—*crazy*. "The ancients locked up strong ego groups right along with weak ones. Today we would lock up those ancient people."

The class agreed silently.

"But there were more and more schizophrenics to lock up. By 1950 the prisons and hospitals were so full of schizophrenic people that the ancients did not have room left to lock up any more. They were beginning to see that soon everyone would be schizophrenic.

"Of course, in the twentieth century, the schizophrenic people were almost as helpless and 'crazy' as the ancient Modern men. Naturally they did not fight wars and lead the silly life of the Moderns, but without proper drugs they couldn't control their ego-shiftability. The personalities in a brain would always be fighting each other. One personality would cut the body or hurt it or make it filthy, so that when the other personality took over the body, it would have to suffer. No, the schizophrenic people of the twentieth century were almost as 'crazy' as the ancient Moderns.

"But then the drugs were invented one by one and the schizophrenic people of the twentieth century were freed of their troubles. With the drugs the personalities of each body were able to live side by side in harmony at last. It turned out that many schizophrenic people, called overendowed personalities, simply had so many talents and viewpoints that it took two or more personalities to handle everything.

"The drugs worked so well that the ancients had to let millions of schizophrenic people out from behind the bars of 'crazy' houses. That was the Great Emancipation of the 1990's. From then on, schizophrenic people had trouble only when they criminally didn't take their drugs. Usually, there are two egos in a schizophrenic person—the hyperalter, or prime ego, and the hypoalter, the alternate ego. There often were more than two, but the Medicorps makes us take our drugs so that won't happen to us.

"At last someone realized that if everyone took the new drugs, the great wars would stop. At the World Congress of 1997, laws were passed to make everyone take the drugs. There were many fights over this because some people wanted to stay Modern and fight wars. The Medicorps was organized and told to kill anyone who wouldn't take their drugs as prescribed. Now the laws are enforced and everybody takes the drugs and the hyperalter and hypoalter are each allowed to have the body for an ego-shift of five days. . . ."

Mary Walden faltered. She looked up at the faces of her classmates, started to turn to Mrs. Harris and felt the sickness growing in her head. Six great waves of crescendo silence washed through her. The silence swept away everything but the terror, which stood in her frail body like a shrieking rock.

Mary heard Mrs. Harris hurry to the shining dispensary along one wall of the classroom and return to stand before her with a swab of antiseptic and a disposable syringe.

Mrs. Harris helped her to a chair. A few minutes after the expert injection, Mary's mind struggled back from its core of silence.

"Mary, dear, I'm sorry. I haven't been watching you closely enough."

"Oh, Mrs. Harris . . ." Mary's chin trembled. "I hope it never happens again."

"Now, child, we all have to go through these things when we're young. You're just a little slower than the others in acclimatizing to the drugs. You'll be fourteen soon and the medicop assures me you'll be over this sort of thing just as the others are."

Mrs. Harris dismissed the class and when they had all filed from the room, she turned to Mary.

"I think, dear, we should visit the clinic together, don't you?"

"Yes, Mrs. Harris." Mary was not frightened now. She was just ashamed to be such a difficult child and so slow to acclimatize to the drugs.

As she and the teacher walked down the long corridor to the clinic, Mary made up her mind to tell the medicop what she thought was wrong.

It was not herself. It was her hypoalter, that nasty little Susan Shorrs. Sometimes, when Susan had the body, the things Susan was doing and thinking came to Mary like what the ancients had called *dreams,* and Mary had never liked this secondary ego whom she could never really know. Whatever was wrong, it was Susan's doing. The filthy creature never took care of her hair, it was always so messy when Susan shifted the body to her.

Mrs. Harris waited while Mary went into the clinic.

Mary was glad to find Captain Thiel, the nice medicop, on duty. But she was silent while the X rays were being taken, and, of course, while he got the blood samples, she concentrated on being brave.

Later, while Captain Thiel looked in her eyes with the bright little light, Mary said calmly, "Do you know my hypoalter, Susan Shorrs?"

The medicop drew back and made some notes on a pad before answering. "Why, yes. She's in here quite often too."

"Does she look like me?"

"Not much. She's a very nice little girl . . ." He hesitated, visibly fumbling.

Mary blurted, "Tell me truly, what's she like?"

Captain Thiel gave her his nice smile. "Well, I'll tell you a secret if you keep it to yourself."

"Oh, I promise."

He leaned over and whispered in her ear and she liked the clean odor of him. "She's not nearly as pretty as you are."

Mary wanted very badly to put her arms around him and hug him. Instead, wondering if Mrs. Harris, waiting outside, had heard, she drew back self-consciously and said, "Susan is the cause of all this trouble, the nasty little thing."

"Oh now!" the medicop exclaimed. "I don't think so, Mary. She's in trouble, too, you know."

"She still eats sauerkraut." Mary was defiant.

"But what's wrong with that?"

"You told her not to last year because it makes me sick on my shift. But it agrees in buckets with a little pig like her."

The medicop took this seriously. He made a note on the pad. "Mary, you should have complained sooner."

"Do you think my father might not like me because Susan Shorrs is my hypoalter?" she asked abruptly.

"I hardly think so, Mary. After all, he doesn't even know her. He's never on her ego-shift."

"A little bit," Mary said, and was immediately frightened.

Captain Thiel glanced at her sharply. "What do you mean by that, child?"

"Oh, nothing," Mary said hastily. "I just thought maybe he was."

"Let me see your pharmacase," he said rather severely.

Mary slipped the pharmacase off the belt at her waist and handed it to him. Captain Thiel extracted the prescription card from the back and threw it away. He slipped a new card in the taping machine on his desk and punched out a new prescription, which he reinserted in the pharmacase. In the space on the front, he wrote directions for Mary to take the drugs numbered from left to right.

Mary watched his serious face and remembered that he had complimented her about being prettier than Susan. "Captain Thiel, is your hypoalter as handsome as you are?"

The young medicop emptied the remains of the old prescription from the pharmacase and took it to the dispensary in the corner, where he slid it into the filing slot. He seemed unmoved by her question and simply muttered, "Much handsomer."

The machine automatically filled the case from the punched card on its back and he returned it to Mary. "Are you taking your drugs exactly as prescribed? You know there are very strict laws about that, and as soon as you are fourteen, you will be held to them."

Mary nodded solemnly. Great strait-jackets, who didn't know there were laws about taking your drugs?

There was a long pause and Mary knew she was supposed to leave. She wanted, though, to stay with Captain Thiel and talk with him. She wondered how it would be if he were appointed her father.

Mary was not hurt that her shy compliment to him had gone unnoticed. She had only wanted something to talk about. Finally she said desperately, "Captain Thiel, how is it possible for a body to change as much from one ego-shift to another as it does between Susan and me?"

"There isn't all the change you imagine," he said. "Have you had your first physiology?"

"Yes. I was very good . . ." Mary saw from his smile that her inadvertent little conceit had trapped her.

"Then, Miss Mary Walden, how do *you* think it is possible?"

Why did teachers and medicops have to be this way? When all you wanted was to have them talk to you, they turned everything around and made you think.

She quoted unhappily from her schoolbook, "The main things in an ego-shift are the two vegetative nervous systems that translate the conditions of either personality to the blood and other organs right from the brain. The vegetative nervous systems change the rate at which the liver burns or stores sugar and the rate at which the kidneys excrete . . ."

Through the closed door to the other room, Mrs. Harris's voice raised at the visiophone and said distinctly, *"But, Mr. Walden . . ."*

"Reabsorb," corrected Captain Thiel.

"What?" She didn't know what to listen to—the medicop or the distant voice of Mrs. Harris.

"It's better to think of the kidneys as reabsorbing salts and nutrients from the filtrated blood."

"Oh."

*"But, Mr. Walden, we can overdo a good thing. The proper amount of neglect is definitely required for full development of some personality types and Mary certainly is one of those. . . ."*

"What about the pituitary gland that's attached to the brain and controls all the other glands during the shift of egos?" pressed Captain Thiel distractingly.

*"But, Mr. Walden, too much neglect at this critical point may cause another personality to split off and we can't have that. Adequate personalities are congenital. A new one now would only rob the present personalities. You are the appointed parent of this child and the Board of Education will enforce your compliance with our diagnosis. . . ."*

Mary's mind leaped to a page in one of her girlhood storybooks. It was an illustration of a little girl resting beneath a great tree that overhung a brook. There were friendly little wild animals about. Mary could see the page clearly and she thought about it very hard instead of crying.

"Aren't you interested any more, Mary?" Captain Thiel was looking at her strangely.

The agitation in her voice was a surprise. "I have to get home. I have a lot of things to do."

Outside, when Mrs. Harris seemed suddenly to realize that something was wrong, and delicately probed to find out whether her angry voice had been overheard, Mary said calmly and as if it didn't matter, "Was my father home when you called him before?"

"Why—yes, Mary. But you mustn't pay any attention to conversations like that, darling."

*You can't force him to like me,* she thought to herself, and she was angry with Mrs. Harris because now her father would only dislike her more.

Neither her father nor her mother was home when Mary walked into the evening-darkened apartment. It was the first day of the family shift, and on that day, for many periods now, they had not been home until late.

Mary walked through the empty rooms, turning on lights. She passed up the electrically heated dinner her father had set out for her. Presently she found herself at the storage room door. She opened it slowly.

After hesitating a while she went in and began an exhausting search for the old storybook with the picture in it.

Finally she knew she could not find it. She stood in the middle of the junk-filled room and began to cry.

The day which ended for Mary Walden in lonely weeping should have been, for Conrad Manz, a pleasant rest day with an hour of rocket racing in the middle of it. Instead, he awakened with a shock to hear his wife actually *talking* while she was *asleep.*

He stood over her bed and made certain that she was asleep. It was as though her mind thought it was somewhere else, doing something else. Vaguely he remembered that the ancients did something called *dreaming* while they slept and the thought made him shiver.

Clara Manz was saying, "Oh, Bill, they'll catch us. We can't pretend any more unless we have drugs. Haven't we any drugs, Bill?"

Then she was silent and lay still. Her breathing was shallow and even in the dawn light her cheeks were deeply flushed against the blonde hair.

Having just awakened, Conrad was on a very low drug level and the incident was unpleasantly disturbing. He picked up his pharmacase from beside his bed and made his way to the bathroom. He took his hypothalamic block and the integration enzymes and returned to the bedroom. Clara was still sleeping.

She had been behaving oddly for some time, but there had never been anything as disturbing as this. He felt that he should call a medicop, but, of course, he didn't want to do anything that extreme. It was probably something with a simple explanation. Clara was a little scatterbrained at times. Maybe she had forgotten to take her sleeping compound and that was what caused *dreaming.* The very word made his powerful body chill.

But if she was neglecting to take any of her drugs and he called in a medicop, it would be serious.

Conrad went into the library and found the *Family Pharmacy*. He switched on a light in the dawn-shrunken room and let his heavy frame into a chair. *A Guide to Better Understanding of Your Family Prescriptions. Official Edition, 2831*. The book was mostly Medicorps propaganda and almost never gave a practical suggestion. If something went wrong, you called a medicop.

Conrad hunted through the book for the section on sleeping compound. It was funny, too, about that name Bill. Conrad went over all the men of their acquaintance with whom Clara had occasional affairs or with whom she was friendly and he couldn't remember a single Bill. In fact, the only man with that name whom he could think of was his own hyperalter, Bill Walden. But that was naturally impossible.

Maybe dreaming was always about imaginary people.

SLEEPING COMPOUND: An official mixture of soporific and hypnotic alkaloids and synthetics. A critical drug; an essential feature in every prescription. Slight deviations in following prescription are unallowable because of the subtle manner in which behavior may be altered over months or years. The first sleeping compound was announced by Thomas Marshall in 1986. The formula has been modified only twice since then.

There followed a tightly packaged description of the chemistry and pharmacology of the various ingredients. Conrad skipped through this.

The importance of sleeping compound in the life of every individual and to society is best appreciated when we recall Marshall's words announcing its initial development:

"It is during so-called *normal* sleep that the vicious unconscious mind responsible for wars and other symptoms of unhappiness develops its resources and its hold on our conscious lives.

"In this *normal* sleep the critical faculties of the cortex are paralyzed. Meanwhile, the infantile unconscious mind expands misinterpreted experience into the toxic patterns of neurosis and psychosis. The conscious mind takes over at morning, unaware that these infantile motivations have been cleverly woven into its very structure.

"Sleeping compound will stop this. There is no unconscious activity after taking this harmless drug. We believe the Medicorps should at once initiate measures to acclimatize every child to its use. In these children, as the years go by, infantile patterns unable to work during sleep will fight a losing battle during waking hours with conscious patterns accumulating in the direction of adulthood."

That was all there was—mostly the Medicorps patting its own back for saving humanity. But if you were in trouble and called a medicop, you'd risk getting into real trouble.

Conrad became aware of Clara standing in the doorway. The flush of her disturbed emotions and the pallor of her fatigue mixed in ragged banners on her cheeks.

Conrad waved the *Family Pharmacy* with a foolish gesture of embarrassment.

"Young lady, have you been neglecting to take your sleeping compound?"

Clara turned utterly pale. "I—I don't understand."

"You were talking in your sleep."

"I—was?"

She came forward so unsteadily that he helped her to a seat. She stared at him. He asked jovially, "Who is this 'Bill' you were so desperately involved with? Have you been having an affair I don't know about? Aren't my friends good enough for you?"

The result of this banter was that she alarmingly began to cry, clutching her robe about her and dropping her blonde head on her knees and sobbing.

Children cried before they were acclimatized to the drugs, but Conrad Manz had never in his life seen an adult cry. Though he had taken his morning drugs and certain disrupting emotions were already impossible, nevertheless this sight was completely unnerving.

In gasps between her sobs, Clara was saying, "Oh, I can't go back to taking them! But I can't keep this up! I just can't!"

"Clara, darling, I don't know what to say or do. I think we ought to call the Medicorps."

Intensely frightened, she rose and clung to him, begging, "Oh, no, Conrad, that isn't necessary! It isn't necessary at all. I've only neglected to take my sleeping compound and it won't happen again. All I need is a sleeping compound. Please get my pharmacase for me and it will be all right."

She was so desperate to convince him that Conrad got the pharmacase and a glass of water for her only to appease the white face of fright.

Within a few minutes of taking the sleeping compound, she was calm. As he put her back to bed, she laughed with a lazy indolence.

"Oh, Conrad, you take it so seriously. I only needed a sleeping compound very badly and now I feel fine. I'll sleep all day. It's a rest day, isn't it? Now go race a rocket and stop worrying and thinking about calling the medicops."

But Conrad did not go rocket racing as he had planned. Clara had been asleep only a few minutes when there was a call on the visiophone; they wanted him at the office. The city of Santa Fe would be completely out of balance within twelve shifts if revised plans were not put into operation immediately. They were to start during the next five days while he would be out of shift. In order to carry on the first day of their next shift, he and the other three traffic managers he worked with would have to come down today and familiarize themselves with the new operations.

There was no getting out of it. His rest day was spoiled. Conrad resented it all the more because Santa Fe was clear out on the edge of their traffic district and could have been revised out of the Mexican offices just as well. But those boys down there rested all five days of their shift.

Conrad looked in on Clara before he left and found her asleep in the total suspension of proper drug level. The unpleasant memory of her behavior made him squirm, but now that the episode was over, it no longer worried him. It was typical of him that, things having been set straight in the proper manner, he did not think of her again until late in the afternoon.

As early as 1950, the pioneer communications engineer Norbert Wiener had pointed out that there might be a close parallel between disassociation of personalities and the disruption of a communication system. Wiener referred back specifically to the first clear description, by Morton Prince, of multiple personalities existing together in the same human body. Prince had described only individual cases and his observations were not altogether acceptable in Wiener's time. Nevertheless, in the schizophrenic society of the twenty-ninth century, a major managerial problem was that of balancing the communicating and noncommunicating populations in a city.

As far as Conrad and the other traffic men present at the conference were concerned, Santa Fe was a resort and retirement area of one hundred thousand human bodies, alive and consuming more than they produced every day of the year. Whatever the representatives of the Medicorps and Communications Board worked out, it would mean only slight changes in the types of foodstuffs, entertainment and so forth moving into Santa Fe, and Conrad could have grasped the entire traffic change in ten minutes after the real problem had been settled. But, as usual, he and the other traffic men had to sit through two hours while small wheels from the Medicorps and Communications acted big about rebalancing a city.

For them, Conrad had to admit, Santa Fe was a great deal more complex than one hundred thousand consuming, moderately producing human bodies. It was two hundred thousand human personalities, two to each body. Conrad wondered sometimes what they would have done if the three and four personality cases so common back in the twentieth and twenty-first centuries had been allowed to reproduce. The two hundred thousand personalities in Santa Fe were difficult enough.

Like all cities, Santa Fe operated in five shifts, A, B, C, D and E.

Just as it was supposed to be for Conrad in his city, today was rest day for the twenty thousand hypoalters on D-shift in Santa Fe. Tonight at around six P.M. they would all go to shifting rooms and be replaced by their hyperalters, who had different tastes in food and pleasure and took different drugs.

Tomorrow would be rest day for the hypoalters on E-shift and in the evening they would turn things over to their hyperalters.

The next day it would be rest for the A-shift hyperalters and three days after that the D-shift hyperalters, including Bill Walden, would rest till evening, when Conrad and the D-shift hypoalters everywhere would again have their five-day use of their bodies.

Right now the trouble with Santa Fe's retired population, which worked only for its own maintenance, was that too many elderly people on the D-shift and E-shift had been dying off. This point was brought out by a deeper young department head from Communications.

Conrad groaned when, as he knew would happen, a Medicorps officer promptly set out on an exhaustive demonstration that Medicorps predictions of deaths for Santa Fe had indicated clearly that Communications should have been moving people from D-shift and E-shift into the area.

Actually, it appeared that someone from Communications had blundered and had overloaded the quota of people on A-shift and B-shift moving to Santa Fe. Thus on one rest day there weren't enough people working to keep things going, and later in the week there were so many available workers that they were clogging the city.

None of this was heated exchange or in any way emotional. It was just interminably, exhaustively logical and boring. Conrad fidgeted through two hours of it, seeing his chance for a rocket race dissolving. When at last the problem of balanced shift-populations for Santa Fe was worked out, it took him and the other traffic men only a few minutes to apply their tables and reschedule traffic to coordinate with the population changes.

Disgusted, Conrad walked over to the Tennis Club and had lunch.

There were still two hours of his rest day left when Conrad Manz realized that Bill Walden was again forcing an early shift. Conrad was in the middle of a volley-tennis game and he didn't like having the shift forced so soon. People generally shifted at their appointed regular hour every five days, and a hyperalter was not supposed to use his power to force shift. It was such an unthinkable thing nowadays that there was occasional talk of abolishing the terms hyperalter and hypoalter because they were somewhat disparaging to the hypoalter, and really designated only the antisocial power of the hyperalter to force the shift.

Bill Walden had been cheating two to four hours on Conrad every shift for several periods back. Conrad could have reported it to the Medicorps, but he himself was guilty of a constant misdemeanor about which Bill had not yet complained. Unlike the sedentary Walden, Conrad Manz enjoyed exercise. He overindulged in violent sports and put off sleep, letting Bill Walden make up the fatigue on his shift. That was undoubtedly why the poor old sucker had started cheating a few hours on Conrad's rest day.

Conrad laughed to himself, remembering the time Bill Walden had registered a long list of sports which he wished Conrad to be restrained from—rocket racing, deep sea exploration, jet-skiing. It had only given Conrad some ideas he hadn't had before. The Medicorps had refused to enforce the list on the basis that danger and violent exercise were a necessary outlet for Conrad's constitution. Then poor old Bill had written Conrad a note threatening to sue him for any injury resulting from such sports. As if he had a chance against the Medicorps ruling!

Conrad knew it was no use trying to finish the volley-tennis game. He lost interest and couldn't concentrate on what he was doing when Bill started forcing the shift. Conrad shot the ball back at his opponent in a blistering curve impossible to intercept.

"So long," he yelled at the man. "I've got some things to do before my shift ends."

He lounged into the locker rooms and showered, put his clothes and belongings, including his pharmacase, in a shipping carton, addressed them to his own home and dropped them in the mail chute.

He stepped with languid nakedness across the hall, pressed his identifying wristband to a lock-face and dialed his clothing sizes.

In this way he procured a neatly wrapped, clean shifting costume from the slot. He put it on without bothering to return to his shower room.

He shouted a loud good-by to no one in particular among the several men and women in the baths and stepped out on to the street.

Conrad felt too good even to be sorry that his shift was over. After all, nothing happened except you came to, five days later, on your next shift. The important thing was the rest day. He had always said the last days of the shift should be a work day; then you would be glad it was over. He guessed the idea was to rest the body before another personality took over. Well, poor old Bill Walden never got a rested body. He probably slept off the first twelve hours.

Walking unhurriedly through the street crowds, Conrad entered a public shifting station and found an empty room. As he started to open the door, a girl came out of the adjoining booth and Conrad hastily averted his glance. She was still rearranging her hair. There were so many rude people nowadays who didn't seem to care at all about the etiquette of shifting, women particularly. They were always redoing their hair or make-up where a person couldn't help seeing them.

Conrad pressed his identifying wristband to the lock and entered the booth he had picked. The act automatically sent the time and his shift number to Medicorps Headquarters.

Once inside the shifting room, Conrad went to the lavatory and turned on the tap of make-up solvent. In spite of losing two hours of his rest day, he decided to be decent to old Bill, though he was half-tempted to leave his make-up on. It was a pretty foul joke, of course, especially on a humorless fellow like poor Walden.

Conrad creamed his face thoroughly and then washed in water and used the automatic dryer. He looked at his strong lined face and features in the mirror. They displayed a less distinct expression of his own personality with the make-up gone.

He turned away from the mirror and it was only then that he remembered he hadn't spoken to his wife before shifting. Well, he couldn't decently call up and let her see him without make-up.

He stepped across to the visiophone and set the machine to deliver his spoken message in type: "Hello, Clara. Sorry I forgot to call you before.

Bill Walden is forcing me to shift early again. I hope you're not still upset about that business this morning. Be a good girl and smile at me on the next shift. I love you. Conrad."

For a moment, when the shift came, the body of Conrad Manz stood moronically uninhabited. Then, rapidly, out of the gyri of its brain, the personality of Bill Walden emerged, replacing the slackly powerful attitude of Conrad by the slightly prim preciseness of Bill's bearing.

The face, just now relaxed with readiness for action, was abruptly pulled into an intellectual mask of tension by habitual patterns of conflict in the muscles. There were also acute momentary signs of clash between the vegetative nervous activity characteristic of Bill Walden and the internal homeostasis Conrad Manz had left behind him. The face paled as hypersensitive vascular beds closed under new vegetative volleys.

Bill Walden grasped sight and sound, and the sharp color of make-up solvent stung his nostrils. He was conscious of only one clamoring, terrifying thought: *They will catch us. It cannot go on much longer without Helen guessing about Clara. She is already angry about Clara delaying the shift, and if she learns from Mary that I am cheating on Conrad's shift. . . . Any time now, perhaps this time, when the shift is over, I will be looking into the face of a medicop who is pulling a needle from my arm, and then it'll all be over.*

So far, at least, there was no medicop. Still feeling unreal but anxious not to lose precious moments, Bill took an individualized kit from the wall dispenser and made himself up. He was sparing and subtle in his use of the make-up, unlike the horrible make-up jobs Conrad Manz occasionally left on. Bill rearranged his hair. Conrad always wore it too short for his taste, but you couldn't complain about everything.

Bill sat in a chair to await some of the slower aspects of the shift. He knew that an hour after he left the booth, his basal metabolic rate would be ten points higher. His blood sugar would go down steadily. In the next five days he would lose six to eight pounds, which Conrad would promptly regain.

Just as Bill was about to leave the booth, he remembered to pick up a news summary. He put his wristband to the switch on the telephoto and a freshly printed summary of the last five days in the world fell into the rack. His wristband, of course, called forth one edited for hyperalters on the D-shift.

It did not mention by name any hypoalter on the D-shift. Should one of them have done something that it was necessary for Bill or other D-shift hyperalters to know about, it would appear in news summaries called forth by their wristbands—but told in such fashion that the personality involved seemed namelessly incidental, while names and pictures of hyperalters and hypoalters on any of the other four shifts naturally were freely used. The purpose was to keep Conrad Manz and all the other hypoalters on the D-shift, one-tenth of the total population, nonexistent as far as their hyperalters were concerned. This convention made it necessary for photo-print summaries to be on light-sensitive paper that blackened illegibly before six hours were up, so that a man might never stumble on news about his hypoalter.

Bill did not even glance at the news summary. He had picked it up only for appearances. The summaries were essential if you were going to start where you left off on your last shift and have any knowledge of the five intervening days. A man just didn't walk out of a shifting room without one. It was failure to do little things like that would start them wondering about him.

Bill opened the door of the booth by applying his wristband to the lock and stepped out into the street.

Late afternoon crowds pressed about him. Across the boulevard, a helicopter landing swarmed with clouds of rising commuters. Bill had some trouble figuring out the part of the city Conrad had left him in and walked two blocks before he understood where he was. Then he got into an idle two-place cab, started the motor with his wristband and hurried the little three-wheeler recklessly through the traffic. Clara was probably already waiting and he first had to go home and get dressed.

The thought of Clara waiting for him in the park near her home was a sharp reminder of his strange situation. He was in a world that was literally not supposed to exist for him for it was the world of his own hypoalter, Conrad Manz.

Undoubtedly, there were people in the traffic up ahead who knew both him and Conrad, people from the other shifts who never mentioned the one to the other except in those guarded, snickering little confidences they couldn't resist telling and you couldn't resist listening to. After all, the most important person in the world was your alter. If he got sick, injured or killed, so would you.

Thus, in moments of intimacy or joviality, an undercover exchange went on. . . . *I'll tell you about your hyperalter if you'll tell me about my hypoalter.* It was orthodox bad manners that left you with shame, and a

fear that the other fellow would tell people you seemed to have a patholog-
ical interest in your alter and must need a change in your prescription.

But the most flagrant abuser of such morbid little exchanges would have
been horrified to learn that right here, in the middle of the daylight traffic,
was a man who was using his antisocial shifting power to meet in secret
the wife of his own hypoalter!

Bill did not have to wonder what the Medicorps would think. Relations
between hyperalters and hypoalters of opposite sex were punishable—
drastically punishable.

When he arrived at the apartment, Bill remembered to order a dinner
for his daughter Mary. His order, dialed from the day's menu, was deliv-
ered to the apartment pneumatically and he set it out over electric warm-
ers. He wanted to write a note to the child, but he started two and threw
both in the basket. He couldn't think of anything to say to her.

Staring at the lonely table he was leaving for Mary, Bill felt his guilt
overwhelming him. He could stop the behavior which led to the guilt by
taking his drugs as prescribed. They would return him immediately to the
sane and ordered conformity of the world. He would no longer have to
carry the fear that the Medicorps would discover he was not taking his
drugs. He would no longer neglect his appointed child. He would no
longer endanger the very life of Conrad's wife Clara and, of course, his
own.

When you took your drugs as prescribed, it was impossible to experience such ancient and primitive emotions as guilt. Even should you
miscalculate and do something wrong, the drugs would not allow any such
emotional reaction. To be free to experience his guilt over the lonely child
who needed him was, for these reasons, a precious thing to Bill. In all the
world, this night, he was undoubtedly the only man who could and did
feel one of the ancient emotions. People felt shame, not guilt; conceit,
not pride; pleasure, not desire. Now that he had stopped taking his drugs
as prescribed, Bill realized that the drugs allowed only an impoverished
segment of a vivid emotional spectrum.

But however exciting it was to live them, the ancient emotions did not
seem to act as deterrents to bad behavior. Bill's sense of guilt did not keep
him from continuing to neglect Mary. His fear of being caught did not
restrain him from breaking every rule of interalter law and loving Clara,
his own hypoalter's wife.

Bill got dressed as rapidly as possible. He tossed the discarded shifting costume into the return chute. He retouched his make-up, trying to eliminate some of the heavy, inexpressive planes of muscularity which were more typical of Conrad than of himself.

The act reminded him of the shame which his wife Helen had felt when she learned, a few years ago, that her own hypoalter, Clara, and his hypoalter, Conrad, had obtained from the Medicorps a special release to marry. Such rare marriages in which the same bodies lived together on both halves of a shift were something to snicker about. They verged on the antisocial, but could be arranged if the batteries of Medicorps tests could be satisfied.

Perhaps it had been the very intensity of Helen's shame on learning of this marriage, the nauseous display of conformity so typical of his wife, that had first given Bill the idea of seeking out Clara, who had dared convention to make such a peculiar marriage. Over the years, Helen had continued blaming all their troubles on the fact that both egos of himself were living with, and intimate with, both egos of herself.

So Bill had started cutting down on his drugs, the curiosity having become an obsession. What was this other part of Helen like, this Clara who was unconventional enough to want to marry only Bill's own hypoalter, in spite of almost certain public shame?

He had first seen Clara's face when it formed on a visiophone, the first time he had forced Conrad to shift prematurely. It was softer than Helen's. The delicate contours were less purposefully set, gayer.

"Clara Manz?" Bill had sat there staring at the visiophone for several seconds, unable to continue. His great fear that she would immediately report him must have been naked on his face.

He had watched an impish suspicion grow in the tender curve of her lips and her oblique glance from the visophone. She did not speak.

"Mrs. Manz," he finally said. "I would like to meet you in the park across from your home."

To this awkward opening he owed the first time he had heard Clara laugh. Her warm, clear laughter, teasing him, tumbled forth like a cloud of gay butterflies.

"Are you afraid to see me here at home because my husband might *walk in on us?*"

Bill had been put completely at ease by this bantering indication that Clara knew who he was and welcomed him as an intriguing diversion.

Quite literally, the one person who could not *walk in on them*, as the ancients thought of it, was his own hypoalter, Conrad Manz.

Bill finished retouching his make-up and hurried to leave the apartment. But this time, as he passed the table where Mary's dinner was set out, he decided to write a few words to the child, no matter how empty they sounded to himself. The note he left explained that he had some early work to do at the microfilm library where he worked.

Just as Bill was leaving the apartment, the visiophone buzzed. In his hurry Bill flipped the switch before he thought. Too late, his hand froze and the implications of this call, an hour before anyone would normally be home, shot a shaft of terror through him.

But it was not the image of a medicop that formed on the screen. The woman introduced herself as Mrs. Harris, one of Mary's teachers.

It was strange that she should have thought he might be home. The shift for children was half a day earlier than for adults, so the parents could have half their rest day free. This afternoon would be for Mary the first classes of her shift, but the teacher must have guessed something was wrong with the shifting schedules in Mary's family. Or had the child told her?

Mrs. Harris explained rather dramatically that Mary was being neglected. What could he say to her? That he was a criminal breaking drug regulations in the most flagrant manner? That nothing, not even the child appointed to him, meant more to him than his wife's own hypoalter? Bill finally ended the hopeless and possibly dangerous conversation by turning off the receiver and leaving the apartment.

Bill realized that now, for both him and Clara, the greatest joy had been those first few times together. The enormous threat of the Medicorps retaliation took the pleasure from their contact and they came together desperately because, having tasted this fantastic nonconformity and the new undrugged intimacy, there was no other way for them. Even now as he drove through the traffic towards where she would be waiting, he was not so much concerned with meeting Clara in their fear-poisoned present as with the vivid, aching remembrance of what those meetings once had really been like.

He recalled an evening they had spent lying on the summer lawn of the park, looking out at the haze-dimmed stars. It had been shortly after Clara joined him in cutting down on the drugs, and the clear memory of their quiet laughter so captured his mind now that Bill almost tangled his car in the traffic.

In memory he kissed her again and, as it had been, the newly cut grass mixed with the exciting fragrance of her skin. After the kiss they continued a mock discussion of the ancient word *sin*. Bill pretended to be trying to explain the meaning of the word to her, sometimes with definitions that kept them laughing and sometimes with demonstrational kisses that stopped their laughter.

He could remember Clara's face turned to him in the evening light with an outrageous parody of interest. He could hear himself saying, "You see, the ancients would say we are not *sinning* because they would disagree with the medicops that you and Helen are two completely different people, or that Conrad and I are not the same person."

Clara kissed him with an air of tentative experimentation. "Mmm, no. I can't say I care for that interpretation."

"You'd rather be sinning?"

"Definitely."

"Well, if the ancients did agree with the medicops that we are distinct from our alters, Helen and Conrad, then they would say we are sinning —but not for the same reasons the Medicorps would give."

"That," asserted Clara, "is where I get lost. If this sinning business is going to be worth anything at all, it has to be something you can identify."

Bill cut his car out of the main stream of traffic and towards the park, without interrupting his memory.

"Well, darling, I don't want to confuse you, but the medicops would say we are sinning only because you are my wife's hypoalter, and I am your husband's hyperalter—in other words for the very reason the ancients would say we are *not* sinning. Furthermore, if either of us were with anyone else, the medicops would think it was perfectly all right, and so would Conrad and Helen. Provided, of course, I took a hyperalter and you took a hypoalter only."

"Of course," Clara said, and Bill hurried over the gloomy fact.

"The ancients, on the other hand, would say we are sinning because we are making love to someone we are not married to."

"But what's the matter with that? Everybody does it."

"The ancient Moderns didn't. Or, that is, they often did, but . . ."

Clara brought her full lips hungrily to his. "Darling, I think the ancient Moderns had the right idea, though I don't see how they ever arrived at it."

Bill grinned. "It was just an invention of theirs, along with the wheel and atomic energy."

That evening was long gone by as Bill stopped the little taxi beside the park and left it there for the next user. He walked across the lawns towards the statue where he and Clara always met. The very thought of entering one's own hypoalter's house was so unnerving that Bill brought himself to do it only by first meeting Clara near the statue. As he walked between the trees, Bill could not again capture the spirit of that evening he had been remembering. The Medicorps was too close. It was impossible to laugh that away now.

Bill arrived at the statue, but Clara was not there. He waited impatiently while a livid sunset coagulated between the branches of the great trees. Clara should have been there first. It was easier for her, because she was leaving her shift, and without doing it prematurely.

The park was like a quiet backwater in the eddying rush of the evening city. Bill felt conspicuous and vulnerable in the gloaming light. Above all, he felt a new loneliness, and he knew that now Clara felt it, too. They needed each other as each had been, before fear had bleached their feeling to white bones of desperation.

They were not taking their drugs as prescribed, and for that they would be horribly punished. That was the only unforgivable *sin* in their world. By committing it, he and Clara had found out what life could be, in the same act that would surely take life from them. Their powerful emotions they had found in abundance simply by refusing to take the drugs, and by being together briefly each fifth day in a dangerous breach of all convention. The closer their discovery and the greater their terror; the more desperately they needed even their terror, and the more impossible became the delight of their first meetings.

Telegraphing bright beads of sound, a night bird skimmed the sunset lawns to the looming statue and skewed around its monolithic base. The bird's piping doubled and then choked off as it veered frantically from Bill. After a while, far off through the park, it released a fading protest of song.

Above Bill, the towering statue of the great Alfred Morris blackened against the sunset. The hollowed granite eyes bore down on him out of an undecipherable dark . . . the ancient, implacable face of the Medicorps. As if to pronounce a sentence on his present crimes by a magical disclosure of the weight of centuries, a pool of sulphurous light and leaf shadows danced on the painted plaque at the base of the statute:

On this spot in the Gregorian year 1996, Alfred Morris announced to an assembly of war survivors the hypothalamic block. His stirring words were, "The new drug selectively halts at the thalamic brain the upward flow of unconscious stimuli and the downward flow of unconscious motivations. It acts as a screen between the cerebrum and the psychosomatic discharge system. Using hypothalamic block, we will not act emotively, we will initiate acts only from the logical demands of situations."

This announcement and the subsequent wholehearted action of the war-weary people made the taking of hypothalamic block obligatory. This put an end to the powerful play of unconscious mind in the public and private affairs of the ancient world. It ended the great paranoid wars and saved mankind.

In the strange evening light, the letters seemed alive, a centuries-old condemnation of any who might try to go back to the ancient pre-pharmacy days. Of course, it was not really possible to go back. Without drugs, everybody and all society would fall apart.

The ancients had first learned to keep endocrine deviates such as the diabetic alive with drugs. Later they learned with other drugs to "cure" the far more prevalent disease, schizophrenia, that was jamming their hospitals. The big change came when the ancients used these same drugs on everyone to control the private and public irrationality of their time and stop the wars.

In this new, drugged world, the schizophrene thrived better than any, and the world became patterned on him. But, just as the diabetic was still diabetic, the schizophrene was still himself, plus the drugs. Meanwhile, everyone had forgotten what it was the drugs did to you—that the emotions experienced were blurred emotions, that insight was at an isolated level of rationality because the drugs kept true feelings from emerging.

How inconceivable it would be to Helen and the other people of this world to live on as little drug as possible . . . to experience the conflicting emotions, the interplay of passion and logic that almost tore you apart! Sober, the ancients called it, and they lived that way most of the time, with only the occasional crude and clublike effects of alcohol or narcotics to relieve their chronic anxiety.

By taking as little hypothalamic block as possible, he and Clara were able to desire their fantastic attachment, to delight in an absolutely illogical situation unheard of in their society. But the society would judge their refusal to take hypothalamic block in only one sense. The weight of this judgment stood before him in the smoldering words, *"It ended the great paranoid wars and saved mankind."*

When Clara did appear, she was searching myopically in the wrong vicinity of the statue. He did not call to her at once, letting the sight of her smooth out the tensions in him, convert all the conflicts into this one intense longing to be with her.

Her halting search for him was deeply touching, like that of a tragic little puppet in a darkening dumbshow. He saw suddenly how like puppets the two of them were. They were moved by the strengthening wires of a new life of feeling to batter clumsily at an implacable stage setting that would finally leave them as bits of wood and paper.

Then suddenly in his arms Clara was at the same time hungrily moving and tense with fear of discovery. Little sounds of love and fear choked each other in her throat. Her blonde head pressed tightly into his shoulder and she clung to him with desperation.

She said, "Conrad was disturbed by my tension this morning and made me take a sleeping compound. I've just awakened."

They walked to her home in silence and even in the darkened apartment they used only the primitive monosyllables of apprehensive need. Beyond these mere sounds of compassion, they had long ago said all that could be said.

Because Bill was the hyperalter, he had no fear that Conrad could force a shift on him. When later they lay in darkness, he allowed himself to drift into a brief slumber. Without the sleeping compound, distorted events came and went without reason. Dreaming, the ancients had called it. It was one of the most frightening things that had begun to happen when he first cut down on the drugs. Now, in the few seconds that he dozed, a thousand fragments of incidental knowledge, historical reading and emotional need melded and, in a strange contrast to their present tranquility, he was dreaming a frightful moment in the twentieth century. *These are the great paranoid wars,* he thought. And it was so because he had thought it.

He searched frantically through the glove compartment of an ancient car. "Wait," he pleaded. "I tell you we have sulphonamide-14. We've been taking it regularly as directed. We took a double dose back in Paterson because there were soft-bombs all through that part of Jersey and we didn't know what would be declared Plague Area now."

Now Bill threw things out of his satchel on to the floor and seat of the car, fumbling deeper by the flashlight Clara held. His heart beat thickly with terror. They remembered sooner about their pharmacases. Bill tore at the belt around his waist.

The Medicorps captain stepped back from the door of their car. He jerked his head at the dark form of the corporal standing in the roadway. "Shoot them. Run the car off the embankment before you burn it."

Bill screamed metallically through the speaker of his radiation mask. "Wait. I've found it." He thrust the pharmacase out the door of the car. "This is a pharmacase," he explained. "We keep our drugs in one of these and it's belted to our waist so we are never without them."

The captain of the Medicorps came back. He inspected the pharmacase and the drugs and returned it. "From now on, keep your drugs handy. Take them without fail according to radio instructions. Do you understand?"

Clara's head pressed heavily against Bill's shoulder, and he could hear the tinny sound of her sobbing through the speaker of her mask.

The captain stepped into the road again. "We'll have to burn your car. You passed through a Plague Area and it can't be sterilized on this route. About a mile up this road you'll come to a sterilization unit. Stop and have your person and belongings rayed. After that, keep walking, but stick to the road. You'll be shot if you're caught off it."

The road was crowded with fleeing people. Their way was lighted by piles of cadavers writhing in gasoline flames. The Medicorps was everywhere. Those who stumbled, those who coughed, the delirious and their helping partners . . . these were taken to the side of the road, shot and burned. And there was bombing again to the south.

Bill stopped in the middle of the road and looked back. Clara clung to him.

"There is a plague here we haven't any drug for," he said, and realized he was crying. "We are all mad."

Clara was crying too. "Darling, what have you done? Where are the drugs?"

The water of the Hudson hung as it had in the late afternoon, ice crystals in the stratosphere. The high, high sheet flashed and glowed in the new bombing to the south, where multicolored pillars of flame boiled into the sky. But the muffled crash of the distant bombing was suddenly the steady click of the urgent signal on a bedside visiophone, and Bill was abruptly awake.

Clara was throwing on her robe and moving towards the machine on terror-rigid limbs. With a scrambling motion, Bill got out of the possible view of the machine and crouched at the end of the room.

Distinctly, he could hear the machine say, "Clara Manz?"

"Yes," Clara's voice was a thin treble that could have been a shriek had it continued.

"This is Medicorps Headquarters. A routine check discloses you have delayed your shift two hours. To maintain the statistical record of deviations, please give us a full explanation."

"I . . ." Clara had to swallow before she could talk. "I must have taken too much sleeping compound."

"Mrs. Manz, our records indicate that you have been delaying your shift consistently for several periods now. We made a check of this as a routine follow up on any such deviation, but the discovery is quite serious." There was a harsh silence, a silence that demanded a logical answer. But how could there be a logical answer.

"My hyperalter hasn't complained and I—well, I have just let a bad habit develop. I'll see that it—doesn't happen again."

The machine voiced several platitudes about the responsibilities of one personality to another and the duty of all to society before Clara was able to shut it off.

Both of them sat as they were for a long, long time while the tide of terror subsided. When at last they looked at each other across the dim and silent room, both of them knew there could be at least one more time together before they were caught.

Five days later, on the last day of her shift, Mary Walden wrote the address of her appointed father's hypoalter, Conrad Manz, with an indelible pencil on the skin just below her armpit.

During the morning, her father and mother had spoiled the family rest day by quarreling. It was about Helen's hypoalter delaying so many shifts. Bill did not think it very important, but her mother was angry and threatened to complain to the Medicorps.

The lunch was eaten in silence, except that at one point Bill said, "It seems to me Conrad and Clara Manz are guilty of a peculiar marriage, not us. Yet they seem perfectly happy with it and you're the one who is made unhappy. The woman has probably just developed a habit of taking too much sleeping compound for her rest-day naps. Why don't you drop her a note?"

Helen made only one remark. It was said through her teeth and very softly. "Bill, I would just as soon the child did not realize her relationship to this sordid situation."

Mary cringed over the way Helen disregarded her hearing, the possibility that she might be capable of understanding or her feelings about being shut out of their mutual world.

After lunch Mary cleared the table, throwing the remains of the meal and the plastiplates into the flash trash disposer. Her father had retreated to the library room and Helen was getting ready to attend a Citizens' Meeting. Mary heard her mother enter the room to say good-by while she was wiping the dining table. She knew that Helen was standing well-dressed and a little impatient, just behind her, but she pretended she did not know.

"Darling, I'm leaving now for the Citizens' Meeting."

"Oh . . . yes."

"Be a good girl and don't be late for your shift. You only have an hour now." Helen's patrician face smiled.

"I won't be late."

"Don't pay any attention to the things Bill and I discussed this morning, will you?"

"No."

And she was gone. She did not say good-by to Bill.

Mary was very conscious of her father in the house. He continued to sit in the library. She walked by the door and she could see him sitting in a chair, staring at the floor. Mary stood in the sun room for a long while. If he had risen from the chair, if he had rustled a page, if he had sighed, she would have heard him.

It grew closer and closer to the time she would have to leave if Susan Shorrs was to catch the first school hours of her shift. Why did children have to shift half a day before adults?

Finally, Mary thought of something to say. She could let him know she was old enough to understand what the quarrel had been about if only it were explained to her.

Mary went into the library and hesitantly sat on the edge of a couch near him. He did not look at her and his face seemed gray in the midday light. Then she knew that he was lonely, too. A great feeling of tenderness for him went through her.

"Sometimes I think you and Clara Manz must be the only people in the world," she said abruptly, "who aren't so silly about shifting right on the dot. Why, I don't *care* if Susan Shorrs *is* an hour late for classes!"

Those first moments when he seized her in his arms, it seemed her heart would shake loose. It was as though she had uttered some magic formula, one that had abruptly opened the doors to his love. It was only after he had explained to her why he was always late on the first day of the family shift that she knew something was wrong. He *did* tell her, over and over, that he knew she was unhappy and that it was his fault. But he was at the same time soothing her, petting her, as if *he was afraid of her.*

He talked on and on. Gradually, Mary understood in his trembling body, in his perspiring palms, in his pleading eyes, that he was afraid of dying, that he was afraid *she* would kill him with the merest thing she said, with her very presence.

This was not painful to Mary, because, suddenly, something came with ponderous enormity to stand before her: *I would just as soon the child did not realize her relationship to this sordid situation.*

Her relationship. It was some kind of relationship to Conrad and Clara Manz, because those were the people they had been talking about.

The moment her father left the apartment, she went to his desk and took out the file of family records. After she found the address of Conrad Manz, the idea occurred to her to write it on her body. Mary was certain that Susan Shorrs never bathed and she thought this a clever idea. Sometime on Susan's rest day, five days from now, she would try to force the shift and go to see Conrad and Clara Manz. Her plan was simple in execution, but totally vague as to goal.

Mary was already late when she hurried to the children's section of a public shifting station. A Children's Transfer B was waiting, and Mary registered on it for Susan Shorrs to be taken to school. After that she found a shifting room and opened it with her wristband. She changed into a shifting costume and sent her own clothes and belongings home.

Children her age did not wear make-up, but Mary always stood at the mirror during the shift. She always tried as hard as she could to see what Susan Shorrs looked like. She giggled over a verse that was scrawled beside the mirror . . .

> Rouge your hair and comb your face;
> Many a third head is lost in this place.

. . . and then the shift came, doubly frightening because of what she knew she was going to do.

Especially if you were a hyperalter like Mary, you were supposed to have some sense of the passage of time while you were out of shift. Of course, you did not know what was going on, but it was as though a more or less accurate chronometer kept running when you went out of shift. Apparently Mary's was highly inaccurate, because, to her horror, she found herself sitting bolt upright in one of Mrs. Harris's classes, not out on the playgrounds, where she had expected Susan Shorrs to be.

Mary was terrified, and the ugly school dress Susan had been wearing accented, by its strangeness, the seriousness of her premature shift. Children weren't supposed to show much difference from hyperalter to hypoalter; but when she raised her eyes, her fright grew. Children did change. She hardly recognized anyone in the room, though most of them must be the alters of her own classmates. Mrs. Harris was a B-shift and overlapped both Mary and Susan, but otherwise Mary recognized only Carl Blair's hypoalter because of his freckles.

Mary knew she had to get out of there or Mrs. Harris would eventually recognize her. If she left the room quietly, Mrs. Harris would not question her unless she recognized her. It was no use trying to guess how Susan would walk.

Mary stood and went towards the door, glad that it turned her back to Mrs. Harris. It seemed to her that she could feel the teacher's eyes stabbing through her back.

But she walked safely from the room. She dashed down the school corridor and out into the street. So great was her fear of what she was doing that her hypoalter's world actually seemed like a different one.

It was a long way for Mary to walk across town, and when she rang the bell, Conrad Manz was already home from work. He smiled at her and she loved him at once.

"Well, what do you want, young lady?" he asked.

Mary couldn't answer him. She just smiled back.

"What's your name, eh?"

Mary went right on smiling, but suddenly he blurred in front of her.

"Here, here! There's nothing to cry about. Come on in and let's see if we can help you. Clara! We have a visitor, a very sentimental visitor."

Mary let him put his big arm around her shoulder and draw her, crying, into the apartment. Then she saw Clara swimming before her, looking like her mother, but . . . no, not at all like her mother.

"Now, see here, chicken, what is it you've come for?" Conrad asked when her crying stopped.

Mary had to stare hard at the floor to be able to say it. "I want to live with you."

Clara was twisting and untwisting a handkerchief. "But, child, we have already had our first baby appointed to us. He'll be with us next shift, and after that I have to bear a baby for someone else to keep. We wouldn't be allowed to take care of you."

"I thought maybe I was your real child." Mary said it helplessly, knowing in advance what the answer would be.

"Darling," Clara soothed, "children don't live with their natural parents. It's neither practical nor civilized. I have had a child conceived and born on my shift, and this baby is my exchange, so you see that you are much too old to be my conception. Whoever your natural parents may be, it is just something on record with the Medicorps Genetic Division and isn't important."

"But you're a special case," Mary pressed. "I thought because it was a special arrangement that you were my real parents." She looked up and she saw that Clara had turned white.

And now Conrad Manz was agitated, too. "What do you mean, we're a special case?" He was staring hard at her.

"Because . . ." And now for the first time Mary realized how special this case was, how sensitive they would be about it.

He grasped her by the shoulders and turned her so she faced his unblinking eyes. "I said, what do you mean, we're a special case? Clara, what in thirty heads does this kid mean?"

His grip hurt her and she began to cry again. She broke away. "You're the hypoalters of my appointed father and mother. I thought maybe when it was like that, I might be your real child . . . and you might want me. I don't want to be where I am. I want somebody . . ."

Clara was calm now, her sudden fear gone. "But, darling, if you're unhappy where you are, only the Medicorps can reappoint you. Besides, maybe your appointed parents are just having some personal problems right now. Maybe if you tried to understand them, you would see that they really love you."

Conrad's face showed that he did not understand. He spoke with a stiff, quiet voice and without taking his eyes from Mary. "What are you doing here? My own hyperalter's kid in my house, throwing it up to me that I'm married to his wife's hypoalter!"

They did not feel the earth move, as she fearfully did. They sat there, staring at her, as though they might sit forever while she backed away, out of the apartment and ran into her collapsing world.

Conrad Manz's rest day fell the day after Bill Walden's kid showed up at his apartment. It was ten days since that strait-jacket of a conference on Santa Fe had lost him a chance to blast off a rocket racer. This time, on the practical knowledge that emergency business conferences were seldom called after lunch, Conrad had placed his reservation for a racer in the afternoon. The visit from Mary Walden had upset him every time he thought of it. Since it was his rest day, he had no intention of thinking about it and Conrad's scrupulously drugged mind was capable of just that.

So now, in the lavish coolness of the lounge at the Rocket Club, Conrad sipped his drink contentedly and made no contribution to the gloomy conversation going on around him.

"Look at it this way," the melancholy face of Alberts, a pilot from England, morosely emphasized his tone. "It takes about ten thousand economic units to jack a forty-ton ship up to satellite level and snap it around the course six times. That's just practice for us. On the other hand, an intellectual fellow who spends his spare time at a microfilm library doesn't use up one thousand units in a year. In fact, his spare-time activity may turn up as units gained. The Economic Board doesn't argue that all pastime should be gainful. They just say rocket racing wastes more economic units than most pilots make on their work days. I tell you the day is almost here when they'll ban the rockets."

"That's just it," another pilot put it. "There was a time when you could show that rocket races were necessary for better spaceship design. Design has gone way beyond that. From their point of view we just burn up units as fast as other people create them. And it's no use trying to argue for the television shows. The board can prove people would rather see a jet-skiing meet at a cost of about one-hundredth that of a rocket race."

Conrad Manz grinned into his drink. He had been aware for several minutes that pert little Angela, Alberts's soft-eyed husky-voiced wife, was trying to catch his eye. But stranded as she was in the buzzing traffic of rockets, she was trying to hail the wrong rescuer. He had about fifteen minutes till the ramp boys would have a ship ready for him. Much as he liked Angela, he wasn't going to miss that race.

Still, he let his grin broaden and, looking up at her, he lied maliciously by nodding. She interpreted this signal as he knew she would. Well, at least he would afford her a graceful exit from the boring conversation.

He got up and went over and took her hand. Her full lips parted a little and she kissed him on the mouth.

Conrad turned to Alberts and interrupted him. "Angela and I would like to spend a little time together. Do you mind?"

Alberts was annoyed at having his train of thought broken and rather snapped out the usual courtesy. "Of course not. I'm glad for both of you."

Conrad looked the group over with a bland stare. "Have you lads ever tried jet-skiing? There's more genuine excitement in ten minutes of it than an hour of rocket racing. Personally, I don't care if the board does ban the rockets soon. I'll just hop out to the Rocky Mountains on rest days."

Conrad knew perfectly well that if he had made this assertion before asking Alberts for his wife, the man would have found some excuse to have her remain. All the faces present displayed the aficionado's disdain for one who has just demonstrated he doesn't *belong*. What the strait-jacket did they think they were—some ancient order of noblemen?

Conrad took Angela's yielding arm and led her serenely away before Alberts could think of anything to detain her.

On the way out of the lounge, she stroked his arm with frank admiration. "I'm so glad you were agreeable. Honestly, Harold could talk rockets till I died."

Conrad bent and kissed her. "Angela, I'm sorry, but this isn't going to be what you think. I have a ship to take off in just a few minutes."

She flared and dug into his arm now. "Oh, Conrad Manz! You . . . you made me believe . . ."

He laughed and grabbed her wrists. "Now, now, I'm neglecting you to fly a rocket, not just to talk about them. I won't let you die."

At last she could not suppress her husky musical laugh. "I found that out the last time you and I were together. Clara and I had a drink the other day at the Citizens' Club. I don't often use dirty language, but I told Clara she must be keeping you in a *strait-jacket* at home."

Conrad frowned, wishing she hadn't brought up the subject. It worried him off and on that something was wrong with Clara, something even worse than that awful *dreaming* business ten days ago. For several shifts now she had been cold, nor was it just a temporary lack of interest in himself, for she was also cold to the men of their acquaintance of whom she was usually quite fond. As for himself, he had had to depend on casual contacts such as Angela. Not that they weren't pleasant, but a man and wife were supposed to maintain a healthy love life between themselves, and it usually meant trouble with the Medicorps when this broke down.

Angela glanced at him. "I didn't think Clara laughed well at my remark. Is something wrong between you?"

"Oh, no," he declared hastily. "Clara is sometimes that way . . . doesn't catch a joke right off."

A page boy approached them where they stood in the rotunda and advised Conrad that his ship was ready.

"Honestly, Angela, I'll make it up, I promise."

"I know you will, darling. And at least I'm grateful you saved me from all those rocket jets in there." Angela raised her lips for a kiss and afterwards, as she pushed him towards the door, her slightly vacant face smiled at him.

Out on the ramp, Conrad found another pilot ready to take off. They made two wagers—first to reach the racing course, and winner in a six-lap heat around the six-hundred-mile hexagonal course.

They fired together and Conrad blasted his ship up on a thunderous column of flame that squeezed him into his seat. He was good at this and he knew he would win the lift to the course. On the course, though, if his opponent was any good at all, Conrad would probably lose, because he enjoyed slamming the ship around the course in his wasteful, swash-buckling style much more than merely winning the heat.

Conrad kept his drive on till the last possible second and then shot out his nose jets. The ship shuddered up through another hundred miles and came to a lolling halt near the starting buoys. The other pilot gasped when Conrad shouted at him over the intership, "The winner by all thirty heads!"

It was generally assumed that a race up to the course consisted of cutting all jets when you had enough lift, and using the nose brakes only to correct any overshot. "What did you do, just keep your power on and flip the ship around?" The other racer coasted up to Conrad's level with a brief forward burst.

They got the automatic signal from the starting buoy and went for the first turn, nose and nose, about half a mile apart. Conrad lost five thousand yards on the first turn by shoving his power too hard against the starboard steering jets.

It made a pretty picture when a racer hammered its way around a turn that way with a fan of outside jets holding it in place. The other fellow made his turns cleanly, using mostly the driving jets for steering. But that didn't look like much to those who happened to flip on their television while this little heat was in progress. On every turn, Conrad lost a little in space, but not in the eye of the automatic televisor on the buoy marking the turn. As usual, he cut closer to the buoys than regulations allowed, to give the folks a show.

Without the slightest regret, Conrad lost the heat by a full two sides of the hexagon. He congratulated his opponent and watched the fellow let his ship down carefully towards earth on its tail jets. For a while Conrad lolled his ship around near the starting buoy and its probably watching eye, flipping through a series of complicated maneuvers with the steering jets.

Conrad did not like the grim countenance of outer space. The lifeless, gemlike blaze of cloud upon cloud of stars in the perspectiveless black repelled him. He liked rocket racing only because of the neat timing necessary, and possibly because the knowledge that he indulged in it scared poor old Bill Walden half to death.

Today the black aspect of the galaxy harried his mind back upon its own problems. A particularly nasty association of Clara with Walden and his sniveling kid kept dogging Conrad's mind and, as soon as stunting had exhausted his excess of fuel, he turned the ship to earth and sent it in with a short, spectacular burst.

Now that he stopped to consider it, Clara's strange behavior had begun at about the same time that Bill Walden started cheating on the shifts. That kid Mary must have known something was going on, or she would not have done such a disgusting thing as to come to their apartment.

Conrad had let the rocket fall nose-down, until now it was screaming into the upper ionosphere. With no time to spare, he swiveled the ship on its guiding jets and opened the drive blast at the uprushing earth. He had just completed this wrenching maneuver when two appalling things happened together.

Conrad suddenly knew, whether as a momentary leak from Bill's mind to his, or as a rapid calculation of his own, that Bill Walden and Clara shared a secret. At the same moment, something tore through his mind like fingers of chill wind. With seven gravities mashing him into the bucketseat, he grunted curses past thin-stretched lips.

"Great blue psychiatrist! What in thirty strait-jackets is that three-headed fool trying to do, kill us both?"

Conrad just managed to raise his leaden hand and set the plummeting racer for automatic pilot before Bill Walden forced him out of the shift. In his last moment of consciousness, and in the shock of his overwhelming shame, Conrad felt the bitter irony that he could not cut the power and kill Bill Walden.

When Bill Walden became conscious of the thunderous clamor of the braking ship and the awful weight of deceleration into which he had shifted, the core of him froze. He was so terrified that he could not have thought of reshifting even had there been time.

His head rolled on the pad in spite of its weight, and he saw the earth coming at him like a monstrous swatter aimed at a fly. Between his fright and the inhuman gravity, he lost consciousness without ever seeing on the control panel the red warning that saved him: *Automatic Pilot.*

The ship settled itself on the ramp in a mushroom of fire. Bill regained awareness several seconds later. He was too shaken to do anything but sit there for a long time.

When at last he felt capable of moving, he struggled with the door till he found how to open it, and climbed down to the still hot ramp he had landed on. It was at least a mile to the Rocket Club across the barren flat of the field, and he set out on foot. Shortly, however, a truck came speeding across to him.

The driver leaned out. "Hey, Conrad, what's the matter? Why didn't you pull the ship over to the hangars?"

With Conrad's make-up on, Bill felt he could probably get by. "Controls aren't working," he offered noncommittally.

At the club, a place he had never been to before in his life, Bill found an unused helicopter and started it with his wristband. He flew the machine into town to the landing station nearest his home.

He was doomed, he knew. Conrad certainly would report him for this. He had not intended to force the shift so early or so violently. Perhaps he had not intended to force it at all this time. But there was something in him more powerful than himself . . . a need to break the shift and be with Clara that now acted almost independently of him and certainly without regard for his safety.

Bill flew his craft carefully through the city traffic, working his way between the widely spaced towers with the uncertain hand of one to whom machines are not an extension of the body. He put the helicopter down at the landing station with some difficulty.

Clara would not be expecting him so early. From his apartment, as soon as he had changed make-up, he visiophoned her. It was strange how long and how carefully they needed to look at each other and how few words they could say.

Afterwards, he seemed calmer and went about getting ready with more efficiency. But when he found himself addressing the package of Conrad's clothes to his home, he chuckled bitterly.

It was when he went back to drop the package in the mail chute that he noticed the storage room door ajar. He disposed of the package and went over to the door. Then he stood still, listening. He had to stop his own breathing to hear clearly.

Bill tightened himself and opened the door. He flipped on the light and saw Mary. The child sat on the floor in the corner with her knees drawn up against her chest. Between the knees and the chest, the frail wrists were crossed, the hands closed limply like—like those of a fetus. The forehead rested on the knees so that, should the closed eyes stay open, they would be looking at the placid hands.

The sickening sight of the child squeezed down on his heart till the color drained from his face. He went forward and knelt before her. His dry throat hammered with the words, *what have I done to you,* but he could not speak. The question of how long she might have been here, he could not bear to think.

He put out his hand, but he did not touch her. A shudder of revulsion shook him and he scrambled to his feet. He hurried back into the apartment with only one thought. He must get someone to help her. Only the Medicorps could take care of a situation like this.

As he stood at the visiophone, he knew that this involuntary act of panic had betrayed all that he had ever thought and done. He had to call the Medicorps. He could not face the result of his own behavior without them. Like a ghostly after-image, he saw Clara's face on the screen. She was lost, cut off, with only himself to depend on.

A part of him, a place where there were no voices and a great tragedy, had been abruptly shut off. He stood stupidly confused and disturbed about something he couldn't recall. The emotion in his body suddenly had no referent. He stood like a badly frightened animal while his heart slowed and blood seeped again into whitened parenchymas, while tides of epinephrine burned lower.

Remembering he must hurry, Bill left the apartment. It was an apartment with its storage room door closed, an apartment without a storage room.

From the moment that he walked in and took Clara in his arms, he was not worried about being caught. He felt only the great need for her. There seemed only one difference from the first time and it was a good difference, because now Clara was so tense and apprehensive. He felt a new tenderness for her, as one might feel for a child. It seemed to him that there was no end to the well of gentleness and compassion that was suddenly in him. He was mystified by the depth of his feeling. He kissed her again and again and petted her as one might a disturbed child.

Clara said, "Oh Bill, we're doing wrong! Mary was here yesterday!"

Whoever she meant, it had no meaning for him. He said, "It's all right. You mustn't worry."

"She needs you, Bill, and I take you away from her."

Whatever it was she was talking about was utterly unimportant beside the fact that she was not happy herself. He soothed her. "Darling, you mustn't worry about it. Let's be happy the way we used to be."

He led her to a couch and they sat together, her head resting on his shoulder.

"Conrad is worried about me. He knows something is wrong. Oh, Bill, if he knew, he'd demand the worst penalty for you."

Bill felt the stone of fear come back in his chest. He thought, too, of Helen, of how intense her shame would be. Medicorps action would be machinelike, logical as a set of equations; they were very likely to take more drastic steps where the complaints would be so strong and no request for leniency forthcoming. Conrad knew now, of course. Bill had felt his hate.

It was nearing the end. Death would come to Bill with electronic fingers. A ghostly probing in his mind and suddenly . . .

Clara's great unhappiness and the way she turned her head into her shoulder to cry forced him to calm the rising panic in himself, and again to caress the fear from her.

Even later, when they lay where the moonlight thrust into the room an impalpable shaft of alabaster, he loved her only as a succor. Carefully, slowly, smoothing out her mind, drawing it away from all the other things, drawing it down into this one thing. Gathering all her mind into her senses and holding it there. Then quickly taking it away from her in a moaning spasm so that now she was murmuring, murmuring, palely drifting. Sleeping like a loved child.

For a long, long time he watched the white moon cut its arc across their window. He listened with a deep pleasure to her evenly breathing sleep.

But slowly he realized that her breath had changed, that the body so close to his was tensing. His heart gave a great bound and tiny moths of horror fluttered along his back. He raised himself and saw that the eyes were open in the silver light. Even through the make-up he saw that they were Helen's eyes.

He did the only thing left for him. He shifted. But in that terrible instant he understood something he had not anticipated. In Helen's eyes there was not only intense shame over shifting into her hypoalter's home; there was not only the disgust with himself for breaking communication codes. He saw that, as a woman of the twentieth century might have felt, Helen hated Clara as a sexual rival. She hated Clara doubly because he had turned not to some other woman, but to the other part of herself whom she could never know.

As she shifted, Bill knew that the next light he saw would be on the adamant face of the Medicorps.

Major Paul Grey, with two other Medicorps officers, entered the Walden apartment about two hours after Bill left it to meet Clara. Major Grey was angry with himself. Important information on a case of communication breaks and drug refusal could be learned by letting it run its course under observation. But he had not intended Conrad Manz's life to be endangered, and certainly he would not have taken the slightest chance on what they found in the Walden apartment if he had expected it this early.

Major Grey blamed himself for what had happened to Mary Walden. He should have had the machines watching Susan and Mary at the same time that they were relaying wristband data for Bill and Conrad and for Helen and Clara to his office.

He had not done this because it was Susan's shift and he had not expected Mary to break it. Now he knew that Helen and Bill Walden had been quarreling over the fact that Clara was cheating on Helen's shifts, and their conversations had directed the unhappy child's attention to the Manz couple. She had broken shift to meet them . . . looking for a loving father, of course.

Still—things would not have turned out so badly if Captain Thiel, Mary's school officer, had not attributed Susan Shorrs's disappearance only to poor drug acclimatization. Captain Thiel had naturally known that Major Grey was in town to prosecute Bill Walden, because the major had called on him to discuss the case. Yet it had not occurred to him, until eighteen hours after Susan's disappearance, that Mary might have forced the shift for some reason associated with her aberrant father.

By the time the captain advised him, Major Grey already knew that Bill had forced the shift on Conrad under desperate circumstances and he had decided to close in. He fully expected to find the father and daughter at the apartment, and now . . . it sickened him to see the child's demented condition and realize that Bill had left her there.

Major Grey could see at a glance that Mary Walden would not be accessible for days even with the best treatment. He left it to the other two officers to hospitalize the child and set out for the Manz apartment.

He used his master wristband to open the door there, and found a woman standing in the middle of the room, wrapped in a sheet. He knew that this must be Helen Walden. It was odd how ill-fitting Clara Manz's softly sensual make-up seemed, even to a stranger, on the more rigidly composed face before him. He guessed that Helen would wear color higher on her cheeks and the mouth would be done in severe lines. Certainly the present haughty face struggled with its incongruous make-up as well as the indignity of her dress.

She pulled the sheet tighter about her and said icily, "I will not wear that woman's clothes."

Major Grey introduced himself and asked, "Where is Bill Walden?"

"He shifted! He left me with . . . Oh, I'm so ashamed!"

Major Grey shared her loathing. There was no way to escape the conditioning of childhood—sex relations between hyperalter and hypoalter were more than outlawed, they were in themselves disgusting. If they were allowed, they could destroy this civilization. These idealists— they were almost all hypoalters, of course—who wanted the old terminology changed didn't take that into account. Next thing they'd want children to live with their actual parents!

Major Grey stepped into the bedroom. Through the bathroom door beyond, he could see Conrad Manz changing his make-up.

Conrad turned and eyed him bluntly. "Would you mind staying out of here till I'm finished? I've had about all I can take."

Major Grey shut the door and returned to Helen Walden. He took a hypothalamic block from his own pharmacase and handed it to her. "Here, you're probably on very low drug levels. You'd better take this." He poured her a glass of wine from a decanter and, while they waited for Conrad, he dialed the nearest shifting station on the visiophone and ordered up an emergency shifting costume for her.

When at last they were both dressed, made up to their satisfaction and drugged to his satisfaction, he had them sit on a couch together across from him. They sat at opposite ends of it, stiff with resentment at each other's presence.

Major Grey said calmly, "You realize that this matter is coming to a Medicorps trial. It will be serious."

Major Grey watched their faces. On hers he saw grim determination. On Conrad's face he saw the heavy movement of alarm. The man loved his wife. That was going to help. "It is necessary in a case such as this for the Medicorps to weigh your decisions along with the scientific evidence we will accumulate. Unfortunately, the number of laymen directly involved in this case—and not on trial—is only two, due to your peculiar marriage. If the hypoalters, Clara and Conrad, were married to other partners, we might call on as many as six involved persons and obtain a more equitable lay judgment. As it stands, the entire responsibility rests on the two of you."

Helen Walden was primly confident. "I don't see how we can fail to treat the matter with perfect logic. After all, it is not *we* who neglect our drug levels . . . They *were* refusing to take their drugs, weren't they?" she asked, hoping for the worst and certain she was right.

"Yes, this is drug refusal." Major Grey paused while she relished the answer. "But I must correct you in one impression. Your proper drug levels do not assure that you will act logically in this matter. The drugged mind *is* logical. However, its fundamental datum is that the drugs and drugged minds must be protected before everything else." He watched Conrad's face while he added, "Because of this, it is possible for you to arrive logically at a conclusion that . . . death is the required solution." He paused, looking at their white lips. Then he said, "Actually, other, more suitable solutions may be possible."

"But they *were* refusing their drugs," she said. "You talk as if you are defending them. Aren't you a Medicorps prosecutor?"

"I do not prosecute *people* in the ancient twentieth century sense, Mrs. Walden. I prosecute the acts of drug refusal and communication breaks. There is quite a difference."

"Well!" she said almost explosively. "I always knew Bill would get into trouble sooner or later with his wild, antisocial ideas. I never *dreamed* the Medicorps would take *his* side."

Major Grey held his breath, almost certain now that she would walk into the trap. If she did, he could save Clara Manz before the trial.

"After all, they have broken every communication code. They have refused the drugs, a defiance aimed at our very lives. They—"

"Shut up!" It was the first time Conrad Manz had spoken since he sat down. "The Medicorps spent weeks gathering evidence and preparing their recommendations. You haven't seen any of that and you've already made up your mind. How logical is that? It sounds as if you *want* your husband dead. Maybe the poor devil had some reason, after all, for what he did." On the man's face there was the nearest approach to hate that the drugs would allow.

Major Grey let his breath out softly. They were split permanently. She would have to trade him a mild decision on Clara in order to save Bill. And even there, if the subsequent evidence gave any slight hope, Major Grey believed now that he could work on Conrad to hang the lay judgment and let the Medicrops scientific recommendation go through unmodified.

He let them stew in their cross-purposed silence for a while and then nailed home a disconcerting fact.

"I think I should remind you that there are a few advantages to having your alter extinguished in the *mnemonic eraser*. A man whose hyperalter has been extinguished must report on his regular shift days to a hospital and be placed for five days in suspended animation. This is not very healthy for the body, but necessary. Otherwise, everyone's natural distaste for his own alter and the understandable wish to spend twice as much time living would generate schemes to have one's alter sucked out by the eraser. That happened extensively back in the twenty-first century before the five-day suspension was required. It was also used as a 'cure' for schizophrenia, but it was, of course, only the brutal murder of innocent personalities."

Major Grey smiled grimly to himself. "Now I will have to ask you both to accompany me to the hospital. I will want you, Mrs. Walden, to shift at once to Mrs. Manz. Mr. Manz, you will have to remain under the close observation of an officer until Bill Walden tries to shift back. We have to catch him with an injection to keep him in shift."

The young medicop put the syringe aside and laid his hand on Bill Walden's forehead. He pushed the hair back out of Bill's eyes.

"There, Mr. Walden, you don't have to struggle now."

Bill let his breath out in a long sigh. "You've caught me. I can't shift any more, can I?"

"That's right, Mr. Walden. Not unless we want you to." The young man picked up his medical equipment and stepped aside.

Bill noticed then the Medicorps officer standing in the background.

The man was watching as though he contemplated some melancholy distance. "I am Major Grey, Bill. I'm handling your case."

Bill did not answer. He lay staring at the hospital ceiling. Then he felt his mouth open in a slow grin.

"What's funny?" Major Grey asked mildly.

"Leaving my hypoalter with my wife," Bill answered candidly. It had already ceased to be funny to him, but he saw Major Grey smile in spite of himself.

"They were quite upset when I found them. It must have been some scramble before that." Major Grey came over and sat in the chair vacated by the young man who had just injected Bill. "You know, Bill, we will need a complete analysis of you. We want to do everything we can to save you, but it will require your cooperation."

Bill nodded, feeling his chest tighten. Here it came. Right to the end they would be tearing him apart to find out what made him work.

Major Grey must have sensed Bill's bitter will to resist. His resonant voice was soft, his face kindly. "We must have your sincere desire to help. We can't force you to do anything."

"Except die," Bill said.

"Maybe helping us get the information that might save your life at the trial isn't worth the trouble to you. But your aberration has seriously disturbed the lives of several people. Don't you think you owe it to them to help us to prevent this sort of thing in the future?" Major Grey ran his hand through his whitening hair. "I thought you would like to know Mary will come through all right. We will begin shortly to acclimatize her to her new appointed parents, who will be visiting her each day. That will accelerate her recovery a great deal. Of course, right now she is still inaccessible."

The brutally clear picture of Mary alone in the storage room crashed back into Bill's mind. After a while, in such slow stages that the beginning was hardly noticeable, he began to cry. The young medicop injected him with a sleeping compound, but not before Bill knew he would do whatever the Medicorps wanted.

The next day was crowded with battery after battery of tests. The interviews were endless. He was subjected to a hundred artificial situations and every reaction from his blood sugar to the frequency ranges of his voice was measured. They gave him only small amounts of drugs in order to test his reaction to them.

Late in the evening, Major Grey came by and interrupted an officer who was taking an electro-encephalogram for the sixth time after injection of a drug.

"All right, Bill, you have really given us cooperation. But after you've had your dinner, I hope you won't mind if I come to your room and talk with you for a little while."

When Bill finished eating, he waited impatiently in his room for the Medicorps officer. Major Grey came soon after. He shook his head at the mute question Bill shot at him.

"No, Bill. We will not have the results of your tests evaluated until late tomorrow morning. I can't tell you a thing until the trial in any case."

"When will that be?"

"As soon as the evaluation of your test is in." Major Grey ran his hand over his smooth chin and seemed to sigh. "Tell me, Bill, how do you feel about your case? How did you get into this situation and what do you think about it now?" The officer sat in the room's only chair and motioned Bill to the cot.

Bill was astonished at his sudden desire to talk about his problem. He had to laugh to cover it up. "I guess I feel as if I am being condemned for trying to stay sober." Bill used the ancient words with a mock tone of righteousness that he knew the major would understand.

Major Grey smiled. "How do you feel when you're sober?"

Bill searched his face. "The way the ancient Moderns did, I guess. I feel what happens to me the *way* it happens to me, not the artificial way the drugs let it happen. I think there is a way for us to live without the drugs and really enjoy life. Have you ever cut down on your drugs, major?"

The officer shook his head.

Bill smiled at him dreamily. "You ought to try it. It's as though a new life has suddenly opened up. Everything looks different to you.

"Look, with an average life span of a hundred years, each of us only lives fifty years and our alter lives the other fifty. Yet even on half-time we experience only about half the living we'd do if we didn't take the drugs. We would be able to feel the loves and hatreds and desires of life. No matter how many mistakes we made, we would be able occasionally to live those intense moments that made the ancients great."

Major Grey said tonelessly. "The ancients were great at killing, cheating and debasing one another. And they were worse sober than *drunk.*" This time he did not smile at the word.

Bill understood the implacable logic before him. The logic that had saved man from himself by smothering his spirit. The carefully achieved logic of the drugs that had seized upon the disassociated personality, and engineered it into a smoothly running machine, where there was no unhappiness because there was no great happiness, where there was no crime except failure to take the drugs or cross the alter sex line. Without drugs, he was capable of fury and he felt it now.

"You should see how foolish these communication codes look when you are undrugged. This stupid hide-and-seek of shifting! These two-headed monsters simpering about their artificial morals and their endless prescriptions! They belong in *crazy* houses! What use is there in such a world? If we are all this sick, we should die . . ."

Bill stopped and there was suddenly a ringing silence in the barren little room.

Finally Major Grey said, "I think you can see, Bill, that your desire to live without drugs is incompatible with this society. It would be impossible for us to maintain in you an artificial need for the drugs that would be healthy. Only if we can clearly demonstrate that this aberration is not an inherent part of your personality can we do something medically or psycho-surgically about it."

Bill did not at first see the implication in this. When he did, he thought of Clara rather than of himself, and his voice was shaken. "Is it a localized aberration in Clara?"

Major Grey looked at him levelly. "I have arranged for you to be with Clara Manz a little while in the morning." He stood up and said good night and was gone.

Slowly, as if it hurt him to move, Bill turned off the light and lay on the cot in the semi-dark. After a while he could feel his heart begin to take hold and he started feeling better. It was as though a man who had thought himself permanently expatriated had been told, "Tomorrow, you walk just over that hill and you will be home."

All through the night he lay awake, alternating between panic and desperate longing in a cycle with which finally he became familiar. At last, as rusty light of dawn reddened his silent room, he fell into a troubled sleep.

He started awake in broad daylight. An orderly was at the door with his breakfast tray. He could not eat, of course. After the orderly left, he hastily changed to a new hospital uniform and washed himself. He redid his make-up with a trembling hand, straightened the bedclothes and then he sat on the edge of the cot.

No one came for him.

The young medicop who had given him the injection that caught him in shift finally entered, and was standing near him before Bill was aware of his presence.

"Good morning, Mr. Walden. How are you feeling?"

Bill's wildly oscillating tensions froze at the point where he could only move helplessly with events and suffer a constant, unchangeable longing.

It was as if in a dream that they moved in silence together down the long corridors of the hospital and took the lift to an upper floor. The medicop opened the door to a room and let Bill enter. Bill heard the door close behind him.

Clara did not turn from where she stood looking out the window. Bill did not care that the walls of the chill little room were almost certainly recording every sight and sound. All his hunger was focused on the back of the girl at the window. The room seemed to ring with his racing blood. But he was slowly aware that something was wrong, and when at last he called her name, his voice broke.

Still without turning, she said in a strained monotone, "I want you to understand that I have consented to this meeting only because Major Grey has assured me it was necessary."

It was a long time before he could speak. "Clara, I need you."

She spun on him. "Have you no shame? You are married to my hyperalter—don't you understand that?" Her face was suddenly wet with tears and the intensity of her shame flamed at him from her cheeks. "How can Conrad ever forgive me for being with his hyperalter and talking about him? Oh, how can I have been so *mad?*"

"They have done something to you," he said, shaking with tension.

Her chin raised at this. She was defiant, he saw, though not towards himself—he no longer existed for her—but towards that part of herself which once had needed him and now no longer existed. "They have cured me," she declared. "They have cured me of everything but my shame, and they will help me get rid of that as soon as you leave this room."

Bill stared at her before leaving. Out in the corridor, the young medicop did not look him in the face. They went back to Bill's room and the officer left without a word. Bill lay down on his cot.

Presently Major Grey entered the room. He came over to the cot. "I'm sorry it had to be this way, Bill."

Bill's words came tonelessly from his dry throat. "Was it necessary to be cruel?"

"It was necessary to test the result of her psycho-surgery. Also, it will help her over her shame. She might otherwise have retained a seed of fear that she still loved you."

Bill did not feel anything any more. Staring at the ceiling, he knew there was no place left for him in this world and no one in it who needed him. The only person who had really needed him had been Mary, and he could not bear to think of how he had treated her. Now the Medicorps was efficiently curing the child of the hurt he had done her. They had already erased from Clara any need for him she had ever felt.

This seemed funny and he began to laugh. "Everyone is being cured of me."

"Yes, Bill. That is necessary." When Bill went on laughing Major Grey's voice turned quite sharp. "Come with me. It's time for your trial."

The enormous room in which they held the trial was utterly barren. At the great oaken table around which they all sat, there were three Medicorps officers in addition to Major Grey.

Helen did not speak to Bill when they brought him in. He was placed on the same side of the table with an officer between them. Two orderlies stood behind Bill's chair. Other than these people, there was no one in the room.

The great windows were high above the floor and displayed only the blissful sky. Now and then Bill saw a flock of pigeons waft aloft on silver-turning wings. Everyone at the table except himself had a copy of his case report and they discussed it with clipped sentences. Between the stone floor and the vaulted ceiling, a subtle echolalia babbled about Bill's problem behind their human talk.

The discussion of the report lulled when Major Grey rapped on the table. He glanced unsmiling from face to face, and his voice hurried the ritualized words: "This is a court of medicine, co-joining the results of medical science and considered lay judgment to arrive at a decision in the case of patient Bill Walden. The patient is hospitalized for a history of drug refusal and communication breaks. We have before us the medical case record of patient Walden. Has everyone present studied this record?"

All at the table nodded.

"Do all present feel competent to pass judgment in this case?"

Again there came the agreement.

Major Grey continued, "It is my duty to advise you, in the presence of the patient, of the profound difference between a trial for simple drug refusal and one in which that aberration is compounded with communication breaks.

"It is true that no other aberration is possible when the drugs are taken as prescribed. After all, the drugs *are* the basis for our schizophrenic society. Nevertheless, simple drug refusal often is a mere matter of physiology, which is easy enough to remedy.

"A far more profound threat to our society is the break in communication. This generally is more deeply motivated in the patient, and is often inaccessible to therapy. Such a patient is driven to emotive explorations which place the various ancient passions, and the infamous art of *historical gesture,* such as 'give me liberty or give me death,' above the welfare of society."

Bill watched the birds flash down the sky, a handful of heavenly coin. Never had it seemed to him so good to look at the sky. *If they hospitalize me,* he thought, *I will be content forever to sit and look from windows.*

"Our schizophrenic society," Major Grey was saying, "holds together and runs smoothly because, in each individual, the personality conflicts have been compartmentalized between hyperalter and hypoalter. On the social level, conflicting personalities are kept on opposite shifts and never contact each other. Or they are kept on shifts where contact is possible no more than one or two days out of ten. Bill Walden's break of shift is the type of behavior designed to reactivate these conflicts, and to generate the destructive passions on which an undrugged mind feeds. Already illness and disrupted lives have resulted."

Major Grey paused and looked directly at Bill. "Exhaustive tests have demonstrated that your entire personality is involved. I might also say that the aberration to live without the drugs and to break communication codes *is* your personality. All these Medicorps officers are agreed on that diagnosis. It remains now for us of the Medicorps to sit with the laymen intimately involved and decide on the action to be taken. The only possible alternatives after that diagnosis are permanent hospitalization or . . . total removal of the personality by mnemonic erasure."

Bill could not speak. He saw Major Grey nod to one of the orderlies and felt the man pushing up his sleeve and injecting his nerveless arm. They were forcing him to shift, he knew, so that Conrad Manz could sit in on the trial and participate.

Helplessly, he watched the great sky blacken and the room dim and disappear.

Major Grey did not avert his face, as did the others, while the shift was in progress. Helen Walden, he saw, was dramatizing her shame at being present during a shift, but the Medicorps officers simply stared at the table. Major Grey watched the face of Conrad Manz take form while the man who was going to be tried faded.

Bill Walden had been without make-up, and as soon as he was sure Manz could hear him, Major Grey apologized. "I hope you won't object to this brief interlude in public without make-up. You are present at the trial of Bill Walden."

Conrad Manz nodded and Major Grey waited another full minute for the shift to complete itself before he continued. "Mr. Manz, during the two days you waited in the hospital for us to catch Walden in shift, I discussed this case quite thoroughly with you, especially as it applied to the case of Clara Manz, on which we were already working.

"You will recall that in the case of your wife, the Medicorps diagnosis was one of a clearly localized aberration. It was quite simple to apply the mnemonic eraser to that small section without distrubing in any way her basic personality. Medicorps agreement was for this procedure and the case did not come to trial, but simply went to operation, because lay agreement was obtained. First yourself and eventually—" Major Grey paused and let the memory of Helen's stubborn insistence that Clara die stir in Conrad's mind—"Mrs. Walden agreed with the Medicorps."

Major Grey let the room wait in silence for awhile. "The case of Bill Walden is quite different. The aberration involves the whole personality, and the alternative actions to be taken are permanent hospitalization or total erasure. In this case, I believe that Medicorps opinion will be divided as to proper action and—" Major Grey paused again and looked levelly at Conrad Manz—"this may be true, also, of the lay opinion."

"How's that, Major?" demanded the highest ranking Medicorps officer present, a colonel named Hart, a tall, handsome man on whom the military air was a becoming skin. "What do you mean about Medicorps opinion being divided?"

Major Grey answered quietly, "I'm holding out for hospitalization."

Colonel Hart's face reddened. He thrust it forward and straightened his back. "That's preposterous! This is a clear-cut case of a dangerous threat to our society, and we, let me remind you, are *sworn* to protect that society."

Major Grey felt very tired. It was, after all, difficult to understand why he always fought so hard against erasure of these aberrant cases. But he began with quiet determination. "The threat to society is effectively removed by either of the alternatives, hospitalization or total erasure. I think you can all see from Bill Walden's medical record that his is a well-rounded personality with a remarkable mind. In the environment of the twentieth century, he would have been an outstanding citizen, and possibly, if there had been more like him, our present society would have been better for it.

"Our history has been one of weeding out all personalities that did not fit easily into our drugged society. Today there are so few left that I have handled only one hundred and thirty-six in my entire career. . . ."

Major Grey saw that Helen Walden was tensing in her chair. He realized suddenly that she sensed better than he the effect he was having on the other men.

"We should not forget that each time we erase one of these personalities," he pressed on relentlessly, "society loses irrevocably a certain capacity for change. If we eliminate all personalities who do not fit, we may find ourselves without any minds capable of meeting future change. Our direct ancestors were largely the inmates of mental hospitals . . . we are fortunate *they* were not erased. Conrad Manz," he asked abruptly, "what is your opinion on the case of Bill Walden?"

Helen Walden started, but Conrad Manz shrugged his muscular shoulders. "Oh, hospitalize the three-headed monster!"

Major Grey snapped his eyes directly past Colonel Hart and fastened them on the Medicorps captain. "Your opinion, captain?"

But Helen Walden was too quick. Before he could rap the table for order, she had her thin words hanging in the echoing room. "Having been Mr. Walden's wife for fifteen years, my sentiments naturally incline me to ask for hospitalization. That is why I may safely say, if Major Grey will pardon me, that the logic of the drugs does not entirely fail us in this situation."

Helen waited while all present got the idea that Major Grey had accused them of being illogical. "Bill's aberration has led to our daughter's illness. And think how quickly it contaminated Clara Manz! I cannot ask that society any longer expose itself, even to the extent of keeping Bill in the isolation of the hospital, for my purely sentimental reasons.

"As for Major Grey's closing remarks, I cannot see how it is fair to bring my husband to trial as a threat to society, if some future change is expected, in which a man of his behavior would benefit society. Surely such a change could only be one that would ruin our present world, or Bill would hardly fit it. I would not want to save Bill or anyone else for such a future."

She did not have to say anything further. Both of the other Medicorps officers were now fully roused to their duty. Colonel Hart, of course, "humphed" at the opinions of a woman and cast his with Major Grey. But the fate of Bill Walden was sealed.

Major Grey sat, weary and uneasy, as the creeping little doubts began. In the end, he would be left with the one big stone-heavy doubt . . . could he have gone through with this if he had not been drugged, and how would the logic of the trial look without drugs?

He became aware of the restiveness in the room. They were waiting for him, now that the decision was irrevocable. Without the drugs, he reflected, they might be feeling—what was the ancient world, *guilt*? No, that was what the criminal felt. *Remorse*? That would be what they should be feeling. Major Grey wished Helen Walden could be forced to witness the erasure. People did not realize what it was like.

What was it Bill had said? "You should see how foolish these communication codes look when you are undrugged. This stupid hide-and-seek of shifting. . . ."

Well, wasn't that a charge to be *inspected* seriously, if you were taking it seriously enough to kill the man for it? As soon as this case was completed, he would have to return to his city and blot himself out so that his own hyperalter, Ralph Singer, a painter of bad pictures and a useless fool, could waste five more days. To that man he lost half his possible living days. What earthly good was Singer?

Major Grey roused himself and motioned the orderly to inject Conrad Manz, so that Bill Walden would be forced back into shift.

"As soon as I have advised the patient of our decision, you will all be dismissed. Naturally, I anticipated this decision and have arranged for immediate erasure. After the erasure, Mr. Manz, you will be instructed to appear regularly for suspended animation."

For some reason, the first thing Bill Walden did when he became conscious of his surroundings was to look out the great window for the flock of birds. But they were gone.

Bill looked at Major Grey and said, "What are you going to do?"

The officer ran his hand back through his whitening hair, but he looked at Bill without wavering. "You will be erased."

Bill began to shake his head. "There is something wrong," he said.

"Bill . . ." the major began.

"There is something wrong," Bill repeated hopelessly. "Why must we be split so there is always something missing in each of us? Why must we be stupefied with drugs that keep us from knowing what we should feel?

I was trying to live a better life. I did not want to hurt anyone."

"But you *did* hurt others," Major Grey said bluntly. "You would do so again if allowed to function in your own way in this society. Yet it would be insufferable to you to be hospitalized. You would be shut off forever from searching for another Clara Manz. And—there is no one else for you, is there?"

Bill looked up, his eyes cringing as though they stared at death. "No one else?" he asked vacantly. "No one?"

The two orderlies lifted him up by his arms, almost carrying him into the operating room. His feet dragged helplessly. He made no resistance as they lifted him on to the operating table and strapped him down.

Beside him was the great panel of the mnemonic eraser with its thousand unblinking eyes. The helmetlike prober cabled to this calculator was fastened about his skull, and he could no longer see the professor who was lecturing in the amphitheater above. But along his body he could see the group of medical students. They were looking at him with great interest, too young not to let the human drama interfere with their technical education.

The professor, however, droned in a purely objective voice. "The mnemonic eraser can selectively shunt from the brain any identifiable category of memory, and erase the synaptic patterns associated with its translation into action. Circulating memory is disregarded. The machine only locates and shunts out those energies present as permanent memory. These are there in part as permanently echoing frequencies in closed cytoplasmic systems. These systems are in contact with the rest of the nervous system only during the phenomenon of remembrance. Remembrance occurs when, at all the synapses in a given network 'y,' the permanently echoing frequencies are duplicated as transient circulating frequencies.

"The objective in a total operation of the sort before us is to distinguish all the stored permanent frequencies, typical of the personality you wish to extinguish, from the frequencies typical of the other personality present in the brain."

Major Grey's face, very tired, but still wearing a mask of adamant reassurance, came into Bill's vision. "There will be a few moments of drug-induced terror, Bill. That is necessary for the operation. I hope knowing it beforehand will help you ride with it. It will not be for long." He squeezed Bill's shoulder and was gone.

"The trick was learned early in our history, when this type of total operation was more often necessary," the professor continued. "It is really quite simple to extinguish one personality while leaving the other undisturbed. The other personality in the case before us has been drug-immobilized to keep this one from shifting. At the last moment, this personality before us will be drug-stimulated to bring it to the highest possible pitch of total activity. This produces utterly disorganized activity, every involved neutron and synapse being activated simultaneously by the drug. It is then a simple matter for the mnemonic eraser to locate all permanently echoing frequencies involved in this personality and suck them into its receiver."

Bill was suddenly aware that a needle had been thrust into his arm. Then it was as though all the terror, panic and traumatic incidents of his whole life leaped into his mind. All the pleasant experiences and feelings he had ever known were there, too, but were transformed into terror.

A bell was ringing with regular strokes. Across the panel of the mnemonic eraser, the tiny counting lights were alive with movement.

There was in Bill a fright, a demand for survival so great that it could not be felt.

It was actually from an island of complete calm that part of him saw the medical students rising dismayed and whitefaced from their seats. It was apart from himself that his body strained to lift some mountain and filled the operating amphitheater with shrieking echoes. And all the time the thousand eyes of the mnemonic eraser flickered in swift patterns, a silent measure of the cells and circuits of his mind.

Abruptly the tiny red counting lights went off, a red beam glowed with a burr of warning. Someone said, "Now!" The mind of Bill Walden flashed along a wire as electrical energy, and, converted on the control panel into mechanical energy, it spun a small ratchet counter.

"Please sit down," the professor said to the shaken students. "The drug that has kept the other personality immobilized is being counteracted by this next injection. Now that the sickly personality has been dissipated, the healthy one can be brought back rapidly.

"As you are aware, the synapse operates on the binary 'yes-no' choice system of an electronic calculator. All synapses which were involved in the diseased personality have now been reduced to an atypical, uniform threshold. Thus they can be reeducated in new patterns by the healthy personality remaining. . . . There, you see the countenance of the healthy personality appearing."

It was Conrad Manz who looked up at them with a wry grin. He rotated his shoulders to loosen them. "How many of you pushed old Bill Walden around? He left me with some sore muscles. Well, I did that often enough to him. . . ."

Major Grey stood over him, face sick and white with the horror of what he had seen. "According to law, Mr. Manz, you and your wife are entitled to five rest days on your next shift. When they are over, you will, of course, report for suspended animation for what would have been your hyperalter's shift."

Conrad Manz's grin shrank and vanished. "*Would* have been? Bill is —gone?"

"Yes."

"I never thought I'd miss him." Conrad looked as sick as Major Grey felt. "It makes me feel—I don't know if I can explain it—sort of *amputated*. As though something's wrong with me because everybody else has an alter and I don't. Did the poor son of a strait-jacket suffer much?"

"I'm afraid he did."

Conrad Manz lay still for a moment with his eyes closed and his mouth thin with pity and remorse. "What will happen to Helen?"

"She'll be all right," Major Grey said. "There will be Bill's insurance, naturally, and she won't have much trouble finding another husband. That kind never seems to."

"Five rest days?" Conrad repeated. "Is that what you said?" He sat up and swung his legs off the table, and he was grinning again. "I'll get in a whole shift of jet-skiing! No, wait—I've got a date with the wife of a friend of mine out at the rocket grounds. I'll take Clara out there; she'll like some of the men."

Major Grey nodded abstractedly. "Good idea." He shook hands with Conrad Manz, wished him fun on his rest shift, and left.

Taking a helicopter back to his city, Major Grey thought of his own hyperalter, Ralph Singer. He'd often wished that the silly fool could be erased. Now he wondered how it would be to have only one personality, and, wondering, realized that Conrad Manz had been right—it *would* be like amputation, the shameful distinction of living in a schizophrenic society with no alter.

No, Bill Walden had been wrong, completely wrong, both about drugs and being split into two personalities. What one made up in pleasure through not taking drugs was more than lost in the suffering of conflict, frustration and hostility. And having an alter—any kind, even one as useless as Singer—meant, actually, *not being alone.*

Major Grey parked the helicopter and found a shifting station. He took off his make-up, addressed and mailed his clothes and waited for the shift to come.

It was a pretty wonderful society he lived in, he realized. He wouldn't trade it for the kind Bill Walden had wanted. Nobody in his right mind would.

JOHN VARLEY

# Equinoctial

*Symbiosis is a controversial subject in biology and zoology, with some authorities claiming that different species live together to their common benefit, others insisting that this only appears to be the case. Science fiction writers have many times examined the problems and rewards of symbiotic relationships, but rarely has symbiosis been so powerfully explored as in John Varley's "Equinoctial," a wonderful and strangely neglected masterpiece.*

Parameter knew she was being followed. They had been behind her for days, always far enough behind that they couldn't get a permanent fix on her, but never so far that she could lose them. She was in danger, but now was not the time to worry about it.

Now was one of the big moments in her life. She proposed to savor it to the full and refused to be distracted by the hunters. She was giving birth to quintuplets.

*Uni, Duo, Tri, Quad . . .* Hopelessly trite. *Doc, Happy, Sneezy, Grumpy* —No, there were seven of those. *Army, Navy, Marine, Airforce, Coastguard?* That was a pentagon, for an interesting pun. But who wanted to be called Coastguard? What *was* a Coastguard, anyway?

She put the naming ordeal out of her mind. It wasn't important; they would pick their own names when the time came. She just thought it might be nice with *five* to have something to tag them with, if only for bookkeeping purposes.

"They just got another sighting," she thought, but it wasn't her own thought. It was the voice of Equinox. Equinox was Parameter's companion, her environment, her space suit, her alter ego; her Symb. She looked in the direction she had come from.

She looked back on the most spectacular scene in the solar system. She was two hundred thirty thousand kilometers from the center of Saturn, according to the figures floating in the upper left corner of her field of vision. To one side of her was the yellow bulk of the giant planet, and all around her was a golden line that bisected the universe. She was inside

55

the second and brightest of the Rings.

But Saturn and the Rings was not all she saw. About ten degrees away from Saturn and in the plane of the Rings was a hazy thing like the bell of a trumpet. It was transparent. The wide end of the bell was facing her. Within this shape were four lines of red that were sharp and well-defined far away but became fuzzy as they neared her. These were the hunters. All around her, but concentrated in the plane of the Rings, were slowly moving lines of all colors, each with an arrow at one end, each shifting perspective in a dazzling 3-D ballet.

None of it—the lines, the bell, the "hunters," even Saturn itself—none of it was any more real than the image in a picture tube. Some of it was even less real than that. The shifting lines, for instance, were vector representations of the large chunks of rock and ice within radar range of Equinox.

The bell was closer than it had been for days. That was bad news, because the space-time event it represented was the approach of the hunters and their possible locations projected from the time of the last fix. The fuzzy part was almost touching her. That meant they could be very close indeed, though it wasn't too likely. They were probably back in the stem where the projection looked almost solid, and almost certainly within the four lines that were their most probable location. But it was still too close.

"Since they know where we are, let's get a fix on *them,*" Parameter decided, and as she thought it, the bell disappeared, to be replaced by four red points that grew tails even as she watched.

"Too close. Way too close." Now they had two fixes on her: one of their own, and the one she had given them by bouncing a signal off them. From this, their Symbs could plot a course; therefore, it was time to alter it.

She couldn't afford to change course in the usual way, by bouncing off a rock. The hunters were close enough that they would detect the change in the rock's velocity and get a better idea of where she was. It was time for thrusters, though she could ill afford the wasted mass.

"Which way?" she asked.

"I suggest you move out of the plane. They won't expect that yet. They don't know you're in labor."

"That's pretty dangerous. There's nothing to hide in out there."

Equinox considered it. "If they get any closer, you'll have to do something at least that drastic, with less chance of success. But I only advise."

"Sure. All right, do it, my green pasture."

The world around her jerked, and all the colored lines started moving down around her, bending as their relative velocity changed. There was a gentle pressure at the small of her back.

"Keep an eye on them. I'm going back to the business of giving birth. How are they doing, by the way?"

"No sweat. One of the girls is in the tube right now—you can feel her—"

"You can tell me *that* three times . . ."

"—and she's a little puzzled by the pressure. But she's taking it well. She tells you not to worry, she'll be all right."

"Can I talk to her yet?"

"Not for another few hours. Be patient."

"Right. It shouldn't be long now."

And that was very true. She felt the wave of sensation as her uterus contracted again. She looked down at herself, absently expecting to see the first head coming out. But she could no longer see that far; her belly stuck out.

Nothing that Parameter saw was real; all was illusion. Her head was completely enclosed in the thick, opaque substance of Equinox, and all the sensory data she received was through the direct connection from Equinox's senses into her own brain. Much of this information was edited and embellished in ways that made it easier for Parameter to interpret.

So it was that when she looked down at herself she saw not the dark green surface of Equinox, but her own brown skin. She had asked for that illusion long ago, when it had become a matter of some importance to her to believe she still had her own body. The illusion was flawless. She could see the fingerprints on her hand, the mole on her knee, the color of her nipples, the sentimental scar on her forearm, all illuminated by the soft diffusion of light from the Rings. But if she tried to touch herself, her hand would be stopped while still a good distance from what she saw as the surface of her body. Equinox was invisible to her, but she was certainly there.

She watched as the contraction caused her stomach to writhe and flow like putty. This was more like it. She remembered her other deliveries, before she married Equinox. One had been "natural," and it hadn't worked all that well. She didn't regret it, but it had been painful, not something she would want to repeat. The other had been under anesthetic, and no fun at all. She might as well not have bothered; there had been no pain, no pleasure, no *sensation*. It was like reading about it in the newspaper. But this one, her third birth, was different. It was intense, so intense she had difficulty concentrating on eluding the hunters. But there was no pain. All she felt was a series of waves of pleasure-pain that didn't hurt, and could be related to no other sensation humans had ever experienced.

One of the lines ahead seemed to point almost directly at her. It was a thick red line, meaning it was 70 percent ice and about a million kilograms in mass. The vector was short. It was moving slowly enough that rendezvous would be easy.

She took the opportunity and altered course slightly with the sure instinct she had developed. The line swung, foreshortened even more, then flashed brighter and began to pulse. This was the collision warning from Equinox's plotting sector.

When the rock was close enough to see as an object rather than a simulated projection, she rotated until her legs pointed at it. She soaked up the shock of the landing, then began to scuttle over the surface in a manner quite astonishing, and with a speed not to be believed. She moved with the coordinated complexity of a spider, all four limbs grasping at the rock and ice.

To an observer, she was a comical sight. She looked like a barbell with arms and legs and a bulge at the top that just might be a head. There were no creases or sharp lines anywhere on the outer surface of Equinox; all was gentle curves, absolutely featureless except for short claws on the hands and feet. At the ends of her legs were grasping appendages more like oversized hands than feet. And her legs bent the wrong way. Her knees were hinged to bend away from each other.

But she swarmed over the rock with effortless ease, not even hampered by her pregnancy, though the labor "pains" were getting intense.

When she was where she wanted to be, she pushed off with both hands and peds, rising rapidly. She was now on a course about ninety degrees away from her pursuers. She hoped they would not be expecting this. Now she had to rely on the screening effect of the billions of tiny rocks and ice crystals around her. For the next few hours she would be vulnerable if they beamed in her direction, but she didn't think it likely they would. Their Symbs would be plotting a course for her almost opposite to the one she was actually taking. If she had continued that way they would certainly have caught her later when she was burdened with five infants. Now was the time for audacity.

Having done that, she put the matter out of her mind again, and none too soon. The first baby had arrived.

The head was just emerging as she pushed off the rock. She savored the delicious agony as the head forced its way through her body, struggling to reach the air. It would never reach it. There was no air out here, just another womb that Equinox had prepared, a womb the baby would live in for the rest of its life. No first breath for Parameter's children; no breath at all.

The babies were not full-term. Each had been growing only seven months and would not be able to survive without extensive care. But Equinox was the world's best incubator. She had counseled, and Parameter had agreed, that it would be best to birth them while they were still small and get them out where Equinox could keep a closer eye on them.

Parameter moved her strangely articulated legs, bringing the handlike peds up to the baby. She pressed slowly and felt the peds sink in as Equinox absorbed the outer covering. Then she felt the head with her own nerve endings. She ran her long fingers over the wet ball. There was another contraction and the baby was out. She was holding it in her peds. She couldn't see much of it, and suddenly she wanted to.

"This is one of the girls, right?"

"Yes. And so are two, three, and five. Navy, Marine and Coastguard, if you want to get more personal."

"Those were just tags," she laughed. "I didn't even like them."

"Until you think of something else, they'll do."

"*They* won't want them."

"Perhaps not. Anyway, I'm thinking of shifting the boy around to fifth position. There's a little tangling of the cords."

"Whatever you want. I'd like to see her. 'Army,' I mean."

"Do you want a picture, or should I move her?"

"Move her." She knew it was only a semantic quibble as to whether she would actually "see" her child. The projection Equinox could provide would look just as real, hanging in space. But she wanted the picture to coincide with the feel she was getting of the baby against her skin.

By undulating the inner surface of her body, Equinox was able to move the infant around the curve of Parameter's belly until she was visible. She was wet, but there was no blood; Equinox had already absorbed it all.

"I want to touch her with my hands," Parameter thought.

"Go ahead. But don't forget there's another coming in a few minutes."

"Hold it up. I want to enjoy this one first."

She put her hands on the invisible surface of Equinox and they sank in until she was holding the child. It stirred and opened its mouth, but no sound came. There seemed to be no trauma involved for the brand-new human being; she moved her arms and legs slowly but seemed content to lie still for the most part. Compared to most human children, she hadn't really been born at all. Parameter tried to interest her in a nipple, but she didn't want it. She was the prettiest thing Parameter had ever seen.

"Let's get the next one out," she said. "This is so extravagant I still can't believe it. Five!"

She drifted into a wonderful haze as the others arrived, each as pretty as the last. Soon she was covered with tiny bodies, each still tied to an umbilicus. The cords would be left in place until Equinox had finished her childbirth and had five semi-autonomous baby Symbs to receive the children. Until then, the children were still a part of her. It was a feeling Parameter loved; she would never be closer to her children.

"Can you hear them yet?" Equinox asked.

"No, not yet."

"You'll have to wait a while longer for mind contact. I'm tuning out. Are you all right? I shouldn't be longer than about two hours."

"Don't worry about me. I'll be fine. In fact, I've never been happier." She stopped verbalizing and let a wave of intense love flood over her; love for her invisible mate. It was answered by such an outpouring of affection that Parameter was in tears. "I love you, earthmother," she said.

"And you, sunshine."

"I hope it'll be as good for you as it was for me."

"I wish I could share it with you. But back to business. I really think we've shaken the hunters. There's been no signal from them for an hour, and their projected path is well away from us. I think we'll be safe, at least for a few hours."

"I hope so. But don't worry about me. I'll get along while you're away. I'm not scared of the dark."

"I know. It won't be for long. See you later."

Parameter felt her mate slipping away. For a moment she *was* afraid, but not of the dark. She was afraid of the loneliness. Equinox would be unavailable to her for the time it took to give birth to her children, and that meant she would be cut off from the outside. That didn't matter, but the absence of Equinox from Parameter's mind was a little frightening. It recalled an unpleasant incident in her past.

But as the lights faded she realized she was not alone. Cut off from sight, sound, smell and taste by the shutdown of Equinox's interpretative faculties, she still had touch, and that was enough.

She floated in total darkness and felt the sharp tingle as a mouth found a nipple and began to suck. Imperceptibly, she drifted into sleep.

She awoke to a vague feeling of discomfort. It was small and nagging, and impossible to ignore. She felt in her mind for Equinox, and couldn't find her. So she was still in the process of giving birth.

But the feeling persisted. She felt helpless in the dark, then she realized it wasn't totally dark. There was a faint pinkness, like looking into closed eyelids. She could not account for it. Then she knew what was wrong, and it was worse than she could have imagined. The babies were gone.

She felt over her body with increasing panic, but they were nowhere to be found. Before her panic overwhelmed her, she tried to think of what could have happened that would have separated them, and all she could come up with was the hunters. But why would they take the babies? Then she lost control; there was nothing she could do in the darkness without Equinox to create the universe for her.

She was drawn back to rationality by a thought so black she could hardly credit it. In torment, she opened her eyes.

She could see.

She was floating in the center of a room hollowed out of bare rock. There was another person in the room, or rather another symbiote; all she could see was the dark green, curved form of the Symb.

"Equinox!" she yelled, and heard herself. In a dream, she looked down at her body and felt the bare reality of it. She touched herself; there was no resistance. She was alone. Half of her was gone.

Her mind was dissolving; she watched it go, and knew it to be preferable to facing life without Equinox. She said good-by to the last shreds of reality, rolled her eyes up into her head, and swallowed her tongue.

The figure looked like a cartoon of a human drawn by a three-year-old, one who was confused about sex. The broad shoulders and bullish neck were ludicrously like the build of a weightlifter, and the narrowing waist and bulbous ass were a moron's idea of a well-built woman. He was green, and featureless except for an oval opening where his mouth should have been.

"Just why do you want to become a Ringer?" The sound issued from the hole in his "face."

Parameter sighed and leaned back in her chair. The operation at Titan was anything but efficient. She had spent three days talking to people who had been no help at all and finally found this man, who seemed to have the authority to give her a Symb. Her patience—never very long—was at an end.

"I should make a tape," she said. "You're the fourth bastard who's asked me that today."

"Nevertheless, I must have your answer. And why don't you keep the smart remarks to yourself? I don't need them. For two cents I'd walk out of here and forget about you."

"Why don't you? I don't think you can even get out of that chair, much less walk out of here. I never expected anything like this. I thought you Consers wanted new people, so why are you giving me such a runaround? I might get up and walk out myself. You people aren't the only Ringers."

He proved her wrong by rising from the chair. He was awkward but steady, and, even more interesting, there was something in his hand that could only be a gun. She was amazed. He was sitting in a bare room, and had been empty-handed. Suddenly there was this gun, out of nowhere.

"If you mean that you're thinking of going over to the Engineers, it's my duty to blow your brains out. You have ten seconds to explain yourself." There was no trace of anger. The gun never wavered.

She swallowed hard, keeping very still.

"Uh, no, that's not what I meant."

The gun dropped slightly.

"It was a foolish remark," she said, her ears burning with shame and anger. "I'm committed to the Conservationists."

The gun vanished into the Symb he was wearing. It could still be in his hand for all she could tell.

"Now you can answer my question."

Keeping her anger rigidly in check, she started her story. She was quite good at it by now, and had it condensed nicely. She recited it in a singsong tone that the interrogator didn't seem to notice.

"I am seventy-seven Earth years old, I was born on Mercury, the Helios Enclave, the child of an extremely wealthy energy magnate. I grew up in the rigid, confining atmosphere that has always existed in Mercury, and I hated it. When I turned twelve, my mother gave me 20 percent of her fortune and said she hoped I'd use it wisely. Luckily for me, I was an adult and beyond her reach, because I disappointed her badly.

"I bought passage on the first ship leaving the planet, which happened to be going to Mars. For the next sixty years I devoted myself to experiencing everything the human organism can experience and still survive.

"It would be tedious and overlong to tell you everything I did, but so you won't think I'm hiding something, I can give you a random sample.

"Drugs: I tried them all. Some only once. Others for years at a time. I had to have my personality rebuilt three times and lost a lot of memory in the process.

"Sex: with two, three, four partners; seven partners; thirty partners; three hundred partners. All-week orgies. Men, women, girls, boys. Infants. Elephants. Pythons. Corpses. I changed sex so many times I'm not sure if I grew up as a male or a female.

"I killed a man. I got away with it. I killed a woman and got away again. I got caught the third time and spent seven years in rehabilitation.

"I traveled. I went to the Belt, to Luna, to the moons of Saturn, Uranus, Neptune. I went to Pluto, and beyond with a holehunter.

"I tried surgery. I joined up with a pair cult and was connected for a year to another woman as a Siamese twin. I tried out weird new organs and sex systems. I tried on extra limbs.

"A few years ago I joined a passivity cult. They believed all action was meaningless, and demonstrated it by having their arms and legs amputated and relying on the mercy of random strangers to feed them and keep them alive. I lay for months in the public square beneath Coprates. Sometimes I went hungry and thirsty. Sometimes I stewed in my own filth; then someone would clean me up, usually with a stern lecture to quit this way of life and go straight. I didn't care.

"But the second time a dog used me for a urinal, I gave it up. I asked someone to carry me to a doctor, and walked out a changed woman. I decided I had *done* everything and had better start looking for an elaborate and original suicide. I was so bored, so jaded, that *breathing* seemed like too much of a bother.

"Then I thought of two places I'd never been: the sun and the Rings. The sun is the fancy suicide I told you about. The only way to get to the Rings is in a Symb. I tend to sympathize with you people over the Engineers. So here I am."

She settled back in her chair. She was not optimistic about being allowed to join the Conservationist Church, and was already planning ways to get over to the Engineers. If there was ever an unprepossessing story, it was hers, and she knew it. These Consers were supposed to be dedicated people, and she knew she couldn't present a very convincing line. In point of fact, she didn't give any thought at all to the Grand Design of the Engineers. Why should she care if a band of religious fanatics were trying to paint one of Saturn's Rings?

"The next to the last statement was a lie," the man informed her.

"Right," she spat. "You self-righteous bastards. It's the custom in polite society to inform someone when they're undergoing a lie-detector test. Even ask their consent." She got up to go.

"Please sit down, Parameter." She hesitated, then did so.

"It's time some false impressions were cleared up. First, this is not 'polite society,' this is war. Religious war, which is the dirtiest kind. We do what we have to in the interests of security. The sole purpose of this interview was to determine if your story was true. We don't care what you have done, as long as you haven't been consorting with our enemy. Have you?"

"No."

"That is a true statement. Now for the other mistake. We are not self-righteous bastards. We're pragmatists. And we're not religious fanatics, not really, though we all come to believe deeply in what we're doing out here. And that brings us to the third mistake. The primary reasons we're out here have little to do with defeating the Engineers. We're all out here for our own personal reasons, too."

"And what are they?"

"They're personal. Each of us had a different reason for coming. You are out here to satisfy the last dregs of a jaded appetite; that's a common reason. You have some surprises coming up, but you'll stay. You'll have to. You won't be able to bear leaving. And you'll like it. You might even help us fight the Engineers."

She looked at him with suspicion.

"We don't care why you're out here. Your story doesn't impress me one way or the other. You probably expected condemnation or contempt. Don't flatter yourself. As long as you're not here to help paint Ring Beta red, we don't care."

"Then when do I get a Symb?"

"As soon as you can undergo a bit of surgery." For the first time he unbent a little. The corners of the slit that covered his mouth bent up in a silly attempt at a smile. "I must confess that I *was* interested by one thing you said. *How* do you have sex with an elephant?"

Parameter kept a perfectly straight face.

"You don't have sex *with* an elephant. The best you can do is have sex *at* an elephant."

The Symb was a soft-looking greenish lump in the center of the room. With the best will in the world, Parameter could not see that it resembled anything so much as a pile of green cow manure. It was smaller than she had expected, but that was because it had no occupant. She was about to remedy that.

She stumped over to it and looked down dubiously. She had no choice but to walk awkwardly; her legs were no longer built for walking. They had been surgically altered so that the best she could do was a grotesque bowlegged prancing, stepping high so her long fingers would clear the floor. She was now ideally suited for a weightless existence. In a gravitational field, she was clumsy beyond belief.

The man who had interviewed her, whom she now knew by the name of Bushwhacker, was the only other occupant of the room. He handled himself better than she did, but only slightly. He was itching to get back to the Rings; this base duty galled him. Gravity was for poor flatfoots.

"Just touch it, that's all?" she said. Now that it had come to it, she was having second thoughts.

"That's right. The Symb will do the rest. It won't be easy. You'll have between six weeks and three months of sensory deprivation while the personality develops. You'd go crazy in two days, but you won't be alone. All you'll have to hang on to will be the mind of the Symb. And it'll be a baby, hard to get along with. You'll grow up together."

She took a deep breath, wondering why she was so reluctant. She had done things easily that were much more repulsive than this. Perhaps it was the dawning realization that this would be much more than a simple lark. It could last a long time.

"Here goes." She lifted her leg and touched one of her ped-fingers to the blob. It stuck. The Symb slowly began stirring.

The Symb was . . . warm? No, at first she thought so, but it would be more accurate to say it was no temperature at all. It was thirty-seven degrees: blood temperature. It oozed up her leg, spreading itself thinner as it came. In a short time it was inching up her neck.

"Inhale," Bushwhacker advised. "It'll help a little."

She did so, just as the Symb moved over her chin. It moved over her mouth and nose, then her eyes.

There was a moment of near-panic when part of her brain told her she *must* take a breath, and she dutifully tried to. Nothing happened, and she wanted to scream. But it was all right. She didn't need to breathe. When she opened her mouth the Symb flowed down her throat and trachea. Soon her lungs were filled with the interface tissue whose function it was to put oxygen in her blood and remove carbon dioxide. It filled her nasal passages, slithered up the eustachian tube to her inner ear. At that point she lost her balance and fell to the floor. Or she thought she did; she could no longer be sure. She had felt no impact. A wave of dizziness swept over her; she wondered what a Symb would do about vomiting. But it didn't happen, and she suspected it never would.

It was a shock, even though she had expected it, when the Symb entered her anus and vagina. Not a *bad* shock. Rather a thrill, actually. It filled the spaces in her uterus, wound into the urethra to fill the bladder, then up the ureter to mingle with the kidneys. Meanwhile another tendril had filled the large and small intestine, consuming the nutrients it found there, and joined with the tendril coming from her mouth. When it was done, she was threaded like the eye of a serpentine needle, and was revealed to any that could see as a topological example of a torus.

The silence closed in. It was absolutely quiet for a period of time she was powerless to measure, but couldn't have been longer than five minutes.

The obvious place where the human brain is accessible without violating any solid membranes is alongside the eyeball and through the supraorbital foramen. But the Symb would not be able to get a very substantial tendril through in the tight confines of the eye. So the genetic engineers, elaborating on the basic design for oxygen breathers received over the Ophiuchi Hotline, had given the Symb the capability of forcing an entry through the top of the skull.

Parameter felt a twinge of pain as a two-centimeter hole was eaten in the top of her head. But it subsided as the Symb began to feel out the proper places to make connections. The Symb was still a mindless thing, but was guided infallibly by the carefully designed instinct built into it.

Suddenly she was surrounded by fear; childish, inconsolable fear that frightened her out of her wits but did not come from her mind. She fought it, but it only became more insistent. In the end, she abandoned herself to it and cried like a baby. She became an infant, sloughing off her seventy-odd years there in the impalpable darkness like they had never happened.

There was nothing; nothing but two very lost voices, crying in the void.

There had been a debate raging for centuries as to whether the Symbiotic Space-Environment Organisms were really a form of artificial intelligence. (Or alien intelligence, depending on your definition.) The people who lived in them were unanimously of the opinion that they were. But the other side—who were mostly psychologists—pointed out that the people who actually *lived* in them were in the worst possible place to judge. Whatever one's opinion on the subject, it was based on personal prejudice, because there could be no objective facts.

The Symbs were genetically tailored organisms that could provide a complete, self-contained environment for a single human being in space. They thrived on human waste products: urine, feces, heat and carbon dioxide.

They contained several chlorophyll-like enzymes and could accomplish photosynthesis utilizing the human's body heat, though at a low efficiency. For the rest of the energy needs of the pair, the Symb could use sunlight. They were very good at storing energy in chemical compounds that could be broken down later at need. Together with a human, a Symb made a self-contained heat engine. They were a closed ecology, neither host nor parasite: a symbiosis.

To the human being, the Symb was a green pasture, a running brook, a fruit tree, an ocean to swim in. To the Symb, the human was rich soil, sunshine, gentle rain, fertilizer, a pollinating bee. It was an ideal team. Without the other, each was at the mercy of elaborate mechanical aids to survive. Humans were adapted to an environment that no longer existed for their use in a natural state; wherever humans lived since the occupation of the Earth, they had to make their own environment. Now the Symbs were to provide that environment free of charge.

But it hadn't worked that way.

The Symbs were more complicated than they looked. Humans were used to taking from their surroundings, bending or breaking them until they fit human needs. The Symbs required more of humanity; they made it necessary to give.

When inside a Symb, a human was cut off entirely from the external universe. The human component of the symbiosis had to rely on the Symb's faculties. And the sensory data were received in an unusual way.

The Symb extended a connection directly into the human brain and fed data into it. In the process, it had to get tied up in the brain in such a way that it could be difficult to say where human left off and Symb began. The Symb reorganized certain portions of the human brain, freeing its tremendous potential for computation and integration, and using those abilities to translate the sensory data into pictures, sounds, tastes, smells and touches, going directly through the sensorium. In the process, a mind was generated.

The Symb had no brain of its own, it merely was able to utilize the human brain on a time-sharing basis, and utilize it better than its original owner had been able to. So it would seem impossible that it could have a mind of its own. But every Ringer in the system would swear it had. And that was the crux of the debate: was it actually an independent mind, parasitically using the human brain as its vehicle for sentient thought, or was it merely schizophrenia, induced by isolation and projection?

It was impossible to decide. Without a human inside it, there is nothing more helpless than a Symb. Without the human brain in combination with the genetic information and enzymatically coded procedures, the Symb can do no more than lie there inert like the green turd it so closely resembles. It has only rudimentary musculature, and doesn't even use that when alone. There is no good analogy for a Symb without a human; nothing else is so dependent on anything else.

Once combined with a human, the pair is transformed, becoming much more than the sum of its parts. The human is protected against the harshest environment imaginable. The livable range with a Symb extends from just outside the orbit of Earth (radiation limit) to the orbit of Neptune (sunlight limit). The pair feed each other, water each other and respirate each other. The human brain is converted into a super-computer. The Symb has radio and radar sender and receiver organs, in addition to sensors for radiation and the electromagnetic spectrum from one thousand to sixteen thousand angstroms. The system can gain mass by ingesting rock and ice and the Symb can retain the valuable minerals and water and discard the rest. About all the pair cannot do is change velocity without a chunk of rock to push against. But it is a small matter to carry a rocket thruster instead of the whole apparatus of a space suit. In the Rings, they didn't even do that. The Symb could manufacture enough gas for attitude control. For major velocity changes, the Ringers carried small bottles of compressed gas.

So why weren't all humans in space installed in Symbs?

The reason was that the Symbs needed more than most people were willing to give. It wasn't a simple matter of putting it on when you needed it and taking it off later. When you took off your Symb, the Symb ceased to exist.

It was probably the heaviest obligation a human ever had to face. Once mated with a Symb, you were mated for life. There had never been a closer relationship; the Symb lived *inside your mind,* was with you even when you slept, moving independently through your dreams. Compared with that, Siamese twins were utter strangers who pass in the night.

It was true that all the humans who had ever tried it swore they hadn't even been alive before they joined their Symb. It looked attractive in some ways, but for most people the imagined liabilities outweighed the gains. Few people are able to make a commitment they *know* will be permanent, not when permanent could mean five or six hundred years.

After an initial rush of popularity the Symb craze had died down. Now all the Symbs in the system were in the Rings, where they had made possible a nomadic existence never before known.

Ringers are loners by definition. Humans meet at long intervals, mate if they are of a mind to and go their separate ways. Ringers seldom see the same person twice in a lifetime.

They are loners who are never alone.

"Are you there?"

?????

"I can sense you. We have to do something. I can't stand this darkness, can you? Listen: *let there be light!*"

?????

"Oh, you're hopeless. Why don't you get lost?"

Sorrow. Deep and childish sorrow. Parameter was drawn into it, cursing herself and the infantile thing she was caught with. She tried for the thousandth time to thrash her legs, to let someone out there know she wanted *out.* But she had lost her legs. She could no longer tell if she was moving them.

From the depths of the Symb's sorrow, she drew herself up and tried to stand away from it. It was no use. With a mental sob, she was swallowed up again and was no longer able to distinguish herself from the infant alien.

Her chest was rising and falling. There was an unpleasant smell in her nostrils. She opened her eyes.

She was still in the same room, but now there was a respirator clamped to her face, forcing air in and out of her lungs. She rolled her eyes and saw the grotesque shape of the other person in the room with her. It floated, bandy legs drawn up, hands and peds clasped together.

A hole formed in the front of the blank face.

"Feeling any better?"

She screamed and screamed until she thankfully faded back into her dream world.

"You're getting it. Keep trying. No, that's the wrong direction; whatever you were doing just then, do the opposite."

It was tentative; Parameter hadn't the foggiest idea of what opposite was, because she hadn't the foggiest idea of what the little Symb was doing in the first place. But it was progress. There was light. Faint, wavering, tentative; but *light.*

The undefined luminance flickered like a candle, shimmered, blew out. But she felt good. Not half as good as the Symb felt; she was flooded by a proud feeling of accomplishment that was not her own. But, she reflected, what does it matter if it's my own or not? It was getting to where she no longer cared to haggle about whether it was she who felt something or the Symb. If they both had to experience it, what difference did it make?

"That was *good.* We're getting there. You and me, kid. We'll go places. We'll get out of this mess yet."

Go? Fear. Go? Sorrow. Go? Anger?

The emotions were coming labeled with words now, and they were extending in range.

"Anger? Anger, did you say? What's this? Of course, I want to get out of here, why do you think we're going through this? It ain't easy, kid. I don't remember anything so hard to get a grip on since I tried to control my alpha waves, years ago. Now wait a minute . . ." Fear, fear, fear. "Don't do that, kid, you scare me. Wait, I didn't mean it . . ." Fear, fear, loneliness, fear, FEAR! "Stop! Stop, you're scaring me to death, you're . . ." Parameter was shivering, becoming a child again.

Black, endless fear. Parameter slipped away from her mind; fused with the other mind; chided herself; consoled herself; comforted herself; loved herself.

"Here, take some water, it'll make you feel better."

"Ggggwwway."

"What?"

"Goway. Gway. Goaway. GO. A. WAY!"

"You'll have to drink some water first. I won't go away until you do."
"Go 'way. Murder. Murder'r."

Parameter was at a loss.
"*Why*, why won't you do it? For me. Do it for Parameter."
Negation.
"You mean 'no.' Where do you get those fancy words?"
Your memory. No. Will not do it.
Parameter sighed, but she had acquired patience, infinite patience. And something else, something that was very like love. At least it was a profound admiration for this spunky kid. But she was still scared, because the Symb was beginning to win her over and it was only with increasing desperation that she hung onto her idea of getting the child to open the outside world so she could tell someone she wanted out.

And the desperation only made matters worse. She couldn't conceal it from the Symb, and the act of experiencing communicated it in all its raw, naked panic.

"Listen to me. We've got to get off this merry-go-round. How can we talk something over intelligently if I keep communicating my fear to you, which makes you scared, which scares me, which makes you panicky, which scares me more, which . . . now stop that!"

Not my fault. Love, love. You need me. You are incomplete without me. I need commitment before I'll cooperate.

"But I can't. Can't you see I have to be *me*? I can't be you. And it's you who's incomplete without me, not the way you said."

Wrong. Both incomplete without the other. It's too late for you. You are no longer you. You are me, I am you.

"I won't believe that. We've been here for centuries, for eons. If I haven't accepted you yet, I never will. I want to be free, in time to see the sun burn out."

Wrong. Here for two months. The sun is still burning.

"Aha! Tricked you, didn't I? You can see out, you're further along than you told me. Why did you trick me like that? Why didn't you tell me you knew what time it was? I've been aching to know that. Why didn't you tell me?"

You didn't ask.

"What kind of answer is that?"

An honest one.

Parameter simmered. She knew it was honest. She knew she was belaboring the child, who couldn't tell a lie any more than she could. But she clung to her anger with the sinking feeling that it was all she had left of herself.

You hurt me. You are angry. I've done nothing to you. Why do you hate me? Why? ????? I love you. I'm afraid you'll leave me.

"I . . . I love you. I love you, Godhelpme, I really do. But that's not me. No! It's something else. I don't know what yet, but I'll hang on. Hang on to it. Hang on to it."

Where are you?

Parameter?

"I'm here. Go away."

"Go away."

"You have to eat something. Please, try this. It's good for you. Really it is. Try it."

"Eat!" She turned in the air with sudden cramps of hunger and revulsion. She retched up stale air and thin fluid. "Get away from me. Don't touch me. Equinox! Equinox!"

The figure touched her with its hand. The hand was hard and cold.

"Your breasts," he said. "They've been oozing milk. I was wondering . . ."

"Gone. All gone."

Parameter.

"What is it? Are you ready to try again with that picture?"

No. No need. You can go.

"Huh?"

You can go. I can't keep you. You think you are self-sufficient; maybe you're right. You can go.

Parameter was confused.

"Why? Why so sudden?"

I've been looking into some of the concepts in your memory. Freedom. Self-determination. Independence. You are free to go.

"You know what I think, what I *really* think about those concepts, too. Unproven at best. Fantasies at worst."

You are cynical. I recognize that they may indeed be real, so you should be free. I am detaining you against your will. This is contrary to most ethical codes, including the ones you accept more than any others. You are free to go.

It was an awkward moment. It hurt more than she would have thought possible. And she was unsure of whose hurt she was feeling. Not that it mattered.

What was she saying? Here was what might be her one and only chance, and she was acknowledging what the kid had said all along, that they were already fused. And the kid had heard it, like she heard everything.

Yes, I heard it. It doesn't matter. I can hear your doubts about many things. I can feel your uncertainty. It will be with you always.

"Yes, I guess it will. But you. I can't feel much from you. Not that I can distinguish."

You feel my death.

"No, no. It isn't that bad. They'll give you another human. You'll get along. Sure you will."

Perhaps. Despair. Disbelief.

Parameter kicked herself in the mental butt; told herself that if she didn't get out now, she never would.

"Okay. Let me out."

Fade. A gradual withdrawal that was painful and slow as the tendril began to disengage. And Parameter felt her mind being drawn in two.

It would always be like that. It would never get any better.

"Wait, kid. Wait!"

The withdrawal continued.

"Listen to me. Really! No kidding, I really want to discuss this with you. Don't go."

It's for the best. You'll get along.

"No! No more than you will. I'll die."

No you won't. It's like you said; if you don't get out now, you never will. You'll . . . all right . . . 'by . . .

"No! You don't understand. I don't want to go anymore. I'm afraid. Don't leave me like this. You can't leave me."

Hesitation.

"Listen to me. Listen. Feel me. Love. Love. Commitment, pure and honest commitment-forever-and-ever-till-death-us-do-part. Feel me."

"I feel you. We are one."

She had eaten, only to bring it back up. But her jailer was persistent. He was not going to let her die.

"Would it be any better if you got inside with me?"

"No. I can't. I'm half gone. It would be no good. Where is Equinox?"

"I told you I don't know. And I don't know where your children are. But you won't believe me."

"That's right. I don't believe you. Murderer."

She listened groggily as he explained how she came to be in this room with him. She didn't believe him, not for a minute.

He said he had found her by following a radio beacon signaling from a point outside the plane of the Rings. He had found a pseudosymb there; a simplified Symb created by budding a normal one without first going through the conjugation process. A pseudo can only do what any other plant can do: that is, ingest carbon dioxide and give out oxygen from its inner surface. It cannot contract into contact with a human body. It remains in the spherical configuration. A human can stay alive in a pseudosymb, but will soon die of thirst.

Parameter had been inside the pseudo, bruised and bleeding from the top of her head and from her genitals. But she had been alive. Even more remarkable, she had lived the five days it had taken to get her to the Conser emergency station. The Consers didn't maintain many of the stations. The ones they had were widely separated.

"You were robbed by Engineers," he said. "There's no other explanation. How long have you been in the Rings?"

After the third repeat of the question, Parameter muttered, "Five years."

"I thought so. A new one. That's why you don't believe me. You don't know much about Engineers, do you? You can't understand why they would take your Symb and leave you alive, with a beacon to guide help to you. It doesn't make sense, right?"

"I . . . no, I don't know. I can't understand. They should have killed me. What they did was more cruel."

No emotion could be read on the man's "face," but he was optimistic for the first time that she might pull through. At least she was talking, if fitfully.

"You should have learned more. I've been fighting for a century, and I still don't know all I'd like to know. They robbed you for your children, don't you see? To raise them as Engineers. That's what the real battle is about: population. The side that can produce the most offspring is the one that gains the advantage."

"I don't want to talk."

"I understand. Will you just listen?"

He took her lack of response to mean she would.

"You've just been drifting through your life. It's easy to do out here; we all just drift from time to time. When you think about the Engineers at all, it's just a question of evading them. That isn't too hard. Considering the cubic kilometers out here, the hunted always has the advantage over the hunter. There are so many places to hide; so many ways to dodge."

"But you've drifted into a rough neighborhood. The Engineers have concentrated a lot of people in this sector. Maybe you've noticed the high percentage of red rocks. They hunt in teams, which is not something we Consers have ever done. We're too loose a group to get together much, and we all know our real fight doesn't begin for another thousand years.

"We are the loosest army in the history of humanity. We're volunteers on both sides, and on our side, we don't require that individuals do anything at *all* to combat the Engineers. So you don't know anything about them, beyond the fact that they've vowed to paint Ring Beta red within twenty-five thousand years."

He at last got a rise out of her.

"I know a little more than that. I know they are followers of Ringpainter the Great. I know he lived almost two hundred years ago. I know he founded the Church of Cosmic Engineering."

"You read all that in a book. Do you know that Ringpainter is still alive? Do you know how they plan to paint the Ring? Do you know what they do to Consers they catch?"

He was selective in his interpretations. This time he took her silence to mean she didn't know.

"He is alive. Only he's a she now. Her 'Population Edict' of fifty years ago decreed that each Engineer shall spend 90 percent of her time as a female, and bear three children every year. If they really do that, we haven't got a chance. The Rings would be solid Engineers in a few centuries."

She was slightly interested for the first time in weeks.

"I didn't know it was such a long-term project."

"The longest ever undertaken by humans. At the present rate of coloring, it would take three million years to paint the entire Ring. But the rate is accelerating."

He waited, trying to draw her out again, but she lapsed back into listlessness. He went on.

"The one aspect of their religion you don't seem to know about is their ban on killing. They won't take a human or Symb life."

That got her attention.

"Equinox! Where . . ." she started shaking again.

"She's almost certainly alive."

"How could they keep her alive?"

"You're forgetting your children. Five of them."

The last thing anyone said to Parameter for two years was, "Take this, you might want to use it. Just press it to a red rock and forget about it. It lasts forever."

She took the object, a thin tube with a yellow bulb on each end. It was a Bacteriophage Applicator, filled with the tailored DNA that attacked and broke down the deposits of red dust left by the Engineers' Ringvirus. Touching the end of it to a coated rock would begin a chain reaction that would end only when all the surface of the rock was restored to its original color.

Parameter absently touched it to her side, where it sank without a trace in the tough integument of Equinox's outer hide. Then she shoved out the airlock and into fairyland.

"I never saw anything like this, Equinox," she said.

"No, you certainly haven't." The Symb had only Parameter's experiences to draw on.

"Where should we go? What's that line around the sky? Which way is it to the Ring?"

Affectionate laughter. "Silly plant-eater. We're *in* the Ring. That's why it stretches all around us. All except over in that direction. The sun is behind that part of the Ring, so the particles are illuminated primarily from the other side. You can see it faintly, by reflected light."

"Where did you learn all that?"

"From your head. The facts are there, and the deductive powers. You just never thought about it."

"I'm going to start thinking a lot more. This is almost frightening. I repeat: where do we go from here?"

"Anywhere at all, as long as it's away from this awful place. I don't think I want to come back to the Ringmarket for about a decade."

"Now, now," Parameter chided her. "Surely we'll have to go back before that. Aren't you feeling the least bit poetic?"

The Ringmarket was the clearinghouse for the wildly variant and irresistibly beautiful art that was the by-product of living a solitary life in the Rings. Art brokers, musicmongers, poetry sellers, editors, moodmusic vendors . . . all the people who made a living by standing between the artist and the audience and raking off a profit as works of art passed through their hands; they all gathered at the Ringmarket bazaar and bought exquisite works for the equivalent of pretty-colored beads. The Ringers had no need of money. All exchanges were straight barter: a fresh gas bottle for a symphony that would crash through the mind with unique rhythms and harmonies. A handful of the mineral pellets the Ringers needed every decade to supply trace elements that were rare in the Rings could buy a painting that would bring millions back in civilization. It was a speculative business. No one could know *which* of the thousands of works would catch the public taste at high tide and run away with it. All the buyers knew was that for unknown reasons the art of the Rings had consistently captured the highest prices and the wildest reviews. It was different. It was from a whole new viewpoint.

"I can't feel poetic back there. Besides, didn't you know that when we start to create, it will be music?"

"I didn't know that. How do you know?"

"Because there's a song in my heart. Off-key. Let's get out of here."

They left the metallic sphere of the market and soon it was only a blue vector line, pointed away from them.

They spent two years just getting used to their environment. The wonder never wore off. When they met others, they avoided them. Neither was ready for companionship; they had all they needed.

She was sinking, and glad of it. Every day without Equinox was torture. She had come to hate her jailer, even if his story was true. He was keeping her alive, which was the cruelest thing he could do. But even her hatred was a weak and fitful thing.

She stared into the imaginary distance and seldom noticed his comings and goings.

Then one day there were two of them. She noted it dispassionately, watched as they embraced each other and began to flow. So the other person was a female; they were going to mate. She turned away and didn't see, as the two Symbs merged in their conjugation process and slowly expanded into a featureless green sphere within which the humans would couple silently and then part, probably forever.

But something nagged at her, and she looked back. A bulge was forming on the side of the sphere that was facing her. It grew outward and began to form another, smaller sphere. A pink line formed the boundary between the two globes.

She looked away again, unable to retain an interest as the Symbs gave birth. But something was still nagging.

"Parameter."

The man (or was it the woman?) was floating beside her, holding the baby Symb.

She froze. Her eyes filled with horror.

"You're out of your mind."

"Maybe. I can't force it on you. But it's here. I'm going now, and you'll never see me again. You can live or die, whichever you choose. I've done all I can."


It was a warm day in the Upper Half. But then it was always a warm day, though some were warmer than others.

Ringography is an easy subject to learn. There are the Rings: Alpha, Beta and the thin Gamma. The divisions are called Cassini and Encke, each having been created by the gravitational tug-of-war between Saturn and the larger moons for possession of the particles that make up the Rings. Beyond that, there is only the Upper Half and the Lower Half, above and below the plane, and Inspace and Outspace. The Ringers never visited Inspace because it included the intense Van Allen–type radiation belts that circle Saturn. Outspace was far from the traveled parts of the Rings, but was a nice place to visit because the Rings were all in one part of the sky from that vantage point. An odd experience for children, accustomed from birth to see the sky cut in half by the Rings.

Parameter was in the Upper Half to feed on the sunlight that was so much more powerful there than in the Ring. Equinox was in her extended configuration. The pair looked like a gauzy parabolic dish, two hundred meters across. The dish was transparent, with veins that made it look like a spider web. The illusion was heightened by the small figure spread-eagled in the center of it, like a fly. The fly was Parameter.

It was delicious to float there. She looked directly at the sun, which was bright even this far away and would have burned her eyes quickly if she had been really looking at it. But she saw only a projection. Equinox's visual senses were not nearly as delicate as human eyes.

The front of her body was bathed in radiance. It was highly sensual, but in a new way. It was the mindless joy of a flower unfolding to the sun that Parameter experienced, not the hotter animal passions she was used to. Energy coursed through her body and out into the light-gathering sheets that Equinox had extended. Her mind was disconnected more completely than she would have believed possible. Her thoughts came hours apart, and were concerned with sluggish, vegetable pleasures. She saw herself as naked, exposed to the light and the wind, floating in the center of a silver circle of life. She could feel the wind on her body in this airless place and wondered vacantly how Equinox could be so utterly convincing in the webs of illusion she spun.

There was a sudden gust.

"Parameter. Wake up, my darling."

"Hmmm?"

"There's a storm coming up. We've got to furl the sails and head into port."

Parameter felt other gusts as she swam through the warm waters back to alertness.

"How far are we from the Ring?"

"We're all right. We can be there in ten minutes if I tack for a bit and then use a few seconds of thrust."

In her extended configuration, Equinox was a moderately efficient solar sail. By controlling the angle she presented to the incoming sunlight she could slowly alter velocity. All Parameter had to do was push off above or below the Rings in a shallow arc. Equinox could bring them back into the Rings in a few days, using solar pressure. But the storm was a danger they had always to keep in mind.

It was the solar wind that Equinox felt, a cloud of particles thrust out from the sun by storms beneath the surface. Her radiation sensors had detected the first speed-of-light gusts of it, and the dangerous stuff would not be far behind.

Radiation was the chief danger of life in the Rings. The outer surface of a Symb was proof against much of the radiation the symbiotic pair would encounter in space. What got through was not enough to worry about, certainly never enough to cause sickness. But stray high-energy particles could cause mutations of the egg and sperm cells of the humans.

The intensity of the wind was increasing as they furled their sails and applied the gas thrusters.

"Did we get moving in time?" Parameter asked.

"There's a good margin. But we can't avoid getting a little hard stuff. Don't worry about it."

"What about children? If I want to have some later, couldn't that be a problem?"

"Naturally. But you'll never give birth to a mutation. I'll be able to see any deviations in the first few weeks and abort it and not even have to tell you."

"But you would tell me, wouldn't you?"

"If you want me to. But it isn't important. No more than the daily control I exert over any of your other bodily processes."

"If you say so."

"I say so. Don't worry, I said. You just handle the motor control and leave the busy work to me. Things don't seem quite real to me unless they're on the molecular level."

Parameter trusted Equinox utterly. So much so that when the really hard wind began buffeting them, she didn't worry for a second. She spread her arms to it, embraced it. It was strange that the "wind" didn't blow her around like a leaf. She would have liked that. All she really missed was her hair streaming around her shoulders. She no longer had any hair at all. It got in the way of the seal between the two of them.

As soon as she thought it, long black hair whipped out behind her, curling into her face and tickling her eyes. She could see it and feel it against her skin, but she couldn't touch it. That didn't surprise her, because it wasn't there.

"Thank you," she laughed. And then she laughed even harder as she looked down at herself. She was covered with hair; long, flowing hair that grew as she watched it.

They reentered the Ring, preceded by a twisting, imaginary train of hair a kilometer long.

Three days later she was still staring at the floating ball.

On the fifth day her hand twitched toward it.

"No. No. Equinox. Where are you?"

The Symb was in its dormant state. Only an infant Symb could exist without a human to feed and water it; once it had become attached to a human, it would die very quickly without one. But in dormancy, they could live for weeks at a low energy level. It only needed the touch of her hand to be triggered into action.

The hunger was eating its way through her body; she ignored it completely. It had become a fact of life, something she clutched to her to forget about the *real* hunger that was in her brain. She would never be forced to accept the Symb from hunger. It didn't even enter the question.

On the ninth day her hand began moving. She watched it, crying for Equinox to stop the movement, to give her strength.

She touched it.

"I think it's time we tried out the new uterus."

"I think you're right."

"If that thing out there is a male, we'll do it."

Equinox had in her complex of capabilities the knack of producing a nodule within her body that could take a cloned cell and nurture it until it grew into a complete organ; any organ she wished. She had done that with one of Parameter's cells. She removed it, cloned it and let it grow into a new uterus. Parameter's old one had run out of eggs long ago and was useless for procreation, but the new one was brimming with life.

She had operated on her mate, taking out the old one and putting in the new. It had been painless and quick; Parameter had not even felt it.

Now they were ready to have a seed planted in it.

"Male," came the voice of the other figure. Before, Parameter would have answered by saying, "Solitude," and he would have gone on his way.

Now she said, "Female."

"Wilderness," he introduced himself.

"Parameter."

The mating ritual over, they fell silent as they drifted closer. She had computed it well, if a little fast. They hit and clung together with all their limbs. Slowly the Symbs melted into each other.

A sensation of pleasure came over Parameter.

"What is it?"

"What do you think? It's heaven. Did you think that because we're sexless, we wouldn't get any pleasure out of conjugation?"

"I guess I hadn't thought about it. It's . . . different. Not bad at all. But nothing like an orgasm."

"Stick around. We're just getting started."

There was a moment of insecurity as Equinox withdrew her connections, leaving only the one into her brain. She shuddered as an unfamiliar feeling passed over her, then realized she was holding her breath. She had to start respirating again. Her chest crackled as she brought long-unused muscles into play, but once the reflex was started she was able to forget about it and let her hindbrain handle the chore.

The inner surface started to phosphoresce, and she made out a shadowy figure floating in front of her. The light got brighter until it reached the level of bright moonlight. She could see him now.

"Hello," she said. He seemed surprised she wanted to talk, but grinned at her.

"Hello. You must be new."

"How did you know?"

"It shows. You want to talk. You probably expect me to go through an elaborate ritual." And with that he reached for her and pulled her toward him.

"Hold on there," she said. "I'd like to know you a little better first."

He sighed, but let her go. "I'm sorry. You don't know yet. All right, what would you like to know about me?"

She looked him over. He was small, slightly smaller than her. He was completely hairless, as was she. There didn't seem to be any way to guess his age; all the proper clues were missing. Growing out of the top of his head was a snaky umbilicus.

She discovered there was really little to ask him, but having made a point of it, she threw in a token question.

"How old are you?"

"Old enough. Fourteen."

"All right, let's do it your way." She touched him and shifted in space to accommodate his entry.

To her pleasant surprise, it lasted longer than the thirty seconds she had expected. He was an accomplished lover; he seemed to know all the right moves. She was warming deliciously when she heard him in her head.

*"Now* you know," he said, and her head was filled with laughter.

Everything before that, good as it was, had been just a warm-up.

Parameter and the baby Symb howled with pain.

"I didn't want you," she cried, hurling waves of rejection at the child and at herself. "All I want is Equinox."

That went on for an endless time. The stars burnt out around them. The galaxy turned like a whirligig. The universe contracted; exploded; contracted again. Exploded. Contracted and gave it up as a waste of time. Time ended as all events came to an end.

The two of them floated, howling at each other.

Wilderness drifted away against the swirling background of stars. He didn't look back, and neither did Parameter. They knew each other too well to need good-bys. They might never meet again, but that didn't matter either, because each carried all they needed of the other.

"In a life full of cheap thrills, I never had anything like that."

Equinox seemed absorbed. She quietly acknowledged that it had, indeed, been superduper, but there was something else. There was a new knowledge.

"I'd like to try something," she said.

"Shoot."

Parameter's body was suddenly caressed by a thousand tiny, wet tongues. They searched out every cranny, all at the same time. They were hot, at least a thousand billion degrees, but they didn't burn; they soothed.

"Where were you keeping *that?*" Parameter quavered when it stopped. "And why did you stop?"

"I just learned it. I was watching while I was experiencing. I picked up a few tricks."

"You've got *more?*"

"Sure. I didn't want to start out with the intense ones until I saw how you liked that one. I thought it was very nice. You shuddered beautifully; the delta waves were fascinating."

Parameter broke up with laughter. "Don't give me that clinical stuff. You liked it so much you scared yourself."

"That comes as close as you can come to describing my reaction. But I was serious about having things I think we'll like even better. I can combine sensations in a novel way. Did you appreciate the subtle way the 'heat' blended into the sensation of feathers with an electric current through them?"

"It sounds hideous when you say it in words. But that was what it was, all right. Electric feathers. But pain had nothing to do with it."

Equinox considered it. "I'm not sure about that. I was deep into the pain-sensation center of you. But I was tickling it in a new way, the same way Wilderness tickled you. There is something I'm discovering. It has to do with the reality of pain. *All* you experience is more a function of your brain than of your nerve endings. Pain is no exception. What I do is connect the two centers—pain and pleasure—and route them through other sensorium pathways, resulting in . . ."

"Equinox."

?????

"Make love to me."

She was in the center of the sun, every atom of her body fusing in heat so hot it was icy. She swam to the surface, taking her time through the plasmic waves of ionized gas, where she grew until she could hold the whole sputtering ball in her hand and rub it around her body. It flicked and fumed and smoked, gigantic prominences responding to her will, wreathing her in fire and smoke that bit and tickled. Flares snaked into her, reaming nerves with needle-sharp pins of gas that were soft as a kiss. She was swallowed whole by something pink that had no name, and slid down the slippery innards to splash in a pool of sweet-smelling sulfur.

It melted her; she melted it. Equinox was there; she picked her up and hurled her and herself in a wave of water, a gigantic wave that was gigatons of pent-up energy, rearing itself into a towering breaker a thousand kilometers high. She crashed on a beach of rubbery skin, which became a forest of snakes that squeezed her until the top of her head blew off and tiny flowers showered around her, all of them Equinox.

She was drawn back together from the far corners of the solar system and put into a form that called itself "Parameter" but would answer to anything at all. Then she was rising on a rocket that thrust deep into her vagina, into recesses that weren't even there but felt like mirrors that showed her own face. She was a fusion warhead of sensation; primed to blow. Sparks whipped around her, and each was a kiss of electric feathers. She was reaching orbital velocity; solar escape velocity; the speed of light. She turned herself inside out and contained the universe. The speed of light was a crawl slower than any snail; she transcended it.

There was an explosion; an implosion. She drew away from herself and fell into herself, and the fragments of her body drifted down to the beach, where she and Equinox gathered them and put them in a pile of quivering parts, each smaller than an atom.

It was a long job. They took their time.

"Next time," Parameter suggested, "try to work in some elephants."

Someone had invented a clock. It ticked.

Parameter woke up.

"Did you do that?"

No answer.

"Shut the damn thing off."

The ticking stopped. She rolled over and went back to sleep. Around her, a trillion years passed.

It was no good; she couldn't sleep.

"Are you there?"

Yes.

"What do you think we ought to do?"

Despair. We've lost Equinox.

"You never knew her."

Part of her will always be with you. Enough to hurt you. We will always hurt.

"I want to live again."

Live with hurt?

"If there's no other way. Come on. Let's start. Try to make a light. Come on, you can do it. I can't tell you how; you have to do that yourself. I love you. Blend with me, wash me clean, wipe out the memory."

Impossible. We cannot alter ourselves. I want Equinox.

"Damn you, you never knew her."

Know her as good as you. Better. In a way, I *am* Equinox. But in another way, I can never be.

"Don't talk in riddles. Merge with me."

Cannot. You do not love me yet.

"You want to sleep on it another few thousand years?"

Yes. You are much nicer when you are asleep.

"Is that an insult?"

No. You have loved me in your sleep. You have talked to me, you have taught me, given me love and guidance, grown me up to an adult. But you still think I'm Equinox. I'm not. I am me.

"Who is that?"

No name. I will have a name when you start really talking to me.

"Go to sleep. You confuse me."

Love. Affection. Rockabye, rockabye, rockabye.

"You have a name yet?"

"Yes. My name is Solstice."

Parameter cried, loud and long, and washed herself clean in her own tears.

It took them four years to work their way around to Ringmarket. They traded a song, one that had taken three years to produce, a sweet-sad dirge that somehow rang with hope, orchestrated for three lutes and synthesizer; traded it and a promise of four more over the next century to a tinpanalley cat for an elephant gun. Then they went out on a trail that was four years cold to stalk the memory of those long-ago pachyderm days.

In the way that an earlier generation of humans had known the shape of a hill, the placement of trees and flowers on it, the smell and feel of it; and another generation could remember at a glance what a street corner looked like; or still another the details of a stretch of corridor beneath the surface of the moon; in that same way, Parameter knew rocks. She would know the rock she had pushed off from on that final day just before Equinox was taken from her, the rock she now knew to have been an Engineer way-station. She knew where it had been going on that day, and how fast, and for how long. She knew where it would be now, and that was where she and Solstice were headed. The neighborhood would be different, but she could find that rock.

They found it, in only three years of search. She knew it instantly, knew every crevice and pit on the side she had landed on. The door was on the other side. They picked a likely rock a few kilometers away and settled down for a long wait.

Seventy-six times Saturn turned below them while they used the telescopic sight of the gun to survey the traffic at the station. By the end of that time, they knew the routine of the place better than the residents did. When the time came for action they had worked over each detail until it was almost a reflex.

A figure came out of the rock and started off in the proper direction. Parameter squinted down the barrel of the gun and drew a bead. The range was extreme, but she had no doubt of a hit. The reason for her confidence was the long red imaginary line that she saw growing from the end of the barrel. It represented the distance the bullet would travel in one-thousandth of a second. The figure she was shooting at also had a line extending in front of it, not nearly so long. All she had to do was bring the ends of the two lines together and squeeze the trigger.

It went as planned. The gun was firing stunbullets, tiny harmonic generators that would knock out the pair for six hours. The outer hide of a Symb was proof against the kinetic energy contained in most projectiles, natural or artificial. She didn't dare use a beam stunner because the Engineers in the station would detect it.

They set out in pursuit of the unconscious pair. There was no hurry; the longer it took to rendezvous, the farther they would be from danger.

It took five hours to reach them. Once in contact, Solstice took over. She had assured Parameter that it would be possible to fuse with an unconscious Symb, and she was right. Soon Parameter was floating in the dark cavity with the Engineer, a female. She put the barrel of the gun under the other's chin and waited.

"I don't know if I can do it, Solstice," she said.

"It won't be something you'll ever be proud of, but you know the reasons as well as I. Just keep thinking of Equinox."

"I wonder if that's a good idea? I'd rather do something for her that I *would* be proud of."

"Want to back out? We can still get away. But if she wakes up and sees us, it could get awkward if we let her live."

"I know. I have to do it. I just don't like it."

The Engineer was stirring. Parameter tightened her grip on the rifle.

She opened her eyes, looked around and seemed to be listening. Solstice was keeping the other Symb from calling for help.

"I won't give you any trouble," the woman said. "But is it asking too much to allow me a few minutes for my death ritual?"

"You can have that and more if you're a fast talker. I don't want to kill you, but I confess I think I'll have to. I want to tell you some things, and to do it, I'll need your cooperation. If you don't cooperate, I can take what I need from you anyway. What I'm hoping is that there'll be some way you can show me that will make your death unnecessary. Will you open your mind to me?"

A light came into the woman's eyes, then was veiled. Parameter was instantly suspicious.

"Don't be nervous," the Engineer said, "I'll do as you ask. It was just something of a surprise." She relaxed, and Parameter eased herself into the arms of Solstice, who took over as go-between.

They had a lot staked on the outcome of this mutual revelation.

It came in a rush, the impalpable weight of the religious fervor and dedication. And above it all, the Great Cause, the project that would go on long after everyone now alive was dead. The audacity of it! The vision of humanity the mover, the controller, the artist; the Engineer. The universe would acknowledge the sway of humanity when it gazed at the wonder that was being wrought in the Rings of Saturn.

Ringpainter the Great was a utopian on a grand scale. He had been bitterly disappointed in the manner in which humanity had invaded the solar system. He thought in terms of terraforming and of shifting planets in their courses. What he saw was burrows in rock.

So he preached, and spoke of Dyson spheres and space arks, of turning stars on and off at will, of remodeling galaxies. To him and his followers, the universe was an immensely complex toy that they could do beautiful things with. They wanted to unscrew a black hole and see what made it tick. They wanted to unshift the red shift. They believed in continuous creation, because the big bang implied an end to all their efforts.

Parameter and Solstice reeled under the force of it; the conviction that this admittedly symbolic act could get humanity moving in the direction Ringpainter wanted. He had an idea that there were beings out there keeping score, and they could be impressed by the Grand Gesture. When they saw what a pretty thing Ring Beta had become, they would step in and give the forces of Ringpainter a hand.

The woman they had captured, whose name they learned was Rosy-Red-Ring 3351, was convinced of the truth of these ideas. She had devoted her life to the furtherance of the Design. But they saw her faith waver as she beheld what they had to show her. She cringed away from the shrunken, hardened, protectively encased memory of the days after the theft of Equinox. They held it up and made her look at it, peeling away the layers of forgetfulness they had protected themselves with and thrusting it at her.

At last they let her go. She crouched, quivering, in the air.

"You've seen what we've been."

"Yes." She was sobbing.

"And you know what we have to do to find Equinox. You saw that in my mind. What I want to know is, can this cup pass from us? Do you know another way? Tell me quick."

"I didn't *know*," she cried. "It's what we do to all the Consers we capture. We can't kill them. It's against the Law. So we separate them, keep the Symb, leave the human to be found. We know most of them are never found, but it's the best we can do. But I didn't know it was so bad. I never thought of it. I almost think—"

"No need to think. You're right. It *would* be more merciful to kill the human. I don't know about the Symb. I'll have to talk to Equinox about that. At first I wanted to kill all the Engineers in the Rings, with a lot of care put into the project so they didn't die too quick. I can't do that any more. I'm not a Conser. I never was. I'm not anything but a seeker, looking for my friend. I don't care if you paint the Ring; go ahead. But I have to find Equinox, and I have to find my children. You have to answer my question now. Can you think of a way I can let you live and still do what I have to do?"

"No. There's no other way."

Parameter sighed. "All right. Get on with your ritual."

"I'm not sure if I want to any more."

"You'd probably better. Your faith has been shaken, but you might be right about the scorekeepers. If you are, I'd hate to be the cause of you going out the wrong way." She was already putting her distance between herself and this woman she would kill. She was becoming an object, something she was going to do something unpleasant to; not a person with a right to live.

Rosy-Red-Ring 3351 gradually calmed as she went through the motions of her auto–extreme unction. By the time she had finished she was as composed as she had been at the start of her ordeal.

"I've experienced the fullness of it," she said quietly. "The Engineers do not claim to know everything. We were wrong about our policy of separating symbiotic pairs. My only regret is that I can't tell anyone about our mistake." She looked doubtfully at Parameter, but knew it was useless. "I forgive you. I love you, my killer. Do the deed." She presented her white neck and closed her eyes.

"Umm," Parameter said. She had not heard her victim's last words; she had cut herself off and could see only the neck. She let Solstice guide her hands. They found the pressure points as if by instinct, pressed hard and it was just like Solstice had said it would be. The woman was unconscious in seconds. Now she must be kept alive for a few minutes while Solstice did what she had to do.

"Got it," came Solstice's shaken thought.

"Was it hard?" Parameter had kept away from it.

"Let's don't talk about it. I'll show it to you in about a decade and we can cry for a year. But I have it."

So the other Symb was already dead, and Solstice had been with it as it died. Parameter's job would not be nearly so hard.

She put her thumbs on the woman's neck again, bent her ear to the chest. She pressed, harder this time. Soon the heartbeat fluttered, raced briefly. There was a convulsion, then she was dead.

"Let's get out of here."

What they had acquired was the Symb-Engineer frequency organ. It was the one way the inhabitants of the Rings had of telling friend from foe. The radio organs of the Symbs were tuned from birth to send on a specific frequency, and the Engineers used one band exclusively. The

Consers employed another, because they had a stake in identifying friends and foes, too. But Parameter no longer identified with either side, and now had the physical resources to back up her lack of conviction. She could send on either band now, according to the needs of the moment, and so could move freely from one society to the other. If caught, she would be seen as a spy by either side, but she didn't think of herself as one.

It had been necessary to kill the Engineer pair because the organ could not be removed without causing the death of the Symb. The organ could be cloned, and that was the escape Parameter had offered the other two. But it had been refused. So now Solstice had two voices; her own, and the one from the other organ which she had already implanted in herself.

In addition to the double voice, they had picked up information about the life of the Engineers without which it would be impossible to function without immediate exposure. They knew the customs and beliefs of the Engineers and could fit in with them as long as they didn't go into sexual rapport. That could get sticky, but they had a dodge. The most reliable way to avoid intercourse was to be pregnant, and that was what they set out to do.

It didn't seem too important, but his name was Appoggiatura. They had encountered him during the third week after the murder. It was a risk —a small one, but a risk all the same. He had been easy about it. He learned all about Parameter's deeds and plans during their intercourse and remained unperturbed. Fanatic dedication was rare among Consers; the only real fanatic Parameter had met was Bushwhacker, who had offered to shoot her at the hint of treason. Parameter and Solstice were aware that what they were doing was treason to the Conser cause. Appoggiatura didn't seem to care, or if he did, he thought it was justified after what they had been through.

"But have you thought about what you'll *do* if you find Equinox? I don't know what you think, but it sounds like a thorny problem to me."

"It's thorny, all right," Solstice agreed. "To me, especially. Don't talk to me about problems until you've gone through the insecurity I've felt when I think about that day."

"It's *my* insecurity, too," Parameter said. "We don't know. But we do know we have to find her. And the children, though that isn't so strong. I only saw them for a few minutes, and they'll be seven years old now. I can't expect much there."

"I wouldn't expect much from Equinox, either," he said. "I know something about what happens to a Symb when it's separated from a human. Something dies; I don't know what. But it has to start over again from the beginning. She'll be a part of one of your children now, whichever one of them she took over when she was separated from you. You won't know her, and she won't know you."

"Still, we have to do this. I want to leave you now."

For six months they drifted, allowing Parameter's body to swell to the point that it would be obvious she was pregnant and not available for sex. During that time they thought.

Countless times they decided they were being foolish; that to complete their search would be to finish their life's mission and be faced with what to do with the next thousand years. But they could not just go through the motions. Perhaps one person could do that, but it wouldn't work with two. There was always that alter ego telling you by her very presence that you were living a lie.

And there was Rosy-Red-Ring 3351. If they quit, her murder would have been for no purpose. That would have been too much to bear. They had her in their memory, always cherishing her, always ashamed of what they had done. And the Symb, whose name Solstice had not yet been able to mention. One day Parameter would have to go through that killing again, but closer. Solstice was, if anything, even more determined than Parameter to verify the necessity of that terrible act.

So they started back to the Engineer-infested sector where so long ago Equinox had been made a prisoner of war.

There was a nervous moment the first time they used the stolen transmitter organ, but it went off smoothly. After that, they were able to move freely in Engineer society. It was a strange world, steeped in ritual that would have instantly confounded a novice. But they had received an instant course in religion and fell back on the memories of Rosy-Red-Ring that were burned into their minds.

They took the name Earth-Revenger 9954f, a common name attached to a random number with the "f" added as a mark of status. Only Engineers who had borne a hundred children were supposed to add the letter to their names. Theoretically, births were supposed to be recorded at Ringpainter Temple, clear across the Ring from them, where what records it was possible to keep in Ring society were stored. But there was no danger once they had verified that their stolen transmitter would fool the Engineers. Even in Engineer society, where social contact was more important than among Consers, the chance of meeting the same person twice was small. The chance of Parameter and Solstice meeting the *real* Earth-Revenger 9954f was not even worth thinking about.

The place they stayed around was the very rock she had pushed off from on the day of her capture, the rock from which Rosy-Red-Ring had left on her final day. It was a communications center, a social hall, a gossip rendezvous; the means by which the Engineers were able to keep their cohesiveness against the formidable odds of empty space.

She took over the job of station manager, a largely informal, voluntary post that meant you stayed in the station and loosely coordinated the activities there. These consisted of posting in written form information that was too important to entrust to word of mouth, and generally trying to pump each incoming Engineer for that type of information. As such, it was ideally suited for what she wanted to do.

There was the problem of her pregnancy. Pregnant women needed a lot of sunshine and rock and ice, and generally didn't take the job. She faced a lot of questions about it, but got away with her story about just plain liking the job so much she didn't want to give it up.

But the problem of getting enough sunlight was real. The location of the station was deep enough inside the Rings by now that the incident sunlight was low. She should have gone above the plane to where the light wasn't scattered off so many rocks, but she couldn't.

She compromised by spending all her free time outside the station with Solstice in her extended configuration.

The prime topic of conversation was the failure of the Pop Edict, and it was this that led her to information about Equinox.

Under the edict, each Engineer was to undergo a sex change and spend nine years as a female for every year as a male. Three children were to be borne each of those years. The figures told a different story.

It was the first resistance to an edict; unorganized, but still disturbing. There was much debate about it, and much solemn rededication. Everyone vowed to bear as many children as she could, but Parameter wondered how sincere it was. Her own sampling of Engineers revealed that females did outnumber males, but only by three to one, not nine to one.

There were several causes discussed for it. One, and the most obvious, was simple preference. Statistically, 90 percent of all people had a preferred sex, and of those, it was evenly divided as to which sex was the preferred one. For the target percentages to be in effect, 35 percent of the Engineers would have to be living as the sex they did not prefer. The actual figures indicated that not many of them were doing so. They were remaining defiantly male.

Then there was the logistical problem. To gain enough useful mass to produce one baby, a Symb-human pair had to ingest almost a thousand kilograms of rock and ice. Only a tiny fraction of it was the chemicals needed to produce a baby. Then, to convert the mass to useful form, energy was required. The pair had to spend long hours in the sunlight. After all that, there was little time for painting the Ring, and that was what most Engineers saw as their prime mission, not becoming baby factories.

It was said that Ringpainter was in meditation, and had been for the past ten years, trying to find a way out of the dilemma. She saw her Grand Gesture being slowed down to the point where it was actually in jeopardy. If, in the far future, the Engineer birthrate didn't outstrip the Conser birthrate, it would mean trouble. The time of the great Conser effort was yet to come. As things now stood, a Conser might not even see a painted rock in three or four days; they were too far apart. But as the number of painted rocks grew, the rate of recoloring would also grow. Then the Engineers would have to depend on the sheer rate of repainting to over-power the negative effect of the Consers. If their populations were nearly equal, it would be a stalemate, and only the Consers could win a stalemate. To accomplish the Grand Design, 90 percent of the rock in Ring Beta must be painted. To reach this figure, the Engineers must outnumber the Consers by ten to one, otherwise the number of painted rocks would stabilize below the target figure. It was a crisis of the first magnitude, though no one alive would see the outcome.

In discussing this with one of the Engineers, a woman named Glorious-Red-Ring 43f, the break came. She was one of the early followers of Ringpainter, had been in the Ring for two hundred years. She had birthed three hundred eighty-nine children, and acknowledged it was below her quota. She was living proof that the goals of Ringpainter were unrealistic, but she had unshakable faith that it was the right policy. She blamed herself that she had not had six hundred children, and had dedicated herself to meeting her quota within the next century. To do that, she must bear five hundred children. Parameter thought she was pathetic. She was pregnant with septuplets.

"I see these young ones coming in here with twins in their wombs and wonder how they can call themselves Engineers," she complained. "Only last month I saw one with a single child on the way. One! Can you imagine? How many do you have there?"

"Three. Maybe it should have been more." Parameter tried to sound guilty about it.

"That's all right. Three is the right number. I won't ask if you had three *last* year.

"And the number of males I see makes me weep. I make it 7.43 to 2.57, female to male." She lapsed into a brooding silence.

"If that wasn't bad enough," Parameter prompted, "I understand the Conser birthrate has equaled ours."

"Has it?" She was concerned at this bit of news, and would have been relieved to learn it was totally spurious. Parameter used that line frequently to lead someone into a discussion of Conser women in general and one Conser in particular who had been captured around here several years ago while birthing quints.

"But it shouldn't surprise me," the Engineer said. "So many of the Consers we've taken lately have been pregnant with three, four, even five."

This was more like it. Parameter considered remarks that might draw the woman out.

"I recall, almost ten years ago . . . or was it five? I get confused. There was this Conser some of our people took. Five children she had just borne."

Parameter was so surprised she almost let the opportunity slip by.

"Five?" she managed to croak. It was enough.

"That's right. How long has it been since you saw one of ours give birth to five? And those anarchists don't even have a Pop Edict to tell them to do it. She was doing it for fun."

"Were you there when it happened? When they captured the woman?"

"I heard about it later. They had the pups around here for a few days. Didn't know what to do with them. No one had heard about the crèche."

"Crèche?"

"You, too. The newsmongering around here has fallen down. It should have been posted and circulated."

"I'll surely see that it's done if you'll tell me about it."

"There's a crèche for POW children about fifty thousand kilometers forward from here. That's where we're supposed to take captured Conser children for indoctrination."

They digested that, didn't like the taste of it.

"The indoctrination's pretty successful, is it?"

"Great Red Ring, I hope so. Haven't been there myself. But we need everything we can get these days."

"Just where is this crèche? I should post the orbital elements around here."

The triplets were a failure. During the tenth month, on the way to the crèche, Solstice notified Parameter that it was hopeless; they hadn't gotten enough energy and raw materials during their stay at the way-station. It was no longer possible to hold their development back, and it was too late to amass the necessary minerals to do the job.

Solstice aborted them and reabsorbed the dead bodies. With the extra energy from the abortion, they were able to make good time to the crèche. It only took two years.

The crèche was deserted; an empty shell. News traveled slowly in the Ring. Inquiring around, Parameter discovered that it had not been operating for fifteen years. So her children had never arrived, though they had set out.

This was the time for despair, but they were beyond despair. Somewhere on the way to the crèche they had stopped believing it was possible to do what they were trying to do. So it wasn't a blow to find the crèche deserted. Still, it was hard to accept that their search ended here; they had been on the trail for nine years.

But the figures were unimpeachable. The volume of Ring Beta was seventy billion cubic kilometers, and any one of them could hide a thousand children.

They hung around the crèche for a few weeks, questioning Engineers, trying to find an angle that would enable them to defeat the statistics. Without a known destination for their children, there was no way out; they could be anywhere, and that was so vast it didn't bear thinking about.

In the end they left, and didn't know where they were bound.

Three days later they encountered another Conser, a male, and mated with him. He was sympathetic to their plight, but agreed with them that there was no chance of finding their children. Solstice carefully saw to it that Parameter was not fertilized. They had had enough of pregnancy for the next century or so.

And after they left the Conser, they found themselves falling asleep. Only they knew it wasn't sleep.

Before she even opened her eyes, Parameter reached frantically for the top of her head.

"Solstice . . ."

"I'm here. Don't make any sudden moves. We've been captured. I don't know by whom, but he's armed."

She opened her eyes. She was in a conjugation sphere and the tendril from Solstice was still firmly planted in her head. There was another person with her, a small person. He waved his gun at her and she nodded.

"Don't be alarmed," he said. "If you can answer a few questions you'll probably come out of this alive."

"You can set your mind at ease. I won't cause any trouble."

She realized he was a child, about eleven years old. But he seemed to know about stunners.

"We've been watching you for about a week," he said. "You talked to Engineers, so we naturally assumed you were one. But just now you spoke to a Conser, and on the Conser frequency. I want an explanation."

"I was originally a Conser. Recently I killed an Engineer and stole her transmitter organ." She knew she couldn't think of a convincing lie quickly enough to be safe from his stunner. She wasn't sure there *was* a convincing lie to cover her situation.

"Which side do you identify with now?"

"Neither side. I want to be independent if anyone will allow that."

He looked thoughtful. "That may be easier than you know. Why did you kill the Engineer?"

"I had to do it so I could move in Engineer society, so I could hunt for my children and the Symb who was taken from me several years ago. I have been—"

"What's your name?"

"Parameter, and Solstice."

"Right. I've got a message for you, Parameter. It's from your children. They're all right, and looking for you around here. We should be able to find them in a few days' search."

The children recognized the awkwardness of the situation. As they joined the group conjugation, emerging from the walls of the slowly enlarging sphere, they limited themselves to a brief kiss, then withdrew into a tangle of small bodies.

Parameter and Solstice were so jittery they could hardly think. The five children they could get to know, but Equinox? What about her?

They got the distinct feeling that the children recognized Parameter, then realized it was possible. Equinox had been talking to them while still in the womb, urging their minds to develop with pictures and sounds. Some of the pictures would have been of Parameter.

Ring children are not like other human children. They are born already knowing most of what they need to survive in the Rings. Then they are able to join with an infant Symb and help guide its development into an adult in a few weeks. From there, the Symb takes over for three years, teaching them and leading them to the places they need to go to grow up strong and healthy. For all practical purposes they are mature at three years. They must be; they cannot count on being with their mother more than the few weeks it takes them to acquire an adult Symb. From that time, they are on their own. Infant physical shortcomings are made up by the guidance and control of the Symb.

Parameter looked at these strange children, these youngsters whose backyard was billions of cubic kilometers wide and whose toys were stars and comets. What did she know of them? They might as well be another species. But that shouldn't matter; so was Solstice.

Solstice was almost hysterical. She was gripped in fear that in some way she couldn't understand she was going to lose Parameter. She was in danger of losing her mind. One part of her loved Equinox as hopelessly as Parameter did; another part knew there was room for only one Symb for any one human. What if it came to a choice? How would they face it?

"Equinox?"

There was a soundless scream from Solstice. "Equinox?"

?????

"Is that you, Equinox?"

The answer was very faint, very far away. They could not hear it.

"It's me. Parameter."

"And Solstice. You don't know me—"

I know you. You are me. I used to be you. I remember both of you. Interesting.

But the voice didn't sound interested. It was cool.

"I don't understand." No one was sure who said it.

But you do. I am gone. There is a new me. There is a new you. It is over.

"We love you."

Yes. Of course you do. But there is no me left to love.

"We're confused."

You will get over it.

The children floated together: quietly, respectfully; waiting for their mother to come to grips with her new reality. At last she stirred.

"Maybe we'll understand it some day," Parameter said.

One of the girls spoke.

"Equinox is no more, mother," she said. "And yet she's still with us. She made a choice when she knew we were going to be captured. She reabsorbed her children and fissioned into five parts. None of us got all of her, but we all got enough."

Parameter shook her head and tried to make sense out of it. The child who had brought her here had not been willing to tell her anything, preferring to wait until her children could be with her.

"I don't understand how you came to find me."

"All it took was patience. We never reached the crèche; we were liberated on the way here by Alphans. They killed all the Engineers who were guarding us and adopted us themselves."

"What's an Alphan?"

"Alphans are the Ringers who live in Ring Alpha, who are neither Conser nor Engineer. They are renegades from both sides who have opted out of the conflict. They took care of us, and helped us when we said we wanted to find you. We knew where we had been going, and knew it was only a matter of time until you showed up here, if you were still alive. So we waited. And you got here in only nine years. You're very resourceful."

"Perhaps." She was looking at her children's legs. They were oddly deformed. And what were those blunt instruments at the ends of them? How odd.

"Feet, mother," the child said. "There are surgeons in Alpha, but we could never afford to go there until we had found you. Now we'll go. We hope you'll go with us."

"Huh? Ah, I guess I should. That's across the Cassini Division, isn't it? And there's no war there? No killing?"

"That's right. We don't care if they paint Ring Beta with stripes and polka dots. They're freaks: Conser and Engineer. We are the true Ring-ers."

"Solstice?"

"Why not?"

"We'll go with you. Say, what are your names?"

"Army," said one of the girls.

"Navy," said another.

"Marine."

"Airforce."

"And Elephant," said the boy.

They laughed all the way to Alpha.

# By His Bootstraps

*Time travel is one of the most popular of science fiction's basic themes because it allows the author the freedom to speculate on both the past and the future from the perspective of the present. It can also provide the author and reader with the opportunity to have some intellectual fun playing with the many time-paradoxes involved—for example, if you went back in time and killed your mother before you were born, would you continue to exist?*

*No one in science fiction has ever engaged these issues with as much throughness as Robert A. Heinlein did in this (paradoxically) rarely reprinted story that is widely considered a classic in the field.*

Bob Wilson did not see the circle grow.

Nor, for that matter, did he see the stranger who stepped out of the circle and stood staring at the back of Wilson's neck—stared, and breathed heavily, as if laboring under strong and unusual emotion.

Wilson had no reason to suspect that anyone else was in his room; he had every reason to expect the contrary. He had locked himself in his room for the purpose of completing his thesis in one sustained drive. He *had* to—tomorrow was the last day for submission, yesterday the thesis had been no more than a title: "An Investigation Into Certain Mathematical Aspects of a Rigor of Metaphysics."

Fifty-two cigarettes, four pots of coffee and thirteen hours of continuous work had added seven thousand words to the title. As to the validity of his thesis he was far too groggy to give a damn. Get it done, was his only thought, get it done, turn it in, take three stiff drinks and sleep for a week.

He glanced up and let his eyes rest on his wardrobe door, behind which he had cached a gin bottle, nearly full. No, he admonished himself, one more drink and you'll never finish it, Bob, old son.

The stranger behind him said nothing.

Wilson resumed typing. "—nor is it valid to assume that a conceivable proposition is necessarily a possible proposition, even when it is possible to formulate mathematics which describes the proposition with exactness.

A case in point is the concept 'time travel.' Time travel may be imagined and its necessities may be formulated under any and all theories of time, formulae which resolve the paradoxes of each theory. Nevertheless, we know certain things about the empirical nature of time which preclude the possibility of the conceivable proposition. Duration is an attribute of consciousness and not of the plenum. It has no *Ding an Sich.* There-fore—"

A key of the typewriter stuck, three more jammed up on top of it. Wilson swore dully and reached forward to straighten out the cantanker-ous machinery. "Don't bother with it," he heard a voice say. "It's a lot of utter hogwash anyhow."

Wilson sat up with a jerk, then turned his head slowly around. He fervently hoped that there was someone behind him. Otherwise—

He perceived the stranger with relief. "Thank God," he said to himself. "For a moment I thought I had come unstuck." His relief turned to extreme annoyance. "What the devil are you doing in my room?" he demanded. He shoved back his chair, got up and strode over to the one door. It was still locked, and bolted on the inside.

The windows were no help; they were adjacent to his desk and three stories above a busy street. "How *did* you get in?" he added.

"Through that," answered the stranger, hooking a thumb toward the circle. Wilson noticed it for the first time, blinked his eyes and looked again. There it hung between them and the wall, a great disk of nothing, of the color one sees when the eyes are shut tight.

Wilson shook his head vigorously. The circle remained. "Gosh," he thought, "I was right the first time. I wonder when I slipped my trolley?" He advanced toward the disk, put out a hand to touch it.

"Don't!" snapped the stranger.

"Why not?" said Wilson edgily. Nevertheless he paused.

"I'll explain. But let's have a drink first." He walked directly to the wardrobe, opened it, reached in and took out the bottle of gin without looking.

"Hey!" yelled Wilson. "What are you doing there? That's *my* liquor."

"*Your* liquor—" The stranger paused for a moment. "Sorry. You don't mind if I have a drink, do you?"

"I suppose not," Bob Wilson conceded in a surly tone. "Pour me one while you're about it."

"Okay," agreed the stranger, "then I'll explain."

"It had better be good," Wilson said ominously. Nevertheless he drank his drink and looked the stranger over.

He saw a chap about the same size as himself and much the same age —perhaps a little older, though a three-day growth of beard may have accounted for that impression. The stranger had a black eye and a freshly cut and badly swollen upper lip. Wilson decided he did not like the chaps' face. Still, there was something familiar about the face; he felt that he should have recognized it, that he had seen it many times before under different circumstances.

"Who are you?" he asked suddenly.

"Me?" said his guest. "Don't you recognize me?"

"I'm not sure," admitted Wilson. "Have I ever seen you before?"

"Well—not exactly," the other temporized. "Skip it—you wouldn't know about it."

"What's your name?"

"My name? Uh . . . just call me Joe."

Wilson set down his glass. "Okay, Joe Whatever-your-name-is, trot out that explanation and make it snappy."

"I'll do that," agreed Joe. "That dingus I came through"—he pointed to the circle—"that's a Time Gate."

"A what?"

"A Time Gate. Time flows along side by side on each side of the Gate, but some thousands of years apart—just how many thousands I don't know. But for the next couple of hours that Gate is open. You can walk into the future just by stepping through that circle." The stranger paused.

Bob drummed on the desk. "Go ahead. I'm listening. It's a nice story."

"You don't believe me, do you? I'll show you." Joe got up, went again to the wardrobe and obtained Bob's hat, his prized and only hat, which he had mistreated into its present battered grandeur through six years of undergraduate and graduate life. Joe chucked it toward the impalpable disk.

It struck the surface, went on through with no apparent resistance, disappeared from sight.

Wilson got up, walked carefully around the circle and examined the bare floor. "A neat trick," he conceded. "Now I'll thank you to return to me my hat."

The stranger shook his head. "You can get it for yourself when you pass through."

"Huh?"

"That's right. Listen—" Briefly the stranger repeated his explanation about the Time Gate. Wilson, he insisted, had an opportunity that comes once in a millennium—if he would only hurry up and climb through that circle. Furthermore, though Joe could not explain in detail at the moment, it was very important that Wilson go through.

Bob Wilson helped himself to a second drink, and then a third. He was beginning to feel both good and argumentative. "Why?" he said flatly.

Joe looked exasperated. "Dammit, if you'd just step through once, explanations wouldn't be necessary. However—" According to Joe, there was an old guy on the other side who needed Wilson's help. With Wilson's help the three of them would run the country. The exact nature of the help Joe could not or would not specify. Instead he bore down on the unique possibilities for high adventure. "You don't want to slave your life away teaching numskulls in some freshwater college," he insisted. "This is your chance. Grab it!"

Bob Wilson admitted to himself that a Ph.D. and an appointment as an instructor was not his idea of existence. Still, it beat working for a living. His eye fell on the gin bottle, its level now deplorably lowered. That explained it. He got up unsteadily.

"No, my dear fellow," he stated, "I'm not going to climb on your merry-go-round. You know why?"

"Why?"

"Because I'm drunk, that's why. You're not there at all. *That* ain't there." He gestured widely at the circle. "There ain't anybody here but me, and I'm drunk. Been working too hard," he added apologetically. "I'm goin' to bed."

"You're not drunk."

"I *am* drunk. Peter Piper pepped a pick of pippered peckles." He moved toward his bed.

Joe grabbed his arm. "You can't do that," he said.

"Let him alone!"

They both swung around. Facing them, standing directly in front of the circle was a third man. Bob looked at the newcomer, looked back at Joe, blinked his eyes and tried to focus them. The two looked a good bit alike, he thought, enough alike to be brothers. Or maybe he was seeing double. Bad stuff, gin. Should 'ave switched to rum a long time ago. Good stuff, rum. You could drink it, or take a bath in it. No, that was gin—he meant Joe.

How silly! Joe was the one with the black eye. He wondered why he had ever been confused.

Then who was this other lug? Couldn't a couple of friends have a quiet drink together without people butting in?

"Who are you?" he said with quiet dignity.

The newcomer turned his head, then looked at Joe. *"He* knows me," he said meaningly.

Joe looked him over slowly. "Yes," he said, "yes, I suppose I do. But what the deuce are you here for? And why are you trying to bust up the plan?"

"No time for long-winded explanations. I know more about it than you do—you'll concede that—and my judgment is bound to be better than yours. He doesn't go through the Gate."

"I don't concede anything of the sort—"

The telephone rang.

"Answer it!" snapped the newcomer.

Bob was about to protest the peremptory tone, but decided he wouldn't. He lacked the phlegmatic temperament necessary to ignore a ringing telephone. "Hello?"

"Hello," he was answered. "Is that Bob Wilson?"

"Yes. Who is this?"

"Never mind. I just wanted to be sure you were there. I *thought* you would be. You're right in the groove, kid, right in the groove."

Wilson heard a chuckle, then the click of the disconnection. "Hello," he said. "Hello!" He jiggled the bar a couple of times, then hung up.

"What was it?" asked Joe.

"Nothing. Some nut with a misplaced sense of humor." The telephone bell rang again. Wilson added, "There he is again," and picked up the receiver. "Listen, you butterfly-brained ape! I'm a busy man, and this is *not* a public telephone."

"Why, Bob!" came a hurt feminine voice.

"Huh? Oh, it's you, Genevieve. Look—I'm sorry. I apologize—"

"Well, I should think you would!"

"You don't understand, honey. A guy has been pestering me over the phone and I thought it was him. You know I wouldn't talk that way to you, babe."

"Well, I should think not. Particularly after all you said to me this afternoon, and all we *meant* to each other."

"Huh? This afternoon? Did you say *this* afternoon?"

"Of course. But what I called up about was this: you left your hat in my apartment. I noticed it a few minutes after you had gone and just thought I'd call and tell you where it is. Anyhow," she added coyly, "it gave me an excuse to hear your voice again."

"Sure. Fine," he said mechanically. "Look, babe, I'm a little mixed up about this. Trouble I've had all day long, and more trouble now. I'll look you up tonight and straighten it out. But I *know* I didn't leave your hat in my apartment—"

"*Your* hat, silly!"

"Huh? Oh, sure! Anyhow, I'll see you tonight. 'By." He rang off hurriedly. Gosh, he thought, that woman is getting to be a problem. Hallucinations. He turned to his two companions.

"Very well, Joe. I'm ready to go if you are." He was not sure just when or why he had decided to go through the time gadget, but he had. Who did this other mug think he was, anyhow, trying to interfere with a man's freedom of choice?

"Fine!" said Joe, in a relieved voice. "Just step through. That's all there is to it."

"No, you don't!" It was the ubiquitous stranger. He stepped between Wilson and the Gate.

Bob Wilson faced him. "Listen, you! You come butting in here like you think I was a bum. If you don't like it, go jump in the lake—and I'm just the kind of guy who can do it! You and who else?"

The stranger reached out and tried to collar him. Wilson let go a swing, but not a good one. It went by nothing faster than parcel post. The stranger walked under it and let him have a mouthful of knuckles—large, hard ones. Joe closed in rapidly, coming to Bob's aid. They traded punches in a free-for-all, with Bob joining in enthusiastically but inefficiently. The only punch he landed was on Joe, theoretically his ally. However, he had intended it for the third man.

It was this faux pas which gave the stranger an opportunity to land a clean left jab on Wilson's face. It was inches higher than the button, but in Bob's bemused condition it was sufficient to cause him to cease taking part in the activities.

Bob Wilson came slowly to awareness of his surroundings. He was seated on a floor which seemed a little unsteady. Someone was bending over him. "Are you all right?" the figure inquired.

"I guess so," he answered thickly. His mouth pained him; he put his hand to it, got it sticky with blood. "My head hurts."

"I should think it would. You came through head over heels. I think you hit your head when you landed."

Wilson's thoughts were coming back into confused focus. Came through? He looked more closely at his succorer. He saw a middle-aged man with gray-shot bushy hair and a short, neatly trimmed beard. He was dressed in what Wilson took to be purple lounging pajamas.

But the room in which he found himself bothered him even more. It was circular and the ceiling was arched so subtly that it was difficult to say how high it was. A steady glareless light filled the room from no apparent source. There was no furniture save for a high dais or pulpit-shaped object near the wall facing him. "Came through? Came through what?"

"The Gate, of course." There was something odd about the man's accent. Wilson could not place it, save for a feeling that English was not a tongue he was accustomed to speaking.

Wilson looked over his shoulder in the direction of the other's gaze, and saw the circle.

That made his head ache even more. "Oh, Lord," he thought, "now I really am nuts. Why don't I wake up?" He shook his head to clear it.

That was a mistake. The top of his head did not quite come off—not quite. And the circle stayed where it was, a simple locus hanging in the air, its flat depth filled with the amorphous colors and shapes of no-vision. "Did I come through that?"

"Yes."

"Where am I?"

"In the Hall of the Gate in the High Palace of Norkaal. But what is more important is *when* you are. You have gone forward a little more than thirty thousand years."

"Now I know I'm crazy," thought Wilson. He got up unsteadily and moved toward the Gate.

The older man put a hand on his shoulder. "Where are you going?"

"Back!"

"Not so fast. You will go back all right—I give you my word on that. But let me dress your wounds first. And you should rest. I have some explanations to make to you, and there is an errand you can do for me when you get back—to our mutual advantage. There is a great future in store for you and me, my boy—a great future!"

Wilson paused uncertainly. The elder man's insistence was vaguely disquieting. "I don't like this."

The other eyed him narrowly. "Wouldn't you like a drink before you go?"

Wilson most assuredly would. Right at the moment a stiff drink seemed the most desirable thing on Earth—or in time. "Okay."

"Come with me." The older man led him back of the structure near the wall and through a door which led into a passageway. He walked briskly; Wilson hurried to keep up.

"By the way," he asked, as they continued down the long passage, "what is your name?"

"My name? You may call me Diktor—everyone else does.

"Okay, Diktor. Do you want my name?"

"Your name?" Diktor chuckled. "I know your name. It's Bob Wilson."

"Huh? Oh—I suppose Joe told you."

"Joe? I know no one by that name."

"You don't? He seemed to know you. Say—maybe you aren't that guy I was supposed to see."

"But I am. I have been expecting you—in a way. Joe . . . Joe—Oh!" Diktor chuckled. "It had slipped my mind for a moment. He told you to call him Joe, didn't he?"

"Isn't it his name?"

"It's as good a name as any other. Here we are." He ushered Wilson into a small, but cheerful, room. It contained no furniture of any sort, but the floor was soft and warm as live flesh. "Sit down. I'll be back in a moment."

Bob looked around for something to sit on, then turned to ask Diktor for a chair. But Diktor was gone, furthermore the door through which they had entered was gone. Bob sat down on the comfortable floor and tried not to worry.

Diktor returned promptly. Wilson saw the door dilate to let him in, but did not catch on to how it was done. Diktor was carrying a carafe, which gurgled pleasantly, and a cup. "Mud in your eye," he said heartily and poured a good four fingers. "Drink up."

Bob accepted the cup. "Aren't you drinking?"

"Presently. I want to attend to your wounds first."

"Okay." Wilson tossed off the first drink in almost indecent haste— it was good stuff, a little like Scotch, he decided, but smoother and not as dry—while Diktor worked deftly with salves that smarted at first, then soothed. "Mind if I have another?"

"Help yourself."

Bob drank more slowly the second cup. He did not finish it; it slipped from relaxed fingers, spilling a ruddy, brown stain across the floor. He snored.

Bob Wilson woke up feeling fine and completely rested. He was cheerful without knowing why. He lay relaxed, eyes still closed, for a few moments and let his soul snuggle back into his body. This was going to be a good day, he felt. Oh, yes—he had finished that double-damned thesis. No, he hadn't either! He sat up with a start.

The sight of the strange walls around him brought him back into continuity. But before he had time to worry—at once, in fact—the door relaxed and Diktor stepped in. "Feeling better?"

"Why, yes, I do. Say, what is this?"

"We'll get to that. How about some breakfast?"

In Wilson's scale of evaluations breakfast rated just after life itself and ahead of the chance of immortality. Diktor conducted him to another room—the first that he had seen possessing windows. As a matter of fact half the room was open, a balcony hanging high over a green countryside. A soft, warm, summer breeze wafted through the place. They broke their fast in luxury, Roman style, while Diktor explained.

Bob Wilson did not follow the explanations as closely as he might have done, because his attention was diverted by the maidservants who served the meal. The first came in bearing a great tray of fruit on her head. The fruit was gorgeous. So was the girl. Search as he would he could discern no fault in her.

Her costume lent itself to the search.

She came first to Diktor, and with a single, graceful movement dropped to one knee, removed the tray from her head, and offered it to him. He helped himself to a small, red fruit and waved her away. She then offered it to Bob in the same delightful manner.

"As I was saying," continued Diktor, "it is not certain where the High Ones came from or where they went when they left Earth. I am inclined to think they went away into Time. In any case they ruled more than twenty thousand years and completely obliterated human culture as you knew it. What is more important to you and to me is the effect they had on the human psyche. One twentieth-century style go-getter can accomplish just about anything he wants to accomplish around here—Aren't you listening?"

"Huh? Oh, yes, sure. Say, that's one mighty pretty girl." His eyes still rested on the exit through which she had disappeared.

"Who? Oh, yes, I suppose so. She's not exceptionally beautiful as women go around here."

"That's hard to believe. I could learn to get along with a girl like that."

"You like her? Very well, she is yours."

"Huh?"

"She's a slave. Don't get indignant. They are slaves by nature. If you like her, I'll make you a present of her. It will make her happy." The girl had just returned. Diktor called to her in a language strange to Bob. "Her name is Arma," he said in an aside, then spoke to her briefly.

Arma giggled. She composed her face quickly, and, moving over to where Wilson reclined, dropped on both knees to the floor and lowered her head, with both hands cupped before her. "Touch her forehead," Diktor instructed.

Bob did so. The girl arose and stood waiting placidly by his side. Diktor spoke to her. She looked puzzled, but moved out of the room. "I told her that, notwithstanding her new status, you wished her to continue serving breakfast."

Diktor resumed his explanations while the service of the meal continued. The next course was brought in by Arma and another girl. When Bob saw the second girl he let out a low whistle. He realized he had been a little hasty in letting Diktor give him Arma. Either the standard of pulchritude had gone up incredibly, he decided, or Diktor went to a lot of trouble in selecting his servants.

"—for that reason," Diktor was saying, "it is necessary that you go back through the Time Gate at once. Your first job is to bring this other chap back. Then there is one other task for you to do, and we'll be sitting pretty. After that it is share and share alike for you and me. And there is plenty to share, I—You aren't listening!"

"Sure I was, chief. I heard every word you said." He fingered his chin. "Say, have you got a razor I could borrow? I'd like to shave."

Diktor swore softly in two languages. "Keep your eyes off those wenches and listen to me! There's work to be done."

"Sure, sure. I understand that—and I'm your man. When do we start?" Wilson had made up his mind some time ago—just shortly after Arma had entered with the tray of fruit, in fact. He felt as if he had walked into some extremely pleasant dream. If cooperation with Diktor would cause that dream to continue, so be it. To hell with an academic career!

Anyhow, all Diktor wanted was for him to go back where he started and persuade another guy to go through the Gate. The worst that could happen was for him to find himself back in the twentieth century. What could he lose?

Diktor stood up. "Let's get on with it," he said shortly, "before you get your attention diverted again. Follow me." He set off at a brisk pace with Wilson behind him.

Diktor took him to the Hall of the Gate and stopped. "All you have to do," he said, "is to step through the Gate. You will find yourself back in your own room, in your own time. Persuade the man you find there to go through the Gate. We have need of him. Then come back yourself."

Bob held up a hand and pinched thumb and forefinger together. "It's in the bag, boss. Consider it done." He started to step through the Gate.

"Wait!" commanded Diktor. "You are not used to time travel. I warn you that you are going to get one hell of a shock when you step through. This other chap—you'll recognize him."

"Who is he?"

"I won't tell you because you wouldn't understand. But you will when you see him. Just remember this—There are some very strange paradoxes connected with time travel. Don't let anything you see throw you. You do what I tell you to and you'll be all right."

"Paradoxes don't worry me," Bob said confidently. "Is that all? I'm ready."

"One minute." Diktor stepped behind the raised dais. His head appeared above the side a moment later. "I've set the controls. Okay. Go!"

Bob Wilson stepped through the locus known as the Time Gate.

There was no particular sensation connected with the transition. It was like stepping through a curtained doorway into a darker room. He paused for a moment on the other side and let his eyes adjust to the dimmer light. He was, he saw, indeed in his own room.

There was a man in it, seated at his own desk. Diktor had been right about that. This, then, was the chap he was to send back through the Gate. Diktor had said he would recognize him. Well, let's see who it is.

He felt a passing resentment at finding someone at *his* desk in *his* room, then thought better of it. After all, it was just a rented room; when he disappeared, no doubt it had been rented again. He had no way of telling how long he had been gone—shucks, it might be the middle of next week!

The chap did look vaguely familiar, although all he could see was his back. Who was it? Should he speak to him, cause him to turn around? He felt vaguely reluctant to do so until he knew who it was. He rationalized the feeling by telling himself that it was desirable to know with whom he was dealing before he attempted anything as outlandish as persuading this man to go through the Gate.

The man at the desk continued typing, paused to snuff out a cigarette by laying it in an ash tray, then stamping it with a paper weight.

Bob Wilson knew that gesture.

Chills trickled down his back. "If he lights his next one," he whispered to himself, "the way I think he is going to—"

The man at the desk took out another cigarette, tamped it on one end, turned it and tamped the other, straightened and crimped the paper on one end carefully against his left thumbnail and placed that end in his mouth.

Wilson felt the blood beating in his neck. *Sitting there with his back to him was himself, Bob Wilson!*

He felt that he was going to faint. He closed his eyes and steadied himself on a chair back. "I knew it," he thought, "the whole thing is absurd. I'm crazy. I know I'm crazy. Some sort of split personality. I shouldn't have worked so hard."

The sound of typing continued.

He pulled himself together, and reconsidered the matter. Diktor had warned him that he was due for a shock, a shock that could not be explained ahead of time, because it could not be believed. "All right— suppose I'm not crazy. If time travel can happen at all, there is no reason why I can't come back and see myself doing something I did in the past. If I'm sane, that is what I'm doing.

"And if I am crazy, it doesn't make a damn bit of difference what I do!

"And furthermore," he added to himself, "if I'm crazy, maybe I can stay crazy and go back through the Gate! No, that does not make sense. Neither does anything else—the hell with it!"

He crept forward softly and peered over the shoulder of his double. "Duration is an attribute of the consciousness," he read, "and not of the plenum."

"That tears it," he thought, "right back where I started, and watching myself write my thesis."

The typing continued. "It has no *Ding an Sich*. Therefore—" A key stuck, and others piled up on top of it. His double at the desk swore and reached out a hand to straighten the keys.

"Don't bother with it," Wilson said on sudden impulse. "It's a lot of utter hogwash anyhow."

The other Bob Wilson sat up with a jerk, then looked slowly around. An expression of surprise gave way to annoyance. "What the devil are you doing in my room?" he demanded. Without waiting for an answer he got up, went quickly to the door and examined the lock. "How did you get in?"

"This," thought Wilson, "is going to be difficult."

"Through that," Wilson answered, pointing to the Time Gate. His double looked where he had pointed, did a double take, then advanced cautiously and started to touch it.

"Don't!" yelled Wilson.

The other checked himself. "Why not?" he demanded.

Just why he must not permit his other self to touch the Gate was not clear to Wilson, but he had had an unmistakable feeling of impending disaster when he saw it about to happen. He temporized by saying, "I'll explain. But let's have a drink." A drink was a good idea in any case. There had never been a time when he needed one more than he did right now. Quite automatically he went to his usual cache of liquor in the wardrobe and took out the bottle he expected to find there.

"Hey!" protested the other. "What are you doing there? That's *my* liquor."

"*Your* liquor—" Hell's bells! It was *his* liquor. No, it wasn't; it was— *their* liquor. Oh, the devil! It was much too mixed up to try to explain. "Sorry. You don't mind if I have a drink, do you?"

"I suppose not," his double said grudgingly. "Pour me one while you're about it."

"Okay," Wilson assented, "then I'll explain." It was going to be much, much too difficult to explain until he had had a drink, he felt. As it was, he couldn't explain it fully to himself.

"It had better be good," the other warned him, and looked Wilson over carefully while he drank his drink.

Wilson watched his younger self scrutinizing him with confused and almost insupportable emotions. Couldn't the stupid fool recognize his own face when he saw it in front of him? If he could not *see* what the situation was, how in the world was he ever going to make it clear to him?

It had slipped his mind that his face was barely recognizable in any case, being decidedly battered and unshaven. Even more important, he failed to take into account the fact that a person does not look at his own face, even in mirrors, in the same frame of mind with which he regards another's face. No sane person ever expects to see his own face hanging on another.

Wilson could see that his companion was puzzled by his appearance, but it was equally clear that no recognition took place. "Who are you?" the other man asked suddenly.

"Me?" replied Wilson. "Don't you recognize me?"

"I'm not sure. Have I ever seen you before?"

"Well—not exactly," Wilson stalled. How did you go about telling another guy that the two of you were a trifle closer than twins? "Skip it —you wouldn't know about it."

"What's your name?"

"My name? Uh—" Oh, oh! This was going to be sticky! The whole situation was utterly ridiculous. He opened his mouth, tried to form the words "Bob Wilson," then gave up with a feeling of utter futility. Like many a man before him, he found himself forced into a lie because the truth simply would not be believed. "Just call me Joe," he finished lamely.

He felt suddenly startled at his own words. It was at this point that he realized that he was *in fact,* "Joe," the Joe whom he had encountered once before. That he had landed back in his own room at the very time at which he had ceased working on his thesis he already realized, but he had not had time to think the matter through. Hearing himself refer to himself as Joe slapped him in the face with the realization that this was not simply a similar scene, but the *same* scene he had lived through once before—save that he was living through it from a different viewpoint.

At least he thought it was the same scene. Did it differ in any respect? He could not be sure as he could not recall, word for word, what the conversation had been.

For a complete transcript of the scene that lay dormant in his memory he felt willing to pay twenty-five dollars cash, plus sales tax.

Wait a minute now—he was under no compulsion. He was sure of that. Everything he did and said was the result of his own free will. Even if he couldn't remember the script, there were some things he *knew* "Joe" hadn't said. "Mary had a little lamb," for example. He would recite a nursery rhyme and get off this damned repetitive treadmill. He opened his mouth—

"Okay, Joe Whatever-your-name-is," his alter ego remarked, setting down a glass which had contained, until recently, a quarter pint of gin, "trot out that explanation and make it snappy."

He opened his mouth again to answer the question, then closed it. "Steady, son, steady," he told himself. "You're a free agent. You want to recite a nursery rhyme—go ahead and do it. Don't answer him; go ahead and recite it—and break this vicious circle."

But under the unfriendly, suspicious eye of the man opposite him he found himself totally unable to recall any nursery rhyme. His mental processes stuck on dead center.

He capitulated. "I'll do that. That dingus I came through—that's a Time Gate."

"A what?"

"A Time Gate. Time flows along side by side on each side—" As he talked he felt sweat breaking out on him; he felt reasonably sure that he was explaining in exactly the same words in which explanation had first been offered to *him.* "—into the future just by stepping through that circle." He stopped and wiped his forehead.

"Go ahead," said the other implacably. "I'm listening. It's a nice story."

Bob suddenly wondered if the other man *could* be himself. The stupid arrogant dogmatism of the man's manner infuriated him. All right, all right! He'd show him. He strode suddenly over to the wardrobe, took out his hat and threw it through the Gate.

His opposite number watched the hat snuff out of existence with expressionless eyes, then stood up and went around in back of the Gate, walking with the careful steps of a man who is a little bit drunk, but determined not to show it. "A neat trick," he applauded, after satisfying himself that the hat was gone, "now I'll thank you to return to me my hat."

Wilson shook his head. "You can get it for yourself when you pass through," he answered absent mindedly. He was pondering the problem of how many hats there were on the other side of the Gate.

"Huh?"

"That's right. Listen—" Wilson did his best to explain persuasively what it was he wanted his earlier *persona* to do. Or rather to cajole. Explanations were out of the question, in any honest sense of the word. He would have preferred attempting to explain tensor calculus to an

Australian aborigine, even though he did not understand that esoteric mathematics himself.

The other man was not helpful. He seemed more interested in nursing the gin than he did in following Wilson's implausible protestations.

"Why?" he interrupted pugnaciously.

"Dammit," Wilson answered, "if you'd just step through once, explanations wouldn't be necessary. However—" He continued with a synopsis of Diktor's proposition. He realized with irritation that Diktor had been exceedingly sketchy with *his* explanations. He was forced to hit only the high spots in the logical parts of his argument, and bear down on the emotional appeal. He was on safe ground there—no one knew better than he did himself how fed up the earlier Bob Wilson had been with the petty drudgery and stuffy atmosphere of an academic career. "You don't want to slave your life away teaching numskulls in some freshwater college," he concluded. "This is your chance. Grab it!"

Wilson watched his companion narrowly and thought he detected a favorable response. He definitely seemed interested. But the other set his glass down carefully, stared at the gin bottle and at last replied:

"My dear fellow, I am not going to climb on your merry-go-round. You know why?"

"Why?"

"Because I'm drunk, that's why. You're not there at all. *That* ain't there." He gestured widely at the Gate, nearly fell and recovered himself with effort. "There ain't anybody here but me, and I'm drunk. Been working too hard," he mumbled, "'m goin' to bed."

"You're not drunk," Wilson protested unhopefully. "Damnation," he thought, "a man who can't hold his liquor shouldn't drink."

"I *am* drunk. Peter Piper pepped a pick of pippered peckles." He lumbered over toward the bed.

Wilson grabbed his arm. "You can't do that."

"Let him alone!"

Wilson swung around, saw a third man standing in front of the Gate —recognized him with a sudden shock. His own recollection of the sequence of events was none too clear in his memory, since he had been somewhat intoxicated—damned near boiled, he admitted—the first time he had experienced this particular busy afternoon. He realized that he should have anticipated the arrival of a third party. But his memory had not prepared him for who the third party would turn out to be.

He recognized himself—another carbon copy.

He stood silent for a minute, trying to assimilate this new fact and force it into some reasonable integration. He closed his eyes helplessly. This was just a little too much. He felt that he wanted to have a few plain words with Diktor.

"Who the hell are you?" He opened his eyes to find that his other self, the drunk one, was addressing the latest edition. The newcomer turned away from his interrogator and looked sharply at Wilson.

*"He* knows me."

Wilson took his time about replying. This thing was getting out of hand. "Yes," he admitted, "yes, I suppose I do. But what the deuce are you here for? And why are you trying to bust up the plan?"

His facsimile cut him short. "No time for long-winded explanations. I know more about it than you do—you'll concede that—and my judgment is bound to be better than yours. He doesn't go through the Gate."

The offhand arrogance of the other antagonized Wilson. "I don't concede anything of the sort—" he began.

He was interrupted by the telephone bell. "Answer it!" snapped Number Three.

The tipsy Number One looked belligerent but picked up the handset. "Hello. . . . Yes. Who is this? . . . Hello. . . . Hello!" He tapped the bar of the instrument, then slammed the receiver back into its cradle.

"Who was that?" Wilson asked, somewhat annoyed that he had not had a chance to answer it himself.

"Nothing. Some nut with a misplaced sense of humor." At that instant the telephone rang again. "There he is again!" Wilson tried to answer it, but his alcoholic counterpart beat him to it, brushed him aside. "Listen, you butterfly-brained ape! I'm a busy man and this is *not* a public telephone. . . . Huh? Oh, it's you, Genevieve. Look—I'm sorry. I apologize — . . . You don't understand, honey. A guy has been pestering me over the phone and I thought it was him. You know I wouldn't talk to you that way, babe. . . . Huh? This afternoon? Did you say *this* afternoon? Sure. Fine. Look, babe, I'm a little mixed up about this. Trouble I've had all day long and more trouble now. I'll look you up tonight and straighten it out. But I *know* I didn't leave your hat in my apartment—. . . Huh? Oh, sure! Anyhow, I'll see you tonight. 'By."

It almost nauseated Wilson to hear his earlier self catering to the demands of that clinging female. Why didn't he just hang up on her? The contrast with Arma—there was a dish!—was acute; it made him more determined than ever to go ahead with the plan, despite the warning of the latest arrival.

After hanging up the phone his earlier self faced him, pointedly ignoring the presence of the third copy. "Very well, Joe," he announced. "I'm ready to go if you are."

"Fine!" Wilson agreed with relief. "Just step through. That's all there is to it."

"No, you don't!" Number Three barred the way.

Wilson started to argue, but his erratic comrade was ahead of him. "Listen, you! You come butting in here like you think I was a bum. If you don't like it, go jump in the lake—and I'm just the kind of a guy who can do it! You and who else?"

They started trading punches almost at once. Wilson stepped in warily, looking for an opening that would enable him to put the slug on Number Three with one decisive blow.

He should have watched his drunken ally as well. A wild swing from that quarter glanced off his already damaged features and caused him excruciating pain. His upper lip, cut, puffy and tender from his other encounter, took the blow and became an area of pure agony. He flinched and jumped back.

A sound cut through his fog of pain, a dull *smack!* He forced his eyes to track and saw the feet of a man disappear through the Gate. Number Three was still standing by the Gate. "Now you've done it!" he said bitterly to Wilson, and nursed the knuckles of his left hand.

The obviously unfair allegation reached Wilson at just the wrong moment. His face still felt like an experiment in sadism. "Me?" he said angrily. "*You* knocked him through. I never laid a finger on him."

"Yes, but it's your fault. If you hadn't interfered, I wouldn't have had to do it."

"*Me* interfere? Why, you bald faced hypocrite—*you* butted in and tried to queer the pitch. Which reminds me—you owe me some explanations and I damn well mean to have 'em. What's the idea of—"

But his opposite number cut in on him. "Stow it," he said gloomily. "It's too late now. He's gone through."

"Too late for what?" Wilson wanted to know.

"Too late to put a stop to this chain of events."

"Why should we?"

"Because," Number Three said bitterly, "Diktor has played me—I mean has played *you* . . . *us*—for a dope, for a couple of dopes. Look, he told you that he was going to set you up as a big shot over *there*"—he indicated the Gate—"didn't he?"

"Yes," Wilson admitted.

"Well, that's a lot of malarkey. All he means to do is to get us so incredibly tangled up in this Time Gate thing that we'll never get straightened out again."

Wilson felt a sudden doubt nibbling at his mind. It *could* be true. Certainly there had not been much sense to what had happened so far. After all, why should Diktor want his help, want it bad enough to offer to split with him, even-steven, what was obviously a cushy spot? "How do you know?" he demanded.

"Why go into it?" the other answered wearily. "Why don't you just take my word for it?"

"Why should I?"

His companion turned a look of complete exasperation on him. "If you can't take my word, whose word can you take?"

The inescapable logic of the question simply annoyed Wilson. He resented this interloping duplicate of himself anyhow; to be asked to follow his lead blindly irked him. "I'm from Missouri," he said. "I'll see for myself." He moved toward the Gate.

"Where are you going?"

"Through! I'm going to look up Diktor and have it out with him."

"Don't!" the other said. "Maybe we can break the chain even now." Wilson felt and looked stubborn. The other sighed. "Go ahead," he surrendered. "It's your funeral. I wash my hands of you."

Wilson paused as he was about to step through the Gate. "It is, eh? H-m-m-m—how can it be *my* funeral unless it's *your* funeral, too?"

The other man looked blank, then an expression of apprehension raced over his face. That was the last Wilson saw of him as he stepped through.

The Hall of the Gate was empty of other occupants when Bob Wilson came through on the other side. He looked for his hat, but did not find it, then stepped around back of the raised platform, seeking the exit he remembered. He nearly bumped into Diktor.

"Ah, there you are!" the older man greeted him. "Fine! Fine! Now there is just one more little thing to take care of, then we will be all squared away. I must say I am pleased with you, Bob, very pleased indeed."

"Oh, you are, are you?" Bob faced him truculently. "Well, it's too bad

I can't say the same about you! I'm not a damn bit pleased. What was the idea of shoving me into that . . . that daisy chain without warning me? What's the meaning of all this nonsense? Why didn't you warn me?"

"Easy, easy," said the older man, "don't get excited. Tell the truth now —if I had told you that you were going back to meet yourself face to face, would you have believed me? Come now, 'fess up."

Wilson admitted that he would not have believed it.

"Well, then," Diktor continued with a shrug, "there was no point in me telling you, was there? If I had told you, you would not have believed me, which is another way of saying that you would have believed false data. Is it not better to be in ignorance than to believe falsely?"

"I suppose so, but—"

"Wait! I did not intentionally deceive you. I did not deceive you at all. But had I told you the full truth, you would have been deceived because you would have rejected the truth. It was better for you to learn the truth with your own eyes. Otherwise—"

"Wait a minute! Wait a minute!" Wilson cut in. "You're getting me all tangled up. I'm willing to let bygones be bygones, if you'll come clean with me. Why did you send me back at all?"

" 'Let bygones be bygones,' " Diktor repeated. "Ah, if we only could! But we can't. That's why I sent you back—in order that you might come through the Gate in the first place."

"Huh? Wait a minute—I already *had* come through the Gate."

Diktor shook his head. "Had you, now? Think a moment. When you got back into your own time and your own place you found your earlier self there, didn't you?"

"Mmmm—yes."

"*He*—your earlier self—had not yet been through the Gate, had he?"

"No. I—"

"How could you have *been* through the Gate, unless you persuaded him to *go* through the Gate?"

Bob Wilson's head was beginning to whirl. He was beginning to wonder who did what to whom and who got paid. "But that's impossible! You are telling me that I did something because I was going to do something."

"Well, didn't you? You were there."

"No, I didn't—no . . . well, maybe I did, but it didn't *feel* like it."

"Why should you expect it to? It was something totally new to your experience."

"But . . . but—" Wilson took a deep breath and got control of himself.

Then he reached back into his academic philosophical concepts and produced the notion he had been struggling to express. "It denies all reasonable theories of causation. You would have me believe that causation can be completely circular. I went through because I came back from going through to persuade myself to go through. That's silly."

"Well, didn't you?"

Wilson did not have an answer ready for that one. Diktor continued with, "Don't worry about it. The causation you have been accustomed to is valid enough in its own field but is simply a special case under the general case. *Causation in a plenum need not be and is not limited by a man's perception of duration.*"

Wilson thought about that for a moment. It sounded nice, but there was something slippery about it. "Just a second," he said. "How about entropy? You can't get around entropy."

"Oh, for heaven's sake," protested Diktor, "shut up, will you? You remind me of the mathematician who proved that airplanes couldn't fly." He turned and started out the door. "Come on. There's work to be done."

Wilson hurried after him. "Dammit, you can't do this to me. What happened to the other two?"

"The other two what?"

"The other two of me? Where are they? How am I ever going to get unsnarled?"

"You aren't snarled up. You don't feel like more than one person, do you?"

"No, but—"

"Then don't worry about it."

"But I've got to worry about it. What happened to the guy that came through just ahead of me?"

"You remember, don't you? However—" Diktor hurried on ahead, led him down a passageway, and dilated a door. "Take a look inside," he directed.

Wilson did so. He found himself looking into a small windowless unfurnished room, a room that he recognized. Sprawled on the floor, snoring steadily, was another edition of himself.

"When you first came through the Gate," explained Diktor at his elbow, "I brought you in here, attended to your hurts and gave you a drink. The drink contained a soporific which will cause you to sleep about thirty-six hours, sleep that you badly needed. When you wake up, I will give you breakfast and explain to you what needs to be done."

Wilson's head started to ache again. "Don't do that," he pleaded. "Don't refer to that guy as if he were me. *This* is *me*, standing here."

"Have it your own way," said Diktor. "That is the man you *were*. You remember the things that are about to happen to him, don't you?"

"Yes, but it makes me dizzy. Close the door, please."

"Okay," said Diktor, and complied. "We've got to hurry, anyhow. Once a sequence like this is established there is no time to waste. Come on." He led the way back to the Hall of the Gate.

"I want you to return to the twentieth century and obtain certain things for us, things that can't be obtained on this side but which will be very useful to us in, ah, developing—yes, that is the word—developing this country."

"What sort of things?"

"Quite a number of items. I've prepared a list for you—certain reference books, certain items of commerce. Excuse me, please. I must adjust the controls of the Gate." He mounted the raised platform from the rear. Wilson followed him and found that the structure was boxlike, open at the top and had a raised floor. The Gate could be seen by looking over the high sides.

The controls were unique.

Four colored spheres the size of marbles hung on crystal rods arranged with respect to each other as the four major axes of a tetrahedron. The three spheres which bounded the base of the tetrahedron were red, yellow and blue; the fourth at the apex was white. "Three spatial controls, one time control," explained Diktor. "It's very simple. Using here-and-now as zero reference, displacing any control away from the center moves the other end of the Gate farther from here-and-now. Forward or back, right or left, up or down, past or future—they are all controlled by moving the proper sphere in or out on its rod."

Wilson studied the system. "Yes," he said, "but how do you tell where the other end of the Gate is? Or when? I don't see any graduations."

"You don't need them. You can see where you are. Look." He touched a point under the control framework on the side toward the Gate. A panel rolled back and Wilson saw there was a small image of the Gate itself. Diktor made another adjustment and Wilson found that he could see through the image.

He was gazing into his own room, as if through the wrong end of a telescope. He could make out two figures, but the scale was too small for him to see clearly what they were doing, nor could he tell which editions of himself were there present—if they were in truth himself! He found it quite upsetting. "Shut it off," he said.

Diktor did so and said, "I must not forget to give you your list." He fumbled in his sleeve and produced a slip of paper which he handed to Wilson. "Here—take it."

Wilson accepted it mechanically and stuffed it into his pocket. "See here," he began, "everywhere I go I keep running into myself. I don't like it at all. It's disconcerting. I feel like a whole batch of guinea pigs. I don't half-understand what this is all about and now you want to rush me through the Gate again with a bunch of half-baked excuses. Come clean. Tell me what it's all about."

Diktor showed temper in his face for the first time. "You are a stupid and ignorant young fool. I've told you all that you are able to understand. This is a period in history entirely beyond your comprehension. It would take weeks before you would even begin to understand it. I am offering you half a world in return for a few hours' cooperation and you stand there arguing about it. Stow it, I tell you. Now—where shall we set you down?" He reached for the controls.

"Get away from those controls!" Wilson rapped out. He was getting the glimmering of an idea. "Who are you, anyhow?"

"Me? I'm Diktor."

"That's not what I mean and you know it. How did you learn English?"

Diktor did not answer. His face became expressionless.

"Go on," Wilson persisted. "You didn't learn it here; that's a cinch. You're from the twentieth century, *aren't you?*"

Diktor smiled sourly. "I wondered how long it would take you to figure that out."

Wilson nodded. "Maybe I'm not bright, but I'm not as stupid as you think I am. Come on. Give me the rest of the story."

Diktor shook his head. "It's immaterial. Besides, we're wasting time."

Wilson laughed. "You've tried to hurry me with that excuse once too often. How can we waste time when we have *that?*" He pointed to the controls and to the Gate beyond it. "Unless you lied to me, we can use any slice of time we want to, any time. No, I think I know why you tried to rush me. Either you want to get me out of the picture here, or there is something devilishly dangerous about the job you want me to do. And I know how to settle it—you're going with me!"

"You don't know what you're saying," Diktor answered slowly. "That's impossible. I've got to stay here and manage the controls."

"That's just what you aren't going to do. You could send me through and lose me. I prefer to keep you in sight."

"Out of the question," answered Diktor. "You'll have to trust me." He bent over the controls again.

"Get away from there!" shouted Wilson. "Back out of there before I bop you one." Under Wilson's menacing fist Diktor withdrew from the control pulpit entirely. "There. That's better," he added when both of them were once more on the floor of the hall.

The idea which had been forming in his mind took full shape. The controls, he knew, were still set on his room in the boardinghouse where he lived—or had lived—back in the twentieth century. From what he had seen through the speculum of the controls, the time control was set to take him right back to the day in 1952 from which he had started. "Stand there," he commanded Diktor, "I want to see something."

He walked over to the Gate as if to inspect it. Instead of stopping when he reached it, he stepped on through.

He was better prepared for what he found on the other side than he had been on the two earlier occasions of time translation—"earlier" in the sense of sequence in his memory track. Nevertheless it is never too easy on the nerves to catch up with one's self.

For he had done it again. He was back in his own room, but there were two of himself there before him. They were very much preoccupied with each other; he had a few seconds in which to get them straightened out in his mind. One of them had a beautiful black eye and a badly battered mouth. Beside that he was very much in need of a shave. That tagged him. He had been through the Gate at least once. The other, though somewhat in need of shaving himself, showed no marks of a fist fight.

He had them sorted out now, and knew where and *when* he was. It was all still mostly damnably confusing, but after former—no, not *former*, he amended—*other* experiences with time translation he knew better what to expect. He was back at the beginning again; this time he would put a stop to the crazy nonsense once and for all.

The other two were arguing. One of them swayed drunkenly toward the bed. The other grabbed him by the arm. "You can't do that," he said.

"Let him alone!" snapped Wilson.

The other two swung around and looked him over. Wilson watched the more sober of the pair size him up, saw his expression of amazement change to startled recognition. The other, the earliest Wilson, seemed to have trouble in focusing on him at all. "This going to be a job," thought Wilson. "The man is positively stinking." He wondered why anyone would be foolish enough to drink on an empty stomach. It was not only stupid, it was a waste of good liquor.

He wondered if they had left a drink for him.

"Who are you?" demanded his drunken double.

Wilson turned to "Joe." "He knows me," he said significantly.

"Joe," studied him. "Yes," he conceded, "yes, I suppose I do. But what the deuce are you here for? And why are you trying to bust up the plan?"

Wilson interrupted him. "No time for long-winded explanations, I know more about it than you do—you'll concede that—and my judgment is bound to be better than yours. He doesn't go through the Gate."

"I don't concede anything of the sort—"

The ringing of the telephone checked the argument. Wilson greeted the interruption with relief, for he realized that he had started out on the wrong tack. Was it possible that he was really as dense himself as this lug appeared to be? Did *he* look that way to other people? But the time was too short for self-doubts and soul-searching. "Answer it!" he commanded Bob (Boiled) Wilson.

The drunk looked belligerent, but acceded when he saw that Bob (Joe) Wilson was about to beat him to it. "Hello. . . . Yes. Who is this? . . . Hello. . . . Hello!"

"Who was that?" asked "Joe."

"Nothing. Some nut with a misplaced sense of humor." The telephone rang again. "There he is again." The drunk grabbed the phone before the others could reach it. "Listen, you butterfly-brained ape! I'm a busy man and this is *not* a public telephone. . . . Huh? Oh, it's you, Genevieve—" Wilson paid little attention to the telephone conversation—he had heard it too many times before, and he had too much on his mind. His earliest *persona* was much too drunk to be reasonable, he realized; he must concentrate on some argument that would appeal to "Joe"—otherwise he was outnumbered. "—Huh? Oh, sure!" the call concluded. "Anyhow, I'll see you tonight. 'By."

Now was the time, thought Wilson, before this dumb yap can open his mouth. What would he say? What would sound convincing?

But the boiled edition spoke first. "Very well, Joe," he stated, "I'm ready to go if you are."

"Fine!" said "Joe." "Just step through. That's all there is to it."

This was getting out of hand, not the way he had planned it at all. "No, you don't!" he barked and jumped in front of the Gate. He would have to make them realize, and quickly.

But he got no chance to do so. The drunk cussed him out, then swung on him; his temper snapped. He knew with sudden fierce exultation that he had been wanting to take a punch at someone for some time. Who did they think they were to be taking chances with his future?

The drunk was clumsy; Wilson stepped under his guard and hit him hard in the face. It was a solid enough punch to have convinced a sober man, but his opponent shook his head and came back for more. "Joe" closed in. Wilson decided that he would have to put his original opponent away in a hurry, and give his attention to "Joe"—by far the more dangerous of the two.

A slight mix-up between the two allies gave him his chance. He stepped back, aimed carefully and landed a long jab with his left, one of the hardest blows he had ever struck in his life. It lifted his target right off his feet.

As the blow landed Wilson realized his orientation with respect to the Gate, knew with bitter certainty that he had again played through the scene to its inescapable climax.

He was alone with "Joe;" their companion had disappeared through the Gate.

His first impulse was the illogical but quite human and very common feeling of look-what-you-made-me-do. "Now you've done it!" he said angrily.

"Me?" "Joe" protested. "You knocked him through. I never laid a finger on him."

"Yes," Wilson was forced to admit. "But it's your fault," he added, "if you hadn't interfered, I wouldn't have had to do it."

"*Me* interfere? Why, you bald faced hypocrite, you butted in and tried to queer the pitch. Which reminds me—you owe me some explanations and I damn well mean to have them. What's the idea of—"

"Stow it," Wilson headed him off. He hated to be wrong and he hated still more to have to admit that he was wrong. It had been hopeless from the start, he now realized. He felt bowed down by the utter futility of it. "It's too late now. He's gone through."

"Too late for what?"

"Too late to put a stop to this chain of events." He was aware now that it always had been too late, regardless of what time it was, what year it was or how many times he came back and tried to stop it. He *remembered* having gone through the first time, he had *seen* himself asleep on the other side. Events would have to work out their weary way.

"Why should we?"

It was not worthwhile to explain, but he felt the need for self-justifica-
tion. "Because," he said, "Diktor has played me—I mean has played *you*
. . . us—for a dope, for a couple of dopes. Look, he told you that he was
going to set you up as a big shot over there, didn't he?"

"Yes—"

"Well, that's a lot of malarkey. All he means to do is to get us so
incredibly tangled up in this Gate thing that we'll never get straightened
out again."

"Joe" looked at him sharply. "How do you know?"

Since it was largely hunch, he felt pressed for reasonable explanation.
"Why go into it?" he evaded. "Why don't you just take my word for it?"

"Why should I?"

"Why should you? Why, you lunk, can't you see? I'm yourself, older
and more experienced—you *have* to believe me." Aloud he answered, "If
you can't take my word, whose word can you take?"

"Joe" grunted. "I'm from Missouri," he said. "I'll see for myself."

Wilson was suddenly aware that "Joe" was about to step through the
Gate. "Where are you going?"

"Through! I'm going to look up Diktor and have it out with him."

"Don't!" Wilson pleaded. "Maybe we can break the chain even now."
But the stubborn sulky look on the other's face made him realize how
futile it was. He was still enmeshed in inevitability; it *had* to happen. "Go
ahead," he shrugged. "It's your funeral. I wash my hands of you."

"Joe" paused at the Gate. "It is, eh? H–m-m-m—how can it be *my*
funeral unless it's *your* funeral, too?"

Wilson stared speechlessly while "Joe" stepped through the Gate.
Whose funeral? He had not thought of it in quite that way. He felt a
sudden impulse to rush through the Gate, catch up with his alter ego and
watch over him. The stupid fool might do anything. Suppose he got
himself killed? Where would that leave Bob Wilson? Dead, of course.

Or would it? Could the death of a man thousands of years in the future
kill *him* in the year 1952? He saw the absurdity of the situation suddenly,
and felt very much relieved. "Joe's" actions could not endanger him; he
remembered everything that "Joe" had done—was going to do. "Joe"
would get into an argument with Diktor and, in due course of events,
would come back through the Time Gate. No, *had* come back through
the Time Gate. He was "Joe." It was hard to remember that.

Yes, he was "Joe." As well as the first guy. They would thread their courses, in and out and roundabout and end up here, with *him*. Had to.

Wait a minute—in that case the whole crazy business was straightened out. He had gotten away from Diktor, had all of his various personalities sorted out and was back where he started from, no worse for the wear except for a crop of whiskers and, possibly, a scar on his lip. Well, he knew when to let well enough alone. Shave, and get back to work, kid.

As he shaved he stared at his face and wondered why he had failed to recognize it the first time. He had to admit that he had never looked at it objectively before. He had always taken it for granted.

He acquired a crick in his neck from trying to look at his own profile through the corner of one eye.

On leaving the bathroom the Gate caught his eye forcibly. For some reason he had assumed that it would be gone. It was not. He inspected it, walked around it, carefully refrained from touching it. Wasn't the damned thing ever going to go away? It had served its purpose; why didn't Diktor shut it off?

He stood in front of it, felt a sudden surge of the compulsion that leads men to jump from high places. What would happen if he went through? What would he find? He thought of Arma. And the other one—what was her name? Perhaps Diktor had not told him. The other maidservant, anyhow, the second one.

But he restrained himself and forced himself to sit back down at the desk. If he was going to stay here—and of course he was, he was resolved on that point—he must finish the thesis. He had to eat; he needed the degree to get a decent job. Now where was he?

Twenty minutes later he had come to the conclusion that the thesis would have to be rewritten from one end to the other. His prime theme, the application of the empirical method to the problems of speculative metaphysics and its expression in rigorous formulae, was still valid, he decided, but he had acquired a mass of new and not yet digested data to incorporate in it. In rereading his manuscript he was amazed to find how dogmatic he had been. Time after time he had fallen into the Cartesian fallacy, mistaking clear reasoning for correct reasoning.

He tried to brief a new version of the thesis, but discovered that there were two problems he was forced to deal with which were decidedly not clear in his mind: the problem of the ego and the problem of free will. When there had been three of him in the room, which one was the ego

—was *himself?* And how was it that he had been unable to change the course of events?

An absurdly obvious answer to the first question occurred to him at once. The ego was himself. Self is self, an unproved and unprovable first statement, directly experienced. What, then, of the other two? Surely they had been equally sure of ego-being—he remembered it. He thought of a way to state it: ego is the point of consciousness, the latest term in a continuously expanding series along the line of memory duration. That sounded like a general statement, but he was not sure; he would have to try to formulate it mathematically before he could trust it. Verbal language had such queer booby traps in it.

The telephone rang.

He answered it absent mindedly. "Yes?"

"Is that you, Bob?"

"Yes. Who is this?"

"Why, it's Genevieve, of course, darling. What's come over you today? That's the second time you've failed to recognize my voice."

Annoyance and frustration rose up in him. Here was another problem he had failed to settle—well, he'd settle it now. He ignored her complaint. "Look here, Genevieve, I've told you not to telephone me while I'm working. Good-by!"

"Well, of all the—You can't talk that way to me, Bob Wilson! In the first place, you weren't working today. In the second place, what makes you think you can use honey and sweet words on me and two hours later snarl at me? I'm not any too sure I want to marry you."

"Marry you? What put that silly idea in your head?"

The phone sputtered for several seconds. When it had abated somewhat he resumed with, "Now just calm down. This isn't the Gay Nineties, you know. You can't assume that a fellow who takes you out a few times intends to marry you."

There was a short silence. "So that's the game, is it?" came an answer at last in a voice so cold and hard and completely shrewish that he almost failed to recognize it. "Well, there's a way to handle men like you. A woman isn't unprotected in this state!"

"You ought to know," he answered savagely. "You've hung around the campus enough years."

The receiver clicked in his ear.

He wiped the sweat from his forehead. That dame, he knew, was quite capable of causing him lots of trouble. He had been warned before he ever started running around with her, but he had been so sure of his own ability to take care of himself. He should have known better—but then he had not expected anything quite as raw as this.

He tried to get back to work on his thesis, but found himself unable to concentrate. The deadline of ten A.M. the next morning seemed to be racing toward him. He looked at his watch. It had stopped. He set it by the desk clock—four fifteen in the afternoon. Even if he sat up all night he could not possibly finish it properly.

Besides there was Genevieve—

The telephone rang again. He let it ring. It continued; he took the receiver off the cradle. He would *not* talk to her again.

He thought of Arma. There was a proper girl with the right attitude. He walked over to the window and stared down into the dusty, noisy street. Half-subconsciously he compared it with the green and placid countryside he had seen from the balcony where he and Diktor had breakfasted. This was a crummy world full of crummy people. He wished poignantly that Diktor had been on the up-and-up with him.

An idea broke surface in his brain and plunged around frantically. The Gate was still open. *The Gate was still open!* Why worry about Diktor? He was his own master. Go back and play it out—everything to gain, nothing to lose.

He stepped up to the Gate, then hesitated. Was he wise to do it? After all, how much did he know about the future?

He heard footsteps climbing the stairs, coming down the hall, no—yes, stopping at his door. He was suddenly convinced that it was Genevieve; that decided him. He stepped through.

The Hall of the Gate was empty on his arrival. He hurried around the control box to the door and was just in time to hear, "Come on. There's work to be done." Two figures were retreating down the corridor. He recognized both of them and stopped suddenly.

That was a near thing, he told himself; I'll just have to wait until they get clear. He looked around for a place to conceal himself, but found nothing but the control box. That was useless; they were coming back. Still—

He entered the control box with a plan vaguely forming in his mind. If he found that he could dope out the controls, the Gate might give him all the advantage he needed. First he needed to turn on the speculum gadget. He felt around where he recalled having seen Diktor reach to turn it on, then reached in his pocket for a match.

Instead he pulled out a piece of paper. It was the list that Diktor had given him, the things he was to obtain in the twentieth century. Up to the present moment there had been too much going on for him to look it over.

His eyebrows crawled up his forehead as he read. It was a funny list, he decided. He had subconsciously expected it to call for technical reference books, samples of modern gadgets, weapons. There was nothing of the sort. Still, there was a sort of mad logic to the assortment. After all, Diktor knew these people better than he did. It might be just what was needed.

He revised his plans, subject to being able to work the Gate. He decided to make one more trip back and do the shopping Diktor's list called for —but for his own benefit, not Diktor's. He fumbled in the semi-darkness of the control booth, seeking the switch or control for the speculum. His hand encountered a soft mass. He grasped it, and pulled it out.

It was his hat.

He placed it on his head, guessing idly that Diktor had stowed it there, and reached again. This time he brought forth a small notebook. It looked like a find—very possibly Diktor's own notes on the operation of the controls. He opened it eagerly.

It was not what he had hoped. But it did contain page after page of handwritten notes. There were three columns to the page; the first was in English, the second in international phonetic symbols, the third in a completely strange sort of writing. It took no brilliance for him to identify it as a vocabulary. He slipped it into a pocket with a broad smile; it might have taken Diktor months or even years to work out the relationship between the two languages; he would be able to ride on Diktor's shoulders in the matter.

The third try located the control and the speculum lighted up. He felt again the curious uneasiness he had felt before, for he was gazing again into his own room and again it was inhabited by two figures. He did not want to break into that scene again, he was sure. Cautiously he touched one of the colored beads.

The scene shifted, panned out through the walls of the boardinghouse and came to rest in the air, three stories above the campus. He was pleased to have gotten the Gate out of the house, but three stories was too much of a jump. He fiddled with the other two colored beads and established that one of them caused the scene in the speculum to move toward him or away from him while the other moved it up or down.

He wanted a reasonably inconspicuous place to locate the Gate, some place where it would not attract the attention of the curious. This bothered him a bit; there was no ideal place, but he compromised on a blind alley, a little court formed by the campus powerhouse and the rear wall of the library. Cautiously and clumsily he maneuvered his flying eye to the neighborhood he wanted and set it down carefully between the two buildings. He then readjusted his position so that he stared right into a blank wall. Good enough!

Leaving the controls as they were, he hurried out of the booth and stepped unceremoniously back into his own period.

He bumped his nose against the brick wall. "I cut that a little too fine," he mused as he slid cautiously out from between the confining limits of the wall and the Gate. The Gate hung in the air, about fifteen inches from the wall and roughly parallel to it. But there was room enough, he decided —no need to go back and readjust the controls. He ducked out of the areaway and cut across the campus toward the Students' Co-op, wasting no time. He entered and went to the cashier's window.

"Hi, Bob."

"H'lo, Soupy. Cash a check for me?"

"How much?"

"Twenty dollars."

"Well—I suppose so. Is it a good check?"

"Not very. It's my own."

"Well, I might invest in it as a curiosity." He counted out a ten, a five and five ones.

"Do that," advised Wilson. "My autographs are going to be rare collectors' items." He passed over the check, took the money and proceeded to the bookstore in the same building. Most of the books on the list were for sale there. Ten minutes later he had acquired title to:

*The Prince*, by Niccolò Machiavelli.

*Behind the Ballots*, by James Farley.

*Mein Kampf* (unexpurgated), by Adolf Schicklgruber.

*How to Make Friends and Influence People*, by Dale Carnegie.

The other titles he wanted were not available in the bookstore; he went from there to the university library where he drew out *Real Estate Broker's Manual*, *History of Musical Instruments* and a quarto titled *Evolution of Dress Styles*. The latter was a handsome volume with beautiful colored plates and was classified as reference. He had to argue a little to get a twenty-four hour permission for it.

He was fairly well-loaded down by then; he left the campus, went to a pawnshop and purchased two used, but sturdy, suitcases into one of which he packed the books. From there he went to the largest music store in the town and spent forty-five minutes in selecting and rejecting phonograph records, with emphasis on swing and torch—highly emotional stuff, all of it. He did not neglect classical and semi-classical, but he applied the same rule to those categories—a piece of music had to be sensuous and compelling, rather than cerebral. In consequence his collection included such strangely assorted items as the "Marseillaise," Ravel's "Bolero," four Cole Porters and "L'Après-midi d'un Faune."

He insisted on buying the best mechanical reproducer on the market in the face of the clerk's insistence that what he needed was an electrical one. But he finally got his own way, wrote a check for the order, packed it all in his suitcases and had the clerk get a taxi for him.

He had a bad moment over the check. It was pure rubber, as the one he had cashed at the Students' Co-op had cleaned out his balance. He had urged them to phone the bank, since that was what he wished them not to do. It had worked. He had established, he reflected, the all-time record for kiting checks—thirty thousand years.

When the taxi drew up opposite the court where he had located the Gate, he jumped out and hurried in.

The Gate was gone.

He stood there for several minutes, whistling softly and assessing—unfavorably—his own abilities, mental processes, et cetera. The consequences of writing bad checks no longer seemed quite so hypothetical.

He felt a touch at his sleeve. "See here, Bud, do you want my hack, or don't you? The meter's still clicking."

"Huh? Oh, sure." He followed the driver, climbed back in.

"Where to?"

That was a problem. He glanced at his watch, then realized that the usually reliable instrument had been through a process which rendered its reading irrelevant. "What time is it?"

"Two fifteen." He reset his watch.

Two fifteen. There would be a jamboree going on in his room at that time of a particularly confusing sort. He did not want to go *there*—not yet. Not until his blood brothers got through playing happy fun games with the Gate.

The Gate!

It would be in his room until sometime after four fifteen. If he timed it right—"Drive to the corner of Fourth and McKinley," he directed, naming the intersection closest to his boardinghouse.

He paid off the taxi driver there, and lugged his bags into the filling station at that corner, where he obtained permission from the attendant to leave them and assurance that they would be safe. He had nearly two hours to kill. He was reluctant to go very far from the house for fear some hitch would upset his timing.

It occurred to him that there was one piece of unfinished business in the immediate neighborhood—and time enough to take care of it. He walked briskly to a point two streets away, whistling cheerfully and turned in at an apartment house.

In response to his knock the door of Apartment 211 was opened a crack, then wider. "Bob darling! I thought you were working today."

"Hi, Genevieve. Not at all—I've got time to burn."

She glanced back over her shoulder. "I don't know whether I should let you come in—I wasn't expecting you. I haven't washed the dishes, or made the bed. I was just putting on my make-up."

"Don't be coy." He pushed the door open wide, and went on in.

When he came out he glanced at his watch. Three thirty—plenty of time. He went down the street wearing the expression of the canary that ate the cat.

He thanked the service station salesman and gave him a quarter for his trouble, which left him with a lone dime. He looked at this coin, grinned to himself and inserted it in the pay phone in the office of the station. He dialed his own number.

"Hello," he heard.

"Hello," he replied. "Is that Bob Wilson?"

"Yes. Who is this?"

"Never mind," he chuckled. "I just wanted to be sure you were there. I *thought* you would be. You're right in the groove, kid, right in the groove." He replaced the receiver with a grin.

At four ten he was too nervous to wait any longer. Struggling under the load of the heavy suitcases he made his way to the boardinghouse. He let himself in and heard a telephone ringing upstairs. He glanced at his watch —four fifteen. He waited in the hall for three interminable minutes, then labored up the stairs and down the upper hallway to his own door. He unlocked the door and let himself in.

The room was empty, the Gate still there.

Without stopping for anything, filled with apprehension lest the Gate should flicker and disappear while he crossed the floor, he hurried to it, took a firm grip on his bags and strode through it.

The Hall of the Gate was empty, to his great relief. What a break, he told himself thankfully. Just five minutes, that's all I ask. Five uninterrupted minutes. He set the suitcases down near the Gate to be ready for a quick departure. As he did so he noticed that a large chunk was missing from a corner of one case. Half a book showed through the opening, sheared as neatly as with a printer's trimmer. He identified it as "Mein Kampf."

He did not mind the loss of the book but the implications made him slightly sick at his stomach. Suppose he had not described a clear arc when he had first been knocked through the Gate, had hit the edge, half in and half out? Man Sawed in Half—and no illusion!

He wiped his face and went to the control booth. Following Diktor's simple instructions he brought all four spheres together at the center of the tetrahedron. He glanced over the side of the booth and saw that the Gate had disappeared entirely. "Check!" he thought. "Everything on zero —no Gate." He moved the white sphere slightly. The Gate reappeared. Turning on the speculum he was able to see that the miniature scene showed the inside of the Hall of the Gate itself. So far so good—but he would not be able to tell what time the Gate was set for by looking into the hall. He displaced a space control slightly; the scene flickered past the walls of the palace and hung in the open air. Returning the white time control to zero he then displaced it very, very slightly. In the miniature scene the sun became a streak of brightness across the sky; the days flickered past like light from a low frequency source of illumination. He increased the displacement a little, saw the ground become sear and brown, then snow covered and finally green again.

Working cautiously, steadying his right hand with his left, he made the seasons march past. He had counted ten winters when he became aware of voices somewhere in the distance. He stopped and listened, then very hastily returned the space controls to zero, leaving the time control as it was—set for ten years in the past—and rushed out of the booth.

He hardly had time to grasp his bags, lift them and swing them through the Gate, himself with them. This time he was exceedingly careful not to touch the edge of the circle.

He found himself, as he had planned to, still in the Hall of the Gate, but, if he had interpreted the controls correctly, ten years away from the events he had recently participated in. He had intended to give Diktor a wider berth than that, but there had been no time for it. However, he reflected, since Diktor was, by his own statement and the evidence of the little notebook Wilson had lifted from him, a native of the twentieth century, it was quite possible that ten years was enough. Diktor might not be in this era. If he was, there was always the Time Gate for a getaway. But it was reasonable to scout out the situation first before making any more jumps.

It suddenly occurred to him that Diktor might be looking at him through the speculum of the Time Gate. Without stopping to consider that speed was no protection—since the speculum could be used to view *any* time sector—he hurriedly dragged his two suitcases into the cover of the control booth. Once inside the protecting walls of the booth he calmed down a bit. Spying could work both ways. He found the controls set at zero; making use of the same process he had used once before, he ran the scene in the speculum forward through ten years, then cautiously hunted with the space controls on zero. It was a very difficult task; the time scale necessary to hunt through several months in a few minutes caused any figure which might appear in the speculum to flash past at an apparent speed too fast for his eye to follow. Several times he thought he detected flitting shadows which might be human beings but he was never able to find them when he stopped moving the time control.

He wondered in great exasperation why whoever had built the double-damned gadget had failed to provide it with graduations and some sort of delicate control mechanism—a vernier, or the like. It was not until much later that it occurred to him that the creator of the Time Gate might have no need of such gross aids to his senses. He would have given up, was about to give up, when, purely by accident, one more fruitless scanning happened to terminate with a figure in the field.

It was himself, carrying two suitcases. He saw himself walking directly into the field of view, grow large, disappear. He looked over the rail, half expecting to see himself step out of the Gate.

But nothing came out of the Gate. It puzzled him, until he recalled that it was the setting at *that* end, ten years in the future, which controlled the time of egress. But he had what he wanted; he sat back and watched. Almost immediately Diktor and another edition of himself appeared in the scene. He recalled the situation when he saw it portrayed in the speculum. It was Bob Wilson Number Three, about to quarrel with Diktor and make his escape back to the twentieth century.

That was that—Diktor had not seen him, did not know that he had made unauthorized use of the Gate, did not know that he was hiding ten years in the "past," would not look for him there. He returned the controls to zero, and dismissed the matter.

But other matters needed his attention—food, especially. It seemed obvious, in retrospect, that he should have brought along food to last him for a day or two at least. And maybe a .45. He had to admit that he had not been very foresighted. But he easily forgave himself—it was hard to be foresighted when the future kept slipping up behind one. "All right, Bob, old boy," he told himself aloud, "let's see if the natives are friendly —as advertised."

A cautious reconnoiter of the small part of the palace with which he was acquainted turned up no human beings or life of any sort, not even insect life. The place was dead, sterile, as static and unlived-in as a window display. He shouted once just to hear a voice. The echoes caused him to shiver; he did not do it again.

The architecture of the place confused him. Not only was it strange to his experience—he had expected that—but the place, with minor exceptions, seemed totally unadapted to the uses of human beings. Great halls large enough to hold ten thousand people at once—had there been floors for them to stand on. For there frequently were no floors in the accepted meaning of a level or reasonably level platform. In following a passageway he came suddenly to one of the great mysterious openings in the structure and almost fell in before he realized that his path had terminated. He crawled gingerly forward and looked over the edge. The mouth of the passage debouched high up on a wall of the place; below him the wall was cut back so that there was not even a vertical surface for the eye to follow. Far below him, the wall curved back and met its mate of the opposite side —not decently, in a horizontal plane, but at an acute angle.

There were other openings scattered around the walls, openings as unserviceable to human beings as the one in which he crouched. "The High Ones," he whispered to himself. All his cockiness was gone out of him. He retraced his steps through the fine dust and reached the almost friendly familiarity of the Hall of the Gate.

On his second try he attempted only those passages and compartments which seemed obviously adapted to men. He had already decided what such parts of the palace must be—servants' quarters, or, more probably, slaves' quarters. He regained his courage by sticking to such areas. Though deserted completely, by contrast with the rest of the great structure a room or a passage which seemed to have been built for men was friendly and cheerful. The sourceless ever-present illuminations and the unbroken silence still bothered him, but not to the degree to which he had been upset by the gargantuan and mysteriously convoluted chambers of the "High Ones."

He had almost despaired of finding his way out of the palace and was thinking of retracing his steps when the corridor he was following turned and he found himself in bright sunlight.

He was standing at the top of a broad steep ramp which spread fanlike down to the base of the building. Ahead of him and below him, distant at least five hundred yards, the pavement of the ramp met the green of sod and bush and tree. It was the same placid, lush and familiar scene he had looked out over when he breakfasted with Diktor—a few hours ago and ten years in the future.

He stood quietly for a short time, drinking in the sunshine, soaking up the heart-lifting beauty of the warm, spring day. "This is going to be all right," he exulted. "It's a grand place."

He moved slowly down the ramp, his eyes searching for human beings. He was halfway down when he saw a small figure emerge from the trees into a clearing near the foot of the ramp. He called out to it in joyous excitement. The child—it was a child he saw—looked up, stared at him for a moment, then fled back into the shelter of the trees.

"Impetuous, Robert—that's what you are," he chided himself. "Don't scare 'em. Take it easy." But he was not made downhearted by the incident. Where there were children there would be parents, society, opportunities for a bright, young fellow who took a broad view of things. He moved on down at a leisurely pace.

A man showed up at the point where the child had disappeared. Wilson stood still. The man looked him over and advanced hesitantly a step or two. "Come here!" Wilson invited in a friendly voice. "I won't hurt you."

The man could hardly have understood his words, but he advanced slowly. At the edge of the pavement he stopped, eyed it and would not proceed farther.

Something about the behavior pattern clicked in Wilson's brain, fitted in with what he had seen in the palace and with the little that Diktor had told him. "Unless," he told himself, "the time I spent in 'Anthropology I' was totally wasted, this palace is tabu, the ramp I'm standing on is tabu, and, by contagion, I'm tabu. Play your cards, son, play your cards!"

He advanced to the edge of the pavement, being careful not to step off it. The man dropped to his knees and cupped his hands in front of him, head bowed. Without hesitation Wilson touched him on the forehead. The man got back to his feet, his face radiant.

"This isn't even sporting," Wilson said. "I ought to shoot him on the rise."

His Man Friday cocked his head, looked puzzled and answered in a deep, melodious voice. The words were liquid and strange and sounded like a phrase from a song. "You ought to commercialize that voice," Wilson said admiringly. "Some stars get by on less. However—Get along now, and fetch something to eat. Food." He pointed to his mouth.

The man looked hesitant, spoke again. Bob Wilson reached into his pocket and took out the stolen notebook. He looked up *eat*, then looked up *food*. It was the same word. "Blellan," he said carefully.

"Blellaaaan?"

"Blellaaaaaaaan," agreed Wilson. "You'll have to excuse my accent. Hurry up." He tried to find *hurry* in the vocabulary, but it was not there. Either the language did not contain the idea or Diktor had not thought it worthwhile to record it. But we'll soon fix that, Wilson thought—if there isn't such a word, I'll give 'em one.

The man departed.

Wilson sat himself down Turk-fashion and passed the time by studying the notebook. The speed of his rise in these parts, he decided, was limited only by the time it took him to get into full communication. But he had only time enough to look up a few common substantives when his first acquaintance returned, in company.

The procession was headed by an extremely elderly man, white-haired but beardless. All of the men were beardless. He walked under a canopy carried by four male striplings. Only he of all the crowd wore enough clothes to get by anywhere but on a beach. He was looking uncomfortable in a sort of toga effect which appeared to have started life as a Roman-striped awning. That he was the head man was evident.

Wilson hurriedly looked up the word for *chief*.

The word for chief was *Diktor*.

It should not have surprised him, but it did. It was, of course, a logical probability that the word *Diktor* was a title rather than a proper name. It simply had not occurred to him.

Diktor—*the* Diktor—had added a note under the word. "One of the few words," Wilson read, "which shows some probability of having been derived from the dead languages. This word, a few dozen others and the grammatical structure of the language itself, appear to be the only link between the language of the 'Forsaken Ones' and the English language."

The chief stopped in front of Wilson, just short of the pavement. "Okay, Diktor," Wilson ordered, "kneel down. You're not exempt." He pointed to the ground. The chief knelt down. Wilson touched his forehead.

The food that had been fetched along was plentiful and very palatable. Wilson ate slowly and with dignity, keeping in mind the importance of face. While he ate he was serenaded by the entire assemblage. The singing was excellent he was bound to admit. Their ideas of harmony he found a little strange and the performance, as a whole, seemed primitive, but their voices were all clear and mellow and they sang as if they enjoyed it.

The concert gave Wilson an idea. After he had satisfied his hunger he made the chief understand, with the aid of the indispensable little notebook, that he and his flock were to wait where they were. He then returned to the Hall of the Gate and brought back from there the phonograph and a dozen assorted records. He treated them to a recorded concert of "modern" music.

The reaction exceeded his hopes. "Begin the Beguine" caused tears to stream down the face of the old chief. The first movement of Tschaikowsky's "Concerto Number One in B Flat Minor" practically stampeded them. They jerked. They held their heads and moaned. They shouted their applause. Wilson refrained from giving them the second movement, tapered them off instead with the compelling monotony of the "Bolero."

"Diktor," he said—he was not thinking of the old chief—"Diktor, old chum, you certainly had these people doped out when you sent me shopping. By the time you show up—if you ever do—I'll own the place."

Wilson's rise to power was more in the nature of a triumphal progress than a struggle for supremacy; it contained little that was dramatic. Whatever it was that the High Ones had done to the human race it had left them with only physical resemblance and with temperament largely changed. The docile friendly children with whom Wilson dealt had little in common with the brawling, vulgar, lusty, dynamic swarms who had once called themselves the people of the United States.

The relationship was like that of Jersey cattle to longhorns, or cocker spaniels to wolves. The fight was gone out of them. It was not that they lacked intelligence, or civilized arts; it was the competitive spirit that was gone, the will-to-power.

Wilson had a monopoly on that.

But even he lost interest in playing a game that he always won. Having established himself as boss man by taking up residence in the palace and representing himself as the viceroy of the departed High Ones, he, for a time, busied himself in organizing certain projects intended to bring the culture "up-to-date"—the reinvention of musical instruments, establishment of a systematic system of mail service, redevelopment of the idea of styles in dress and a tabu against wearing the same fashion more than one season. There was cunning in the latter project. He figured that arousing a hearty interest in display in the minds of the womenfolk would force the men to hustle to satisfy their wishes. What the culture lacked was drive—it was slipping downhill. He tried to give them the drive they lacked.

His subjects cooperated with his wishes, but in a bemused fashion, like a dog performing a trick, not because he understands it, but because his master and god desires it.

He soon tired of it.

But the mystery of the High Ones, and especially the mystery of their Time Gate, still remained to occupy his mind. His was a mixed nature, half-hustler, half-philosopher. The philosopher had his inning.

It was intellectually necessary to him that he be able to construct in his mind a physio-mathematical model for the phenomena exhibited by the Time Gate. He achieved one, not a good one perhaps, but one which satisfied all of the requirements. Think of a plane surface, a sheet of paper or, better yet, a silk handkerchief—silk, because it has no rigidity, folds easily, while maintaining all of the relative attributes of a two-dimensional continuum on the surface of the silk itself. Let the threads of the woof be the dimension—or direction—of time; let the threads of the woof represent all three of the space dimensions.

An ink spot on the handkerchief becomes the Time Gate. By folding the handkerchief that spot may be superposed on any other spot on the silk. Press the two spots together between thumb and forefinger; the controls are set, the Time Gate is open, a microscopic inhabitant of this piece of silk may crawl from one fold to the other without traversing any other part of the cloth.

The model is imperfect; the picture is static—but a physical picture is necessarily limited by the sensory experience of the person visualizing it.

He could not make up his mind whether or not the concept of folding the four-dimensional continuum—three of space, one of time—back on itself so that the Gate was "open" required the concept of higher dimensions through which to fold it. It seemed so, yet it might simply be an intellectual shortcoming of the human mind. Nothing but empty space was required for the "folding," but "empty space" was itself a term totally lacking in meaning—he was enough of a mathematician to know that.

If higher dimensions were required to "hold" a four-dimensional continuum, then the number of dimensions of space and of time were necessarily infinite; each order requires the next higher order to maintain it.

But "infinite" was another meaningless term. "Open series" was a little better, but not much.

Another consideration forced him to conclude that there was probably at least one more dimension than the four his senses could perceive—the Time Gate itself. He became quite skilled in handling its controls, but he never acquired the foggiest notion of how it worked, or how it had been built. It seemed to him that the creatures who built it must necessarily have been able to stand outside the limits that confined him in order to anchor the Gate to the structure of space time. The concept escaped him.

He suspected that the controls he saw were simply the ones that stuck through into the space he knew. The very palace itself might be no more than a three-dimensional section of a more involved structure. Such a condition would help to explain the otherwise inexplicable nature of its architecture.

He became possessed of an overpowering desire to know more about these strange creatures, the "High Ones," who had come and ruled the human race and built this palace and this Gate, and gone away again— and in whose backwash he had been flung out of his setting some thirty millennia. To the human race they were no more than a sacred myth, a contradictory mass of tradition. No picture of them remained, no trace of their writing, nothing of their works save the High Palace of Norkaal and the Gate. And a sense of irreparable loss in the hearts of the race they had ruled, a loss expressed by their own term for themselves—the Forsaken Ones.

With controls and speculum he hunted back through time, seeking the Builders. It was slow work, as he had found before. A passing shadow, a tedious retracing—and failure.

Once he was sure that he had seen such a shadow in the speculum. He set the controls back far enough to be sure that he had repassed it, armed himself with food and drink and waited.

He waited three weeks.

The shadow might have passed during the hours he was forced to take out for sleep. But he felt sure that he was in the right period; he kept up the vigil.

He saw it.

It was moving toward the Gate.

When he pulled himself together he was halfway down the passageway leading away from the hall. He realized that he had been screaming. He still had an attack of the shakes.

Somewhat later he forced himself to return to the hall, and, with eyes averted, enter the control booth and return the spheres to zero. He backed out hastily and left the hall for his apartment. He did not touch the controls or enter the hall for more than two years.

It had not been fear of physical menace that had shaken his reason, nor the appearance of the creature—he could recall nothing of *how* it looked. It had been a feeling of sadness infinitely compounded which had flooded through him at the instant, a sense of tragedy, of grief insupportable and unescapable, of infinite weariness. He had been flicked with emotions many times too strong for his spiritual fiber and which he was no more fitted to experience than an oyster is to play a violin.

He felt that he had learned all about the High Ones a man could learn and still endure. He was no longer curious. The shadow of that vicarious emotion ruined his sleep, brought him sweating out of dreams.

One other problem bothered him—the problem of himself and his meanders through time. It still worried him that he had met himself coming back, so to speak, had talked with himself, fought with himself.

Which one was *himself*?

He was all of them, he knew, for he remembered being each one. How about the times when there had been more than one present?

By sheer necessity he was forced to expand the principle of nonidentity —"Nothing is identical with anything else, not even with itself"—to include the ego. In a four-dimensional continuum each event is an absolute individual, it has its space coordinates and its date. The Bob Wilson he was right now was *not* the Bob Wilson he had been ten minutes ago. Each was a discrete section of a four-dimensional process. One resembled the other in many particulars, as one slice of bread resembles the slice next to it. But they were *not* the same Bob Wilson—they differed by a length of time.

When he had doubled back on himself, the difference had become apparent, for the separation was now in space rather than in time, and he happened to be so equipped as to be able to *see* a space length, whereas

he could only remember a time difference. Thinking back he could remember a great many different Bob Wilsons, baby, small child, adoles-
cent, young man. They were all different—he knew that. The only thing
that bound them together into a feeling of identity was continuity of
memory.

And that was the same thing that bound together the three—no, four,
Bob Wilsons on a certain crowded afternoon, a memory track that ran
through all of them. The only thing about it that remained remarkable
was time travel itself.

And a few other little items—the nature of "free will," the problem of
entropy, the law of the conservation of energy and mass. The last two,
he now realized, needed to be extended or generalized to include the cases
in which the Gate, or something like it, permitted a leak of mass, energy
or entropy from one neighborhood in the continuum to another. They
were otherwise unchanged and valid. Free will was another matter. It
could not be laughed off, because it could be directly experienced—yet
his own free will had worked to create the same scene over and over again.
Apparently human will must be considered as one of the factors which
make up the processes in the continuum—"free" to the ego, mechanistic
from the outside.

And yet his last act of evading Diktor had apparently changed the
course of events. He was here and running the country, had been for many
years, but Diktor had not showed up. Could it be that each act of "true"
free will created a new and different future? Many philosophers had
thought so.

This future appeared to have no such person as Diktor—*the* Diktor—
in it, anywhere or anywhen.

As the end of his first ten years in the future approached, he became
more and more nervous, less and less certain of his opinion. Damnation,
he thought, if Diktor is going to show up it was high time that he did
so. He was anxious to come to grips with him, establish which was to be
boss.

He had agents posted throughout the country of the Forsaken Ones
with instructions to arrest any man with hair on his face and fetch him
forthwith to the palace. The Hall of the Gate he watched himself.

He tried fishing the future for Diktor, but had no significant luck. He
thrice located a shadow and tracked it down; each time it was himself.
From tedium and partly from curiosity he attempted to see the other end

of the process; he tried to relocate his original home, thirty thousand years in the past.

It was a long chore. The further the time button was displaced from the center, the poorer the control became. It took patient practice to be able to stop the image within a century or so of the period he wanted. It was in the course of this experimentation that he discovered what he had once looked for, a fractional control—a vernier, in effect. It was as simple as the primary control, but twist the bead instead of moving it directly.

He steadied down on the twentieth century, approximated the year by the models of automobiles, types of architecture and other gross evidence, and stopped in what he believed to be 1952. Careful displacement of the space controls took him to the university town where he had started— after several false tries; the image did not enable him to read road signs.

He located his boardinghouse, brought the Gate into his own room. It was vacant, no furniture in it.

He panned away from the room, and tried again, a year earlier. Success —his own room, his own furniture, but empty. He ran rapidly back, looking for shadows.

There! He checked the swing of the image. There were three figures in the room, the image was too small, the light too poor for him to be sure whether or not one of them was himself. He leaned over and studied the scene.

He heard a dull thump outside the booth. He straightened up and looked over the side.

Sprawled on the floor was a limp human figure. Near it lay a crushed and battered hat.

He stood perfectly still for an uncounted time, staring at the two redundant figures, hat and man, while the winds of unreason swept through his mind and shook it. He did not need to examine the unconscious form to identify it. He knew . . . *he knew*—it was his younger self, knocked willy-nilly through the Time Gate.

It was not that fact in itself which shook him. He had not particularly expected it to happen, having come tentatively to the conclusion that he was living in a different, an alternative, future from the one in which he had originally transitted the Time Gate. He had been aware that it might happen nevertheless, that it did happen did not surprise him.

When it did happen, *he himself had been the only spectator!*

He was Diktor. He was *the* Diktor. He was *the only* Diktor!

He would never find Diktor, or have it out with him. He need never fear his coming. There never had been, never would be, any other person called Diktor, because Diktor never had been or ever would be anyone but himself.

In review, it seemed obvious that he must be Diktor, there were so many bits of evidence pointing to it. And yet it had not been obvious. Each point of similarity between himself and the Diktor, he recalled, had arisen from rational causes—usually from his desire to ape the gross characteristics of the "other" and thereby consolidate his own position of power and authority before the "other" Diktor showed up. For that reason he had established himself in the very apartments that "Diktor" had used—so that they would be "his" first.

To be sure his people called him Diktor, but he had thought nothing of that—they called anyone who ruled by that title, even the little sub-chieftains who were his local administrators.

He had grown a beard, such as Diktor had worn, partly in imitation of the "other" man's precedent, but more to set him apart from the hairless males of the Forsaken Ones. It gave him prestige, increased his tabu. He fingered his bearded chin. Still, it seemed strange that he had not recalled that his own present appearance checked with the appearance of "Diktor." "Diktor" had been an older man. He himself was only thirty-two, ten here, twenty-two *there.*

Diktor he had judged to be about forty-five. Perhaps an unprejudiced witness would believe himself to be that age. His hair and beard were shot with gray—had been, ever since the year he had succeeded too well in spying on the High Ones. His face was lined. Uneasy lies the head and so forth. Running a country, even a peaceful Arcadia, will worry a man, keep him awake nights.

Not that he was complaining—it had been a good life, a grand life, and it beat anything the ancient past had to offer.

In any case, he had been looking for a man in his middle forties, whose face he remembered dimly after ten years and whose picture he did not have. It had never occurred to him to connect that blurred face with his present one. Naturally not.

But there were other little things. Arma, for example. He had selected a likely-looking lass some three years back and made her one of his household staff, renaming her Arma in sentimental memory of the girl he had once fancied. It was logically necessary that they were the same girl, not two Armas, but one.

But, as he recalled her, the "first" Arma had been much prettier.

H–m–m–m—it must be his own point of view that had changed. He admitted that he had had much more opportunity to become bored with exquisite female beauty than his young friend over there on the floor. He recalled with a chuckle how he had found it necessary to surround himself with an elaborate system of tabus to keep the nubile daughters of his subjects out of his hair—most of the time. He had caused a particular pool in the river adjacent to the palace to be dedicated to his use in order that he might swim without getting tangled up in mermaids.

The man on the floor groaned, but did not open his eyes.

Wilson, the Diktor, bent over him but made no effort to revive him. That the man was not seriously injured he had reason to be certain. He did not wish him to wake up until he had had time to get his own thoughts entirely in order.

For he had work to do, work which must be done meticulously, without mistake. Everyone, he thought with a wry smile, makes plans to provide for their future.

He was about to provide for his past.

There was the matter of the setting of the Time Gate when he got around to sending his early self back. When he had tuned in on the scene in his room a few minutes ago, he had picked up the action just before his early self had been knocked through. In sending him back he must make a slight readjustment in the time setting to an instant around two o'clock of that particular afternoon. That would be simple enough; he need only search a short sector until he found his early self alone and working at his desk.

But the Time Gate had appeared in that room at a later hour; he had just caused it to do so. He felt confused.

Wait a minute, now—if he changed the setting of the time control, the Gate would appear in his room at the earlier time, remain there and simply blend into its "reappearance" an hour or so later. Yes, that was right. To a person in the room it would simply be as if the Time Gate had been there all along, from about two o'clock.

Which it had been. He would see to that.

Experienced as he was with the phenomena exhibited by the Time Gate, it nevertheless required a strong and subtle intellectual effort to think other than in durational terms, to take an *eternal* viewpoint.

And there was the hat. He picked it up and tried it on. It did not fit very well, no doubt because he was wearing his hair longer now. The hat must be placed where it would be found—Oh, yes, in the control booth. And the notebook, too.

The notebook, the notebook—Mm-m-m—Something funny, there. When the notebook he had stolen had become dog-eared and tattered almost to illegibility some four years back, he had carefully recopied its contents in a new notebook—to refresh his memory of English rather than from any need for it as a guide. The worn-out notebook he had destroyed; it was the new one he intended to obtain, and leave to be found.

In that case, *there never had been two notebooks.* The one he had now would become, after being taken through the Gate to a point ten years in the past, the notebook from which he had copied it. They were simply different segments of the same physical process, manipulated by means of the Gate to run concurrently, side by side, for a certain length of time.

As he had himself—one afternoon.

He wished that he had not thrown away the worn-out notebook. If he had it at hand, he could compare them and convince himself that they were identical save for the wear and tear of increasing entropy.

But when had he learned the language, in order that he might prepare such a vocabulary? To be sure, when he copied it he then *knew* the language—copying had not actually been necessary.

But he *had* copied it.

The physical process he had all straightened out in his mind, but the intellectual process it represented was completely circular. His older self had taught his younger self a language which the older self knew because the younger self, after being taught, grew up to be the older self and was, therefore, capable of teaching.

But where had it started?

Which comes first, the hen or the egg?

You feed the rats to the cats, skin the cats, and feed the carcasses of the cats to the rats who are in turn fed to the cats. The perpetual motion fur farm.

If God created the world, who created God?

Who wrote the notebook? Who started the chain?

He felt the intellectual desperation of any honest philosopher. He knew that he had about as much chance of understanding such problems as a collie has of understanding how dog food gets into cans. Applied psychology was more his size—which reminded him that there were certain books which his early self would find very useful in learning how to deal with the political affairs of the country he was to run. He made a mental note to make a list.

The man on the floor stirred again, sat up. Wilson knew that the time had come when he must insure his past. He was not worried; he felt the sure confidence of the gambler who is "hot," who *knows* what the next roll of the dice will show.

He bent over his alter ego. "Are you all right?" he asked.

"I guess so," the younger man mumbled. He put his hand to his bloody face. "My head hurts."

"I should think it would," Wilson agreed. "You came through head over heels. I think you hit your head when you landed."

His younger self did not appear fully to comprehend the words at first. He looked around dazedly, as if to get his bearings. Presently he said, "Came through? Came through what?"

"The Gate, of course," Wilson told him. He nodded his head toward the Gate, feeling that the sight of it would orient the still groggy younger Bob.

Young Wilson looked over his shoulder in the direction indicated, sat up with a jerk, shuddered and closed his eyes. He opened them again after what seemed to be a short period of prayer, looked again, and said, "Did I come through that?"

"Yes," Wilson assured him.

"Where am I?"

"In the Hall of the Gate in the High Palace of Norkaal. But what is more important," Wilson added, "is *when* you are. You have gone forward a little more than thirty thousand years."

The knowledge did not seem to reassure him. He got up and stumbled toward the Gate. Wilson put a restraining hand on his shoulder. "Where are you going?"

"Back!"

"Not so fast." He did not dare let him go back yet, not until the Gate had been reset. Besides he was still drunk—his breath was staggering. "You will go back all right—I give you my word on that. But let me dress your wounds first. And you should rest. I have some explanations to make to you, and there is an errand you can do for me when you get back— to our mutual advantage. There is a great future in store for you and me, my boy—a great future!"

A great future!

THEODORE STURGEON

# The Golden Helix

*Science fiction is frequently described as a form of prophecy, and readers are quick to remind the uninitiated of SF's having "predicted" atomic energy, the submarine, travel to the moon, subliminal advertising and much else that has come to pass in the "real" world. Yet, science fiction's record as prophetic literature is really very mixed—surprisingly few of the many thousands of inventions and developments predicted by SF writers have actually taken place. "The Golden Helix"—an intriguing mystery and a terrific adventure story—is an example of a science fiction writer anticipating one of the most important breakthroughs in the history of science.*

I

Tod awoke first, probably because he was so curious, so deeply alive; perhaps because he was (or had been) seventeen. He fought back, but the manipulators would not be denied. They bent and flexed his arms and legs, squeezed his chest, patted and rasped and abraded him. His joints creaked, his sluggish blood clung sleepily to the walls of his veins, reluctant to move after so long.

He gasped and shouted as needles of cold played over his body, gasped again and screamed when his skin sensitized and the tingling intensified to a scald. Then he fainted, and probably slept, for he easily reawoke when someone else started screaming.

He felt weak and ravenous, but extraordinarily well-rested. His first conscious realization was that the manipulators had withdrawn from his body, as had the needles from the back of his neck. He put a shaky hand back there and felt the traces of spot-tape, already half-fused with his healing flesh.

He listened comfortably to this new screaming, satisfied that it was not his own. He let his eyes open, and a great wonder came over him when he saw that the lid of his Coffin stood open.

He clawed upward, sat a moment to fight a vicious swirl of vertigo, vanquished it and hung his chin on the edge of the Coffin.

149

The screaming came from April's Coffin. It was open too. Since the two massive boxes touched and their hinges were on opposite sides, he could look down at her. The manipulators were at work on the girl's body, working with competent violence. She seemed to be caught up in some frightful nightmare, lying on her back, dreaming of riding a runaway bicycle with an off-center pedal sprocket and epicyclic hubs. And all the while her arms seemed to be flailing at a cloud of dream-hornets round her tossing head. The needle-cluster rode with her head, fanning out behind the nape like the mechanical extrapolation of an Elizabethan collar.

Tod crawled to the end of his Coffin, stood up shakily and grasped the horizontal bar set at chest level. He got an arm over it and snugged it close under his armpit. Half-suspended, he could then manage one of his feet over the edge, then the other, to the top step. He lowered himself until he sat on it, outside the Coffin at last, and slumped back to rest. When his furious lungs and battering heart calmed themselves, he went down the four steps one at a time, like an infant, on his buttocks.

April's screams stopped.

Tod sat on the bottom step, jackknifed by fatigue, his feet on the metal floor, his knees in the hollows between his pectorals and his shoulders. Before him, on a low pedestal, was a cube with a round switch-disk on it. When he could, he inched a hand forward and let it fall on the disk. There was an explosive tinkle and the front panel of the cube disappeared, drifting slowly away as a fine glittering dust. He lifted his heavy hand and reached inside. He got one capsule, two, carried them to his lips. He rested, then took a beaker from the cube. It was three-quarters full of purple crystals. He bumped it on the steel floor. The beaker's cover powdered and fell in, and the crystals were suddenly a liquid, effervescing violently. When it subsided, he drank it down. He belched explosively, and then his head cleared, his personal horizons expanded to include the other Coffins, the compartment walls, the ship itself and its mission.

Out there somewhere—somewhere close, now—was Sirius and its captive planet, Terra Prime. Earth's first major colony, Prime would one day flourish as Earth never had, for it would be a planned and tailored planet. Eight and a half light-years from Earth, Prime's population was composed chiefly of Earth immigrants, living in pressure domes and slaving to alter the atmosphere of the planet to Earth normal. Periodically there must be an infusion of Earth blood to keep the strain as close as possible on both planets, for unless a faster-than-light drive could be developed, there could be no frequent interchange between the worlds. What took light eight years took humans half a lifetime. The solution was the Coffins—the marvelous machine in which a man could slip into a sleep which was more than sleep while still on Earth, and awake years later in space, near his destination, subjectively only a month or so older. Without the Coffins there could be only divergence, possibly mutation. Humanity wanted to populate the stars—but with humanity.

Tod and his five shipmates were hand-picked. They had superiorities —mechanical, mathematical and artistic aptitudes. But they were not all completely superior. One does not populate a colony with leaders alone and expect it to live. They, like the rest of their cargo (machine designs, microfilms of music and art, technical and medical writings, novels and entertainment) were neither advanced nor extraordinary. Except for Teague, they were the tested median, the competent; they were basic blood for a mass, rather than an elite.

Tod glanced around the blank walls and into the corner where a thin line delineated the sealed door. He ached to fling it open and skid across the corridor, punch the control which would slide away the armor which masked the port and soak himself in his first glimpse of outer space. He had heard so much about it, but he had never seen it—they had all been deep in their timeless sleep before the ship had blasted off.

But he sighed and went instead to the Coffins.

Alma's was still closed, but there was sound and motion, in varying degrees, from all the others.

He glanced first into April's Coffin. She seemed to be asleep now. The needle-cluster and manipulators had withdrawn. Her skin glowed; it was alive and as unlike its former monochrome waxiness as it could be. He smiled briefly and went to look at Teague.

Teague, too, was in real slumber. The fierce vertical line between his brows was shallow now, and the hard, deft hands lax and uncharacteristically purposeless. Tod had never seen him before without a focus for those narrow, blazing green eyes, without decisive spring and balance in his pose. It was good, somehow, to feel that for all his responsibilities, Teague could be as helpless as anyone.

Tod smiled as he passed Alma's closed Coffin. He always smiled at Alma when he saw her, when he heard her voice, when she crossed his thoughts. It was possible to be very brave around Alma, for gentleness and comfort were so ready that it was almost not necessary to call upon them.

One could bear anything, knowing she was there.

Tod crossed the chamber and looked at the last pair. Carl was a furious blur of motion, his needle-cluster swinging free, his manipulators in the final phase. He grunted instead of screaming, a series of implosive, startled gasps. His eyes were open but only the whites showed.

Moira was quite relaxed, turned on her side, poured out on the floor of the Coffin like a long golden cat. She seemed in a contented abandonment of untroubled sleep.

He heard a new sound and went back to April. She was sitting up, cross-legged, her head bowed apparently in deep concentration. Tod understood; he knew that sense of achievement and the dedication of an entire psyche to the proposition that these weak and trembling arms which hold one up shall *not* bend.

He reached in and gently lifted the soft white hair away from her face. She raised the albino's fathomless ruby eyes to him and whimpered.

"Come on," he said quietly. "We're here." When she did not move, he balanced on his stomach on the edge of the Coffin and put one hand between her shoulder blades. "Come on."

She pitched forward but he caught her so that she stayed kneeling. He drew her up and forward and put her hands on the bar. "Hold tight, Ape," he said. She did, while he lifted her thin body out of the Coffin and stood her on the top step. "Let go now. Lean on me."

Mechanically she obeyed, and he brought her down until she sat, as he had, on the bottom step. He punched the switch at her feet and put the capsules in her mouth while she looked up at him numbly, as if hypnotized. He got her beaker, thumped it, held it until its foaming subsided, and then put an arm around her shoulders while she drank. She closed her eyes and slumped against him, breathing deeply at first, and later, for a moment that frightened him, not at all. Then she sighed. "Tod . . . ."

"I'm here, Ape."

She straightened up, turned and looked at him. She seemed to be trying to smile, but she shivered instead. "I'm cold."

He rose, keeping one hand on her shoulder until he was sure she could sit up unassisted, and then brought her a cloak from the clips outside the Coffin. He helped her with it, knelt and put on her slippers for her. She sat quite still, hugging the garment tight to her. At last she looked around and back; up, around and back again. "We're—there!" she breathed.

"We're *here,*" he corrected.

"Yes, here. Here. How long do you suppose we . . ."

"We won't know exactly until we can take some readings. Twenty-five, twenty-seven years—maybe more."

She said, "I could be old, old—" She touched her face, brought her fingertips down to the sides of her neck. "I could be forty, even!"

He laughed at her, and then a movement caught the corner of his eye. "Carl!"

Carl was sitting sidewise on the edge of his Coffin, his feet still inside. Weak or no, bemused as could be expected, Carl should have grinned at Tod, should have made some healthy, swaggering gesture. Instead he sat still, staring about him in utter puzzlement. Tod went to him. "Carl! Carl, we're here!"

Carl looked at him dully. Tod was unaccountably disturbed. Carl always shouted, always bounced; Carl had always seemed to be just a bit larger inside than he was outside, ready to burst through, always thinking faster, laughing more quickly than anyone else.

He allowed Tod to help him down the steps, and sat heavily while Tod got his capsules and beaker for him. Waiting for the liquid to subside, he looked around numbly. Then drank, and almost toppled. April and Tod held him up. When he straightened again, it was abruptly. "Hey!" he roared. "We're here!" He looked up at them. "April! Tod-o! Well what do you know—how are you, kids?"

"Carl?" The voice was the voice of a flute, if a flute could whisper. They looked up. There was a small golden surf of hair tumbled on and over the edge of Moira's Coffin.

Weakly, eagerly, they clambered up to Moira and helped her out. Carl breathed such a sigh of relief that Tod and April stopped to smile at him, at each other.

Carl shrugged out of his weakness as if it were an uncomfortable garment and went to be close to Moira, to care about Moira and nothing else.

A deep labored voice called, "Who's up?"

"Teague! It's Teague . . . all of us, Teague," called Tod. "Carl and Moira and April and me. All except Alma."

Slowly Teague's great head rose out of the Coffin. He looked around with the controlled motion of a radar sweep. When his head stopped its one turning, the motion seemed relayed to his body, which began to move steadily upward. The four who watched him knew intimately what this cost him in sheer willpower, yet no one made any effort to help. Unasked, one did not help Teague.

One leg over, the second. He ignored the bar and stepped down to seat himself on the bottom step as if it were a throne. His hands moved very slowly but without faltering as he helped himself to the capsules, then the beaker. He permitted himself a moment of stillness, eyes closed, nostrils pinched; then life coursed strongly into him. It was as if his muscles visibly filled out a little. He seemed heavier and taller, and when he opened his eyes, they were the deeply vital, commanding light-sources which had drawn them, linked them, led them all during their training.

He looked toward the door in the corner. "Has anyone—"

"We were waiting for you," said Tod. "Shall we . . . can we go look now? I want to see the stars."

"We'll see to Alma first." Teague rose, ignoring the lip of his Coffin and the handhold it offered. He went to Alma's. With his height, he was the only one among them who could see through the top plate without mounting the steps.

Then, without turning, he said, "Wait."

The others, half across the room from him, stopped. Teague turned to them. There was no expression on his face at all. He stood quite motionless for perhaps ten seconds, and then quietly released a breath. He mounted the steps of Alma's Coffin, reached and the side nearest his own machine sank silently into the floor. He stepped down, and spent a long moment bent over the body inside. From where they stood, tense and frightened, the others could not see inside. They made no effort to move closer.

"Tod," said Teague, "get the kit. Surgery Lambda. Moira, I'll need you."

The shock of it went to Tod's bones, regenerated, struck him again; yet so conditioned was he to Teague's commands that he was on his feet and moving before Teague had stopped speaking. He went to the after bulkhead and swung open a panel, pressed a stud. There was a metallic whisper, and the heavy case slid out at his feet. He lugged it over to Teague, and helped him rack it on the side of the Coffin. Teague immediately plunged his hands through the membrane at one end of the kit, nodding to Moira to do likewise at the other. Tod stepped back, studiously avoiding a glance in at Alma, and returned to April. She put both her hands tight around his left biceps and leaned close. "Lambda. . . ." she whispered. "That's . . . parturition, isn't it?"

He shook his head. "Parturition is Surgery Kappa," he said painfully. He swallowed. "Lambda's Caesarian."

Her crimson eyes widened. "Caesarian? *Alma?* She'd never need a Caesarian!"

He turned to look at her, but he could not see, his eyes stung so. "Not while she lived, she wouldn't," he whispered. He felt the small white hands tighten painfully on his arm. Across the room, Carl sat quietly. Tod squashed the water out of his eyes with the heel of his hand. Carl began pounding knuckles, very slowly, against his own temple.

Teague and Moira were busy for a long time.

## II

Tod pulled in his legs and lowered his head until the kneecaps pressed cruelly against his eyebrow ridges. He hugged his shins, ground his back into the wall panels and in this red-spangled blackness he let himself live back and back to Alma and joy, Alma and comfort, Alma and courage.

He had sat once, just this way, twisted by misery and anger, blind and helpless, in a dark corner of an equipment shed at the spaceport. The rumor had circulated that April would not come after all, because albinism and the Sirius Rock would not mix. It turned out to be untrue, but that did not matter at the time. He had punched her, punched *Alma!* because in all the world he had been given nothing else to strike out at, and she had found him and had sat down to be with him. She had not even touched her face, where the blood ran; she simply waited until at last he flung himself on her lap and wept like an infant. And no one but he and Alma ever knew of it. . . .

He remembered Alma with the spaceport children, rolling and tumbling on the lawn with them, and in the pool; and he remembered Alma, her face still, looking up at the stars with her soft and gentle eyes, and in those eyes he had seen a challenge as implacable and pervasive as space itself. The tumbling on the lawn, the towering dignity—these coexisted in Alma without friction. He remembered things she had said to him; for each of the things he could recall the kind of light, the way he stood, the very smell of the air at the time. "Never be afraid, Tod. Just think of the worst possible thing that might happen. What you're afraid of will probably not be *that* bad—and anything else just has to be better." And she said once, "Don't confuse logic and truth, however good the logic. You can stick one end of logic in solid ground and throw the other end clear out of the cosmos without breaking it. Truth's a little less flexible." And, "Of *course* you need to be loved, Tod! Don't be ashamed of that, or try to change it. It's not a thing you have to worry about, ever. You are loved. April loves you. And I love you. Maybe I love you even more than April, because she loves everything you are, but I love everything you were and ever will be."

And some of the memories were deeper and more important even than these, but were memories of small things—the meeting of eyes, the touch of a hand, the sound of laughter or a snatch of song, distantly.

Tod descended from memory into a blackness that was only loss and despair, and then a numbness, followed by a reluctant awareness. He became conscious of what, in itself, seemed the merest of trifles: that there was a significance in his pose there against the bulkhead. Unmoving, he considered it. It was comfortable, to be so turned in upon oneself, and so protected, unaware . . . and Alma would have hated to see him this way.

He threw up his head, and self-consciously straightened from his fetal posture. *That's over now,* he told himself furiously, and then, dazed, wondered what he had meant.

He turned to look at April. She was huddled miserably against him, her face and body lax, stopped, disinterested. He thumped his elbow into her ribs, hard enough to make her remember she had ribs. She looked up into his eyes and said, "How? How could . . ."

Tod understood. Of the three couples standard for each ship of the Sirian project, one traditionally would beget children on the planet; one, earlier, as soon as possible after awakening; and one still earlier, for conception would take place within the Coffin. But—not *before* awakening, and surely not long enough before to permit of gestation. It was an impossibility; the vital processes were so retarded within the Coffin that, effectively, there would be no stirring of life at all. So—"How?" April pleaded. "How could. . . ."

Tod gazed upon his own misery, then April's, and wondered what it must be that Teague was going through.

Teague, without looking up, said, "Tod."

Tod patted April's shoulder, rose and went to Teague. He did not look into the Coffin. Teague, still working steadily, tilted his head to one side to point. "I need a little more room here."

Tod lifted the transparent cube Teague had indicated and looked at the squirming pink bundle inside. He almost smiled. It was a nice baby. He took one step away and Teague said, "Take 'em all, Tod."

He stacked them and carried them to where April sat. Carl rose and came over, and knelt. The boxes hummed—a vibration which could be felt, not heard—as nutrient-bearing air circulated inside and back to the power-packs. "A nice normal deliv—I mean, a nice normal batch o' brats," Carl said. "Four girls, one boy. Just right."

Tod looked up at him. "There's one more, I think."

There was—another girl. Moira brought it over in the sixth box. "Sweet," April breathed, watching them. "They're sweet."

Moira said, wearily, "That's all."

Tod looked up at her.

"Alma . . . ?"

Moira waved laxly toward the neat stack of incubators. "That's all," she whispered tiredly, and went to Carl.

*That's all there is of Alma,* Tod thought bitterly. He glanced across at Teague. The tall figure raised a steady hand, wiped his face with his upper arm. His raised hand touched the high end of the Coffin, and for an instant held a grip. Teague's face lay against his arm, pillowed, hidden and still. Then he completed the wiping motion and began stripping the sterile plastic skin from his hands. Tod's heart went out to him, but he bit the insides of his cheeks and kept silent. *A strange tradition,* thought Tod, *that makes it impolite to grieve. . . .*

Teague dropped the shreds of plastic into the disposal slot and turned to face them. He looked at each in turn, and each in turn found some measure of control. He turned then, and pulled a lever, and the side of Alma's Coffin slid silently up.

*Good-by. . . .*

Tod put his back against the bulkhead and slid down beside April. He put an arm over her shoulders. Carl and Moira sat close, holding hands. Moira's eyes were shadowed but very much awake. Carl bore an expression almost of sullenness. Tod glanced, then glared at the boxes. Three of the babies were crying, though of course they could not be heard through the plastic incubators. Tod was suddenly conscious of Teague's eyes upon him. He flushed, and then let his anger drain to the capacious inner reservoir which must hold it and all his grief as well.

When he had their attention, Teague sat crosslegged before them and placed a small object on the floor.

Tod looked at the object. At first glance it seemed to be a metal spring about as long as his thumb, mounted vertically on a black base. Then he realized that it was an art object of some kind, made of a golden substance which shimmered and all but flowed. It was an interlocked double spiral; the turns went round and up, round and down, round and up again, the texture of the gold clearly indicating, in a strange and alive way, which symbolized a rising and falling flux. Shaped as if it had been wound on a cylinder and the cylinder removed, the thing was formed of a continuous wire or rod which had no beginning and no end, but which turned and rose and turned and descended again in an exquisite continuity. . . . Its base was formless, an almost-smoke just as the gold showed an almost-flux; and it was as lightless as ylem.

Teague said, "This was in Alma's Coffin. It was not there when we left Earth."

"It must have been," said Carl flatly.

Teague silently shook his head. April opened her lips, closed them again. Teague said, "Yes, April?"

April shook her head. "Nothing, Teague. Really nothing." But because Teague kept looking at her, waiting, she said, "I was going to say . . . it's beautiful." She hung her head.

Teague's lips twitched. Tod could sense the sympathy there. He stroked April's silver hair. She responded, moving her shoulder slightly under his hand. "What is it, Teague?"

When Teague would not answer, Moira asked, "Did it . . . had it anything to do with Alma?"

Teague picked it up thoughtfully. Tod could see the yellow loom it cast against his throat and cheek, the golden points it built in his eyes. "Something did." He paused. "You know she was supposed to conceive on awakening. But to give birth—"

Carl cracked a closed hand against his forehead. "She must have been awake for anyway two hundred and eighty days!"

"Maybe she made it," said Moira.

Tod watched Teague's hand half-close on the object as if it might be precious now. Moira's was a welcome thought, and the welcome could be read on Teague's face. Watching it, Tod saw the complicated spoor of a series of efforts—a gathering of emotions, a determination; the closing of certain doors, the opening of others.

Teague rose. "We have a ship to inspect, sights to take, calculations . . . we've got to tune in Terra Prime, send them a message if we can. Tod, check the corridor air."

"The stars—we'll see the stars!" Tod whispered to April, the heady thought all but eclipsing everything else. He bounded to the corner where the door controls waited. He punched the test button, and a spot of green appeared over the door, indicating that with their awakening, the evacuated chambers, the living and control compartments, had been flooded with air and warmed. "Air okay."

"Go on then."

They crowded around Tod as he grasped the lever and pushed. *I won't wait for orders,* Tod thought. *I'll slide right across the corridor and open the guard plate and there it'll be—space, and the stars!*

The door opened.

There was no corridor, no bulkhead, no armored porthole, no—

No *ship!*

There was a night out there, dank, warm. It was wet. In it were hooked, fleshy leaves and a tangle of roots; a thing with legs which hopped up on the sill and shimmered its wings for them; a thing like a flying hammer which crashed in and smote the shimmering one and was gone with it, leaving a stain on the deck-plates. There was a sky aglow with a ghastly green. There was a thrashing and a scream out there, a pressure of growth and a wrongness.

Blood ran down Tod's chin. His teeth met through his lower lip. He turned and looked past three sets of terrified eyes to Teague, who said, "Shut it!"

Tod snatched at the control. It broke off in his hand. . . .

How long does a thought, a long thought, take?

Tod stood with the fractured metal in his hand and thought:

*We were told that above all things we must adapt. We were told that perhaps there would be a thin atmosphere by now, on Terra Prime, but that in all likelihood we must live a new kind of life in pressure-domes. We were warned that what we might find would be flash-mutation, where the people could be more or less than human. We were warned, even, that there might be no life on Prime at all. But look at me now—look at all of us. We weren't meant to adapt to this! And we can't . . .*

Somebody shouted while somebody shrieked, each sound a word, each destroying the other. Something thick as a thumb, long as a hand, with a voice like a distant airhorn, hurtled through the door and circled the room. Teague snatched a folded cloak from the clothing rack and, poising just a moment, batted it out of the air. It skittered, squirming, across the metal door. He threw the cloak on it to capture it. "Get that door closed."

Carl snatched the broken control lever out of Tod's hand and tried to fit it back into the switch mounting. It crumbled as if it were dried bread. Tod stepped outside, hooked his hands on the edge of the door and pulled. It would not budge. A lizard as long as his arm scuttled out of the twisted grass and stopped to stare at him. He shouted at it, and with forelegs much too long for such a creature, it pressed itself upward until its body was forty-five degrees from the horizontal, it flicked the end of its long tail upward, and something flew over its head toward Tod, buzzing angrily. Tod turned to see what it was, and as he did the lizard struck from one side and April from the other.

April succeeded and the lizard failed, for its fangs clashed and it fell forward, but April's shoulder had taken Tod on the chest and, off balance as he was, he went flat on his back. The cold, dry, pulsing tail swatted his hand. He gripped it convulsively, held on tight. Part of the tail broke off and buzzed, flipping about on the ground like a click-beetle. But the rest held. Tod scuttled backward to pull the lizard straight as it began to turn on him, got his knees under him, then his feet. He swung the lizard twice around his head and smashed it against the inside of the open door. The part of the tail he was holding then broke off, and the scaly thing thumped inside and slid, causing Moira to leap so wildly to get out of its way that she nearly knocked the stocky Carl off his feet.

Teague swept away the lid of the Surgery Lambda kit, inverted it, kicked the clutter of instruments and medicaments aside and clapped the inverted box over the twitching, scaly body.

"April!" Tod shouted. He ran around in a blind semi-circle, saw her struggling to her feet in the grass, snatched her up and bounded inside with her. "Carl!" he gasped, "Get the door. . . ."

But Carl was already moving forward with a needle torch. With two deft motions he sliced out a section of the power-arm which was holding the door open. He swung the door to, yelling, "Parametal!"

Tod, gasping, ran to the lockers and brought a length of the synthetic. Carl took the wide ribbon and with a snap of the wrists broke it in two. Each half he bent (for it was very flexible when moved slowly) into a U. He placed one against the door and held out his hand without looking.

Tod dropped the hammer into it. Carl tapped the parametal gently and it adhered to the door. He turned his face away and struck it sharply. There was a blue white flash and the U was rigid and firmly welded to the door. He did the same thing with the other U, welding it to the nearby wall plates. Into the two gudgeons thus formed, Moira dropped a luxalloy bar, and the door was secured.

"Shall I sterilize the floor?" Moira asked.

"No," said Teague shortly.

"But—bacteria . . . spores . . ."

"Forget it," said Teague.

April was crying. Tod held her close, but made no effort to stop her. Something in him, deeper than panic, more essential than wonderment, understood that she could use this circumstance to spend her tears for Alma, and that these tears must be shed now or swell and burst her heart. *So cry,* he pled silently, *cry for both of us, all of us.*

With the end of action, belated shock spread visibly over Carl's face. "The ship's gone," he said stupidly. "We're on a planet." He looked at his hands, turned abruptly to the door, stared at it and began to shiver. Moira went to him and stood quietly, not touching him—just being near, in case she should be needed. April grew gradually silent. Carl said, "I—" and then shook his head.

*Click. Shh. Clack, click.* Methodically Teague was stacking the scattered contents of the medical kit. Tod patted April's shoulder and went to help. Moira glanced at them, peered closely into Carl's face, then left him and came to lend a hand. April joined them, and at last Carl. They swept up, and tracked and stored the clutter, and when Teague lowered a table, they helped get the dead lizard on it and pegged out for dissection. Moira cautiously disentangled the huge insect from the folds of the cloak and clapped a box over it, slid the lid underneath to bring the feebly squirming thing to Teague. He studied it for a long moment, then set it down and peered at the lizard. With forceps he opened the jaws and bent close. He grunted. "April. . . ."

She came to look. Teague touched the fangs with the tip of a scalpel. "Look there."

"Grooves," she said. "Like a snake."

Teague reversed the scalpel and with the handle he gingerly pressed upward, at the root of one of the fangs. A cloudy yellow liquid beaded, ran down the groove. He dropped the scalpel and slipped a watch-glass under the tooth to catch the droplet. "Analyze that later," he murmured. "But I'd say you saved Tod from something pretty nasty."

"I didn't even think," said April. "I didn't . . . I never knew there was any animal life on Prime. I wonder what they call this monster."

"The honors are yours, April. You name it."

"They'll have a classification for it already!"

"Who?"

Everyone started to talk, and abruptly stopped. In the awkward silence Carl's sudden laugh boomed. It was a wondrous sound in the frightened chamber. There was comprehension in it, and challenge, and above all, Carl himself—boisterous and impulsive, quick, sure. The laugh was triggered by the gush of talk and its sudden cessation, a small thing in itself. But its substance was understanding, and with that an emotional surge, and with that, the choice of the one emotional expression Carl would always choose.

"Tell them, Carl," Teague said.

Carl's teeth flashed. He waved a thick arm at the door. "That isn't Sirius Prime. Or Earth. Go ahead, April—name your pet."

April, staring at the lizard, said, "*Crotalidus,* then, because it has a rattle and fangs like a diamondback." Then she paled and turned to Carl, as the full weight of his statement came on her. "Not—*not Prime?*"

Quietly, Teague said, "Nothing like these ever grew on Earth. And Prime is a cold planet. It could never have a climate like that," he nodded toward the door, "no matter how much time has passed."

"But what . . . where . . ." It was Moira.

"We'll find out when we can. But the instruments aren't here—they were in the ship."

"But if it's a new . . . another planet, why didn't you let me sterilize? What about airborne spores? Suppose it had been methane out there or—"

"We've obviously been conditioned to anything in the atmosphere. As to its composition—well, it isn't poisonous, or we wouldn't be standing here talking about it. Wait!" He held up a hand and quelled the babble of questions before it could fully start. "Wondering is a luxury like worrying. We can't afford either. We'll get our answers when we get more evidence."

"What shall we do?" asked April faintly.

"Eat," said Teague. "Sleep." They waited. Teague said, "Then we go outside."

## III

There were stars like daisies in a field, like dust in a sunbeam and like flying, flaming mountains; near ones, far ones, stars of every color and every degree of brilliance. And there were bands of light which must be stars too distant to see. And something was stealing the stars, not taking them away, but swallowing them up, coming closer and closer, eating as it came. And at last there was only one left. Its name was Alma, and it was gone, and there was nothing left but an absorbent blackness and an aching loss.

In this blackness Tod's eyes snapped open, and he gasped, frightened and lost.

"You awake, Tod?" April's small hand touched his face. He took it and drew it to his lips, drinking comfort from it.

From the blackness came Carl's resonant whisper, "We're awake. Teague? . . ."

The lights flashed on, dim first, brightening swiftly, but not so fast as to dazzle unsuspecting eyes. Tod sat up and saw Teague at the table. On it was the lizard, dissected and laid out as neatly as an exploded view in a machine manual. Over the table, on a gooseneck, was a floodlamp with its lens masked by an infrared filter. Teague turned away from the table, pushing up his "black-light" goggles, and nodded to Tod. There were shadows under his eyes, but otherwise he seemed the same as ever. Tod wondered how many lonely hours he had worked while the two couples slept, doing that meticulous work under the irritating glow so that they would be undisturbed.

Tod went to him. "Has my playmate been talking much?" He pointed at the remains of the lizard.

"Yes and no," said Teague. "Oxygen-breather, all right, and a true lizard. He had a secret weapon—that tail segment he flips over his head toward his victims. It has primitive ganglia like an Earth salamander's, so that the tail segment trembles and squirms, sounding the rattles, after he throws it. He also has a skeleton that—but all this doesn't matter. Most important is that he's the analogue of our early Permian life, which means (unless he's an evolutionary dead-end like a cockroach) that this planet is a billion years old at the least. And the little fellow here—" he touched the flying thing—"bears this out. It's not an insect, you know. It's an arachnid."

"With *wings?*"

Teague lifted the slender, scorpion like pincers of the creature and let them fall. "Flat chitinous wings are no more remarkable a leg adaptation than those things. Anyway, in spite of the ingenuity of his engineering, internally he's pretty primitive. All of which lets us hypothesize that we'll find fairly close analogues of what we're used to on Earth."

"Teague," Tod interrupted, his voice lowered, his eyes narrowed to contain the worry that threatened to spill over, "Teague, what's happened?"

"The temperature and humidity here seem to be exactly the same as that outside," Teague went on, in precisely the same tone as before. "This would indicate either a warm planet, or a warm season on a temperate planet. In either case it is obvious that—"

"But, *Teague*—"

"—that a good deal of theorizing is possible with very little evidence, and we need not occupy ourselves with anything else but that evidence."

"Oh," said Tod. He backed off a step. "Oh," he said again, "sorry, Teague." He joined the others at the food dispensers, feeling like a cuffed puppy. *But he's right,* he thought. *As Alma said . . . of the many things which might have happened, only one actually has. Let's wait then, and worry about that one thing when we can name it.*

There was a pressure on his arm. He looked up from his thoughts and into April's searching eyes. He knew that she had heard, and he was unreasonably angry at her. "Damm it, he's so cold-blooded," he blurted defensively, but in a whisper.

April said, "He has to stay with things he can understand, every minute." She glanced swiftly at the closed Coffin. "Wouldn't you?"

There was a sharp pain and a bitterness in Tod's throat as he thought about it. He dropped his eyes and mumbled, "No, I wouldn't. I don't think I could." There was a difference in his eyes as he glanced back at Teague. *But it's so easy, after all, for strong people to be strong,* he thought.

"Teague, what'll we wear?" Carl called.

"Skinflex."

"Oh, no!" cried Moira. "It's so clingy and hot!"

Carl laughed at her. He swept up the lizard's head and opened its jaws. "Smile at the lady. She wouldn't put any tough old skinflex in the way of your pretty teeth!"

"Put it down," said Teague sharply, though there was a flicker of amusement in his eyes. "It's still loaded with God-knows-what alkaloid. Moira, he's right. Skinflex just doesn't puncture."

Moira looked respectfully at the yellow fangs and went obediently to storage, where she pulled out the suits.

"We'll keep close together, back to back," said Teague as they helped each other into the suits. "All the weapons are . . . were . . . in the forward storage compartment, so we'll improvise. Tod, you and the girls each take a globe of anesthene. It's the fastest anesthetic we have and it ought to take care of anything that breathes oxygen. I'll take scalpels. Carl—"

"The hammer," Carl grinned. His voice was fairly thrumming with excitement.

"We won't attempt to fasten the door from outside. I don't mean to go farther than ten meters out, this first time. Just—you, Carl—lift off the bar as we go out, get the door shut as quickly as possible and prop it there. Whatever happens, do not attack anything out there unless you are attacked first, or unless I say so."

Hollow-eyed, steady, Teague moved to the door with the others close around him. Carl shifted the hammer to his left hand, lifted the bar and stood back a little, holding it like a javelin. Teague, holding a glittering lancet lightly in each hand, pushed the door open with his foot. They boiled through, stepped aside for Carl as he butted the rod deep into the soil and against the closed door. "All set."

They moved as a unit for perhaps three meters, and stopped.

It was daytime now, but such a day as none of them had dreamed of. The light was green, very nearly a lime green, and the shadows were purple. The sky was more lavender than blue. The air was warm and wet.

They stood at the top of a low hill. Before them a tangle of jungle tumbled up at them. So vital, so completely alive, it seemed to move by its own power of growth. Stirring, murmuring, it was too big, too much, too wide and deep and intertwined to assimilate at a glance; the thought, *this is a jungle,* was a pitiable understatement.

To the left, savannahlike grassland rolled gently down to the choked margins of a river—calmfaced, muddy and secretive. It too seemed astir with inner growings. To the right, more jungle. Behind them, the bland and comforting wall of their compartment.

Above—

It may have been April who saw it first; in any case, Tod always associated the vision with April's scream.

They moved as she screamed, five humans jerked back then like five dolls on a single string, pressed together and to the compartment wall by an overwhelming claustrophobia. They were ants under a descending heel, flies on an anvil . . . together their backs struck the wall and they cowered there, looking up.

And it was not descending. It was only—big. It was just that it was there, over them.

April said, later, that it was like a cloud. Carl would argue that it was cylindrical, with flared ends and a narrow waist. Teague never attempted to describe it, because he disliked inaccuracies, and Moira was too awed to try. To Tod, the object had no shape. It was a luminous opacity between him and the sky, solid, massive as mountains. There was only one thing they agreed on, and that was that it was a ship.

And out of the ship came the golden ones.

They appeared under the ship as speckles of light, and grew in size as they descended, so that the five humans must withstand a second shock: they had known the ship was huge, but had not known until now how very high above them it hung.

Down they came, dozens, hundreds. They filled the sky over the jungle and around the five, moving to make a spherical quadrant from the horizontal to the zenith, a full hundred and eighty degrees from side to side—a radiant floating shell with its concave surface toward, around, above them. They blocked out the sky and the jungle-tops, cut off most of the strange green light, replacing it with their own—for each glowed coolly.

Each individual was distinct and separate. Later, they would argue about the form and shape of the vessel, but the exact shape of these golden things was never even mentioned. Nor did they ever agree on a name for them. To Carl they were an army, to April, angels. Moira called them (secretly) "the seraphim," and to Tod they were masters. Teague never named them.

For measureless time they hung there, with the humans gaping up at them. There was no flutter of wings, no hum of machinery to indicate how they stayed aloft, and if each individual had a device to keep him afloat, it was of a kind the humans could not recognize. They were beautiful, awesome, uncountable.

And nobody was afraid.

Tod looked from side to side, from top to bottom of this incredible formation, and became aware that it did not touch the ground. Its lower edge was exactly horizontal, at his eye level. Since the hill fell away on all sides, he could see under this lower edge, here the jungle, there down across the savannah to the river. In a new amazement he saw eyes, and protruding heads.

In the tall grass at the jungle margin was a scurry and cease, scurry and cease, as newtlike animals scrambled not quite into the open and froze, watching. Up in the lower branches of the fleshy, hook-leaved trees, the heavy scaly heads of leaf-eaters showed, and here and there was the armed head of a lizard with catlike tearing tusks.

Leather-winged fliers flapped clumsily to rest in the branches, hung for a moment for all the world like broken umbrellas, then achieved balance and folded their pinions. Something slid through the air, almost caught a branch, missed it and tumbled end-over-end to the ground, resolving itself into a broad-headed scaly thing with wide membranes between fore and hind legs. And Tod saw his acquaintance of the night before, with its serrated tail and needle fangs.

And though there must have been eater and eaten here, hunter and hunted, they all watched silently, turned like living compass-needles to the airborne mystery surrounding the humans. They crowded together like a nightmare parody of the Lion and the Lamb, making a constellation, a galaxy of bright and wondering eyes; their distance from each other being, in its way, cosmic.

Tod turned his face into the strange light, and saw one of the golden beings separate from the mass and drift down and forward and stop. Had this living shell been a segment of curving mirror, this one creature would have been at its focal point. For a moment there was complete stillness, a silent waiting. Then the creature made a deep . . . *gesture.* Behind it, all the others did the same.

If ten thousand people stand ten thousand meters away, and if, all at once, they kneel, it is hardly possible to see just what it is they have done; yet the aspect of their mass undergoes a definite change. So it was with the radiant shell—it changed, all of it, without moving. There was no mistaking the nature of the change, though its meaning was beyond knowing. It was an obeisance. It was an expression of profound respect, first to the humans themselves, next, and hugely, to something the humans represented. It was unquestionably an act of worship.

*And what,* thought Tod, *could we symbolize to these shining ones?* He was a scarab beetle or an Egyptian cat, a Hindu cow or a Teuton tree, told suddenly that it was sacred.

All the while there flooded down the thing which Carl had tried so

ineptly to express: *"We're sorry. But it will be all right. You will be glad.
You can be glad now."*

At last there was a change in the mighty formation. The center rose
and the wings came in, the left one rising and curling to tighten the curve,
the right one bending inward without rising. In a moment the formation
was a column, a hollow cylinder. It began to rotate slowly, divided into
a series of close-set horizontal rings. Alternate rings slowed and stopped
and began a counter-rotation, and with a sudden shift, became two interlocked spirals. Still the overall formation was a hollow cylinder, but now
it was composed of an upward and a downward helix.

The individuals spun and swirled down and down, up and up, and kept
this motion within the cylinder, and the cylinder quite discrete, as it began
to rise. Up and up it lifted, brilliantly, silently, the living original of that
which they had found by Alma's body . . . up and up, filling the eye and
the mind with its complex and controlled ascent, its perfect continuity;
for here was a thing with no beginning and no end, all flux and balance
where each rising was matched by a fall and each turn by its counterpart.

High, and higher, and at last it was a glowing spot against the hovering
shadow of the ship, which swallowed it up. The ship left then, not moving,
but fading away like the streamers of an aurora, but faster. In three
heartbeats it was there, perhaps it was there, it was gone.

Tod closed his eyes, seeing that dynamic double helix. The tip of his
mind was upon it; he trembled on the edge of revelation. He *knew* what
that form symbolized. He knew it contained the simple answer to his life
and their lives, to this planet and its life and the lives which were brought
to it. If a cross is more than an instrument of torture, more than the
memento of an event; if the *crux ansata*, the Yin-and-Yang, David's star
and all such crystallizations were but symbols of great systems of philosophy, then this dynamic intertwined spiral, this free-flowing, rigidly choreo-
graphed symbol was . . . was—

Something grunted, something screamed, and the wondrous answer
turned and rose spiraling away from him to be gone in three heartbeats.
Yet in that moment he knew it was there for him when he had the time,
the phasing, the bringing-together of whatever elements were needed. He
could not use it yet but he had it. He had it.

Another scream, an immense thrashing all about. The spell was broken
and the armistice over. There were chargings and fleeings, cries of death-
agony and roaring challenges in and over the jungle, through the grasses

to the suddenly boiling river. Life goes on, and death with it, but there must be more death than life when too much life is thrown together.

## IV

It may be that their five human lives were saved, in that turbulent reawakening, only by their alienness, for the life around them was cheek-and-jowl with its familiar enemy, its familiar quarry, its familiar food, and there need be no experimenting with the five soft containers of new rich juices standing awestruck with their backs to their intrusive shelter.

Then slowly they met one another's eyes. They cared enough for each other so that there was a gladness of sharing. They cared enough for themselves so that there was also a sheepishness, a troubled self-analysis: *What did I do while I was out of my mind?*

They drew together before the door and watched the chase and slaughter around them as it subsided toward its usual balance of hunting and killing, eating and dying. Their hands began to remember the weapons they held, their minds began to reach for reality.

"They were angels," April said, so softly that no one but Tod heard her. Tod watched her lips tremble and part, and knew that she was about to speak the thing he had almost grasped, but then Teague spoke again, and Tod could see the comprehension fade from her and be gone. "Look! Look there!" said Teague, and moved down the wall to the corner.

What had been an inner compartment of their ship was now an isolated cube, and from its back corner, out of sight until now, stretched another long wall. At regular intervals were doors, each fastened by a simple outside latch of parametal.

Teague stepped to the first door, the others crowding close. Teague listened intently, then stepped back and threw the door open.

Inside was a windowless room, blazing with light. Around the sides, machines were set. Tod instantly recognized their air cracker, the water purifiers, the protein converter and one of the auxiliary power plants. In the center was a generator coupled to a light-metal fusion motor. The output buses were neatly insulated, coupled through fuseboxes and resistance controls to a "Christmas tree" multiple outlet. Cables ran through the wall to the Coffin compartment and to the line of unexplored rooms to their left.

"They've left us power, at any rate," said Teague. "Let's look down the line."

*Fish,* Tod snarled silently. *Dead man! After what you've just seen you should be on your knees with the weight of it, you should put out your eyes to remember better. But all you can do is take inventory of your nuts and bolts.*

Tod looked at the others, at their strained faces and their continual upward glances, as if the bright memory had magnetism for them. He could see the dream fading under Teague's untimely urgency. *You couldn't let us live with it quietly, even for a moment.* Then another inward voice explained to him, *But you see, they killed Alma.*

Resentfully he followed Teague.

Their ship had been dismantled, strung out along the hilltop like a row of shacks. They were interconnected, wired up, restacked, ready and reeking with efficiency—the lab, the library, six chambers full of mixed cargo, then—then the noise Teague made was as near to a shout of glee as Tod had ever heard from the man. The door he had just opened showed their instruments inside, all the reference tapes and tools and manuals. There was even a dome in the roof, and the refractor was mounted and waiting.

"April?" Tod looked, looked again. She was gone. "April!"

She emerged from the library, three doors back. "Teague!"

Teague pulled himself away from the array of instruments and went to her. "Teague," she said, "every one of the reels has been read."

"How do you know?"

"None of them are rewound."

Teague looked up and down the row of doors. "That doesn't sound like the way they—" The unfinished sentence was enough. Whoever had built this from their ship's substance worked according to function and with a fine efficiency.

Teague entered the library and picked a tape reel from its rack. He inserted the free end of film into a slot and pressed a button. The reel spun and the film disappeared inside the cabinet.

Teague looked up and back. Every single reel was inside out on the clips. "They could have rewound them," said Teague, irritated.

"Maybe they wanted us to know that they'd read them," said Moira.

"Maybe they did," Teague murmured. He picked up a reel, looked at it, picked up another and another. "Music. A play. And here's our personal stuff—behavior film, training records, everything."

Carl said, "Whoever read through all this knows a lot about us."

Teague frowned. "Just us?"

"Who else?"

"Earth," said Teague. "All of it."

"You mean we were captured and analyzed so that whoever they are could get a line on Earth? You think they're going to attack Earth?"

" 'You mean . . . You think . . .' " Teague mimicked coldly. "I mean nothing and I think nothing! Tod, would you be good enough to explain to this impulsive young man what you learned from me earlier? That we need concern ourselves only with evidence?"

Tod shuffled his feet, wishing not to be made an example for anyone, especially Carl, to follow. Carl flushed and tried to smile. Moira took his hand secretly and squeezed it. Tod heard a slight exhalation beside him and looked quickly at April. She was angry. There were times when he wished she would not be angry.

She pointed. "Would you call *that* evidence, Teague?"

They followed her gesture. One of the tape-readers stood open. On its reelshelf stood the counterpart of the strange object they had seen twice before—once, in miniature, found in Alma's Coffin; once again, huge in the sky. This was another of the miniatures.

Teague stared at it, then put out his hand. As his fingers touched it, the pilot-jewel on the tape-reader flashed on, and a soft, clear voice filled the room.

Tod's eyes stung. He had thought he would never hear that voice again. As he listened, he held to the lifeline of April's presence, and felt his lifeline tremble.

Alma's voice said:

> *"They made some adjustments yesterday with the needle-clusters in my Coffin, so I think they will put me back into it . . . Teague, oh, Teague, I'm going to die!*
>
> *"They brought me the recorder just now. I don't know whether it's for their records or for you. If it's for you, then I must tell you . . . how can I tell you?*
>
> *"I've watched them all this time . . . how long? Months . . . I don't know. I conceived when I awoke, and the babies are coming very soon now; it's been long enough for that; and yet—how can I tell you?*

*"They boarded us, I don't know how, I don't know why, or where . . . outside, space is strange, wrong. It's all misty, without stars, crawling with blurs and patches of light.*

*"They understand me; I'm sure of that—what I say, what I think. I can't understand them at all. They radiate feelings—sorrow, curiosity, confidence, respect. When I began to realize I would die, they gave me a kind of regret. When I broke and cried and said I wanted to be with you, Teague, they reassured me, they said I would. I'm sure that's what they said. But how could that be?*

*"They are completely dedicated in what they are doing. Their work is a religion to them, and we are part of it. They . . . value us, Teague. They didn't just find us. They chose us. It's as if we were the best part of something even they consider great.*

*"The best . . . ! Among them I feel like an amoeba. They're beautiful, Teague. Important. Very sure of what they are doing. It's that certainty that makes me believe what I have to believe; I am going to die, and you will live, and you and I will be together. How can that be? How can that be?*

*"Yet it is true, so believe it with me, Teague. But—find out how!*

*"Teague, every day they have put a machine on me, radiating. It has to do with the babies. It isn't done to harm them. I'm sure of that. I'm their mother and I'm sure of it. They won't die.*

*"I will. I can feel their sorrow.*

*"And I will be with you, and they are joyous about that. . . .*

*"Teague—find out how!"*

Tod closed his eyes so that he would not look at Teague, and wished with all his heart that Teague had been alone to hear that ghostly voice. As to what it had said, the words stood as a frame for a picture he could not see, showing him only where it was, not what it meant. Alma's voice had been tremulous and unsure, but he knew it well enough to know that joy and certitude had lived with her as she spoke. There was wonderment, but no fear.

Knowing that it might be her only message to them, should she not have told them more—facts, figures, measurements?

Then an old, old tale flashed into his mind, an early thing from the ancient Amerenglish, by Hynlen (Henlyne, was it? no matter) about a man who tried to convey to humanity a description of the super-beings who had captured him, with only his body as a tablet and his nails as a stylus. Perhaps he was mad by the time he finished, but his message was clear at least to him: *"Creation took eight days."* How would he, Tod, describe an association with the ones he had seen in the sky outside, if he had been with them for nearly three hundred days?

April tugged gently at his arm. He turned toward her, still avoiding the sight of Teague. April inclined her shining white head to the door. Moira and Carl already stood outside. They joined them, and waited wordlessly until Teague came out.

When he did, he was grateful, and he need not say so. He came out, a great calm in his face and voice, passed them and let them follow him to his methodical examination of the other compartments, to finish his inventory.

Food stores, cable and conduit, metal and parametal rod and sheet stock, tools and tool-making matrices and dies. A hangar, in which lay their lifeboat, fully equipped.

But there was no long-range communication device, and no parts for one.

And there was no heavy space-drive mechanism, or tools to make one, or fuel if they should make the tools.

Back in the instrument room, Carl grunted. "Somebody means for us to stick around."

"The boat—"

Teague said, "I don't think they'd have left us the boat if Earth was in range."

"We'll build a beacon," Tod said suddenly. "We'll get a rescue ship out to us."

"Out where?" asked Teague drily.

They followed his gaze. Bland and silent, merciless, the decay chronometer stared back at them. Built around a standard radioactive, it had two dials—one which measured the amount of energy radiated by the material, and one which measured the loss mass. When they checked, the reading was correct. They checked, and the reading was sixty-four.

"Sixty-four years," said Teague. "Assuming we averaged as much as one-half light speed, which isn't likely, we must be thirty light-years away from Earth. Thirty years to get a light-beam there, sixty or more to get a ship back, plus time to make the beacon and time for Earth to understand the signal and prepare a ship. . . ." He shook his head.

"Plus the fact," Tod said in a strained voice, "that there is no habitable planet in a thirty-year radius from Sol. Except Prime."

Shocked, they gaped silently at this well-known fact. A thousand years of scrupulous search with the best instruments could not have missed a planet like this at such a distance.

"Then the chronometer's wrong!"

"I'm afraid not," said Teague. "It's sixty-four years since we left Earth, and that's that."

"And this planet doesn't exist," said Carl with a sour smile, "and I suppose that is also that."

"Yes, Teague," said Tod. "One of those two facts can't exist with the other."

"They can because they do," said Teague. "There's a missing factor. Can a man breathe under water, Tod?"

"If he has a diving helmet."

Teague spread his hands. "It took sixty-four years to get to this planet *if*. We have to find the figurative diving helmet." He paused. "The evidence in favor of the planet's existence is fairly impressive," he said wryly. "Let's check the other fact."

"How?"

"The observatory."

They ran to it. The sky glowed its shimmering green, but through it the stars had begun to twinkle. Carl got to the telescope first, put a big hand on the swing-controls, and said, "Where first?" He tugged at the instrument. "Hey!" He tugged again.

"Don't!" said Teague sharply. Carl let go and backed away. Teague switched on the lights and examined the instrument. "It's already connected to the compensators," he said. "Hmp! Our hosts are most helpful." He looked at the setting of the small motors which moved the instrument to cancel diurnal rotation effects. "Twenty-eight hours, thirteen minutes plus. Well, if that's correct for this planet, it's proof that this isn't Earth or Prime—if we needed proof." He touched the controls lightly. "Carl, what's the matter here?"

Carl bent to look. There were dabs of dull silver on the threads of the adjusting screws. He touched them. "Parametal," he said. "Unflashed, but it has adhered enough to jam the threads. Take a couple days to get it off without jarring it. Look here—they've done the same thing with the objective screws!"

"We look at what they want us to see, and like it," said Tod.

"Maybe it's something we want to see," said April gently.

Only half-teasing, Tod said, "Whose side are you on, anyway?"

Teague put his eye to the instrument. His hands, by habit, strayed to the focusing adjustment, but found it locked the same way as the others. "Is there a Galactic Atlas?"

"Not in the rack," said Moira a moment later.

"Here," said April from the chart table. Awed, she added, "Open."

Tensely they waited while Teague took his observation and referred to the atlas and to the catalogue they found lying under it. When at last he lifted his face from the calculations, it bore the strangest expression Tod had ever seen there.

"Our diving helmet," he said at last, very slowly, too evenly, "—that is, the factor which rationalizes our two mutually exclusive facts—is simply that our captors have a faster-than-light drive."

"But according to theory—"

"According to our telescope," Teague interrupted, "through which I have just seen Sol, and these references so thoughtfully laid out for us . . ." Shockingly, his voice broke. He took two deep breaths, and said, "Sol is two hundred and seventeen light-years away. That sun which set a few minutes ago is Beta Librae." He studied their shocked faces, one by one. "I don't know what we shall eventually call this place," he said with difficulty, "but we had better get used to calling it home."

They called the planet Viridis ("the greenest name I can think of," Moira said) because none among them had ever seen such a green. It was more than the green of growing, for the sunlight was green-tinged and at night the whole sky glowed green, a green as bright as the brightest silver of Earth's moon, as water molecules, cracked by the star's intense ultraviolet, celebrated their nocturnal reunion.

They called the moons Wynken, Blynken and Nod, and the sun they called—the sun.

They worked like slaves, and then like scientists, which is a change of occupation but not a change of pace. They built a palisade of a cypresslike, straight-grained wood, each piece needle-pointed, double-laced with parametal wire. It had a barred gate and peepholes with periscopes and permanent swivel-mounts for the needle-guns they were able to fabricate from tube-stock and spare solenoids. They roofed the enclosure with parametal mesh which, at one point, could be rolled back to launch the lifeboat.

They buried Alma.

They tested and analyzed, classified, processed, researched everything in the compound and within easy reach of it—soil, vegetation, fauna. They developed an insect-repellent solution to coat the palisade and an insecticide with an automatic spray to keep the compound clear of the creatures, for they were numerous, large and occasionally downright dangerous, like the "flying caterpillar" which kept its pseudopods in its winged form and enthusiastically broke them off in the flesh of whatever attacked them, leaving an angry rash and suppurating sores. They discovered three kinds of edible seed and another which yielded a fine hydrocarbonic oil much like soy, and a flower whose calyces, when dried and then soaked and broiled, tasted precisely like crabmeat.

For a time they were two separate teams, virtually isolated from each other. Moira and Teague collected minerals and put them through the mass spectroscope and the radioanalyzers, and it fell to April to classify the life-forms, with Carl and Tod competing mightily to bring in new ones. Or at least photographs of new ones. Two-ton *Parametrodon*, familiarly known as dopey—a massive herbivore with just enough intelligence to move its jaws—was hardly the kind of thing to be carried home under one's arm, and *Felodon*, the scaly carnivore with the catlike tusks, though barely as long as a man, was about as friendly as a half-starved wolverine.

*Tetrapodys* (Tod called it "umbrellabird") turned out to be a rewarding catch. They stumbled across a vine which bore foul-smelling pods; these the clumsy amphibious bats found irresistible. Carl synthesized the evil stuff and improved upon it, and they smeared it on tree-boles by the river. *Tetrapodys* came there by the hundreds, and laid eggs apparently in sheer frustration. These eggs were camouflaged by a frilly green membrane, for all the world like the ground-buds of the giant water-fern. The green shoots tasted like shallots and were fine for salad when raw and excellent as onion soup when stewed. The half-hatched *Tetrapodys* yielded ligaments which when dried made excellent self-baited fish-hooks. The wing muscles of the adult tasted like veal cutlet with fish sauce, and the inner, or main shell of the eggs afforded them an amazing shoe-sole—light, tough and flexible, which, for some unknown reason, *Felodon* would not track.

*Pteronauchis*, or "flapping frog," was the gliding newt they had seen on that first day. Largely nocturnal, it was phototropic; a man with a strong light could fill a bushel with the things in minutes. Each specimen yielded twice as many, twice as large and twice as good frog-legs as a Terran frog.

There were no mammals.

There were flowers in profusion—white (a sticky green in that light), purple, brown, blue and, of course, the ubiquitous green. No red—as a matter of fact, there was virtually no red anywhere on the planet. April's eyes became a feast for them all. It is impossible to describe the yearning one can feel for an absent color. And so it was that a legend began with them. Twice Tod had seen a bright red growth. The first time he thought it was a mushroom, the second it seemed more of a lichen. The first time it was surrounded by a sea of crusher ants on the move—a fearsome carpet which even *Parametrodon* respected. The second time he had seen it from twenty meters away and had just turned toward it when not one, but three *Felodons* came hurtling through the undergrowth at him.

He came back later, both times, and found nothing. And once Carl swore he saw a brilliant red plant move slowly into a rock crevice as he approached. The thing became their *edelweiss*—very nearly their Grail.

Rough diamonds lay in the streambeds and emeralds glinted in the night-glow, and for the Terran-oriented mind there was incalculable treasure to be scratched up just below the steaming humus: iridium, ruthenium, metallic neptunium-237. There was an unaccountable (at first) shift toward the heavier metals. The ruthenium-rhodium-palladium group was as plentiful on Viridis as the iron-nickel-cobalt series on Earth; cadmium was actually more plentiful here than its relative, zinc. Technetium was present, though rare, on the crust, while Earth's had long since decayed.

Vulcanism was common on Viridis, as could be expected in the presence of so many radioactives. From the lifeboat they had seen bald spots where there were particularly high concentrations of "hot" material. In some of these there was life.

At the price of a bout of radiation sickness, Carl went into one such area briefly for specimens. What he found was extraordinary—a tree which was warm to the touch, which used minerals and water at a profligate pace and which, when transplanted outside an environment which destroyed cells almost as fast as they developed, went cancerous, grew enormously and killed itself with its own terrible viability. In the same lethal areas lived a primitive worm which constantly discarded segments to keep pace with its rapid growth, and which also grew visibly and died of living too fast when taken outside.

The inclination of the planet's axis was less than two degrees, so that there were virtually no seasons, and very little variation in temperature from one latitude to another. There were two continents and an equatorial sea, no mountains, no plains and few large lakes. Most of the planet was gently rolling hill country and meandering rivers, clothed in thick jungle or grass. The spot where they had awakened was as good as any other, so there they stayed, wandering less and less as they amassed information. Nowhere was there an artifact of any kind, or any slightest trace of previous habitation. Unless, of course, one considered the existence itself of life on this planet. For Permian life can hardly be expected to develop in less than a billion years; yet the irreproachable calendar inherent in the radioactive bones of Viridis insisted that the planet was no more than thirty-five million years old.

## V

When Moira's time came, it went hard with her, and Carl forgot to swagger because he could not help. Teague and April took care of her, and Tod stayed with Carl, wishing for the right thing to say and not finding it, wanting to do something for this new strange man with Carl's face, and the unsure hands which twisted each other, clawed the ground, wiped cruelly at the scalp, at the shins, restless, terrified. Through Carl, Tod learned a little more of what he never wanted to know—what it must have been like for Teague when he lost Alma.

Alma's six children were toddlers by then, bright and happy in the only world they had ever known. They had been named for moons—Wynken, Blynken and Nod, Rhea, Callisto and Titan. Nod and Titan were the boys, and they and Rhea had Alma's eyes and hair and sometimes Alma's odd, brave stillness—a sort of suspension of the body while the mind went out to grapple and conquer instead of fearing. If the turgid air and the radiant ground affected them, they did not show it, except perhaps in their rapid development.

They heard Moira cry out. It was like laughter, but it was pain. Carl sprang to his feet. Tod took his arm and Carl pulled it away. "Why can't I do something? Do I have to just *sit* here?"

"Shh. She doesn't feel it. That's a tropism. She'll be all right. Sit down, Carl. Tell you what you can do—you can name them. Think. Think of a nice set of names, all connected in some way, Teague used moons. What are you going to—"

"Time enough for that," Carl grunted. "Tod . . . do you know what I'll . . . I'd be if she—if something happened?"

"Nothing's going to happen."

"I'd just cancel out. I'm not Teague. I couldn't carry it. How does Teague do it? . . ." Carl's voice lapsed to a mumble.

"Names," Tod reminded him. "Seven, eight of 'em. Come on, now."

"Think she'll have eight?"

"Why not? She's normal." He nudged Carl. "Think of names. I know! How many of the old signs of the zodiac would make good names?"

"Don't remember 'em."

"I do. Aries, that's good. Taurus. Gem—no; you wouldn't want to call a child 'Twins.' Leo—that's *fine!*"

"Libra," said Carl, "for a girl. Aquarius, Sagittarius—how many's that?"

Tod counted on his fingers. "Six. Then, Virgo and Capricorn. And you're all set!" But Carl wasn't listening. In two long bounds he reached April, who was just stepping into the compound. She looked tired. She looked more than tired. In her beautiful eyes was a great pity, the color of a bleeding heart.

"Is she all right? Is she?" They were hardly words, those hoarse, rushed things.

April smiled with her lips, while her eyes poured pity. "Yes, yes, she'll be all right. It wasn't too bad."

Carl whooped and pushed past her. She caught his arm, and for all her frailty, swung him around.

"Not yet, Carl. Teague says to tell you first—"

"The babies? What about them? How many, April?"

April looked over Carl's shoulder at Tod. She said, "Three."

Carl's face relaxed, numb, and his eyes went round. "Th—what? Three so far, you mean. There'll surely be more. . . ."

She shook her head.

Tod felt the laughter explode within him, and he clamped his jaws on it. It surged at him, hammered in the back of his throat. And then he caught April's pleading eyes. He took strength from her, and bottled up a great bray of merriment.

Carl's voice was the last fraying thread of hope. "The others died, then."

She put a hand on his cheek. "There were only three. Carl . . . don't be mean to Moira."

"Oh, I won't," he said with difficulty. "She couldn't . . . I mean it wasn't her doing." He flashed a quick, defensive look at Tod, who was glad now he had controlled himself. What was in Carl's face meant murder for anyone who dared laugh.

April said, "Not your doing either, Carl. It's this planet. It must be."

"Thanks, April," Carl muttered. He went to the door, stopped, shook himself like a big dog. He said again, "Thanks," but this time his voice didn't work and it was only a whisper. He went inside.

Tod bolted for the corner of the building, whipped around it and sank to the ground, choking. He held both hands over his mouth and laughed until he hurt. When at last he came to a limp silence, he felt April's presence. She stood quietly watching him, waiting.

"I'm sorry," he said. "I'm sorry. But . . . it *is* funny."

She shook her head gravely. "We're not on Earth, Tod. A new world means new manners, too. That would apply even on Terra Prime if we'd gone there."

"I suppose," he said, and then repressed another giggle.

"I always thought it was a silly kind of joke anyway," she said primly. "Judging virility by the size of a brood. There isn't any scientific basis for it. Men are silly. They used to think that virility could be measured by the amount of hair on their chests, or how tall they were. There's nothing wrong with having only three."

"Carl?" grinned Tod. "The big ol' swashbuckler?" He let the grin fade. "All right, Ape, I won't let Carl see me laugh. Or you either. All right?" A peculiar expression crossed his face. "What was that you said? April! Men never had hair on their chests!"

"Yes they did. Ask Teague."

"I'll take your word for it." He shuddered. "I can't imagine it unless a man had a tail too. And bony ridges over his eyes."

"It wasn't so long ago that they had. The ridges, anyway. Well—I'm glad you didn't laugh in front of him. You're nice, Tod."

"You're nice too." He pulled her down beside him and hugged her gently. "Bet you'll have a dozen."

"I'll try." She kissed him.

When specimen-hunting had gone as far as it could, classification became the settlement's main enterprise. And gradually, the unique pattern of Viridian life began to emerge.

Viridis had its primitive fish and several of the mollusca, but the fauna was primarily arthropods and reptiles. The interesting thing about each of the three branches was the close relationship between species. It was almost as if evolution took a major step with each generation, instead of bumbling along as on Earth, where certain stages of development are static for thousands, millions of years. *Pterodon,* for example, existed in three varieties, the simplest of which showed a clear similarity to *Pteronauchis,* the gliding newt. A simple salamander could be shown to be the common ancestor of both the flapping frog and massive *Parametrodon,* and there were strong similarities between this salamander and the worm which fathered the arthropods.

They lived close to the truth for a long time without being able to see it, for man is conditioned to think of evolution from simple to complex, from ooze to animalcule to mollusk to ganoid; amphibid to monotreme to primate to tinker . . . losing the significance of the fact that all these coexist. Was the vertebrate eel of prehistory a *higher* form of life than his simpler descendant? The whale lost his legs; this men call recidivism, a sort of backsliding in evolution, and treat it as a kind of illegitimacy.

Men are oriented out of simplicity toward the complex, and make of the latter a goal. Nature treats complex matters as expediencies and so is never confused. It is hardly surprising, then, that the Viridis colony took so long to discover their error, for the weight of evidence was in error's favor. There was indeed an unbroken line from the lowest forms of life to the highest, and to assume that they had a common ancestor was a beautifully consistent hypothesis, of the order of accuracy an archer might display in hitting dead center, from a thousand paces, a bowstring with the nock of his arrow.

The work fell more and more on the younger ones. Teague isolated himself, not by edict, but by habit. It was assumed that he was working along his own lines; and then it became usual to proceed without him, until finally he was virtually a hermit in their midst. He was aging rapidly; perhaps it hurt something in him to be surrounded by so much youth. His six children thrived, and, with Carl's three, ran naked in the jungle armed only with their sticks and their speed. They were apparently immune to practically everything Viridis might bring against them, even *Crotalidus's* fangs, which gave them the equivalent of a severe bee sting (as opposed to what had happened to Moira once, when they had had to reactivate one of the Coffins to keep her alive).

Tod would come and sit with him sometimes, and as long as there was no talk the older man seemed to gain something from the visits. But he preferred to be alone, living as much as he could with memories for which not even a new world could afford a substitute.

Tod said to Carl, "Teague is going to wither up and blow away if we can't interest him in something."

"He's interested enough to spend a lot of time with whatever he's thinking about," Carl said bluntly.

"But I'd like it better if he was interested in something here, now. I wish we could . . . I wish—" But he could think of nothing, and it was a constant trouble to him.

Little Titan was killed, crushed under a great clumsy *Parametrodon* which slid down a bank on him while the child was grubbing for the scarlet cap of the strange red mushroom they had glimpsed from time to time. It was in pursuit of one of these that Moira had been bitten by the *Crotalidus*. One of Carl's children was drowned—just how, no one knew. Aside from these tragedies, life was easy and interesting. The compound began to look more like a *kraal* as they acclimated, for although the adults never adapted as well as the children, they did become far less sensitive to insect bites and the poison weeds which first troubled them.

It was Teague's son Nod who found what was needed to bring Teague's interest back, at least for a while. The child came back to the compound one day, trailed by two slinking *Felodons* who did not catch him because they kept pausing and pausing to lap up gouts of blood which marked his path. Nod's ear was torn and he had a green-stick break in his left ulna, and a dislocated wrist. He came weeping, weeping tears of joy. He shouted as he wept, great proud noises. Once in the compound he collapsed, but he would not lose consciousness, or his grip on his prize, until Teague came. Then he handed Teague the mushroom and fainted.

The mushroom was and was not like anything on Earth. Earth has a fungus called *schizophyllum*, not uncommon but most strange. Though not properly a fungus, the red "mushroom" of Viridis had many of the functions of *schizophyllum*.

*Schizophyllum* produces spores of four distinct types, each of which grows into a genetically distinct, completely dissimilar plant. Three of these are sterile. The fourth produces *schizophyllum*.

The red mushroom of Viridis also produced four distinct heterokaryons or genetically different types, and the spores of one of these produced the mushroom.

Teague spent an engrossing Earth-year in investigating the other three.

# VI

Sweating and miserable in his integument of skinflex, Tod hunched in the crotch of a finger-tree. His knees were drawn up and his head was down; his arms clasped his shins and he rocked slightly back and forth. He knew he would be safe here for some time—the fleshy fingers of the tree were clumped at the slender, swaying ends of the branches and never turned back toward the trunk. He wondered what it would be like to be dead. Perhaps he would be dead soon, and then he'd know. He might as well be.

The names he'd chosen were perfect and all of a family: Sol, Mercury, Venus, Terra, Mars, Jupiter . . . eleven of them. And he could think of a twelfth if he had to.

For what?

He let himself sink down again into the blackness wherein nothing lived but the oily turning of *what's it like to be dead?*

Quiet, he thought. *No one would laugh.*

Something pale moved on the jungle floor below him. He thought instantly of April, and angrily put the thought out of his mind. April would be sleeping now, having completed the trifling task it had taken her so long to start. Down there, that would be Blynken, or maybe Rhea. They were very alike.

It didn't matter, anyway.

He closed his eyes and stopped rocking. He couldn't see anyone, no one could see him. That was the best way. So he sat, and let time pass, and when a hand lay on his shoulder, he nearly leaped out of the tree. "Damn it, Blynken—"

"It's me. Rhea." The child, like all of Alma's daughters, was large for her age and glowing with health. How long had it been? Six, eight . . . nine Earth years since they had landed.

"Go hunt mushrooms," Tod growled. "Leave me alone."

"Come back," said the girl.

Tod would not answer. Rhea knelt beside him, her arm around the primary branch, her back, with his, against the trunk. She bent her head and put her cheek against his. "Tod."

Something inside him flamed. He bared his teeth and swung a heavy fist. The girl doubled up soundlessly and slipped out of the tree. He stared down at the lax body and at first could not see it for the haze of fury which blew and whirled around him. Then his vision cleared and he moaned, tossed his club down and dropped after it. He caught up the club and whacked off the tree-fingers which probed toward them. He swept up the child and leapt clear, and sank to his knees, gathering her close.

"Rhea, I'm sorry, I'm sorry . . . I wasn't . . . I'm not—*Rhea!* Don't be dead!"

She stirred and made a tearing sound with her throat. Her eyelids trembled and opened, uncovering pain-blinded eyes. "Rhea!"

"It's all right," she whispered, "I shouldn't't've bothered you. Do you want me to go away?"

"No," he said, "No." He held her tight. *Why not let her go away?* a part of him wondered, and another part, frightened and puzzled, cried, *No! No!* He had an urgent, half-hysterical need to explain. *Why explain to her, a child? Say you're sorry, comfort her, heal her, but don't expect her to understand.* Yet he said, "I can't go back. There's nowhere else to go. So what can I do?"

Rhea was quiet, as if waiting. A terrible thing, a wonderful thing, to have someone you have hurt wait patiently like that while you find a way to explain. Even if you only explain it to yourself . . . "What could I do if I went back? They—they'll never—they'll laugh at me. They'll all laugh. They're laughing now." Angry again, plaintive no more, he blurted, "April! *Damn* April! She's made a eunuch out of me!"

"Because she had only one baby?"

"Like a savage."

"It's a beautiful baby. A boy."

"A man, a real man, fathers six or eight."

She met his eyes gravely. "That's silly."

"What's happening to us on this crazy planet?" he raged. "Are we evolving backward? What comes next—one of you kids hatching out some amphibids?"

She said only, "Come back, Tod."

"I can't," he whispered. "They'll think I'm . . . that I can't . . ." Helplessly, he shrugged. "They'll laugh."

"Not until you do, and then they'll laugh *with* you. Not at you, Tod."

Finally, he said it, "April won't love me; she'll never love a weakling."

She pondered, holding him with her clear gaze. "You really need to be loved a whole lot."

Perversely, he became angry again. "I can get along!" he snapped.

And she smiled and touched the nape of his neck. "You're loved," she assured him. "Gee, you don't have to be mad about that. I love you, don't I? April loves you. Maybe I love you even more than she does. She loves everything you are, Tod. I love everything you ever were and everything you ever will be."

He closed his eyes and a great music came to him. A long, long time ago he had attacked someone who came to comfort him, and she had let him cry, and at length she had said . . . not exactly these words, but— it was the same.

"Rhea."

He looked at her. "You said all that to me before."

A puzzled small crinkle appeared between her eyes and she put her fingers on it. "Did I?"

"Yes," said Tod, "but it was before you were even born."

He rose and took her hand, and they went back to the compound, and whether he was laughed at or not he never knew, for he could think of nothing but his full heart and of April. He went straight in to her and kissed her gently and admired his son, whose name was Sol, and who had been born with hair and two tiny incisors, and who had heavy bony ridges over his eyes. . . .

"A fantastic storage capacity," Teague remarked, touching the top of the scarlet mushroom. "The spores are almost microscopic. The thing doesn't seem to want them distributed, either. It positively hoards them, millions of them."

"Start over, please," April said. She shifted the baby in her arms. He was growing prodigiously. "Slowly. I used to know something about biology—or so I thought. But *this*—"

Teague almost smiled. It was good to see. The aging face had not had so much expression in it in five Earth-years. "I'll get as basic as I can, then, and start from there. First of all, we call this thing a mushroom, but it isn't. I don't think it's a plant, though you couldn't call it an animal, either."

"I don't think anybody ever told me the real difference between a plant and an animal," said Tod.

"Oh . . . well, the most convenient way to put it—it's not strictly accurate, but it will do—is that plants make their own food and animals subsist on what others have made. This thing does both. It has roots, but—" he lifted an edge of the skirted stem of the mushroom—"it can move them. Not much, not fast; but if it wants to shift itself, it can."

April smiled, "Tod, I'll give you basic biology any time. Do go on, Teague."

"Good. Now, I explained about the heterokaryons—the ability this thing has to produce spores which grow up into four completely different plants. One is a mushroom just like this. Here are the other three."

Tod looked at the box of plants. "Are they really all from the mushroom spores?"

"Don't blame you," said Teague, and actually chuckled. "I didn't believe it myself at first. A sort of pitcher plant, half full of liquid. A thing like a cactus. And this one. It's practically all underground, like a truffle, although it has these cilia. You wouldn't think it was anything but a few horsehairs stuck in the ground."

"And they're all sterile," Tod recalled.

"They're not," said Teague, "and that's what I called you in here to tell you. They'll yield if they are fertilized."

"Fertilized how?"

Instead of answering, Teague asked April, "Do you remember how far back we traced the evolution of Viridian life?"

"Of course. We got the arthropods all the way back to a simple segmented worm. The insects seemed to come from another worm, with pseudopods and a hard carapace."

"A caterpillar," Tod interpolated.

"Almost," said April, with a scientist's nicety. "And the most primitive reptile we could find was a little gymnoderm you could barely see without a glass."

"Where did we find it?"

"Swimming around in—oh! In those pitcher plant things!"

"If you won't take my word for this," said Teague, a huge enjoyment glinting between his words, "you'll just have to breed these things yourself. It's a lot of work, but this is what you'll discover.

"An adult gymnoderm—a male—finds this pitcher and falls in. There's plenty of nutriment for him, you know, and he's a true amphibian. He fertilizes the pitcher. Nodules grow under the surface of the liquid inside there—" he pointed "—and bud off. The buds are mobile. They grow into wrigglers, miniature tadpoles. Then into lizards. They climb out and go about the business of being—well, lizards."

"All males?" asked Tod.

"No," said Teague, "and that's an angle I haven't yet investigated. But apparently some males breed with females, which lay eggs, which hatch into lizards, and some find plants to fertilize. Anyway, it looks as if this plant is actually the progenitor of all the reptiles here; you know how clear the evolutionary lines are to all the species."

"What about the truffle with the horsehairs?" asked Tod.

"A pupa," said Teague, and to the incredulous expression on April's face, he insisted, "Really—a pupa. After nine weeks or so of dormance, it hatches out into what you almost called a caterpillar."

"And then into all the insects here," said April, and shook her head in wonderment. "And I suppose that cactus-thing hatches out the nematodes, the segmented ones that evolve into arthropods?"

Teague nodded. "You're welcome to experiment," he said again, "but believe me—you'll only find out I'm right: it really happens."

"Then this scarlet mushroom is the beginning of everything here."

"I can't find another theory," said Teague.

"I can," said Tod.

They looked at him questioningly, and he rose and laughed. "Not yet. I have to think it through." He scooped up the baby and then helped April to her feet. "How do you like our Sol, Teague?"

"Fine," said Teague. "A fine boy." Tod knew he was seeing the heavy occipital ridges, the early teeth, and saying nothing. Tod was aware of a faint inward surprise as the baby reached toward April and he handed him over. He should have resented what might be in Teague's mind, but he did not. The beginnings of an important insight welcomed criticism of the child, recognized its hairiness, its savagery, and found these things good. But as yet the thought was too nebulous to express, except by a smile. He smiled, took April's hand and left.

"That was a funny thing you said to Teague," April told him as they walked toward their quarters.

"Remember, April, the day we landed? Remember—" he made a gesture that took in a quadrant of sky—"Remember how we all felt . . . good?"

"Yes," she murmured. "It was like a sort of compliment, and a reassurance. How could I forget?"

"Yes. Well . . ." He spoke with difficulty but his smile stayed. "I have a thought, and it makes me feel like that. But I can't get it into words," After a thoughtful pause, he added, "Yet."

She shifted the baby. "He's getting so heavy."

"I'll take him." He took the squirming bundle with the deep-set, almost humorous eyes. When he looked up from them, he caught an expression on April's face which he hadn't seen in years. "What is it, Ape?"

"You—*like* him."

"Well, sure."

"I was afraid. I was afraid for a long time that you . . . he's ours, but he isn't exactly a pretty baby."

"I'm not exactly a pretty father."

"You know how precious you are to me?" she whispered.

He knew, for this was an old intimacy between them. He laughed and followed the ritual: "How precious?"

She cupped her hands and brought them together, to make of them an ivory box. She raised the hands and peeped into them, between the thumbs, as if at a rare jewel, then clasped the magic tight and hugged it to her breast, raising tear-filled eyes to him. "That precious," she breathed.

He looked at the sky, seeing somewhere in it the many peak moments of their happiness when she had made that gesture, feeling how each one, meticulously chosen, brought all the others back. "I used to hate this place," he said, "I guess it's changed."

"You've changed."

*Changed how?* he wondered. He felt the same, even though he knew he looked older. . . .

The years passed, and the children grew. When Sol was fifteen Earth-years old, short, heavy-shouldered, powerful, he married Carl's daughter Libra. Teague, turning to parchment, had returned to his hermitage from the temporary stimulation of his researches on what they still called "the mushroom." More and more the colony lived off the land and out of the jungle, not because there was any less to be synthesized from their compact machines, but out of preference; it was easier to catch flapping frogs or umbrellabirds and cook them than to bother with machine settings and check analyses, and, somehow, a lot more fun to eat them, too.

It seemed to them safer, year by year. *Felodon*, unquestionably the highest form of life on Viridis, was growing scarce, being replaced by a smaller, more timid carnivore April called *Vulpidus* (once, for it seemed not to matter much any more about keeping records) and everyone ultimately called "fox," for all the fact that it was a reptile. *Pterodon* was disappearing too, as were all the larger forms. More and more they strayed after food, not famine-driven, but purely for variety; more and more they found themselves welcome and comfortable away from the compound. Once Carl and Moira drifted off for nearly a year. When they came back they had another child—a silent, laughing little thing with oddly long arms and heavy teeth.

The warm days and the glowing nights passed comfortably and the stars no longer called. Tod became a grandfather and was proud. The child, a girl, was albino like April, and had exactly April's deep red eyes. Sol and Libra named her Emerald, a green name and a ground-term rather than a sky-term, as if in open expression of the slow spell worked on them all by Viridis. She was mute—but so were almost all the new children, and it seemed not to matter. They were healthy and happy.

Tod went to tell Teague, thinking it might cheer the old one up a little. He found him lying in what had once been his laboratory, thin and placid and disinterested, absently staring down at one of the arthropodal flying creatures that had once startled them so by zooming into the Coffin chamber. This one had happened to land on Teague's hand, and Teague was laxly waiting for it to fly off again, out through the unscreened window, past the unused sprays, over the faint tumble of rotted spars which had once been a palisade.

"Teague, the baby's come!"

Teague sighed, his tired mind detaching itself from memory episode by episode. His eyes rolled toward Tod and finally he turned his head. "Which one would that be?"

Tod laughed. "My grandchild, a girl. Sol's baby."

Teague let his lids fall. He said nothing.

"Well, aren't you glad?"

Slowly a frown came to the papery brow. "Glad." Tod felt he was looking at the word as he had stared at the arthropod, wondering limply when it might go away. "What's the matter with it?"

"What?"

Teague sighed again, a weary, impatient sound. "What does it look like?" he said slowly, emphasizing each one-syllabled word.

"Like April. Just like April."

Teague half sat up, and blinked at Tod. "You don't mean it."

"Yes, eyes red as—" The image of an Earth sunset flickered near his mind but vanished as too hard to visualize. Tod pointed at the four red-capped "mushrooms" that had stood for so many years in the test-boxes in the laboratory. "Red as those."

"Silver hair," said Teague.

"Yes, beau—"

"All over," said Teague flatly.

"Well, yes."

Teague let himself fall back on the cot and gave a disgusted snort. "A monkey."

*"Teague!"*

"Ah-h-h . . . go 'way," growled the old man. "I long ago resigned myself to what was happening to us here. A human being just can't adapt to the kind of radioactive ruin this place is for us. Your monsters'll breed monsters, and the monsters'll do the same if they can, until pretty soon they just won't breed any more. And that will be the end of that, and good riddance. . . ." His voice faded away. His eyes opened, looking on distant things, and gradually found themselves focused on the man who stood over him in shocked silence. "But the one thing I can't stand is to have somebody come in here saying, 'Oh, joy, oh happy day!' "

"Teague . . ." Tod swallowed heavily.

"Viridis eats ambition; there was going to be a city here," said the old man indistinctly. "Viridis eats humanity; there were going to be people here." He chuckled gruesomely. "All right, all right, accept it if you have to—and you have to. But don't come around here celebrating."

Tod backed to the door, his eyes horror-round, then turned and fled.

## VII

April held him as he crouched against the wall, rocked him slightly, made soft unspellable mother-noises to him.

"Shh, he's all decayed, all lonesome and mad," she murmured. "Shh. Shh."

Tod felt half-strangled. As a youth he had been easily moved, he recalled; he had that tightness of the throat for sympathy, for empathy, for injustices he felt the Universe was hurling at him out of its capacious store. But recently life had been placid, full of love and togetherness and a widening sense of membership with the earth and the air and all the familiar things which walked and flew and grew and bred in it. And his throat was shaped for laughter now; these feelings hurt him.

"But he's right," he whispered. "Don't you see? Right from the beginning it . . . it was . . . remember Alma had six children, April? And a little later, Carl and Moira had three? And you, only one . . . how long is it since the average human gave birth to only one?"

"They used to say it was humanity's last major mutation," she admitted, "Multiple births . . . these last two thousand years. But—"

"Eyebrow ridges," he interrupted. "Hair . . . that skull, Emerald's skull, slanting back like that; did you see the tusks on that little . . . *baboon* of Moira's?"

"Tod! *Don't!*"

He leaped to his feet, sprang across the room and snatched the golden helix from the shelf where it had gleamed its locked symbolism down on them ever since the landing. "Around and down!" he shouted. "Around and around and down!" He squatted beside her and pointed furiously. "Down and down into the blackest black there is; down into *nothing.*" He shook his fist at the sky. "You see what they do? They find the highest form of life they can and plant it here and watch it slide down into the muck!" He hurled the artifact away from him.

"But it goes up too, round and up. Oh, Tod!" she cried. "Can you remember them, what they looked like, the way they flew, and say these things about them?"

"I can remember Alma," he gritted, "conceiving and gestating alone in space, while they turned their rays on her every day. You know *why?*" With the sudden thought, he stabbed a finger down at her. "To give her babies a head start on Viridis, otherwise they'd have been born normal here; it would've taken another couple of generations to start them downhill, and they wanted us all to go together."

"No, Tod, no!"

"Yes, April, yes. How much proof do you need?" He whirled on her. "Listen—remember that mushroom Teague analyzed? He had to *pry* spores out of it to see what it yielded. Remember the three different plants he got? Well, I was just there; I don't know how many times before I've seen it, but only now it makes sense. He's got four mushrooms now; do you see? Do you see? Even back as far as we can trace the bugs and newts on this green hell-pit, Viridis won't let anything climb; it must fall."

"I don't—"

"You'll give me basic biology any time," he quoted sarcastically. "Let me tell you some biology. That mushroom yields three plants, and the plants yield animal life. Well, when the animal life fertilized those hetero-whatever—"

"Heterokaryons."

"Yes. Well, you don't get animals that can evolve and improve. You get one pitiful generation of animals which breeds back into a mushroom, and there it sits hoarding its spores. Viridis wouldn't let one puny newt, one primitive pupa build! It snatches 'em back, locks 'em up. That mushroom isn't the beginning of everything here—*it's the end!*"

April got to her feet slowly, looking at Tod as if she had never seen him before, not in fear, but with a troubled curiosity. She crossed the room and picked up the artifact, stroked its gleaming golden coils. "You could be right," she said in a low voice. "But that can't be all there is to it." She set the helix back in its place. "They *wouldn't.*"

She spoke with such intensity that for a moment that metrical formation, mighty and golden, rose again in Tod's mind, up and up to the measureless cloud which must be a ship. He recalled the sudden shift, like a genuflection, directed at them, at *him,* and for that moment he could find no evil in it. Confused, he tossed his head, found himself looking out the door, seeing Moira's youngest ambling comfortably across the compound.

"They *wouldn't?*" he snarled. He took April's slender arm and whirled her to the door. "You know what I'd do before I'd father another one like *that?*" He told her specifically what he would do. "A lemur next, hm? A spider, an oyster, a jellyfish!"

April whimpered and ran out. "Know any lullabies to a tapeworm?" he roared after her. She disappeared into the jungle, and he fell back, gasping for breath. . . .

Having no stomach for careful thought or careful choosing, having Teague for an example to follow, Tod too turned hermit. He could have survived the crisis easily perhaps, with April to help, but she did not come back. Moira and Carl were off again, wandering; the children lived their own lives, and he had no wish to see Teague. Once or twice Sol and Libra came to see him, but he snarled at them and they left him alone. It was no sacrifice. Life on Viridis was very full for the contented ones.

He sulked in his room or poked about the compound by himself. He activated the protein converter once, but found its products tasteless, and never bothered with it again. Sometimes he would stand near the edge of the hilltop and watch the children playing in the long grass, and his lip would curl.

*Damn Teague!* He'd been happy enough with Sol all those years, for all the boy's bulging eyebrow ridges and hairy body. He had been about to accept the silent, silver Emerald, too, when the crotchety old man had dropped his bomb. Once or twice Tod wondered detachedly what it was in him that was so easily reached, so completely insecure, that the suggestion of abnormality should strike so deep.

Somebody once said, *"You really need to be loved, don't you, Tod?"*

No one would love this tainted thing, father of savages who spawned animals. He didn't deserve to be loved.

He had never felt so alone. *"I'm going to die. But I will be with you too."* That had been Alma. Huh! There was old Teague, tanning his brains in his own sour acids. Alma had believed something or other . . . and what had come of it? That wizened old crab lolling his life away in the lab.

Tod spent six months that way.

"Tod!" He came out of sleep reluctantly, because in sleep an inner self still lived with April where there was no doubt and no fury; no desertion, no loneliness.

He opened his eyes and stared dully at the slender figure silhouetted against Viridis's glowing sky. "April?"

"Moira," said the figure. The voice was cold.

"Moira!" he said, sitting up. "I haven't seen you for a year. More. Wh—"

"Come," she said. "Hurry."

"Come where?"

"Come by yourself or I'll get Carl and he'll carry you." She walked swiftly to the door.

He reeled after her. "You can't come in here and—"

"Come on." The voice was edged and slid out from between clenched teeth. A miserable part of him twitched in delight and told him that he was important enough to be hated. He despised himself for recognizing the twisted thought, and before he knew what he was doing he was following Moira at a steady trot.

"Where are—" he gasped, and she said over her shoulder, "If you don't talk you'll go faster."

At the jungle margin a shadow detached itself and spoke. "Got him?"
"Yes, Carl."

The shadow became Carl. He swung in behind Tod, who suddenly realized that if he did not follow the leader, the one behind would drive. He glanced back at Carl's implacable bulk, and then put down his head and jogged doggedly along as he was told.

They followed a small stream, crossed it on a fallen tree and climbed a hill. Just as Tod was about to accept the worst these determined people might offer in exchange for a moment to ease his fiery lungs, Moira stopped. He stumbled into her. She caught his arm and kept him on his feet.

"In there," she said, pointing.

"A finger tree."

"You know how to get inside," Carl growled.

Moira said, "She begged me not to tell you, ever. I think she was wrong."

"Who? What is—"

"Inside," said Carl, and shoved him roughly down the slope.

His long conditioning was still with him, and reflexively he sidestepped the fanning fingers which swayed to meet him. He ducked under them, batted aside the inner phalanx and found himself in the clear space underneath. He stopped there, gasping.

Something moaned.

He bent, fumbled cautiously in the blackness. He touched something smooth and alive, recoiled, touched it again. A foot.

Someone began to cry harshly, hurtfully, the sound exploding as if through clenched hands.

"*April!*"

"I told them not to. . . ." and she moaned.

"April, what is it, what's happened?"

"You needn't . . . be," she said, sobbed a while, and went on, ". . . angry. It didn't live."

"What didn't . . . you mean you . . . April, you—"

"It wouldn't've been a tapeworm," she whispered.

"Who—" he fell to his knees, found her face. "When did you—"

"I was going to tell you that day, that very same day, and when you came in so angry at what Teague told you, I specially wanted to, I thought you'd . . . be glad."

"April, why didn't you come back? If I'd known. . . ."

"You *said* what you'd do if I ever . . . if you ever had another . . . you meant it, Tod."

"It's this place, this Viridis," he said sadly. "I went crazy."

He felt her wet hand on his cheek.

"It's all right. I just didn't want to make it worse for you," April said.

"I'll take you back."

"No, you can't. I've been . . . I've lost a lot of . . . just stay with me a little while."

"Moira should have—"

"She just found me," said April. "I've been alone all the—I guess I made a noise. I didn't mean to. Tod . . . don't quarrel. Don't go into a lot of . . . It's all right."

Against her throat he cried. *"All right!"*

"When you're by yourself," she said faintly, "you think; you think better. Did you ever think of—"

"April!" he cried in anguish, the very sound of her pale, pain-wracked voice making this whole horror real.

"Shh, sh. Listen," she said rapidly, "There isn't time, you know, Tod. Tod, did you ever think of us all, Teague and Alma and Moira and Carl and us, what we are?"

"I know what I am."

*"Shh.* Altogether we're a leader and mother; a word and a shield; a doubter, a mystic. . . ." Her voice trailed off. She coughed and he could feel the spastic jolt shoot through her body. She panted lightly for a moment and went on urgently, "Anger and prejudice and stupidity, courage, laughter, love, music . . . it was all aboard that ship and it's all here on Viridis. Our children and theirs—no matter what they look like, Tod, no matter how they live or what they eat—they have that in them. Humanity isn't just a way of walking, merely a kind of skin. It's what we had together and what we gave Sol. It's what the golden ones found in us and wanted for Viridis. You'll see. You'll see."

"Why Viridis?"

"Because of what Teague said—what you said." Her breath puffed out in the ghost of a laugh. "Basic biology . . . ontogeny follows phylogeny. The human fetus is a cell, an animalcule, a gilled amphibian . . . all up the line. It's there in us; Viridis makes it go backward."

"To what?"

"The mushroom. The spores. We'll be spores, Tod. Together . . . Alma

*said* she could be dead, and together with Teague! That's why I said
. . . it's all right. This doesn't matter, what's happened. We live in Sol,
we live in Emerald with Carl and Moira, you see? Closer, nearer than
we've ever been."

Tod took a hard hold on his reason. "But back to spores—why? What
then?"

She sighed. It was unquestionably a happy sound. "They'll be back for
the reaping, and they'll have us, Tod, all we are and all they worship:
goodness and generosity and the urge to build; mercy; kindness."

"They're needed too," she whispered. "And the spores make mushrooms, and the mushrooms make the heterokaryons; and from those, away
from Viridis, come the life-forms to breed us—*us*, Tod! into whichever
form is dominant. And there we'll be, that flash of old understanding of
a new idea . . . the special pressure on a painter's hand that makes him
a Rembrandt, the sense of architecture that turns a piano-player into a
Bach. Three billion extra years of evolution, ready to help wherever it can
be used. On every Earth-type planet, Tod—millions of us, blowing about
in the summer wind, waiting to give. . . ."

"Give! Give what Teague is now, rotten and angry?"

"That isn't Teague. That will die off. Teague lives with Alma in their
children, and in theirs . . . she *said* she'd be with him!"

"Me . . . what about me?" he breathed. "What I did to you. . . ."

"Nothing, you did nothing. You live in Sol, in Emerald. Living, conscious, alive . . . with me. . . ."

He said, "You mean . . . you could talk to me from Sol?"

I think I might." With his forehead, bent so close to her, he felt her
smile. "But I don't think I would. Lying so close to you, why should I
speak to an outsider?"

Her breathing changed and he was suddenly terrified. "April, don't
die."

"I won't," she said. "Alma didn't." She kissed him gently and died.


It was a long darkness, with Tod hardly aware of roaming and raging
through the jungle, of eating without tasting, of hungering without knowing of it. Then there was a twilight, many months long, soft and still, with
restfulness here and a promise soon. Then there was the compound again,
found like a dead memory, learned again just a little more readily than
something new. Carl and Moira were kind, knowing the nature of justice
and the limits of punishment, and at last Tod was alive again.

He found himself one day down near the river, watching it and thinking back without fear of his own thoughts, and a growing wonder came to him. His mind had for so long dwelt on his own evil that it was hard to break new paths. He wondered with an awesome effort what manner of creatures might worship humanity for itself, and what manner of creatures humans were to be so worshipped. It was a totally new concept to him, and he was completely immersed in it, so that when Emerald slid out of the grass and stood watching him, he was frightened and shouted.

She did not move. There was little to fear now on Viridis. All the large reptiles were gone, and there was room for the humans, the humanoids, the primates, the . . . children. In his shock the old reflexes played. He stared at her, her square stocky body, the silver hair which covered it all over except for the face, the palms, the soles of the feet. *"A monkey!"* he spat, in Teague's tones, and the shock turned to shame. He met her eyes, April's deep glowing rubies, and they looked back at him without fear.

He let a vision of April grow and fill the world. The child's rare red eyes helped (there was so little, so very little red on Viridis). He saw April at the spaceport, holding him in the dark shadows of the blockhouse while the sky flamed above them. *We'll go out like that soon, soon, Tod. Squeeze me, squeeze me . . . Ah,* he'd said, *who needs a ship?*

Another April, part of her in a dim light as she sat writing; her hair, a crescent of light loving her cheek, a band of it on her brow; then she had seen him and turned, rising, smothered his first word with her mouth. Another April wanting to smile, waiting; and April asleep, and once April sobbing because she could not find a special word to tell him what she felt for him. . . . He brought his mind back from her in the past, from her as she was, alive in his mind, back to here, to the bright mute with the grave red eyes who stood before him, and he said, "How precious?"

The baby kept her eyes on his, and slowly raised her silken hands. She cupped them together to make a closed chamber, looked down at it, opened her hands slightly and swiftly to peer inside, rapt at what she pretended to see; closed her hands again to capture the treasure, whatever it was, and hugged it to her breast. She looked up at him slowly, and her eyes were full of tears, and she was smiling.

He took his grandchild carefully in his arms and held her gently and strongly. Monkey?

"April," he gasped. "Little Ape. Little Ape."

Viridis is a young planet which bears (at first glance) old life-forms. Come away and let the green planet roll around its sun; come back in a while—not long, as astronomical time goes.

The jungle is much the same, the sea, the rolling savannahs. But the life. . . .

Viridis was full of primates. There were blunt-toothed herbivores and long-limbed tree-dwellers, gliders and burrowers. The fish-eaters were adapting the way all Viridis life must adapt, becoming more fit by becoming simpler, or go to the wall. Already the sea-apes had rudimentary gills and had lost their hair. Already tiny forms competed with the insects on their own terms.

On the banks of the wandering rivers, monotremes with opposed toes dredged and paddled, and sloths and lemurs crept at night. At first they had stayed together, but they were soon too numerous for that; and a half-dozen generations cost them the power of speech, which was, by then, hardly a necessity. Living was good for primates on Viridis, and became better each generation.

Eating and breeding, hunting and escaping filled the days and the cacophonous nights. It was hard in the beginning to see a friend cut down, to watch a slender silver shape go spinning down a river and know that with it went some of your brother, some of your mate, some of yourself. But as the hundreds became thousands and the thousands millions, witnessing death became about as significant as watching your friend get his hair cut. The basic ids each spread through the changing, mutating population like a stain, crossed and recrossed by the strains of the others, coexisting, eating each other and being eaten and all the while passing down through the generations.

There was a cloud over the savannah, high over the ruins of the compound. It was a thing of many colors and of no particular shape, and it was bigger than one might imagine, not knowing how far away it was.

From it dropped a golden spot that became a thread, and down came a golden mass. It spread and swung, exploded into a myriad of individuals. Some descended on the compound, erasing and changing, lifting, breaking—always careful to kill nothing. Others blanketed the planet, streaking silently through the green aisles, flashing unimpeded through the tangled thickets. They combed the riverbanks and the half-light of hill waves, and everywhere they went they found and touched the mushroom and stripped it of its spores, the compaction and multiplication of what had once been the representatives of a very high reptile culture.

Primates climbed and leaped, crawled and crept to the jungle margins to watch. Eater lay by eaten; the hunted stood on the hunter's shoulder, and a platypoid laid an egg in the open which nobody touched.

Simian forms hung from the trees in loops and ropes, in swarms and beards, and more came all the time, brought by some ineffable magnetism to watch at the hill. It was a fast and a waiting, with no movement but jostling for position, a crowding forward from behind and a pressing back from the slightest chance of interfering with the golden visitors.

Down from the polychrome cloud drifted a mass of the golden beings, carrying with them a huge sleek ship. They held it above the ground, sliced it, lifted it apart, set down this piece and that until a shape began to grow. Into it went bales and bundles, stocks and stores, and then the open tops were covered. It was a much bigger installation than the one before.

Quickly, it was done, and the golden cloud hung waiting.

The jungle was trembling with quiet.

In one curved panel of the new structure, something spun, fell outward, and out of the opening came a procession of stately creatures, long-headed, bright-eyed, three-toed, richly plumed and feathered. They tested their splendid wings, then stopped suddenly, crouched and looking upward.

They were given their obeisance by the golden ones, and after there appeared in the sky the exquisite symbol of a beauty that rides up and up, turns and spirals down again only to rise again; the symbol of that which has no beginning and no end, and the sign of those whose worship and whose work it is to bring to all the Universe that which has shown itself worthy in parts of it.

Then they were gone, and the jungle exploded into killing and flight, eating and screaming, so that the feathered ones dove back into their shelter and closed the door. . . .

And again to the green planet (when the time was right) came the cloud-ship, and found a world full of birds, and the birds watched in awe while they harvested their magic dust, and built a new shelter. In this they left four of their own for later harvesting, and this was to make of Viridis a most beautiful place.

From Viridis, the ship vaulted through the galaxies, searching for worlds worthy of what is human in humanity, whatever their manner of being alive. These they seeded, and of these, perhaps one would produce something new, something which could be reduced to the dust of Viridis, and from dust return.

ROBERT SILVERBERG

# Born With the Dead

*Science fiction has been called "contemporary mythology" and SF (like much of literature) has borrowed heavily from ancient mythology for its themes and plots. This is particularly true of the popular quest story and of works which recapitulate the myth of Prometheus.*

*Here, Robert Silverberg blends the story of Orpheus and his travels into something as science fictional as it is beautiful.*

*M.H.G.*

1.

And what the dead had no speech for, when living,
They can tell you, being dead: the communication
Of the dead is tongued with fire beyond the language of the living.

T.S. Eliot: *Little Gidding*

Supposedly his late wife Sybille was on her way to Zanzibar. That was what they told him, and he believed it. Jorge Klein had reached that stage in his search when he would believe anything, if belief would only lead him to Sybille. Anyway, it wasn't so absurd that she would go to Zanzibar. Sybille had always wanted to go there. In some unfathomable obsessive way the place had seized the center of her consciousness long ago. When she was alive it hadn't been possible for her to go there, but now, loosed from all bonds, she would be drawn toward Zanzibar like a bird to its nest, like Ulysses to Ithaca, like a moth to a flame.

The plane, a small Air Zanzibar Havilland FP-803, took off more than half-empty from Dar es Salaam at 0915 on a mild bright morning, gaily circled above the dense masses of mango trees, red-flowering flamboyants and tall coconut palms along the aquamarine shores of the Indian Ocean, and headed northward on the short hop across the strait to Zanzibar. This day—Tuesday, the ninth of March, 1993—would be an unusual one for Zanzibar: five deads were aboard the plane, the first of their kind ever to

200

visit that fragrant isle. Daud Mahmoud Barwani, the health officer on duty that morning at Zanzibar's Karume Airport, had been warned of this by the emigration officials on the mainland. He had no idea how he was going to handle the situation, and he was apprehensive: these were tense times in Zanzibar. Times are always tense in Zanzibar. Should he refuse them entry? Did deads pose any threat to Zanzibar's ever-precarious political stability? What about subtler menaces? Deads might be carriers of dangerous spiritual maladies. Was there anything in the Revised Administrative Code about refusing visas on grounds of suspected contagions of the spirit? Daud Mahmoud Barwani nibbled moodily at his breakfast —a cold *chapatti,* a mound of cold curried potato—and waited without eagerness for the arrival of the deads.

Almost two and a half years had passed since Jorge Klein had last seen Sybille: the afternoon of Saturday, October 13, 1990, the day of her funeral. That day she lay in her casket as though merely asleep, her beauty altogether unmarred by her final ordeal: pale skin, dark lustrous hair, delicate nostrils, full lips. Iridescent gold and violet fabric enfolded her serene body; a shimmering electrostatic haze, faintly perfumed with a jasmine fragrance, protected her from decay. For five hours she floated on the dais while the rites of parting were read and the condolences were offered—offered almost furtively, as if her death were a thing too monstrous to acknowledge with a show of strong feeling; then, when only a few people remained, the inner core of their circle of friends, Klein kissed her lightly on the lips and surrendered her to the silent dark-clad men whom the Cold Town had sent. She had asked in her will to be rekindled; they took her away in a black van to work their magic on her corpse. The casket, retreating on their broad shoulders, seemed to Klein to be disappearing into a throbbing gray vortex that he was helpless to penetrate. Presumably he would never hear from her again. In those days the deads kept strictly to themselves, sequestered behind the walls of their self-imposed ghettos; it was rare ever to see one outside the Cold Towns, rare even for one of them to make oblique contact with the world of the living.

So a redefinition of their relationship was forced on him. For nine years it had been Jorge and Sybille, Sybille and Jorge, I and thou forming *we,* above all *we,* a transcendental *we.* He had loved her with almost painful intensity. In life they had gone everywhere together, had done everything together, shared research tasks and classroom assignments, thought interchangeable thoughts, expressed tastes that were nearly always identical, so completely had each permeated the other. She was a part of him, he of her, and until the moment of her unexpected death he had assumed it would be like that forever. They were still young, he thirty-eight, she thirty-four, decades to look forward to. Then she was gone. And now they were mere anonymities to one another, she not Sybille but only a dead, he not Jorge but only a warm. She was somewhere on the North American continent, walking about, talking, eating, reading, and yet she was gone, lost to him, and it behooved him to accept that alteration in his life, and outwardly he did accept it, but yet, though he knew he could never again have things as they once had been, he allowed himself the indulgence of a lingering wistful hope of regaining her.

Shortly the plane was in view, dark against the brightness of the sky, a suspended mote, an irritating fleck in Barwani's eye, growing larger, causing him to blink and sneeze. Barwani was not ready for it. When Ameri Kombo, the flight controller in the cubicle next door, phoned him with the routine announcement of the landing, Barwani replied, "Notify the pilot that no one is to debark until I have given clearance. I must consult the regulations. There is possibly a peril to public health." For twenty minutes he let the plane sit, all hatches sealed, on the quiet runway. Wandering goats emerged from the shrubbery and inspected it. Barwani consulted no regulations. He finished his modest meal; then he folded his arms and sought to attain the proper state of tranquility. These deads, he told himself, could do no harm. They were people like all other people, except that they had undergone extraordinary medical treatment. He must overcome his superstitious fear of them: he was no peasant, no silly clove-picker, nor was Zanzibar an abode of primitives. He would admit them, he would give them their antimalaria tablets as though they were ordinary tourists, he would send them on their way. Very well. Now he was ready. He phoned Ameri Kombo. "There is no danger," he said. "The passengers may exit."

There were nine altogether, a sparse load. The four warms emerged first, looking somber and a little congealed, like people who had had to travel with a party of uncaged cobras. Barwani knew them all: the German consul's wife, the merchant Chowdhary's son and two Chinese engineers, all returning from brief holidays in Dar. He waved them through the gate without formalities. Then came the deads, after an interval of half a minute: probably they had been sitting together at one end of the nearly empty plane and the others had been at the other. There were two women, three men, all of them tall and surprisingly robust-looking. He had expected them to shamble, to shuffle, to limp, to falter, but they moved with aggressive strides, as if they were in better health now than when they had been alive. When they reached the gate Barwani stepped forward to greet them, saying softly, "Health regulations, come this way, kindly." They were breathing, undoubtedly breathing: he tasted an emanation of liquor from the big red-haired man, a mysterious and pleasant sweet flavor, perhaps anise, from the dark-haired woman. It seemed to Barwani that their skins had an odd waxy texture, an unreal glossiness, but possibly that was his imagination; white skins had always looked artificial to him. The only certain difference he could detect about the deads was in their eyes, a way they had of remaining unnervingly fixed in a single intense gaze for many seconds before shifting. Those were the eyes, Barwani thought, of people who had looked upon the Emptiness without having been swallowed into it. A turbulence of questions erupted within him: what is it like, how do you feel, what do you remember, where did you go? He left them unspoken. Politely he said, "Welcome to the isle of cloves. We ask you to observe that malaria has been wholly eradicated here through extensive precautionary measures, and to prevent recurrence of unwanted disease we require of you that you take these tablets before proceeding further." Tourists often objected to that; these people swallowed their pills without a word of protest. Again Barwani yearned to reach toward them, to achieve some sort of contact that might perhaps help him to transcend the leaden weight of being. But an aura, a shield of strangeness, surrounded these five, and, though he was an amiable man who tended to fall into conversations easily with strangers, he passed them on in silence to Mponda the immigration man. Mponda's high forehead was shiny with sweat, and he chewed at his lower lip; evidently he was as disturbed by the deads as Barwani. He fumbled forms, he stamped a visa in the wrong place, he stammered while telling the deads that he must keep their passports overnight. "I shall post them by messenger to your hotel in the morning." Mponda promised them, and sent the visitors onward to the baggage pickup area with undue haste.

Klein had only one friend with whom he dared talk about it, a colleague of his at UCLA, a sleek little Parsee sociologist from Bombay named Framji Jijibhoi, who was as deep into the elaborate new subculture of the deads as a warm could get. "How can I accept this?" Klein demanded. "I can't accept it at all. She's out there somewhere, she's alive, she's—"

Jijibhoi cut him off with a quick flick of his fingertips. "No, dear friend," he said sadly, "not alive, not alive at all, merely rekindled. You must learn to grasp the distinction." Klein could not learn to grasp anything having to do with Sybille's death. He could not bear to think that she had passed into another existence from which he was totally excluded. To find her, to speak with her, to participate in her experience of death and whatever lay beyond death, became his only purpose. He was inextricably bound to her, as though she were still his wife, as though Jorge-and-Sybille still existed in any way.

He waited for letters from her, but none came. After a few months he began trying to trace her, embarrassed by his own compulsiveness and by his increasingly open breaches of the etiquette of this sort of widower-hood. He traveled from one Cold Town to another—Sacramento, Boise, Ann Arbor, Louisville—but none would admit him, none would even answer his questions. Friends passed on rumors to him, that she was living among the deads of Tucson, of Roanoke, of Rochester, of San Diego, but nothing came of these tales; then Jijibhoi, who had tentacles into the world of the rekindled in many places, and who was aiding Klein in his quest even though he disapproved of its goal, brought him an authoritia-tive-sounding report that she was at Zion Cold Town in southeastern Utah. They turned him away there too, but not entirely cruelly, for he did manage to secure plausible evidence that that was where Sybille really was.

In the summer of '92 Jijibhoi told him that Sybille had emerged from Cold Town seclusion. She had been seen, he said, in Newark, Ohio, touring the municipal golf course at Octagon State Memorial in the company of a swaggering red-haired archaeologist named Kent Zacharias, also a dead, formerly a specialist in the mound-building Hopewellian cultures of the Ohio Valley. "It is a new phase," said Jijibhoi, "not unanticipated. The deads are beginning to abandon their early philosophy of total separatism. We have started to observe them as tourists visiting our world—exploring the life-death interface, as they like to term it. It will be very interesting, dear friend." Klein flew at once to Ohio and, without ever actually seeing her, tracked her from Newark to Chillicothe, from Chillicothe to Marietta, from Marietta into West Virginia, where he lost her trail somewhere between Moundsville and Wheeling. Two months later she was said to be in London, then in Cairo, then Addis Ababa. Early in '93 Klein learned, via the scholarly grapevine—an ex-Californian now at Nyerere University in Arusha—that Sybille was on safari in Tanzania and was planning to go, in a few weeks, across to Zanzibar.

Of course. For ten years she had been working on a doctoral thesis on the establishment of the Arab Sultanate in Zanzibar in the early nineteenth century—studies unavoidably interrupted by other academic chores, by love affairs, by marriage, by financial reverses, by illnesses, death and other responsibilities—and she had never actually been able to visit the island that was so central to her. Now she was free of all entanglements. Why shouldn't she go to Zanzibar at last? Why not? Of course: she was heading for Zanzibar. And so Klein would go to Zanzibar too, to wait for her.

As the five disappeared into taxis, something occurred to Barwani. He asked Mponda for the passports and scrutinized the names. Such strange ones: Kent Zacharias, Nerita Tracy, Sybille Klein, Anthony Gracchus, Laurence Mortimer. He had never grown accustomed to the names of Europeans. Without the photographs he would be unable to tell which were the women, which the men. Zacharias, Tracy, Klein . . . ah. *Klein.* He checked a memo, two weeks old, tacked to his desk. Klein, yes. Barwani telephoned the Shirazi Hotel—a project that consumed several minutes—and asked to speak with the American who had arrived ten days before, that slender man whose lips had been pressed tight in tension, whose eyes had glittered with fatigue, the one who had asked a little service of Barwani, a special favor, and had dashed him a much-needed hundred shillings as payment in advance. There was a lengthy delay, no doubt while porters searched the hotel, looking in the men's room, the bar, the lounge, the garden, and then the American was on the line. "The person about whom you inquired has just arrived, sir," Barwani told him.

· 2 ·

The dance begins. Worms underneath fingertips, lips beginning to pulse, heartache and throat-catch. All slightly out of step and out of key, each its own tempo and rhythm. Slowly, connections. Lip to lip, heart to heart, finding self in other, dreadfully, tentatively, burning . . . notes finding themselves in chords in sequence, cacophony turning to polyphonous contrapuntal chorus, a diapason of celebration.

R.D. Laing: *The Bird of Paradise*

Sybille stands timidly at the edge of the municipal golf course at Octagon State Memorial in Newark, Ohio, holding her sandals in her hand and surreptitiously working her toes into the lush, immaculate carpet of dense, close-cropped lime green grass. It is a summer afternoon in 1992, very hot; the air, beautifully translucent, has that timeless midwestern shimmer, and the droplets of water from the morning sprinkling have not yet burned off the lawn. Such extraordinary grass! She hadn't often seen grass like that in California, and certainly not at Zion Cold Town in thirsty Utah. Kent Zacharias, towering beside her, shakes his head sadly. "A golf course!" he mutters. "One of the most important prehistoric sites in North America and they make a golf course out of it! Well, I suppose it could have been worse. They might have bulldozed the whole thing and turned it into a municipal parking lot. Look, there, do you see the earthworks?"

She is trembling. This is her first extended journey outside the Cold Town, her first venture into the world of the warms since her rekindling, and she is picking up threatening vibrations from all the life that burgeons about her. The park is surrounded by pleasant little houses, well-kept. Children on bicycles rocket through the streets. In front of her, golfers are merrily slamming away. Little yellow golf carts clamber with lunatic energy over the rises and dips of the course. There are platoons of tourists who, like herself and Zacharias, have come to see the Indian mounds. There are dogs running free. All this seems menacing to her. Even the vegetation—the thick grass, the manicured shrubs, the heavy-leafed trees with low-hanging boughs—disturbs her. Nor is the nearness of Zacharias reassuring, for he too seems inflamed with undeadlike vitality; his face is florid, his gestures are broad and overanimated, as he points out the low flat-topped mounds, the grassy bumps and ridges making up the giant joined circle and octagon of the ancient monument. Of course, these mounds are the mainspring of his being, even now, five years post mortem. Ohio is his Zanzibar.

"—once covered four square miles. A grand ceremonial center, the Hopewellian equivalent of Chichen Itza, of Luxor, of—" He pauses. Awareness of her distress has finally filtered through the intensity of his archeological zeal. "How are you doing?" he asks gently.

She smiles a brave smile. Moistens her lips. Inclines her head toward the golfers, toward the tourists, toward the row of darling little houses outside the rim of the park. Shudders.

"Too cheery for you, is it?"

"Much," she says.

Cheery. Yes. A cheery little town, a magazine-cover town, a chamber-of-commerce town. Newark lies becalmed on the breast of the sea of time: but for the look of the automobiles, this could be 1980 or 1960 or perhaps 1940. Yes. Motherhood, baseball, apple pie, church every Sunday. Yes. Zacharias nods and makes one of the signs of comfort at her. "Come," he whispers. "Let's go toward the heart of the complex. We'll lose the twentieth century along the way."

With brutal imperial strides he plunges into the golf course. Long-legged Sybille must work hard to keep up with him. In a moment they are within the embankment, they have entered the sacred octagon, they have penetrated the vault of the past, and at once Sybille feels they have achieved a successful crossing of the interface between life and death. How still it is here! She senses the powerful presence of the forces of death, and those dark spirits heal her unease. The encroachments of the world of the living on these precincts of the dead become insignificant: the houses outside the park are no longer in view, the golfers are mere foolish incorporeal shadows, the bustling yellow golf carts become beetles, the wandering tourists are invisible.

She is overwhelmed by the size and symmetry of the ancient site. What spirits sleep here? Zacharias conjures them, waving his hands like a magician. She has heard so much from him already about these people, these Hopewellians—what did they call themselves? how can we ever know?—who heaped up these ramparts of earth twenty centuries ago. Now he brings them to life for her with gestures and low urgent words. He whispers fiercely:

—Do you see them?

And she does see them. Mists descend. The mounds reawaken; the mound-builders appear. Tall, slender, swarthy, nearly naked, clad in shining copper breastplates, in necklaces of flint disks, in bangles of bone and mica and tortoiseshell, in heavy chains of bright lumpy pearls, in rings of stone and terra-cotta, in armlets of bears' teeth and panthers' teeth, in spool-shaped metal ear ornaments, in furry loincloths. Here are priests in intricately woven robes and awesome masks. Here are chieftains with crowns of copper rods, moving in frosty dignity along the long earthen-walled avenue. The eyes of these people glow with energy. What an enormously vital, enormously profligate culture they sustain here! Yet Sybille is not alienated by their throbbing vigor, for it is the vigor of the dead, the vitality of the vanished.

Look, now. Their painted faces, their unblinking gazes. This is a funeral procession. The Indians have come to these intricate geometrical enclosures to perform their acts of worship, and now, solemnly parading along the perimeters of the circle and the octagon, they pass onward, toward the mortuary zone beyond. Zacharias and Sybille are left alone in the middle of the field. He murmurs to her:

—Come. We'll follow them.

He makes it real for her. Through his cunning craft she has access to this community of the dead. How easily she has drifted backward across time! She learns here that she can affix herself to the sealed past at any point; it's only the present, open-ended and unpredictable that is troublesome. She and Zacharias float through the misty meadow, no sensation of feet touching ground; leaving the octagon, they travel now down a long grassy causeway to the place of the burial mounds, at the edge of a dark forest of wide-crowned oaks. They enter a vast clearing. In the center the ground has been plastered with clay, then covered lightly with sand and fine gravel; on this base the mortuary house, a roofless four-sided structure with walls consisting of rows of wooden palisades, has been erected. Within this is a low clay platform topped by a rectangular tomb of log cribbing, in which two bodies can be seen: a young man, a young woman, side by side, bodies fully extended, beautiful even in death. They wear copper breastplates, copper ear ornaments, copper bracelets, necklaces of gleaming yellowish bears' teeth.

Four priests station themselves at the corners of the mortuary house. The faces are covered by grotesque wooden masks topped by great antlers, and they carry wands two feet long, effigies of the death-cup mushroom in wood sheathed with copper. One priest commences a harsh, percussive chant. All four lift their wands and abruptly bring them down. It is a signal; the depositing of grave-goods begins. Lines of mourners bowed under heavy sacks approach the mortuary house. They are unweeping, even joyful, faces ecstatic, eyes shining, for these people know what later cultures will forget, that death is no termination but rather a natural continuation of life. Their departed friends are to be envied. They are honored with lavish gifts, so that they may live like royalty in the next world: out of the sacks come nuggets of copper, meteoric iron, and silver, thousands of pearls, shell beads, beads of copper and iron, buttons of wood and stone, heaps of metal ear-spools, chunks and chips of obsidian, animal effigies carved from slate and bone and tortoiseshell, ceremonial copper axes and knives, scrolls cut from mica, human jawbones inlaid with turquoise, dark coarse pottery, needles of bone, sheets of woven cloth, coiled serpents fashioned from dark stone, a torrent of offerings, heaped up around and even upon the two bodies.

At length the tomb is choked with gifts. Again there is a signal from the priests. They elevate their wands and the mourners, drawing back to the borders of the clearing, form a circle and begin to sing a somber, throbbing funereal hymn. Zacharias, after a moment, sings with them, wordlessly embellishing the melody with heavy melismas. His voice is a rich *basso cantante,* so unexpectedly beautiful that Sybille is moved almost to confusion by it, and looks at him in awe. Abruptly he breaks off, turns to her, touches her arm, leans down to say:

—You sing too.

Sybille nods hesitantly. She joins the song, falteringly at first, her throat constricted by self-consciousness; then she finds herself becoming part of the rite, somehow, and her tone becomes more confident. Her high clear soprano soars brilliantly above the other voices.

Now another kind of offering is made: boys cover the mortuary house with heaps of kindling—twigs, dead branches, thick boughs, all sorts of combustible debris—until it is quite hidden from sight, and the priests cry a halt. Then, from the forest, comes a woman bearing a blazing firebrand, a girl, actually, entirely naked, her sleek fair-skinned body painted with bizarre horizontal stripes of red and green on breasts and buttocks and thighs, her long glossy black hair flowing like a cape behind her as she runs. Up to the mortuary house she sprints; breathlessly she touches the firebrand to the kindling, here, here, here, performing a wild dance as she goes, and hurls the torch into the center of the pyre. Skyward leap the flames in a ferocious rush. Sybille feels seared by the blast of heat. Swiftly the house and tomb are consumed.

While the embers still glow, the bringing of earth gets under way. Except for the priests, who remained rigid at the cardinal points of the site, and the girl who wielded the torch, who lies like discarded clothing at the edge of the clearing, the whole community takes part. There is an open pit behind a screen of nearby trees; the worshippers, forming lines, go to it and scoop up soil, carrying it to the burned mortuary house in baskets, in buckskin aprons, in big moist clods held in their bare hands. Silently they dump their burdens on the ashes and go back for more.

Sybille glances at Zacharias; he nods; they join the line. She goes down into the pit, gouges a lump of moist black clayey soil from its side, takes it to the growing mound. Back for another, back for another. The mound rises rapidly, two feet above ground level now, three, four, a swelling circular blister, its outlines governed by the unchanging positions of the four priests, its tapering contours formed by the tamping of scores of bare feet. Yes, Sybille thinks, this is a valid way of celebrating death, this is a fitting rite. Sweat runs down her body, her clothes become stained and muddy, and still she runs to the earth-quarry, runs from there to the mound, runs to the quarry, runs to the mound, runs, runs, transfigured, ecstatic.

Then the spell breaks. Something goes wrong, she does not know what, and the mists clear, the sun dazzles her eyes, the priests and the mound-builders and the unfinished mound disappear. She and Zacharias are once again in the octagon, golf carts roaring past them on every side. Three children and their parents stand just a few feet from her, staring, staring, and a boy about ten years old points to Sybille and says in a voice that reverberates through half of Ohio, "Dad, what's wrong with those people? Why do they look so weird?" Mother gasps and cries, "*Quiet*, Tommy, don't you have any manners?" Dad, looking furious, gives the boy a stinging blow across the face with the tips of his fingers, seizes him by the wrist, tugs him toward the other side of the park, the whole family following in their wake.

Sybille shivers convulsively. She turns away, clasping her hand to her betraying eyes. Zacharias embraces her. "It's all right," he says tenderly. "The boy didn't know any better. It's all right."

"Take me away from here!"

"I want to show you—"

"Some other time. Take me away. To the motel. I don't want to see anything. I don't want anybody to see me."

He takes her to the motel. For an hour she lies face down on the bed, racked by dry sobs. Several times she tells Zacharias she is unready for this tour, she wants to go back to the Cold Town, but he says nothing, simply strokes the tense muscles of her back, and after a while the mood passes. She turns to him and their eyes meet and he touches her and they make love in the fashion of the deads.

3.

Newness is renewal: *ad hoc enim venit, ut renovemur in illo;* making it new again, as on the first day; *herrlich wie am ersten Tag.* Reforma-

tion, or renaissance; rebirth. Life is Phoenix-like, always being born
again out of its own death. The true nature of life is resurrection; all
life is life after death, a second life, reincarnation. *Totus hic ordo
revolubilis testatio est resurrectionis mortuorum.* The universal pattern of recurrence bears witness to the resurrection of the dead.

Norman O. Brown: *Love's Body*

"The rains shall be commencing shortly, gentleman and lady," the taxi
driver said, speeding along the narrow highway to Zanzibar Town. He had
been chattering steadily, wholly unafraid of his passengers. He must not
know what we are, Sybille decided. "Perhaps in a week or two they begin.
These shall be the long rains. The short rains come in the last of November and December."

"Yes, I know," Sybille said.

"Ah, you have been to Zanzibar before?"

"In a sense," she replied. In a sense she had been to Zanzibar many
times, and how calmly she was taking it now that the true Zanzibar was
beginning to superimpose itself on the template in her mind, on that
dream-Zanzibar she had carried about so long! She took everything calmly
now; nothing excited her, nothing aroused her. In her former life the delay
at the airport would have driven her into a fury: a ten-minute flight, and
then to be trapped on the runway twice as long! But she had remained
tranquil throughout it all, sitting almost immobile, listening vaguely to
what Zacharias was saying and occasionally replying as if sending messages
from some other planet. And now Zanzibar, so placidly accepted. In the
old days she had felt a sort of paradoxical amazement whenever some
landmark familiar from childhood geography lessons or the movies or
travel posters—the Grand Canyon, the Manhattan skyline, Taos Pueblo
—turned out in reality to look exactly as she imagined it would; but now
here was Zanzibar, unfolding predictably and unsurprisingly before her,
and she observed it with a camera's cool eye, unmoved, unresponsive.

The soft, steamy air was heavy with a burden of perfumes, not only the
expected pungent scent of cloves but also creamier fragrances which
perhaps were those of hibiscus, frangipani, jacaranda, bougainvillea, pene-
trating the cab's open window like probing tendrils. The imminence of
the long rains was a tangible pressure, a presence, a heaviness in the
atmosphere: at any moment a curtain might be drawn aside and the
torrents would start. The highway was lined by two shaggy green walls of
palms broken by tin-roofed shacks; behind the palms were mysterious dark

groves, dense and alien. Along the edge of the road was the usual tropical array of obstacles: chickens, goats, naked children, old women with shrunken, toothless faces, all wandering around untroubled by the taxi's encroachment on their right-of-way. On through the rolling flatlands the cab sped, out onto the peninsula on which Zanzibar Town sits. The temperature seemed to be rising perceptibly minute by minute; a fist of humid heat was clamping tight over the island. "Here is the waterfront, gentleman and lady," the driver said. His voice was an intrusive hoarse purr, patronizing, disturbing. The sand was glaringly white, the water a dazzling glassy blue; a couple of dhows moved sleepily across the mouth of the harbor, their lateen sails bellying slightly as the gentle sea breeze caught them. "On this side, please—" An enormous white wooden building, four stories high, a wedding cake of long verandas and cast-iron railings, topped by a vast cupola. Sybille, recognizing it, anticipated the driver's spiel, hearing it like a subliminal pre–echo: "Beit al-Ajaib, the House of Wonders, former government house. Here the sultan was often make great banquets, here the famous of all Africa came homaging. No longer in use. Next door the old Sultan's Palace, now Palace of People. You wish to go in House of Wonders? Is open: we stop, I take you now."

"Another time," Sybille said faintly. "We'll be here a while."

"You not here just a day like most?"

"No, a week or more. I've come to study the history of your island. I'll surely visit the Beit al-Ajaib. But not today."

"Not today, no. Very well: you call me, I take you anywhere. I am Ibuni." He gave her a gallant toothy grin over his shoulder and swung the cab inland with a ferocious lurch, into the labyrinth of winding streets and narrow alleys that was Stonetown, the ancient Arab quarter.

All was silent here. The massive white stone buildings presented blank faces to the streets. The windows, mere slits, were shuttered. Most doors —the famous paneled doors of Stonetown, richly carved, studded with brass, cunningly inlaid, each door an ornate Islamic masterpiece—were closed and seemed to be locked. The shops looked shabby, and the small display windows were speckled with dust. Most of the signs were so faded Sybille could barely make them out:

PREMCHAND'S EMPORIUM
MONJI'S CURIOS
ABDULLAH'S BROTHERHOOD STORE
MOTILAL'S BAZAAR

The Arabs were long since gone from Zanzibar. So were most of the Indians, though they were said to be creeping back. Occasionally, as it pursued its intricate course through the maze of Stonetown, the taxi passed elongated black limousines, probably of Russian or Chinese make, chauffeur-driven, occupied by dignified self-contained dark-skinned men in white robes. Legislators, so she supposed them to be, en route to meetings of state. There were no other vehicles in sight, and no pedestrians except for a few women, robed entirely in black, hurrying on solitary errands. Stonetown had none of the vitality of the countryside; it was a place of ghosts, she thought, a fitting place for vacationing deads. She glanced at Zacharias, who nodded and smiled, a quick quirky smile that acknowledged her perception and told her that he too had had it. Communication was swift among the deads and the obvious rarely needed voicing.

The route to the hotel seemed extraordinarily involuted, and the driver halted frequently in front of shops, saying hopefully, "You want brass chests, copper pots, silver curios, gold chains from China?" Though Sybille gently declined his suggestions, he continued to point out bazaars and emporiums, offering earnest recommendations of quality and moderate price, and gradually she realized, getting her bearings in the town, that they had passed certain corners more than once. Of course: the driver must be in the pay of shopkeepers who hired him to lure tourists. "Please take us to our hotel," Sybille said, and when he persisted in his huckstering —"Best ivory here, best lace"—she said it more firmly, but she kept her temper. Jorge would have been pleased by her transformation, she thought; he had all too often been the immediate victim of her fiery impatience. She did not know the specific cause of the change. Some metabolic side-effect of the rekindling process, maybe, or maybe her two years of communion with Guidefather at the Cold Town, or was it, perhaps, nothing more than the new knowledge that all of time was hers, that to let oneself feel hurried now was absurd?

"Your hotel is this," Ibuni said at last.

It was an old Arab mansion—high arches, innumerable balconies, musty air, electric fans turning sluggishly in the dark hallways. Sybille and Zacharias were given a sprawling suite on the third floor, overlooking a courtyard lush with palms, vermilion nandi, kapok trees, poinsettia and agapanthus. Mortimer, Gracchus and Nerita had long since arrived in the other cab and were in an identical suite one floor below. "I'll have a bath," Sybille told Zacharias. "Will you be in the bar?"

"Very likely. Or strolling in the garden."

He went out. Sybille quickly shed her travel-sweaty clothes. The bathroom was a Byzantine marvel, elaborate swirls of colored tile, an immense yellow tub standing high on bronze eagle-claw-and-globe legs. Lukewarm water dribbled in slowly when she turned the tap. She smiled at her reflection in the tall oval mirror. There had been a mirror somewhat like it at the rekindling house. On the morning after her awakening, five or six deads had come into her room to celebrate with her her successful transition across the interface, and they had had that big mirror with them; delicately, with great ceremoniousness, they had drawn the coverlet down to show herself to her in it, naked, slender, narrow-waisted, high-breasted, the beauty of her body unchanged, marred neither by dying nor by rekindling, indeed enhanced by it, so that she had become more youthful-looking and even radiant in her passage across that terrible gulf.

—You're a very beautiful woman.

That was Pablo. She would learn his name and all the other names later.

—I feel such a flood of relief. I was afraid I'd wake up and find myself a shriveled ruin.

—That could not have happened, Pablo said.

—And never will happen, said a young woman. Nerita, she was.

—But deads do age, don't they?

—Oh, yes, we age, just as the warms do. But not *just* as.

—More slowly?

—Very much more slowly. And differently. All our biological processes operate more slowly, except the functions of the brain, which tend to be quicker than they were in life.

—Quicker?

—You'll see.

—It all sounds ideal.

—We are extremely fortunate. Life has been kind to us. Our situation is, yes, ideal. We are the new aristocracy.

—The new aristocracy—

Sybille slipped slowly into the tub, leaning back against the cool porcelain, wriggling a little, letting the tepid water slide up as far as her throat. She closed her eyes and drifted peacefully. All of Zanzibar was waiting for her. *Streets I never thought I should visit.* Let Zanzibar wait. Let Zanzibar wait. *Words I never thought to speak. When I left my body on a distant shore.* Time for everything, everything in its due time.

*—You're a very beautiful woman,* Pablo had told her, not meaning to flatter.

Yes. She had wanted to explain to them, that first morning, that she didn't really care all that much about the appearance of her body, that her real priorities lay elsewhere, were "higher," but there hadn't been any need to tell them that. They understood. They understood everything. Besides, she *did* care about her body. Being beautiful was less important to her than it was to those women for whom physical beauty was their only natural advantage, but her appearance mattered to her; her body pleased her and she knew it was pleasing to others, it gave her access to people, it was a means of making connections, and she had always been grateful for that. In her other existence her delight in her body had been flawed by the awareness of the inevitability of its slow steady decay, the certainty of the loss of that accidental power that beauty gave her, but now she had been granted exemption from that: she would change with time but she would not have to feel as warms must feel, that she was gradually falling apart. Her rekindled body would not betray her by turning ugly. No.

*—We are the new aristocracy—*

After her bath she stood a few minutes by the open window, naked to the humid breeze. Sounds came to her: distant bells, the bright chatter of tropical birds, the voices of children singing in a language she could not identify. Zanzibar! Sultans and spices, Livingstone and Stanley, Tippu Tib the slaver, Sir Richard Burton spending a night in this very hotel room, perhaps. There was a dryness in her throat, a throbbing in her chest: a little excitement coming alive in her after all. She felt anticipation, even eagerness. All Zanzibar lay before her. Very well. Get moving, Sybille, put some clothes on, let's have lunch, a look at the town.

She took a light blouse and shorts from her suitcase. Just then Zacharias returned to the room, and she said, not looking up, "Kent, do you think it's all right for me to wear these shorts here? They're—" A glance at his face and her voice trailed off. "What's wrong?"

"I've just been talking to your husband."

"He's *here?*"

"He came up to me in the lobby. Knew my name. 'You're Zacharias,' he said, with a Bogarty little edge to his voice, like a deceived movie husband confronting the other man. 'Where is she? I have to see her.' "

"Oh, no, Kent."

"I asked him what he wanted with you. 'I'm her husband,' he said, and I told him, 'Maybe you were her husband once, but things have changed,' and then—"

"I can't imagine Jorge talking tough. He's such a *gentle* man, Kent! How did he look?"

"Schizoid," Zacharias said. "Glassy eyes, muscles bunching in his jaws, signs of terrific pressure all over him. He knows he's not supposed to do things like this, doesn't he?"

"Jorge knows exactly how he's supposed to behave. Oh, Kent, what a stupid mess! Where is he now?"

"Still downstairs. Nerita and Laurence are talking to him. You don't want to see him, do you?"

"Of course not."

"Write him a note to that effect and I'll take it down to him. Tell him to clear off."

Sybille shook her head. "I don't want to hurt him."

"Hurt him? He's followed you halfway around the world like a lovesick boy, he's tried to violate your privacy, he's disrupted an important trip, he's refused to abide by the conventions that govern the relationships of warms and deads, and you—"

"He loves me, Kent."

"He loved you. All right, I concede that. But the person he loved doesn't exist any more. He has to be made to realize that."

Sybille closed her eyes. "I don't want to hurt him. I don't want you to hurt him either."

"I won't hurt him. Are you going to see him?"

"No," she said. She grunted in annoyance and threw her shorts and blouse into a chair. There was a fierce pounding at her temples, a sensation of being challenged, of being threatened, that she had not felt since that awful day at the Newark mounds. She strode to the window and looked out, half expecting to see Jorge arguing with Nerita and Laurence in the courtyard. But there was no one down there except a houseboy who looked up as if her bare breasts were beacons and gave her a broad dazzling smile. Sybille turned her back to him and said dully, "Go back down. Tell him that it's impossible for me to see him. Use that word. Not that I *won't* see him, not that I *don't want* to see him, not that it isn't *right* for me to see him, just that it's impossible. And then phone the airport. I want to go back to Dar on the evening plane."

"But we've only just arrived!"

"No matter. We'll come back some other time. Jorge is very persistent; he won't accept anything but a brutal rebuff, and I can't do that to him. So we'll leave."

Klein had never seen deads at close range before. Cautiously, uneasily, he stole quick intense looks at Kent Zacharias as they sat side by side on rattan chairs among the potted palms in the lobby of the hotel. Jijibhoi had told him that it hardly showed, that you perceived it more subliminally than by any outward manifestation, and that was true; there was a certain look about the eyes, of course, the famous fixity of the deads, and there was something oddly pallid about Zacharias' skin *beneath* the florid complexion, but if Klein had not known what Zacharias was he might not have guessed it. He tried to imagine this man, this red-haired redfaced dead archeologist, this digger of dirt mounds, in bed with Sybille. Doing with her whatever it was that the deads did in their couplings. Even Jijibhoi wasn't sure. Something with hands, with eyes, with whispers and smiles, not at all genital—so Jijibhoi believed. *This is Sybille's lover I'm talking to. This is Sybille's lover.* How strange that it bothered him so. She had had affairs when she was living; so had he; so had everyone; it was the way of life. But he felt threatened, overwhelmed, defeated, by this walking corpse of a lover.

Klein said, "Impossible?"

"That was the word she used."

"Can't I have ten minutes with her?"

"Impossible."

"Would she let me see her for a few moments, at least? I'd just like to find out how she looks."

"Don't you find it humilating, doing all this scratching around just for a glimpse of her?"

"Yes."

"And you still want it?"

"Yes."

Zacharias sighed. "There's nothing I can do for you. I'm sorry."

"Perhaps Sybille is tired from having done so much traveling. Do you think she might be in a more receptive mood tomorrow?"

"Maybe," Zacharias said. "Why don't you come back then?"

"You've been very kind."

"*De nada.*"

"Can I buy you a drink?"

"Thanks, no," Zacharias said. "I don't indulge any more. Not since—"
He smiled.

Klein could smell whiskey on Zacharias's breath. All right, though. All
right. He would go away. A driver waiting outside the hotel grounds poked
his head out of his cab window and said hopefully, "Tour of the island,
gentleman? See the clove plantations, see the athlete stadium?"

"I've seen them already," Klein said. He shrugged. "Take me to the
beach."

He spent the afternoon watching turquoise wavelets lapping pink sand.
The next morning he returned to Sybille's hotel, but they were gone, all
five of them, gone on last night's flight to Dar, said the apologetic desk
clerk. Klein asked if he could make a telephone call, and the clerk showed
him an ancient instrument in an alcove near the bar. He phoned Barwani.
"What's going on?" he demanded. "You told me they'd be staying at least
a week!"

"Oh, sir, things change," Barwani said softly.

4.

What portends? What will the future bring? I do not know, I have
no presentiment. When a spider hurls itself down from some fixed
point, consistently with its nature, it always sees before it only an
empty space wherein it can find no foothold however much it sprawls.
And so it is with me: always before me an empty space; what drives
me forward is a consistency which lies behind me. This life is topsy-
turvy and terrible, not to be endured.

Soren Kierkegaard: *Either/Or*

Jijibhoi said, "In the entire question of death who is to say what is right,
dear friend? When I was a boy in Bombay it was not unusual for our
Hindu neighbors to practice the rite of suttee, that is, the burning of the
widow on her husband's funeral pyre, and by what presumption may we
call them barbarians? Of course"—his dark eyes flashed mischievously—
"we *did* call them barbarians, though never when they might hear us.
Will you have more curry?"

Klein repressed a sigh. He was getting full, and the curry was fiery stuff,
of an incandescence far beyond his usual level of tolerance; but Jijibhoi's
hospitality, unobtrusively insistent, had a certain hieratic quality about it

that made Klein feel like a blasphemer whenever he refused anything in his home. He smiled and nodded, and Jijibhoi, rising, spooned a mound of rice into Klein's plate, buried it under curried lamb, bedecked it with chutneys and sambals. Silently, unbidden, Jijibhoi's wife went to the kitchen and returned with a cold bottle of Heineken's. She gave Klein a shy grin as she set it down before him. They worked well together, these two Parsees, his hosts.

They were an elegant couple—striking, even. Jijibhoi was a tall, erect man with a forceful aquiline nose, dark Levantine skin, jet black hair, a formidable mustache. His hands and feet were extraordinarily small; his manner was polite and reserved; he moved with a quickness of action bordering on nervousness. Klein guessed that he was in his early forties, though he suspected his estimate could easily be off by ten years in either direction. His wife—strangely, Klein had never been told her name—was younger than her husband, nearly as tall, fair of complexion—a light olive tone—and voluptuous of figure. She dressed invariably in flowing silken saris; Jijibhoi affected Western business dress, suits and ties in styles twenty years out of date. Klein had never seen either of them bareheaded: she wore a kerchief of white linen, he a brocaded skullcap that might lead people to mistake him for an Oriental Jew. They were childless and self-sufficient, forming a closed dyad, a perfect unit, two segments of the same entity, conjoined and indivisible, as Klein and Sybille once had been. Their harmonious interplay of thought and gesture made them a trifle disconcerting, even intimidating, to others. As Klein and Sybille once had been.

Klein said, "Among your people—"

"Oh, very different, very different, quite unique. You know of our funeral custom?"

"Exposure of the dead, isn't it?"

Jijibhoi's wife giggled. "A very ancient recycling scheme!"

"The Towers of Silence," Jijibhoi said. He went to the dining room's vast window and stood with his back to Klein, staring out at the dazzling lights of Los Angeles. The Jijibhois' house, all redwood and glass, perched precariously on stilts near the crest of Benedict Canyon, just below Mulholland: the view took in everything from Hollywood to Santa Monica. "There are five of them in Bombay," said Jijibhoi, "on Malabar Hill, a rocky ridge overlooking the Arabian Sea. They are centuries old, each one circular, several hundred feet in circumference, surrounded by a stone wall twenty or thirty feet high. When a Parsee dies—do you know of this?"

"Not as much as I'd like to know."

"When a Parsee dies, he is carried to the towers on an iron bier by professional corpse-bearers; the mourners follow in procession, two by two, joined hand to hand by holding a white handkerchief between them. A beautiful scene, dear Jorge. There is a doorway in the stone wall through which the corpse-bearers pass, carrying their burden. No one else may enter the tower. Within is a circular platform paved with large stone slabs and divided into three rows of shallow, open receptacles. The outer row is used for the bodies of males, the next for those of females, the innermost one for children. The dead one is given a resting place; vultures rise from the lofty palms in the gardens adjoining the towers; within an hour or two, only bones remain. Later, the bare, sun-dried skeleton is cast into a pit at the center of the tower. Rich and poor crumble together there into dust."

"And all Parsees are—ah—buried in this way?"

"Oh, no, no, by no means," Jijibhoi said heartily. "All ancient traditions are in disrepair nowadays, do you not know? Our younger people advocate cremation or even conventional interment. Still, many of us continue to see the beauty of our way."

"—beauty?—"

Jijibhoi's wife said in a quiet voice, "To bury the dead in the ground, in a moist tropical land where diseases are highly contagious, seems not sanitary to us. And to burn a body is to waste its substance. But to give the bodies of the dead to the efficient hungry birds—quickly, cleanly, without fuss—is to us a way of celebrating the economy of nature. To have one's bones mingle in the pit with the bones of the entire community is, to us, the ultimate democracy."

"And the vultures spread no contagions themselves, feeding as they do on the bodies of—"

"Never," said Jijibhoi firmly. "Nor do they contract our ills."

"And I gather that you both intend to have your bodies returned to Bombay when you—" Aghast, Klein paused, shook his head, coughed in embarrassment, forced a weak smile. "You see what this radioactive curry of yours has done to my manners? Forgive me. Here I sit, a guest at your dinner table, quizzing you about your funeral plans!"

Jijibhoi chuckled. "Death is not frightening to us, dear friend. It is— one hardly needs say it, does one?—it is a natural event. For a time we are here, and then we go. When our time ends, yes, she and I will give ourselves to the Towers of Silence."

His wife added sharply, "Better there than the Cold Towns! Much better!"

Klein had never observed such vehemence in her before.

Jijibhoi swung back from the window and glared at her. Klein had never seen that before either. It seemed as if the fragile web of elaborate courtesy that he and these two had been spinning all evening was suddenly unraveling, and that even the bonds between Jijibhoi and his wife were undergoing strain. Agitated now, fluttery, Jijibhoi began to collect the empty dishes, and after a long awkward moment said, "She did not mean to give offense."

"Why should I be offended?"

"A person you love chose to go to the Cold Towns. You might think there was implied criticism of her in my wife's expression of distaste for —"

Klein shrugged. "She's entitled to her feelings about rekindling. I wonder, though—"

He halted, uneasy, fearing to probe too deeply.

"Yes?"

"It was irrelevant."

"Please," Jijibhoi said. "We are old friends."

"I was wondering," said Klein slowly, "if it doesn't make things hard for you, spending all your time among deads, studying them, mastering their ways, devoting your whole career to them, when your wife evidently despises the Cold Towns and everything that goes on in them. If the theme of your work repels her you must not be able to share it with her."

"Oh," Jijibhoi said, tension visibly going from him, "if it comes to that, I have even less liking for the entire rekindling phenomenon than she."

"You do?" This was a side of Jijibhoi that Klein had never suspected. "It repels you? Then why did you choose to make such an intensive survey of it?"

Jijibhoi looked genuinely amazed. "What? Are you saying one must have personal allegiance to the subject of one's field of scholarship?" He laughed. "You are of Jewish birth, I think, and yet your doctoral thesis was concerned, was it not, with the early phases of the Third Reich?"

Klein winced. "Touché!"

"I find the subculture of the deads irresistible, as a sociologist," Jijibhoi went on. "To have such a radical new aspect of human existence erupt during one's career is an incredible gift. There is no more fertile field for me to investigate. Yet I have no wish, none at all, ever to deliver myself up for rekindling. For me, for my wife, it will be the Towers of Silence, the hot sun, the obliging vultures—and finish, the end, no more, terminus."

"I had no idea you felt this way. I suppose if I'd known more about Parsee theology, I might have realized—"

"You misunderstand. Our objections are not theological. It is that we share a wish, an idiosyncratic whim, not to continue beyond the allotted time. But also I have serious reservations about the impact of rekindling on our society. I feel a profound distress at the presence among us of these deads, I feel a purely private fear of these people and the culture they are creating, I feel even an abhorrence for—" Jijibhoi cut himself short. "Your pardon. That was perhaps too strong a word. You see how complex my attitudes are toward this subject, my mixture of fascination and repulsion? I exist in constant tension between those poles. But why do I tell you all this, which if it does not disturb you must surely bore you? Let us hear about your journey to Zanzibar."

"What can I say? I went, I waited a couple of weeks for her to show up, I wasn't able to get near her at all, and I came home. All the way to Africa and I never even had a glimpse of her."

"What a frustration, dear Jorge!"

"She stayed in her hotel room. They wouldn't let me go upstairs to her."

"They?"

"Her entourage," Klein said, "She was traveling with four other deads, a woman and three men. Sharing her room with the archaeologist, Zacharias. He was the one who shielded her from me, and did it very cleverly, too. He acts as though he owns her. Perhaps he does. What can you tell me, Framji? Do the deads marry? Is Zacharias her new husband?"

"It is very doubtful. The terms *wife* and *husband* are not in use among the deads. They form relationships, yes, but pair-bonding seems to be uncommon among them, possibly altogether unknown. Instead they tend to create supportive pseudofamilial groupings of three or four or even more individuals, who—"

"Do you mean that all four of her companions in Zanzibar are her lovers?"

Jijibhoi gestured eloquently. "Who can say? If you mean in a physical sense, I doubt it, but one can never be sure. Zacharias seems to be her special companion, at any rate. Several of the others may be part of her pseudofamily also, or all, or none. I have reason to think that at certain times every dead may claim a familial relationship to all others of his kind. Who can say? We perceive the doings of these people, as they say, through a glass, darkly."

"I don't see Sybille even that well. I don't even know what she looks like now."

"She has lost none of her beauty."

"So you've told me before. But I want to see her myself. You can't really comprehend, Framji, how much I want to see her. The pain I feel, not able—"

"Would you like to see her right now?"

Klein shook in a convulsion of amazement. "What? What do you mean? Is she—"

"Hiding in the next room? No, no, nothing like that. But I do have a small surprise for you. Come into the library." Smiling expansively, Jijibhoi led the way from the dining room to the small study adjoining it, a room densely packed from floor to ceiling with books in an astonishing range of languages—not merely English, French and German, but also Sanskrit, Hindi, Gujarati, Farsi, the tongues of Jijibhoi's polyglot upbringing among the tiny Parsee colony of Bombay, a community in which no language once cherished was ever discarded. Pushing aside a stack of dog-eared professional journals, he drew forth a glistening picture-cube, activated its inner light with a touch of this thumb, and handed it to Klein.

The sharp, dazzling holographic image showed three figures in a broad grassy plain that seemed to have no limits and was without trees, boulders or other visual interruptions, an endlessly unrolling green carpet under a blank death-blue sky. Zacharias stood at the left, his face averted from the camera; he was looking down, tinkering with the action of an enormous rifle. At the far right stood a stocky, powerful-looking dark-haired man whose pale, harsh-featured face seemed all beard and nostrils. Klein recognized him: Anthony Gracchus, one of the deads who had accompanied Sybille to Zanzibar. Sybille stood beside him, clad in khaki slacks and a crisp white blouse. Gracchus's arm was extended; evidently he had just pointed out a target to her, and she was intently aiming a gun nearly as big as Zacharias's.

Klein shifted the cube about, studying her face from various angles, and the sight of her made his fingers grow thick and clumsy, his eyelids to quiver. Jijibhoi had spoken truly: she had lost none of her beauty. Yet she was not at all the Sybille he had known. When he had last seen her, lying in her casket, she had seemed to be a flawless marble image of herself, and she had that same surreal statuary appearance now. Her face was an expressionless mask, calm, remote, aloof; her eyes were glossy mysteries; her lips registered a faint, enigmatic, barely perceptible smile. It frightened him to behold her this way, so alien, so unfamiliar. Perhaps it was the intensity of her concentration that gave her that forbidding marmoreal look, for she seemed to be pouring her entire being into the task of taking aim. By tilting the cube more extremely, Klein was able to see what she was aiming at: a strange awkward bird moving through the grass at the lower left, a bird larger than a turkey, round as a sack, with ash gray plumage, a whitish breast and tail, yellow white wings and short, comical yellow legs. Its head was immense and its black bill ended in a great snubbed hook. The creature seemed solemn, rather dignified and faintly absurd; it showed no awareness that its doom was upon it. How odd that Sybille should be about to kill it, she who had always detested the taking of life: Sybille the huntress now, Sybille the lunar goddess, Sybille-Diana!

Shaken, Klein looked up at Jijibhoi and said, "Where was this taken? On that safari in Tanzania, I suppose."

"Yes. In February. This man is the guide, the white hunter."

"I saw him in Zanzibar. Gracchus, his name is. He was one of the deads traveling with Sybille."

"He operates a hunting preserve not far from Kilimanjaro," Jijibhoi said, "that is set aside exclusively for the use of the deads. One of the more bizarre manifestations of their subculture, actually. They hunt only those animals which—"

Klein said impatiently, "How did you get this picture?"

"It was taken by Nerita Tracy, who is one of your wife's companions."

"I met her in Zanzibar too. But how—"

"A friend of hers is an acquaintance of mine, one of my informants, in fact, a valuable connection in my researches. Some months ago I asked him if he could obtain something like this for me. I did not tell him, of course, that I meant it for you." Jijibhoi looked close. "You seem troubled, dear friend."

Klein nodded. He shut his eyes as though to protect them from the glaring surfaces of Sybille's photograph. Eventually he said in a flat, toneless voice, "I have to get to see her."

"Perhaps it would be better for you if you would abandon—"

"No."

"Is there no way I can convince you that it is dangerous for you to pursue your fantasy of—"

"No," Klein said. "Don't even try. It's necessary for me to reach her. Necessary."

"How will you accomplish this, then?"

Klein said mechanically, "By going to Zion Cold Town."

"You have already done that. They would not admit you."

"This time they will. They don't turn away deads."

The Parsee's eyes widened. "You will surrender your own life? Is this your plan? What are you saying, Jorge?"

Klein, laughing, said, "That isn't what I meant at all."

"I am bewildered."

"I intend to infiltrate. I'll disguise myself as one of them. I'll slip into the Cold Town the way an infidel slips into Mecca." He seized Jijibhoi's wrist. "Can you help me? Coach me in their ways, teach me their jargon?"

"They'll find you out instantly."

"Maybe not. Maybe I'll get to Sybille before they do."

"This is insanity," Jijibhoi said quietly.

"Nevertheless. You have the knowledge. Will you help me?"

Gently Jijibhoi withdrew his arm from Klein's grasp. He crossed the room and busied himself with an untidy bookshelf for some moments, fussily arranging and rearranging. At length he said, "There is little I can do for you myself. My knowledge is broad but not deep, not deep enough. But if you insist on going through with this, Jorge, I can introduce you to someone why may be able to assist you. He is one of my informants, a dead, a man who has rejected the authority of the Guidefathers, a person who is *of* the deads but not *with* them. Possibly he can instruct you in what you would need to know."

"Call him," Klein said.

"I must warn you he is unpredictable, turbulent, perhaps even treacherous. Ordinary human values are without meaning to him in his present state."

"Call him."

"If only I could discourage you from—"

"Call him."

5.

Quarreling brings trouble. These days lions roar a great deal. Joy follows grief. It is not good to beat children much. You had better go away now and go home. It is impossible to work today. You should go to school every day. It is not advisable to follow this path, there is water in the way. Never mind, I shall be able to pass. We had better go back quickly. These lamps use a lot of oil. There are no mosquitoes in Nairobi. There are no lions here. There are people here, looking for eggs. Is there water in the well? No, there is none. If there are only three people, work will be impossible today.

D. V. Perrott: *Teach Yourself Swahili*

Gracchus signals furiously to the porters and bellows, *"Shika njia hii hii!"* Three turn, two keep trudging along. *"Ninyi nyote!"* he calls. *"Fanga kama hivi!"* He shakes his head, spits, flicks sweat from his forehead. He adds, speaking in a lower voice and in English, taking care that they will not hear him. "Do as I say, you malevolent black bastards, or you'll be deader than I am before sunset!"

Sybille laughs nervously. "Do you always talk to them like that?"

"I try to be easy on them. But what good does it do, what good does any of it do? Come on, let's keep up with them."

It is less than an hour after dawn but already the sun is very hot, here in the flat dry country between Kilimanjaro and Serengeti. Gracchus is leading the party northward across the high grass, following the spoor of what he thinks is a quagga, but breaking a trail in the high grass is hard work and the porters keep veering away toward a ravine that offers the tempting shade of a thicket of thorn trees, and he constantly has to harass them in order to hold them to the route he wants. Sybille has noticed that Gracchus shouts fiercely to his blacks, as if they were no more than recalcitrant beasts, and speaks of them behind their backs with a rough contempt, but it all seems done for show, all part of his white-hunter role: she has also noticed, at times when she was not supposed to notice, that privately Gracchus is in fact gentle, tender, even loving among the porters, teasing them—she supposes—with affectionate Swahili banter and playful mock-punches. The porters are role-players too: they behave in the traditional manner of their profession, alternately deferential and patronizing to the clients, alternately posing as all-knowing repositories of the lore of the bush and as simple, guileless savages fit only for carrying burdens. But the clients they serve are not quite like the sportsmen of Hemingway's time, since they are deads, and secretly the porters are terrified of the strange beings whom they serve. Sybille has seen them muttering prayers and fondling amulets whenever they accidentally touch one of the deads, and has occasionally detected an unguarded glance conveying unalloyed fear, possibly revulsion. Gracchus is no friend of theirs, however jolly he may get with them: they appear to regard him as some sort of monstrous sorcerer and the clients as fiends made manifest.

Sweating, saying little, the hunters move in single file, first the porters with the guns and supplies, then Gracchus, Zacharias, Sybille, Nerita constantly clicking her camera and Mortimer. Patches of white cloud drift slowly across the immense arch of the sky. The grass is lush and thick, for the short rains were unusually heavy in December. Small animals scurry through it, visible only in quick flashes, squirrels and jackals and guinea-fowl. Now and then larger creatures can be seen: three haughty ostriches, a pair of snuffling hyenas, a band of Thomson gazelles flowing like a tawny river across the plain. Yesterday Sybille spied two warthogs, some giraffes and a serval, an elegant big-eared wildcat, that slithered along like a miniature cheetah. None of these beasts may be hunted, but only those special ones that the operators of the preserve have introduced for the special needs of their clients; anything considered native African wildlife, which is to say anything that was living here before the deads leased this tract from the Masai, is protected by government decree. The Masai themselves are allowed to do some lion-hunting, since this is their reservation, but there are so few Masai left that they can do little harm. Yesterday, after the warthogs and before the giraffes, Sybille saw her first Masai, five lean, handsome, long-bodied men, naked under skimpy red robes, drifting silently through the bush, pausing frequently to stand thoughtfully on one leg, propped against their spears. At close range they were less handsome—toothless, fly-specked, herniated. They offered to sell their spears and their beaded collars for a few shillings, but the safarigoers had already stocked up on Masai artifacts in Nairobi's curio shops, at astonishingly higher prices.

All through the morning they stalk the quagga, Gracchus pointing out hoofprints here, fresh dung there. It is Zacharias who has asked to shoot a quagga. "How can you tell we're not following a zebra?" he asks peevishly.

Gracchus winks. "Trust me. We'll find zebras up ahead too. But you'll get your quagga. I guarantee it."

Ngiri, the head porter, turns and grins. *"Piga quagga m'uzuri, bwana,"* he says to Zacharias, and winks also, and then—Sybille sees it plainly—his jovial confident smile fades as though he has had the courage to sustain it only for an instant, and a veil of dread covers his dark glossy face.

"What did he say?" Zacharias asks.

"That you'll shoot a fine quagga," Gracchus replies.

Quaggas. The last wild one was killed about 1870, leaving only three in the world, all females, in European zoos. The Boers had hunted them to the edge of extinction in order to feed their tender meat to Hottentot slaves and to make from their striped hides sacks for Boer grain, leather *veldschoen* for Boer feet. The quagga of the London zoo died in 1872, that in Berlin in 1875, the Amsterdam quagga in 1883, and none was seen alive again until the artificial revival of the species through breedback selection and genetic manipulation in 1990, when this hunting preserve was opened to a limited and special clientele.

It is nearly noon, now, and not a shot has been fired all morning. The animals have begun heading for cover; they will not emerge until the shadows lengthen. Time to halt, pitch camp, break out the beer and sandwiches, tell tall tales of harrowing adventures with maddened buffaloes and edgy elephants. But not quite yet. The marchers come over a low hill and see, in the long sloping hollow beyond, a flock of ostriches and several hundred grazing zebras. As the humans appear, the ostriches begin slowly and warily to move off, but the zebras, altogether unafraid, continue to graze. Ngiri points and says, *"Piga quagga, bwana."*

"Just a bunch of zebras," Zacharias says.

Gracchus shakes his head. "No. Listen. You hear the sound?"

At first no one perceives anything unusual. But then, yes, Sybille hears it: a shrill barking neigh, very strange, a sound out of lost time, the cry of some beast she has never known. It is a song of the dead. Nerita hears it too, and Mortimer, and finally Zacharias. Gracchus nods toward the far side of the hollow. There, among the zebras, are half a dozen animals that might almost be zebras, but are not—unfinished zebras, striped only on their heads and foreparts; the rest of their bodies are yellowish brown, their legs are white, their manes are dark brown with pale stripes. Their coats sparkle like mica in the sunshine. Now and again they lift their heads, emit that weird percussive whistling snort, and bend to the grass again. Quaggas. Strays out of the past, relicts, rekindled specters. Gracchus signals and the party fans out along the peak of the hill. Ngiri hands Zacharias his colossal gun. Zacharias kneels, sights.

"No hurry," Gracchus murmurs. "We have all afternoon."

"Do I seem to be hurrying?" Zacharias asks. The zebras now block the little group of quaggas from his view, almost as if by design. He must not shoot a zebra, of course, or there will be trouble with the rangers. Minutes go by. Then the screen of zebras abruptly parts and Zacharias squeezes his trigger. There is a vast explosion; zebras bolt in ten directions, so that the eye is bombarded with dizzying stroboscopic waves of black and white; when the convulsive confusion passes, one of the quaggas is lying on its side, alone in the field, having made the transition across the interface. Sybille regards it calmly. Death once dismayed her, death of any kind, but no longer.

"*Piga m'uzuri!*" the porters cry exultantly.

"*Kufa,*" Gracchus says. "Dead. A neat shot. You have your trophy."

Ngiri is quick with the skinning knife. That night, camping below Kilimanjaro's broad flank, they dine on roast quagga, deads and porters alike. The meat is juicy, robust, faintly tangy.

Late the following afternoon, as they pass through cooler stream-broken country thick with tall, scrubby gray green vase-shaped trees, they come upon a monstrosity, a shaggy shambling thing twelve or fifteen feet high, standing upright on ponderous hind legs and balancing itself on an incredibly thick, heavy tail. It leans against a tree, pulling at its top branches with long forelimbs that are tipped with ferocious claws like a row of sickles; it munches voraciously on leaves and twigs. Briefly it notices them, and looks around, studying them with small stupid yellow eyes; then it returns to its meal.

"A rarity," Gracchus says. "I know hunters who have been all over this park without ever running into one. Have you ever seen anything so ugly?"

"What is it?" Sybille asks.

"Megatherium. Giant ground sloth. South American, really, but we weren't fussy about geography when we were stocking this place. We have only four of them, and it costs God knows how many thousands of dollars to shoot one. Nobody's signed up for a ground sloth yet. I doubt anyone will."

Sybille wonders where the beast might be vulnerable to a bullet: surely not in its dim peanut-sized brain. She wonders, too, what sort of sportsman would find pleasure in killing such a thing. For a while they watch as the sluggish monster tears the tree apart. Then they move on.

Gracchus shows them another prodigy at sundown: a pale dome, like some huge melon, nestling in a mound of dense grass beside a stream. "Ostrich egg?" Mortimer guesses.

"Close. Very close. It's a moa egg. World's biggest bird. From New

Zealand, extinct since about the eighteenth century."

Nerita crouches and lightly taps the egg. "What an omelet we could make!"

"There's enough there to feed seventy-five of us," Gracchus says. "Two gallons of fluid, easy. But of course we mustn't meddle with it. Natural increase is very important in keeping this park stocked."

"And where's mama moa?" Sybille asks. "Should she have abandoned the egg?"

"Moas aren't very bright," Gracchus answers. "That's one good reason why they became extinct. She must have wandered off to find some dinner. And—"

"Good God," Zacharias blurts.

The moa has returned, emerging suddenly from a thicket. She stands like a feathered mountain above them, limned by the deep blue of twilight: an ostrich, more or less, but a magnified ostrich, an ultimate ostrich, a bird a dozen feet high, with a heavy rounded body and a great thick hose of a neck and taloned legs sturdy as saplings. Surely this is Sinbad's rukh, that can fly off with elephants in its grasp! The bird peers at them, sadly contemplating the band of small beings clustered about her egg; she arches her neck as though readying for attack, and Zacharias reaches for one of the rifles, but Gracchus checks his hand, for the moa is merely rearing back to protest. It utters a deep mournful mooing sound and does not move. "Just back slowly away," Gracchus tells them. "It won't attack. But keep away from the feet; one kick can kill you."

"I was going to apply for a license on a moa," Mortimer says.

"Killing them's a bore," Gracchus tells him. "They just stand there and let you shoot. You're better off with what you signed up for."

What Mortimer has signed up for is an aurochs, the vanished wild ox of the European forests, known to Caesar, known to Pliny, hunted by the hero Siegfried, altogether exterminated by the year 1627. The plains of East Africa are not a comfortable environment for the aurochs and the herd that has been conjured by the genetic necromancers keeps to itself in the wooded highlands, several days' journey from the haunts of quaggas and ground sloths. In this dark grove the hunters come upon troops of chattering baboons and solitary big-eared elephants and, in a place of broken sunlight and shadow, a splendid antelope, a bull bongo with a fine curving pair of horns. Gracchus leads them onward, deeper in. He seems tense: there is peril here. The porters slip through the forest like black wraiths, spreading out in arching crab-claw patterns, communicating with one another and with Gracchus by whistling. Everyone keeps weapons ready in here. Sybille half-expects to see leopards draped on overhanging branches, cobras slithering through the undergrowth. But she feels no fear.

They approach a clearing.

"Aurochs," Gracchus says.

A dozen of them are cropping the shrubbery: big short-haired long-horned cattle, muscular and alert. Picking up the scent of the intruders, they lift their heavy heads, sniff, glare. Gracchus and Ngiri confer with eyebrows. Nodding, Gracchus mutters to Mortimer, "Too many of them. Wait for them to thin off." Mortimer smiles. He looks a little nervous. The aurochs has a reputation for attacking without warning. Four, five, six of the beasts slip away, and the others withdraw to the edge of the clearing, as if to plan strategy; but one big bull, sour-eyed and grim, stands his ground, glowering. Gracchus rolls on the balls of his feet. His burly body seems, to Sybille, a study in mobility, in preparedness.

"Now," he says.

In the same moment the bull aurochs charges, moving with extraordinary swiftness, head lowered, horns extended like spears. Mortimer fires. The bullet strikes with a loud whonking sound, crashing into the shoulder of the aurochs, a perfect shot, but the animal does not fall, and Mortimer shoots again, less gracefully ripping into the belly, and then Gracchus and Ngiri are firing also, not at Mortimer's aurochs but over the heads of the others, to drive them away, and the risky tactic works, for the other animals go stampeding off into the woods. The one Mortimer has shot continues toward him, staggering now, losing momentum, and falls practically at his feet, rolling over, knifing the forest floor with its hooves.

"*Kufa,*" Ngiri says. "*Piga nyati m'uzuri, bwana.*" Mortimer grins. "*Piga,*" he says.

Gracchus salutes him. "More exciting than moa," he says.

"And these are mine," says Nerita three hours later, indicating a tree at the outer rim of the forest. Several hundred large pigeons nest in its boughs, so many of them that the tree seems to be sprouting birds rather than leaves. The females are plain—light brown above, gray below—but the males are flamboyant, with rich, glossy blue plumage on their wings and backs, breasts of a wine red chestnut color, iridescent spots of bronze and green on their necks and weird, vivid eyes of a bright, fiery orange.

Gracchus says, "Right. You've found your passenger pigeons."

"Where's the thrill in shooting pigeons out of a tree?" Mortimer asks.

Nerita gives him a withering look. "Where's the thrill in gunning down a charging bull?" She signals to Ngiri, who fires a shot into the air. The startled pigeons burst from their perches and fly in low circles. In the old days, a century and a half ago in the forests of North America, no one troubled to shoot passenger pigeons on the wing: the pigeons were food, not sport, and it was simpler to blast them as they sat, for that way a single hunter might kill thousands of birds in one day. Thus it took only fifty years to reduce the passenger pigeon population from uncountable sky-blackening billions to zero. Nerita is more sporting. This is a test of her skill, after all. She aims her shotgun, shoots, pumps, shoots, pumps. Stunned birds drop to the ground. She and her gun are a single entity, sharing one purpose. In moments it is all over. The porters retrieve the fallen birds and snap their necks. Nerita has the dozen pigeons her license allows: a pair to mount, the rest for tonight's dinner. The survivors have returned to their tree and stare placidly, unreproachfully, at the hunters. "They breed so damned fast," Gracchus mutters. "If we aren't careful, they'll be getting out of the preserve and taking over all of Africa."

Sybille laughs. "Don't worry. We'll cope. We wiped them out once and we can do it again, if we have to."

Sybille's prey is a dodo. In Dar, when they were applying for their licenses, the others mocked her choice: a fat flightless bird, unable to run or fight, so feeble of wit that it fears nothing. She ignored them. She wants a dodo because to her it is the essence of extinction, the prototype of all that is dead and vanished. That there is no sport in shooting foolish dodos means little to Sybille. Hunting itself is meaningless for her.

Through this vast park she wanders as in a dream. She sees ground sloths, great auks, quaggas, moas, heath hens, Javan rhinos, giant armadillos and many other rarities. The place is an abode of ghosts. The ingenuities of the genetic craftsmen are limitless; someday, perhaps, the preserve will offer trilobites, tyrannosaurs, mastodons, saber-toothed cats, baluchitheria, even—why not?—packs of australopithecines, tribes of Neanderthals. For the amusement of the deads, whose games tend to be somber. Sybille wonders whether it can really be considered killing, this slaughter of laboratory-spawned novelties. Are these animals real or artificial? Living things, or cleverly animated constructs? Real, she decides. Living. They eat, they metabolize, they reproduce. They must seem real to themselves, and so they are real, realer, maybe, than dead human beings who walk again in their own cast-off bodies.

"Shotgun," Sybille says to the closest porter.

There is the bird, ugly, ridiculous, waddling laboriously through the tall grass. Sybille accepts a weapon and sights along its barrel. "Wait," Nerita says. "I'd like to get a picture of this." She moves slantwise around the group, taking exaggerated care not to frighten the dodo, but the dodo does not seem to be aware of any of them. Like an emissary from the realm of darkness, carrying good news of death to those creatures not yet extinct, it plods diligently across their path. "Fine," Nerita says. "Anthony, point at the dodo will you, as if you've just noticed it? Kent, I'd like you to look down at your gun, study its bolt or something. Fine. And Sybille, just hold that pose—aiming—yes—"

Nerita takes the picture.

Calmly Sybille pulls the trigger.

*"Kazi imekwisha,"* Gracchus says. "The work is finished."


6.

> Although to be driven back upon oneself is an uneasy affair at best, rather like trying to cross a border with borrowed credentials, it seems to be now the one condition necessary to the beginnings of real self-respect. Most of our platitudes notwithstanding, self-deception remains the most difficult deception. The tricks that work on others count for nothing in that very well-lit back alley where one keeps assignations with oneself: no winning smiles will do here, no prettily drawn lists of good intentions.
>
> Joan Didion: *On Self-Respect*


"You better believe what Jeej is trying to tell you," Dolorosa said. "Ten minutes inside the Cold Town, they'll have your number. Five minutes."

Jijibhoi's man was small, rumpled-looking, forty or fifty years old, with untidy long dark hair and wide-set smoldering eyes. His skin was sallow and his face was gaunt. Such other deads as Klein had seen at close range had about them an air of unearthly serenity, but not this one: Dolorosa was tense, fidgety, a knuckle-cracker, a lip-gnawer. Yet somehow there could be no doubt he was a dead, as much a dead as Zacharias, as Gracchus, as Mortimer.

"They'll have my what?" Klein asked.

"Your number. Your number. They'll know you aren't a dead, because it can't be faked. Jesus, don't you even speak English? Jorge, that's a foreign name. I should have known. Where are you from?"

"Argentina, as a matter of fact, but I was brought to California when I was a small boy. In 1955. Look, if they catch me, they catch me. I just want to get in there and spend half an hour talking with my wife."

"Mister, you don't have any wife any more."

"With Sybille," Klein said, exasperated. "To talk with Sybille, my—my former wife."

"All right. I'll get you inside."

"What will it cost?"

"Never mind that," Dolorosa said. "I owe Jeej here a few favors. More than a few. So I'll get you the drug—"

"Drug?"

"The drug the Treasury agents use when they infiltrate the Cold Towns. It narrows the pupils, contracts the capillaries, gives you that good old Zombie look. The agents always get caught and thrown out, and so will you, but at least you'll go in there feeling that you've got a convincing disguise. Little oily capsule, one every morning before breakfast."

Klein looked at Jijibhoi. "Why do Treasury agents infiltrate the Cold Towns?"

"For the same reasons they infiltrate anywhere else," Jijibhoi said. "To spy. They are trying to compile dossiers on the financial dealings of the deads, you see, and until proper life-defining legislation is approved by Congress there is no precise way of compelling a person who is deemed legally dead to divulge—"

Dolorosa said, "Next, the background. I can get you a card of residence from Albany Cold Town in New York. You died last December, okay, and they rekindled you back East because—let's see—"

"I could have been attending the annual meeting of the American Historical Association in New York," Klein suggested. "That's what I do, you understand, professor of contemporary history at UCLA. Because of the Christmas holiday my body couldn't be shipped back to California, no room on any flight, and so they took me to Albany. How does that sound?"

Dolorosa smiled. "You really enjoy making up lies, professor, don't you? I can dig that quality in you. Okay, Albany Cold Town, and this is your first trip out of there, your drying-off trip—that's what it's called, drying-off—you come out of the Cold Town like a new butterfly just out of its cocoon, all soft and damp, and you're on your own in a strange place. Now, there's a lot of stuff you'll need to know about how to behave, little mannerisms, social graces, that kind of crap, and I'll work on that with you tomorrow and Wednesday and Friday, three sessions; that ought to be enough. Meanwhile let me give you the basics. There are only three things you really have to remember while you're inside:

"1) Never ask a direct question.
"2) Never lean on anybody's arm. You know what I mean?
"3) Keep in mind that to a dead the whole universe is plastic, nothing's real, nothing matters a hell of a lot, it's all only a joke. Only a joke, friend, only a joke."

Early in April he flew to Salt Lake City, rented a car, and drove out past Moab into the high plateau rimmed by red-rock mountains where the deads had built Zion Cold Town. This was Klein's second visit to the necropolis. The other had been in the late summer of '91, a hot, parched season when the sun filled half the sky and even the gnarled junipers looked dazed from thirst; but now it was a frosty afternoon, with faint pale light streaming out of the wintry western hills and occasional gusts of light snow whirling through the iron blue air. Jijibhoi's route instructions pulsed from the memo screen on his dashboard. Fourteen miles from town, yes, narrow paved lane turns off highway, yes, discreet little sign announcing PRIVATE ROAD, NO ADMITTANCE, yes, a second sign a thousand yards in, ZION COLD TOWN, MEMBERS ONLY, yes, and then just beyond that the barrier of green light across the road, the scanner system, the road-blocks sliding like scythes out of the underground installations, a voice on an invisible loudspeaker saying, "If you have a permit to enter Zion Cold Town, please place it under your left-hand windshield wiper."

That other time he had had no permit, and he had gone no farther than this, though at least he had managed a little colloquy with the unseen gatekeeper out of which he had squeezed the information that Sybille was indeed living in that particular Cold Town. This time he affixed Dolorosa's forged card of residence to his windshield, and waited tensely, and in thirty seconds the roadblocks slid from sight. He drove on, along a winding road that followed the natural contours of a dense forest of scrubby conifers, and came at last to a brick wall that curved away into the trees as though it encircled the entire town. Probably it did. Klein had an overpowering sense of the Cold Town as a hermetic city, ponderous and sealed as old Egypt. There was a metal gate in the brick wall; green electronic eyes surveyed him, signaled their approval, and the wall rolled open.

He drove slowly toward the center of town, passing through a zone of what he supposed were utility buildings—storage depots, a power substation, the municipal waterworks, whatever, a bunch of grim windowless one-story cinderblock affairs—and then into the residential district, which was not much lovelier. The streets were laid out on a rectangular grid; the buildings were squat, dreary, impersonal, homogeneous. There was practically no automobile traffic, and in a dozen blocks he saw no more than ten pedestrians, who did not even glance at him. So this was the environment in which the deads chose to spend their second lives. But why such deliberate bleakness? "You will never understand us," Dolorosa had warned. Dolorosa was right. Jijibhoi had told him that Cold Towns were something less than charming, but Klein had not been prepared for this. There was a glacial quality about the place, as though it were wholly entombed in a block of clear ice: silence, sterility, a mortuary clam. Cold Town, yes, aptly named. Architecturally, the town looked like the worst of all possible cheap-and-sleazy tract developments, but the psychic texture it projected was even more depressing, more like that of one of those ghastly retirement communities, one of the innumerable Leisure Worlds or Sun Manors, those childless joyless retreats where colonies of that other kind of living dead collected to await the last trumpet. Klein shivered.

At last, another few minutes deeper into the town, a sign of activity, if not exactly of life: a shopping center, flat-topped brown stucco buildings around a U-shaped courtyard, a steady flow of shoppers moving about. All right. His first test was about to commence. He parked his car near the mouth of the U and strolled uneasily inward. He felt as if his forehead were a beacon, flashing glowing betrayals at rhythmic intervals:

FRAUD INTRUDER INTERLOPER SPY

Go ahead, he thought, seize me, seize the impostor, get it over with, throw me out, string me up, crucify me. But no one seemed to pick up the signals. He was altogether ignored. Out of courtesy? Or just contempt? He stole what he hoped were covert glances at the shoppers, half-expecting to run across Sybille right away. They all looked like sleepwalkers, moving in glazed silence about their errands. No smiles, no chatter: the icy aloofness of these self-contained people heightened the familiar suburban atmosphere of the shopping center into surrealist intensity, Norman Rockwell with an overlay of Dali or De Chirico. The shopping center looked like all other shopping centers: clothing stores, a bank, a record shop, snack bars, a florist, a TV-stereo outlet, a theater, a five-and-dime. One difference, though, became apparent as Klein wandered from shop to shop: the whole place was automated. There were no clerks anywhere, only the ubiquitous data screens, and no doubt a battery of hidden scanners to discourage shoplifters. (Or did the impulse toward petty theft perish with the body's first death?) The customers selected all the merchandise themselves, checked it out via data screens, touched their thumbs to charge-plates to debit their accounts. Of course. No one was going to waste his precious rekindled existence standing behind a counter to sell tennis shoes or cotton candy. Nor were the dwellers in the Cold Towns likely to dilute their isolation by hiring a labor force of imported warms. Somebody here had to do a little work, obviously—how did the merchandise get into the stores?—but, in general, Klein realized, what could not be done here by machines would not be done at all.

For ten minutes he prowled the center. Just when he was beginning to think he must be entirely invisible to these people, a short, broad-shouldered man, bald but with oddly youthful features, paused in front of him and said, "I am Pablo. I welcome you to Zion Cold Town." This unexpected puncturing of the silence so startled Klein that he had to fight to retain appropriate deadlike imperturbability. Pablo smiled warmly and touched both his hands to Klein's in friendly greeting, but his eyes were frigid, hostile, remote, a terrifying contradiction. "I've been sent to bring you to the lodging place. Come: your car."

Other than to give directions, Pablo spoke only three times during the five-minute drive. "Here is the rekindling house," he said. A five-story building, as inviting as a hospital, with walls of dark bronze and windows black as onyx. "This is Guidefather's house," Pablo said a moment later. A modest brick building, like a rectory, at the edge of a small park. And, finally: "This is where you will stay. Enjoy your visit." Abruptly he got out of the car and walked rapidly away.

This was the house of strangers, the hotel for visiting deads, a long low cinderblock structure, functinal and unglamourous, one of the least seductive buildings in this city of stark disagreeable buildings. However else it might be with the deads, they clearly had no craving for fancy architecture. A voice out of a data screen in the spartan lobby assigned him to a room: a white-walled box, square, high of ceiling. He had his own toilet, his own data screen, a narrow bed, a chest of drawers, a modest closet, a small window that gave him a view of a neighboring building just as drab as this. Nothing had been said about rental; perhaps he was a guest of the city. Nothing had been said about anything. It seemed that he had been accepted. So much for Jijibhoi's gloomy assurance that he would instantly be found out, so much for Dolorosa's insistence that they would have his number in ten minutes or less. He had been in Zion Cold Town for half an hour. Did they have his number?

"Eating isn't important among us," Dolorosa had said.

"But you do eat?"

"Of course we eat. It just isn't *important.*"

It was important to Klein, though. Not haute cuisine, necessarily, but some sort of food, preferably three times a day. He was getting hungry now. Ring for room service? There were no servants in this city. He turned to the data screen. Dolorosa's first rule: *Never ask a direct question.* Surely that didn't apply to the data screen, only to his fellow deads. He didn't have to observe the niceties of etiquette when talking to a computer. Still, the voice behind the screen might not be that of a computer after all, so he tried to employ the oblique, elliptical conversational style that Dolorosa said the deads favored among themselves:

"Dinner?"

"Commissary."

"Where?"

"Central Four," said the screen.

Central Four? All right. He would find the way. He changed into fresh clothing and went down the long vinyl-floored hallway to the lobby. Night had come; streetlamps were glowing; under cloak of darkness the city's ugliness was no longer so obtrusive, and there was even a kind of controlled beauty about the brutal regularity of its streets.

The streets were unmarked, though, and deserted. Klein walked at random for ten minutes, hoping to meet someone heading for the Central Four commissary. But when he did come upon someone, a tall and regal woman well advanced in years, he found himself incapable of approaching her. *(Never ask a direct question. Never lean on anybody's arm.)* He walked alongside her, in silence and at a distance, until she turned suddenly to enter a house. For ten minutes more he wandered alone again. This is ridiculous, he thought: dead or warm, I'm a stranger in town, I should be entitled to a little assistance. Maybe Dolorosa was just trying to complicate things. On the next corner, when Klein caught sight of a man hunched away from the wind, lighting a cigarette, he went boldly over to him.

"Excuse me, but—"

The other looked up. "Klein?" he said. "Yes. Of course. Well, so you've made the crossing too!"

He was one of Sybille's Zanzibar companions, Klein realized. The quick-eyed, sharp-edged one—Mortimer. A member of her pseudo familial grouping, whatever that might be. Klein stared sullenly at him. This had to be the moment when his imposture would be exposed, for only some six weeks had passed since he had argued with Mortimer in the gardens of Sybille's Zanzibar hotel, not nearly enough time for someone to have died and been rekindled and gone through his drying-off. But a moment passed and Mortimer said nothing. At length Klein said, "I just got here. Pablo showed me to the house of strangers and now I'm looking for the commissary."

"Central Four? I'm going there myself. How lucky for you." No sign of suspicion in Mortimer's face. Perhaps an elusive smile revealed his awareness that Klein could not be what he claimed to be. *Keep in mind that to a dead the whole universe is plastic, it's all only a joke.* "I'm waiting for Nerita," Mortimer said. "We can all eat together."

Klein said heavily, "I was rekindled in Albany Cold Town. I've just emerged."

"How nice," Mortimer said.

Nerita Tracy stepped out of a building just beyond the corner—a slim athletic-looking woman, about forty, with short reddish brown hair. As she swept toward them Mortimer said, "Here's Klein, who we met in Zanzibar. Just rekindled, out of Albany."

"Sybille will be amused."

"Is she in town?" Klein blurted.

Mortimer and Nerita exchanged sly glances. Klein felt abashed. *Never ask a direct question.* Damn Dolorosa!

Nerita said, "You'll see her before long. Shall we go to dinner?"

The commissary was less austere than Klein had expected: actually quite an inviting restaurant, elaborately constructed on five or six levels divided by lustrous dark hangings into small, secluded dining areas. It had the warm, rich look of a tropical resort. But the food, which came auto-mat-style out of revolving dispensers, was prefabricated and cheerless—another jarring contradiction. *Only a joke, friend, only a joke.* In any case he was less hungry than he had imagined at the hotel. He sat with Mortimer and Nerita, picking at his meal, while their conversation flowed past him at several times the speed of thought. They spoke in fragments and ellipses, in periphrastics and aposiopeses, in a style abundant in chiasmus, metonymy, meiosis, oxymoron and zeugma; their dazzling rhetorical techniques left him baffled and uncomfortable, which beyond much doubt was their intention. Now and again they would dart from a thicket of indirection to skewer him with a quick corroborative stab: isn't that so, they would say, and he would smile and nod, nod and smile, saying, Yes, yes, absolutely. Did they know he was a fake, and were they merely playing with him, or had they, somehow, impossibly, accepted him as one of them? So subtle was their style that he could not tell. A very new member of the society of the rekindled, he told himself, would be nearly as much at sea here as a warm in deadface.

Then Nerita said—no verbal games, this time—"You still miss her terribly, don't you?"

"I do. Some things evidently never perish."

"Everything perishes," Mortimer said. "The dodo, the aurochs, the Holy Roman Empire, the T'ang Dynasty, the walls of Byzantium, the language of Mohenjodaro."

"But not the Great Pyramid, the Yangtze, the coelacanth or the skullcap of Pithecanthropus," Klein countered. "Some things persist and endure. And some can be regenerated. Lost languages have been deciphered. I believe the dodo and the aurochs are hunted in a certain African park in this very era."

"Replicas," Mortimer said.

"Convincing replicas. Simulations as good as the original."

"Is that what you want?" Nerita asked.

"I want what's possible to have."

"A convincing replica of lost love?"

"I might be willing to settle for five minutes of conversation with her."

"You'll have it. Not tonight. See? There she is. But don't bother her now." Nerita nodded across the gulf in the center of the restaurant; on the far side, three levels up from where they sat, Sybille and Kent Zacharias had appeared. They stood for a brief while at the edge of their dining alcove, staring blandly and emotionlessly into the restaurant's central well. Klein felt a muscle jerking uncontrollably in his cheek, a damning revelation of undeadlike uncoolness, and pressed his hand over it, so that it twanged and throbbed against his palm. She was like a goddess up there, manifesting herself in her sanctum to her worshippers, a pale shimmering figure, more beautiful even than she had become to him through the anguished enhancements of memory, and it seemed impossible to him that that being had ever been his wife, that he had known her when her eyes were puffy and reddened from a night of study, that he had looked down at her face as they made love and had seen her lips pull back in that spasm of ecstasy that is so close to a grimace of pain, that he had known her crochety and unkind in her illness, short-tempered and impatient in health, a person of flaws and weaknesses, of odors and blemishes, in short a human being, this goddess, this unreal rekindled creature, this object of his quest, this Sybille. Serenely she turned, serenely she vanished into her cloaked alcove. "She knows you're here," Nerita told him. "You'll see her. Perhaps tomorrow." Then Mortimer said something maddeningly oblique, and Nerita replied with the same off-center mystification, and Klein once more was plunged into the river of their easy dancing wordplay, down into it, down and down and down, and as he struggled to keep from drowning, as he fought to comprehend their interchanges, he never once looked toward the place where Sybille sat, not even once, and congratulated himself on having accomplished that much at least in his masquerade.

That night, lying alone in his room at the house of strangers, he wonders what he will say to Sybille when they finally meet, and what she will say to him. Will he dare bluntly to ask her to describe to him the quality of her new existence? That is all that he wants from her, really, that knowledge, that opening of an aperture into her transfigured self; that is as much as he hopes to get from her, knowing as he does that there is scarcely a chance of regaining her, but will he dare to ask, will he dare even that? Of course his asking such things will reveal to her that he is still a warm, too dense and gross of perception to comprehend the life of a dead; but he is certain she will sense that anyway, instantly. What will he say, what will he say? He plays out an imagined script of their conversation in the theater of his mind:

—Tell me what it's like, Sybille, to be the way you are now.
—Like swimming under a sheet of glass.
—I don't follow.
—Everything is quiet where I am, Jorge. There's a peace that passeth

all understanding. I used to feel sometimes that I was caught up in a great storm, that I was being buffeted by every breeze, that my life was being consumed by agitations and frenzies, but now, now, I'm at the eye of the storm, at the place where everything is always calm. I observe rather than let myself be acted upon.

—But isn't there a loss of feeling that way? Don't you feel that you're wrapped in an insulating layer? Like swimming under glass, you say—that conveys being insulated, being cut off, being almost numb.

—I suppose you might think so. The way it is is that one no longer is affected by the unnecessary.

—It sounds to me like a limited existence.

—Less limited than the grave, Jorge.

—I never understood why you wanted rekindling. You were such a world-devourer, Sybille, you lived with such intensity, such passion. To settle for the kind of existence you have now, to be only half-alive—

—Don't be a fool, Jorge. To be half alive is better than to be rotting in the ground. I was so young. There was so much else still to see and do.

—But to see it and do it half-alive?

—Those were your words, not mine. I'm not alive at all. I'm neither less nor more than the person you knew. I'm another kind of being altogether. Neither less nor more, only different.

—Are all your perceptions different?

—Very much so. My perspective is broader. Little things stand revealed as little things.

—Give me an example, Sybille.

—I'd rather not. How could I make anything clear to you? Die and be with us, and you'll understand.

—You know I'm not dead?

—Oh, Jorge, how funny you are!

—How nice that I can still amuse you.

—You look so hurt, so tragic. I could almost feel sorry for you. Come: ask me anything.

—Could you leave your companions and live in the world again?

—I've never considered that.

—Could you?

—I suppose I could. But why should I? This is my world now.

—This ghetto.

—Is that how it seems to you?

—You lock yourselves into a closed society of your peers, a tight subcul-

ture. Your own jargon, your own wall of etiquette and idiosyncrasy. Designed, I think, mainly to keep the outsiders off balance, to keep them
feeling like outsiders. It's a defensive thing. The hippies, the blacks, the
gays, the deads—same mechanism, same process.

—The Jews, too. Don't forget the Jews.

—All right, Sybille, the Jews. With their little tribal jokes, their special
holidays, their own mysterious language, yes, a good case in point.

—So I've joined a new tribe. What's wrong with that?

—Did you need to be part of a tribe?

—What did I have before? The tribe of Californians? The tribe of
academics?

—The tribe of Jorge and Sybille Klein.

—Too narrow. Anyway, I've been expelled from that tribe. I needed
to join another one.

—Expelled?

—By death. After that there's no going back.

—You could go back. Any time.

—Oh, no, no, no, Jorge, I can't, I can't, I'm not Sybille Klein any more.
I never will be again. How can I explain it to you? There's no way. Death
brings on changes. Die and see, Jorge. Die and see.

Nerita said, "She's waiting for you in the lounge."

It was a big, coldly furnished room at the far end of the other wing of
the house of strangers. Sybille stood by a window through which pale,
chilly morning light was streaming. Mortimer was with her, and also Kent
Zacharias. The two men favored Klein with mysterious oblique smiles—
courteous or derisive, he could not tell which. "Do you like our town?"
Zacharias asked. "Have you been seeing the sights?" Klein chose not to
reply. He acknowledged the question with a faint nod and turned to
Sybille. Strangely, he felt altogether calm at this moment of attaining a
years-old desire: he felt nothing at all in her presence, no panic, no
yearning, no dismay, no nostalgia, nothing, nothing. As though he were
truly a dead. He knew it was the tranquility of utter terror.

"We'll leave you two alone," Zacharias said. "You must have so much
to tell each other." He went out, with Nerita and Mortimer. Klein's eyes
met Sybille's and lingered there. She was looking at him coolly, in a kind
of impersonal appraisal. That damnable smile of hers, Klein thought:
dying turns them all into Mona Lisas.

She said, "Do you plan to stay here long?"

"Probably not. A few days, maybe a week." He moistened his lips. "How have you been, Sybille? How has it been going?"

"It's all been about as I expected."

*What do you mean by that? Can you give me some details? Are you at all disappointed? Have there been any surprises? What has it been like for you, Sybille? Oh, Jesus—*

*—Never ask a direct question—*

He said, "I wish you had let me visit with you in Zanzibar."

"That wasn't possible. Let's not talk about it now." She dismissed the episode with a casual wave. After a moment she said, "Would you like to hear a fascinating story I've uncovered about the early days of Omani influence in Zanzibar?"

The impersonality of the question startled him. How could she display such absolute lack of curiosity about his presence in Zion Cold Town, his claim to be a dead, his reasons for wanting to see her? How could she plunge so quickly, so coldly, into a discussion of archaic political events in Zanzibar?

"I suppose so," he said weakly.

"It's a sort of Arabian Nights story, really. It's the story of how Ahmad the Sly overthrew Abdullah ibn Muhammad Alawi."

The names were strange to him. He had indeed taken some small part in her historical researches, but it was years since he had worked with her, and everything had drifted about in his mind, leaving a jumbled residue of Ahmads and Hasans and Abdullahs. "I'm sorry," he said. "I don't recall who they were."

Unperturbed, Sybille said, "Certainly you remember that in the eighteenth and early nineteenth centuries the chief power in the Indian Ocean was the Arab state of Oman, ruled from Muscat on the Persian Gulf. Under the Busaidi dynasty, founded in 1744 by Ahmad ibn Said al-Busaidi, the Omani extended their power to East Africa. The logical capital for their African empire was the port of Mombasa, but they were unable to evict a rival dynasty reigning there, so the Busaidi looked toward nearby Zanzibar—a cosmopolitan island of mixed Arab, Indian and African population. Zanzibar's strategic placement on the coast and its spacious and well-protected harbor made it an ideal base for the East African slave trade that the Busaidi of Oman intended to dominate."

"It comes back to me now, I think."

"Very well. The founder of the Omani Sultanate of Zanzibar was Ahmad ibn Majid the Sly, who came to the throne of Oman in 1811—

do you remember?—upon the death of his uncle Abd-er-Rahman al-Busaidi.

"The names sound familiar," Klein said doubtfully.

"Seven years later," Sybille continued, "seeking to conquer Zanzibar without the use of force, Ahmad the Sly shaved his beard and moustache and visited the island disguised as a soothsayer, wearing yellow robes and a costly emerald in his turban. At that time most of Zanzibar was governed by a native ruler of mixed Arab and African blood, Abdullah ibn Muhammad Alawi, whose hereditary title was Mwenyi Mkuu. The Mwenyi Mkuu's subjects were mainly Africans, members of a tribe called the Hadimu. Sultan Ahmad, arriving in Zanzibar Town, gave a demonstration of his soothsaying skills on the waterfront and attracted so much attention that he speedily gained an audience at the court of the Mwenyi Mkuu. Ahmad predicted a glowing future for Abdullah, declaring that a powerful prince famed throughout the world would come to Zanzibar, make the Mwenyi Mkuu his high lieutenant and would confirm him and his descendants as lords of Zanzibar forever.

" 'How do you know these things?' asked the Mwenyi Mkuu.

" 'There is a potion I drink,' Sultan Ahmad replied, 'that enables me to see what is to come. Do you wish to taste of it?'

" 'Most surely I do,' Abdullah said, and Ahmad thereupon gave him a drug that sent him into rapturous transports and showed him visions of paradise. Looking down from his place near the footstool of Allah, the Mwenyi Mkuu saw a rich and happy Zanzibar governed by his children's children's children. For hours he wandered in fantasies of almighty power.

"Ahmad then departed, and let his beard and moustache grow again, and returned to Zanzibar ten weeks later in his full regalia as sultan of Oman, at the head of an imposing and powerful armada. He went at once to the court of the Mwenyi Mkuu and proposed, just as the soothsayer had prophesied, that Oman and Zanzibar enter into a treaty of alliance under which Oman would assume responsibility for much of Zanzibar's external relations—including the slave trade—while guaranteeing the authority of the Mwenyi Mkuu over domestic affairs. In return for his partial abdication of authority, the Mwenyi Mkuu would receive financial compensation from Oman. Remembering the vision the soothsayer had revealed to him, Abdullah at once signed the treaty, thereby legitimizing what was, in effect, the Omani conquest of Zanzibar. A great feast was held to celebrate the treaty, and, as a mark of honor, the Mwenyi Mkuu offered Sultan Ahmad a rare drug used locally, known as *borgash*, or 'the flower of truth.' Ahmad only pretended to put the pipe to his lips, for he loathed all mind-altering drugs, but Abdullah, as the flower of truth possessed him, looked at Ahmad and recognized the outlines of the soothsayer's face behind the sultan's new beard. Realizing that he had been deceived, the Mwenyi Mkuu thrust his dagger, the tip of which was poisoned, deep into the sultan's side and fled the banquet hall, taking up residence on the neighboring island of Pemba. Ahmad ibn Majid survived, but the poison consumed his vital organs and the remaining ten years of his life were spent in constant agony. As for the Mwenyi Mkuu, the sultan's men hunted him down and put him to death along with ninety members of his family, and native rule in Zanzibar was therewith extinguished.' "

Sybille paused. "Is that not a gaudy and wonderful story?" she asked at last.

"Fascinating," Klein said. "Where did you find it?"

"Unpublished memoirs of Claude Richburn of the East India Company. Buried deep in the London archives. Strange that no historian ever came upon it before, isn't it? The standard texts simply say that Ahmad used his navy to bully Abdullah into signing the treaty, and then had the Mwenyi Mkuu assassinated at the first convenient moment."

"Very strange," Klein agreed. But he had not come here to listen to romantic tales of visionary potions and royal treacheries. He groped for some way to bring the conversation to a more personal level. Fragments of his imaginary dialogue with Sybille floated through his mind. *Everything is quiet where I am, Jorge. There's a peace that passeth all understanding. Like swimming under a sheet of glass. The way it is is that one no longer is affected by the unnecessary. Little things stand revealed as little things. Die and be with us, and you'll understand.* Yes. Perhaps. But did she really believe any of that? He had put all the words in her mouth; everything he had imagined her to say was his own construct, worthless as a key to the true Sybille. Where would he find the key, though?

She gave him no chance. "I will be going back to Zanzibar soon," she said. "There's much I want to learn about this incident from the people in the back country—old legends about the last days of the Mwenyi Mkuu, perhaps variants on the basic story—"

"May I accompany you?"

"Don't you have your own research to resume, Jorge?" she asked, and did not wait for an answer. She walked briskly toward the door of the lounge and went out, and he was alone.

7.

I mean what they and their hired psychiatrists call "delusional systems." Needless to say, "delusions" are always officially defined. We
don't have to worry about questions of real or unreal. They only talk
out of expediency. It's the *system* that matters. How the data arrange
themselves inside it. Some are consistent, others fall apart.

Thomas Pynchon: *Gravity's Rainbow*

Once more the deads, this time only three of them coming over on the
morning flight from Dar. Three was better than five, Daud Mahmoud
Barwani supposed, but three was still more than a sufficiency. Not that
those others, two months back, had caused any trouble, staying just the
one day and flitting off to the mainland again, but it made him uncomfortable to think of such creatures on the same small island as himself. With
all the world to choose, why did they keep coming to Zanzibar?

"The plane is here," said the flight controller.

Thirteen passengers. The health officer let the local people through the
gate first—two newspapermen and four legislators coming back from the
Pan-African Conference in Capetown—and then processed a party of
four Japanese tourists, unsmiling owlish men festooned with cameras. And
then the deads: and Barwani was surprised to discover that they were the
same ones as before, the red-haired man, the brown-haired man without
the beard, the black-haired woman. Did deads have so much money that
they could fly from America to Zanzibar every few months? Barwani had
heard a tale to the effect that each new dead, when he rose from his coffin,
was presented with bars of gold equal to his own weight, and now he
thought he believed it. No good will come of having such beings loose in
the world, he told himself, and certainly none from letting them into
Zanzibar. Yet he had no choice. "Welcome once again to the isle of
cloves," he said unctuously, and smiled a bureaucratic smile, and wondered, not for the first time, what would become of Daud Mahmoud
Barwani once his days on earth had reached their end.

"—Ahmad the Sly versus Abdullah Something," Klein said. "That's all
she would talk about. The history of Zanzibar." He was in Jijibhoi's study.
The night was warm and a late-season rain was falling, blurring the million
sparkling lights of the Los Angeles basin. "It would have been, you know,
gauche to ask her any direct questions. Gauche. I haven't felt so gauche

since I was fourteen. I was helpless among them, a foreigner, a child."

"Do you think they saw through your disguise?" Jijibhoi asked.

"I can't tell. They seemed to be toying with me, to be having sport with me, but that may just have been their general style with any newcomer. Nobody challenged me. Nobody hinted I might be an impostor. Nobody seemed to care very much about me or what I was doing there or how I had happened to become a dead. Sybille and I stood face to face, and I wanted to reach out to her, I wanted her to reach out to me, and there was no contact, none, none at all, it was as though we had just met at some academic cocktail party and the only thing on her mind was the new nugget of obscure history she had just unearthed, and so she told me all about how Sultan Ahmad outfoxed Abdullah and Abdullah stabbed the sultan." Klein caught sight of a set of familiar books on Jijibhoi's crowded shelves—Oliver and Mathew, *History of East Africa,* books that had traveled everywhere with Sybille in the years of their marriage. He pulled forth Volume I, saying, "She claimed that the standard histories give a sketchy and inaccurate description of the incident and that she's only now discovered the true story. For all I know, she was just playing a game with me, telling me a piece of established history as though it were something nobody knew till last week. Let me see—Ahmad, Ahmad, Ahmad—"

He examined the index. Five Ahmads were listed, but there was no entry for a Sultan Ahmad ibn Majid the Sly. Indeed an Ahmad ibn Majid was cited, but he was mentioned only in a footnote and appeared to be an Arab chronicler. Klein found three Abdullahs, none of them a man of Zanzibar. "Something's wrong," he murmured.

"It does not matter, dear Jorge," Jijibhoi said mildly.

"It does. Wait a minute." He prowled the listings. Under *Zanzibar, Rulers,* he found no Ahmads, no Abdullahs; he did discover a Majid ibn Said, but when he checked the reference he found that he had reigned somewhere in the second half of the nineteenth century. Desperately Klein flipped pages, skimming, turning back, searching. Eventually he looked up and said, "It's all wrong!"

"The Oxford History of East Africa?"

"The details of Sybille's story. Look, she said this Ahmad the Sly gained the throne of Oman in 1811, and seized Zanzibar seven years later. But the book says that a certain Seyyid Said al-Busaidi became sultan of Oman in 1806, and ruled for *fifty years.* He was the one, not this nonexistent Ahmad the Sly, who grabbed Zanzibar, but he did it in 1828, and the ruler he compelled to sign a treaty with him, the Mwenyi Mkuu, was named

Hasan ibn Ahmad Alawi, and—" Klein shook his head. "It's an altogether different cast of characters. No stabbings, no assassinations, the dates are entirely different, the whole thing—"

Jijibhoi smiled sadly. "The deads are often mischievous."

"But why would she invent a complete fantasy and palm it off as a sensational new discovery? Sybille was the most scrupulous scholar I ever knew! She would never—"

"That was the Sybille you knew, dear friend. I keep urging you to realize that this is another person, a new person, within her body."

"A person who would lie about history?"

"A person who would tease," Jijibhoi said.

"Yes," Klein muttered. "Who would tease." *Keep in mind that to a dead the whole universe is plastic, nothing's real, nothing matters a hell of a lot.* "Who would tease a stupid, boring, annoyingly persistent ex-husband who has shown up in her Cold Town, wearing a transparent disguise and pretending to be a dead. Who would invent not only an anecdote but even its principals, as a joke, a game, a *jeu d'esprit.* Oh, God. Oh, God, how cruel she is, how foolish I was! It was her way of telling me she knew I was a phony dead. *Quid pro quo,* fraud for fraud!"

"What will you do?"

"I don't know," Klein said.

What he did, against Jijibhoi's strong advice and his own better judgment, was to get more pills from Dolorosa and return to Zion Cold Town. There would be a fitful joy, like that of probing the socket of a missing tooth, in confronting Sybille with the evidence of her fictional Ahmad, her imaginary Abdullah. Let there be no more games between us, he would say. Tell me what I need to know, Sybille, and then let me go away; but tell me only truth. All the way to Utah he rehearsed his speech, polishing and embellishing. There was no need for it, though, since this time the gate of Zion Cold Town would not open for him. The scanners scanned his forged Albany card and the loudspeaker said, "Your credentials are invalid."

Which could have ended it. He might have returned to Los Angeles and picked up the pieces of his life. All this semester he had been on sabbatical leave, but the summer term was coming and there was work to do. He did return to Los Angeles, but only long enough to pack a somewhat larger suitcase, find his passport and drive to the airport. On a sweet May evening a BOAC jet took him over the Pole to London, where, barely pausing for coffee and buns at an airport shop, he boarded another plane that carried him southeast toward Africa. More asleep than awake he watched the dreamy landmarks drifting past: the Mediterranean, coming and going with surprising rapidity, and the tawny carpet of the Libyan Desert and the mighty Nile, reduced to a brown thread's thickness when viewed from a height of ten miles. Suddenly Kilimanjaro, mist-wrapped, snowbound, loomed like a giant double-headed blister to his right, far below, and he thought he could make out to his left the distant glare of the sun on the Indian Ocean. Then the big needle-nosed plane began its abrupt swooping descent, and he found himself, soon after, stepping out into the warm humid air and dazzling sunlight of Dar es Salaam.

Too soon, too soon. He felt unready to go on to Zanzibar. A day or two of rest, perhaps: he picked a Dar hotel at random, the Agip, liking the strange sound of its name, and hired a taxi. The hotel was sleek and clean, a streamlined affair in the glossy 1960's style, much cheaper than the Kilimanjaro where he had stayed briefly on the other trip, and located in a pleasant leafy quarter of the city, near the ocean. He strolled about for a short while, discovered that he was altogether exhausted, returned to his room for a nap that stretched on for nearly five hours, and, awaking groggy, showered and dressed for dinner. The hotel's dining room was full of beefy redfaced fair-haired men, jacketless and wearing open-throated white shirts, all of whom reminded him disturbingly of Kent Zacharias; but these were warms, Britishers from their accents, engineers, he suspected, from their conversation. They were building a dam and a power plant somewhere up the coast, it seemed, or perhaps a power plant without a dam; it was hard to follow what they said. They drank a good deal of gin and spoke in hearty booming shouts. There were also a good many Japanese businessmen, of course, looking trim and restrained in dark blue suits and narrow ties, and at the table next to Klein's were five tanned curly-haired men talking in rapid Hebrew—Israelis, surely. The only Africans in sight were waiters and bartenders. Klein ordered Mombasa oysters, steak and a carafe of red wine, and found the food unexpectedly good, but left most of it on his plate. It was late evening in Tanzania, but for him it was ten o'clock in the morning, and his body was confused. He tumbled into bed, meditated vaguely on the probable presence of Sybille just a few air-minutes away in Zanzibar and dropped into a sound sleep from which he awakened, what seemed like many hours later, to discover that it was still well before dawn.

He dawdled away the morning sightseeing in the old native quarter, hot and dusty, with unpaved streets and rows of tin shacks, and at midday returned to his hotel for a shower and lunch. Much the same national distribution in the restaurant—British, Japanese, Israeli—though the faces seemed different. He was on his second beer when Anthony Gracchus came in. The white hunter, broad-shouldered, pale, densely bearded, clad in khaki shorts, khaki shirt, seemed almost to have stepped out of the picture-cube Jijibhoi had once shown him. Instinctively Klein shrank back, turning toward the window, but too late: Gracchus had seen him. All chatter came to a halt in the restaurant as the dead man strode to Klein's table, pulled out a chair unasked, and seated himself; then, as though a motion picture projector had been halted and started again, the British engineers resumed their shouting, sounding somewhat strained now. "Small world," Gracchus said. "Crowded one, anyway. On your way to Zanzibar, are you, Klein?"

"In a day or so. Did you know I was here?"

"Of course not." Gracchus' harsh eyes twinkled slyly. "Sheer coincidence is what this is. She's there already."

"She is?"

"She and Zacharias and Mortimer. I hear you wiggled your way into Zion."

"Briefly," Klein said. "I saw Sybille. Briefly."

"Unsatisfactorily. So once again you've followed her here. Give it up, man. Give it up."

"I can't."

"*Can't!*" Gracchus scowled. "A neurotic's word, *can't*. What you mean is *won't*. A mature man can do anything he wants to that isn't a physical impossibility. Forget her. You're only annoying her, this way, interfering with her work, interfering with her—" Gracchus smiled. "With her life. She's been dead almost three years, hasn't she? Forget her. The world's full of other women. You're still young, you have money, you aren't ugly, you have professional standing—"

"Is this what you were sent here to tell me?"

"I wasn't sent here to tell you anything, friend. I'm only trying to save you from yourself. Don't go to Zanzibar. Go home and start your life again."

"When I saw her at Zion," Klein said, "she treated me with contempt. She amused herself at my expense. I want to ask her why she did that."

"Because you're a warm and she's a dead. To her, you're a clown. To all of us you're a clown. It's nothing personal, Klein. There's simply a gulf in attitudes, a gulf too wide for you to cross. You went to Zion drugged up like a Treasury man, didn't you? Pale face, bulgy eyes? You didn't fool anyone. You certainly didn't fool *her*. The game she played with you was her way of telling you that. Don't you know that?"

"I know it, yes."

"What more do you want, then? More humiliation?"

Klein shook his head wearily and stared at the tablecloth. After a moment he looked up, and his eyes met those of Gracchus, and he was astounded to realize that he trusted the hunter, that for the first time in his dealings with the deads he felt he was being met with sincerity. He said in a low voice, "We were very close, Sybille and I, and then she died, and now I'm nothing to her. I haven't been able to come to terms with that. I need her, still. I want to share my life with her, even now."

"But you can't."

"I know that. And still I can't help doing what I've been doing."

"There's only one thing you *can* share with her," Gracchus said. "That's your death. She won't descend to your level: you have to climb to hers."

"Don't be absurd."

"Who's absurd, me or you? Listen to me, Klein. I think you're a fool, I think you're a weakling, but I don't dislike you, I don't hold you to blame for your own foolishness. And so I'll help you, if you'll allow me." He reached into his breast pocket and withdrew a tiny metal tube with a safety catch at one end. "Do you know what this is?" Gracchus asked. "It's a self-defense dart, the kind all the women in New York carry. A good many deads carry them, too, because we never know when the reaction will start, when the mobs will turn against us. Only we don't use anesthetic drugs in ours. Listen, we can walk into any tavern in the native quarter and have a decent brawl going in five minutes, and in the confusion I'll put one of these darts into you, and we'll have you in Dar General Hospital fifteen minutes after that, crammed into a deep-freeze unit, and for a few thousand dollars we can ship you unthawed to California, and this time Friday night you'll be undergoing rekindling in, say, San Diego Cold Town. And when you come out of it you and Sybille will be on the same side of the gulf, do you see? If you're destined to get back together with her, ever, that's the only way. That way you have a chance. This way you have none."

"It's unthinkable," Klein said.

"Unacceptable, maybe. But not unthinkable. Nothing's unthinkable once somebody's thought it. You think it some more. Will you promise me that? Think about it before you get aboard that plane for Zanzibar. I'll be staying here tonight and tomorrow, and then I'm going out to Arusha to meet some deads coming in for the hunting, and any time before then I'll do it for you if you say the word. Think about it. Will you think about it? Promise me that you'll think about it."

"I'll think about it," Klein said.

"Good. Good. Thank you. Now let's have lunch and change the subject. Do you like eating here?"

"One thing puzzles me. Why does this place have a clientele that's exclusively non-African? Does it dare to discriminate against blacks in a black republic?"

Gracchus laughed. "It's the blacks who discriminate, friend. This is considered a second-class hotel. All the blacks are at the Kilimanjaro or the Nyerere. Still, it's not such a bad place. I recommend the fish dishes, if you haven't tried them, and there's a decent white wine from Israel that—"

8.

O Lord, methought what pain it was to drown!
What dreadful noise of water in mine ears!
What sights of ugly death within mine eyes!
Methought I saw a thousand fearful wracks;
A thousand men that fishes gnawed upon;
Wedges of gold, great anchors, heaps of pearl,
Inestimable stones, unvalued jewels,
All scatt'red in the bottom of the sea.
Some lay in dead men's skulls, and in the holes
Where eyes did once inhabit there were crept,
As 'twere in scorn of eyes, reflecting gems
That wooed the slimy bottom of the deep
And mocked the dead bones that lay scatt'red by.
Shakespeare: *Richard III*

"—Israeli wine," Mick Dongan was saying. "Well, I'll try anything once, especially if there's some neat little irony attached to it. I mean, there we were in Egypt, in *Egypt*, at this fabulous dinner party in the hills at Luxor, and our host is a Saudi prince, no less, in full tribal costume right down to the sunglasses, and when they bring out the roast lamb he grins devilishly and says, Of course we could always drink Mouton-Rothschild, but I do happen to have a small stock of select Israeli wines in my cellar, and because I think you are, like myself, a connoisseur of small incongruities I've asked my steward to open a bottle or two of—Klein, do you see that girl who just came in?" It is January, 1981, early afternoon, a fine drizzle in the air. Klein is lunching with six colleagues from the history department of the Hanging Gardens atop the Westwood Plaza. The hotel is a huge ziggurat on stilts; the Hanging Gardens is a rooftop restaurant, ninety stories up, in freaky neo-Babylonian decor, all winged bulls and snorting dragons of blue and yellow tile, waiters with long curly beards and scimitars at their hips—gaudy nightclub by dark, campy faculty hangout by day. Klein looks to his left. Yes, a handsome woman, mid-twenties, coolly beautiful, serious-looking, taking a seat by herself, putting a stack of books and cassettes down on the table before her. Klein does not pick up strange girls: a matter of moral policy, and also a matter of innate shyness. Dongan teases him. "Go on over, will you? She's your type, I swear. Her eyes are the right color for you, aren't they?"

Klein has been complaining, lately, that there are too many blue-eyed girls in Southern California. Blue eyes are disturbing to him, somehow, even meanacing. His own eyes are brown. So are hers: dark, warm, sparkling. He thinks he has seen her occasionally in the library. Perhaps they have even exchanged brief glances. "Go on," Dongan says. "Go *on*, Jorge. Go." Klein glares at him. He will not go. How can he intrude on this woman's privacy? To force himself on her—it would almost be like rape. Dongan smiles complacently; his bland grin is a merciless prod. Klein refuses to be stampeded. But then, as he hesitates, the girl smiles too, a quick shy smile, gone so soon he is not altogether sure it happened at all, but he is sure enough, and he finds himself rising, crossing the alabaster floor, hovering awkwardly over her, searching for some inspired words with which to make contact, and no words come, but still they make contact the old-fashioned way, eye to eye, and he is stunned by the intensity of what passes between them in that first implausible moment.

"Are you waiting for someone?" he mutters, stunned.

"No." The smile again, far less tentative. "Would you like to join me?"

She is a graduate student, he discovers quickly. Just got her master's, beginning now on her doctorate—the nineteenth-century East African slave trade, particular emphasis on Zanzibar. "How romantic," he says. "Zanzibar! Have you been there?"

"Never. I hope to go some day. Have you?"

"Not ever. But it always interested me, ever since I was a small boy collecting stamps. It was the last country in my album."

"Not in mine," she says. "Zululand was."

She knows him by name, it turns out. She had even been thinking of enrolling in his course on Nazism and Its Offspring. "Are you South American?" she asks.

"Born there. Raised here. My grandparents escaped to Buenos Aires in '37."

"Why Argentina? I thought that was a hotbed of Nazis."

"Was. Also full of German-speaking refugees, though. All their friends went there. But it was too unstable. My parents got out in '55, just before one of the big revolutions, and came to California. What about you?"

"British family. I was born in Seattle. My father's in the consular service. He—"

A waiter looms. They order sandwiches offhandedly. Lunch seems very unimportant now. The contact still holds. He sees Conrad's *Nostromo* in her stack of books; she is halfway through it, and he has just finished it, and the coincidence amuses them. Conrad is one of her favorites, she says. One of his, too. What about Faulkner? Yes, and Mann, and Virginia Woolf, and they share even a fondness for Hermann Broch, and a dislike for Hesse. How odd. Operas? *Freischütz, Holländer, Fidelio*, yes. "We have very Teutonic tastes," she observes. "We have very similar tastes," he adds. He finds himself holding her hand. "Amazingly similar," she says. Mick Dongan leers at him from the far side of the room; Klein gives him a terrible scowl. Dongan winks. "Let's get out of here," Klein says, just as she starts to say the same thing.

They talk half the night and make love until dawn. "You ought to know," he tells her solemnly over breakfast, "that I decided long ago never to get married and certainly never to have a child."

"So did I," she says. "When I was fifteen."

They were married four months later. Mick Dongan was his best man.

Gracchus said, as they left the restaurant, "You will think things over, won't you?"

"I will," Klein said. "I promise you that."

He went to his room, packed his suitcase, checked out and took a cab to the airport, arriving in plenty of time for the afternoon flight to Zanzibar. The same melancholy little man was on duty as health officer when he landed, Barwani. "Sir, you have come back," Barwani said. "I thought you might. The other people have been here several days already."

"The other people?"

"When you were here last, sir, you kindly offered me a retainer in order that you might be informed when a certain person reached this island." Barwani's eyes gleamed. "That person, with two of her former companions, is here now."

Klein carefully placed a twenty-shilling note on the health officer's desk. "At which hotel?"

Barwani's lips quirked. Evidently twenty shillings fell short of expectations. But Klein did not take out another banknote, and after a moment Barwani said, "As before. The Zanzibar House. And you, sir?"

"As before," Klein said. "I'll be staying at the Shirazi."

Sybille was in the garden of the hotel, going over that day's research notes, when the telephone call came from Barwani. "Don't let my papers blow away," she said to Zacharias, and went inside. When she returned, looking bothered, Zacharias said, "Is there trouble?"

She sighed. "Jorge. He's on his way to his hotel now."

"What a bore," Mortimer murmured. "I thought Gracchus might have brought him to his senses."

"Evidently not," Sybille said. "What are we going to do?"

"What would you like to do?" Zacharias asked.

She shook her head. "We can't allow this to go on, can we?"

The evening air was humid and fragrant. The long rains had come and gone, and the island was in the grip of the new season's lunatic fertility: outside the window of Klein's hotel room some vast twining vine was putting forth monstrous trumpet-shaped yellow flowers, and all about the hotel grounds everything was in blossom, everything was in a frenzy of moist young leaves. Klein's sensibility reverberated to that feeling of universal vigorous thrusting newness; he paced the room, full of energy, trying to devise some feasible stratagem. Go immediately to see Sybille?

Force his way in, if necessary, with shouts and alarums, and demand to know why she had told him that fantastic tale of imaginary sultans? No. No. He would do no more confronting, no more lamenting; now that he was here, now that he was close by her, he would seek her out calmly, he would talk quietly, he would invoke memories of their old love, he would speak of Rilke and Woolf and Broch, of afternoons in Puerto Vallarta and nights in Santa Fe, of music heard and caresses shared, he would rekindle not their marriage, for that was impossible, but merely the remembrance of the bond that once had existed, he would win from her some acknowledgment of what had been, and then he would soberly and quietly exorcise that bond, he and she together, they would work to free him by speaking softly of the change that had come over their lives, until, after three hours or four or five, he had brought himself with her help to an acceptance of the unacceptable. That was all. He would demand nothing, he would beg for nothing, except only that she assist him for one evening in ridding his soul of this useless destructive obsession. Even a dead, even a capricious, wayward, volatile, whimsical, wanton dead, would surely see the desirability of that, and would freely give him her cooperation. Surely. And then home, and then new beginnings, too long postponed.

He made ready to go out.

There was a soft knock at the door. "Sir? Sir? You have visitors downstairs."

"Who?" Klein asked, though he knew the answer.

"A lady and two gentlemen," the bellhop replied. "The taxi has brought them from the Zanzibar House. They wait for you in the bar."

"Tell them I'll be down in a moment."

He went to the iced pitcher on the dresser, drank a glass of cold water mechanically, unthinkingly, poured himself a second, drained that too. This visit was unexpected; and why had she brought her entourage along? He had to struggle to regain that centeredness, that sense of purpose understood, which he thought he had attained before the knock. Eventually he left the room.

They were dressed crisply and impeccably this damp night, Zacharias in a tawny frock coat and pale green trousers, Mortimer in a belted white caftan trimmed with intricate brocade, Sybille in a simple lavender tunic. Their pale faces were unmarred by perspiration; they seemed perfectly composed, models of poise. No one sat near them in the bar. As Klein entered, they stood to greet him, but their smiles appeared sinister, having nothing of friendliness in them. Klein clung tight to his intended calmness. He said quietly, "It was kind of you to come. May I buy drinks for you?"

"We have ours already," Zacharias pointed out. "Let us be your hosts. What will you have?"

"Pimm's Number Six," Klein said. He tried to match their frosty smiles. "I admire your tunic, Sybille. You all look so debonair tonight that I feel shamed."

"You never were famous for your clothes," she said.

Zacharias returned from the counter with Klein's drink. He took it and toasted them gravely.

After a short while Klein said, "Do you think I could talk privately with you, Sybille?"

"There's nothing we have to say to one another that can't be said in front of Kent and Laurence."

"Nevertheless."

"I prefer not to, Jorge."

"As you wish," Klein peered straight into her eyes and saw nothing there, nothing, and flinched. All that he had meant to say fled his mind. Only churning fragments danced there; Rilke, Broch, Puerto Vallarta. He gulped at his drink.

Zacharias said, "We have a problem to discuss, Klein."

"Go on."

"The problem is you. You're causing great distress to Sybille. This is the second time, now, that you've followed her to Zanzibar, to the literal end of the earth, Klein, and you've made several attempts besides to enter a closed sanctuary in Utah under false pretenses, and this is interfering with Sybille's freedom, Klein, it's an impossible, intolerable interference."

"The deads are dead," Mortimer said. "We understand the depths of your feelings for your late wife, but this compulsive pursuit of her must be brought to an end."

"It will be," Klein said, staring at a point on the stucco wall midway between Zacharias and Sybille. "I want only an hour or two of private conversation with my—with Sybille, and then I promise you that there will be no further—"

"Just as you promised Anthony Gracchus," Mortimer said, "not to go to Zanzibar."

"I wanted—"

"We have our rights," said Zacharias. "We've gone through hell, literally through hell, to get where we are. You've infringed on our right to be left alone. You bother us. You bore us. You annoy us. We hate to be annoyed." He looked toward Sybille. She nodded. Zacharias' hand vanished into the breast pocket of his coat. Mortimer seized Klein's wrist with astonishing suddenness and jerked his arm forward. A minute metal tube glistened in Zacharias's huge fist. Klein had seen such a tube in the hand of Anthony Gracchus only the day before.

"No," Klein gasped. "I don't believe—*no!*"

Zacharias plunged the cold tip of the tube quickly into Klein's forearm.

"The freezer unit is coming," Mortimer said. "It'll be here in five minutes or less."

"What if it's late?" Sybille asked anxiously. "What if something irreversible happens to his brain before it gets here?"

"He's not even entirely dead yet," Zacharias reminded her. "There's time. There's ample time. I spoke to the doctor myself, a very intelligent Chinese, flawless command of English. He was most sympathetic. They'll have him frozen within a couple of minutes of death. We'll book cargo passage aboard the morning plane for Dar. He'll be in the United States within twenty-four hours, I guarantee that. San Diego will be notified. Everything will be all right, Sybille!"

Jorge Klein lay slumped across the table. The bar had emptied the moment he had cried out and lurched forward: the half-dozen customers had fled, not caring to mar their holidays by sharing an evening with the presence of death, and the waiters and bartenders, big-eyed, terrified, lurked in the hallway. A heart attack, Zacharias had announced, some kind of sudden attack, maybe a stroke, where's the telephone? No one had seen the tiny tube do its work.

Sybille trembled. "If anything goes wrong—"

"I hear the sirens now," Zacharias said.

From his desk at the airport Daud Mahmoud Barwani watched the bulky refrigerated coffin being loaded by grunting porters aboard the morning plane for Dar. And then, and then, and then? They would ship the dead man to the far side of the world, to America, and breathe new life into him, and he would go once more among men. Barwani shook his head. These people! The man who was alive is now dead, and these dead ones, who knows what they are? Who knows? Best that the dead remain dead, as was intended in the time of first things. Who could have foreseen a day when the dead returned from the grave? Not I. And who can foresee what we will all become, a hundred years from now? Not I. Not I. A hundred years from now I will sleep, Barwani thought. I will sleep, and it will not matter to me at all what sort of creatures walk the earth.

9.

We die with the dying: See, they depart, and we go with them. We are born with the dead: See, they return, and bring us with them.
> T. S. Eliot: *Little Gidding*

On the day of his awakening he saw no one except the attendants at the rekindling house, who bathed him and fed him and helped him to walk slowly around his room. They said nothing to him, nor he to them; words seemed irrelevant. He felt strange in his skin, too snugly contained, as though all his life he had worn ill-fitting clothes and now had for the first time encountered a competent tailor. The images that his eyes brought him were sharp, unnaturally clear and faintly haloed by prismatic colors, an effect that imperceptibly vanished as the day passed. On the second day he was visited by the San Diego Guidefather, not at all the formidable patriarch he had imagined, but rather a cool efficient executive, about fifty years old, who greeted him cordially and told him briefly of the disciplines and routines he must master before he could leave the Cold Town. "What month is this?" Klein asked, and Guidefather told him it was June, the seventeenth of June, 1993. He had slept four weeks.

Now it is the morning of the third day after his awakening, and he has guests: Sybille, Nerita, Zacharias, Mortimer, Gracchus. They file into his room and stand in an arc at the foot of his bed, radiant in the glow of light that pierces the narrow windows. Like demigods, like angels, glittering with a dazzling inward brilliance, and now he is of their company. Formally they embrace him, first Gracchus, then Nerita, then Mortimer. Zacharias advances next to his bedside, Zacharias who sent him into death, and he smiles at Klein and Klein returns the smile, and they embrace. Then it is Sybille's turn: she slips her hand between his, he draws her close, her lips brush his cheek, his touch hers, his arm encircles her shoulders.

"Hello," she whispers.

"Hello," he says.

They ask him how he feels, how quickly his strength is returning, whether he has been out of bed yet, how soon he will commence his drying-off. The style of their conversation is the oblique, elliptical style favored by the deads, but not nearly so clipped and cryptic as the way of speech they normally would use among themselves; they are favoring him, leading him inch by inch into their customs. Within five minutes he thinks he is getting the knack.

He says, using their verbal shorthand, "I must have been a great burden to you."

"You were, you were," Zacharias agrees. "But all that is done with now."

"We forgive you," Mortimer says.

"We welcome you among us," declares Sybille.

They talk about their plans for the months ahead. Sybille is nearly finished with her work on Zanzibar; she will retreat to Zion Cold Town for the summer months to write her thesis. Mortimer and Nerita are off to Mexico to tour the ancient temples and pyramids; Zacharias is going to Ohio, to his beloved mounds. In the autumn they will reassemble at Zion and plan the winter's amusement: a tour of Egypt, perhaps, or Peru, the heights of Machu Picchu. Ruins, archaeological sites, delight them; in the places where death has been busiest, their joy is most intense. They are flushed, excited, verbose—virtually chattering, now. Away we will go, to Zimbabwe, to Palenque, to Angkor, to Knossos, to Uxmal, to Nineveh, to Mohenjodaro. And as they go on and on, talking with hands and eyes and smiles and even words, even words, torrents of words, they blur and become unreal to him, they are mere dancing puppets jerking about a badly painted stage, they are droning insects, wasps or bees or mosquitoes, with all their talk of travels and festivals, of Boghazköy and Babylon, of Megiddo and Masada, and he ceases to hear them, he tunes them out, he lies there smiling, eyes glazed, mind adrift. It perplexes him that he has so little interest in them. But then he realizes that it is a mark of his liberation. He is freed of old chains now. Will he join their set? Why should he? Perhaps he will travel with them, perhaps not, as the whim takes him. More likely not. Almost certainly not. He does not need their company. He has his own interests. He will follow Sybille about no longer. He does not need, he does not want, he will not seek. Why should he become one of them, rootless, an amoral wanderer, a ghost made flesh? Why should he embrace the values and customs of these people who had given him to death as dispassionately as they might swat an insect, only because he had bored them, because he had annoyed them? He does not hate them for what they did to him, he feels no resentment that he can identify, he merely chooses to detach himself from them. Let them float on from ruin to ruin, let them pursue death from continent to continent; he will go his own way. Now that he has crossed the interface he finds that Sybille no longer matters to him.

—*Oh, sir, things change*—

"We'll go now," Sybille says softly.

He nods. He makes no other reply.

"We'll see you after your drying-off," Zacharias tells him, and touches him slightly with his knuckles, a farewell gesture used only by the deads.

"See you," Mortimer says.

"See you," says Gracchus.

"Soon," Nerita says.

Never, Klein says, saying it without words, but so they will understand. Never. Never. Never. I will never see any of you. I will never see you, Sybille. The syllables echo through his brain, and the word, *never, never, never*, rolls over him like the breaking surf, cleansing him, purifying him, healing him. He is free. He is alone.

"Goodby," Sybille calls from the hallway.

"Goodby," he says.

It was years before he saw her again. But they spent the last days of '99 together, shooting dodos under the shadow of mighty Kilimanjaro.

CHARLES V. DE VET and KATHERINE MACLEAN

# Second Game

*The modern spy story has moved closer to science fiction in recent years, and books like Ian Fleming's* Moonraker *are as much science fiction as Robert A. Heinlein's* The Moon Is a Harsh Mistress. *Indeed, the whole subgenre becoming known as "near-future" fiction would have been considered "regular" science fiction only a few years ago.*

*"Second Game" is an excellent example of the science fictional spy story, an intellectual treat for those who enjoy the skillful working out of a genuine puzzle.*

The sign was big, with black letters that read: I'LL BEAT YOU THE SECOND GAME.

I eased myself into a seat behind the play board, straightened the pitchman's cloak about my shoulders, took a final deep breath, let it out —and waited.

A nearby fair visitor glanced at the sign as he hurried by. His eyes widened with anticipated pleasure and he shifted his gaze to me, weighing me with the glance.

I knew I had him.

The man changed direction and came over to where I sat. "Are you giving any odds?" he asked.

"Ten to one," I answered.

"A dronker." He wrote on a blue slip with a white stylus, dropped it at my elbow and sat down.

"We play the first game for feel," I said. "Second game pays."

Gradually I let my body relax. Its weight pulled at the muscles of my back and shoulders, and I slouched into a half-slump. I could feel my eyelids droop as I released them, and the corners of my mouth pulled down. I probably appeared tired and melancholy. Or like a man operating in a gravity heavier than was normal for him. Which I was.

I had come to this world called Velda two weeks earlier. My job was to find why its humanlike inhabitants refused all contacts with the Federation.

Earth's colonies had expanded during the last several centuries until they now comprised a loose alliance known as the Ten Thousand Worlds. They were normally peaceful—and wanted peace with Velda. But you cannot talk peace with a people who won't talk back. Worse, they had obliterated the fleet bringing our initial peace overtures. As a final gesture I had been smuggled in—in an attempt to breach that standoff stubbornness. This booth at their fair was my best chance—as I saw it—to secure audience with the men in authority. And with luck it would serve a double purpose.

Several Veldians gathered around the booth and watched with interest as my opponent and I chose colors. He took the red; I the black. We arranged our fifty-two pieces on their squares and I nodded to him to make the first move.

He was an anemic oldster with an air of nervous energy, and he played the same way, with intense concentration. By the fourth move I knew he would not win. On each play he had to consult the value board suspended between us before deciding what his next move would be. On a play board with one hundred and sixty-nine squares, each with a different value—in fact one set of values for offense, and another for defense—only a brilliant player could keep them all in mind. But no man without that ability was going to beat me.

I let him win the first game. Deliberately. The "second game counts" gimmick was not only to attract attention, but to give me a chance to test a player's strength—and find his weakness.

At the start of the second game, the oldster moved his front row center pukt three squares forward and one left oblique. I checked it with an end pukt, and waited.

The contest was not going to be exacting enough to hold my complete attention. Already an eidetic portion of my mind—which I always thought of as a small machine, ticking away in one corner of my skull, independent of any control or direction from me—was moving its interest out to the spectators around my booth.

It caught a half-completed gesture of admiration at my last move from a youth directly ahead of me. And with the motion, and the glimpse of the youth's face, something slipped into place in my memory. Some subconscious counting finished itself, and I knew that there had been too many of these youths, with faces like this one, finely boned and smooth, with slender delicate necks and slim hands and movements that were cool and detached. Far too many to be a normal number in a population of adults and children.

As if drawn, my glance went past the forms of the watchers around the booth and plumbed the passing crowd to the figure of a man; a magnificent masculine type of the Veldian race, thick-shouldered and strong, thoughtful in motion, yet with something of the swagger of a gladiator, who, as he walked, spoke to the woman who held his arm, leaning toward her cherishingly as if he protected a great prize.

She was wearing a concealing cloak, but her face was beautiful, her hair semi-long, and in spite of the cloak I could see that her body was full-fleshed and almost voluptuously feminine. I had seen few such women on Velda.

Two of the slim, delicately built youths went by arm in arm, walking with a slight defiant sway of bodies, and looked at the couple as they passed, with a pleasure in the way the man's fascinated attention clove to the woman, and looked at the beauty of the woman possessively without lust, and passed by, their heads held higher in pride as if they shared a secret triumph with her. Yet they were strangers.

I had an answer to my counting. The "youths" with the large eyes and smooth delicate heads, with the slim straight asexual bodies, thought of themselves as women. I had not seen them treated with the subdued attraction and conscious avoidance one sex gives another, but by numbers . . . my memory added the number of these "youths" to the numbers of figures and faces that had been obviously female. It totaled to almost half the population I had seen. No matter what the biological explanation, it seemed reasonable that half . . .

I bent my head, to not see the enigma of the boy-woman face watching me, and braced my elbow to steady my hand as I moved. For two weeks I had been on Velda and during the second week I had come out of hiding and passed as a Veldian. It was incredible that I had been operating under a misunderstanding as to which were women, and which men, and not blundered openly. The luck that had saved me had been undeserved.

Opposite me, across the board, the bleach-skinned hand of the oldster was beginning to waver with indecision as each pukt was placed. He was seeing defeat, and not wishing to see it.

In eight more minutes I completed the rout of his forces and closed out the game. In winning I had lost only two pukts. The other's defeat was crushing, but my ruthlessness had been deliberate. I wanted my reputation to spread.

My sign, and the game in progress, by now had attracted a line of challengers, but as the oldster left the line broke and most of them shook their heads and moved back, then crowded around the booth and good-naturedly elbowed their way to positions of better vantage.

I knew then that I had set my lure with an irresistible bait. On a world where the game was played from earliest childhood—was in fact a vital aspect of their culture—my challenge could not be ignored. I pocketed the loser's blue slip and nodded to the first in line of the four men who still waited to try me.

This second man played a better game than the old one. He had a fine tight-knit offensive, with a good grasp of values, but his weakness showed early in the game when I saw him hesitate before making a simple move in a defensive play. He was not skilled in the strategy of retreat and defense, or not suited to it by temperament. He would be unable to cope with a swift forward press, I decided.

I was right.

Some of the challengers bet more, some less, all lost on the second game. I purchased a nut and fruit confection from a passing food vender and ate it for a sparse lunch while I played through the late afternoon hours.

By the time Velda's distant sun had begun to print long shadows across the fairgrounds, I was certain that word of my booth had spread well.

The crowd about the railing of my stand was larger—but the players were fewer. Sometimes I had a break of several minutes before one made a decision to try his skill. And there were no more challenges from ordinary players. Still the results were the same. None had sufficient adroitness to give me more than a passing contest.

Until Caertin Vlosmin made his appearance.

Vlosmin played a game intended to be impregnably defensive, to remain untouchable until an opponent made a misplay or an overzealous drive, of which he would then take advantage. But his mental prowess was not quite great enough to be certain of a sufficiently concealed or complex weakness in the approach of an adversary, and he would not hazard an attack on an uncertainty. Excess caution was his weakness.

During our play I sensed that the crowd about us was very intent and still. On the outskirts, newcomers inquiring cheerfully were silenced by whispered exclamations.

Though it required all my concentration the game was soon over. I looked at Vlosmin as he rose to his feet, and noted with surprise that a fine spotting of moisture brightened his upper lip. Only then did I recognize the strain and effort he had invested into the attempt to defeat me.

"You are an exceptional craftsman," he said. There was a grave emphasis he put on the "exceptional" which I could not miss, and I saw that his face was whiter.

His formal introduction of himself earlier as Caertin Vlosmin had meant something more than I had realized at the time.

I had just played against, and defeated, one of the Great Players!

The sun set a short time later and floating particles of light-reflecting air-foam drifted out over the fairgrounds. Some way they were held suspended above the ground while air currents tossed them about and intermingled them in the radiance of vari-hued spotlights. The area was still as bright as day, but filled with pale, shifting, shadows that seemed to heighten the byplay of sound and excitement coming from the fair visitors.

Around my booth all was quiet; the spectators were subdued—as though waiting for the next act in a tense drama. I was very tired now, but I knew by the tenseness I observed around me that I did not have much longer to wait.

By the bubbles' light I watched new spectators take their positions about my booth. And as time went by I saw that some of them did not move on, as my earlier visitors had done.

The weight that rode my stomach muscles grew abruptly heavier. I had set my net with all the audacity of a spider waiting for a fly, yet I knew that when my anticipated victim arrived he would more likely resemble a spider hawk. Still the weight was not caused by fear: it was excitement —the excitement of the larger game about to begin.

I was playing an opponent of recognizably less ability than Vlosmin when I heard a stirring and murmuring in the crowd around my stand. The stirring was punctuated by my opponent rising to his feet.

I glanced up.

The big man who had walked into my booth was neither arrogant nor condescending, yet the confidence in his manner was like an aura of strength. He had a deep reserve of vitality, I noted as I studied him carefully, but it was a leashed, controlled vitality. Like most of the men of the Veldian race he wore a uniform, cut severely plain, and undecorated. No flowing robes or tunics for these men. They were a warrior race, unconcerned with the aesthetic touches of personal dress, and left that strictly to their women.

The newcomer turned to my late opponent. His voice was impressive, controlled. "Please finish your game," he said courteously.

The other shook his head. "The game is already as good as over. My sword is broken. You are welcome to my place."

The tall man turned to me. "If you don't mind?"

"My pleasure," I answered. "Please be seated."

This was it.

My visitor shrugged his close-wrapped cloak back from his shoulders and took the chair opposite me. "I am Kalin Trobt," he said. As if he knew I had been expecting him.

In reply I came near to telling him my correct name. But Robert O. Lang was a name that would have been alien to Velda. Using it would have been as good as a confession. "Claustil Anteer," I said, giving a name I had invented earlier.

We played the first game as children play it, taking each other's pukts as the opportunity presented, making no attempt at finesse. Trobt won, two up. Neither of us had made mention of a wager. There would be more than money involved in this game.

I noticed, when I glanced up before the second game, that the spectators had been cleared from around the booth. Only the inner, unmoving, ring I had observed earlier remained now. They watched calmly—professionally.

Fortunately I had no intention of trying to escape.

During the early part of the second game Trobt and I tested each other carefully, as skilled swordsmen, probing, feinting and shamming attack, but never actually exposing ourselves. I detected what could have been a slight tendency to gamble in Trobt's game, but there was no concrete situation to confirm it.

My first moves were entirely passive. Alertly passive. If I had judged correctly the character of the big man opposite me, I had only to ignore the bait he offered to draw me out, to disregard his openings and apparent —too apparent—errors, until he became convinced that I was unshakably cautious, and not to be tempted into making the first thrusts. For this was his weakness as I had guessed it: that his was a gambling temperament —that when he saw an opportunity he would strike—without the caution necessary to insure safety.

Pretending to move with timidity, and pausing with great deliberation over even the most obvious plays, I maneuvered only to defend. Each time Trobt shifted to a new position of attack I covered—until finally I detected the use of slightly more arm force than necessary when he moved a pukt. It was the only sign of impatience he gave, but I knew it was there.

Then it was that I left one—thin—opening.

Trobt streaked a pukt through and cut out one of my middle defenders.

Instead of making the obvious counter of taking his piece, I played a pukt far removed from his invading man. He frowned in concentration, lifted his arm—and his hand hung suspended over the board.

Suddenly his eyes widened. His glance swept upward to my face and what he saw there caused his expression to change to one of mingled dismay and astonishment. There was but one move he could make. When he made it his entire left flank would be exposed. He had lost the game.

Abruptly he reached forward, touched his index finger to the tip of my nose and pressed gently.

After a minute during which neither of us spoke, I said, "You know?"

He nodded. "Yes," he said. "You're a human."

There was a stir and rustle of motion around me. The ring of spectators had leaned forward a little as they heard his words. I looked up and saw that they were smiling, inspecting me with curiosity and something that could have been called admiration. In the dusk the clearest view was the ring of teeth, gleaming—the view a rabbit might get of a circle of grinning foxes. Foxes might feel friendly toward rabbits, and admire a good big one. Why not?

I suppressed an ineffectual impulse to deny what I was. The time was past for that. "How did you find out?" I asked Trobt.

"Your game. No one could play like that and not be well known. And now your nose."

"My nose?" I repeated.

"Only one physical difference between a human and a Veldian is apparent on the surface. The nose cartilage. Yours is split—mine is single." He rose to his feet. "Will you come with me, please?"

It was not a request.

My guards walked singly and in couples, sometimes passing Trobt and myself, sometimes letting us pass them and sometimes lingering at a booth, like any other walkers, and yet, unobtrusively they held me encircled, always in the center of the group. I had already learned enough of the Veldian personality to realize that this was simply a habit of tact. Tact to prevent an arrest from being conspicuous, so as not to add the gaze of his fellows to whatever punishment would be decided for a culprit's offense. Apparently they considered humiliation too deep a punishment to use indiscriminately.

At the edge of the fairgrounds some of the watchers bunched around me while others went to get the tricars. I stood and looked across the park to The City. That was what it was called, The City, The Citadel, The Hearthplace, the home place where one's family is kept safe, the sanctuary whose walls have never been pierced. All those connotations had been in the name and the use of the name; in the voices of those who spoke it. Sometimes they called it The Hearth, and sometimes The Market, always *The* as if it were the only one.

Though the speakers lived in other places and named them as the homes of their ancestors, most of the Veldians were born here. Their history was colored, I might say even shaped, by their long era of struggle with the dleeth, a four-footed, hairy carnivore, physically little different from the big cats of Earth, but intelligent. They had battled the Veldians in a struggle for survival from the Veldians' earliest memories until a couple of centuries before my visit. Now the last few surviving dleeth had found refuge in the frigid region of the north pole. With their physical superiority they probably would have won the struggle against the Veldians, except that their instincts had been purely predatory, and they had no hands and could not develop technology.

The City had been the one strong point that the dleeth had never been able to breach. It had been held by one of the stronger clans, and there was seldom unity among the tribes, yet any family about to bear a child was given sanctuary within its walls.

The clans were nomads—made so by the aggression of the dleeth—but they always made every effort to reach The City when childbirth was imminent. This explained, at least partly, why even strangers from foreign areas regarded The City as their home place.

I could see the Games Building from where I stood. In the walled city called Hearth it was the highest point. Big and red, it towered above the others, and the city around it rose to it like a wave, its consort of surrounding smaller buildings matched to each other in size and shape in concentric rings. Around each building wound the ramps of elevator runways, harmonious and useful, each of different colored stone, lending variety and warmth. Nowhere was there a clash of either proportion or color.

Sometimes I wondered if the Veldians did not build more for the joy of creating symmetry than because of utilitarian need.

I climbed into Trobt's three-wheeled car as it stopped before me, and the minute I settled into the bucket seat and gripped the bracing handles, Trobt spun the car and it dived into the highway and rushed toward the city. The vehicle seemed unstable, being about the width of a motorbike, with side car in front, and having nothing behind except a metal box that must have housed a powerful battery, and a shaft with the rear wheel that did the steering. It was an arrangement that made possible sudden wrenching turns that were battering to any passenger as unused to it as I. To my conditioning it seemed that the Veldians on the highway drove like madmen, the traffic rules were incomprehensible or nonexistent and all drivers seemed determined to drive only in gull-like sweeping lines, giving no obvious change of course for other such cars, brushing by tricars from the opposite direction with an inch or less of clearance.

Apparently the maneuverability of the cars and the skill of the drivers were enough to prevent accidents, and I had to force my totally illogical driver's reflexes to relax and stop tensing against the nonexistent peril.

I studied Trobt as he drove, noting the casual way he held the wheel, and the assurance in the set of his shoulders. I tried to form a picture in my mind of the kind of man he was, and just what were the motivations that would move or drive him.

Physically he was a long-faced man, with a smooth muscular symmetry, and an Asiatic cast to his eyes. I was certain that he excelled at whatever job he held. In fact I was prepared to believe that he would excel at anything he tried. He was undoubtedly one of those amazing men for whom the exceptional was mere routine. If he were to be cast in the role of my opponent: be the person in whom the opposition of this race would be actualized—as I now anticipated—I would not have wanted to bet against him.

The big skilled man was silent for several minutes, weaving the tricar with smooth swerves through a three-way tangle at an intersection, but twice he glanced at my expression with evident curiosity. Finally, as a man would state an obvious fact he said, "I presume you know you will be executed."

Trobt's face reflected surprise at the shock he must have read in mine. I had known the risk I would be taking in coming here, of course, and of the very real danger that it might end in my death. But this had come up on me too fast. I had not realized that the affair had progressed to the point where my death was already assured. I had thought that there would be negotiations, consultations and perhaps ultimatums. But only if they failed did I believe that the repercussions might carry me along to my death.

However, there was the possibility that Trobt was merely testing my courage. I decided on boldness. "No," I said. "I do not expect to be executed."

Trobt raised his eyebrows and slowed, presumably to gain more time to talk. With a sudden decision he swung the tricar from the road into one of the small parks spread at regular intervals along the highway.

"Surely you don't think we would let you live? There's a state of war between Velda and your Ten Thousand Worlds. You admit that you're human, and obviously you are here to spy. Yet when you're captured, you do not expect to be executed?"

"Was I captured?" I asked, emphasizing the last word.

He pondered on that a moment, but apparently did not come up with an answer that satisfied him. "I presume your question means something," he said.

"If I had wanted to keep my presence here a secret, would I have set up a booth at the fair and invited inspection?" I asked.

He waved one hand irritably, as though to brush aside a picayune argument. "Obviously you did it to test yourself against us, to draw the great under your eye and perhaps become a friend, treated as an equal with access to knowledge of our plans and weapons. Certainly! Your tactic drew two members of the council into your net before it was understood. If we had accepted you as a previously unknown Great, you would have won. You are a gambling man, and you played a gambler's hand. You lost."

Partly he was right.

"My deliberate purpose was to reach you," I said, "or someone else with sufficient authority to listen to what I have to say."

Trobt pulled the vehicle deeper into the park. He watched the cars of our escort settling to rest before and behind us. I detected a slight unease and rigidity in his stillness as he said, "Speak then. I'm listening."

"I've come to negotiate," I told him.

Something like a flash of puzzlement crossed his features before they returned to tighter immobility. Unexpectedly he spoke in Earthian, my own language. "Then why did you choose this method? Would it not have been better simply to announce yourself?"

This was the first hint he had given that he might have visited our worlds before I visited his. Though we had suspected before I came that some of them must have. They probably knew of our existence years before we discovered them.

Ignoring his change of language, I replied, still speaking Veldian, "Would it have been that simple? Or would some minor official, on capturing me, perhaps have had me imprisoned, or tortured to extract information?"

Again the suppressed puzzlement in the shift of position as he looked at me. "They would have treated you as an envoy, representing your Ten Thousand Worlds. You could have spoken to the council immediately." He spoke in Veldian now.

"I did not know that," I said. "You refused to receive our fleet envoys; why should I expect you to accept me any more readily?"

Trobt started to speak, stopped and turned in his seat to regard me levelly and steadily, his expression unreadable. "Tell me what you have to say then. I will judge whether or not the council will listen."

"To begin with—" I looked away from the expressionless eyes, out the windshield, down the vistas of brown short trees that grew between each small park and the next. "Until an exploring party of ours found signs of extensive mining operations on a small metal-rich planet, we knew nothing of your existence. We were not even aware that another race in the galaxy had discovered faster-than-light space travel. But after the first clue we were alert for other signs, and found them. Our discovery of your planet was bound to come. However, we did not expect to be met on our first visit with an attack of such hostility as you displayed."

"When we learned that you had found us," Trobt said, "we sent a message to your Ten Thousand Worlds, warning them that we wanted no contact with you. Yet you sent a fleet of spaceships against us."

I hesitated before answering. "That phrase, 'sent against us,' is hardly the correct one," I said. "The fleet was sent for a diplomatic visit, and was not meant as an aggressive action." I thought, *But obviously the display of force was intended "diplomatically" to frighten you people into being polite.* In diplomacy the smile, the extended hand—and the big stick visible in the other hand—had obviated many a war, by giving the stranger a chance to choose a hand, in full understanding of the alternative. *We showed our muscle to your little planet—you showed your muscle. And now we are ready to be polite.*

I hoped these people would understand the face-saving ritual of negotiation, the disclaimers of intent, that would enable each side to claim that there had been no war, merely accident.

"We did not at all feel that you were justified in wiping the fleet from space," I said. "But it was probably a legitimate misunderstanding—"

"You had been warned!" Trobt's voice was grim, his expression not inviting of further discussion. I thought I detected a bunching of the muscles in his arms.

For a minute I said nothing, made no gesture. Apparently this angle of approach was unproductive—and probably explosive. Also, trying to explain and justify the behavior of the Federation politicos could possibly become rather taxing.

"Surely you don't intend to postpone negotiations indefinitely?" I asked tentatively. "One planet cannot conquer the entire Federation."

The bunched muscles of his arms strained until they pulled his shoulders, and his lips whitened with the effort of controlling some savage anger. Apparently my question had impugned his pride.

This, I decided quickly, was not the time to make an enemy. "I apologize if I have insulted you," I said in Earthian. "I do not yet always understand what I am saying, in your language."

He hesitated, made some kind of effort and shifted to Earthian. "It is not a matter of strength, or weakness," he said, letting his words ride out on his released breath, "but of behavior, courtesy. We would have left you alone, but now it is too late. We will drive your faces into the ground. I am certain that we can, but if we could not, still we would try. To imply that we would not try, from fear, seems to me words to soil the mouth, not worthy of a man speaking to a man. We are converting our ships of commerce to war. Your people will see soon that we will fight."

"Is it too late for negotiation?" I asked.

His forehead wrinkled into a frown and he stared at me in an effort of concentration. When he spoke it was with a considered hesitation. "If I make a great effort I can feel that you are sincere, and not speaking to mock or insult. It is strange that beings who look so much like ourselves can"—he rubbed a hand across his eyes—"pause a moment. When I say 'yag loogt'-n'balt' what does it mean to you in Earthish?"

"I must play." I hesitated as he turned one hand palm down, signifying that I was wrong. "I must duel," I said, finding another meaning in the way I had heard the phrase expressed. It was a strong meaning, judging by the tone and inflection the speaker had used. I had mimicked the tone without full understanding. The verb was perhaps stronger than *must*, meaning something inescapable, fated, but I could find no Earthian verb for it. I understood why Trobt dropped his hand to the seat without turning it palm up to signify that I was correct.

"There may be no such thought on the human worlds," he said resignedly. "I have to explain as to a child or a madman. I cannot explain in Veldian, for it has no word to explain what needs no explanation."

He shifted to Earthian, his controlled voice sounding less controlled when moving with the more fluid inflections of my own tongue. "We said we did not want further contact. Nevertheless you sent the ships—deliberately in disregard of our expressed desire. That was an insult, a deep insult, meaning we have not strength to defend our word, meaning we are so helpless that we can be treated with impoliteness, like prisoners, or infants.

"Now we must show you which of us is helpless, which is the weakling. Since you would not respect our wishes, then in order to be no further insulted we must make of your people a captive or a child in helplessness, so that you will be without power to affront us another time."

"If apologies are in order—"

He interrupted with raised hand, still looking at me very earnestly with forehead wrinkled, thought half-turned inward in difficult introspection of his own meaning, as well as a grasping for my viewpoint.

"The insult of the fleet can only be wiped out in the blood of testing —of battle—and the test will not stop until one or the other shows that he is too weak to struggle. There is no other way."

He was demanding total surrender!

I saw it was a subject that could not be debated. The Federation had taken on a bearcat this time!

"I stopped because I wanted to understand you," Trobt resumed. "Because the others will not understand how you could be an envoy—how your Federation could send an envoy—except as an insult. I have seen enough of human strangeness to be not maddened by the insolence of an emissary coming to us, or by your people expecting us to exchange words when we carry your first insult still unwashed from our face. I can even see how it could perhaps be considered *not* an insult, for I have seen your people living on their planets and they suffered insult from each other without striking, until finally I saw that they did not know when they were insulted, as a deaf man does not know when his name is called."

I listened to the quiet note of his voice, trying to recognize the attitude that made it different from his previous tones—calm and slow and deep. Certainty that what he was saying was important . . . conscious tolerance . . . generosity.

Trobt turned on the tricar's motor and put his hands on the steering shaft. "You are a man worthy of respect," he said, looking down the dark empty road ahead. "I wanted you to understand us. To see the difference between us. So that you will not think us without justice." The car began to move.

"I wanted you to understand why you will die."

I said nothing—having nothing to say. But I began immediately to bring my report up to date, recording the observations during the games, and recording with care this last conversation, with the explanation it carried of the Veldian reactions that had been previously obscure.

I used nerve-twitch code, "typing" on a tape somewhere inside myself the coded record of everything that had passed since the last time I brought the report up to date. The typing was easy, like flexing a finger in code jerks, but I did not know exactly where the recorder was located. It was some form of transparent plastic which would not show up on X ray. The surgeons had imbedded it in my flesh while I was unconscious, and had implanted a mental block against my noticing which small muscle had been linked into the contrivance for the typing.

If I died before I was able to return to Earth, there were several capsuled chemicals buried at various places in my body, that intermingled, would temporarily convert my body to a battery for a high-powered broadcast of the tape report, destroying the tape and my body together. This would go into action only if my temperature fell fifteen degrees below the temperature of life.

I became aware that Kalin Trobt was speaking again, and that I had let my attention wander while recording and taping some subjective material. The code twitches easily became an unconscious accompaniment to memory and thought, and this was the second time I had found myself recording more than necessary.

Trobt watched the dark road, threading among buildings and past darkened vehicles. His voice was thoughtful. "In the early days, Miklas of Danlee, when he had the Ornan family surrounded and outnumbered, wished not to destroy them, for he needed good warriors, and in another circumstance they could have been his friends. Therefore he sent a slave to them with an offer of terms of peace. The Ornan family had the slave skinned while alive, smeared with salt and grease so that he would not bleed and sent back, tied in a bag of his own skin, with a message of no. The chroniclers agree that since the Ornan family was known to be honorable, Miklas should not have made the offer.

"In another time and battle, the Cheldos were offered terms of surrender by an envoy. Nevertheless they won against superior forces, and gave their captives to eat a stew whose meat was the envoy of the offer to surrender. Being given to eat their own words as you'd say in Earthish. Such things are not done often, because the offer is not given."

He wrenched the steering post sideways and the tricar turned almost at right angles, balanced on one wheel for a dizzy moment and fled up a great spiral ramp winding around the outside of the red Games Building.

Trobt still looked ahead, not glancing at me. "I understand, from observing them, that you Earthians will lie without soiling the mouth. What are you here for, actually?"

"I came from interest, but I intend, given the opportunity, to observe and to report my observations back to my government. They should not enter a war without knowing anything about you."

"Good." He wrenched the car around another abrupt turn into a red archway in the side of the building, bringing it to a stop inside. The sound of the other tricars entering the tunnel echoed hollowly from the walls and died as they came to a stop around us. "You are a spy then."

"Yes," I said, getting out. I had silently resigned my commission as envoy some five minutes earlier. There was little point in delivering political messages, if they have no result except to have one skinned or made into a stew.

A heavy door with the seal of an important official engraved upon it opened before us. In the forepart of the room we entered, a slim-bodied creature with the face of a girl sat with crossed legs on a platform like a long coffee table, sorting vellum marked with the dots and dashes, arrows and pictures, of the Veldian language.

She had green eyes, honeyed olive complexion, a red mouth and purple black hair. She stopped to work an abacus, made a notation on one of the stiff sheets of vellum, then glanced up to see who had come in. She saw us, and glanced away again, as if she had coolly made a note of our presence and gone back to her work, sorting the vellum sheets and stacking them in thin shelves with quick, graceful motions.

"Kalin Trobt of Pagael," a man on the far side of the room said, a man sitting cross-legged on a dais covered with brown fur and scattered papers.

He accepted the hand Trobt extended and they gripped wrists in a locked gesture of friendship. "And how survive the other sons of the citadel of Pagael?"

"Well, and continuing in friendship to the house of Lyagin," Trobt replied carefully. "I have seen little of my kin. There are many farlanders all around us, and between myself and my hearthfolk swarm the adopted."

"It is not like the old days, Kalin Trobt. In a dream I saw a rock sink from the weight of sons, and I longed for the sight of a land that is without strangers."

"We are all kinfolk now, Lyagin."

"My hearth pledged it."

Lyagin put his hand on a stack of missives which he had been considering, his face thoughtful, sparsely fleshed, mostly skull and tendon, his hair bound back from his face, and wearing a short white cotton dress beneath a light fur cape.

He was an old man, already in his senility, and now he was lost in a lapse of awareness of what he had been doing a moment before. By no sign did Trobt show impatience, or even consciousness of the other's lapse.

Lyagin raised his head after a minute and brought his rheumy eyes into focus on us. "You bring someone in regard to an inquiry?" he asked.

"The one from the Ten Thousand Worlds," Trobt replied.

Lyagin nodded apologetically. "I received word that he would be brought," he said. "How did you capture him?"

"He came."

The expression must have had some connotation that I did not recognize for the official let his glance cross mine, and I caught one slight flicker of interest in his eyes. "You say these humans lie?" he asked Trobt.

"Frequently. It is considered almost honorable to lie to an enemy in circumstances where one may profit by it."

"You brought back from his worlds some poison which insures their speaking the truth, I believe?"

"Not a poison, something they call drugs, which affects one like strong drink, dulling a man and changing what he might do. Under its influence he loses his initiative of decision."

"You have this with you?"

"Yes." Trobt was going to waste no time getting from me anything I had that might be of value to them.

"It will be interesting having an enemy cooperate," Lyagin said. "If he finds no way to kill himself, he can be very useful to us." So far my contact with the Veldians had not been going at all as I had hoped and planned.

The boy-girl at the opposite side of the room finished a problem on the abacus, noted the answer and glanced directly at my face, at my expression, then locked eyes with me for a brief moment. When she glanced down to the vellum again it was as if she had seen whatever she had looked up to see, and was content. She sat a little straighter as she worked, and moved with an action that was a little less supple and compliant.

I believe she had seen me as a man.

During the questioning I made no attempt to resist the drug's influence. I answered truthfully—but literally. Many times my answers were undecidable—because I knew not the answers, or I lacked the data to give them. And the others were cloaked under a full literal subtlety that made them useless to the Veldians. Questions such as the degree of unity existing between the Worlds: I answered—truthfully—that they were united under an authority with supreme power of decision. The fact that that authority had no actual force behind it; that it was subject to the whims and fluctuations of sentiment and politics of intra-alliances; that it had deteriorated into a mere supernumerary body of impractical theorists that occupied itself, in a practical sphere, only with picayune matters, I did not explain. It was not asked of me.

Would our worlds fight? I answered that they would fight to the death to defend their liberty and independence. I did not add that that will to fight would evidence itself first in internecine bickering, procrastinations and jockeying to avoid the worst thrusts of the enemy—before it finally resolved itself into a united front against attack.

By early morning Trobt could no longer contain his impatience. He stepped closer. "We're going to learn one thing," he said, and his voice was harsh. "Why did you come here?"

"To learn all that I could about you," I answered.

"You came to find a way to whip us!"

It was not a question and I had no necessity to answer.

"Have you found the way?"

"No."

"If you do, and you are able, will you use that knowledge to kill us?"

"No."

Trobt's eyebrows raised. "No?" he repeated. "Then why do you want it?"

"I hope to find a solution that will not harm either side."

"But if you found that a solution was not possible, you would be willing to use your knowledge to defeat us?"

"Yes."

"Even if it meant that you had to exterminate us—man, woman and child?"

"Yes."

"Why? Are you so certain that you are right, that you walk with God, and that we are knaves?"

"If the necessity to destroy one civilization or the other arose, and the decision were mine to make, I would rule against you because of the number of sentient beings involved."

Trobt cut the argument out from under me. "What if the situation were reversed, and your side was in the minority? Would you choose to let them die?"

I bowed my head as I gave him the truthful answer. "I would choose for my own side, no matter what the circumstances."

The interrogation was over.

On the drive to Trobt's home I was dead tired, and must have slept for a few minutes with my eyes open. With a start I heard Trobt say, " . . . that a man with ability enough to be a games—chess—master is given no authority over his people, but merely consulted on occasional abstract questions of tactics."

"It is the nature of the problem." I caught the gist of his comment from his last words and did my best to answer it. I wanted nothing less than to engage in conversation, but I realized that the interest he was showing now was just the kind I had tried to guide him to, earlier in the evening. If I could get him to understand us better, our motivations and ideals, perhaps even our frailties, there would be more hope for a compatible meeting of minds. "Among peoples of such mixed natures, such diverse histories and philosophies and different ways of life, most administrative problems are problems of a choice of whims, of changing and conflicting goals; not *how* to do what a people want done, but *what* they want done, and whether their next generation will want it enough to make work on it, now, worthwhile."

"They sound insane," Trobt said. "Are your administrators supposed to serve the flickering goals of demented minds?"

"We must weigh values. What is considered good may be a matter of viewpoint, and may change from place to place, from generation to generation. In determining what people feel and what their unvoiced wants are, a talent of strategy, and an impatience with the illogic of others, are not qualifications."

"The good is good, how can it change?" Trobt asked. "I do not understand."

I saw that truly he could not understand, since he had seen nothing of the clash of philosophies among a mixed people. I tried to think of ways it could be explained; how to show him that a people who let their emotions control them more than their logic, would unavoidably do many things they could not justify or take pride in—but that that emotional predominance was what had enabled them to grow, and spread throughout their part of the galaxy—and be, in the main, happy.

I was tired, achingly tired. More, the events of the long day, and Velda's heavier gravity had taken me to the last stages of exhaustion. Yet I wanted to keep that weakness from Trobt. It was possible that he, and the other Veldians, would judge the humans by what they observed in me.

Trobt's attention was on his driving and he did not notice that I followed his conversation only with difficulty. "Have you had only the two weeks of practice in the game, since you came?" he asked.

I kept my eyes open with an effort and breathed deeply. Velda's one continent, capping the planet on its upper third, merely touched what would have been a temperate zone. During its short summer its mean temperature hung in the low sixties. At night it dropped to near freezing. The cold night air bit into my lungs and drove the fog of exhaustion from my brain.

"No," I answered Trobt's question. "I learned it before I came. A chess adept wrote me, in answer to an article on chess, that a man from one of the out-worlds had shown him a game of greater richness and flexibility than chess, with much the same feeling to the player, and had beaten him in three games of chess after only two games to learn it, and had said that on his own planet this chesslike game was the basis for the amount of authority with which a man is invested. The stranger would not name his planet.

"I hired an investigating agency to learn the whereabouts of this planet. There was none in the Ten Thousand Worlds. That meant that the man had been a very ingenious liar, or—that he had come from Velda."

"It was I, of course," Trobt acknowledged.

"I realized that from your conversation. The sender of the letter," I resumed, "was known to me as a chess champion of two Worlds. The matter tantalized my thoughts for weeks, and finally I decided to try to arrange a visit to Velda. If you had this game, I wanted to try myself against your skilled ones."

"I understand that desire very well," Trobt said. "The same temptation caused me to be indiscreet when I visited your worlds. I have seldom been able to resist the opportunity for an intellectual gambit."

"It wasn't much more than a guess that I would find the game on Velda," I said. "But the lure was too strong for me to pass it by."

"Even if you came intending to challenge, you had little enough time to learn to play as you have—against men who have spent lifetimes learning. I'd like to try you again soon, if I may."

"Certainly." I was in little mood or condition to welcome any further polite conversation. And I did not appreciate the irony of his request—to the best of my knowledge I was still under a sentence of early death.

Trobt must have caught the bleakness in my reply for he glanced quickly over his shoulder at me. "There will be time," he said, gently for him. "Several days at least. You will be my guest." I knew that he was doing his best to be kind. His decision that I must die had not been prompted by any meanness of nature: to him it was only—inevitable.

The next day I sat at one end of a games table in a side wing of his home while Trobt leaned against the wall to my left. "Having a like nature I can well understand the impulse that brought you here," he said. "The supreme gamble. Playing—with your life the stake in the game. Nothing you've ever experienced can compare with it. And even now—when you have lost, and will die—you do not regret it, I'm certain."

"I'm afraid you're overestimating my courage, and misinterpreting my intentions," I told him, feeling instinctively that this would be a good time to again present my arguments. "I came because I hoped to reach a better understanding. We feel that an absolutely unnecessary war, with its resulting death and destruction, would be foolhardy. And I fail to see your viewpoint. Much of it strikes me as stupid racial pride."

Trobt ignored the taunt. "The news of your coming is the first topic of conversation in The City," he said. "The clans understand that you have come to challenge; one man against a nation. They greatly admire your audacity."

"Look," I said, becoming angry and slipping into Earthian. "I don't know whether you consider me a damn fool or not. But if you think I came here expecting to die; that I'm looking forward to it with pleasure—"

He stopped me with an idle gesture of one hand.

"You deceive yourself if you believe what you say," he commented. "Tell me this: would you have stayed away if you had known just how great the risk was to be?"

I was surprised to find that I did not have a ready answer to his question.

"Shall we play?" Trobt asked.

We played three games; Trobt with great skill, employing diversified and ingenious attacks. But he still had that bit too much audacity in his execution. I won each time.

"You're undoubtedly a master," Trobt said at the end of the third game. "But that isn't all of it. Would you like me to tell you why I can't beat you?"

"Can you?" I asked.

"I think so," he said. "I wanted to try against you again and again, because each time it did not seem that you had defeated me, but only that I had played badly, made childish blunders, and that I lost each game before we ever came to grips. Yet when I entered the duel against you a further time, I'd begin to blunder again."

He shoved his hands more deeply under his weapons belt, leaning back and observing me with his direct inspection. "My blundering then has to do with you, rather than myself," he said. "Your play is excellent, of course, but there is more beneath the surface than above. This is your talent: you lose the first game to see an opponent's weakness—and play it against him."

I could not deny it. But neither would I concede it. Any small advantage I might hold would be sorely needed later.

"I understand humans a little," Trobt said. "Enough to know that very few of them would come to challenge us without some other purpose. They have no taste for death, with glory or without."

Again I did not reply.

"I believe," Trobt said, "that you came here to challenge in your own way, which is to find any weakness we might have, either in our military, or in some odd way, in our very selves."

Once again—with a minimum of help from me—he had arrived in his reasoning at a correct answer. From here on—against this man—I would have to walk a narrow line.

"I think," Trobt said more slowly, glancing down at the board between us, then back at my expression, "that this may be the first game, and that you are more dangerous than you seem, that you are accepting the humiliation of allowing yourself to be thought of as weaker than you are, in actuality. You intend to find our weakness, and you expect somehow to tell your states what you find."

I looked across at him without moving. "What weakness do you fear I've seen?" I countered.

Trobt placed his hands carefully on the board in front of him and rose to his feet. Before he could say what he intended a small boy pulling something like a toy riding-horse behind him came into the game room and grabbed Trobt's trouser leg. He was the first blonde child I had seen on Velda.

The boy pointed at the swords on the wall. "Da," he said beseechingly, making reaching motions. "Da."

Trobt kept his attention on me. After a moment a faint humorless smile moved his lips. He seemed to grow taller, with the impression a strong man gives when he remembers his strength. "You will find no weakness," he said. He sat down again and placed the child on his lap.

The boy grabbed immediately at the abacus hanging on Trobt's belt and began playing with it, while Trobt stroked his hair. All the Veldians dearly loved children, I had noticed.

"Do you have any idea how many of our ships were used to wipe out your fleet?" he asked abruptly.

As I allowed myself to show the interest I felt he put a hand on the boy's shoulder and leaned forward. "One," he said.

I very nearly called Trobt a liar—one ship obliterating a thousand—before I remembered that Veldians were not liars, and that Trobt obviously was not lying. Somehow this small under-populated planet had developed a science of weapons that vastly exceeded that of the Ten Thousand Worlds.

I had thought that perhaps my vacation on this games-mad planet would result in some mutual information that would bring quick negotiation or conciliation: that players of a chesslike game would be easy to approach: that I would meet men intelligent enough to see the absurdity of such an ill-fated war against the overwhelming odds of the Ten Thousand Worlds Federation. Intelligent enough to foresee the disaster that would result from such a fight. It began to look as if the disaster might be to the Ten Thousand and not to the one.

Thinking, I walked alone in Trobt's roof garden.

Walking in Velda's heavy gravity took more energy than I cared to expend, but too long a period without exercise brought a dull ache to the muscles of my shoulders and at the base of my neck.

This was my third evening in the house. I had slept at least ten hours each night since I arrived, and found myself exhausted at day's end, unless I was able to take a nap or lie down during the afternoon.

The flowers and shrubbery in the garden seemed to feel the weight of gravity also, for most of them grew low, and many sent creepers out along the ground. Overhead strange formations of stars clustered thickly and shed a glow on the garden very like Earth's moonlight.

I was just beginning to feel the heavy drag in my leg tendons when a woman's voice said, "Why don't you rest a while?" It spun me around as I looked for the source of the voice.

I found her in a nook in the bushes, seated on a contour chair that allowed her to stretch out in a half-reclining position. She must have weighed near to two hundred—Earth-weight—pounds.

But the thing that had startled me more than the sound of her voice was that she had spoken in the universal language of the Ten Thousand Worlds. And without accent!

"You're—?" I started to ask.

"Human," she finished for me.

"How did you get here?" I inquired eagerly.

"With my husband." She was obviously enjoying my astonishment. She was a beautiful woman, in a gentle bovine way, and very friendly. Her blonde hair was done up in tight ringlets.

"You mean . . . Trobt?" I asked.

"Yes." As I stood trying to phrase my wonderment into more questions, she asked, "You're the Earthman, aren't you?"

I nodded. "Are you from Earth?"

"No," she answered. "My home world is Mandel's Planet, in the Thumb group."

She indicated a low hassock of a pair, and I seated myself on the lower and leaned an elbow on the higher, beginning to smile. It would have been difficult not to smile in the presence of anyone so contented. "How did you meet Trobt?" I asked.

"It's a simple love story. Kalin visited Mandel—without revealing his true identity of course—met, and courted me. I learned to love him, and agreed to come to his world as his wife."

"Did you know that he wasn't . . . That he . . ." I stumbled over just how to phrase the question. And wondered if I should have started it.

Her teeth showed white and even as she smiled. She propped a pillow under one plump arm and finished my sentence for me. ". . . That he wasn't human?" I was grateful for the way she put me at ease—almost as though we had been old friends.

I nodded.

"I didn't know." For a moment she seemed to draw back into her thoughts, as though searching for something she had almost forgotten. "He couldn't tell me. It was a secret he had to keep. When I arrived here and learned that his planet wasn't a charted world, was not even human, I was a little uncertain and lonesome. But not frightened. I knew Kalin would never let me be hurt. Even my lonesomeness left quickly. Kalin and I love each other very deeply. I couldn't be more happy than I am now."

She seemed to see I did not consider that my question had been answered—completely. "You're wondering still if I mind that he isn't human, aren't you?" she asked. "Why should I? After all, what does it mean to be 'human'? It is only a word that differentiates one group of people from another. I seldom think of the Veldians as being different—and certainly never that they're beneath me."

"Does it bother you—if you'll pardon this curiosity of mine—that you will never be able to bear Kalin's children?"

"The child you saw the first morning is my son," she answered complacently.

"But that's impossible," I blurted.

"Is it?" she asked. "You saw the proof."

"I'm no expert at this sort of thing," I said slowly, "but I've always understood that the possibility of two separate species producing offspring was a million to one."

"Greater than that, probably," she agreed. "But whatever the odds, sooner or later the number is bound to come up. This was it."

I shook my head, but there was no arguing a fact. "Wasn't it a bit unusual that Kalin didn't marry a Veldian woman?"

"He has married—two of them," she answered. "I'm his third wife."

"Then they do practice polygamy," I said. "Are you content with such a marriage?"

"Oh, yes," she answered. "You see, besides being very much loved, I occupy a rather enviable position here. I, ah . . ." She grew slightly flustered. "Well . . . the other women—the Veldian women—can bear children only once every eight years, and during the other seven . . ." She hesitated again and I saw a tinge of red creep into her cheeks. She was obviously embarrassed, but she laughed and resolutely went on.

"During the other seven, they lose their feminine appearance, and don't think of themselves as women. While I . . ." I watched with amusement as her color deepened and her glance dropped. "I am always of the same sex, as you might say, always a woman. My husband is the envy of all his friends."

After her first reticence she talked freely, and I learned then the answer to the riddle of the boy-girls of Velda. And at least one reason for their great affection for children.

One year of fertility in eight . . .

Once again I saw the imprint of the voracious dleeth on this people's culture. In their age-old struggle with their cold planet and its short growing seasons—and more particularly with the dleeth—the Veldian women had been shaped by evolution to better fit their environment. The women's strength could not be spared for frequent childbearing—so childbearing had been limited. Further, one small child could be carried in the frequent flights from the dleeth, but not more than one. Nature had done its best to cope with the problem: in the off seven years she tightened the women's flesh, atrophying glands and organs—making them nonfunctional—and changing their bodies to be more fit to labor and survive—and to fight, if necessary. It was an excellent adaptation— for a time and environment where a low birthrate was an asset to survival.

But this adaptation had left only a narrow margin for race perpetuation. Each woman could bear only four children in her lifetime. That, I realized as we talked, was the reason why the Veldians had not colonized other planets, even though they had spaceflight—and why they probably never would, without a drastic change in their biological make-up. That left so little ground for a quarrel between them and the Ten Thousand Worlds. Yet here we were, poised to spring into a death struggle.

"You are a very unusual woman." My attention returned to Trobt's wife. "In a very unusual situation."

"Thank you," she accepted it as a compliment. She made ready to rise. "I hope you enjoy your visit here. And that I may see you again before you return to Earth."

I realized then that she did not know of my peculiar position in her home. I wondered if she knew even of the threat of war between us and her adopted people. I decided not, or she would surely have spoken of it.

Either Trobt had deliberately avoided telling her, perhaps to spare her the pain it would have caused, or she had noted that the topic of my presence was disturbing to him and had tactfully refrained from inquiring. For just a moment I wondered if I should explain everything to her, and have her use the influence she must have with Trobt. I dismissed the idea as unworthy—and useless.

"Good night," I said.

The next evening as we rode in a tricar Trobt asked if I would like to try my skill against a better games player.

"I had assumed you were the best," I said.

"Only the second best," he answered. "It would be interesting to compare your game with that of our champion. If you can whip him, perhaps we will have to revise our opinion of you humans."

He spoke as though in jest, but I saw more behind his words than he intended me to see. Here at last might be a chance to do a positive service for my side. "I would be happy to play," I said.

Trobt parked the tricar on a side avenue and we walked perhaps a hundred yards. We stopped at the door of a small one-story stone house and Trobt tapped with his fingernails on a hollow gong buried in the wood.

After a minute a curtain over the door glass was drawn back and an old woman with straggly gray hair peered out at us. She recognized Trobt and opened the door.

We went in. Neither Trobt nor the old woman spoke. She turned her back after closing the door and went to stir embers in a stone grate.

Trobt motioned with his head for me to follow and led the way into a back room.

"Robert O. Lang," he said, "I would like you to meet Yondtl."

I looked across the room in the direction Trobt had indicated. My first impression was of a great white blob, propped up on a couch and supported by the wall at its back.

Then the thing moved. Moved its eyes. It was alive. Its eyes told me also that it was a man. If I could call it a man.

His head was large and bloated, with blue eyes, washed almost colorless, peering out of deep pouches of flesh. He seemed to have no neck; almost as though his great head were merely an extension of the trunk, and separated only by puffy folds of fat. Other lappings of flesh hung from his body in great thick rolls.

It took another minute of fascinated inspection before I saw that he had no arms, and that no legs reached from his body to the floor. The entire sight of him made me want to leave the room and be sick.

"Robert O. Lang is an Earthian who would challenge you sir," Trobt addressed the monstrosity.

The other gave no sign that I could see but Trobt went to pull a games table at the side of the room over toward us. "I will serve as his hands," Trobt said.

The pale blue eyes never left my face.

I stood without conscious thought until Trobt pushed a chair under me. Mentally I shook myself. With unsteady hands—I had to do something with them—I reached for the pukts before me. "Do you . . . do you have a choice . . . of colors, sir?" I stammered, trying to make up for my earlier rudeness of staring.

The lips of the monstrosity quivered, but he made no reply.

All this while Trobt had been watching me with amusement. "He is deaf and speechless," Trobt said. "Take either set. I will place the other before him."

Absently I pulled the red pieces toward me and placed them on their squares.

"In deference to you as a visitor, you will play 'second game counts,' " Trobt continued. He was still enjoying my consternation. "He always allows his opponent the first move. You may begin when you are ready."

With an effort I forced myself to concentrate on the playing board. My start, I decided, must be orthodox. I had to learn something of the type of game this . . . Yondtl . . . played. I moved the first row right-hand pukt its two oblique and one left squares.

Yondtl inclined his head slightly. His lips moved. Trobt put his hand to a pukt and pushed it forward. Evidently Trobt read his lips. Very probably Yondtl could read ours also.

We played for almost an hour with neither of us losing a man.

I had tried several gambits; gambits that invited a misplay on Yondtl's part. But he made none. When he offered I was careful to make no mistakes of my own. We both played as though this first game were the whole contest.

Another hour went by. I deliberately traded three pukts with Yondtl, in an attempt to trick him into a misplay. None came.

I tried a single decoy gambit, and when nothing happened, followed with a second decoy. Yondtl countered each play. I marveled that he gave so little of his attention to the board. Always he seemed to be watching me. I played. He played. He watched me.

I sweated.

Yondtl set up an overt side pass that forced me to draw my pukts back into the main body. Somehow I received the impression that he was teasing me. It made me want to beat him down.

I decided on a crossed-force, double decoy gambit. I had never seen it employed. Because, I suspect, it is too involved, and open to error by its user. Slowly and painstakingly I set it up and pressed forward.

The Caliban in the seat opposite me never paused. He matched me play for play. And though Yondtl's features had long since lost the power of expression, his pale eyes seemed to develop a blue luster. I realized, almost with a shock of surprise, that the fat monstrosity was happy—intensely happy.

I came out of my brief reverie with a start. Yondtl had made an obvious play. I had made an obvious counter. I was startled to hear him sound a cry somewhere between a muffled shout and an idiot's laugh, and my attention jerked back to the board. I had lost the game!

My brief moment of abstraction had given Yondtl the opportunity to make a pass too subtle to be detected with part of my faculties occupied elsewhere.

I pushed back my chair. "I've had enough for tonight," I told Trobt. If I were to do the humans a service, I would need rest before trying Yondtl in the second game.

We made arrangements to meet again the following evening, and let ourselves out. The old woman was nowhere in sight.

The following evening when we began play I was prepared to give my best. I was rested and eager. And I had a concrete plan. Playing the way I had been doing I would never beat Yondtl, I'd decided after long thought. A stand off was the best I could hope for. Therefore the time had come for more consummate action. I would engage him in a triple decoy gambit!

I had no illusion that I could handle it—the way it should be handled. I doubt that any man, human or Veldian, could. But at least I would play it with the greatest skill I had, giving my best to every move, and push the game up the scale of reason and involution—up and up—until either Yondtl or I became lost in its innumerable complexities, and fell.

As I attacked, the complexes and complications would grow gradually more numerous, become more and more difficult, until they embraced a span greater than one of us had the capacity to encompass, and the other would win.

The game began and I forced it into the pattern I had planned. Each play, and each maneuver, became all important, and demanding of the greatest skill I could command. Each pulled at the core of my brain, dragging out the last iota of sentient stuff that writhed there. Yondtl stayed with me, complex gambit through complex gambit.

When the strain became too great I forced my mind to pause, to rest and to be ready for the next clash. At the first break I searched the annotator. It was working steadily, with an almost smooth throb of efficiency, keeping the position of each pukt—and its value—strong in the forefront of visualization. But something was missing!

A minute went by before I spotted the fault. The move of each pukt involved so many possibilities, so many avenues of choice, that no exact answer was predictable on any one. The number and variation of gambits open on every play, each subject to the multitude of Yondtl's counter-moves, stretched the possibilities beyond prediction. The annotator was a harmonizing perceptive force, but not a creative, initiating one. It operated in a statistical manner, similar to a computer, and could not perform effectively where a crucial factor or factors were unknown, or concealed, as they were here.

My greatest asset was negated.

At the end of the third hour I began to feel a steady pain in my temples, as though a tight metal band pressed against my forehead and squeezed it inward. The only reaction I could discern in Yondtl was that the blue glint in his eyes had become brighter. All his happiness seemed gathered there.

Soon my pauses became more frequent. Great waves of brain weariness had to be allowed to subside before I could play again.

And at last it came.

Suddenly, unexpectedly, Yondtl threw a pukt across the board and took my second decoy—and there was no way for me to retaliate! Worse, my entire defense was smashed.

I felt a kind of calm dismay. My shoulders sagged and I pushed the board away from me and slumped in my chair.

I was beaten.

The next day I escaped from Trobt. It was not difficult. I simply walked away.

For three days I followed the wall of The City, looking for a way out. Each gate was guarded. I watched unobserved and saw that a permit was necessary when leaving. If I found no other way I would make a run for it. The time of decision never came.

Meanwhile to obtain food I was forced into some contact with The City's people, and learned to know them better. Adding this new knowledge to the old I decided that I liked them.

Their manners and organization—within the framework of their culture—was as simple and effective as their architecture. There was a strong emphasis on pride, on strength and honor, on skill and on living a dangerous life with a gambler's self-command, on rectitude, on truth and the unbreakable bond of loyalty among family and friends. Lying, theft and deceit were practically unknown.

I did detect what might have been a universal discontent in their young men. They had a warrior heritage and nature which, with the unity of the tribes and the passing of the dleeth—and no one to fight except themselves—had left them with an unrecognized futility of purpose. They had not quite been able to achieve a successful sublimation of their post-warrior need to fight in the games. Also, the custom of polygamy—necessary in the old days, and desired still by those able to attain it—left many sexually frustrated.

I weighed all these observations in my reactions to the Veldians, and toward the end a strange feeling—a kind of wistfulness—came as I observed. I felt kin to them, as if these people had much in common with myself. And I felt that it was too bad that life was not fundamentally so simple that one could discard the awareness of other ways of life, of other values and philosophies that bid against one another, and against one's attention, and make one cynical of the philosophy one lives by, and dies for. Too bad that I could not see and take life as that direct, and as that simple.

The third day I climbed a spiral ramp to the top of a tower that rose above the walls of Hearth and gazed out over miles of swirling red sand. Directly beneath me stretched a long concrete ribbon of road. On the road were dozens of slowly crawling vehicles that might have been caterpillar trucks of Earth!

In my mind the pattern clicked into place. Hearth was not typical of the cities of Velda!

It was an anachronism, a revered homeplace, a symbol of their past, untainted by the technocracy that was pursued elsewhere. This was the capital city, from which the heads of the government still ruled, perhaps for sentimental reasons, but it was not typical.

My stay in Hearth was cut short when I descended from the tower and found Trobt waiting for me.

As I might have expected, he showed no sign of anger with me for having fled into The City. His was the universal Veldian viewpoint. To them all life was the game. With the difference that it was played on an infinitely larger board. Every man, and every woman, with whom the player had contact, direct or indirect, were pukts on the board. The player made his decisions, and his plays, and how well he made them determined whether he won or lost. His every move, his every joining of strength with those who could help him, his every maneuver against those who would oppose him, was his choice to make, and he rose or fell on the wisdom of the choice. Game, in Velda, means duel, means struggle and the test of man against the opponent, life. I had made my escape as the best play as I saw it. Trobt had no recriminations.

The evening of the next day Trobt woke me. Something in his constrained manner brought me to my feet. "Not what you think," he said, "but we must question you again. We will try our own methods this time."

"Torture?"

"You will die under the torture, of course. But for the questioning it will not be necessary. You will talk."

The secret of their method was very simple. Silence. I was led to a room within a room within a room. Each with very thick walls. And left alone. Here time meant nothing.

Gradually I passed from boredom to restlessness, to anxiety, briefly through fear, to enervating frustration, and finally to stark apathy.

When Trobt and his three accompanying guardsmen led me into the blinding daylight I talked without hesitation or consideration of consequences.

"Did you find any weakness in the Veldians?"

"*Yes.*"

I noted then a strange thing. It was the annotator—the thing in my brain that was a part of me, and yet apart from me—that had spoken. It was not concerned with matters of emotion; with sentiments of patriotism, loyalty, honor and self-respect. It was interested only in my—and its own—survival. Its logic told it that unless I gave the answers my questioner wanted I would die. That, it intended to prevent.

I made one last desperate effort to stop that other part of my mind from assuming control—and sank lower into my mental impotence.

"What is our weakness?"

*"Your society is doomed."* With the answer I realized that the annotator had arrived at another of its conclusions.

"Why?"

*"There are many reasons."*

"Give one."

*"Your culture is based on a need for struggle, for combat. When there is no one to fight it must fall."*

Trobt was dealing with a familiar culture now. He knew the questions to ask.

"Explain that last statement."

*"Your culture is based on its impetuous need to battle . . . it is armed and set against dangers and the expectation of danger . . . fostering the pride of courage under stress. There is no danger now . . . nothing to fight, no place to spend your overaggressiveness, except against each other in personal duels. Already your decline is about to enter the bloody circus and religion stage, already crumbling in the heart while expanding at the outside. And this is your first civilization . . . like a boy's first love . . . you have no experience of a fall in your history before to have recourse to—no cushioning of philosophy to accept it . . ."*

For a time Trobt maintained a puzzled silence. I wondered if he had the depth of understanding to accept the truth and significance of what he had heard. "Is there no solution?" he asked at last.

*"Only a temporary one."* Now it was coming.

"Explain."

*"War with the Ten Thousand Worlds."*

"Explain."

*"Your willingness to hazard, and eagerness to battle is no weakness when you are armed with superior weapons, and are fighting against an opponent as disorganized, and as incapable of effective organization as the Ten Thousand Worlds, against your long-range weapons and subtle traps."*

"Why do you say the solution is only temporary?"

*"You cannot win the war. You will seem to win, but it will be an illusion. You will win the battles, kill billions, rape worlds, take slaves and destroy*

*ships and weapons. But after that you will be forced to hold the subjection. Your numbers will not be expendable. You will be spread thin, exposed to other cultures that will influence you, change you. You will lose skirmishes, and in the end you will be forced back. Then will come a loss of old ethics, corruption and opportunism will replace your honor and you will know unspeakable shame and dishonor . . . your culture will soon be weltering back into a barbarism and disorganization which in its corruption and despair will be nothing like the proud tribal primitive life of its first barbarism. You will be aware of the difference and unable to return."*

I understood Trobt's perplexity as I finished. He could not accept what I told him because to him winning was only a matter of a military victory, a victory of strength; Velda had never experienced defeat as a weakness from within. My words made him uneasy, but he did not understand. He shrugged. "Do we have any other weakness?" he asked.

*"Your women."*

"Explain."

*"They are 'set' for the period when they greatly outnumbered their men. Your compatible ratio is eight women to one man. Yet now it is one to one. Further, you produce too few children. Your manpower must ever be in small supply. Worse, your shortage of women sponsors a covert despair and sadism in your young men . . . a hunger and starvation to follow instinct, to win women by courage and conquest and battle against danger . . . that only a war can restrain.*

"The solution?"

*"Beat the Federation. Be in a position to have free access to their women."*

Came the final ingnominy. "Do you have a means of reporting back to the Ten Thousand Worlds?"

*"Yes. Buried somewhere inside me is a nerve-twitch tape. Flesh pockets of chemicals are stored there also. When my body temperature drops fifteen degrees below normal the chemicals will be activated and will use the tissues of my body for fuel and generate sufficient energy to transmit the information on the tape back to the Ten Thousand Worlds."*

That was enough.


"Do you still intend to kill me?" I asked Trobt the next day as we walked in his garden.

"Do not fear," he answered. "You will not be cheated of an honorable death. All Velda is as eager for it as you."

"Why?" I asked. "Do they see me as a madman?"

"They see you as you are. They cannot conceive of one man challenging a planet, except to win himself a bright and gory death on a page of history, the first man to deliberately strike and die in the coming war—not an impersonal clash of battleships, but a *man* declaring personal battle against men. We would not deprive you of that death. Our admiration is too great. We want the symbolism of your blood now just as greatly as you want it yourself. Every citizen is waiting to watch you die—gloriously."

I realized now that all the while he had interpreted my presence here in this fantastic way. And I suspected that I had no arguments to convince him differently.

Trobt had hinted that I would die under torture. I thought of the old histories of Earth that I had read. Of the warrior race of North American Indians. A captured enemy must die. But if he had been an honorable enemy he was given an honorable death. He was allowed to die under the stress most familiar to them. Their strongest ethic was a cover-up for the defeated, the universal expressionless suppressal of reaction in conquering or watching conquest, so as not to shame the defeated. Public torture—with the women, as well as warriors, watching—the chance to exhibit fortitude, all the way to the breaking point, and beyond. That was considered the honorable death, while it was a shameful trick to quietly slit a man's throat in his sleep without giving him a chance to fight—to show his scorn of flinching under the torture.

Here I was the Honorable Enemy who had exhibited courage. They would honor me, and satisfy their hunger for an enemy, by giving me the breaking point test.

But I had no intention of dying!

"You will not kill me," I addressed Trobt. "And there will be no war."

He looked at me as though I had spoken gibberish.

My next words, I knew, would shock him. "I'm going to recommend unconditional surrender," I said.

Trobt's head, which he had turned away, swiveled sharply back to me. His mouth opened and he made several motions to speak before succeeding. "Are you serious?"

"Very," I answered.

Trobt's face grew gaunt and the skin pressed tight against his cheekbones—almost as though he were making the surrender rather than I. "Is this decision dictated by your logic," he asked dryly, "or by faintness of heart?"

I did not honor the question enough to answer.

Neither did he apologize. "You understand that unconditional surrender is the only kind we will accept?"

I nodded wearily.

"Will they agree to your recommendation?"

"No," I answered. "Humans are not cowards, and they will fight—as long as there is any slightest hope of success. I will not be able to convince them that their defeat is inevitable. But I can prepare them for what is to come. I hope to shorten the conflict immeasurably."

"I can do nothing but accept," Trobt said after a moment of thought. "I will arrange transportation back to Earth for you tomorrow." He paused and regarded me with expressionless eyes. "You realize that an enemy who surrenders without a struggle is beneath contempt?"

The blood crept slowly into my cheeks. It was difficult to ignore his taunt. "Will you give me six months before you move against us?" I asked. "The Federation is large. I will need time to bring my message to all."

"You have your six months." Trobt was still not through with me, personally. "On the exact day that period ends I will expect your return to Velda. We will see if you have any honor left."

"I will be back," I said.

During the next six months I spread my word throughout the Ten Thousand Worlds. I met disbelief everywhere. I had not expected otherwise. The last day I returned to Velda.

Two days later Velda's Council acted. They were going to give the humans no more time to organize counteraction. I went in the same spaceship that carried Trobt. I intended to give him any advice he needed about the worlds. I asked only that his first stop be at the Jason's Fleece fringe.

Beside us sailed a mighty armada of warships, spaced in a long line that would encompass the entire portion of the galaxy occupied by the Ten Thousand Worlds. For an hour we moved ponderously forward, then the stars about us winked out for an instant. The next moment a group of worlds became visible on the ship's vision screen. I recognized them as Jason's Fleece.

One world expanded until it appeared the size of a baseball. "Quagman," Trobt said.

Quagman, the trouble spot of the Ten Thousand Worlds. Dominated by an unscrupulous clique that ruled by vendetta, it had been the source of much trouble and vexation to the other worlds. Its leaders were considered little better than brigands. They had received me with much apparent courtesy. In the end they had even agreed to surrender to the Veldians —when and if they appeared. I had accepted their easy concurrence with suspicion, but they were my main hope.

Two Veldians left our ship in a scooter. We waited ten long, tense hours. When word finally came back it was from the Quagmans themselves. The Veldian envoys were being held captive. They would be released upon the delivery of two billion dollars—in the currency of any recognized world—and the promise of immunity.

The fools!

Trobt's face remained impassive as he received the message.

We waited several more hours. Both Trobt and I watched the green mottled baseball on the vision screen. It was Trobt who first pointed out a small, barely discernible, black spot on the upper left-hand corner of Quagman.

As the hours passed, and the black spot swung slowly to the right as the planet revolved, it grew almost imperceptibly larger. When it disappeared over the edge of the world we slept.

In the morning the spot appeared again, and now it covered half the face of the planet. Another ten hours and the entire planet became a blackened cinder.

Quagman was dead.

The ship moved next to Mican.

Mican was a sparsely populated prison planet. Criminals were usually sent to newly discovered worlds on the edge of the human expansion circle, and allowed to make their own adjustments toward achieving a stable government. Men with the restless natures that made them criminals on their own highly civilized worlds made the best pioneers. However, it always took them several generations to work their way up from anarchy to a cooperative government. Mican had not yet had that time. I had done my best in the week I spent with them to convince them to organize, and to be prepared to accept any terms the Veldians might offer. The gesture, I feared, was useless but I had given all the arguments I knew.

A second scooter left with two Veldian representatives. When it returned Trobt left the control room to speak with them.

He returned, and shook his head. I knew it was useless to argue.

Mican died.

At my request Trobt agreed to give the remaining Jason's Fleece Worlds a week to consider—on the condition that they made no offensive forays. I wanted them to have time to fully assess what had happened to the other two worlds—to realize that that same stubbornness would result in the same disaster for them.

At the end of the third twenty-four hour period the Jason's Fleece Worlds surrendered—unconditionally. They had tasted blood; and recognized futility when faced with it. That had been the best I had been able to hope for, earlier.

Each sector held off surrendering until the one immediately ahead had given in. But the capitulation was complete at the finish. No more blood had had to be shed.

The Veldians' terms left the worlds definitely subservient, but they were neither unnecessarily harsh, nor humiliating. Velda demanded specific limitations on weapons and war-making potentials; the obligation of reporting all technological and scientific progress; and colonial expansion only by prior consent.

There was little actual occupation of the Federation worlds, but the Veldians retained the right to inspect any and all functions of the various governments. Other aspects of social and economic methods would be subject only to occasional checks and investigation. Projects considered questionable would be supervised by the Veldians at their own discretion.

The one provision that caused any vigorous protest from the worlds was the Veldian demand for human women. But even this was a purely emotional reaction, and died as soon as it was more fully understood. The Veldians were not barbarians. They used no coercion to obtain our women. They only demanded the same right to woo them as the citizens of the worlds had. No woman would be taken without her free choice. There would be no valid protest to that.

In practice it worked quite well. On nearly all the worlds there were more women than men, so that few men had to go without mates because of the Veldians' inroads. And—by human standards—they seldom took our most desirable women. Because the acquiring of weight was corollary with the Veldian women becoming sexually attractive, their men had an almost universal preference for fleshy women. As a result many of our women who would have had difficulty securing human husbands found themselves much in demand as mates of the Veldians.

Seven years passed after the worlds' surrender before I saw Kalin Trobt again.

The pact between the Veldians and the worlds had worked out well, for both sides. The demands of the Veldians involved little sacrifice by the Federation, and the necessity of reporting to a superior authority made for less wrangling and jockeying for advantageous position among the worlds themselves.

The fact that the Veldians had taken more than twenty million of our women—it was the custom for each Veldian to take a human woman for one mate—caused little dislocation or discontent. The number each lost did less than balance the ratio of the sexes.

For the Veldians the pact solved the warrior-set frustrations, and the unrest and sexual starvation of their males. Those men who demanded action and adventure were given supervisory posts on the worlds as an outlet for their drives. All could now obtain mates; mates whose biological make-up did not necessitate an eight to one ratio.

Each year it was easier for the humans to understand the Veldians and to meet them on common grounds socially. Their natures became less rigid, and they laughed more—even at themselves, when the occasion demanded.

This was especially noticeable among the younger Veldians, just reaching an adult status. In later years when the majority of them would have a mixture of human blood, the difference between us would become even less pronounced.

Trobt had changed little during those seven years. His hair had grayed some at the temples, and his movements were a bit less supple, but he looked well. Much of the intensity had left his aquiline features, and he seemed content.

We shook hands with very real pleasure. I led him to chairs under the shade of a tree in my front yard and brought drinks.

"First, I want to apologize for having thought you a coward," he began, after the first conventional pleasantries. "I know now I was very wrong. I did not realize for years, however, just what had happened." He gave his wry smile. "You know what I mean, I presume?"

I looked at him inquiringly.

"There was more to your decision to capitulate than was revealed. When you played the game your forte was finding the weakness of an opponent. And winning the second game. You made no attempt to win the first. I see now, that as on the board, your surrender represented only the conclusion of the first game. You were keeping our weakness to yourself, convinced that there would be a second game. And that your Ten Thousand Worlds would win it. As you have."

"What would you say your weakness was?" By now I suspected he knew everything, but I wanted to be certain.

"Our desire and need for human women, of course."

There was no need to dissemble further. "The solution first came to me," I explained, "when I remembered a formerly independent Earth country named China. They lost most of their wars, but in the end they always won."

"Through their women?"

"Indirectly. Actually it was done by absorbing their conquerors. The situation was similar between Velda and the Ten Thousand Worlds. Velda won the war, but in a thousand years there will be no Veldians—racially."

"That was my first realization," Trobt said. "I saw immediately then how you had us hopelessly trapped. The marriage of our men to your women will blend our bloods until—with your vastly greater numbers—in a dozen generations there will be only traces of our race left.

"And what can we do about it?" Trobt continued. "We can't kill our beloved wives—and our children. We can't stop further acquisition of human women without disrupting our society. Each generation the tie between us will become closer, our blood thinner, yours more dominant, as the intermingling continues. We cannot even declare war against the people who are doing this to us. How do you fight an enemy that has surrendered unconditionally?"

"You do understand that for your side this was the only solution to the imminent chaos that faced you?" I asked.

"Yes." I watched Trobt's swift mind go through its reasoning. I was certain he saw that Velda was losing only an arbitrary distinction of race, very much like the absorbing of the early clans of Velda into the family of the Danlee. Their dislike of that was very definitely only an emotional consideration. The blending of our bloods would benefit both; the resultant new race would be better and stronger because of that blending.

With a small smile Trobt raised his glass. "We will drink to the union of two great races," he said. "And to you—the winner of the second game!"

# The Dead Past

*A dream of all historians is the ability to go back in time and experience first-hand the events they have studied. History is frequently a form of speculative fiction, an abstraction from sketchy and uncertain facts, as historians know all too well. What exciting discoveries await the first time travelers who journey back and visit with the great figures of history.*

*But, as Isaac Asimov shows us in "The Dead Past," some unexpected problems may be encountered on such a journey of discovery.*

Arnold Potterley, Ph.D., was a professor of ancient history. That, in itself, was not dangerous. What changed the world beyond all dreams was the fact that he *looked* like a professor of ancient history.

Thaddeus Araman, department head of the Division of Chronoscopy, might have taken proper action if Dr. Potterley had been owner of a large, square chin, flashing eyes, aquiline nose and broad shoulders.

As it was, Thaddeus Araman found himself staring over his desk at a mild-mannered individual, whose faded blue eyes looked at him wistfully from either side of a low-bridged button nose; whose small, neatly dressed figure seemed stamped "milk-and-water" from thinning brown hair to the neatly brushed shoes that completed a conservative middle-class costume.

Araman said pleasantly, "And now what can I do for you, Dr. Potterley?"

Dr. Potterley said in a soft voice that went well with the rest of him, "Mr. Araman, I came to you because you're top man in chronoscopy."

Araman smiled. "Not exactly. Above me is the World Commissioner of Research and above him is the Secretary-General of the United Nations. And above both of them, of course, are the sovereign peoples of Earth."

Dr. Potterley shook his head. "They're not interested in chronoscopy. I've come to you, sir, because for two years I have been trying to obtain permission to do some time viewing—chronoscopy, that is—in connection with my researches on ancient Carthage. I can't obtain such permission. My research grants are all proper. There is no irregularity in any of my intellectual endeavors and yet—"

"I'm sure there is no question of irregularity," said Araman soothingly. He flipped the thin reproduction sheets in the folder to which Potterley's name had been attached. They had been produced by Multivac, whose vast analogical mind kept all the department records. When this was over, the sheets could be destroyed, then reproduced on demand in a matter of minutes.

And while Araman turned the pages, Dr. Potterley's voice continued in a soft monotone.

The historian was saying, "I must explain that my problem is quite an important one. Carthage was ancient commercialism brought to its zenith. Pre-Roman Carthage was the nearest ancient analogue to pre-atomic America, at least insofar as its attachment to trade, commerce and business in general was concerned. They were the most daring seamen and explorers before the Vikings; much better at it than the overrated Greeks.

"To know Carthage would be very rewarding, yet the only knowledge we have of it is derived from the writings of its bitter enemies, the Greeks and Romans. Carthage itself never wrote in its own defense or, if it did, the books did not survive. As a result, the Carthaginians have been one of the favorite sets of villains of history and perhaps unjustly so. Time viewing may set the record straight."

He said much more.

Araman said, still turning the reproduction sheets before him, "You must realize, Dr. Potterley, that chronoscopy, or time viewing, if you prefer, is a difficult process."

Dr. Potterley, who had been interrupted, frowned and said, "I am asking for only certain selected views at times and places I would indicate."

Araman sighed. "Even a few views, even one . . . It is an unbelievably delicate art. There is the question of focus getting the proper scene in view and holding it. There is the synchronization of sound, which calls for completely independent circuits."

"Surely my problem is important enough to justify considerable effort."

"Yes, sir. Undoubtedly," said Araman at once. To deny the importance of someone's research problem would be unforgivably bad manners. "But you must understand how long-drawn-out even the simplest view is. And there is a long waiting line for the chronoscope and an even longer waiting line for the use of Multivac which guides us in our use of the controls."

Potterley stirred unhappily. "But can nothing be done? For two years—"

"A matter of priority, sir. I'm sorry. . . . Cigarette?"

The historian started back at the suggestion, eyes suddenly widening as he stared at the pack thrust out toward him. Araman looked surprised, withdrew the pack, made a motion as though to take a cigarette for himself and thought better of it.

Potterley drew a sigh of unfeigned relief as the pack was put out of sight. He said, "Is there any way of reviewing matters, putting me as far forward as possible. I don't know how to explain—"

Araman smiled. Some had offered money under similar circumstances which, of course, had gotten them nowhere, either. He said, "The decisions on priority are computer–processed. I could in no way alter those decisions arbitrarily."

Potterley rose stiffly to his feet. He stood five and a half feet tall. "Then, good day, sir."

"Good day, Dr. Potterley. And my sincerest regrets."

He offered his hand and Potterley touched it briefly.

The historian left, and a touch of the buzzer brought Araman's secretary into the room. He handed her the folder.

"These," he said, "may be disposed of."

Alone again, he smiled bitterly. Another item in his quarter-century's service to the human race. Service through negation.

At least this fellow had been easy to dispose of. Sometimes academic pressure had to be applied and even withdrawal of grants.

Five minutes later, he had forgotten Dr. Potterley. Nor, thinking back on it later, could he remember feeling any premonition of danger.

During the first year of his frustration, Arnold Potterley had experienced only that—frustration. During the second year, though, his frustration gave birth to an idea that first frightened and then fascinated him. Two things stopped him from trying to translate the idea into action, and neither barrier was the undoubted fact that his notion was a grossly unethical one.

The first was merely the continuing hope that the government would finally give its permission and make it unnecessary for him to do anything more. That hope had perished finally in the interview with Araman just completed.

The second barrier had been not a hope at all but a dreary realization of his own incapacity. He was not a physicist and he knew no physicists from whom he might obtain help. The Department of Physics at the university consisted of men well-stocked with grants and well-immersed in specialty. At best, they would not listen to him. At worst, they would report him for intellectual anarchy and even his basic Carthaginian grant might easily be withdrawn.

That he could not risk. And yet chronoscopy was the only way to carry on his work. Without it, he would be no worse off if his grant were lost.

The first hint that the second barrier might be overcome had come a week earlier than his interview with Araman, and it had gone unrecognized at the time. It had been at one of the faculty teas. Potterley attended these sessions unfailingly because he conceived attendance to be a duty, and he took his duties seriously. Once there, however, he conceived it to be no responsibility of his to make light conversation or new friends. He sipped abstemiously at a drink or two, exchanged a polite word with the dean or such department heads as happened to be present, bestowed a narrow smile on others and finally left early.

Ordinarily, he would have paid no attention, at that most recent tea, to a young man standing quietly, even diffidently, in one corner. He would never have dreamed of speaking to him. Yet a tangle of circumstance persuaded him this once to behave in a way contrary to his nature.

That morning at breakfast, Mrs. Potterley had announced somberly that once again she had dreamed of Laurel; but this time a Laurel grown up, yet retaining the three-year-old face that stamped her as their child. Potterley had let her talk. There had been a time when he fought her too-frequent preoccupation with the past and death. Laurel would not come back to them, either through dreams or through talk. Yet if it appeased Caroline Potterley—let her dream and talk.

But when Potterley went to school that morning, he found himself for once affected by Caroline's inanities. Laurel grown up! She had died nearly twenty years ago; their only child, then and ever. In all that time, when he thought of her, it was as a three-year-old.

Now he thought: but if she were alive now, she wouldn't be three, she'd be nearly twenty-three.

Helplessly, he found himself trying to think of Laurel as growing progressively older; as finally becoming twenty-three. He did not quite succeed.

Yet he tried. Laurel using make-up. Laurel going out with boys. Laurel —getting married!

So it was that when he saw the young man hovering at the outskirts of the coldly circulating group of faculty men, it occurred to him quixotically that, for all he knew, a youngster just such as this might have married Laurel. That youngster himself, perhaps. . . .

Laurel might have met him, here at the university, or some evening when he might be invited to dinner at the Potterleys'. They might grow interested in one another. Laurel would surely have been pretty and this youngster looked well. He was dark in coloring, with a lean intent face and an easy carriage.

The tenuous daydream snapped, yet Potterley found himself staring foolishly at the young man, not as a strange face but as a possible son-in-law in the might-have-been. He found himself threading his way toward the man. It was almost a form of autohypnotism.

He put out his hand. "I am Arnold Potterley of the History Department. You're new here, I think?"

The youngster looked faintly astonished and fumbled with his drink, shifting it to his left hand in order to shake with his right. "Jonas Foster is my name, sir. I'm a new instructor in physics. I'm just starting this semester."

Potterley nodded. "I wish you a happy stay here and great success."

That was the end of it, then. Potterley had come uneasily to his senses, found himself embarrassed and moved off. He stared back over his shoulder once, but the illusion of relationship had gone. Reality was quite real once more and he was angry with himself for having fallen prey to his wife's foolish talk about Laurel.

But a week later, even while Araman was talking, the thought of that young man had come back to him. An instructor in physics. A new instructor. Had he been deaf at the time? Was there a short circuit between ear and brain? Or was it an automatic self-censorship because of the impending interview with the head of chronoscopy?

But the interview failed, and it was the thought of the young man with whom he had exchanged two sentences that prevented Potterley from elaborating his pleas for consideration. He was almost anxious to get away.

And in the autogiro express back to the university, he could almost wish he was superstitious. He could then console himself with the thought that the casual meaningless meeting had really been directed by a knowing and purposeful fate.

Jonas Foster was not new to academic life. The long and rickety struggle for the doctorate would make anyone a veteran. Additional work as a postdoctorate teaching fellow acted as a booster shot.

But now he was Instructor Jonas Foster. Professional dignity lay ahead. And he now found himself in a new sort of relationship toward other professors.

For one thing, they would be voting on future promotions. For another, he was in no position to tell so early in the game which particular member of the faculty might or might not have the ear of the dean or even of the university president. He did not fancy himself as a campus politician and was sure he would make a poor one, yet there was no point in kicking his own rear into blisters just to prove that to himself.

So Foster listened to this mild-mannered historian who, in some vague way, seemed nevertheless to radiate tension, and did not shut him up abruptly and toss him out. Certainly that was his first impulse.

He remembered Potterley well enough. Potterley had approached him at that tea (which had been a grisly affair). The fellow had spoken two sentences to him stiffly, somehow glassy-eyed, had then come to himself with a visible start and hurried off.

It had amused Foster at the time, but now . . .

Potterley might have been deliberately trying to make his acquaintance, or, rather, to impress his own personality on Foster as that of a queer sort of duck, eccentric but harmless. He might now be probing Foster's views, searching for unsettling opinions. Surely, they ought to have done so before granting him his appointment. Still . . .

Potterley might be serious, might honestly not realize what he was doing. Or he might realize quite well what he was doing; he might be nothing more or less than a dangerous rascal.

Foster mumbled, "Well, now—" to gain time, and fished out a package of cigarettes, intending to offer one to Potterley and to light it and one for himself very slowly.

But Potterley said at once, "Please, Dr. Foster. No cigarettes."

Foster looked startled. "I'm sorry, sir."

"No. The regrets are mine. I cannot stand the odor. An idiosyncrasy. I'm sorry."

He was positively pale. Foster put away the cigarettes.

Foster, feeling the absence of the cigarette, took the easy way out. "I'm flattered that you ask my advice and all that, Dr. Potterley, but I'm not a neutrinics man. I can't very well do anything professional in that direction. Even stating an opinion would be out of line, and frankly, I'd prefer that you didn't go into any particulars."

The historian's prim face set hard. "What do you mean, you're not a neutrinics man? You're not anything yet. You haven't received any grant, have you?"

"This is only my first semester."

"I know that. I imagine you haven't even applied for any grant yet."

Foster half-smiled. In three months at the university, he had not succeeded in putting his initial requests for research grants into good enough shape to pass on to a professional science writer, let alone to the Research Commission.

(His department head, fortunately, took it quite well. "Take your time now, Foster," he said, "and get your thoughts well-organized. Make sure you know your path and where it will lead, for, once you receive a grant, your specialization will be formally recognized and, for better or for worse, it will be yours for the rest of your career." The advice was trite enough, but triteness has often the merit of truth, and Foster recognized that.)

Foster said, "By education and inclination, Dr. Potterley, I'm a hyperoptics man with a gravitics minor. It's how I described myself in applying for this position. It may not be my official specialization yet, but it's going to be. It can't be anything else. As for neutrinics, I never even studied the subject."

"Why not?" demanded Potterley at once.

Foster stared. It was the kind of rude curiosity about another man's professional status that was always irritating. He said, with the edge of his own politeness just a trifle blunted, "A course in neutrinics wasn't given at my university."

"Good Lord, where did you go?"

"MIT," said Foster quietly.

"And they don't teach neutrinics?"

"No, they don't." Foster felt himself flush and was moved to a defense. "It's a highly specialized subject with no great value. Chronoscopy, perhaps, has some value, but it is the only practical application and that's a dead end."

The historian stared at him earnestly. "Tell me this. Do you know where I can find a neutrinics man?"

"No, I don't," said Foster bluntly.

"Well, then, do you know a school which teaches neutrinics?"

"No, I don't."

Potterley smiled tightly and without humor.

Foster resented that smile, found he detected insult in it and grew sufficiently annoyed to say, "I would like to point out, sir, that you're stepping out of line."

"What?"

"I'm saying that, as a historian, your interest in any sort of physics, your *professional* interest, is—" He paused, unable to bring himself quite to say the word.

"Unethical?"

"That's the word, Dr. Potterley."

"My researches have driven me to it," said Potterley in an intense whisper.

"The Research Commission is the place to go. If they permit—"

"I have gone to them and have received no satisfaction."

"Then obviously you must abandon this." Foster knew he was sounding stuffily virtuous, but he wasn't going to let this man lure him into an expression of intellectual anarchy. It was too early in his career to take stupid risks.

Apparently, though, the remark had its effect on Potterley. Without any warning, the man exploded into a rapid-fire verbal storm of irresponsibility.

Scholars, he said, could be free only if they could freely follow their own free-swinging curiosity. Research, he said, forced into a predesigned pattern by the powers that held the purse strings became slavish and had to stagnate. No man, he said, had the right to dictate the intellectual interest of another.

Foster listened to all of it with disbelief. None of it was strange to him. He had heard college boys talk so in order to shock their professors and he had once or twice amused himself in that fashion, too. Anyone who studied the history of science knew that many men had once thought so.

Yet it seemed strange to Foster, almost against nature, that a modern man of science could advance such nonsense. No one would advocate running a factory by allowing each individual worker to do whatever pleased him at the moment, or of running a ship according to the casual and conflicting motions of each individual crewman. It would be taken for granted that some sort of centralized supervisory agency must exist in each case. Why should direction and order benefit a factory and a ship but not scientific research?

People might say that the human mind was somehow qualitatively different from a ship or factory but the history of intellectual endeavor proved the opposite.

When science was young and the intricacies of all or most of the known was within the grasp of an individual mind, there was no need for direction, perhaps. Blind wandering over the uncharted tracts of ignorance could lead to wonderful ends by accident.

But as knowledge grew, more and more data had to be absorbed before worthwhile journeys into ignorance could be organized. Men had to specialize. The researcher needed the resources of a library he himself could not gather, then of instruments he himself could not afford. More and more, the individual researcher gave way to the research team and the research institution.

The funds necessary for research grew greater as tools grew more numerous. What college was so small today as not to require at least one nuclear micro-reactor and at least one three-stage computer?

Centuries before, private individuals could no longer subsidize research. By 1940, only the government, large industries and large universities or research institutions could properly subsidize basic research.

By 1960, even the largest universities depended entirely upon government grants, while research institutions could not exist without tax concessions and public subscriptions. By 2000, the industrial combines had become a branch of the world government and, thereafter, the financing of research and therefore its direction naturally became centralized under a department of the government.

It all worked itself out naturally and well. Every branch of science was fitted neatly to the needs of the public, and the various branches of science were coordinated decently. The material advance of the last half-century was argument enough for the fact that science was not falling into stagnation.

Foster tried to say a very little of this and was waved aside impatiently by Potterley who said, "You are parroting official propaganda. You're sitting in the middle of an example that's squarely against the official view. Can you believe that?"

"Frankly, no."

"Well, why do you say time viewing is a dead end? Why is neutrinics unimportant? You say it is. You say it categorically. Yet you've never studied it. You claim complete ignorance of the subject. It's not even given in your school—"

"Isn't the mere fact that it isn't given proof enough?"

"Oh, I see. It's not given because it's unimportant. And it's unimportant because it's not given. Are you satisfied with that reasoning?"

Foster felt a growing confusion. "It's in the books."

"That's all. The books say neutrinics is unimportant. Your professors tell you so because they read it in the books. The books say so because professors write them. Who says it from personal experience and knowledge? Who does research in it? Do you know of anyone?"

Foster said, "I don't see that we're getting anywhere, Dr. Potterley. I have work to do—"

"One minute. I just want you to try this on. See how it sounds to you. I say the government is actively suppressing basic research in neutrinics and chronoscopy. They're suppressing application of chronoscopy."

"Oh, no."

"Why not? They could do it. There's your centrally directed research. If they refuse grants for research in any portion of science, that portion dies. They've killed neutrinics. They can do it and have done it."

"But why?"

"I don't know why. I want you to find out. I'd do it myself if I knew enough. I came to you because you're a young fellow with a brand-new education. Have your intellectual arteries hardened already? Is there no curiosity in you? Don't you want to *know?* Don't you want *answers?*"

The historian was peering intently into Foster's face. Their noses were only inches apart, and Foster was so lost that he did not think to draw back.

He should, by rights, have ordered Potterley out. If necessary, he should have thrown Potterley out.

It was not respect for age and position that stopped him. It was certainly not that Potterley's arguments had convinced him. Rather, it was a small point of college pride.

Why didn't MIT give a course in neutrinics? For that matter, now that he came to think of it, he doubted that there was a single book on neutrinics in the library. He could never recall having seen one.

He stopped to think about that.

And that was ruin.

Caroline Potterley had once been an attractive woman. There were occasions, such as dinners or university functions, when, by considerable effort, remnants of the attraction could be salvaged.

On ordinary occasions, she sagged. It was the word she applied to herself in moments of self-abhorrence. She had grown plumper with the years, but the flaccidity about her was not a matter of fat entirely. It was as though her muscles had given up and grown limp so that she shuffled when she walked while her eyes grew baggy and her cheeks jowly. Even her graying hair seemed tired rather than merely stringy. Its straightness seemed to be the result of a supine surrender to gravity, nothing else.

Caroline Potterley looked at herself in the mirror and admitted this was one of her bad days. She knew the reason, too.

It had been the dream of Laurel. The strange one, with Laurel grown up. She had been wretched ever since.

Still, she was sorry she had mentioned it to Arnold. He didn't say anything; he never did any more; but it was bad for him. He was particularly withdrawn for days afterward. It might have been that he was getting ready for that important conference with the big government official (he kept saying he expected no success), but it might also have been her dream.

It was better in the old days when he would cry sharply at her, "Let the dead past *go*, Caroline! Talk won't bring her back, and dreams won't either."

It had been bad for both of them. Horribly bad. She had been away from home and had lived in guilt ever since. If she had stayed at home, if she had not gone on an unnecessary shopping expedition, there would have been two of them available. One would have succeeded in saving Laurel.

Poor Arnold had not managed. Heaven knew he tried. He had nearly died himself. He had come out of the burning house, staggering in agony, blistered, choking, half-blinded, with the dead Laurel in his arms.

The nightmare of that lived on, never lifting entirely.

Arnold slowly grew a shell about himself afterward. He cultivated a low-voiced mildness through which nothing broke, no lightning struck. He grew puritanical and even abandoned his minor vices, his cigarettes, his penchant for an occasional profane exclamation. He obtained his grant for the preparation of a new history of Carthage and subordinated everything to that.

She tried to help him. She hunted up his references, typed his notes and microfilmed them. Then that ended suddenly.

She ran from the desk suddenly one evening, reaching the bathroom in bare time and retching abominably. Her husband followed her in confusion and concern.

"Caroline, what's wrong?"

It took a drop of brandy to bring her around. She said, "Is it true? What they did?"

"Who did?"

"The Carthaginians."

He stared at her and she got it out by indirection. She couldn't say it right out.

The Carthaginians, it seemed, worshiped Moloch, in the form of a hollow, brazen idol with a furnace in its belly. At times of national crisis, the priests and the people gathered, and infants, after the proper ceremonies and invocations, were dextrously hurled, alive, into the flames.

They were given sweetmeats just before the crucial moment, in order that the efficacy of the sacrifice not be ruined by displeasing cries of panic. The drums rolled just after the moment, to drown out the few seconds of infant shrieking. The parents were present, presumably gratified, for the sacrifice was pleasing to the gods. . . .

Arnold Potterley frowned darkly. Vicious lies, he told her, on the part of Carthage's enemies. He should have warned her. After all, such propagandistic lies were not uncommon. According to the Greeks, the ancient Hebrews worshiped an ass's head in their Holy of Holies. According to the Romans, the primitive Christians were haters of all men who sacrificed pagan children in the catacombs.

"Then they didn't do it?" asked Caroline.

"I'm sure they didn't. The primitive Phoenicians may have. Human sacrifice is commonplace in primitive cultures. But Carthage in her great days was not a primitive culture. Human sacrifice often gives way to symbolic actions such as circumcision. The Greeks and Romans might have mistaken some Carthaginian symbolism for the original full rite, either out of ignorance or out of malice."

"Are you sure?"

"I can't be sure yet, Caroline, but when I've got enough evidence, I'll apply for permission to use chronoscopy, which will settle the matter once and for all."

"Chronoscopy?"

"Time viewing. We can focus on ancient Carthage at some time of crisis, the landing of Scipio Africanus in 202 B.C., for instance, and see with our own eyes exactly what happens. And you'll see, I'll be right."

He patted her and smiled encouragingly, but she dreamed of Laurel every night for two weeks thereafter and she never helped him with his

Carthage project again. Nor did he ever ask her to.

But now she was bracing herself for his coming. He had called her after arriving back in town, told her he had seen the government man and that it had gone as expected. That meant failure, and yet the little telltale sign of depression had been absent from his voice and his features had appeared quite composed in the teleview. He had another errand to take care of, he said, before coming home.

It meant he would be late, but that didn't matter. Neither one of them was particular about eating hours or cared when packages were taken out of the freezer or even which packages or when the self-warming mechanism was activated.

When he did arrive, he surprised her. There was nothing untoward about him in any obvious way. He kissed her dutifully and smiled, took off his hat and asked if all had been well while he was gone. It was all almost perfectly normal. Almost.

She had learned to detect small things, though, and his pace in all this was a trifle hurried. Enough to show her accustomed eye that he was under tension.

She said, "Has something happened?"

He said, "We're going to have a dinner guest night after next, Caroline. You don't mind?"

"Well, no. Is it anyone I know?"

"No. A young instructor. A newcomer. I've spoken to him." He suddenly whirled toward her and seized her arms at the elbow, held them a moment, then dropped them in confusion as though disconcerted at having shown emotion.

He said, "I almost didn't get through to him. Imagine that. Terrible, *terrible*, the way we have all bent to the yoke; the affection we have for the harness about us."

Mrs. Potterley wasn't sure she understood, but for a year she had been watching him grow quietly more rebellious, little by little more daring in his criticism of the government. She said, "You haven't spoken foolishly to him, have you."

"What do you mean, foolishly? He'll be doing some neutrinics for me."

"Neutrinics" was trisyllabic nonsense to Mrs. Potterley, but she knew it had nothing to do with history. She said faintly, "Arnold, I don't like you to do that. You'll lose your position. It's—"

"It's intellectual anarchy, my dear," he said. "That's the phrase you want. Very well. I am an anarchist. If the government will not allow me to push my researches, I will push them on my own. And when I show the way, others will follow. . . . And if they don't, it makes no difference. It's Carthage that counts and human knowledge, not you and I."

"But you don't know this young man. What if he is an agent for the Commissioner of Research."

"Not likely and I'll take that chance." He made a fist of his right hand and rubbed it gently against the palm of his left. "He's on my side now. I'm sure of it. He can't help but be. I can recognize intellectual curiosity when I see it in a man's eyes and face and attitude, and it's a fatal disease for a tame scientist. Even today it takes time to beat it out of a man and the young ones are vulnerable. . . . Oh, why stop at anything? Why not build our own chronoscope and tell the government to go to—"

He stopped abruptly, shook his head and turned away.

"I hope everything will be all right," said Mrs. Potterley, feeling helplessly certain that everything would not be, and frightened, in advance, for her husband's professorial status and the security of their old age.

It was she alone, of them all, who had a violent presentiment of trouble. Quite the wrong trouble, of course.

Jonas Foster was nearly half an hour late in arriving at the Potterleys' off-campus house. Up to that very evening, he had not quite decided he would go. Then, at the last moment, he found he could not bring himself to commit the social enormity of breaking a dinner appointment an hour before the appointed time. That, and the nagging of curiosity.

The dinner itself passed interminably. Foster ate without appetite. Mrs. Potterley sat in distant absentmindedness, merging out of it only once to ask if he were married and to make a deprecating sound at the news that he was not. Dr. Potterley himself asked neutrally after his professional history and nodded his head primly.

It was as staid, stodgy—boring, actually—as anything could be.

Foster thought: he seems so harmless.

Foster had spent the last two days reading up on Dr. Potterley. Very casually, of course, almost sneakily. He wasn't particularly anxious to be seen in the Social Science Library. To be sure, history was one of those borderline affairs and historical works were frequently read for amusement or edification by the general public.

Still, a physicist wasn't quite the "general public." Let Foster take to reading histories and he would be considered queer, sure as relativity, and after a while the head of the department would wonder if his new instructor were really "the man for the job."

So he had been cautious. He sat in the more secluded alcoves and kept his head bent when he slipped in and out at odd hours.

Dr. Potterley, it turned out, had written three books and some dozen articles on the ancient Mediterranean worlds, and the later articles (all in "Historical Reviews") had all dealt with pre-Roman Carthage from a sympathetic viewpoint.

That, at least, checked with Potterley's story and had soothed Foster's suspicions somewhat. . . . And yet Foster felt that it would have been much wiser, much safer, to have scotched the matter at the beginning.

A scientist shouldn't be too curious, he thought in bitter dissatisfaction with himself. It's a dangerous trait.

After dinner, he was ushered into Potterley's study and he was brought up sharply at the threshold. The walls were simply lined with books.

Not merely films. There were films, of course, but these were far outnumbered by the books—print on paper. He wouldn't have thought so many books would exist in usable condition.

That bothered Foster. Why should anyone want to keep so many books at home? Surely all were available in the university library, or, at the very worst, at the Library of Congress, if one wished to take the minor trouble of checking out a microfilm.

There was an element of secrecy involved in a home library. It breathed of intellectual anarchy. That last thought had calmed Foster. He would rather Potterley be an authentic anarchist than a play-acting *agent provocateur.*

And now the hours began to pass quickly and astonishingly.

"You see," Potterley said, in a clear, unflurried voice. It was a matter of finding, if possible, someone who had once used chronoscopy in his work. Naturally, I couldn't ask baldly, since that would be unauthorized research."

"Yes," said Foster dryly. He was a little surprised such a small consideration would stop the man.

"I used indirect methods—"

He had. Foster was amazed at the volume of correspondence dealing with small disputed points of ancient Mediterranean culture which somehow managed to elicit the casual remark over and over again: "Of course, having never made use of chronoscopy—" or, "Pending approval of my request for chronoscopic data, which appears unlikely at the moment—"

"Now these aren't blind questionings," said Potterley. There's a monthly booklet put out by the Institute for Chronoscopy in which items concerning the past as determined by time viewing are printed. Just one or two items.

"What impressed me first was the triviality of most of the items, their insipidity. Why should such researches get priority over my work? So I wrote to people who would be most likely to do research in the directions described in the booklet. Uniformly, as I have shown you, they did *not* make use of the chronoscope. Now let's go over it point by point."

At last Foster, his head swimming with Potterley's meticulously gathered details, asked, "But why?"

"I don't know why," said Potterley, "but I have a theory. The original invention of the chronoscope was by Sterbinski—you see, I know that much—and it was well-publicized. But then the government took over the instrument and decided to suppress further research in the matter or any use of the machine. But then, people might be curious as to why it wasn't being used. Curiosity is such a vice, Dr. Foster." Yes, agreed the physicist to himself.

"Imagine the effectiveness, then," Potterley went on, "of pretending that the chronoscope was being used. It would then be not a mystery, but a commonplace. It would no longer be a fitting object for legitimate curiosity or an attractive one for illicit curiosity."

"You were curious," pointed out Foster.

Potterley looked a trifle restless. "It was different in my case," he said angrily. "I have something that *must* be done, and I wouldn't submit to the ridiculous way in which they kept putting me off."

A bit paranoid, too, thought Foster gloomily.

Yet he had ended up with something, paranoid or not. Foster could no longer deny that something peculiar was going on in the matter of neutrinics.

But what was Potterley after? That still bothered Foster. If Potterley didn't intend this as a test of Foster's ethics, what *did* he want?

Foster put it to himself logically. If an intellectual anarchist with a touch of paranoia wanted to use a chronoscope and was convinced that the powers-that-be was deliberately standing in his way, what would he do?

Supposing it were I, he thought. What would I do?

He said slowly, "Maybe the chronoscope doesn't exist at all?"

Potterley started. There was almost a crack in his general calmness. For an instant, Foster found himself catching a glimpse of something not at all calm.

But the historian kept his balance and said, "Oh, no, there *must* be a chronoscope."

"Why? Have you seen it? Have I? Maybe that's the explanation of everything. Maybe they're not deliberately holding out on a chronoscope they've got. Maybe they haven't got it in the first place."

"But Sterbinski lived. He built a chronoscope. That much is a fact."

"The books say so," said Foster coldly.

"Now listen." Potterley actually reached over and snatched at Foster's jacket sleeve. "I need the chronoscope. I must have it. Don't tell me it doesn't exist. What we're going to do is find out enough about neutrinics to be able to—"

Potterley drew himself up short.

Foster drew his sleeve away. He needed no ending to that sentence. He supplied it himself. He said, "Build one of our own?"

Potterley looked sour as though he would rather not have said it point-blank. Nevertheless, he said, "Why not?"

"Because that's out of the question," said Foster. "If what I've read is correct, then it took Sterbinski twenty years to build his machine and several millions in composite grants. Do you think you and I can duplicate that illegally? Suppose we had the time, which we haven't, and suppose I could learn enough out of books, which I doubt, where would we get the money and equipment? The chronoscope is supposed to fill a five-story building, for heaven's sake."

"Then you won't help me?"

"Well, I'll tell you what. I have one way in which I may be able to find out something—"

"What is that?" asked Potterley at once.

"Never mind. That's not important. But I may be able to find out enough to tell you whether the government is deliberately suppressing research by chronoscope. I may confirm the evidence you already have or I may be able to prove that your evidence is misleading. I don't know what good it will do you in either case, but it's as far as I can go. It's my limit."

Potterley watched the young man go finally. He was angry with himself. Why had he allowed himself to grow so careless as to permit the fellow to guess that he was thinking in terms of a chronoscope of his own. That was premature.

But then why did the young fool have to suppose that a chronoscope might not exist at all?

It *had* to exist. It *had* to. What was the use of saying it didn't?"

And why couldn't a second one be built? Science had advanced in the fifty years since Sterbinski. All that was needed was knowledge.

Let the youngster gather knowledge. Let him think a small gathering would be his limit. Having taken the path to anarchy, there would be no limit. If the boy were not driven onward by something in himself, the first steps would be error enough to force the rest. Potterley was quite certain he would not hesitate to use blackmail.

Potterley waved a last good-by and looked up. It was beginning to rain. Certainly! Blackmail if necessary, but he would not be stopped.

Foster steered his car across the bleak outskirts of town and scarcely noticed the rain.

He *was* a fool, he told himself, but he couldn't leave things as they were. He had to know. He damned his streak of undisciplined curiosity, but he had to know.

But he would go no further than Uncle Ralph. He swore mightily to himself that it would stop there. In that way, there would be no evidence against him, no real evidence. Uncle Ralph would be discreet.

In a way, he was secretly ashamed of Uncle Ralph. He hadn't mentioned him to Potterley partly out of caution and partly because he did not wish to witness the lifted eyebrow, the inevitable half-smile. Professional science writers, however useful, were a little outside the pale, fit only for patronizing contempt. The fact that, as a class, they made more money than did research scientists only made matters worse, of course.

Still, there were times when a science writer in the family could be a convenience. Not being really educated, they did not have to specialize. Consequently, a good science writer knew practically everything. . . . And Uncle Ralph was one of the best.

Ralph Nimmo had no college degree and was rather proud of it. "A degree," he once said to Jonas Foster, when both were considerably younger, "is a first step down a ruinous highway. You don't want to waste it so you go on to graduate work and doctoral research. You end up a thoroughgoing ignoramus on everything in the world except for one subdivisional sliver of nothing.

"On the other hand, if you guard your mind carefully and keep it blank of any clutter of information till maturity is reached, filling it only with intelligence and training it only in clear thinking, you then have a powerful instrument at your disposal and you can become a science writer."

Nimmo received his first assignment at the age of twenty-five, after he had completed his apprenticeship and been out in the field for less than three months. It came in the shape of a clotted manuscript whose language would impart no glimmering of understanding to any reader, however qualified, without careful study and some inspired guesswork. Nimmo took it apart and put it together again (after five long and exasperating interviews with the authors, who were biophysicists), making the language taut and meaningful and smoothing the style to a pleasant gloss.

"Why not?" he would say tolerantly to his nephew, who countered his strictures on degrees by berating him with his readiness to hang on the fringes of science. "The fringe is important. Your scientists can't write. Why should they be expected to? They aren't expected to be grand masters at chess or virtuosos at the violin, so why expect them to know how to put words together? Why not leave that for specialists, too?

"Good Lord, Jonas, read your literature of a hundred years ago. Discount the fact that the science is out of date and that some of the expressions are out of date. Just try to read it and make sense out of it. It's just jaw-cracking, amateurish. Pages are published uselessly; whole articles which are either noncomprehensible or both."

"But you don't get recognition, Uncle Ralph," protested young Foster, who was getting ready to start his college career and was rather starry-eyed about it. "You could be a terrific researcher."

"I get recognition," said Nimmo. "Don't think for a minute I don't. Sure, a biochemist or a strato-meteorologist won't give me the time of day, but they pay me well enough. Just find out what happens when some first-class chemist finds the commission has cut his year's allowance for science writing. He'll fight harder for enough funds to afford me, or someone like me, than to get a recording ionograph."

He grinned broadly and Foster grinned back. Actually, he was proud of his paunchy, round-faced, stub-fingered uncle, whose vanity made him brush his fringe of hair futilely over the desert on his pate and made him dress like an unmade haystack because such negligence was his trademark. Ashamed, but proud, too.

And now Foster entered his uncle's cluttered apartment in no mood at all for grinning. He was nine years older now and so was Uncle Ralph. For nine more years, papers in every branch of science had come to him for polishing and a little of each had crept into his capacious mind.

Nimmo was eating seedless grapes, popping them into his mouth one at a time. He tossed a bunch to Foster who caught them by a hair, then bent to retrieve individual grapes that had torn loose and fallen to the floor.

"Let them be. Don't bother," said Nimmo carelessly. "Someone comes in here to clean once a week. What's up? Having trouble with your grant application write-up?"

"I haven't really got into that yet."

"You haven't? Get a move on, boy. Are you waiting for me to offer to do the final arrangement?"

"I couldn't afford you, uncle."

"Aw, come on. It's all in the family. Grant me all popular publication rights and no cash need change hands."

Foster nodded. "If you're serious, it's a deal."

"It's a deal."

It was a gamble, of course, but Foster knew enough of Nimmo's science writing to realize it could pay off. Some dramatic discovery of public interest on primitive man or on a new surgical technique, or on any branch of spationautics could mean a very cash-attracting article in any of the mass media of communication.

It was Nimmo, for instance, who had written up, for scientific consumption, the series of papers by Bryce and co-workers that elucidated the fine structure of two cancer viruses, for which job he asked the picayune payment of fifteen hundred dollars, provided popular publication rights were included. He then wrote up, exclusively, the same work in semi-dramatic form for use in trimensional video for a twenty-thousand-dollar advance plus rental royalties that were still coming in after five years.

Foster said bluntly, "What do you know about neutrinics, uncle?"

"Neutrinics?" Nimmo's small eyes looked surprised. "Are you working in that? I thought it was pseudo-gravitic optics."

"It is p.g.o. I just happen to be asking about neutrinics."

"That's a devil of a thing to be doing. You're stepping out of line. You know that, don't you?"

"I don't expect you to call the commission because I'm a little curious about things."

"Maybe I should before you get into trouble. Curiosity is an occupational danger with scientists. I've watched it work. One of them will be moving quietly along on a problem, then curiosity leads him up a strange creek. Next thing you know they've done so little on their proper problem, they can't justify for a project renewal. I've seen more—"

"All I want to know," said Foster patiently, "is what's been passing through your hands lately on neutrinics."

Nimmo leaned back, chewing at a grape thoughtfully. "Nothing. Nothing ever. I don't recall ever getting a paper on neutrinics."

"What!" Foster was openly astonished. "Then who does get the work?"

"Now that you ask," said Nimmo, "I don't know. Don't recall anyone talking about it at the conventions. I don't think much work is being done there."

"Why not?"

"Hey, there, don't bark. I'm not doing anything. My guess would be —"

Foster was exasperated. "Don't you know?"

"Hmp. I'll tell you what I know about neutrinics. It concerns the applications of neutrino movements and the forces involved—"

"Sure. Sure. Just as electronics deals with the applications of electron movements and the forces involved, and pseudo-gravitics deals with the applications of artificial gravitational fields. I didn't come to you for that. Is that all you know?"

"And," said Nimmo with equanimity, "neutrinics is the basis of time viewing and that *is* all I know."

Foster slouched back in his chair and massaged one lean cheek with great intensity. He felt angrily dissatisfied. Without formulating it explicitly in his own mind, he had felt sure, somehow, that Nimmo would come up with some late reports, bring up interesting facets of modern neutrinics, send him back to Potterley able to say that the elderly historian was mistaken, that his data was misleading, his deductions mistaken.

Then he could have returned to his proper work.

But now . . .

He told himself angrily: so they're not doing much work in the field. Does that make it deliberate suppression? What if neutrinics is a sterile discipline? Maybe it is. I don't know. Potterley doesn't. Why waste the intellectual resources of humanity on nothing? Or the work might be secret for some legitimate reason. It might be . . .

The trouble was, he had to know. He couldn't leave things as they were now. *He couldn't!*

He said, "Is there a text on neutrinics, Uncle Ralph? I mean a clear and simple one. An elementary one."

Nimmo thought, his plump cheeks puffing out with a series of sighs. "You ask the damnedest questions. The only one I ever heard of was Sterbinski and somebody. I've never seen it, but I viewed something about it once. . . . Sterbinski and LaMarr, that's it."

"Is that the Sterbinski who invented the chronoscope?"

"I think so. Proves the book ought to be good."

"Is there a recent edition? Sterbinski died thirty years ago."

Nimmo shrugged and said nothing.

"Can you find out?"

They sat in silence for a moment, while Nimmo shifted his bulk to the creaking tune of the chair he sat on. Then the science writer said, "Are you going to tell me what this is all about?"

"I can't. Will you help me anyway, Uncle Ralph? Will you get me a copy of the text?"

"Well, you've taught me all I know on pseudo-gravitics. I should be grateful. Tell you what—I'll help you on one condition."

"Which is?"

The older man was suddenly very grave. "That you be careful, Jonas. You're obviously way out of line whatever you're doing. Don't blow up your career just because you're curious about something you haven't been assigned to and which is none of your business. Understand?"

Foster nodded, but he hardly heard. He was thinking furiously.

A full week later, Ralph Nimmo eased his rotund figure into Jonas Foster's on-campus two-room combination and said, in a hoarse whisper, "I've got something."

"What?" Foster was immediately eager.

"A copy of Sterbinski and LaMarr." He produced it, or rather a corner of it, from his ample topcoat.

Foster almost automatically eyed door and windows to make sure they were closed and shaded respectively, then held out his hand.

The film case was flaking with age, and when he cracked it the film was faded and growing brittle. He said sharply "Is this all?"

"Gratitude, my boy, gratitude!" Nimmo sat down with a grunt, and reached into a pocket for an apple.

"Oh, I'm grateful, but it's so old."

"And lucky to get it at that. I tried to get a film run from the Congressional Library. No go. The book was restricted."

"Then how did you get this?"

"Stole it." He was biting crunchingly around the core. "New York Public."

"What?"

"Simple enough. I had access to the stacks, naturally. So I stepped over a chained railing when no one was around, dug this up and walked out with it. They're very trusting out there. Meanwhile, they won't miss it in years. . . . Only you'd better not let anyone see it on you, nephew."

Foster stared at the film as though it were literally hot.

Nimmo discarded the core and reached for a second apple. "Funny thing, now. There's nothing more recent in the whole field of neutrinics. Not a monograph, not a paper, not a progress note. Nothing since the chronoscope."

"Uh-huh," said Foster absently.

Foster worked evenings in the Potterley home. He could not trust his own on-campus rooms for the purpose. The evening work grew more real to him than his own grant applications. Sometimes he worried about it but then that stopped, too.

His work consisted, at first, simply in viewing and reviewing the text film. Later it consisted in thinking (sometimes while a section of the book ran itself through the pocket projector, disregarded).

Sometimes Potterley would come down to watch, to sit with prim, eager eyes, as though he expected thought processes to solidify and become visible in all their convolutions. He interfered in only two ways. He did not allow Foster to smoke and sometimes he talked.

It wasn't conversation talk, never that. Rather it was a low-voiced monologue with which, it seemed, he scarcely expected to command attention. It was much more as though he were relieving a pressure within himself.

Carthage! Always Carthage!

Carthage, the New York of the ancient Mediterranean. Carthage, commercial empire and queen of the seas. Carthage, all that Syracuse and Alexandria pretended to be. Carthage, maligned by her enemies and inarticulate in her own defense.

She had been defeated once by Rome and then driven out of Sicily and Sardinia, but came back to more than recoup her losses by new dominions in Spain, and raised up Hannibal to give the Romans sixteen years of terror.

In the end, she lost again a second time, reconciled herself to fate and built again with broken tools a limping life in shrunken territory, succeeding so well that jealous Rome deliberately forced a third war. And then Carthage, with nothing but bare hands and tenacity, built weapons and forced Rome into a two-year war that ended only with complete destruction of the city, the inhabitants throwing themselves into their flaming houses rather than surrender.

"Could people fight so for a city and a way of life as bad as the ancient writers painted it? Hannibal was a better general than any Roman and his soldiers were absolutely faithful to him. Even his bitterest enemies praised him. There was a Carthaginian. It is fashionable to say that he was an atypical Carthaginian, better than the others, a diamond placed in garbage. But then why was he so faithful to Carthage, even to his death after years of exile? They talk of Moloch—"

Foster didn't always listen but sometimes he couldn't help himself and he shuddered and turned sick at the bloody tale of child sacrifice.

But Potterley went on earnestly, "Just the same, it isn't true. It's a twenty-five-hundred-year-old canard started by the Greeks and Romans. They had their own slaves, their crucifixions and torture, their gladiatorial contests. They weren't holy. The Moloch story is what later ages would have called war propaganda, the big lie. I can prove it was a lie. I can prove and, by heaven, I will—I will—"

He would mumble that promise over and over again in his earnestness.

Mrs. Potterley visited him also, but less frequently, usually on Tuesdays and Thursdays when Dr. Potterley himself had an evening course to take care of and was not present.

She would sit quietly, scarcely talking, face slack and doughy, eyes blank, her whole attitude distant and withdrawn.

The first time, Foster tried, uneasily, to suggest that she leave.

She said tonelessly, "Do I disturb you?"

"No, of course not," lied Foster restlessly. "It's just that—that—" He couldn't complete the sentence.

She nodded, as though accepting an invitation to stay. Then she opened a cloth bag she had brought with her and took out a quire of vitron sheets which she proceeded to weave together by rapid, delicate movements of a pair of slender, tetra-faceted depolarizers, whose battery-fed wires made her look as though she were holding a large spider.

One evening, she said softly, "My daughter, Laurel, is your age."

Foster started, as much at the sudden unexpected sound of speech as at the words. He said, "I didn't know you had a daughter, Mrs. Potterley."

"She died. Years ago."

The vitron grew under the deft manipulations into the uneven shape of some garment Foster could not yet identify. There was nothing left for him to do but mutter inanely, "I'm sorry."

Mrs. Potterley sighed. "I dream about her often." She raised her blue, distant eyes to him.

Foster winced and looked away.

Another evening she asked, pulling at one of the vitron sheets to loosen its gentle clinging to her dress, "What is time viewing anyway?"

That remark broke into a particularly involved chain of thought, and Foster said snappishly, "Dr. Potterley can explain."

"He's tried to. Oh, my, yes. But I think he's a little impatient with me. He calls it chronoscopy most of the time. Do you actually see things in the past, like the trimensionals? Or does it jus† make little dot patterns like the computer you use?"

Foster stared at his hand computer with distaste. It worked well enough, but every operation had to be manually controlled and the answers were obtained in code. Now if he could use the school computer ... well, why dream, he felt conspicuous enough, as it was, carrying a hand computer under his arm every evening as he left his office.

He said, "I've never seen the chronoscope myself, but I'm under the impression that you actually see pictures and hear sound."

"You can hear people talk, too?"

"I think so." Then, half in desperation, "Look here, Mrs. Potterley, this must be awfully dull for you. I realize you don't like to leave a guest all to himself, but really, Mrs. Potterley, you mustn't feel compelled—"

"I don't feel compelled," she said. "I'm sitting here, waiting."

"Waiting? For what?"

She said composedly, "I listened to you that first evening. The time you first spoke to Arnold. I listened at the door."

He said, "You did?"

"I know I shouldn't have, but I was awfully worried about Arnold. I had a notion he was going to do something he oughtn't and I wanted to hear what. And then when I heard—" She paused, bending close over the vitron and peering at it.

"Heard what, Mrs. Potterley?"

"That you wouldn't build a chronoscope."

"Well, of course not."

"I thought maybe you might change your mind."

Foster glared at her. "Do you mean you're coming down here hoping I'll build a chronoscope, waiting for me to build one?"

"I hope you do, Dr. Foster. Oh, I hope you do."

It was as though, all at once, a fuzzy veil had fallen off her face, leaving all her features clear and sharp, putting color into her cheeks, life into her eyes, the vibrations of something approaching excitement into her voice.

"Wouldn't it be wonderful," she whispered, "to have one? People of the past could live again. Pharaohs and kings and—just people. I hope you build one, Dr. Foster. I really—hope—"

She choked, it seemed, on the intensity of her own words and let the vitron sheets slip off her lap. She rose and ran up the basement stairs, while Foster's eyes followed her awkwardly fleeing body with astonishment and distress.

It cut deeper into Foster's nights and left him sleepless and painfully stiff with thought. It was almost a mental indigestion.

His grant requests went limping in, finally, to Ralph Nimmo. He scarcely had any hope for them. He thought numbly: they won't be approved.

If they weren't, of course, it would create a scandal in the department and probably mean his appointment at the university would not be renewed, come the end of the academic year.

He scarcely worried. It was the neutrino, the neutrino, only the neutrino. Its trail curved and veered sharply and led him breathlessly along uncharted pathways that even Sterbinski and LaMarr did not follow.

He called Nimmo. "Uncle Ralph, I need a few things. I'm calling from off the campus."

Nimmo's face in the video plate was jovial, but his voice was sharp. He said, "What you need is a course in communication. I'm having a hell of a time pulling your application into one intelligible piece. If that's what you're calling about—"

Foster shook his head impatiently. "That's *not* what I'm calling about. I need these." He scribbled quickly on a piece of paper and held it up before the receiver.

Nimmo yiped. "Hey, how many tricks do you think I can wangle?"

"You can get them, uncle. You know you can."

Nimmo reread the list of items with silent motions of his plump lips and looked grave.

"What happens when you put those things together?" he asked. Foster shook his head. "You'll have exclusive popular publication rights to whatever turns up, the way it's always been. But please don't ask any questions now."

"I can't do miracles, you know."

"Do this one. You've got to. You're a science writer, not a research man. You don't have to account for anything. You've got friends and connections. They can look the other way, can't they, to get a break from you next publication time?"

"Your faith, nephew, is touching. I'll try."

Nimmo succeeded. The material and equipment were brought over late one evening in a private touring car. Nimmo and Foster lugged it in with the grunting of men unused to manual labor.

Potterley stood at the entrance of the basement after Nimmo had left. He asked softly, "What's this for?"

Foster brushed the hair off his forehead and gently massaged a sprained wrist. He said, "I want to conduct a few simple experiments."

"Really?" The historian's eyes glittered with excitement.

Foster felt exploited. He felt as though he were being led along a dangerous highway by the pull of pinching fingers on his nose; as though he could see the ruin clearly that lay in wait at the end of the path, yet walked eagerly and determinedly. Worst of all, he felt the compelling grip on his nose to be his own.

It was Potterley who began it, Potterley who stood there now, gloating; but the compulsion was his own.

Foster said sourly, "I'll be wanting privacy now, Potterley. I can't have you and your wife running down here and annoying me."

He thought: if that offends him, let him kick me out. Let him put an end to this.

In his heart, though, he did not think being evicted would stop anything.

But it did not come to that. Potterley was showing no signs of offense. His mild gaze was unchanged. He said, "Of course, Dr. Foster, of course. All the privacy you wish."

Foster watched him go. He was left still marching along the highway, perversely glad of it and hating himself for being glad.

He took to sleeping over on a cot in Potterley's basement and spending his weekends there entirely.

During that period, preliminary word came through that his grants (as doctored by Nimmo) had been approved. The department head brought the word and congratulated him.

Foster stared back distantly and mumbled, "Good. I'm glad," with so little conviction that the other frowned and turned away without another word.

Foster gave the matter no further thought. It was a minor point, worth no notice. He was planning something that really counted, a climactic test for that evening.

One evening, a second and third and then, haggard and half-beside himself with excitement, he called in Potterley.

Potterley came down the stairs and looked about at the homemade gadgetry. He said, in his soft voice, "The electric bills are quite high. I don't mind the expense, but the city may ask questions. Can anything be done?"

It was a warm evening, but Potterley wore a tight collar and a semi-jacket. Foster, who was in his undershirt, lifted bleary eyes and said shakily, "It won't be for much longer, Dr. Potterley. I've called you down to tell you something. A chronoscope can be built. A small one, of course, but it can be built."

Potterley seized the railing. His body sagged. He managed a whisper. "Can it be built here?"

"Here in the basement," said Foster wearily.

"Good Lord. You said—"

"I know what I said," cried Foster impatiently. "I said it couldn't be done. I didn't know anything then. Even Sterbinski didn't know anything."

Potterley shook his head. "Are you sure? You're not mistaken, Dr. Foster? I couldn't endure it if—"

Foster said, "I'm not mistaken. Damn it, sir, if just theory had been enough, we could have had a time viewer over a hundred years ago, when the neutrino was first postulated. The trouble was, the original investigators considered it only a mysterious particle without mass or charge that could not be detected. It was just something to even up the bookkeeping and save the law of conservation of mass energy."

He wasn't sure Potterley knew what he was talking about. He didn't care. He needed a breather. He had to get some of this out of his clotting thoughts. . . . And he needed background for what he would have to tell Potterley next.

He went on. "It was Sterbinski who first discovered that the neutrino broke through the space-time cross-sectional barrier, that it traveled through time as well as through space. It was Sterbinski who first devised a method for stopping neutrinos. He invented a neutrino recorder and learned how to interpret the pattern of the neutrino stream. Naturally, the stream had been affected and deflected by all the matter it had passed through in its passage through time, and the deflections could be analyzed and converted into the images of the matter that had done the deflecting. Time viewing was possible. Even air vibrations could be detected in this way and converted into sound."

Potterley was definitely not listening. He said, "Yes. Yes. But when can you build a chronoscope?"

Foster said urgently, "Let me finish. Everything depends on the method used to detect and analyze the neutrino stream. Sterbinski's method was difficult and roundabout. It required mountains of energy. But I've studied pseudo-gravitics, Dr. Potterley, the science of artificial gravitational fields. I've specialized in the behavior of light in such fields. It's a new science. Sterbinski knew nothing of it. If he had, he would have seen—anyone would have—a much better and more efficient method of detecting neutrinos using a pseudo-gravitic field. If I had known more neutrinics to begin with, I would have seen it at once."

Potterley brightened a bit. "I knew it," he said. "Even if they stop research in neutrinics there is no way the government can be sure that discoveries in other segments of science won't reflect knowledge on neutrinics. So much for the value of centralized direction of science. I thought this long ago, Dr. Foster, before you ever came to work here."

"I congratulate you on that," said Foster, "but there's one thing—"

"Oh, never mind all this. Answer me. Please. When can you build a chronoscope?"

"I'm trying to tell you something, Dr. Potterley. A chronoscope won't do you any good." (This is it, Foster thought.)

Slowly, Potterley descended the stairs. He stood facing Foster. "What do you mean? Why won't it help me?"

"You won't see Carthage. It's what I've got to tell you. It's what I've been leading up to. You can never see Carthage."

Potterley shook his head slightly. "Oh, no, you're wrong. If you have the chronoscope, just focus it properly—"

"No, Dr. Potterley. It's not a question of focus. There are random factors affecting the neutrino stream, as they affect all subatomic particles. What we call the uncertainty principle. When the stream is recorded and interpreted, the random factor comes out as fuzziness, or 'noise' as the communications boys speak of it. The further back in time you penetrate, the more pronounced the fuzziness, the greater the noise. After a while, the noise drowns out the picture. Do you understand?"

"More power," said Potterley in a dead kind of voice.

"That won't help. When the noise blurs out detail, magnifying detail magnifies the noise, too. You can't see anything in a sun-burned film by enlarging it, can you? Get this through your head, now. The physical nature of the universe sets limits. The random thermal motions of air molecules set limits to how weak a sound can be detected by any instrument. The length of a light wave or of an electron wave sets limits to the size of objects that can be seen by any instrument. It works that way in chronoscopy, too. You can only time view so far."

"How far? How far?"

Foster took a deep breath. "A century and a quarter. That's the most."

"But the monthly bulletin the commission puts out deals with ancient history almost entirely." The historian laughed shakily. "You must be wrong. The government has data as far back as 3000 B.C."

"When did you switch to believing them?" demanded Foster, scornfully. "You began this business by proving they were lying; that no historian had made use of the chronoscope. Don't you see why now? No historian, except one interested in contemporary history, could. No chronoscope can possibly see back in time further than 1920 under any conditions."

"You're wrong. You don't know everything," said Potterley.

"The truth won't bend itself to your convenience either. Face it. The government's part in this is to perpetuate a hoax."

"Why?"

"I don't know why."

Potterley's snubby nose was twitching. His eyes were bulging. He pleaded, "It's only theory, Dr. Foster. Build a chronoscope. Build one and try."

Foster caught Potterley's shoulder in a sudden, fierce grip. "Do you think I haven't? Do you think I would tell you this before I had checked it every way I knew? I *have* built one. It's all around you. Look!"

He ran to the switches at the power leads. He flicked them on, one by one. He turned a resistor, adjusted other knobs, put out the cellar lights. "Wait. Let it warm up."

There was a small glow near the center of one wall. Potterley was gibbering incoherently, but Foster only cried again, "Look!"

The light sharpened and brightened, broke up into a light-and-dark pattern. Men and women! Fuzzy. Features blurred. Arms and legs mere streaks. An old-fashioned ground car, unclear but recognizable as one of the kind that had once used gasoline-powered internal-combustion engines, sped by.

Foster said, "Mid-twentieth century, somewhere. I can't hook up an audio yet so this is soundless. Eventually, we can add sound. Anyway, mid-twentieth is almost as far back as you can go. Believe me, that's the best focusing that can be done."

Potterley said, "Build a larger machine, a stronger one. Improve your circuits."

"You can't lick the Uncertainty Principle, man, any more than you can live on the sun. There are physical limits to what can be done."

"You're lying. I won't believe you. I—"

A new voice sounded, raised shrilly to make itself heard.

"Arnold! Dr. Foster!"

The young physicist turned at once. Dr. Potterley froze for a long moment, then said, without turning, "What is it, Caroline? Leave us."

"No!" Mrs. Potterley descended the stairs. "I heard. I couldn't help hearing. Do you have a time viewer here, Dr. Foster? Here in the basement?"

"Yes, I do, Mrs. Potterley. A kind of time viewer. Not a good one. I can't get sound yet and the picture is darned blurry, but it works."

Mrs. Potterley clasped her hands and held them tightly against her breast. "How wonderful. How wonderful."

"It's not at all wonderful," snapped Potterley. "The young fool can't reach further back than—"

"Now, look," began Foster in exasperation. . . .

"Please!" cried Mrs. Potterley. "Listen to me. Arnold, don't you see that as long as we can use it for twenty years back, we can see Laurel once again? What do we care about Carthage and ancient times? It's Laurel we can see. She'll be alive for us again. Leave the machine here, Dr. Foster. Show us how to work it."

Foster stared at her then at her husband. Dr. Potterley's face had gone white. Though his voice stayed low and even, its calmness was somehow gone. He said, "You're a fool!"

Caroline said weakly, "Arnold!"

"You're a fool, I say. What will you see? The past. The dead past. Will

Laurel do one thing she did not do? Will you see one thing you haven't seen? Will you live three years over and over again, watching a baby who'll never grow up no matter how you watch?"

His voice came near to cracking, but held. He stepped closer to her, seized her shoulder and shook her roughly. "Do you know what will happen to you if you do that? They'll come to take you away because you'll go mad. Yes, mad. Do you want mental treatment? Do you want to be shut up, to undergo the psychic probe?"

Mrs. Potterley tore away. There was no trace of softness or vagueness about her. She had twisted into a virago. "I want to see my child, Arnold. She's in that machine and I want her."

"She's *not* in the machine. An image is. Can't you understand? An image! Something that's not real!"

"I want my child. Do you hear me?" She flew at him, screaming, fists beating. *"I want my child."*

The historian retreated at the fury of the assault, crying out. Foster moved to step between them, when Mrs. Potterley dropped, sobbing wildly, to the floor.

Potterley turned, eyes desperately seeking. With a sudden heave, he snatched at a Lando-rod, tearing it from its support, and whirling away before Foster, numbed by all that was taking place, could move to stop him.

"Stand back!" gasped Potterley, "or I'll kill you. I swear it."

He swung with force, and Foster jumped back.

Potterley turned with fury on every part of the structure in the cellar, and Foster, after the first crash of glass, watched dazedly.

Potterley spent his rage and then he was standing quietly amid shards and splinters, with a broken Lando-rod in his hand. He said to Foster in a whisper, "Now get out of here! Never come back! If any of this cost you anything, send me a bill and I'll pay for it. I'll pay double."

Foster shrugged, picked up his shirt and moved up the basement stairs. He could hear Mrs. Potterley sobbing loudly, and, as he turned at the head of the stairs for a last look, he saw Dr. Potterley bending over her, his face convulsed with sorrow.

Two days later, with the school day drawing to a close, and Foster looking wearily about to see if there were any data on his newly approved projects that he wished to take home, Dr. Potterley appeared once more. He was standing at the open door of Foster's office.

The historian was neatly dressed as ever. He lifted his hand in a gesture that was too vague to be a greeting, too abortive to be a plea. Foster stared stonily.

Potterley said, "I waited till five, till you were . . . May I come in?"

Foster nodded.

Potterley said, "I suppose I ought to apologize for my behavior. I was dreadfully disappointed; not quite master of myself. Still, it was inexcusable."

"I accept your apology," said Foster. "Is that all?"

"My wife called you, I think."

"Yes, she has."

"She has been quite hysterical. She told me she had but I couldn't be quite sure—"

"She has called me."

"Could you tell me—would you be so kind as to tell me what she wanted?"

"She wanted a chronoscope. She said she had some money of her own. She was willing to pay."

"Did you—make any commitments?"

"I said I wasn't in the manufacturing business."

"Good," breathed Potterley, his chest expanding with a sigh of relief. "Please don't take any calls from her. She's not—quite—"

"Look, Dr. Potterley," said Foster, "I'm not getting into any domestic quarrels, but you'd better be prepared for something. Chronoscopes can be built by anybody. Given a few simple parts that can be bought through some etherics sales center, it can be built in the home workshop. The video part anyway."

"But no one else will think of it beside you, will they? No one has."

"I don't intend to keep it secret."

"But you can't publish. It's illegal research."

"That doesn't matter any more, Dr. Potterley. If I lose my grants, I lose them. If the university is displeased, I'll resign. It just doesn't matter."

"But you can't do that!"

"Till now," said Foster, "you didn't mind my risking loss of grants and position. Why do you turn so tender about it now? Now let me explain something to you. When you first came to me, I believed in organized and directed research. The situation as it existed, in other words. I considered you an intellectual anarchist, Dr. Potterley, and dangerous. But, for one reason or another, I've been an anarchist myself for months now and I have achieved great things.

"Those things have been achieved not because I am a brilliant scientist. Not at all. It was just that scientific research had been directed from above and holes were left that could be filled in by anyone who looked in the right direction. And anyone might have if the government hadn't actively tried to prevent it.

"Now understand me. I still believe directed research can be useful. I'm not in favor of a retreat to total anarchy. But there must be a middle ground. Directed research can retain flexibility. A scientist must be allowed to follow his curiosity, at least in his spare time."

Potterley sat down. He said ingratiatingly, "Let's discuss this, Foster. I appreciate your idealism. You're young. You want the moon. But you can't destroy yourself through fancy notions of what research must consist of. I got you into this. I am responsible and I blame myself bitterly. I was acting emotionally. My interest in Carthage blinded me and I was a damned fool."

Foster broke in. "You mean you've changed completely in two days? Carthage is nothing? Government suppression of research is nothing?"

"Even a damned fool like myself can learn, Foster. My wife taught me something. I understand the reason for government suppression of neutrinics now. I didn't two days ago. And, understanding, I approve. You saw the way my wife reacted to the news of a chronoscope in the basement. I had envisioned a chronoscope used for research purposes. All *she* could see was the personal pleasure of returning neurotically to a personal past, a dead past. The pure researcher, Foster, is in the minority. People like my wife would outweigh us.

"For the government to encourage chronoscopy would have meant that everyone's past would be visible. The government officers would be subjected to blackmail and improper pressure, since who on Earth has a past that is absolutely clean? Organized government might become impossible."

Foster licked his lips. "Maybe the government has some justification in its own eyes. Still, there's an important principle involved here. Who knows what other scientific advances are being stymied because scientists are being stifled into walking a narrow path? If the chronoscope becomes the terror of a few politicians, it's a price that must be paid. The public must realize that science must be free and there is no more dramatic way of doing it than to publish my discovery, one way or another, legally or illegally."

Potterley's brow was damp with perspiration, but his voice remained even. "Oh, not just a few politicians, Dr. Foster. Don't think that. It would be my terror, too. My wife would spend her time living with our dead daughter. She would retreat further from reality. She would go mad living the same scenes over and over. And not just my terror. There would be others like her. Children searching for their dead parents or their own youth. We'll have a whole world living in the past. Midsummer madness."

Foster said, "Moral judgments can't stand in the way. There isn't one advance at any time in history that mankind hasn't had the ingenuity to pervert. Mankind must also have the ingenuity to prevent. As for the chronoscope, your delvers into the dead past will get tired soon enough. They'll catch their loved parents in some of the things their loved parents did and they'll lose their enthusiasm for it all. But all this is trivial. With me, it's a matter of important principle."

Potterley said, "Hang your principle. Can't you understand men and women as well as principle? Don't you understand that my wife will live through the fire that killed our baby? She won't be able to help herself. I know her. She'll follow through each step, trying to prevent it. She'll live it over and over again, hoping each time that it won't happen. How many times do you want to kill Laurel?" A huskiness had crept into his voice.

A thought crossed Foster's mind. "What are you really afraid she'll find out, Dr. Potterley? What happened the night of the fire?"

The historian's hands went up quickly to cover his face and they shook with his dry sobs. Foster turned away and stared uncomfortably out the window.

Potterley said after a while, "It's a long time since I've had to think of it. Caroline was away. I was baby-sitting. I went into the baby's bedroom mid-evening to see if she had kicked off the bedclothes. I had my cigarette with me . . . I smoked in those days. I must have stubbed it out before putting it in the ashtray on the chest of drawers. I was always careful. The baby was all right. I returned to the living room and fell asleep before the video. I awoke, choking, surrounded by fire. I don't know how it started."

"But you think it may have been the cigarette, is that it?" said Foster. "A cigarette which, for once, you forgot to stub out?"

"I don't know. I tried to save her, but she was dead in my arms when I got out."

"You never told your wife about the cigarette, I suppose."

Potterley shook his head. "But I've lived with it."

"Only now, with a chronoscope, she'll find out. Maybe it wasn't the cigarette. Maybe you did stub it out. Isn't that possible?"

The scant tears had dried on Potterley's face. The redness had subsided. He said, "I can't take the chance . . . But it's not just myself, Foster. The past has its terrors for most people. Don't loose those terrors on the human race."

Foster paced the floor. Somehow, this explained the reason for Potterley's rabid, irrational desire to boost the Carthaginians, deify them, most of all disprove the story of their fiery sacrifices to Moloch. By freeing them of the guilt of infanticide by fire, he symbolically freed himself of the same guilt.

So the same fire that had driven him on to causing the construction of a chronoscope was now driving him on to the destruction.

Foster looked sadly at the older man. "I see your position, Dr. Potterley, but this goes above personal feelings. I've got to smash this throttling hold on the throat of science."

Potterley said, savagely, "You mean you want the fame and wealth that goes with such a discovery."

"I don't know about the wealth, but that, too, I suppose. I'm no more than human."

"You won't suppress your knowledge?"

"Not under any circumstances."

"Well, then—" and the historian got to his feet and stood for a moment, glaring.

Foster had an odd moment of terror. The man was older than he, smaller, feebler, and he didn't look armed. Still . . .

Foster said, "If you're thinking of killing me or anything insane like that, I've got the information in a safety-deposit vault where the proper people will find it in case of my disappearance or death."

Potterley said, "Don't be a fool," and stalked out.

Foster closed the door, locked it and sat down to think. He felt silly. He had no information in any safety-deposit vault, of course. Such a melodramatic action would not have occurred to him ordinarily. But now it had.

Feeling even sillier, he spent an hour writing out the equations of the application of pseudo-gravitic optics to neutrinic recording, and some diagrams for the engineering details of construction. He sealed it in an envelope and scrawled Ralph Nimmo's name over the outside.

He spent a rather restless night and the next morning, on the way to school, dropped the envelope off at the bank, with appropriate instructions to an official, who made him sign a paper permitting the box to be opened after his death.

He called Nimmo to tell him of the existence of the envelope, refusing querulously to say anything about its contents.

He had never felt so ridiculously self-conscious as at that moment.

That night and the next, Foster spent in only fitful sleep, finding himself face to face with the highly practical problem of the publication of data unethically obtained.

The "Proceedings of the Society for Pseudo-Gravitics," which was the journal with which he was best acquainted, would certainly not touch any paper that did not include the magic footnote: "The work described in this paper was made possible by Grant No. so-and-so from the Commission of Research of the United Nations."

Nor, doubly so, would the "Journal of Physics."

There were always the minor journals who might overlook the nature of the article for the sake of the sensation, but that would require a little financial negotiation on which he hesitated to embark. It might, on the whole, be better to pay the cost of publishing a small pamphlet for general distribution among scholars. In that case, he would even be able to dispense with the services of a science writer, sacrificing polish for speed. He would have to find a reliable printer. Uncle Ralph might know one.

He walked down the corridor to his office and wondered anxiously if perhaps he ought to waste no further time, give himself no further chance to lapse into indecision and take the risk of calling Ralph from his office phone. He was so absorbed in his own heavy thoughts that he did not notice that his room was occupied until he turned from the clothes closet and approached his desk.

Dr. Potterley was there and a man whom Foster did not recognize.

Foster stared at them. "What's this?"

Potterley said, "I'm sorry, but I had to stop you."

Foster continued staring. "What are you talking about?"

The stranger said, "Let me introduce myself." He had large teeth, a little uneven, and they showed prominently when he smiled. "I am Thaddeus Araman, department head of the Divison of Chronoscopy. I am here to see you concerning information brought to me by Professor Arnold Potterley and confirmed by our own sources—"

Potterley said breathlessly, "I took all the blame, Dr. Foster. I explained that it was I who persuaded you against your will into unethical practices. I have offered to accept full responsibility and punishment. I don't wish you harmed in any way. It's just that chronoscopy must not be permitted!"

Araman nodded. "He has taken the blame as he says, Dr. Foster, but this thing is out of his hands now."

Foster said, "So? What are you going to do? Blackball me from all consideration for research grants?"

"This is in my power," said Araman.

"Order the university to discharge me?"

"That, too, is in my power."

"All right, go ahead. Consider it done. I'll leave my office now, with you. I can send for my books later. If you insist, I'll leave my books. Is that all?"

"Not quite," said Araman. "You must engage to do no further research in chronoscopy, to publish none of your findings in chronoscopy and, of course, to build no chronoscope. You will remain under surveillance indefinitely to make sure you keep that promise."

"Supposing I refuse to promise? What can you do? Doing research out of my field may be unethical, but it isn't a criminal offense."

"In the case of chronoscopy, my young friend," said Araman patiently, "it is a criminal offense. If necessary, you will be put in jail and kept there."

"Why?" shouted Foster. "What's magic about chronoscopy?"

Araman said, "That's the way it is. We cannot allow further developments in the field. My own job is, primarily, to make sure of that, and I intend to do my job. Unfortunately, I had no knowledge, nor did anyone in the department, that the optics of pseudo-gravity fields had such immediate application to chronoscopy. Score one for general ignorance, but henceforward research will be steered properly in that respect, too."

Foster said, "That won't help. Something else may apply that neither you nor I dream of. All science hangs together. It's one piece. If you want to stop one part, you've got to stop it all."

"No doubt that is true," said Araman, "in theory. On the practical side, however, we have managed quite well to hold chronoscopy down to the original Sterbinski level for fifty years. Having caught you in time, Dr.

Foster, we hope to continue doing so indefinitely. And we wouldn't have come this close to disaster, either, if I had accepted Dr. Potterley at something more than face value."

He turned toward the historian and lifted his eyebrows in a kind of humorous self-deprecation. "I'm afraid, sir, that I dismissed you as a history professor and no more on the occasion of our first interview. Had I done my job properly and checked on you, this would not have happened."

Foster said abruptly, "Is anyone allowed to use the government chronoscope?"

"No one outside our division under any pretext. I say that since it is obvious to me that you have already guessed as much. I warn you, though, that any repetition of that fact will be a criminal, not an ethical, offense."

"And your chronoscope doesn't go back more than a hundred twenty-five years or so, does it?"

"It doesn't."

"Then your bulletin with its stories of time viewing ancient times is a hoax?"

Araman said coolly, "With the knowledge you now have, it is obvious you know that for a certainty. However, I confirm your remark. The monthly bulletin is a hoax."

"In that case," said Foster, "I will not promise to suppress my knowledge of chronoscopy. If you wish to arrest me, go ahead. My defense at the trial will be enough to destroy the vicious card house of directed research and bring it tumbling down. Directing research is one thing; suppressing it and depriving mankind of its benefits is quite another."

Araman said, "Oh, let's get something straight, Dr. Foster. If you do not cooperate, you will go to jail directly. You will *not* see a lawyer, you will *not* be charged, you will *not* have a trial. You will simply stay in jail."

"Oh, no," said Foster, "you're bluffing. This is not the twentieth century, you know."

There was a stir outside the office, the clatter of feet, a high-pitched shout that Foster was sure he recognized. The door crashed open, the lock splintering, and three intertwined figures stumbled in.

As they did so, one of the men raised a blaster and brought its butt down hard on the skull of another.

There was a whoosh of expiring air, and the one whose head was struck went limp.

"Uncle Ralph!" cried Foster.

Araman frowned. "Put him down in that chair," he ordered, "and get some water."

Ralph Nimmo, rubbing his head with a gingerly sort of disgust, said, "There was no need to get rough, Araman."

Araman said, "The guard should have been rough sooner and kept you out of here, Nimmo. You'd have been better off."

"You know each other?" asked Foster.

"I've had dealings with the man," said Nimmo, still rubbing. "If he's here in your office, nephew, you're in trouble."

"And you, too," said Araman angrily. "I know Dr. Foster consulted you on neutrinics literature."

Nimmo corrugated his forehead, then straightened it with a wince as though the action had brought pain. "So?" he said. "What else do you know about me?"

"We will know everything about you soon enough. Meanwhile, that one item is enough to implicate you. What are you doing here?"

"My dear Dr. Araman," said Nimmo, some of his jauntiness restored, "day after yesterday, my jackass of a nephew called me. He had placed some mysterious information—"

"Don't tell him! Don't say anything!" cried Foster.

Araman glanced at him coldly. "We know all about it, Dr. Foster. The safety-deposit box has been opened and its contents removed."

"But how can you know—" Foster's voice died away in a kind of furious frustration.

"Anyway," said Nimmo, "I decided the net must be closing around him and, after I took care of a few items, I came down to tell him to get off this thing he's doing. It's not worth his career."

"Does that mean you know what he's doing?" asked Araman.

"He never told me," said Nimmo, "but I'm a science writer with a hell of a lot of experience. I know which side of an atom is electronified. The boy, Foster, specializes in pseudo-gravitic optics and coached me on the stuff himself. He got me to get him a textbook on neutrinics and I kind of skip-viewed it myself before handing it over. I can put the two together. He asked me to get him certain pieces of physical equipment, and that was evidence, too. Stop me if I'm wrong, but my nephew has built a semi-portable, low-power chronoscope. Yes, or—yes?"

"Yes." Araman reached thoughtfully for a cigarette and paid no attention to Dr. Potterley (watching silently, as though all were a dream) who shied away, gasping, from the white cylinder. "Another mistake for me.

I ought to resign. I should have put tabs on you, too, Nimmo, instead of concentrating too hard on Potterley and Foster. I didn't have much time of course and you've ended up safely here, but that doesn't excuse me. You're under arrest, Nimmo."

"What for?" demanded the science writer.

"Unauthorized research."

"I wasn't doing any. I can't, not being a registered scientist. And even if I did, it's not a criminal offense."

Foster said savagely, "No use, Uncle Ralph. This bureaucrat is making his own laws."

"Like what?" demanded Nimmo.

"Like life imprisonment without trial."

"Nuts," said Nimmo. "This isn't the twentieth cen—"

"I tried that," said Foster. "It doesn't bother him."

"Well, nuts," shouted Nimmo. "Look here, Araman. My nephew and I have relatives who haven't lost touch with us, you know. The professor has some also, I imagine. You can't just make us disappear. There'll be questions and a scandal. This *isn't* the twentieth century. So if you're trying to scare us, it isn't working."

The cigarette snapped between Araman's fingers and he tossed it away violently. He said, "Damn it, I don't know *what* to do. It's never been like this before. . . . Look! You three fools know nothing of what you're trying to do. You understand nothing. Will you listen to me?"

"Oh, we'll listen," said Nimmo grimly.

(Foster sat silently, eyes angry, lips compressed. Potterley's hands writhed like two intertwined snakes.)

Araman said, "The past to you is the dead past. If any of you have discussed the matter, it's dollars to nickels you've used that phrase. The dead past. If you knew how many times I've heard those three words, you'd choke on them, too.

"When people think of the past, they think of it as dead, far away and gone, long ago. We encourage them to think so. When we report time viewing, we always talk of views centuries in the past, even though you gentlemen know seeing more than a century or so is impossible. People accept it. The past means Greece, Rome, Carthage, Egypt, the Stone Age. The deader the better.

"Now you three know a century or a little more is the limit, so what does the past mean to you? Your youth. Your first girl. Your dead mother. Twenty years ago. Thirty years ago. Fifty years ago. The deader the better. . . . But when does the past really begin?"

He paused in anger. The others stared at him and Nimmo stirred uneasily.

"Well," said Araman, "when did it begin? A year ago? Five minutes ago? One second ago? Isn't it obvious that the past begins an instant ago? The dead past is just another name for the living present. What if you focus the chronoscope in the past of one-hundredth of a second ago? Aren't you watching the present? Does it begin to sink in?"

Nimmo said, "Damnation."

"Damnation," mimicked Araman. "After Potterley came to me with his story night before last, how do you suppose I checked up on both of you? I did it with the chronoscope, spotting key moments to the very instant of the present."

"And that's how you knew about the safety-deposit box?" said Foster.

"And every other important fact. Now what do you suppose would happen if we let news of a home chronoscope get out? People might start out by watching their youth, their parents and so on, but it wouldn't be long before they'd catch on to the possibilities. The housewife will forget her poor, dead mother and take to watching her neighbor at home and her husband at the office. The businessman will watch his competitor; the employer his employee.

"There will be no such thing as privacy. The party line, the prying eye behind the curtain will be nothing compared to it. The video stars will be closely watched at all times by everyone. Every man his own peeping Tom and there'll be no getting away from the watcher. Even darkness will be no escape because chronoscopy can be adjusted to the infrared and human figures can be seen by their own body heat. The figures will be fuzzy, of course, and the surroundings will be dark, but that will make the titillation of it all the greater, perhaps. . . . Hmp, the men in charge of the machine now experiment sometimes in spite of the regulations against it."

Nimmo seemed sick. "You can always forbid private manufacture—"

Araman turned on him fiercely. "You can, but do you expect it to do good? Can you legislate successfully against drinking, smoking, adultery or gossiping over the back fence? And this mixture of nosiness and prurience will have a worse grip on humanity than any of those. Good Lord, in a thousand years of trying we haven't even been able to wipe out the heroin traffic and you talk about legislating against a device for watching anyone you please at any time you please that can be built in a home workshop."

Foster said suddenly, "I won't publish."

Potterley burst out, half in sobs, "None of us will talk. I regret—"

Nimmo broke in. "You said you didn't tab me on the chronoscope, Araman."

"No time," said Araman wearily. "Things don't move any faster on the chronoscope than in real life. You can't speed it up like the film in a book review. We spent a full twenty-four hours trying to catch the important moments during the last six months of Potterley and Foster. There was no time for anything else and it was enough."

"It wasn't," said Nimmo.

"What are you talking about?" There was a sudden infinite alarm on Araman's face.

"I told you my nephew, Jonas, had called me to say he had put important information in a safety-deposit box. He acted as though he were in trouble. He's my nephew. I had to try to get him off the spot. It took a while, then I came here to tell him what I had done. I told you when I got here, just after your man conked me, that I had taken care of a few items."

"What? For heaven's sake—"

"Just this: I sent the details of the portable chronoscope off to half a dozen of my regular publicity outlets."

Not a word. Not a sound. Not a breath. They were all past any demonstration.

"Don't stare like that," cried Nimmo. "Don't you see my point? I had popular publication rights. Jonas will admit that. I knew he couldn't publish scientifically in any legal way. I was sure he was planning to publish illegally and was preparing the safety-deposit box for that reason. I thought if I put through the details prematurely, all the responsibility would be mine. His career would be saved. And if I were deprived of my science-writing license as a result, my exclusive possession of the chronometric data would set me up for life. Jonas would be angry, I expected that, but I could explain the motive and we would split the take fifty-fifty. . . . Don't stare at me like that. How did I know—"

"Nobody knew anything," said Araman bitterly, "but you all just took it for granted that the government was stupidly bureaucratic, vicious, tyrannical, given to suppressing research for the hell of it. It never occurred to any of you that we were trying to protect mankind as best we could."

"Don't sit there talking," wailed Potterley. "Get the names of the people who were told—"

"Too late," said Nimmo, shrugging. "They've had better than a day. There's been time for the word to spread. My outfits will have called any number of physicists to check my data before going on with it and they'll call one another to pass on the news. Once scientists put neutrinics and pseudo-gravitics together, home chronoscopy becomes obvious. Before the week is out, five hundred people will know how to build a small chronoscope and how will you catch them all?" His plump cheeks sagged. "I suppose there's no way of putting the mushroom cloud back into that nice, shiny uranium sphere."

Araman stood up. "We'll try, Potterley, but I agree with Nimmo. It's too late. What kind of a world we'll have from now on, I don't know, I can't tell, but the world we know has been destroyed completely. Until now, every custom, every habit, every tiniest way of life has always taken a certain amount of privacy for granted, but that's all gone now."

He saluted each of the three with elaborate formality.

"You have created a new world among the three of you. I congratulate you. Happy goldfish bowl to you, to me, to everyone, and may each of you fry in hell forever. Arrest rescinded."

ARTHUR C. CLARKE

# The Road to the Sea

*Science fiction constantly speculates about the future of human civilization. In this beautiful story, Arthur C. Clarke shows us a future in which mankind has divided into two major groups—a static civilization and a more dynamic component that has reached out to the stars. Here the two branches meet after a separation lasting thousands of years.*

THE FIRST LEAVES OF AUTUMN WERE FALLING WHEN Durven met his brother on the headland beside the Golden Sphinx. Leaving his flier among the shrubs by the roadside, he walked to the brow of the hill and looked down upon the sea. A bitter wind was toiling across the moors, bearing the threat of early frost, but down in the valley Shastar the Beautiful was still warm and sheltered in its crescent of hills. Its empty quays lay dreaming in the pale, declining sunlight, the deep blue of the sea washing gently against their marble flanks. As he looked down once more into the hauntingly familiar streets and gardens of his youth, Durven felt his resolution failing. He was glad he was meeting Hannar here, a mile from the city, and not among the sights and sounds that would bring his childhood crowding back upon him.

Hannar was a small dot far down the slope, climbing in his old unhurried, leisurely fashion. Durven could have met him in a moment with the flier, but he knew he would receive little thanks if he did. So he waited in the lee of the great sphinx, sometimes walking briskly to and fro to keep warm. Once or twice he went to the head of the monster and stared up at the still face brooding upon the city and the sea. He remembered how as a child in the gardens of Shastar he had seen the crouching shape upon the skyline, and had wondered if it was alive.

Hannar looked no older than he had seemed at their last meeting, twenty years before. His hair was still dark and thick, and his face unwrinkled, for few things ever disturbed the tranquil life of Shastar and its people. It seemed bitterly unfair, and Durven, gray with the years of unrelenting toil, felt a quick spasm of envy stab through his brain.

Their greetings were brief, but not without warmth. Then Hannar

346

walked over to the ship, lying in its bed of heather and crumpled gorse bushes. He rapped his stick upon the curving metal and turned to Durven.

"It's very small. Did it bring you all the way?"

"No: only from the moon. I came back from the project in a liner a hundred times the size of this."

"And where is the project—or don't you want us to know?"

"There's no secret about it. We're building the ships out in space beyond Saturn, where the sun's gravitational gradient is almost flat and it needs little thrust to send them right out of the solar system."

Hannar waved his stick toward the blue waters beneath them, the colored marble of the little towers and the wide streets with their slowly moving traffic.

"Away from all this, out into the darkness and loneliness—in search of what?"

Durven's lips tightened into a thin, determined line.

"Remember," he said quietly, "I have already spent a lifetime away from Earth."

"And has it brought you happiness?" continued Hannar remorselessly.

Durven was silent for a while.

"It has brought me more than that," he replied at last. "I have used my powers to the utmost, and have tasted triumphs that you can never imagine. The day when the First Expedition returned to the solar system was worth a lifetime in Shastar."

"Do you think," asked Hannar, "that you will build fairer cities than this beneath those strange suns, when you have left our world forever?"

"If we feel that impulse, yes. If not, we will build other things. But build we must; and what have your people created in the last hundred years?"

"Because we have made no machines, because we have turned our backs upon the stars and are content with our own world, don't think we have been completely idle. Here in Shastar we have evolved a way of life that I do not think has ever been surpassed. We have studied the art of living; ours is the first aristocracy in which there are no slaves. That is our achievement, by which history will judge us."

"I grant you this," replied Durven, "but never forget that your paradise was built by scientists who had to fight as we have done to make their dreams come true."

"They have not always succeeded. The planets defeated them once; why should the worlds of other suns be more hospitable?"

It was a fair question. After five hundred years, the memory of that first failure was still bitter. With what hopes and dreams had man set out for the planets, in the closing years of the twentieth century—only to find them not merely barren and lifeless, but fiercely hostile! From the sullen fires of the Mercurian lava seas to Pluto's creeping glaciers of solid nitrogen, there was nowhere that he could live unprotected beyond his own world; and to his own world, after a century of fruitless struggle, he had returned.

Yet the vision had not wholly died; when the planets had been abandoned, there were still some who dared to dream of the stars. Out of that dream had come at last the Transcendental Drive, the First Expedition —and now the heady wine of long-delayed success.

"There are fifty solar-type stars within ten years' flight of Earth," Durven replied, "and almost all of them have planets. We believe now that the possession of planets is almost as much a characteristic of a G-type star as its spectrum, though we don't know why. So the search for worlds like Earth was bound to be successful in time; I don't think that we were particularly lucky to find Eden so soon."

"Eden? Is that what you've called your new world?"

"Yes; it seemed appropriate."

"What incurable romantics you scientists are! Perhaps the name's too well-chosen; all the life in that first Eden wasn't friendly to man, if you remember."

Durven gave a bleak smile.

"That, again, depends on one's viewpoint," he replied. He pointed toward Shastar, where the first lights had begun to glimmer. "Unless our ancestors had eaten deeply from the Tree of Knowledge, you would never have had this."

"And what do you suppose will happen to it now?" asked Hannar bitterly. "When you have opened the road to the stars, all the strength and vigor of the race will ebb away from Earth as from an open wound."

"I do not deny it. It has happened before, and it will happen again. Shastar will go the way of Babylon and Carthage and New York. The future is built on the rubble of the past; wisdom lies in facing that fact, not in fighting against it. I have loved Shastar as much as you have done —so much so that now, though I shall never see it again, I dare not go down once more into its streets. You ask me what will become of it, and I will tell you. What we are doing will merely hasten the end. Even twenty years ago, when I was last here, I felt my will being sapped by the aimless ritual of your lives. Soon it will be the same in all the cities of Earth, for every one of them apes Shastar. I think the drive has come none too soon; perhaps even you would believe me if you had spoken to the men who have come back from the stars, and felt the blood stirring in your veins once more after all these centuries of sleep. For your world is dying, Hannar; what you have now you may hold for ages yet, but in the end it will slip from your fingers. The future belongs to us; we will leave you to your dreams. We also have dreamed, and now we go to make our dreams come true."

The last light was catching the brow of the sphinx as the sun sank into the sea and left Shastar to night but not to darkness. The wide streets were luminous rivers carrying a myriad of moving specks; the towers and pinnacles were jeweled with colored lights, and there came a faint sound of wind-borne music as a pleasure boat put slowly out to sea. Smiling a little, Durven watched it draw away from the curving quay. It had been five hundred years or more since the last merchant ship had unloaded its cargo, but while the sea remained, men would still sail upon it.

There was little more to say; and presently Hannar stood alone upon the hill, his head tilted up toward the stars. He would never see his brother again; the sun, which for a few hours had gone from his sight, would soon have vanished from Durven's forever as it shrank into the abyss of space.

Unheeding, Shastar lay glittering in the darkness along the edge of the sea. To Hannar, heavy with foreboding, its doom seemed already almost upon it. There was truth in Durven's words; the exodus was about to begin.

Ten thousand years ago other explorers had set out from the first cities of mankind to discover new lands. They had found them, and had never returned, and time had swallowed their deserted homes. So must it be with Shastar the Beautiful.

Leaning heavily on his stick, Hannar walked slowly down the hillside toward the lights of the city. The sphinx watched him dispassionately as his figure vanished into the distance and the darkness.

It was still watching, five thousand years later.

Brant was not quite twenty when his people were expelled from their homes and driven westward across two continents and an ocean, filling the ether with piteous cries of injured innocence. They received scant sympathy from the rest of the world, for they had only themselves to blame, and could scarcely pretend that the Supreme Council had acted harshly. It had sent them a dozen preliminary warnings and no fewer than four positively final ultimatums before reluctantly taking action. Then one day a small ship with a very large acoustic radiator had suddenly arrived a thousand feet above the village and started to emit several kilowatts of raw noise. After a few hours of this, the rebels had capitulated and begun to pack their belongings. The transport fleet had called a week later and carried them, still protesting shrilly, to their new homes on the other side of the world.

And so the law had been enforced, the law which ruled that no community could remain on the same spot for more than three lifetimes. Obedience meant change, the destruction of traditions and the uprooting of ancient and well-loved homes. That had been the very purpose of the law when it was framed, four thousand years ago; but the stagnation it had sought to prevent could not be warded off much longer. One day there would be no central organization to enforce it, and the scattered villages would remain where they were until time engulfed them as it had the earlier civilizations of which they were the heirs.

It had taken the people of Chaldis the whole of three months to build new homes, remove a square mile of forest, plant some unnecessary crops of exotic and luxurious fruits, re-lay a river and demolish a hill which offended their aesthetic sensibilities. It was quite an impressive performance, and all was forgiven when the local supervisor made a tour of inspection a little later. Then Chaldis watched with great satisfaction as the transports, the digging machines and all the paraphernalia of a mobile and mechanized civilization climbed away into the sky. The sound of their departure had scarcely faded when, as one man, the village relaxed once more into the sloth that it sincerely hoped nothing would disturb for another century at least.

Brant had quite enjoyed the whole adventure. He was sorry, of course, to lose the home that had shaped his childhood; and now he would never climb the proud, lonely mountain that had looked down upon the village of his birth. There were no mountains in this land—only low, rolling hills and fertile valleys in which forests had run rampant for millennia, since agriculture had come to an end. It was warmer, too, than in the old country, for they were nearer the equator and had left behind them the fierce winters of the North. In almost every respect the change was for the good; but for a year or two the people of Chaldis would feel a comfortable glow of martyrdom.

These political matters did not worry Brant in the least. The entire sweep of human history from the dark ages into the unknown future was considerably less important at the moment than the question of Yradne and her feelings toward him. He wondered what Yradne was doing now, and tried to think of an excuse for going to see her. But that would mean meeting her parents, who would embarrass him by their hearty pretense that his call was simply a social one.

He decided to go to the smithy instead, if only to make a check on Jon's movements. It was a pity about Jon; they had been such good friends only a short while ago. But love was friendship's deadliest enemy, and until Yradne had chosen between them they would remain in a state of armed neutrality.

The village sprawled for about a mile along the valley, its neat, new houses arranged in calculated disorder. A few people were moving around in no particular hurry, or gossiping in little groups beneath the trees. To Brant it seemed that everyone was following him with their eyes and talking about him as he passed—an assumption that, as it happened, was perfectly correct. In a closed community of fewer than a thousand highly intelligent people, no one could expect to have any private life.

The smithy was in a clearing at the far end of the village, where its general untidiness would cause as little offense as possible. It was surrounded by broken and half-dismantled machines that Old Johan had not got around to mending. One of the community's three fliers was lying, its bare ribs exposed to the sunlight, where it had been dumped weeks ago with a request for immediate repair. Old Johan would fix it one day, but in his own time.

The wide door of the smithy was open, and from the brilliantly lit interior came the sound of screaming metal as the automatic machines fashioned some new shape to their master's will. Brant threaded his way carefully past the busy slaves and emerged into the relative quiet at the back of the shop.

Old Johan was lying in an excessively comfortable chair, smoking a pipe and looking as if he had never done a day's work in his life. He was a neat little man with a carefully pointed beard, and only his brilliant, ceaselessly roaming eyes showed any signs of animation. He might have been taken for a minor poet—as indeed he fancied himself to be—but never for a village blacksmith.

"Looking for Jon?" he said between puffs. "He's around somewhere, making something for that girl. Beats me what you two see in her."

Brant turned a slight pink and was about to make some sort of reply when one of the machines started calling loudly for attention. In a flash

Old Johan was out of the room, and for a minute strange crashings and bangings and much bad language floated through the doorway. Very soon, however, he was back again in his chair, obviously not expecting to be disturbed for quite a while.

"Let me tell you something, Brant," he continued, as if there had been no interruption. "In twenty years she'll be exactly like her mother. Ever thought of that?"

Brant hadn't, and quailed slightly. But twenty years is an eternity to youth; if he could win Yradne in the present, the future could take care of itself. He told Johan as much.

"Have it your own way," said the smith, not unkindly. "I suppose if we'd all looked that far ahead the human race would have died out a million years ago. Why don't you play a game of chess, like sensible people, to decide who'll have her first?"

"Brant would cheat," answered Jon, suddenly appearing in the entrance and filling most of it. He was a large, well-built youth, in complete contrast to his father, and was carrying a sheet of paper covered with engineering sketches. Brant wondered what sort of present he was making for Yradne.

"What are you doing?" he asked, with a far from disinterested curiosity.

"Why should I tell you?" asked Jon good-naturedly. "Give me one good reason."

Brant shrugged his shoulders.

"I'm sure it's not important—I was only being polite."

"Don't overdo it," said the smith. "The last time you were polite to Jon, you had a black eye for a week. Remember?" He turned to his son, and said brusquely: "Let's see those drawings, so I can tell you why it can't be done."

He examined the sketches critically, while Jon showed increasing signs of embarrassment. Presently Johan snorted disapprovingly and said: "Where are you going to get the components? They're all nonstandard, and most of them are submicro."

Jon looked hopefully around the workshop.

"There aren't very many of them," he said. "It's a simple job, and I was wondering . . ."

". . . if I'd let you mess up the integrators to try to make the pieces? Well, we'll see about that. My talented son, Brant, is trying to prove that he possesses brains as well as brawn, by making a toy that's been obsolete for about fifty centuries. I hope you can do better than that. Now when I was your age . . ."

His voice and his reminiscences trailed off into silence. Yradne had drifted in from the clangorous bustle of the machine shop, and was watching them from the doorway with a faint smile on her lips.

It is probable that if Brant and Jon had been asked to describe Yradne, it would have seemed as if they were speaking of two entirely different people. There would have been superficial points of resemblance, of course. Both would have agreed that her hair was chestnut, her eyes large and blue and her skin that rarest of colors—an almost pearly white. But to Jon she seemed a fragile little creature, to be cherished and protected; while to Brant her self-confidence and complete assurance were so obvious that he despaired of ever being of any service to her. Part of that difference in outlook was due to Jon's extra six inches of height and nine inches of girth, but most of it came from profounder psychological causes. The person one loves never really exists, but is a projection focused through the lens of the mind onto whatever screen it fits with least distortion. Brant and Jon had quite different ideals, and each believed that Yradne embodied them. This would not have surprised her in the least, for few things ever did.

"I'm going down to the river," she said. "I called for you on the way, Brant, but you were out."

That was a blow at Jon, but she quickly equalized.

"I thought you'd gone off with Lorayne or some other girl, but I knew I'd find Jon at home."

Jon looked very smug at this unsolicited and quite inaccurate testimonial. He rolled up his drawings and dashed off into the house, calling happily over his shoulder: "Wait for me—I won't be long!"

Brant never took his eyes off Yradne as he shifted uncomfortably from one foot to the other. She hadn't actually invited *anyone* to come with her, and until definitely ordered off, he was going to stand his ground. But he remembered that there was a somewhat ancient saying to the effect that if two were company, three were the reverse.

Jon returned, resplendent in a surprising green cloak with diagonal explosions of red down the sides. Only a very young man could have got away with it, and even Jon barely succeeded. Brant wondered if there was time for him to hurry home and change into something still more startling, but that would be too great a risk to take. It would be flying in the face of the enemy; the battle might be over before he could get his reinforcements.

"Quite a crowd," remarked Old Johan unhelpfully as they departed. "Mind if I come along too?" The boys looked embarrassed, but Yradne gave a gay little laugh that made it hard for him to dislike her. He stood in the outer doorway for a while, smiling as they went away through the trees and down the long, grass-covered slope to the river. But presently his eyes ceased to follow them, as he lost himself in dreams as vain as any that can come to man—the dreams of his own departed youth. Very soon he turned his back upon the sunlight and, no longer smiling now, disappeared into the busy tumult of the workshop.

Now the northward-climbing sun was passing the equator, the days would soon be longer than the nights and the rout of winter was complete. The countless villages throughout the hemisphere were preparing to greet the spring. With the dying of the great cities and the return of man to the fields and woods, he had returned also to many of the ancient customs that had slumbered through a thousand years of urban civilization. Some of those customs had been deliberately revived by the anthropologists and social engineers of the third millennium, whose genius had sent so many patterns of human culture safely down the ages. So it was that the spring equinox was still welcomed by rituals which, for all their sophistication, would have seemed less strange to primitive man than to the people of the industrial cities whose smoke had once stained the skies of Earth.

The arrangements for the Spring Festival were always the subject of much intrigue and bickering between neighboring villages. Although it involved the disruption of all other activities for at least a month, any village was greatly honored to be chosen as host for the celebrations. A newly settled community, still recovering from transplantation, would not, of course, be expected to take on such a responsibility. Brant's people, however, had thought of an ingenious way of regaining favor and wiping out the stain of their recent disgrace. There were five other villages within a hundred miles, and all had been invited to Chaldis for the festival.

The invitation had been very carefully worded. It hinted delicately that, for obvious reasons, Chaldis couldn't hope to arrange as elaborate a ceremonial as it might have wished, and thereby implied that if the guests wanted a really good time they had better go elsewhere. Chaldis expected one acceptance at the most, but the inquisitiveness of its neighbors had overcome their sense of moral superiority. They had all said that they would be delighted to come; and there was no possible way in which Chaldis could now evade its responsibities.

There was no night and little sleep in the valley. High above the trees a row of artificial suns burned with a steady, blue white brilliance, banishing the stars and the darkness and throwing into chaos the natural routine of all the wild creatures for miles around. Through lengthening days and shortening nights, men and machines were battling to make ready the great amphitheater needed to hold some four thousand people. In one respect at least, they were lucky: there was no need for a roof or any artificial heating in this climate. In the land they had so reluctantly left, the snow would still be thick upon the ground at the end of March.

Brant woke early on the great day to the sound of aircraft falling down from the skies above him. He stretched himself wearily, wondering when he would get to bed again, and then climbed into his clothes. A kick with his foot at a concealed switch and the rectangle of yielding foam rubber, an inch below floor level, was completely covered by a rigid plastic sheet that had unrolled from within the wall. There was no bed linen to worry about because the room was kept automatically at body temperature. In many such ways Brant's life was simpler than those of his remote ancestors —simpler through the ceaseless and almost forgotten efforts of five thousand years of science.

The room was softly lit by light pouring through one translucent wall, and was quite incredibly untidy. The only clear floor space was that concealing the bed, and probably this would have to be cleared again by nightfall. Brant was a great hoarder and hated to throw anything away. This was a very unusual characteristic in a world where few things were of value because they could be made so easily, but the objects Brant collected were not those that the integrators were used to creating. In one corner a small tree trunk was propped against the wall, partly carved into a vaguely anthropomorphic shape. Large lumps of sandstone and marble were scattered elsewhere over the floor, until such time as Brant decided to work on them. The walls were completely covered with paintings, most of them abstract in character. It would have needed very little intelligence to deduce that Brant was an artist; it was not so easy to decide if he was a good one.

He picked his way through the debris and went in search of food. There was no kitchen; some historians maintained that it had survived until as late as A.D. 2500, but long before then most families made their own meals about as often as they made their own clothes. Brant walked into the main living room and went across to a metal box set in the wall at chest level. At its center was something that would have been quite familiar to every human being for the last fifty centuries—a ten-digit impulse dial. Brant called a four-figure number and waited. Nothing whatsoever happened. Looking a little annoyed, he pressed a concealed button and the front of the apparatus slid open, revealing an interior which should, by all the rules, have contained an appetizing breakfast. It was completely empty.

Brant could call up the central food machine to demand an explanation, but there would probably be no answer. It was quite obvious what had happened—the catering department was so busy preparing for the day's overload that he'd be lucky if he got any breakfast at all. He cleared the circuit, then tried again with a little-used number. This time there was a gentle purr, a dull click, and the doors slid open to reveal a cup of some dark, steaming beverage, a few not-very-exciting-looking sandwiches and a large slice of melon. Wrinkling up his nose, and wondering how long mankind would take to slip back to barbarism at this rate, Brant started on his substitute meal and very soon polished it off.

His parents were still asleep as he went quietly out of the house into the wide, grass-covered square at the center of the village. It was still very early and there was a slight chill in the air, but the day was clear and fine, with that freshness which seldom lingers after the last dew has gone. Several aircraft were lying on the green, disgorging passengers, who were milling around in circles or wandering off to examine Chaldis with critical eyes. As Brant watched, one of the machines went humming briskly up into the sky, leaving a faint trail of ionization behind it. A moment later the others followed; they could carry only a few dozen passengers and would have to make many trips before the day was out.

Brant strolled over to the visitors, trying to look self-assured yet not so aloof as to discourage all contacts. Most of the strangers were about his own age—the older people would be arriving at a more reasonable time.

They looked at him with a frank curiosity which he returned with interest. Their skins were much darker than his, he noticed, and their voices were softer and less modulated. Some of them even had a trace of accent, for despite a universal language and instantaneous communication, regional variations still existed. At least, Brant assumed that they were the ones with accents; but once or twice he caught them smiling a little as he spoke.

Throughout the morning the visitors gathered in the square and made their way to the great arena that had been ruthlessly carved out of the forest. There were tents and bright banners here, and much shouting and laughter, for the morning was for the amusement of the young. Though Athens had swept like a dwindling but never-dying beacon for ten thousand years down the river of time, the pattern of sport had scarcely changed since those first Olympic days. Men still ran and jumped and wrestled and swam; but they did all these things a good deal better now than their ancestors. Brant was a fair sprinter over short distances and managed to finish third in the hundred meters. His time was just over eight seconds, which was not very good, because the record was less than seven. Brant would have been much amazed to learn that there was a time when no one in the world could have approached this figure.

Jon enjoyed himself hugely, bouncing youths even larger than himself onto the patient turf, and when the morning's results were added up, Chaldis had scored more points than any of the visitors, although it had been first in relatively few events.

As noon approached, the crowd began to flow amoebalike down to Five Oaks Glade, where the molecular synthesizers had been working since the early hours to cover hundreds of tables with food. Much skill had gone into preparing the prototypes which were being reproduced with absolute fidelity down to the last atom; for though the mechanics of food production had altered completely, the art of the chef had survived, and had even gone forward to victories in which nature had played no part at all.

The main feature of the afternoon was a long poetic drama—a pastiche put together with considerable skill from the works of poets whose very names had been forgotten ages since. On the whole Brant found it boring, though there were some fine lines here and there that had stuck in his memory:

> For winter's rains and ruins are over,
> And all the season of snows and sins . . .

Brant knew about snow, and was glad to have left it behind. Sin, however, was an archaic word that had dropped out of use three or four thousand years ago; but it had an ominous and exciting ring.

He did not catch up with Yradne until it was almost dusk, and the dancing had begun. High above the valley, floating lights had started to burn, flooding the woods with ever-changing patterns of blue and red and gold. In twos and threes and then in dozens and hundreds, the dancers moved out into the great oval of the amphitheater, until it became a sea of laughing, whirling forms. Here at last was something at which Brant could beat Jon handsomely, and he let himself be swept away on the tide of sheer physical enjoyment.

The music ranged through the whole spectrum of human culture. At one moment the air pulsed to the throb of drums that might have called from some primeval jungle when the world was young; and a little later, intricate tapestries of quarter-tones were being woven by subtle electronic skills. The stars peered down wanly as they marched across the sky, but no one saw them and no one gave any thought to the passage of time.

Brant had danced with many girls before he found Yradne. She looked very beautiful, brimming over with the enjoyment of life, and she seemed in no hurry to join him when there were so many others to choose from. But at last they were circling together in the whirlpool, and it gave Brant no small pleasure to think that Jon was probably watching them glumly from afar.

They broke away from the dance during a pause in the music, because Yradne announced that she was a little tired. This suited Brant admirably, and presently they were sitting together under one of the great trees, watching the ebb and flow of life around them with that detachment that comes in moments of complete relaxation.

It was Brant who broke the spell. It had to be done, and it might be a long time before such an opportunity came again.

"Yradne," he said, "why have you been avoiding me?"

She looked at him with innocent, open eyes.

"Oh, Brant," she replied, "what an unkind thing to say; you know it isn't true! I wish you weren't so jealous: you can't expect me to be following you around *all* the time."

"Oh, very well!" said Brant weakly, wondering if he was making a fool of himself. But he might as well go on now he had started.

"You know, *some* day you'll have to decide between us. If you keep putting it off, perhaps you'll be left high and dry like those two aunts of yours."

Yradne gave a tinkling laugh and tossed her head with great amusement at the thought that she could ever be old and ugly.

"Even if you're too impatient," she replied, "I think I can rely on Jon. Have you seen what he's given me?"

"No," said Brant, his heart sinking.

"You *are* observant, aren't you! Haven't you noticed this necklace?"

On her breast Yradne was wearing a large group of jewels, suspended from her neck by a thin golden chain. It was quite a fine pendant, but there was nothing particularly unusual about it, and Brant wasted no time in saying so. Yradne smiled mysteriously and her fingers flickered toward her throat. Instantly the air was suffused with the sound of music, which first mingled with the background of the dance and then drowned it completely.

"You see," she said proudly, "wherever I go now I can have music with me. Jon says there are so many thousands of hours of it stored up that I'll never know when it repeats itself. Isn't it clever?"

"Perhaps it is," said Brant grudgingly, "but it isn't exactly new. Everyone used to carry this sort of thing once, until there was no silence anywhere on Earth and they had to be forbidden. Just think of the chaos if we all had them!"

Yradne broke away from him angrily.

"There you go again—always jealous of something you can't do yourself. What have you ever given me that's half as clever or useful as this? I'm going—and don't try to follow me!"

Brant stared open-mouthed as she went, quite taken aback by the violence of her reaction. Then he called after her, "Hey, Yradne, I didn't mean . . ." But she was gone.

He made his way out of the amphitheater in a very bad temper. It did him no good at all to rationalize the cause of Yradne's outburst. His remarks, though rather spiteful, had been true, and sometimes there is nothing more annoying than the truth. Jon's gift was an ingenious but trivial toy, interesting only because it now happened to be unique.

One thing she had said still rankled in his mind. What *was* there he had ever given Yradne? He had nothing but his paintings, and they weren't really very good. She had shown no interest in them at all when he had offered her some of his best, and it had been very hard to explain that he wasn't a portrait painter and would rather not try to make a picture of her. She had never really understood this, and it had been very difficult not to hurt her feelings. Brant liked taking his inspiration from nature, but he never copied what he saw. When one of his pictures was finished (which occasionally happened), the title was often the only clue to the original source.

The music of the dance still throbbed around him, but he had lost all interest; the sight of other people enjoying themselves was more than he could stand. He decided to get away from the crowd, and the only peaceful place he could think of was down by the river, at the end of the shining carpet of freshly planted glow-moss that led through the wood.

He sat at the water's edge, throwing twigs into the current and watching them drift downstream. From time to time other idlers strolled by, but they were usually in pairs and took no notice of him. He watched them enviously and brooded over the unsatisfactory state of his affairs.

It would almost be better, he thought, if Yradne did make up her mind to choose Jon, and so put him out of his misery. But she showed not the slightest sign of preferring one to the other. Perhaps she was simply enjoying herself at their expense, as some people—particularly Old Johan —maintained; though it was just as likely that she was genuinely unable to choose. What was wanted, Brant thought morosely, was for one of them to do something really spectacular which the other could not hope to match.

"Hello," said a small voice behind him. He twisted around and looked over his shoulder. A little girl of eight or so was staring at him with her head slightly on one side, like an inquisitive sparrow.

"Hello," he replied without enthusiasm. "Why aren't you watching the dance?"

"Why aren't you in it?" she replied promptly.

"I'm tired," he said, hoping that this was an adequate excuse. "You shouldn't be running around by yourself. You might get lost."

"I am lost," she replied happily, sitting down on the bank beside him. "I like it that way." Brant wondered which of the other villages she had come from; she was quite a pretty little thing, but would look prettier with less chocolate on her face. It seemed that his solitude was at an end.

She stared at him with that disconcerting directness which, perhaps fortunately, seldom survives childhood. "*I* know what's the matter with you," she said suddenly.

"Indeed?" queried Brant with polite skepticism.

"You're in love!"

Brant dropped the twig he was about to throw into the river, and turned to stare at his inquisitor. She was looking at him with such solemn sympathy that in a moment all his morbid self-pity vanished in a gale of laughter. She seemed quite hurt, and he quickly brought himself under control.

"How could you tell?" he asked with profound seriousness.

"I've read all about it," she replied solemnly. "And once I saw a picture play and there was a man in it and he came down to a river and sat there just like you and presently he jumped into it. There was some awful pretty music then."

Brant looked thoughtfully at this precocious child and felt relieved that she didn't belong to his own community.

"I'm sorry I can't arrange the music," he said gravely, "but in any case the river isn't really deep enough."

"It is farther along," came the helpful reply. "This is only a baby river here—it doesn't grow up until it leaves the woods. I saw it from the flier."

"What happens to it then?" asked Brant, not in the least interested, but thankful that the conversation had taken a more innocuous turn. "I suppose it reaches the sea?"

She gave an unladylike sniff of disgust.

"Of course not, silly. All the rivers this side of the hills go to the Great Lake. I know that's as big as a sea, but the *real* sea is on the other side of the hills."

Brant had learned very little about the geographical details of his new home, but he realized that the child was quite correct. The ocean was less than twenty miles to the north, but separated from them by a barrier of low hills. A hundred miles inland lay the Great Lake, bringing life to lands that had been desert before the geological engineers had reshaped this continent.

The child genius was making a map out of twigs and patiently explaining these matters to her rather dull pupil.

"Here we are," she said, "and here's the river, and the hills, and the lake's over there by your foot. The sea goes along here—and I'll tell you a secret."

"What's that?"

"You'll never guess!"

"I don't suppose I will."

Her voice dropped to a confidential whisper. "If you go along the coast —it isn't very far from here—you'll come to Shastar."

Brant tried to look impressed, but failed.

"I don't believe you've ever heard of it!" she cried, deeply disappointed.

"I'm sorry," replied Brant. "I suppose it was a city, and I know I've heard of it somewhere. But there were such a lot of them, you know— Carthage and Chicago and Babylon and Berlin—you simply can't remember them all. And they've all gone now, anyway."

"Not Shastar. It's still there."

"Well, some of the later ones are still standing, more or less, and people often visit them. About five hundred miles from my old home there was quite a big city once, called . . ."

"Shastar isn't just *any* old city," interrupted the child mysteriously. "My grandfather told me about it: he's been there. It hasn't been spoiled at all and it's still full of wonderful things that no one has any more."

Brant smiled inwardly. The deserted cities of Earth had been the breeding places of legends for countless centuries. It would be four—no, nearer five—thousand years since Shastar had been abandoned. If its buildings were still standing, which was of course quite possible, they would certainly have been stripped of all valuables ages ago. It seemed that Grandfather had been inventing some pretty fairy stories to entertain the child. He had Brant's sympathy.

Heedless of his skepticism, the girl prattled on. Brant gave only half his mind to her words, interjecting a polite "Yes" or "Fancy that" as occasion demanded. Suddenly, silence fell.

He looked up and found that his companion was staring with much annoyance toward the avenue of trees that overlooked the view.

"Good-by," she said abruptly. "I've got to hide somewhere else—here comes my sister."

She was gone as suddenly as she had arrived. Her family must have a busy time looking after her, Brant decided: but she had done him a good turn by dispelling his melancholy mood.

Within a few hours, he realized that she had done very much more than that.

Simon was leaning against his doorpost watching the world go by when Brant came in search of him. The world usually accelerated slightly when it had to pass Simon's door, for he was an interminable talker and once he had trapped a victim there was no escape for an hour or more. It was most unusual for anyone to walk voluntarily into his clutches, as Brant was doing now.

The trouble with Simon was that he had a first-class mind, and was too lazy to use it. Perhaps he might have been luckier had he been born in a more energetic age; all he had ever been able to do in Chaldis was to sharpen his wits at other people's expense, thereby gaining more fame than popularity. But he was quite indispensable, for he was a storehouse of knowledge, the greater part of it perfectly accurate.

"Simon," began Brant without any preamble. "I want to learn something about this country. The maps don't tell me much—they're too new. What was here, back in the old days?"

Simon scratched his wiry beard.

"I don't suppose it was very different. How long ago do you mean?"

"Oh, back in the time of the cities."

"There weren't so many trees, of course. This was probably agricultural land, used for food production. Did you see that farming machine they dug up when the amphitheater was being built? It must have been old; it wasn't even electric."

"Yes," said Brant impatiently. "I saw it. But tell me about the cities around here. According to the map, there was a place called Shastar a few hundred miles west of us along the coast. Do you know anything about it?"

"Ah, Shastar," murmured Simon, stalling for time. "A very interesting place; I think I've even got a picture of it around somewhere. Just a moment while I go and see."

He disappeared into the house and was gone for nearly five minutes. In that time he made a very extensive library search, though a man from the age of books would hardly have guessed this from his actions. All the records Chaldis possessed were in a metal case a meter on a side; it contained, locked perpetually in subatomic patterns, the equivalent of a billion volumes of print. Almost all the knowledge of mankind, and the whole of its surviving literature, lay here concealed.

It was not merely a passive storehouse of wisdom, for it possessed a librarian. As Simon signaled his request to the tireless machine, the search went down, layer by layer, through the almost infinite network of circuits. It took only a fraction of a second to locate the information he needed, for he had given the name and the approximate date. Then he relaxed as the mental images came flooding into his brain, under the lightest of self-hypnosis. The knowledge would remain in his possession for a few hours only—long enough for his purpose—and would then fade away. Simon had no desire to clutter up his well-organized mind with irrelevancies, and to him the whole story of the rise and fall of the great cities was a historical digression of no particular importance. It was an interesting, if a regrettable, episode, and it belonged to a past that had irretrievably vanished.

Brant was still waiting patiently when he emerged, looking very wise.

"I couldn't find any pictures," he said. "My wife has been tidying up again. But I'll tell you what I can remember about Shastar."

Brant settled himself down as comfortably as he could; he was likely to be here for some time.

"Shastar was one of the very last cities that man ever built. You know, of course, that cities arose quite late in human culture—only about twelve thousand years ago. They grew in number and importance for several thousand years, until at last there were some containing millions of people. It is very hard for us to imagine what it must have been like to live in such places—deserts of steel and stone with not even a blade of grass for miles. But they were necessary, before transport and communication had been perfected, and people had to live near each other to carry out all the intricate operations of trade and manufacture upon which their lives depended.

"The really great cities began to disappear when air transport became universal. The threat of attack in those far-off, barbarous days also helped to disperse them. But for a long time . . ."

"I've studied the history of that period," interjected Brant, not very truthfully. "I know all about . . ."

". . . for a long time there were still many small cities which were held together by cultural rather than commercial links. They had populations of a few score thousand and lasted for centuries after the passing of the giants. That's why Oxford and Princeton and Heidelberg still mean something to us, while far larger cities are no more than names. But even these were doomed when the invention of the integrator made it possible for any community, however small, to manufacture without effort everything it needed for civilized living.

"Shastar was built when there was no longer any need, technically, for cities, but before people realized that the culture of cities was coming to its end. It seems to have been a conscious work of art, conceived and designed as a whole, and those who lived there were mostly artists of some kind. But it didn't last very long; what finally killed it was the exodus."

Simon became suddenly quiet, as if brooding on those tumultuous centuries when the road to the stars had been opened up and the world was torn in twain. Along that road the flower of the race had gone, leaving the rest behind; and thereafter it seemed that history had come to an end on Earth. For a thousand years or more the exiles had returned fleetingly to the solar system, wistfully eager to tell of strange suns and far planets and the great empire that would one day span the galaxy. But there are gulfs that even the swiftest ships can never cross; and such a gulf was opening now between Earth and her wandering children. They had less and less in common; the returning ships became ever more infrequent, until at last generations passed between the visits from outside. Simon had not heard of any such for almost three hundred years.

It was unusual when one had to prod Simon into speech, but presently Brant remarked: "Anyway, I'm more interested in the place itself than its history. Do you think it's still standing?"

"I was coming to that," said Simon, emerging from his reverie with a start. "Of course it is; they built well in those days. But why are you so interested, may I ask? Have you suddenly developed an overwhelming passion for archaeology? Oh, I think I understand!"

Brant knew perfectly well the uselessness of trying to conceal anything from a professional busybody like Simon.

"I was hoping," he said defensively, "that there might still be things worth going to find, even after all this time."

"Perhaps," said Simon doubtfully. "I must visit it one day. It's almost on our doorstep, as it were. But how are *you* going to manage? The village will hardly let you borrow a flier! And you can't walk. It would take you at least a week to get there."

But that was exactly what Brant intended to do. As, during the next few days, he was careful to point out to almost everyone in the village, a thing wasn't worth doing unless one did it the hard way. There was nothing like making a virtue out of a necessity.

Brant's preparations were carried out in an unprecedented blaze of secrecy. He did not wish to be too specific about his plans, such as they were, in case any of the dozen or so people in Chaldis who had the right to use a flier decided to look at Shastar first. It was, of course, only a matter of time before this happened, but the feverish activity of the past months had prevented such explorations. Nothing would be more humiliating than to stagger into Shastar after a week's journey, only to be coolly greeted by a neighbor who had made the trip in ten minutes.

On the other hand, it was equally important that the village in general, and Yradne in particular, should realize that he was making some exceptional effort. Only Simon knew the truth, and he had grudgingly agreed to keep quiet for the present. Brant hoped that he had managed to divert attention from his true objective by showing a great interest in the country to the *east* of Chaldis, which also contained several archaeological relics of some importance.

The amount of food and equipment one needed for a two or three weeks' absence was really astonishing, and his first calculations had thrown Brant into a state of considerable gloom. For a while he had even thought of trying to beg or borrow a flier, but the request would certainly not be granted—and would indeed defeat the whole object of his enterprise. Yet it was quite impossible for him to carry everything he needed for the journey.

The solution would have been perfectly obvious to anyone from a less mechanized age, but it took Brant some little time to think of it. The flying machine had killed all forms of land transport save one, the oldest and most versatile of all—the only one that was self-perpetuating and could manage very well, as it had done before, with no assistance at all from man.

Chaldis possessed six horses, rather a small number for a community of its size. In some villages the horses outnumbered the humans, but Brant's people, living in a wild and mountainous region, had so far had little opportunity for equitation. Brant himself had ridden a horse only two or three times in his life, and then for exceedingly short periods.

The stallion and five mares were in the charge of Treggor, a snarled little man who had no discernible interest in life except animals. His was not one of the outstanding intellects of Chaldis, but he seemed perfectly happy running his private menagerie, which included dogs of many shapes and sizes, a couple of beavers, several monkeys, a lion cub, two bears, a young crocodile and other beasts more usually admired from a distance. The only sorrow that had ever clouded his placid life arose from the fact that he had so far failed to obtain an elephant.

Brant found Treggor, as he expected, leaning on the gate of the paddock. There was a stranger with him, who was introduced to Brant as a horse fancier from a neighboring village. The curious similarity between the two men, extending from the way they dressed even to their facial expressions, made this explanation quite unnecessary.

One always feels a certain nervousness in the presence of undoubted experts, and Brant outlined his problem with some diffidence. Treggor listened gravely and paused for a long time before replying.

"Yes," he said slowly, jerking his thumb toward the mares, "any of them would do—if you knew how to handle 'em." He looked rather doubtfully at Brant.

"They're like human beings, you know; if they don't like you, you can't do a thing with them."

"Not a thing," echoed the stranger, with evident relish.

"But surely you could teach me how to handle them?"

"Maybe yes, maybe no. I remember a young fellow just like you, wanted to learn to ride. Horses just wouldn't let him get near them. Took a dislike to him—and that was that."

"Horses can *tell,*" interjected the other darkly.

"That's right," agreed Treggor. "You've got to be sympathetic. Then you've nothing to worry about."

There was, Brant decided, quite a lot to be said for the less temperamental machine after all.

"I don't want to ride," he answered with some feeling. "I only want a horse to carry my gear. Or would it be likely to object to that?"

His mild sarcasm was quite wasted. Treggor nodded solemnly.

"That wouldn't be any trouble," he said. "They'll all let you lead them with a halter—all except Daisy, that is. You'd never catch *her.*"

"Then do you think I could borrow one of the—er, more amendable ones—for a while?"

Treggor shuffled around uncertainly, torn between two conflicting desires. He was pleased that someone wanted to use his beloved beasts, but nervous lest they come to harm. Any damage that might befall Brant was of secondary importance.

"Well," he began doubtfully, "it's a bit awkward at the moment. . . ."

Brant looked at the mares more closely, and realized why. Only one of them was accompanied by a foal, but it was obvious that this deficiency would soon be rectified. Here was another complication he had overlooked.

"How long will you be away?" asked Treggor.

"Three weeks, at the most: perhaps only two."

Treggor did some rapid gynecological calculations.

"Then you can have Sunbeam," he concluded. "She won't give you any trouble at all—best-natured animal I've ever had."

"Thank you very much," said Brant. "I promise I'll look after her. Now would you mind introducing us?"

"I don't see why I should do this," grumbled Jon good-naturedly, as he adjusted the panniers on Sunbeam's sleek sides, "especially since you won't even tell me where you're going or what you expect to find."

Brant couldn't have answered the last question even had he wished. In his more rational moments he knew that he would find nothing of value in Shastar. Indeed, it was hard to think of anything that his people did not already possess, or could not obtain instantly if they wished. But the journey itself would be the proof—the most convincing he could imagine —of his love for Yradne.

There was no doubt that she was quite impressed by his preparations, and he had been careful to underline the dangers he was about to face. It would be very uncomfortable sleeping in the open, and he would have a most monotonous diet. He might even get lost and never be seen again. Suppose there were still wild beasts—dangerous ones—up in the hills or in the forests?

Old Johan, who had no feeling for historical traditons, had protested at the indignity of a blacksmith having anything to do with such a primitive survival as a horse. Sunbeam had nipped him delicately for this, with great skill and precision, while he was bending to examine her hoofs. But he had rapidly manufactured a set of panniers in which Brant could put everything he needed for the journey—even his drawing materials, from which he refused to be separated. Treggor had advised on the technical details of the harness, producing ancient prototypes consisting largely of string.

It was still early morning when the last adjustments had been completed; Brant had intended making his departure as unobtrusive as possible, and his complete success was slightly mortifying. Only Jon and Yradne came to see him off.

They walked in thoughtful silence to the end of the village and crossed the slim metal bridge over the river. Then Jon said gruffly: "Well, don't go and break your silly neck," shook hands, and departed, leaving him alone with Yradne. It was a very nice gesture, and Brant appreciated it.

Taking advantage of her master's preoccupation, Sunbeam began to browse among the long grass by the river's edge. Brant shifted awkwardly from foot to foot for a moment, then said half-heartedly:

"I suppose I'd better be going."

"How long will you be away?" asked Yradne. She wasn't wearing Jon's present: perhaps she had grown tired of it already. Brant hoped so—then realized she might lose interest equally quickly in anything he brought back for her.

"Oh, about a fortnight—if all goes well," he added darkly.

"Do be careful," said Yradne, in tones of vague urgency, "and don't do anything rash."

"I'll do my best," answered Brant, still making no move to go, "but one has to take risks sometimes."

This disjointed conversation might have lasted a good deal longer had Sunbeam not taken charge. Brant's arm received a sudden jerk and he was dragged away at a brisk walk. He had regained his balance and was about to wave farewell when Yradne came flying up to him, gave him a large kiss and disappeared toward the village before he could recover.

She slowed down to a walk when Brant could no longer see her. Jon was still a good way ahead, but she made no attempt to overtake him. A curiously solemn feeling, out of place on this bright spring morning, had overcome her. It was very pleasant to be loved, but it had its disadvantages if one stopped to look beyond the immediate moment. For a fleeting instant Yradne wondered if she had been fair to Jon, to Brant—even to herself. One day the decision would have to be made; it could not be postponed forever. Yet she could not for the life of her decide which of the boys she liked the better; and she did not know if she loved either.

No one had ever told her, and she had not yet discovered, that when one has to ask "Am I really in love?" the answer is always "No."

Beyond Chaldis the forest stretched for five miles to the east, then faded out into the great plain which spanned the remainder of the continent. Six thousand years ago this land had been one of the mightiest deserts in the world, and its reclamation had been among the first achievements of the Atomic Age.

Brant intended to go east until he was clear of the forest, and then to turn toward the high land of the North. According to the maps, there had once been a road along the spine of the hills, linking together all the cities on the coast in a chain that ended at Shastar. It should be easy to follow its track, though Brant did not expect that much of the road itself would have survived the centuries.

He kept close to the river, hoping that it had not changed its path since the maps were made. It was both his guide and his highway through the forest; when the trees were too thick, he and Sunbeam could always wade in the shallow water. Sunbeam was quite cooperative; there was no grass here to distract her, so she plodded methodically along with little prompting.

Soon after midday the trees began to thin out. Brant had reached the frontier that, century by century, had been on the march across the lands that man no longer wished to hold. A little later the forest was behind him and he was out in the open plain.

He checked his position from the map, and noted that the trees had advanced an appreciable distance eastward since it was drawn. But there was a clear route north to the low hills along which the ancient road had run, and he should be able to reach them before evening.

At this point certain unforeseen difficulties of a technical nature arose. Sunbeam, finding herself surrounded by the most appetizing grass she had seen for a long time, was unable to resist pausing every three or four steps to collect a mouthful. As Brant was attached to her bridle by a rather short rope, the resulting jerk almost dislocated his arm. Lengthening the rope made matters even worse, because he then had no control at all.

Now Brant was quite fond of animals, but it soon became apparent to him that Sunbeam was simply imposing on his good nature. He put up with it for half a mile, and then steered a course toward a tree which seemed to have particularly slender and lissom branches. Sunbeam watched him warily out of the corners of her limpid brown eyes as he cut a fine, resilient switch and attached it ostentatiously to his belt. Then she set off so briskly that he could scarcely keep pace with her.

She was undoubtedly, as Treggor had claimed, a singularly intelligent beast.

The range of hills that was Brant's first objective was less than two thousand feet high, and the slope was very gentle. But there were numerous annoying foothills and minor valleys to be surmounted on the way to the crest, and it was well toward evening before they had reached the highest point. To the south Brant could see the forest through which he had come, and which could now hinder him no more. Chaldis was somewhere in its midst, though he had only a rough idea of its location; he was surprised to find that he could see no signs of the great clearings that his people had made. To the southeast the plain stretched endlessly away, a level sea of grass dotted with little clumps of trees. Near the horizon Brant could see tiny, creeping specks, and guessed that some great herd of wild animals was on the move.

Northward lay the sea, only a dozen miles away down the long slope and across the lowlands. It seemed almost black in the falling sunlight, except where tiny breakers dotted it with flecks of foam.

Before nightfall Brant found a hollow out of the wind, anchored Sunbeam to a stout bush and pitched the little tent that Old Johan had contrived for him. This was, in theory, a very simple operation, but, as a good many people had found before, it was one that could tax skill and temper to the utmost. At last everything was finished, and he settled down for the night.

There are some things that no amount of pure intelligence can anticipate, but which can only be learned by bitter experience. Who would have guessed that the human body was so sensitive to the almost imperceptible slope on which the tent had been pitched? More uncomfortable still were the minute thermal differences between one point and another, presumably caused by the draughts that seemed to wander through the tent at will. Brant could have endured a uniform temperature gradient, but the unpredictable variations were maddening.

He woke from his fitful sleep a dozen times, or so it seemed, and toward dawn his morale had reached its lowest ebb. He felt cold and miserable and stiff, as if he had not slept properly for days, and it would have needed very little persuasion to have made him abandon the whole enterprise. He was prepared—even willing—to face danger in the cause of love; but lumbago was a different matter.

The discomforts of the night were soon forgotten in the glory of the new day. Here on the hills the air was fresh with the tang of salt, borne by the wind that came climbing up from the sea. The dew was everywhere, hanging thickly on each bent blade of grass—but so soon to be destroyed beyond all trace by the steepening sun. It was good to be alive; it was better to be young; it was best of all to be in love.

They came upon the road very soon after they had started the day's journey. Brant had missed it before because it had been farther down the seaward slope, and he had expected to find it on the crest of the hill. It had been superbly built, and the millennia had touched it lightly. Nature had tried in vain to obliterate it; here and there she succeeded in burying a few meters with a light blanket of earth, but then her servants had turned against her and the wind and the rain had scoured it clean once more. In a great jointless band, skirting the edge of the sea for more than a thousand miles, the road still linked the cities that man had loved in his childhood.

It was one of the great roads of the world. Once it had been no more than a footpath along which savage tribes had come down to the sea, to barter with wily, bright-eyed merchants from distant lands. Then it had known new and more exacting masters; the soldiers of a mighty empire had shaped and hewn the road so skillfully along the hills that the path they gave it had remained unchanged down all the ages. They had paved it with stone so that their armies could move more swiftly than any that the world had known; and along the road their legions had been hurled like thunderbolts at the bidding of the city whose name they bore. Centuries later, that city had called them home in its last extremity; and the road had rested then for five hundred years.

But other wars were still to come; beneath crescent banners the armies

of the Prophet were yet to storm westward into Christendom. Later still
—centuries later—the tide of the last and greatest of conflicts was to turn
here, as steel monsters clashed together in the desert, and the sky itself
rained death.

The centurions, the paladins, the armored divisions—even the desert
—all were gone. But the road remained, of all man's creations the most
enduring. For ages enough it had borne his burdens; and now along its
whole thousand miles it carried no more traffic than one boy and a horse.

Brant followed the road for three days, keeping always in sight of the
sea. He had grown used to the minor discomforts of a nomadic existence,
and even the nights were no longer intolerable. The weather had been
perfect—long, warm days and mild nights—but the fine spell was coming
to an end.

He estimated that he was less than five miles from Shastar on the
evening of the fourth day. The road was now turning away from the coast
to avoid a great headland jutting out to sea. Beyond this was the sheltered
bay along whose shores the city had been built; when it had bypassed the
high ground, the road would sweep northward in a great curve and come
down upon Shastar from the hills.

Toward dusk it was clear that Brant could not hope to see his goal that
day. The weather was breaking, and thick, angry clouds had been gathering swiftly from the west. He was climbing now—for the road was rising
slowly as it crossed the last ridge—in the teeth of a gale. He would have
pitched camp for the night if he could have found a sheltered spot, but
the hill was bare for miles behind him and there was nothing to do but
to struggle onward.

Far ahead, at the very crest of the ridge, something low and dark was
silhouetted against the threatening sky. The hope that it might provide
shelter drove Brant onward: Sunbeam, head well down against the wind,
plodded steadily beside him with equal determination.

They were still a mile from the summit when the rain began to fall,
first in single, angry drops and then in blinding sheets. It was impossible
to see more than a few paces ahead, even when one could open one's eyes
against the stinging rain. Brant was already so wet that any additional
moisture could add nothing to his discomfort; indeed, he had reached that
sodden state when the continuing downpour almost gave him a masochis-
tic pleasure. But the sheer physical effort of fighting against the gale was
rapidly exhausting him.

It seemed ages before the road leveled out and he knew he had reached the summit. He strained his eyes into the gloom and could see, not far ahead, a great dark shape, which for a moment he thought might be a building. Even if it was in ruins, it would give him shelter from the storm.

The rain began to slacken as he approached the object; overhead, the clouds were thinning to let through the last fading light of the western sky. It was just sufficient to show Brant that what lay ahead of him was no building at all, but a great stone beast, crouching upon the hilltop and staring out to sea. He had no time to examine it more closely, but hurriedly pitched his tent in its shelter, out of reach of the wind that still raved angrily overhead.

It was completely dark when he had dried himself and prepared a meal. For a while he rested in his warm little oasis, in that state of blissful exhaustion that comes after hard and successful effort. Then he roused himself, took a hand-torch and went out into the night.

The storm had blown away the clouds and the night was brilliant with stars. In the west a thin crescent moon was sinking, following hard upon the footsteps of the sun. To the north Brant was aware—though how, he could not have said—of the sleepless presence of the sea. Down there in the darkness Shastar was lying, the waves marching forever against it; but strain his eyes as he might, he could see nothing at all.

He walked along the flanks of the great statue, examining the stonework by the light of his torch. It was smooth and unbroken by any joints or seams, and although time had stained and discolored it, there was no sign of wear. It was impossible to guess its age; it might be older than Shastar or it might have been made only a few centuries ago. There was no way of telling.

The hard, blue white beam of the torch flickered along the monster's wetly gleaming sides and came to rest upon the great, calm face and the empty eyes. One might have called it a human face, but thereafter words faltered and failed. Neither male nor female, it seemed at first sight utterly indifferent to all the passions of mankind; then Brant saw that the storms of ages had left their mark behind them. Countless raindrops had coursed down those adamantine cheeks, until they bore the stains of Olympian tears—tears, perhaps, for the city whose birth and death now seemed almost equally remote.

Brant was so tired that when he awoke the sun was already high. He lay for a moment in the filtered half-light of the tent, recovering his senses and remembering where he was. Then he rose to his feet and went blinking into the daylight, shielding his eyes from the dazzling glare.

The sphinx seemed smaller than by night, though it was impressive enough. It was colored, Brant saw for the first time, a rich, autumnal gold, the color of no natural rock. He knew from this that it did not belong, as he had half-suspected, to any prehistoric culture. It had been built by science from some inconceivably stubborn, synthetic substance, and Brant guessed that its creation must lie almost midway in time between him and the fabulous original which had inspired it.

Slowly, half-afraid of what he might discover, he turned his back upon the sphinx and looked to the north. The hill fell away at his feet and the road went sweeping down the long slope as if impatient to greet the sea; and there at its end lay Shastar.

It caught the sunlight and tossed it back to him, tinted with all the colors of its makers' dreams. The spacious buildings lining the wide streets seemed unravished by time; the great band of marble that held the sea at bay was still unbreached; the parks and gardens, though long overgrown with weeds, were not yet jungles. The city followed the curve of the bay for perhaps two miles, and stretched half that distance inland; by the standards of the past, it was very small indeed. But to Brant it seemed enormous, a maze of streets and squares intricate beyond unraveling. Then he began to discern the underlying symmetry of its design, to pick out the main thoroughfares and to see the skill with which its makers had avoided both monotony and discord.

For a long time Brant stood motionless on the hilltop, conscious only of the wonder spread beneath his eyes. He was alone in all that landscape, a tiny figure lost and humble before the achievements of greater men. The sense of history, the vision of the long slope up which man had been toiling for a million years or more, was almost overwhelming. In that moment it seemed to Brant that from his hilltop he was looking over time rather than space: and in his ears there whispered the soughing of the winds of eternity as they sweep into the past.

Sunbeam seemed very nervous as they approached the outskirts of the city. She had never seen anything like this before in her life, and Brant could not help sharing her disquiet. However unimaginative one may be, there is something ominous about buildings that have been deserted for centuries—and those of Shastar had been empty for the better part of five thousand years.

The road ran straight as an arrow between two tall pillars of white metal; like the sphinx, they were tarnished but unworn. Brant and Sunbeam passed beneath these silent guardians and found themselves before a long, low building which must have served as some kind of reception point for visitors to the city.

From a distance it had seemed that Shastar might have been abandoned only yesterday, but now Brant could see a thousand signs of desolation and neglect. The colored stone of the buildings was stained with the patina of age; the windows were gaping, skull-blank eyes, with here and there a miraculously preserved fragment of glass.

Brant tethered Sunbeam outside the first building and made his way to the entrance across the rubble and thickly piled dirt. There was no door, if indeed there had ever been one, and he passed through the high, vaulted archway into a hall which seemed to run the full length of the structure. At regular intervals there were openings into further chambers, and immediately ahead of him a wide flight of stairs rose to the single floor above.

It took him almost an hour to explore the building, and when he left he was infinitely depressed. His careful search had revealed absolutely nothing. All the rooms, great and small, were completely empty; he had felt like an ant crawling through the bones of a clean-picked skeleton.

Out in the sunlight, however, his spirits revived a little. This building was probably only some sort of administrative office and would never have contained anything but records and information machines; elsewhere in the city, things might be different. Even so, the magnitude of the search appalled him.

Slowly he made his way toward the sea front, moving awestruck through the wide avenues and admiring the towering façades on either side. Near the center of the city he came upon one of its many parks. It was largely overgrown with weeds and shrubs, but there were still considerable areas of grass, and he decided to leave Sunbeam here while he continued his explorations. She was not likely to move very far away while there was plenty to eat.

It was so peaceful in the park that for a while Brant was loath to leave it to plunge again into the desolation of the city. There were plants here unlike any that he had ever seen before, the wild descendants of those which the people of Shastar had cherished ages since. As he stood among the high grasses and unknown flowers, Brant heard for the first time, stealing through the calm stillness of the morning, the sound he was always to link with Shastar. It came from the sea, and though he had never heard it before in all his life, it brought a sense of aching recognition into his heart. Where no other voices sounded now, the lonely sea gulls were still calling sadly across the waves.

It was quite clear that many days would be needed to make even the most superficial examination of the city, and the first thing to do would be to find somewhere to live. Brant spent several hours searching for the residential district before it began to dawn on him that there was something very peculiar about Shastar. All the buildings he entered were, without exception, designed for work, entertainment or similar purposes; but none of them had been designed *to live in.* The solution came to him slowly. As he grew to know the pattern of the city, he noticed that at almost every street intersection there were low, single-storied structures of nearly identical form. They were circular or oval, and had many openings leading into them from all directions. When Brant entered one of them, he found himself facing a line of great metal gates, each with a vertical row of indicator lamps by its side. And so he knew where the people of Shastar had lived.

At first the idea of underground homes was completely repellent to him. Then he overcame his prejudice, and realized how sensible, as well as how inevitable, this was. There was no need to clutter up the surface, and to block the sunlight, with buildings designed for the merely mechanical processes of sleeping and eating. By putting all these things underground, the people of Shastar had been able to build a noble and spacious city—and yet keep it so small that one could walk its whole length within an hour.

The elevators were, of course, useless, but there were emergency stairways winding down into the darkness. Once all this underworld must have been a blaze of light, but Brant hesitated now before he descended the steps. He had his torch, but he had never been underground before and had a horror of losing his way in some subterranean catacombs. Then he shrugged his shoulders and started down the steps; after all, there was no danger if he took the most elementary precautions—and there were hundreds of other exits even if he did lose his way.

He descended to the first level and found himself in a long, wide corridor stretching as far as his beam could penetrate. On either side were rows of numbered doors, and Brant tried nearly a dozen before he found one that opened. Slowly, even reverently, he entered the little home that had been deserted for almost half the span of recorded history.

It was clean and tidy, for there had been no dust or dirt to settle here. The beautifully proportioned rooms were bare of furniture; nothing of value had been left behind in the leisurely, age-long exodus. Some of the semi-permanent fittings were still in position; the food distributor, with its familiar selector dial, was so strikingly like the one in Brant's own home that the sight of it almost annihilated the centuries. The dial still turned, though stiffly, and he would scarcely have been surprised to see a meal appear in the materialization chamber.

Brant explored several more homes before he returned to the surface. Though he found nothing of value, he felt a growing sense of kinship toward the people who had lived here. Yet he still thought of them as his inferiors, for to have lived in a city—however beautiful, however brilliantly designed—was to Brant one of the symbols of barbarism.

In the last home he entered he came across a brightly colored room with a fresco of dancing animals around the walls. The pictures were full of a whimsical humor that must have delighted the hearts of the children for whom they had been drawn. Brant examined the paintings with interest, for they were the first works of representative art he had found in Shastar. He was about to leave when he noticed a tiny pile of dust in one corner of the room, and bending down to investigate found himself looking at the still-recognizable fragments of a doll. Nothing solid remained save a few colored buttons, which crumbled to powder in his hand when he picked them up. He wondered why this sad little relic had been left behind by its owner; then he tiptoed away and returned to the surface and the lonely but sunlit streets. He never went to the underground city again.

Toward evening he revisited the park to see that Sunbeam had been up to no mischief, and prepared to spend the night in one of the numerous small buildings scattered through the gardens. Here he was surrounded by flowers and trees, and could almost imagine he was home again. He slept better than he had done since he had left Chaldis, and for the first time for many days, his last waking thoughts were not of Yradne. The magic of Shastar was already working upon his mind; the infinite complexity of the civilization he had affected to despise was changing him more swiftly than he could imagine. The longer he stayed in the city, the more remote he would become from the naïve yet self-confident boy who had entered it only a few hours before.

The second day confirmed the impressions of the first. Shastar had not died in a year, or even in a generation. Slowly its people had drifted away as the new—yet how old!—pattern of society had been evolved and humanity had returned to the hills and the forests. They had left nothing behind them, save these marble monuments to a way of life that was gone forever. Even if anything of value had remained, the thousands of curious explorers who had come here in the fifty centuries since would have taken it long ago. Brant found many traces of his predecessors; their names were carved on walls throughout the city, for this is one kind of immortality that men have never been able to resist.

Tired at last by his fruitless search, he went down to the shore and sat on the wide stonework of the breakwater. The sea lying a few feet beneath him was utterly calm and of a cerulean blue; it was so still and clear that he could watch the fish swimming in its depths, and at one spot could see a wreck lying on its side with the seaweed streaming straight up from it like long, green hair. Yet there must be times, he knew, when the waves came thundering over these massive walls; for behind him the wide parapet was strewn with a thick carpet of stones and shells, tossed there by the gales of centuries.

The enervating peacefulness of the scene, and the unforgettable object lesson in the futility of ambition that surrounded him on every side, took away all sense of disappointment or defeat. Though Shastar had given him nothing of material value, Brant did not regret his journey. Sitting here on the sea wall, with his back to the land and his eyes dazzled by that blinding blue, he already felt remote from his old problems, and could look back with no pain at all, but only a dispassionate curiosity, on all the heartache and the anxiety that had plagued him these last few months.

He went slowly back into the city, after walking a little way along the sea front so that he could return by a new route. Presently he found himself before a large circular building whose roof was a shallow dome of some translucent material. He looked at it with little interest, for he was emotionally exhausted, and decided that it was probably yet another theater or concert hall. He had almost passed the entrance when some obscure impulse diverted him and he went through the open doorway.

Inside, the light filtered through the ceiling with such little hindrance that Brant almost had the impression of being in the open air. The entire building was divided into numerous large halls whose purpose he realized with a sudden stir of excitement. The telltale rectangles of discoloration showed that the walls had once been almost covered with pictures; it was just possible that some had been left behind, and it would be interesting to see what Shastar could offer in the way of serious art. Brant, still secure in his consciousness of superiority, did not expect to be unduly impressed; and so the shock was all the greater when it came.

The blaze of color along the whole length of the great wall smote him like a fanfare of trumpets. For a moment he stood paralyzed in the doorway, unable to grasp the pattern or meaning of what he saw. Then, slowly, he began to unravel the details of the tremendous and intricate mural that had burst suddenly upon his vision.

It was nearly a hundred feet long, and was incomparably the most wonderful thing that Brant had ever seen in his life. Shastar had awed and overwhelmed him, yet its tragedy had left him curiously unmoved. But this struck straight at his heart and spoke in a language he could understand; and as it did so, the last vestiges of his condescension toward the past were scattered like leaves before a gale.

The eye moved naturally from left to right across the painting, to follow the curve of tension to its moment of climax. On the left was the sea, as deep a blue as the water that beat against Shastar; and moving across its face was a fleet of strange ships, driven by tiered banks of oars and by billowing sails that strained toward the distant land. The painting covered not only miles of space but perhaps years of time; for now the ships had reached the shore, and there on the wide plain an army lay encamped, its banners and tents and chariots dwarfed by the walls of the fortress city it was beleaguering. The eye scaled those still inviolate walls and came to rest, as it was meant to do, upon the woman who stood upon them, looking down at the army that had followed her across the ocean.

She was leaning forward to peer over the battlements, and the wind was catching her hair so that it formed a golden mist about her head. Upon her face was written a sadness too deep for words, yet one that did nothing to mar the unbelievable beauty of her face—a beauty that held Brant spellbound, for long unable to tear away his eyes. When at last he could do so, he followed her gaze down those seemingly impregnable walls, to the group of soldiers toiling in their shadow. They were gathered around something so foreshortened by perspective that it was some time before Brant realized what it was. Then he saw that it was an enormous image of a horse, mounted on rollers so that it could be easily moved. It roused no echoes in his mind, and he quickly returned to the lonely figure on the wall, around whom, as he now saw, the whole great design was balanced and pivoted. For as the eye moved on across the painting, taking the mind with it into the future, it came upon ruined battlements, the smoke of the burning city staining the sky and the fleet returning homeward, its mission done.

Brant left only when the light was so poor that he could no longer see.

When the first shock had worn off, he had examined the great painting more closely; and for a while he had searched, but in vain, for the signature of the artist. He also looked for some caption or title, but it was clear that there had never been one—perhaps because the story was too well known to need it. In the intervening centuries, however, some other visitor to Shastar had scratched two lines of poetry on the wall:

> Is this the face that launched a thousand ships
> And burned the topless towers of Ilium?

Ilium! It was a strange and magical name; but it meant nothing to Brant. He wondered whether it belonged to history or to fable, not knowing how many before him had wrestled with that same problem.

As he emerged into the luminous twilight, he still carried the vision of that sad, ethereal loveliness before his eyes. Perhaps if Brant had not himself been an artist, and had been in a less susceptible state of mind, the impression would not have been so overwhelming. Yet it was the impression that the unknown master had set out to create, phoenixlike, from the dying embers of a great legend. He had captured, and held for all future ages to see, that beauty whose service is the purpose of life, and its sole justification.

For a long time Brant sat under the stars, watching the crescent moon sink behind the towers of the city, and haunted by questions to which he could never know the answers. All the other pictures in these galleries had gone, scattered beyond tracing, not merely throughout the world, but throughout the universe. How had they compared with the single work of genius that now must represent forever the art of Shastar?

In the morning Brant returned, after a night of strange dreams. A plan had been forming in his mind; it was so wild and ambitious that at first he tried to laugh it away, but it would give him no peace. Almost reluctantly, he set up his little folding easel and prepared his paints. He had found one thing in Shastar that was both unique and beautiful; perhaps he had the skill to carry some faint echo of it back to Chaldis.

It was impossible, of course, to copy more than a fragment of the vast design, but the problem of selection was easy. Though he had never attempted a portrait of Yradne, he would now paint a woman who, if indeed she had ever existed, had been dust for five thousand years.

Several times he stopped to consider this paradox, and at last thought he had resolved it. He had never painted Yradne because he doubted his own skill, and was afraid of her criticism. There would be no problem here, Brant told himself. He did not stop to ask how Yradne would react when he returned to Chaldis carrying as his only gift the portrait of another woman.

In truth, he was painting for himself, and for no one else. For the first time in his life he had come into direct contact with a great work of classic art, and it had swept him off his feet. Until now he had been a dilettante; he might never be more than this, but at least he would make the effort.

He worked steadily all through the day, and the sheer concentration of his labors brought him a certain peace of mind. By evening he had sketched in the palace walls and battlements, and was about to start on the portrait itself. That night, he slept well.

He lost most of his optimism the next morning. His food supply was running low, and perhaps the thought that he was working against time had unsettled him. Everything seemed to be going wrong; the colors would not match, and the painting, which had shown such promise the day before, was becoming less and less satisfactory every minute.

To make matters worse, the light was failing, though it was barely noon, and Brant guessed that the sky outside had become overcast. He rested for a little while in the hope that it might clear again, but since it showed no signs of doing so, he recommenced work. It was now or nothing; unless he could get that hair right he would abandon the whole project. . . .

The afternoon waned rapidly, but in his fury of concentration Brant scarcely noticed the passage of time. Once or twice he thought he noticed distant sounds and wondered if a storm was coming up, for the sky was still very dark.

There is no experience more chilling than the sudden, the utterly unexpected knowledge that one is no longer alone. It would be hard to say what impulse made Brant slowly lay down his brush and turn, even more slowly, toward the great doorway forty feet behind him. The man standing there must have entered almost soundlessly, and how long he had been watching him Brant had no way of guessing. A moment later he was joined by two companions, who also made no attempt to pass the doorway.

Brant rose slowly to his feet, his brain whirling. For a moment he almost imagined that ghosts from Shastar's past had come back to haunt him. Then reason reasserted itself. After all, why should he not meet other visitors here, when he was one himself?

He took a few paces forward, and one of the strangers did likewise. When they were a few yards apart, the other said in a very clear voice, speaking rather slowly: "I hope we haven't disturbed you."

It was not a very dramatic conversational opening, and Brant was somewhat puzzled by the man's accent—or, more accurately, by the exceedingly careful way he was pronouncing his words. It almost seemed that he did not expect Brant to understand him otherwise.

"That's quite all right," Brant replied, speaking equally slowly. "But you gave me a surprise—I hardly expected to meet anyone here."

"Neither did we," said the other with a slight smile. "We had no idea that anyone still lived in Shastar."

"But I don't," explained Brant. "I'm just a visitor like you."

The three exchanged glances, as if sharing some secret joke. Then one of them lifted a small metal object from his belt and spoke a few words into it, too softly for Brant to overhear. He assumed that other members of the party were on the way, and felt annoyed that his solitude was to be so completely shattered.

Two of the strangers had walked over to the great mural and begun to examine it critically. Brant wondered what they were thinking; somehow he resented sharing his treasure with those who would not feel the same reverence toward it—those to whom it would be nothing more than a pretty picture. The third man remained by his side comparing, as unobtrusively as possible, Brant's copy with the original. All three seemed to be deliberately avoiding further conversation. There was a long and embarrassing silence: then the other two men rejoined them.

"Well, Erlyn, what do you think of it?" said one, waving his hand toward the painting. They seemed for the moment to have lost all interest in Brant.

"It's a very fine late third-millennium primitive, as good as anything we have. Don't you agree, Latvar?"

"Not exactly. I wouldn't say it's late third. For one thing, the subject . . ."

"Oh, you and your theories! But perhaps you're right. It's too good for the last period. On second thoughts, I'd date it around 2500. What do you say, Trescon?"

"I agree. Probably Aroon or one of his pupils."

"Rubbish!" said Latvar.

"Nonsense!" snorted Erlyn.

"Oh, very well," replied Trescon good-naturedly. "I've only studied this period for thirty years, while you've just looked it up since we started. So I bow to your superior knowledge."

Brant had followed this conversation with growing surprise and a rapidly mounting sense of bafflement.

"Are all three of you artists?" he blurted out at last.

"Of course," replied Trescon grandly. "Why else would we be here?"

"Don't be a damned liar," said Erlyn, without even raising his voice. "You won't be an artist if you live a thousand years. You're merely an expert, and you know it. Those who can—do: those who can't—criticize."

"Where have you come from?" asked Brant, a little faintly. He had never met anyone quite like these extraordinary men. They were in late middle age, yet seemed to have an almost boyish gusto and enthusiasm. All their movements and gestures were just a little larger than life, and when they were talking to each other they spoke so quickly that Brant found it difficult to follow them.

Before anyone could reply, there was a further interruption. A dozen men appeared in the doorway—and were brought to a momentary halt by their first sight of the great painting. Then they hurried to join the little group around Brant, who now found himself the center of a small crowd.

"Here you are, Kondar," said Trescon, pointing to Brant. "We've found someone who can answer your questions."

The man who had been addressed looked at Brant closely for a moment, glanced at his unfinished painting and smiled a little. Then he turned to Trescon and lifted his eyebrows in interrogation.

"No," said Trescon succinctly.

Brant was getting annoyed. Something was going on that he didn't understand, and he resented it.

"Would you mind telling me what this is all about?" he said plaintively.

Kondar looked at him with an unfathomable expression. Then he said quietly: "Perhaps I could explain things better if you came outside."

He spoke as if he never had to ask twice for a thing to be done; and Brant followed him without a word, the others crowding close behind him. At the outer entrance Kondar stood aside and waved Brant to pass.

It was still unnaturally dark, as if a thundercloud had blotted out the sun; but the shadow that lay the full length of Shastar was not that of any cloud.

A dozen pairs of eyes were watching Brant as he stood staring at the sky, trying to gauge the true size of the ship floating above the city. It was so close that the sense of perspective was lost; one was conscious only of sweeping metal curves that dwindled away to the horizon. There should have been some sound, some indication of the energies holding that stupendous mass at rest above Shastar; but there was only a silence deeper than any that Brant had ever known. Even the crying of the sea gulls had ceased, as if they, too, were overawed by the intruder who had usurped their skies.

At last Brant turned toward the men gathered behind him. They were waiting, he knew, for his reactions; and the reason for their curiously aloof yet not unfriendly behavior became suddenly clear. To these men, rejoicing in the powers of gods, he was little more than a savage who happened to speak the same language—a survival from their own half-forgotten past, reminding them of the days when their ancestors had shared the Earth with his.

"Do you understand, now, who we are?" asked Kondar.

Brant nodded. "You have been gone a long time," he said. "We had almost forgotten you."

He looked up again at the great metal arch spanning the sky, and thought how strange it was that the first contact after so many centuries should be here, in this lost city of mankind. But it seemed that Shastar was well-remembered among the stars, for certainly Trescon and his friends had appeared perfectly familiar with it.

And then, far to the north, Brant's eye was caught by a sudden flash of reflected sunlight. Moving purposefully across the band of sky framed beneath the ship was another metal giant that might have been its twin, dwarfed though it was by distance. It passed swiftly across the horizon and within seconds was gone from sight.

So this was not the only ship; and how many more might there be? Somehow the thought reminded Brant of the great painting he had just left, and of the invading fleet moving with such deadly purpose toward the doomed city. And with that thought there came into his soul, creeping out from the hidden caves of racial memory, the fear of strangers that once had been the curse of all mankind. He turned to Kondar and cried accusingly:

"You're invading Earth!"

For a moment no one spoke. Then Trescon said, with a slight touch of malice in his voice:

"Go ahead, commander—you've got to explain it sooner or later. Now's a good time to practice."

Commander Kondar gave a worried little smile that first reassured Brant, then filled him with yet deeper forebodings.

"You do us an injustice, young man," he said gravely. "We're not invading Earth. We're evacuating it."

"I hope," said Trescon, who had taken a patronizing interest in Brant, "that *this* time the scientists have learned a lesson—though I doubt it. They just say, 'Accidents will happen,' and when they've cleaned up one mess, they go on to make another. The Sigma Field is certainly their most spectacular failure so far, but progress never ceases."

"And if it does hit Earth—what will happen?"

"The same thing that happened to the control apparatus when the field got loose—it will be scattered uniformly throughout the cosmos. And so will you be, unless we get you out in time."

"Why?" asked Brant.

"You don't really expect a technical answer, do you? It's something to do with uncertainty. The Ancient Greeks—or perhaps it was the Egyptians—discovered that you can't define the position of any atom with absolute accuracy; it has a small but finite probability of being anywhere in the universe. The people who set up the field hoped to use it for propulsion. It would change the atomic odds, as it were, so that a spaceship orbiting Vega would suddenly decide that it really ought to be circling Betelgeuse.

"Well, it seems that the Sigma Field does only half the job. It merely *multiplies* probabilities—it doesn't organize them. And now it's wandering at random through the stars, feeding on interstellar dust and the occasional sun. No one's been able to devise a way of neutralizing it—though there's a horrible suggestion that a twin should be created and a collision arranged. If they try that, I know just what will happen."

"I don't see why we should worry," said Brant. "It's still ten light-years away."

"Ten light-years is much too close for a thing like the Sigma Field. It's zigzagging at random, in what the mathematicians call the Drunkard's Walk. If we're unlucky, it'll be here tomorrow. But the chances are twenty to one that the Earth will be untouched; in a few years, you'll be able to go home again, just as if nothing had ever happened."

"As if nothing had ever happened!" Whatever the future brought, the old way of life was gone forever. What was taking place in Shastar must now be occurring in one form or another, over all the world. Brant watched wide-eyed as strange machines rolled down the splendid streets, clearing away the rubble of ages and making the city fit for habitation again. As an almost extinct star may suddenly blaze up in one last hour of glory, so for a few months Shastar would be one of the capitals of the world, housing the army of scientists, technicians and administrators that had descended upon it from space.

Brant was growing to know the invaders very well. Their vigor, the lavishness of everything they did and the almost childlike delight they took in their superhuman powers never ceased to astonish him. These, his cousins, were the heirs to all the universe; and they had not yet begun to exhaust its wonders or to tire of its mystery. For all their knowledge, there was still a feeling of experimentation, even of cheerful irresponsibility, about many of the things they did. The Sigma Field itself was an example of this; they had made a mistake, they did not seem to mind in the least and they were quite sure that sooner or later they would put things right.

Despite the tumult that had been loosed upon Shastar, as indeed upon the entire planet, Brant had remained stubbornly at his task. It gave him something fixed and stable in a world of shifting values, and as such he clung to it desperately. From time to time Trescon or his colleagues would visit him and proffer advice—usually excellent advice, though he did not always take it. And occasionally, when he was tired and wished to rest his eyes or brain, he would leave the great empty galleries and go out into the transformed streets of the city. It was typical of its new inhabitants that, though they would be here for no more than a few months, they had spared no efforts to make Shastar clean and efficient, and to impose upon it a certain stark beauty that would have surprised its first builders.

At the end of four days—the longest time he had ever devoted to a single work—Brant slowed to a halt. He could go on tinkering indefinitely, but if he did he would only make things worse. Not at all displeased with his efforts, he went in search of Trescon.

He found the critic, as usual, arguing with his colleagues over what should be saved from the accumulated art of mankind. Latvar and Erlyn had threatened violence if one more Picasso was taken aboard, or another Fra Angelico thrown out. Not having heard of either, Brant had no compunction in pressing his own claim.

Trescon stood in silence before the painting, glancing at the original from time to time. His first remark was quite unexpected.

"Who's the girl?" he said.

"You told me she was called Helen—" Brant started to answer.

"I mean the one you've *really* painted."

Brant looked at his canvas, then back at the original. It was odd that he hadn't noticed those differences before, but there were undoubtedly traces of Yradne in the woman he had shown on the fortress walls. This was not the straightforward copy he had set out to make. His own mind and heart had spoken through his fingers.

"I see what you mean," he said slowly. "There's a girl back in my village; I really came here to find a present for her—something that would impress her."

"Then you've been wasting your time," Trescon answered bluntly. "If she really loves you, she'll tell you soon enough. If she doesn't, you can't make her. It's as simple as that."

Brant did not consider that at all simple, but decided not to argue the point.

"You haven't told me what you think about it," he complained.

"It shows promise," Trescon answered cautiously. "In another thirty—well, twenty—years you may get somewhere, if you keep at it. Of course the brushwork is pretty crude, and that hand looks like a bunch of bananas. But you have a nice bold line, and I think more of you for not making a carbon copy. Any fool can do that—this shows you've some originality. What you need now is more practice—and above all, more experience. Well, I think we can provide you with that."

"If you mean going away from Earth," said Brant, "that's not the sort of experience I want."

"It will do you good. Doesn't the thought of traveling out of the stars arouse any feelings of excitement in your mind?"

"No; only dismay. But I can't take it seriously; because I don't believe you'll be able to make us go."

Trescon smiled, a little grimly.

"You'll move quickly enough when the Sigma Field sucks the starlight from the sky. And it may be a good thing when it comes: I have a feeling we were just in time. Though I've often made fun of the scientists, they've freed us forever from the stagnation that was overtaking your race.

"You have to get away from Earth, Brant; no man who has lived all his life on the surface of a planet has ever seen the stars, only their feeble ghosts. Can you imagine what it means to hang in space amid one of the great multiple systems, with colored suns blazing all around you? I've done that; and I've seen stars floating in rings of crimson fire, like your planet Saturn, but a thousand times greater. And can you imagine night on a world near the heart of the galaxy, where the whole sky is luminous with star mist that has not yet given birth to suns? Your Milky Way is only a scattered handful of third-rate suns; wait until you see the Central Nebula!

"These are the great things, but the small ones are just as wonderful. Drink your fill of all that the universe can offer; and if you wish, return to Earth with your memories. *Then* you can begin to work; then, and no sooner, you'll know if you are an artist."

Brant was impressed, but not convinced.

"According to *that* argument," he said "real art couldn't have existed before space travel."

"There's a whole school of criticism based on that thesis; certainly space travel was one of the best things that ever happened to art. Travel, exploration, contact with other cultures—that's the great stimulus for all intellectual activity." Trescon waved at the mural blazing on the wall behind them. "The people who created that legend were seafarers, and the traffic of half a world came through their ports. But after a few thousand years, the sea was too small for inspiration or adventure, and it was time to go into space. Well, the time's come for you, whether you like it or not."

"I don't like it. I want to settle down with Yradne."

"The things that people want and the things that are good for them are very different. I wish you luck with your painting; I don't know whether to wish you luck in your other endeavor. Great art and domestic bliss are mutually incompatible. Sooner or later, you'll have to make your choice."

*Sooner or later, you'll have to make your choice.* Those words still echoed in Brant's mind as he trudged toward the brow of the hill, and the wind came down the great road to meet him. Sunbeam resented the termination of her holiday, so they moved even more slowly than the gradient demanded. But gradually the landscape widened around them, the horizon moved farther out to sea and the city began to look more and more like a toy built from colored bricks—a toy dominated by the ship that hung effortlessly, motionlessly above it.

For the first time Brant was able to see it as a whole, for it was now floating almost level with his eyes and he could encompass it at a glance. It was roughly cylindrical in shape, but ended in complex polyhedral structures whose functions were beyond conjecture. The great curving back bristled with equally mysterious bulges, fluting and cupolas. There was power and purpose here, but nothing of beauty, and Brant looked upon it with distaste.

This brooding monster usurping the sky—if only it would vanish, like the clouds that drifted past its flanks! But it would not disappear because he willed it; against the forces that were gathering now, Brant knew that he and his problems were of no importance. This was the pause when history held its breath, the hushed moment between the lightning flash and the advent of the first concussion. Soon the thunder would be rolling round the world; and soon there might be no world at all, while he and his people would be homeless exiles among the stars. That was the future he did not care to face—the future he feared more deeply than Trescon and his fellows, to whom the universe had been a plaything for five thousand years, could ever understand.

It seemed unfair that this should have happened in his time, after all these centuries of rest. But men cannot bargain with fate, and choose peace or adventure as they wish. Adventure and change had come to the world again, and he must make the best of it—as his ancestors had done when the age of space had opened, and their first frail ships had stormed the stars.

For the last time he saluted Shastar, then turned his back upon the sea. The sun was shining in his eyes, and the road before him seemed veiled with a bright, shimmering mist, so that it quivered like a mirage, or the track of the moon upon troubled waters. For a moment Brant wondered if his eyes had been deceiving him; then he saw that it was no illusion.

As far as the eye could see, the road and the land on either side of it were draped with countless strands of gossamer, so frail and fine that only the glancing sunlight revealed their presence. For the last quarter-mile he had been walking through them, and they had resisted his passage no more than coils of smoke.

Throughout the morning, the wind-borne spiders must have been falling in millions from the sky; and as he stared up into the blue, Brant could still catch momentary glimpses of sunlight upon drifting silk as belated voyagers went sailing by. Not knowing whither they would travel, these tiny creatures had ventured forth into an abyss more friendless and more fathomless than any he would face when the time came to say farewell to Earth. It was a lesson he would remember in the weeks and months ahead.

Slowly the sphinx sank into the skyline as it joined Shastar beyond the eclipsing crescent of the hills. Only once did Brant look back at the crouching monster, whose age-long vigil was now drawing to its close. Then he walked slowly forward into the sun, while ever and again impalpable fingers brushed his face, as the strands of silk came drifting down the wind that blew from home.

# The Star Pit

*Our species has discovered numerous ways to define us. These range from family, clan and tribe to nationality, nation-state and ideological bloc. Indeed, the conflicts between and among these groupings has characterized much of human history. Science fiction has often addressed these conflicts and posited new ways of self-definition. One of the most common is the idea of genetically gifted or "special" people on the one hand and the ordinary "normals" on the other.*

*Here the gifted Samuel R. Delany takes this favorite theme and transforms it into something special and remarkable.*

Two glass panes with dirt between and little tunnels from cell to cell: when I was a kid I had an ant colony.

But once some of our four-to-six-year-olds built an ecologarium with six-foot plastic panels and grooved aluminum bars to hold corners and top down. They put it out on the sand.

There was a mud puddle against one wall so you could see what was going on underwater. Sometimes segment worms crawling through the reddish earth hit the side so their tunnels were visible for a few inches. In hot weather the inside of the plastic got coated with mist and droplets. The small round leaves on the litmus vines changed from blue to pink, blue to pink as clouds coursed the sky and the pH of the photosensitive soil shifted slightly.

The kids would run out before dawn and belly down naked in the cool sand with their chins on the backs of their hands and stare in the half-dark till the red mill wheel of Sigma lifted over the bloody sea. The sand was maroon then, and the flowers of the crystal plants looked like rubies in the dim light of the giant sun. Up the beach the jungle would begin to whisper while somewhere an ani-wort would start warbling. The kids would giggle and poke each other and crowd closer.

Then Sigma-prime, the second member of the binary, would flare like thermite on the water, and crimson clouds would bleach from coral, through peach, to foam. The kids, half on top of each other, now lay like a pile of copper ingots with sun streaks in their hair—even on little Antoni, my oldest, whose hair was black and curly like bubbling oil (like his mother's), the down on the small of his two-year-old back was a white haze across the copper if you looked that close to see.

More children came to squat and lean on their knees, or kneel with their noses an inch from the walls, to watch, like young magicians, as things were born, grew, matured and other things were born. Enchanted at their own construction, they stared at the miracles in their live museum.

A small, red seed lay camouflaged in the silt by the lake/puddle. One evening as white Sigma-prime left the sky violet, it broke open into a brown larva as long and of the same color as the first joint of Antoni's thumb. It flipped and swirled in the mud a couple of days, then crawled to the first branch of the nearest crystal plant to hang, exhausted, head down, from the tip. The brown flesh hardened, thickened, grew shiny, black. Then one morning the children saw the onyx chrysalis crack, and by second dawn there was an emerald-eyed flying lizard buzzing at the plastic panels.

"Oh, look, da!" they called to me. "It's trying to get out!"

The speed-hazed creature butted at the corner, for a few days, then settled at last to crawling around the broad leaves of the miniature shade palms.

When the season grew cool and there was the annual debate over whether the kids should put tunics on—they never stayed in them more than twenty minutes anyway—the jewels of the crystal plant misted, their facets coarsened, and they fell like gravel.

There were little four-cupped sloths, too, big as a six-year-old's fist. Most of the time they pressed their velvety bodies against the walls and stared longingly across the sand with their retractable eye-clusters. Then two of them swelled for about three weeks. We thought at first it was some bloating infection. But one evening there were a couple of litters of white velvet balls half-hidden by the low leaves of the shade palms. The parents were occupied now and didn't pine to get out.

There was a rock half-in and half-out of the puddle, I remember, covered with what I'd always called mustard-moss when I saw it in the wild. Once it put out a brush of white hairs. And one afternoon the children ran to collect all the adults they could drag over. "Look, oh da, da, ma, look!" The hairs had detached themselves and were walking around the water's edge, turning end over end along the soft soil.

I had to leave for work in a few minutes and haul some spare drive parts out to Tau Ceti. But when I got back five days later, the hairs had taken root, thickened, and were already putting out the small round leaves of litmus vines. Among the new shoots, lying on her back, claws curled over her wrinkled belly, eyes cataracted like the foggy jewels of the crystal plant —she'd dropped her wings like cellophane days ago—was the flying lizard. Her pearl throat still pulsed, but as I watched, it stopped. Before she died, however, she had managed to deposit, nearly camouflaged in the silt by the puddle, a scattering of red seeds.

I remember getting home from another job where I'd been doing the maintenance on the shuttle-boats for a crew putting up a ring station to circle a planet itself circling Aldebaran. I was gone a long time on that one. When I left the landing complex and wandered out toward the tall weeds at the edge of the beach, I still didn't see anybody.

Which was just as well because the night before I'd put on a real winner with the crew to celebrate the completion of the station. That morning I'd taken a couple more drinks at the landing bar to undo last night's damage. Never works.

The swish of frond on frond was like clashed rasps. Sun on the sand reached out fingers of pure glare and tried to gouge my eyes. I was glad the home-compound was deserted because the kids would have asked questions I didn't want to answer; the adults wouldn't ask anything, which was even harder to answer.

Then, down by the ecologarium, a child screeched. And screeched again. Then Antoni came hurtling toward me, half-running, half on all fours, and flung himself on my leg. "Oh, da! Da! Why, oh why, da?"

I'd kicked my boots off and shrugged my shirt back at the compound porch, but I still had my overalls on. Antoni had two fists full of my pants leg and wouldn't let go. "Hey, kid-boy, what's the matter?"

When I finally got him on my shoulder he butted his blubber wet face against my collarbone. "Oh, da! Da! It's crazy, it's all cra*aaa-zy!*" His voice rose to lose itself in sobs.

"What's crazy, kid-boy? Tell da."

Antoni held my ear and cried while I walked down to the plastic enclosure.

They'd put a small door in one wall with a two-number combination lock that was supposed to keep this sort of thing from happening. I guess Antoni learned the combination from watching the older kids, or maybe he just figured it out.

One of the young sloths had climbed out and wandered across the sand about three feet.

"See, da! It crazy, it bit me. Bit me, da!" Sobs became sniffles as he showed me a puffy, bluish place on his wrist centered on which was a tiny crescent of pinpricks. Then he pointed jerkily to the creature.

It was shivering, and bloody froth spluttered from its lip flaps. All the while it was digging futilely at the sand with its clumsy cups, eyes retracted. Now it fell over, kicked, tried to right itself, breath going like a flutter valve. "It can't take the heat," I explained, reaching down to pick it up.

It snapped at me, and I jerked back. "Sunstroke, kid-boy. Yeah, it is crazy."

Suddenly it opened its mouth wide, let out all its air and didn't take in any more. "It's all right now," I said.

Two more of the baby sloths were at the door, front cups over the sill, staring with bright, black eyes. I pushed them back with a piece of seashell and closed the door. Antoni kept looking at the white fur ball on the sand. "Not crazy now?"

"It's dead," I told him.

"Dead because it went outside, da?"

I nodded.

"And crazy?" He made a fist and ground something already soft and wet around his upper lip.

I decided to change the subject, which was already too close to something I didn't like to think about. "Who's been taking care of you, anyway?" I asked. "You're a mess, kid-boy. Let's go and fix up that arm. They shouldn't leave a fellow your age all by himself." We started back to the compound. Those bites infect easily, and this one was swelling.

"Why it go crazy? Why it die when it go outside, da?"

"Can't take the light," I said as we reached the jungle. "They're animals that live in shadow most of the time. The plastic cuts out the ultraviolet rays, just like the leaves that shade them when they run loose in the jungle. Sigma-prime's high on ultraviolet. That's why you're so good-looking, kid-boy. I think your ma told me their nervous systems are on the surface, all that fuzz. Under the ultraviolet, the enzymes break down so quickly that—does this mean anything to you at all?"

"Uh-uh." Antoni shook his head. Then he came out with, "Wouldn't it be nice, da—" he admired his bite while we walked "—if some of them could go outside, just a few?"

That stopped me. There were sunspots on his blue black hair. Fronds reflected faint green on his brown cheek. He was grinning, little and wonderful. Something that had been anger in me a lot of times momentarily melted to raging tenderness, whirling about him like the dust in the light striking down at my shoulders, raging to protect my son. "I don't know about that, kid-boy."

"Why not?"

"It might be pretty bad for the ones who had to stay inside," I told him. "I mean after a while."

"Why?"

I started walking again. "Come on, let's fix your arm and get you cleaned up."

I washed the wet stuff off his face, and scraped the dry stuff from beneath it which had been there at least two days. Then I got some antibiotic into him.

"You smell funny, da."

"Never mind how I smell. Let's go outside again." I put down a cup of black coffee too fast, and it and my hangover had a fight in my stomach. I tried to ignore it and do a little looking around. But I still couldn't find anybody. That got me mad. I mean he's independent, sure: he's mine. But he's only two.

Back on the beach we buried the dead sloth in sand; then I pointed out the new, glittering stalks of the tiny crystal plants. At the bottom of the pond, in the jellied mass of ani-wort eggs, you could see the tadpole forms quivering already. An orange-fringed shelf fungus had sprouted nearly eight inches since it had been just a few black spores on a pile of dead leaves two weeks back.

"Grow up," Antoni chirped with nose and fists against the plastic. "Everything grow up, and up."

"That's right."

He grinned at me. "I grow!"

"You sure as hell do."

"You grow?" Then he shook his head, twice: once to say no, and the second time because he got a kick from shaking his hair around—there was a lot of it. "You don't grow. You don't get any bigger. Why don't you grow?"

"I do too," I said indignantly. "Just very slowly."

Antoni turned around, leaned on the plastic and moved one toe at a time in the sand—I can't do that—watching me.

"You have to grow all the time," I said. "Not necessarily get bigger. But inside your head you have to grow, kid-boy. For us human-type people that's what's important. And that kind of growing never stops. At least it shouldn't. You can grow, kid-boy, or you can die. That's the choice you've got, and it goes on all of your life."

He looked back over his shoulder. "Grow up, all the time, even if they can't get out."

"Yeah," I said. And was uncomfortable all over again. I started pulling off my overalls for something to do. "Even—" The zipper got stuck. "God *damn* it—if you can't get out." *Rnrnrnrnrn*—it came loose.

The rest got back that evening. They'd been on a group trip around the foot of the mountain. I did a little shouting to make sure my point got across about leaving Antoni alone. Didn't do much good. You know how family arguments go:

He didn't want to come. We weren't going to force—

So what. He's got to learn to do things he doesn't want—

Like some other people I could mention!

Now look—

It's a healthy group. Don't you want him to grow up a healthy—

I'll be happy if he just grows up period. No food, no medical—

But the server was chock full of food. He knows how to use it—

Look, when I got home the kid's arm was swollen all the way up to his elbow!

And so on and so forth, with Antoni sitting in the middle looking confused. When he got confused enough, he ended it all by announcing matter-of-factly: "Da smell funny when he came home."

Everyone got quiet. Then someone said, "Oh, Vyme, you didn't come home that way again! I mean, in front of the children . . ."

I said a couple of things I was sorry for later and stalked off down the beach—on a four-mile hike.

Times I got home from work? The ecologarium? I guess I'm just leading up to this one.

The particular job had taken me a hectic week to get. It was putting back together a battleship that was gutted somewhere off Aurigae. Only when I got there, I found I'd already been laid off. That particular war was over—they're real quick now. So I scraped and lied and browned my way into a repair gang that was servicing a traveling replacement station, generally had to humiliate myself to get the job because every other drive mechanic from the battleship fiasco was after it too. Then I got canned the first day because I came to work smelling funny. It took me another week to hitch a ride back to Sigma. Didn't even have enough to pay passage, but I made a deal with the pilot I'd do half the driving for him.

We were an hour out, and I was at the controls when something I'd never heard of happening, happened. We came *this* close to ramming another ship. Consider how much empty space there is; the chances are infinitesimal. And on top of that, every ship should be broadcasting an identification beam at all times.

But this big, bulbous keeler-intergalactic slid by so close I could *see* her through the front viewport. Our inertia system went nuts. We jerked around in the stasis whirl from the keeler. I slammed on the video-intercom and shouted, "You great big stupid . . . *stupid* . . ." so mad and scared I couldn't say anything else.

The golden piloting the ship stared at me from the viewscreen with mildly surprised annoyance. I remember his face was just slightly more Negroid than mine.

Our little Serpentina couldn't hurt him. But had we been even a hundred meters closer we might have ionized. The other pilot came bellowing from behind the sleeper curtain and started cursing me out.

"Damm it," I shouted, "it was one of those . . ." and lost all the profanity I know to my rage, ". . . golden . . ."

"This far into galactic center? Come off it. They should be hanging out around the Star-pit!"

"It was a keeler drive," I insisted. "It came right in front of us." I stopped because the control stick was shaking in my hand. You know the Serpentina colophon? They have it in the corner of the view screen and raised in plastic on the head of the control knobs. Well, it got pressed into the ham of my thumb so you could make it out for an hour, I was squeezing the control rod that tight.

When he set me down, I went straight to the bar to cool off. And got in a fight. When I reached the beach I was broke, I had a bloody nose, I was sick, and furious.

It was just after first sunset, and the kids were squealing around the ecologarium. Then one little girl I didn't even recognize ran up to me and jerked my arm. "Da, oh, da! Come look! The ani-worts are just about to—"

I pushed her, and she sat down, surprised, on the sand.

I just wanted to get to the water and splash something cold on my face, because every minute or so it would start to burn.

Another bunch of kids grabbed me, shouting, "Da, da, the ani-worts, da!" and tried to pull me over.

First I took two steps with them. Then I just swung my arms out. I didn't make a sound. But I put my head down and barreled against the plastic wall. Kids screamed. Aluminum snapped; the plastic cracked and went down. My boots were still on, and I kicked and kicked at red earth and sand. Shade palms went down and the leaves tore under my feet. Crystal plants broke like glass rods beneath a piece of plastic. A swarm of lizards flittered up around my head. Some of the red was Sigma, some was what burned behind my face.

I remember I was still shaking and watching water run out of the broken lake over the sand, then soak in so that the wet tongue of sand expanded a little, raised just a trifle around the edge. Then I looked up to see the kids coming back down the beach, crying, shouting, afraid and clustered around Antoni's ma. She walked steadily toward me—steady because she was a woman and they were children. But I saw the same fear in her face. Antoni was on her shoulder. Other grown-ups were coming behind her.

Antoni's ma was a biologist, and I think she had suggested the ecologarium to the kids in the first place. When she looked up from the ruin I'd made, I knew I'd broken something of hers too.

An odd expression got caught in the features of her—I remember it oh so beautiful—face, with compassion alongside the anger, contempt alongside the fear. "Oh, for pity's sake, Vyme," she cried, not loudly at all. "Won't you ever grow up?"

I opened my mouth, but everything I wanted to say was too big and stayed wedged in my throat.

"Grow up?" Antoni repeated and reached for a lizard that buzzed his head. "Everything stop growing up, now." He looked down again at the wreck I'd made. "All broken. Everything get out."

"He didn't mean to break it," she said to the others for me, then knifed my gratitude with a look. "We'll put it back together."

She put Antoni on the sand and picked up one of the walls.

After they got started, they let me help. A lot of the plants were broken. And only the ani-worts who'd completed metamorphosis could be saved. The flying lizards were too curious to get far away, so we—they netted them and got them back inside. I guess I didn't help that much. And I wouldn't say I was sorry.

They got just about everything back except the sloths.

We couldn't find them. We searched for a long time, too.

The sun was down so they should have been all right. They can't negotiate the sand with any speed so couldn't have reached the jungle.

But there were no tracks, no nothing. We even dug in the sand to see if they'd buried themselves. It wasn't till more than a dozen years later I discovered where they went.

For the present I accepted Antoni's mildly adequate, "They just must of got out again."

Not too long after that I left the procreation group. Went off to work one day, didn't come back. But like I said to Antoni, you either grow or die. I didn't die.

Once I considered returning. But there was another war, and suddenly there wasn't anything to return to. Some of the group got out alive. Antoni and his ma didn't. I mean there wasn't even any water left on the planet.

When I finally came to the Star-pit, myself, I hadn't had a drink in years. But working there out on the galaxy's edge did something to me —something to the part that grows I'd once talked about on the beach with Antoni.

If it did it to me, it's not surprising it did it to Ratlit and the rest.

(And I remember a black-eyed creature pressed against the plastic wall, staring across impassable sands.)

Perhaps it was knowing this was as far as you could go.

Perhaps it was the golden.

Golden? I hadn't even joined the group yet when I first heard the word. I was sixteen and a sophomore at Luna Vocational. I was born in a city called New York on a planet called Earth. Luna is its one satellite. You've heard of the system, I'm sure; that's where we all came from. A few other things about it are well known. Unless you're an anthropologist, though, I doubt you've ever been there. It's way the hell off the main trading routes and pretty primitive. I was a drive-mechanics major, on scholarship, living in and studying hard. All morning in Practical Theory (a ridiculous name for a ridiculous class, I thought then) we'd been putting together a model keeler-intergalactic drive. Throughout those dozens of helical inserts and superinertia organus sensitives, I had been silently cursing my teacher, thinking, about like everyone else in the class, "So what if they can fly these jalopies from one galaxy to another. Nobody will ever be able to ride in them. Not with the Psychic and Physiologic shells hanging around this cluster of the universe."

Back in the dormitory I was lying on my bed, scraping graphite lubricant from my nails with the end of my slide rule and half reading at a folded-back copy of "The Young Mechanic" when I saw the article and the pictures.

Through some freakish accident, two people had been discovered who didn't crack up at twenty thousand light-years off the galactic rim, who didn't die at twenty-five thousand.

They were both psychological freaks with some incredible hormone imbalance in their systems. One was a little Oriental girl; the other was an older man, blonde and big-boned, from a cold planet circling Cygnus-beta: golden. They looked sullen as hell, both of them.

Then there were more articles, more pictures, in the economic journals, the sociology student-letters, the legal bulletins, as various fields began acknowledging the impact that the golden and the sudden birth of inter-galactic trade were having on them. The head of some commission summed it up with the statement: "Though interstellar travel has been with us for three centuries, intergalactic trade has been an impossibility, not because of mechanical limitations, but rather because of barriers that till now we have not even been able to define. Some psychic shock causes insanity in any human—or for that matter, any intelligent species or perceptual machine or computer—that goes more than twenty thousand light-years from the galactic rim; then complete physiological death, as well as recording breakdown in computers that might replace human crews. Complex explanations have been offered, none completely satisfactory, but the base of the problem seems to be this: as the nature of space and time are relative to the concentration of matter in a given area of the continuum, the nature of reality itself operates by the same, or similar laws. The averaged mass of all the stars in our Galaxy controls the 'reality' of our microsector of the universe. But as a ship leaves the galactic rim, 'reality' breaks down and causes insanity and eventual death for any crew, even though certain mechanical laws—though not all—appear to remain, for reasons we don't understand, relatively constant. Save for a few bar-baric experiments done with psychedelics at the dawn of spatial travel, we have not even developed a vocabulary that can deal with 'reality' apart from its measurable, physical expression. Yet, just when we had to face the black limit of intergalactic space, bright resources glittered within. Some few of us whose sense of reality has been shattered by infantile, childhood or prenatal trauma, whose physiological orientation makes life in our interstellar society painful or impossible—not all, but a few of these golden . . ." at which point there was static, or the gentleman coughed, ". . . can make the crossing and return."

The name golden, sans noun, stuck.

*Few* was the understatement of the millennium. Slightly less than one human being in thirty-four thousand is a golden. A couple of people had pictures of emptying all mental institutions by just shaking them out over the galactic rim. Didn't work like that. The particular psychosis and endocrine setup was remarkably specialized. Still, back then there was excitement, wonder, anticipation, hope, admiration in the word: admiration for the ones who could get out.

"Golden?" Ratlit said when I asked him. He was working as a grease monkey out here in the Star-pit over a Poloscki's. "Born with the word. Grew up with it. Weren't no first time with me. Though I remember when I was about six, right after the last of my parents was killed, and I was hiding out with a bunch of other lice in a broke-open packing crate in an abandoned freight yard near the ruins of Helios on Creton VII— that's where I was born, I think. Most of the city had been starved out by then, but somebody was getting food to us. There was this old crook-back character who was hiding too. He used to sit on the top of the packing crate and bang his heels on the aluminum slats and tell us stories about the stars. Had a couple of rags held with twists of wire for clothes, missing two fingers off one hand; he kept plucking the loose skin under his chin with those grimy talons. And he talked about them. So I asked, 'Golden what, sir?' He leaned forward so that his face was like a mahogany bruise on the sky, and croaked, 'They've been *out*, I tell you, seen more than ever you or I. Human and inhuman, kid-boy, mothered by women and fathered by men, still they live by their own laws and walk their own ways!' " Ratlit and I were sitting under a streetlamp with our feet over the Edge where the fence had broken. His hair was like breathing flame in the wind, his single earring glittered. Star-flecked infinity dropped away below our boot soles, and the wind created by the stasis field that held our atmosphere down—we call it the "world-wind" out here because it's never cold and never hot and like nothing on any world—whipped his black shirt back from his bony chest as we gazed on galactic night between our knees. "I guess that was back during the second Kyber war," he concluded.

"Kyber war?" I asked. "Which one was that?"

He shrugged. "I just know it was fought over possession of couple of tons of di-allium; that's the polarized element the golden brought back from Lupe-galaxy. They used y-adna ships to fight it—that's why it was such a bad war. I mean worse than usual."

"Y-adna? That's a drive I don't know anything about."

"Some golden saw the plans for them in a civilization in Magellanic-9."

"Oh," I said. "And what was Kyber?"

"It was a weapon, a sort of fungus the golden brought back from some overrun planet on the rim of Andromeda. It's deadly. Only they were too stupid to bring back the antitoxin."

"That's golden for you."

"Yeah. You ever notice about golden, Vyme? I mean just the word. I found out all about it from my publisher, once. It's semantically unsettling."

"Really?" I said. "So are they. Unsettling I mean."

I'd just finished a rough, rough day installing a rebuilt keeler in a quantum transport hull that just wasn't big enough. The golden having the job done stood over my shoulder the whole time, and every hour he'd come out with the sort of added instruction that would make the next sixty-one minutes miserable. But I did it. The golden paid me in cash and without a word climbed into the lift, and two minutes later, while I was still washing the grease off, the damn five-hundred-ton hulk began to whistle for takeoff.

Sandy, a young fellow who'd come looking for a temporary mechanic's job three months back, but hadn't given me cause to fire him yet, barely had time to pull the big waldoes out of the way and go scooting into the shock chamber when the three-hundred-meter doofus tore loose from the grapplers. And Sandy, who, like a lot of these youngsters drifting around from job to job, is usually sort of quiet and vague, got loud and specific. ". . . two thousand pounds of non shockproof equipment out there . . . ruin it all if he could . . . I'm not expendable, I don't care what a . . . these golden out here . . ." while the ship hove off where only the golden go. I just flipped on the "not-open" sign, left the rest of the grease where it was, left the hanger and hunted up Ratlit.

So there we were, under that streetlamp, sitting on the Edge, in the world-wind.

"Golden," Ratlit said under the roar. "It would be much easier to take if it were grammatically connected to something: golden ones, golden people. Or even one gold, two golden."

"Male golden, female goldene?"

"Something like that. It's not an adjective, it's not a noun. My publisher told me that for a while it was written with a dash after it that stood for whatever it might modify."

I remembered the dash. It was an uneasy joke, a fill-in for that cough. Golden *what?* People had already started to feel uncomfortable. Then it went past joking and back to just "golden."

"Think about that, Vyme. Just golden: one, two or three of them."

"That's something to think about, kid-boy," I said.

Ratlit had been six during the Kyber war. Square that and add it once again for my age now. Ratlit's? Double six and add one. I like kids, and they like me. But that may be because my childhood left me a lot younger at forty-two than I should be. Ratlit's had left him a lot older than any thirteen-year-old has a right to be.

"No golden took part in the war," Ratlit said.

"They never do." I watched his thin fingers get all tangled together.

After two divorces, my mother ran off with a salesman and left me and four siblings with an alcoholic aunt for a year. Yeah, they still have divorces, monogamous marriages and stuff like that where I was born. Like I say, it's pretty primitive. I left home at fifteen, made it through vocational school on my own, and learned enough about what makes things fly to end up—after that disastrous marriage I told you about earlier—with my own repair hangar on the Star-pit.

Compared with Ratlit I had a stable childhood.

That's right, he lost the last parent he remembered when he was six. At seven he was convicted of his first felony—after escaping from Creton VII. But part of his treatment at hospital *cum* reform school *cum* prison was to have the details lifted from his memory. "Did something to my head back there. That's why I never could learn to read, I think." For the next couple of years he ran away from one foster group after the other. When he was eleven, some guy took him home from Play Planet where he'd been existing under the boardwalk on discarded hot dogs, souvlakia and falafel. "Fat, smoked perfumed cigarettes; name was Vivian?" Turned out to be the publisher. Ratlit stayed for three months, during which time he dictated a novel to Vivian. "Protecting my honor," Ratlit explained. "I had to do *something* to keep him busy."

The book sold a few hundred thousand copies as a precocious curiosity among many. But Ratlit had split. The next years he was involved as a shill in some illegality I never understood. He didn't either. "But I bet I made a million, Vyme! I earned at least a million." It's possible. At thirteen he still couldn't read or write, but his travels had gained him fair fluency in three languages. A couple of weeks ago he'd wandered off a stellar tramp, dirty and broke, here at the Star-pit. And I'd gotten him a job as grease monkey over at Poloscki's.

He leaned his elbows on his knees, his chin in his hands. "Vyme, it's a shame."

"What's a shame, kid-boy?"

"To be washed up at my age. A has-been! To have to grapple with the fact that this—" he spat at a star "—is it."

He was talking about golden again.

"You still have a chance." I shrugged. "Most of the time it doesn't come out till puberty."

He cocked his head up at me. "I've been pubescent since I was nine, buster."

"Ex*cuse* me."

"I feel cramped in, Vyme. There's all that night out there to grow up in, to explore."

"There was a time," I mused, "when the whole species was confined to the surface, give or take a few feet up or down, of a single planet. You've got the whole galaxy to run around in. You've seen a lot of it, yeah. But not all."

"But there are billions of galaxies out there. I want to see them. In all the stars around here there hasn't been one life form discovered that's based on anything but silicon or carbon. I overheard two golden in a bar once, talking: there's something in some galaxy out there that's big as a star, neither dead nor alive, and sings. I want to hear it, Vyme!"

"Ratlit, you can't fight reality."

"Oh, go to sleep, grandpa!" He closed his eyes and bent his head back until the cords of his neck quivered. "What is it that makes a golden? A combination of physiological and psychological . . . what?"

"It's primarily some sort of hormonal imbalance as well as an environmentally conditioned thalamic/personality response—"

"Yeah. Yeah." His head came down. "And that X-chromosome heredity nonsense they just connected up with it a few years back. But all I know is *they* can take the stasis shift from galaxy to galaxy, where you and I, Vyme, if we get more then twenty thousand light-years off the rim, we're dead."

"Insane at twenty thousand," I corrected. "Dead at twenty-five."

"Same difference." He opened his eyes. They were large, green and mostly pupil. "You know, I stole a golden belt once? Rolled it off a staggering slob about a week ago who came out of a bar and collapsed on the corner. I went across the Pit to Calle-J where nobody knows me and wore it around for a few hours, just to see if I felt different."

"You did?" Ratlit had lengths of gut that astounded me about once a day.

"I didn't. But people walking around me did. Wearing that two-inch band of yellow metal around my waist, nobody in the worlds could tell I wasn't a golden, just walking by on the street, without talking to me awhile, or making hormone tests. And wearing that belt, I learned just how much I hated golden. Because I could suddenly see, in almost everybody who came by, how much they hated me while I had that metal belt on. I threw it over the Edge." Suddenly he grinned. "Maybe I'll steal another one."

"You really hate them, Ratlit?"

He narrowed his eyes at me and looked superior.

"Sure, I talk about them," I told him. "Sometimes they're a pain to work for. But it's not their fault we can't take the reality shift."

"I'm just a child," he said evenly, "incapable of such fine reasoning. I hate them." He looked back at the night. "How can you stand to be trapped by anything, Vyme?"

Three memories crowded into my head when he said that.

First: I was standing at the railing of the East River—runs past this New York I was telling you about—at midnight, looking at the il-luminated dragon of the Manhattan Bridge that spanned the water, then at the industrial fires flickering in bright, smoky Brooklyn and then at the template of mercury streetlamps behind me bleaching out the playground and most of Houston Street; then, at the reflections in the water, here like crinkled foil, there like glistening rubber; at last, looked up at the mid-night sky itself. It wasn't black but dead pink, without a star. This glitter-ing world made the sky a roof that pressed down on me so I almost screamed. . . . That time the next night I was twenty-seven light-years away from Sol on my first star-run.

Second: I was visiting my mother after my first few years out. I was looking in the closet for something when this contraption of plastic straps and buckles fell on my head.

"What's this, ma?" And she smiled with a look of idiot nostalgia and crooned, "Why that's your little harness, Vymey. Your first father and I would take you on picnics up at Bear Mountain and put you in that and tie you to a tree with about ten feet of cord so you wouldn't get—" I didn't hear the rest because of the horror that suddenly flooded me, thinking of myself tied up in that thing. Okay, I was twenty and had just joined that beautiful procreation group a year back on Sigma and was the proud father of three and expecting two more. The hundred and sixty-three of us had the whole beach and nine miles of jungle and half a mountain to ourselves; maybe I was seeing Antoni caught up in that thing, trying to catch a bird or a beetle or a wave—with only ten feet of cord. I hadn't worn clothes for anything but work in a twelvemonth, and I was chomping to get away from that incredible place I had grown up in called an apartment and back to wives, husbands, kids and civilization. Anyway, it was pretty terrible.

The third? After I had left the proke-group—fled them, I suppose, guilty and embarrassed over something I couldn't name, still having nightmares once a month that woke me screaming about what was going to happen to the kids, even though I knew one point of group marriage was to prevent the loss of one, two or three parents being traumatic—still wondering if I wasn't making the same mistakes my parents made, hoping my brood wouldn't turn out like me, or worse like the kids you sometimes read about in the paper (like Ratlit, though I hadn't met him yet), horribly suspicious that no matter how different I tried to be from my sires, it was just the same thing all over again. . . . Anyway, I was on the ship bringing me to the Star-pit for the first time. I'd gotten talking to a golden who, as golden go, was a pretty regular gal. We'd been discussing inter- and intra-galactic drives. She was impressed I knew so much. I was impressed that she could use them and know so little. She was digging in a very girl-way the six-foot-four, two-hundred-and-ten-pound drive mechanic with mildly grimy fingernails that was me. I was digging in a very boy-way the slim, amber-eyed young lady who had seen it *all.* From the view deck we watched the immense, artificial disk of the Star-pit approach, when she turned to me and said, in a voice that didn't sound cruel at all, "This is as far as you go, isn't it?" And I was frightened all over again, because I knew that on about nine different levels she was right.

Ratlit said: "I know what you're thinking." A couple of times when he'd felt like being quiet and I'd felt like talking I may have told him more than I should. "Well, cube that for me, dad. That's how trapped I feel!"

I laughed, and Ratlit looked very young again. "Come on," I said. "Let's take a walk."

"Yeah." He stood. The wind fingered at our hair. "I want to go see Alegra."

"I'll walk you as far as Calle-G," I told him. "Then I'm going to go to bed."

"I wonder what Alegra thinks about this business? I always find Alegra a very good person to talk to," he said sagely. "Not to put you down, but her experiences are a little more up to date than yours. You have to admit she has a modern point of view. Plus the fact that she's older." Than Ratlit anyway. She was fifteen.

"I don't think being 'trapped' ever really bothered her," I said. "Which may be a place to take a lesson from."

By Ratlit's standards Alegra had a few things over me. In my youth kids took to dope in their teens, twenties. Alegra was born with a three-hundred-milligram-a-day habit on a bizarre narcotic that combined the psychedelic qualities of the most powerful hallucinogens with the addictiveness of the strongest depressants. I can sympathize. Alegra's mother was addicted, and the tolerance was passed with the blood plasma through the placental wall. Ordinarily a couple of complete transfusions at birth would have gotten the newborn child straight. But Alegra was also a highly projective telepath. She projected the horrors of birth, the glories of her infantile hallucinated world on befuddled doctors; she was given her drug. Without too much difficulty she managed to be given her drug every day since.

Once I asked Alegra when she'd first heard of golden, and she came back with this horror story. A lot were coming back from Tiber-44 cluster with psychic shock—the mental condition of golden is pretty delicate, and sometimes very minor conflicts nearly ruin them. Anyway, the government that was sponsoring the importation of micro-micro surgical equipment from some tiny planet in that galaxy, to protect its interests, hired Alegra, age eight, as a psychiatric therapist. "I'd concretize their fantasies and make them work 'em through. In just a couple of hours I'd have 'em back to their old, mean, stupid selves again. Some of them were pretty nice when they came to me." But there was a lot of work for her; projective telepaths are rare. So they started withholding her drug to force her to work harder, then rewarding her with increased dosage. "Up till then," she told me, "I might have kicked it. But when I came away, they had me on double what I used to take. They pushed me past the point where withdrawal would be fatal. But I *could* have kicked it, up till then, Vyme." That's right. Age eight.

Oh yeah. The drug was imported by golden from Cancer-9, and most of it goes through the Star-pit. Alegra came here because illegal imports are easier to come by, and you can get it for just about nothing—if you want it. Golden don't use it.

The wind lessened as Ratlit and I started back. Ratlit began to whistle. In Calle-K the first night lamp had broken so that the level street was a tunnel of black.

"Ratlit?" I asked. "Where do you think you'll be, oh, in say five years?"

"Quiet," he said. "I'm trying to get to the end of the street without bumping into the walls, tripping on something or some other catastrophe. If we get through the next five minutes all right, I'll worry about the next five years." He began whistling again.

"Trip? Bump the walls?"

"I'm listening for echoes." Again he commenced the little jets of music.

I put my hands in my overall pouch and went on quietly while Ratlit did the bat bit. Then there was a catastrophe. Though I didn't realize it at the time.

Into the circle of light from the remaining lamp at the other end of the street walked a golden.

His hands went up to his face, and he was laughing. The sound skittered in the street. His belt was low on his belly the way the really down and broke—

I just thought of a better way to describe him; the resemblance struck me immediately. He looked like Sandy, my mechanic, who is short, twenty-four years old, muscled like an ape and wears his worn-out work clothes even when he's off duty. ("I just want this job for a while, boss. I'm not staying out here at the Star-pit. As soon as I save up a little, I'm gonna make it back in toward galactic center. It's funny out here, like dead." He gazes up through the opening in the hangar roof where there are no clouds and no stars either. "Yeah. I'm just gonna be here for a little while.")

("Fine with me, kid-boy.")

(That was three months back, like I say. He's still with me. He works hard too, which puts him a cut above a lot of characters out here. Still, there was something about Sandy . . .) On the other hand Sandy's face is also hacked up with acne. His hair is always nap short over his wide head. But in these aspects, the golden was exactly Sandy's opposite, come to think of it. Still, there was something about the golden . . .

He staggered, went down on his knees still laughing, then collapsed. By the time we reached him, he was silent. With the toe of his boot Ratlit nudged the hand from the belt buckle.

It flopped, palm up, on the pavement. The little fingernail was three quarters of an inch long, the way a lot of the golden wear it. (Like his face, the tips of Sandy's fingers are all masticated wrecks. Still, something . . .)

"Now isn't that something." Ratlit shook his head. "What do you want to do with him, Vyme?"

"Nothing," I said. "Let him sleep it off."

"Leave him so somebody can come along and steal his belt?" Ratlit grinned. "I'm not that nasty."

"Weren't you just telling me how much you hated golden?"

"I'd be nasty to whoever stole the belt and wore it. Nobody but a golden should be hated that much."

"Ratlit, let's go."

But he had already kneeled down and was shaking the golden's shoulder. "Let's get him to Alegra's and find out what's the matter with him."

"He's just drunk."

"Nope," Ratlit said. "Cause he don't smell funny."

"Look. Get back." I hoisted the golden up and laid him across my neck, fireman's carry. "Start moving," I told Ratlit. "I think you're crazy."

Ratlit grinned. "Thanks. Maybe he'll be grateful and lay some lepta on me for taking him in off the street."

"You don't know golden," I said. "But if he does, split it with me."

"Sure."

Two blocks later we reached Alegra's place. (But like I say, Sandy, though well-built, is little; so I didn't have much trouble carrying him.) Halfway up the tilting stairs Ratlit said, "She's in a good mood."

"I guess she is." The weight across my shoulders was becoming pleasant.

I can't describe Alegra's place. I can describe a lot of places like it; and I can describe it before she moved in because I knew a derelict named Drunk-roach who slept on that floor before she did. You know what never-wear plastics look like when they wear out? What nonrust metals look like when they rust through? It was a shabby crack-walled cubicle with dirt in the corners and scars on the windowpane when Drunk-roach had his pile of blankets in the corner. But since the hallucinating projective telepath took it over, who knows what it had become.

Ratlit opened the door on an explosion of classical beauty. "Come in," she said, accompanied by symphonic arrangement scored on twenty-four staves, with full chorus. "What's that you're carrying, Vyme? Oh, it's a golden!" And before me, dizzying tides of yellow.

"Put him down, put him down quick and let's see what's wrong!" Hundreds of eyes, spotlights, glittering lenses; I lowered him to the mattress in the corner. "Ohhh . . ." breathed Alegra.

And the golden lay on orange silk pillows in a teak barge drawn by swans, accompanied by flutes and drums.

"Where did you find him?" she hissed, circling against the ivory moon on her broom. We watched the glowing barge, hundreds of feet below, sliding down the silvered waters between the crags.

"We just picked him up off the street," Ratlit said. "Vyme thought he was drunk. But he don't smell."

"Was he laughing?" Alegra asked. Laughter rolled and broke on the rocks.

"Yeah," Ratlit said. "Just before he collapsed."

"Then he must be from the Un-dok expedition that just got back." Mosquitoes darted at us through wet fronds. The insects reeled among the leaves, upsetting droplets that fell like glass as, barely visible beyond the palms, the barge drifted on the bright, sweltering river.

"That's right," I said, backpaddling frantically to avoid a hippopotamus that threatened to upset my kayak. "I'd forgotten they'd just come in."

"Okay," Ratlit's breath clouded his lips. "I'm out of it. Let me in. Where did they come back from?" The snow hissed beneath the runners, as we looked after the barge, nearly at the white horizon.

"Un-dok, of course," Alegra said. The barking grew fainter. "Where did you think?"

White eclipsed to black, and the barge was a spot gleaming in galactic night, flown on by laboring comets.

"Un-dok is the furthest galaxy reached yet," I told Ratlit. "They just got back last week."

"Sick," Alegra added.

I dug my fingers against my abdomen to grab the pain.

"They all came back sick—"

Fever heated blood-bubbles in my eyes: I slipped to the ground, my mouth wide, my tongue like paper on my lips . . .

Ratlit coughed. "All *right*, Alegra. Cut it out! You don't have to be so dramatic!"

"Oh, I'm dreadfully sorry Ratty, Vyme." Coolth, water. Nausea swept away as solicitous nurses hastily put the pieces back together until everything was beautiful, or so austerely horrible it could be appreciated as beauty. "Anyway," she went on, "they came back with some sort of disease they picked up out there. Apparently it's not contagious, but they're stuck with it for the rest of their lives. Every few days they suddenly have a blackout. It's preceded by a fit of hysterics. It's just one of those stupid things they can't do anything about yet. It doesn't hurt their being golden."

Ratlit began to laugh. Suddenly he asked, "How long are they passed out for?"

"Only a few hours." Alegra said. "It must be terribly annoying." And I began to feel mildly itchy in all sorts of unscratchable places, my shoulder blades, somewhere down my ear, the roof of my mouth. Have you ever tried to scratch the roof of your mouth?

"Well," Ratlit said, "let's sit down and wait it out."

"We can talk," Alegra said, patly. "That way it won't seem like such a long . . ." and hundreds of years later she finished ". . . time."

"Good," Ratlit said. "I wanted to talk to you. That's why I came up here in the first place."

"Oh, fine!" Alegra said. "I love to talk. I want to talk about love. Loving someone" (an incredible yearning twisted my stomach, rose to block my throat) "I mean really loving someone" (the yearning brushed the edge of agony) "means you are willing to admit the person you love is not what you first fell in love with, not the image you first had; and you must be able to like them still for being as close to that image as they are, and avoid disliking them for being so far away."

And through the tenderness that suddenly obliterated all hurt, Ratlit's voice came from the jeweled mosaics shielding him: "Alegra, I want to talk about loneliness."

"I'm on my way home, kids," I said. "Tell me what happens with Prince Charming when he wakes up." They kept on talking while I went through the difficulties of finding my way out without Alegra's help. When my head cleared, halfway down the stairs, I couldn't tell you if I'd been there five minutes or five years.

When I got to the hangar next morning Sandy was filing the eight-foot prongs on the conveyer. "You got a job coming in about twenty minutes," he called down from the scaffold.

"I hope it's not another of those rebuilt jobs."

"Yep."

"Hell," I said. "I don't want to see another one for six weeks."

"All he wants is a general tune-up. Maybe two hours."

"Depends on where it's been," I said. "Where *has* it been?"

"Just back from—"

"Never mind." I started toward the office cubicle. "I think I'll put the books in order for the last six months. Can't let it go forever."

"Boss!" Sandy protested. "That'll take all day!"

"Then I better get started." I leaned back out the door. "Don't disturb me."

Of course as soon as the shadow of the hull fell over the office window I came out in my coveralls, after giving Sandy five minutes to get it grappled and himself worried. I took the lift up to the one-fifty catwalk. When I stepped out, Sandy threw me a grateful smile from his scar-ugly face. The golden had already started his instructions. When I reached them and coughed, the golden turned to me and continued talking, not bothering to fill me in on what he had said before, figuring Sandy and I would put it together. You could tell this golden had made his pile. He wore an immaculate blue tunic, with bronze codpiece, bracelets and earrings. His hair was the same bronze, his skin was burned red black and his blue gray eyes and tight-muscled mouth were proud, proud, proud. While I finished getting instructions, Sandy quietly got started unwelding the eight-foot seal of the organum so we could get to the checkout circuits.

Finally the golden stopped talking—that's the only way you could tell he was finished—and leaned his angular six and a half feet against the railing, clicking his glossy, manicured nails against the pipe a few times. He had that same sword-length pinky nail, all white against his skin. I climbed out on the rigging to help Sandy.

We had been at work ten minutes when a kid, maybe eighteen or nineteen, barefoot and brown, black hair hacked off shoulder length, a rag that didn't fit tucked around under his belt, and dirty, came wandering down the catwalk. His thumbs were hooked under the metal links: golden.

First I thought he'd come from the ship. Then I realized he'd just stalked into the hangar from outside and come up on the lift.

"Hey, brother!" The kid who was golden hooked his thumbs in his belt, as Sandy and I watched the dialogue from the rigging on the side of the hull. "I'm getting tired of hanging around this Star-pit. Just about broke as well. Where you running to?"

The man who was golden clicked his nails again. "Go away, distant cousin."

"Come on, brother, give me a berth on your lifeboat out of this dung-heap to someplace worthwhile."

"Go away, or I'll kill you."

"Now, brother, I'm just a youngster adrift in this forsaken quarter of the sky. Come on, now—"

Suddenly the blonde man whirled from the railing, grabbed up a four-foot length of pipe leaning beside him and swung it so hard it hissed. The black-haired ragamuffin leapt back and from under his rag snatched something black that, with a flick of that long nail, grew seven inches of blade. The bar swung again, caught the shoulder of the boy, then clattered against the hull. He shrieked and came straight forward. The two bodies locked, turned, fell. A gurgle, and the man's hands slipped from the neck of the ragamuffin. The boy scrambled back to his feet. Blood bubbled and popped on the hot blade.

A last spasm caught the man; he flipped over, smearing the catwalk, rolled once more, this time under the rail, and dropped—two hundred and fifty feet to the cement flooring.

Flick. Off went the power in the knife. The golden wiped powdered blood on his thigh, spat over the rail and said softly, "No relative of mine." Flick. The blade itself disappeared. He started down the catwalk.

"Hey!" Sandy called, when he got his voice back up into his throat, "what about . . . I mean you . . . well, your ship!" There are no familial inheritance laws among golden—only rights of plunder.

The golden glanced back. "I give it to you," he sneered. His shoulder must have been killing him, but he stepped into the lift like he was walking into a phone booth. That's a golden for you.

Sandy was horrified and bewildered. Behind his pitted ugliness there was that particularly wretched amazement only the totally vulnerable get when hurt.

"That's the first time you've ever seen an incident like that?" I felt sorry for him.

"Well, I wandered into Gerg's Bar a couple of hours after they had that massacre. But the ones who started it were drunk."

"Drunk or sober," I said. "Believe me, it doesn't mean that much difference to the way a man acts." I shook my head. "I keep forgetting you've only been here three months."

Sandy, upset, looked down at the body on the flooring. "What about him? And the ship, boss?"

"I'll call the wagon to come scrape him up. The ship is yours."

"Huh?"

"He gave it to you. It'll stand up in court. It just takes one witness. Me."

"What am I gonna do with it? I mean I would have to haul it to a junk station to get the salvage. Look, boss, I'm gonna give it to you. Sell it or something. I'd feel sort of funny with it anyway."

"I don't want it. Besides, then I'd be involved in the transaction and couldn't be a witness."

"I'll be a witness." Ratlit stepped from the lift. "I caught the whole bit when I came in the door. Great acoustics in this place." He whistled again. The echo came back. Ratlit closed his eyes for a moment. "Ceiling is . . . a hundred and twenty feet overhead, more or less. How's that, huh?"

"Hundred and twenty-seven," I said.

Ratlit shrugged. "I need more practice. Come on, Sandy, you give it to him, and I'll be a witness."

"You're a minor," Sandy said. Sandy didn't like Ratlit, I used to think it was because Ratlit was violent and flamboyant where Sandy was stolid and ugly. Even though Sandy kept protesting the temporariness of his job to me, I remember, when I first got to the Star-pit, those long-dying thoughts I'd had about leaving. It was a little too easy to see Sandy a mechanic here thirty years from now. I wasn't the only one it had happened to. Ratlit had been a grease monkey here three weeks. You tell me where he was going to be in three more. "Aren't you supposed to be working at Poloscki's?" Sandy said, turning back to the organum.

"Coffee break," Ratlit said. "If you're going to give it away, Sandy, can I have it?"

"So you can claim salvage? Hell, no!"

"I don't want it for salvage. I want it for a present." Sandy looked up again. "Yeah. To give to someone else. Finish the tune-up and give it to me, okay?"

"You're nuts, kid-boy," Sandy said. "Even if I gave you the ship, what you gonna pay for the work with?"

"Aw, it'll only take a couple of hours. You're half-done anyway. I figured you'd throw in the tune-up along with it. If you really want the money, I'll get it to you a little at a time. Vyme, what sort of professional discount will you give me? I'm just a grease monkey, but I'm still in the business."

I whacked the back of his red head between a-little-too-playfully and not-too-hard. "Come on, kid-boy," I said. "Help me take care of puddles downstairs. Sandy, finish it up, huh?"

Sandy grunted and plunged both hands back into the organum.

As soon as the lift door closed, Ratlit demanded, "You gonna give it to me, Vyme?"

"It's Sandy's ship," I said.

"You tell him, and he will."

I laughed. "You tell me how your golden turned out when he came to. I assume that's who you want the ship for. What sort of fellow was he?"

Ratlit hooked his fingers in the mesh wall of the lift cage and leaned back. "They're only two types of golden." He began to swing from side to side. "Mean ones and stupid ones." He was repeating a standard line around the Star-pit.

"I hope yours is stupid." I said, thinking of the two who'd just ruined Sandy's day and upset mine.

"Which is worse?" Ratlit shrugged. That is the rest of the line. When a golden isn't being outright mean, he exhibits the sort of nonthinkingness that gets other people hurt—you remember the one that nearly rammed my ship, or the ones who didn't bother to bring back the Kyber antitoxin? "But this one—" Ratlit stood up "—is unbelievably stupid."

"Yesterday you hated them. Today you want to give one a ship?"

"He doesn't have one," Ratlit explained calmly, as though that warranted all change of attitude. "And because he's sick, it'll be hard for him to find work unless he has one of his own."

"I see." We bounced on the silicon cushion. I pushed open the door and started for the office. "What all went on after I left? I must have missed the best part of the evening."

"You did. Will I really need that much more sleep when I pass thirty-five?"

"Cut the cracks and tell me what happened."

"Well—" Ratlit leaned against the office door jamb while I dialed necrotics. "Alegra and I talked a little after you left, till finally we realized the golden was awake and listening. Then he told us we were beautiful."

I raised an eyebrow. "Mmmm?"

"That's what we said. And he said it again, that watching us talk and think and build was one of the most beautiful things he'd ever seen. 'What have you seen?' we asked him. And he began to tell us." Ratlit stopped breathing, something built up, then, at once, it came out. "Oh, Vyme, the places he's been! The things he's done! The landscapes he's starved in, the hells where he's had to lie down and go to sleep he was that tired, or the heavens he's soared through screaming! Oh, the things he told us about! And Alegra made them almost real so we could all be there again, just like she used to do when she was a psychiatrist! The stories, the places, the things . . ."

"Sounds like it was really something."

"It was nothing!" he came back vehemently. "It was all in the tears that wash your eyes, in the humming in your ears, in the taste of your own saliva. It was just a hallucination, Vyme! It wasn't real." Here his voice started cracking between the two octaves that were after it. "But that thing I told you about . . . huge . . . alive and dead at the same time, like a star . . . way in another galaxy. Well, he's seen it. And last night, but it wasn't real of course, but . . . I almost heard it . . . singing!" His eyes were huge and green and bright. I felt envious of anyone who could pull this reaction from kids like Alegra and Ratlit.

"So, we decided—" his voice fixed itself on the proper side of middle C—"after he went back to sleep, and we lay awake talking a while longer, that we'd try and help him get back out there. Because it's . . . wonderful!"

"That's fascinating." When I finished my call, I stood up from the desk. I'd been sitting on the corner. "After work I'll buy you dinner and you can tell me all about the things he showed you."

"He's still there, at Alegra's," Ratlit said—helplessly, I realized after a moment. "I'm going back there right after work."

"Oh," I said. I didn't seem to be invited.

"It's just a shame," Ratlit said when we came out of the office, "that he's so stupid." He glanced at the mess staining the concrete and shook his head.

I'd gone back to the books when Sandy stepped in. "All finished. What say we knock off for a beer or something, huh, boss?"

"All right," I said, surprised. Sandy was usually as social as he was handsome. "Want to talk about something?"

"Yeah." He looked relieved.

"That business this morning got to your head, huh?"

"Yeah," he repeated.

"There is a reason," I said as I made ready to go. "It's got something to do with the psychological part of being a golden. Meanness and stupidity, like everyone says. But however it makes them act here, it protects them from complete insanity at the twenty thousand light-year limit."

"Yeah. I know, I know." Sandy had started stepping uncomfortably from one boot to the other. "But that's not what I wanted to talk about."

"It isn't?"

"Um-um."

"Well?" I asked after a moment.

"It's that kid, the one you're gonna give the ship to."

"Ratlit?"

"Yeah."

"I haven't made up my mind about giving him the ship," I lied. "Besides, legally it's yours."

"You'll give it to him," Sandy said. "And I don't care, I mean not about the ship. But, boss, I gotta talk to you about that kid-boy."

Something about Sandy . . .

I'd never realized he'd thought of Ratlit as more than a general nuisance. Also, he seemed sincerely worried about me. I was curious. It took him all the way to the bar and through two beers—while I drank hot milk with honey—before he tongued and chewed what he wanted to say into shape.

"Boss, understand, I'm nearer Ratlit than you. Not only my age. My life's been more like his than yours has. You look at him like a son. To me, he's a younger brother: I taught him all the tricks. I don't understand him completely but I see him clearer than you do. He's had a hard time, but not as hard as you think. He's gonna take you—and I don't mean money—for everything he can."

Where the hell that came from I didn't know and didn't like. "He won't take anything I don't want to give."

"Boss?" Sandy suddenly asked. "You got kids of your own?"

"Nine," I said. "Did have. I don't see the ones who're left now, for which their parents have always been just as happy—except one. And she was sensible enough to go along with the rest, while she was alive."

"Oh." Sandy got quiet again. Suddenly he went scrambling in his overall pouch and pulled out a three-inch porta-pix. Those great, greasy hands that I was teaching to pick up an eggshell through a five-hundred-to-one-ratio waldo were clumsily fumbling at the push-pull levers. "I got kids," he said. "See. Seven of them."

And on the porta-pix screen was a milling, giggling group of little apes that couldn't have been anybody else's. All the younger ones lacked was acne. They even shuffled back and forth from one foot to the other. They began to wave, and the speaker in the back chirped: "Hi, da! Hello, da! Da, mommy says to say we love you! Da, da, come home soon!"

"I'm not with them now," he said throatily. "But I'm going back soon as I get enough money so I can take them all out of that hell hole they're in now and get the whole family with a decent-sized proke-group. They're only twenty-three adults there now, and things were beginning to rub. That's why I left in the first place. It was getting so nobody could talk to anyone else. That's pretty rough on all our kids, thirty-two when I left. But soon I'll be able to fix that."

"On the salary I'm paying you?" This was the first I'd heard of any of this; that was my first reaction. My second, which I didn't voice, was: then why the hell don't you take that ship and sell it somehow! Over forty and self-employed, the most romantic become monetarily practical.

Sandy's fist came down hard on the bar. "That's what I'm trying to say to you, boss! About you, about Ratlit. You've all got it in your heads that this, out here, is it! The end! Sure, you gotta accept limitations, but the right ones. Sure, you have to admit there are certain directions in which you cannot go. But once you do that, you find there are others where you can go as far as you want. Look, I'm not gonna hang around the Star-pit all my life! And if I make my way back toward galactic center, make enough money so I can go home, raise my family the way I want, that's going forward, forward even from here. Not back."

"All right," I said. Quiet Sandy surprised me. I still wondered why he wasn't breaking his tail to get salvage on that ship that had just fallen into his hands, if getting back home with money in his pocket was that important. "I'm glad you told me about yourself. Now how does it all tie up with Ratlit?"

"Yeah. Ratlit." He put the porta-pix back in his overall pouch. "Boss, Ratlit is the kid your own could be. You want to give him the advice, friendship and concern he's never had, that you couldn't give yours. But Ratlit is also the kid I was about ten years ago, started no place, with no destination, and no values to help figure out the way, mixed up in all the wrong things, mainly because he's not sure where the right ones are."

"I don't think you're that much like Ratlit," I told him. "I think you may wish you were. You've done a lot of the things Ratlit's done? Ever write a novel?"

"I tried to write a trilogy," Sandy said. "It was lousy. But it pushed some things off my chest. So I got something out of it, even if nobody else did, which is what's important. Because now I'm a better mechanic for it, boss. Until I admit to myself what I can't do, it's pretty hard to work on what I can. Same goes for Ratlit. You too. That's growing up. And one thing you can't do is help Ratlit by giving him a ship he can't fly."

*Growing up* brought back the picture. "Sandy, did you ever build an ecologarium when you were a kid?"

"No." The word had the puzzled inflection that means, Don't-even-know-what-one-is.

"I didn't either," I told him. Then I grinned and punched him on the shoulder. "Maybe you're a little like me, too? Let's get back to work."

"Another thing," Sandy said, not looking very happy as he got off the stool. "Boss, that kid's gonna hurt you. I don't know how, but it's gonna seem like he hunted for how to make it hurt most, too. That's what I wanted to tell you, boss."

I was going to urge him to take the ship, but he handed me the keys back in the hangar before I could say anything, and walked away. When people who should be clearing up their own problems start giving you advice . . . well, there was something about Sandy I didn't like.

If I can't take long walks at night with company, I take them by myself. I was strolling by the Edge, the world-wind was low, and the Stellarplex, the huge heat-gathering mirror that's hung nine thousand miles off the pit, was out. It looks vaguely like the moon used to look from Earth, only twice as big, perfectly silver, and during the three and a half days it faces us it's always full.

Then, up ahead where the fence was broken, I saw Ratlit kicking gravel over the Edge. He was leaning against a lamppost, his shirt ballooning and collapsing at his back.

"Hey, kid-boy! Isn't the golden still at Alegra's?"

Ratlit saw me and shrugged.

"What's the matter?" I asked when I reached him. "Ate dinner yet?"

He shrugged again. His body had the sort of ravenous metabolism that shows twenty-four hours without food. "Come on. I promised you a meal. Why so glum?"

"Make it something to drink."

"I know about your phony ID," I told him. "But we're going to eat. You can have milk, just like me."

No protests, no dissertation on the injustice of liquor laws. He started walking with me.

"Come on, kid-boy, talk to gramps. Don't you want your ship any more?"

Suddenly he clutched my forearm with white, bony fingers. My forearm is pretty thick, and he couldn't get his hands around it. "Vyme, you've got to make Sandy give it to me now! You've got to!"

"Kid-boy, talk to me."

"Alegra." He let go. "And the golden. Hate golden, Vyme. Always hate them. Because if you start to like one, and then start hating again, it's worse."

"What's going on? What are they doing?"

"He's talking. She's hallucinating. And neither one pays any attention to me."

"I see."

"You don't see. You don't understand about Alegra and me."

Then I was the only one who'd met the both of them who didn't. "I know you're very fond of each other." More could be said.

Ratlit said more. "We don't even like each other that much, Vyme. But we need each other. Since she's been here, I get her medicine for her. She's too sick to go out much now. And when I have bad changes, or sometimes bright recognitions, it doesn't matter, I bring them to her, and she builds pictures of them for me, and we explore them together and . . . learn about things. When she was a psychiatrist for the government, she learned an awful lot about how people tick. And she's got an awful lot to teach me, things I've got to know." Fifteen-year-old ex-psychiatrist drug addicts? Same sort of precocity that produces thirteen-year-old novelists. Get used to it. "I need her now almost as much as she needs her . . . medicine."

"Have you told the golden you've got him a ship?"

"You didn't say I could have it yet."

"Well, I say so right now. Why don't we go back there and tell him he can be on his way? If we put it a little more politely, don't you think that'll do the trick?"

He didn't say anything. His face just got back a lot of its life.

"We'll go right after we eat. What the hell, I'll buy you a drink. I may even have one with you."

Alegra's was blinding when we arrived. "Ratlit, oh, you're back! Hello, Vyme! I'm so glad you're both here! Everything is beautiful tonight!"

"The golden," Ratlit said. "Where's the golden?"

"He's not here." A momentary throb of sadness dispelled with tortuous joy. "But he's coming back!"

"Oh," Ratlit said. His voice echoed through the long corridors of golden absence winding the room. " 'Cause I got a ship for him. All his. Just had a tune-up. He can leave any time he wants to."

"Here're the keys," I said, taking them from my pouch for dramatic effect. "Happen to have them right here."

As I handed them to Ratlit there were fireworks, applause, a fanfare of brasses. "Oh, that's wonderful. Wonderful! Because guess what, Ratlit? Guess what, Vyme?"

"I don't know," Ratlit said. "What?"

"I'm a golden guy." Alegra cried from the shoulders of the cheering crowd that pushed its way through more admiring thousands.

"Huh?"

"I, me, myself am actually an honest-to-goodness golden. I just found out today."

"You can't be," Ratlit said. "You're too old for it just to show up now."

"Something about my medicine," Alegra explained. "It's dreadfully complicated." The walls were papered with anatomical charts, music by Stockhausen. "Something in my medicine kept it from coming out until now, until a golden could come to me, drawing it up and out of the depths of me, till it burst out, beautiful and wonderful and . . . golden! Right now he's gone off to Carlson Labs with a urine sample for a final hormone check. They'll let him know in an hour, and he'll bring back my golden belt. But he's sure already. And when he comes back with it, I'm going to go with him to the galaxies, as his apprentice. We're going to find a cure for his sickness and something that will make it so I won't need my medicine any more. He says if you have all the universe to roam around in, you can find anything you look for. But you need it *all*—not just a cramped little cluster of a few billion stars off in a corner by itself. Oh, I'm free, Ratlit, like you always wanted to be! While you were gone, he . . . well, did something to me that was . . . *golden!* It triggered my hormonal imbalance." The image came in through all five senses. Breaking the melodious ecstasy came the clatter of keys as Ratlit hurled them at the wall.

I left feeling pretty odd. Ratlit had started to go too, but Alegra called him back. "Oh, now don't go on like that, Ratty! Act your age. Won't you stay and do me one little last favor?"

So he stayed. When I untangled myself from the place and was walking home, I kept on remembering what Alegra had said about love.

Work next day went surprisingly smoothly. Poloscki called me up about ten and asked if I knew where Ratlit was because he hadn't been at work that day. "You're sure the kid isn't sick?"

I said I'd seen him last night and that he was probably all right. Poloscki made a disgusted sound and hung up.

Sandy left a few minutes early, as he'd been doing all week, to run over to the post office before it closed. He was expecting a letter from his group, he said. I felt strange about having given the ship away out from under him. It was sort of an immature thing to do. But he hadn't said anything about wanting it, and Ratlit was still doing Alegra favors, so maybe it would all work out for the best.

I thought about visiting Alegra that evening. But there was the last six month's paperwork, still not finished. I went into the office, plugged in the computer and got ready to work late.

I was still at it sometime after eleven when the entrance light blinked, which meant somebody had opened the hangar door. I'd locked it. Sandy had the keys so he could come in early. So it was Sandy. I was ready for a break and all set to jaw with him awhile. He was always coming back to do a little work at odd hours. I waited for him to come into the office. But he didn't.

Then the needle on the power gauge, which had been hovering near zero with only the drain of the little office computer, swung up to seven. One of the big pieces of equipment had been cut in.

There was some cleanup work to do, but nothing for a piece that size. Frowning, I switched off the computer and stepped out of the office. The first great opening in the hangar roof was mostly blocked with the bulk of Ratlit's/Sandy's/my ship. Stellarplex light curved smoothly over one side, then snarled in the fine webbing of lifts, catwalks, haul-lines and grappler rigging. The other two openings were empty, and hundred-meter circles of silver dropped through assembly riggings to the concrete floor. Then I saw Sandy.

He stood just inside the light from the last opening, staring up at the Stellarplex, its glare lost in his ruined face. As he raised his left hand—when it started to move I thought it looked too big—light caught on the silver joints of the master-gauntlet he was wearing. I knew where the power was going.

As his hand went above his head, a shadow fell over him as a fifteen-foot slave talon swung from the darkness, its movement aping the master-glove. He dropped his hand in front of his face, fingers curved. Metal claws lowered about him, beginning to quiver. Something about . . . he was trying to kill himself!

I started running toward those hesitant, gaping claws, leaped into the grip, and reached over his shoulder to slap my forearm into the control glove, just as he squeezed. Like I said, my forearm is big, but when those claws came together, it was a tight fit. Sandy was crying.

"You stupid," I shouted, "inconsiderate, bird-brained, infantile—" at last I got the glove off "—puerile . . ." Then I said, "What the hell is the matter with you?"

Sandy was sitting on the floor now, his head hung between his shoulders. He stank.

"Look," I said, maneuvering the talon back into place with the gross-motion controls on the gauntlet's wrist, "if you want to go jump off the Edge, that's fine with me. Half the gate's down anyway. But don't come here and mess up my tools. You can squeeze your own head up a little, but you're not going to bust up my glove here. You're fired. Now tell me what's wrong."

"I knew it wasn't going to work. Wasn't even worth trying. I knew . . ." His voice was getting all mixed up with the sobs. "But I thought maybe . . ." Beside his left hand was the porta-pix, its screen cracked. And a crumpled piece of paper.

I turned off the glove, and the talons stopped humming twenty feet overhead. I picked up the paper and smoothed it out. I didn't mean to read it all the way through.

Dear Sanford,

Things have been difficult since you left but not too hard and I guess a lot of pressure is off everybody since you went away and the kids are getting used to your not being here though Bobbi-D cried a lot at first. She doesn't now. We got your letter and were glad to hear things had begun to settle down for you though Hank said you should have written before this and was very mad though Mary tried to calm him down but he just said, "When he married you all he married me too, damn it, and I've got just as much right to be angry at him as you have," which is true, Sanford, but I tell you what he said because it's a quote and I think you should know exactly what's being said, especially since it expresses something we all feel on one level or another. You said you might be able to send us a little money, if we wanted you home, which I think would be very good, the money I mean, though Laura said if I put that in the letter she would divorce us, but she won't, and like Hank I've got a right to say what I feel which is, Yes I think you should send money, especially after that unpleasant business just before you left. But we are all agreed we do not want you to come back. And would rather not have the money if that's what it meant.

That is hard but true. As you can gather your letter caused quite an upset here. I would like—which makes me different from the others but is why they wanted me to write this letter—to hear from you again and keep track of what you are doing because I used to love you very much and I never could hate you. But like Bobbi-D, I have stopped crying.

Sincerely—

The letter was signed "Joseph." In the lower corner were the names of the rest of the men and women of the group.

"Sandy?"

"I knew they wouldn't take me back. I didn't even really try, did I? But—"

"Sandy, get up."

"But the *children*" he whispered. "What's gonna happen to the children?"

And there was a sound from the other end of the hangar. Three stories up the side of the ship in the open hatchway, silvered by Stellarplex light, stood the golden, the one Ratlit and I had found on the street. You remember what he looked like. He and Alegra must have sneaked in while Sandy and I were struggling with the waldo. Probably they wanted to get away as soon as possible before Ratlit made real trouble, or before I changed my mind and got the keys back. All this ship-giving had been done without witnesses. The sound was the lift rising toward the hatchway. "The children . . ." Sandy whispered again.

The door opened, and a figure stepped out in the white light. Only it was Ratlit! It was Ratlit's red hair, his gold earring, his bouncy run as he started for the hatch. And there were links of yellow metal around his waist.

Baffled, I heard the golden call: "Everything checks out inside, brother. She'll fly us anywhere."

And Ratlit cried, "I got the grapples all released, brother. Let's go!" Their voices echoed down through the hangar. Sandy raised his head, squinting.

As Ratlit leapt into the hatch, the golden caught his arm around the boy's shoulder. They stood a moment, gazing at one another, then Ratlit turned to look down into the hangar, back on the world he was about to leave. I couldn't tell if he knew we were there or not. Even as the hatch swung closed, the ship began to whistle.

I hauled Sandy back into the shock chamber. I hadn't even locked the door when the thunder came and my ears nearly split. I think the noise surprised Sandy out of himself. It broke something up in my head, but the pieces were falling wrong.

"Sandy," I said, "we've got to get going!"

"Huh?" He was fighting the drunkenness and probably his stomach too.

"I don't wanna go nowhere."

"You're going anyway. I'm sure as hell not going to leave you alone."

When we were halfway up the stairs I figured she wasn't there. I felt just the same. Was she with them in the ship?

"My medicine. Please can't you get my medicine? I've got to have my medicine, please, please . . . please." I could just hear the small, high voice when I reached the door. I pushed it open.

Alegra lay on the mattress, pink eyes wide, white hair frizzled around her balding skull. She was incredibly scrawny, her uncut nails black as Sandy's nubs without the excuse of hours in a graphite-lubricated gauntlet. The translucency of her pigmentless skin under how-many-days of dirt made my flesh crawl. Her face drew in around her lips like the flesh about a scar. "My medicine. Vyme, is that you? You'll get my medicine for me, Vyme? Won't you get my medicine?" Her mouth wasn't moving, but the voice came on. She was too weak to project on any but the aural level. It was the first time I'd seen Alegra without her cloak of hallucination, and it brought me up short.

"Alegra," I said when I got hold of myself. "Ratlit and the golden went off on the ship!"

"Ratlit. Oh, nasty Ratty, awful little boy! He wouldn't get my medicine. But you'll get it for me, won't you, Vyme? I'm going to die in about ten minutes, Vyme. I don't want to die. Not like this. The world is so ugly and painful now. I don't want to die here."

"Don't you have any?" I stared around the room I hadn't seen since Drunk-roach lived there. It was a lot worse. Dried garbage, piled first in one corner, now covered half the floor. The rest was littered with papers, broken glass and a spilled can of something unrecognizable for the mold.

"No. None here. Ratlit gets it from a man who hangs out in Gerg's over on Calle-X. Oh, Ratlit used to get it for me every day, such a nice little boy, every day he would bring me my lovely medicine, and I never had to leave my room at all. You go get it for me, Vyme!"

"It's the middle of the night, Alegra! Gerg's is closed, and Calle-X is all the way across the pit anyway. Couldn't even get there in ten minutes, much less find this character and come back!"

"If I were well, Vyme, I'd fly you there in a cloud of light pulled by peacocks and porpoises, and you'd come back to hautboys and tambourines, bringing my beautiful medicine to me, in less than an eye's blink. But I'm sick now. And I'm going to die."

There was a twitch in the crinkled lid of one pink eye.

"Alegra, what happened!"

"Ratlit's insane!" she projected with shocking viciousness. I heard Sandy behind me catch his breath. "Insane at twenty thousand light-years, dead at twenty-five."

"But his golden belt . . ."

"It was mine! It was my belt and he stole it. And he wouldn't get my medicine. Ratlit's not a golden. I'm a golden, Vyme! I can go anywhere, anywhere at all! I'm a golden golden golden . . . But I'm sick now. I'm so sick."

"But didn't the golden know the belt was yours?"

"Him? Oh, he's so incredibly stupid! He would believe anything. The golden went to check some papers and get provisions and was gone all day, to get my belt. But you were here that night. I asked Ratlit to go get my medicine and take another sample to Carlson's for me. But neither of them came back till I was very sick, very weak. Ratlit found the golden, you see, told him that I'd changed my mind about going, and that he, Ratlit, was a golden as well, that he'd just been to Carlson's. So the golden gave him my belt and off they went."

"But how in the world would he believe a kid with a story like that?"

"You know how stupid a golden can be, Vyme. As stupid as they can be mean. Besides, it doesn't matter to him if Ratlit dies. He doesn't care if Ratlit was telling the truth or not. The golden will live. When Ratlit starts drooling, throwing up blood, goes deaf first and blind last and dies, the golden won't even be sad. He's too stupid to feel sad. That's the way golden are. But I'm sad, Vyme, because no one will bring me my medicine."

My frustration had to lash at something; she was there. "You mean you didn't know what you were doing to Ratlit by leaving, Alegra? You mean you didn't know how much he wanted to get out, and how much he needed you at the same time? You couldn't see what it would do to him if you deprived him of the thing he needed and rubbed his nose in the thing he hated both at once? You couldn't guess that he'd pull something crazy? Oh, kid-girl, you talk about golden. You're the stupid one!"

"Not stupid," she projected quietly. *"Mean,* Vyme. I knew he'd try to do something. I just didn't think he'd succeed. Ratlit is really such a child."

The frustration, spent, became rolling sadness. "Couldn't you have waited just a little longer, Alegra? Couldn't you have worked out the leaving some other way, not hurt him so much?"

"I wanted to get out, Vyme, to keep going and not be trapped, to be free. Like Ratlit wanted, like you want, like Sandy wants, like golden. Only I was cruel. I had the chance to do it and I took it. Why is that bad, Vyme? Unless, of course, that's what being free means."

A twitch in the eyelid again. It closed. The other stayed open.

"Alegra—"

"I'm a golden, Vyme. A golden. And that's how golden are. But don't be mad at me, Vyme. Don't. Ratlit was mean too, not to give me my medi—"

The other eye closed. I closed mine too and tried to cry, but my tongue was pushing too hard on the roof of my mouth.

Sandy came to work the next day, and I didn't mention his being fired. The teletapes got hold of it, and the leadlines tried to make the thing as sordid as possible:

X-CON TEENAGER (they didn't mention his novel)
SLAYS JUNKY SWEETHEART! DIES HORRIBLY!

They didn't mention the golden either. They never do.

Reporters pried around the hangar awhile, trying to get us to say the ship was stolen. Sandy came through pretty well. "It was his ship," he grunted, putting lubricant in the gauntlets. "I gave it to him."

"What are you gonna give a kid like that a ship for? Maybe you loaned it to him. 'Dies horrible death in borrowed ship.' That sound okay."

"Gave it to him. Ask the boss." He turned back toward the scaffolding. "He witnessed."

"Look, even if you liked the kid, you're not saving him anything by covering up."

"I didn't like him," Sandy said. "but I gave him the ship."

"Thanks," I told Sandy when they left, not sure what I was thanking him for but still feeling very grateful. "I'll do you a favor back."

A week later Sandy came in and said, "Boss, I want my favor."

I narrowed my eyes against his belligerent tone. "So you're gonna quit at last. Can you finish out the week?"

He looked embarrassed, and his hands started moving around in his overall pouch. "Well, yeah. I am gonna leave. But not right away, boss. It is getting a little hard for me to take, out here."

"You'll get used to it," I said. "You know there's something about you that's, well, a lot like me. I learned. You will too."

Sandy shook his head. "I don't think I want to." His hand came out of his pocket. "See, I got a ticket." In his dirty fingers was a metal-banded card. "In four weeks I'm going back in from the Star-pit. Only I didn't want to tell you just now, because, well, I did want this favor, boss."

I was really surprised. "You're not going back to your group," I said. "What are you going to do?"

He shrugged. "Get a job, I don't know. There're other groups. Maybe I've grown up a little bit." His fists went way down into his pouch, and he started to shift his weight back and forth on his feet. "About that favor, boss."

"What is it?"

"I got to talking to this kid outside. He's really had it rough, Vyme." That was the first and last time Sandy ever called me by name, though I'd asked him to enough times before. "And he could use a job."

A laugh got all set to come out of me. But it didn't, because the look on his ugly face, behind the belligerence, was so vulnerable and intense. Vulnerable? But Sandy had his ticket; Sandy was going on.

"Send him to Poloscki's," I said. "Probably needs an extra grease monkey. Now let me get back to work, huh?"

"Could you take him over there?" Sandy said very quickly. "That's the favor, boss."

"Sandy, I'm awfully busy." I looked at him again. "Oh, all right."

"Hey, boss," Sandy said as I slid from behind the desk, "remember that thing you asked me if I ever had when I was a kid?"

It took a moment to come back to me. "You mean an ecologarium?"

"Yeah. That's the word." He grinned. "The kid-boy's got one. He's right outside, waiting for you."

"He's got it with him?"

Sandy nodded.

I walked toward the hangar door picturing some kid lugging around a six-by-six plastic cage.

Outside the boy was sitting on a fuel hydrant. I'd put a few trees there, and the "day"-light from the illumination tubes arcing the street dappled the gravel around him.

He was about fourteen, with copper skin and curly black hair. I saw why Sandy wanted me to go with him about the job. Around his waist, as he sat hunched over on the hydrant with his toes spread on the metal base-flange, was a wide-linked, yellow belt: golden.

He was looking through an odd jewel-and-brass thing that hung from a chain around his neck.

"Hey."

He looked up. There were spots of light on his blue black hair.

"You need a job?"

He blinked.

"My name's Vyme. What's yours?"

"You call me An." The voice was even, detached, with an inflection that is golden.

I frowned. "Nickname?"

He nodded.

"And really?"

"Androcles."

"Oh." My oldest kid is dead. I know it because I have all sorts of official papers saying so. But sometimes it's hard to remember. And it doesn't matter whether the hair is black, white or red. "Well, let's see if we can put you to work somewhere. Come on." An stood up, eyes fixed on me, suspicion hiding behind high glitter. "What's the thing around your neck?"

His eyes struck it and bounced back to my face. "Cousin?" he asked.

"Huh?" Then I remembered the golden slang. "Oh, sure. First cousins. Brothers if you want."

"Brother," An said. Then a smile came tumbling out of his face, silent and volcanic. He began loping beside me as we started off toward Po-loscki's. "This—" he held up the thing on the chain "—is an ecologarium. Want to see?" His diction was clipped, precise and detached. But when an expression caught on his face, it was unsettlingly intense.

"Oh, a little one. With microorganisms?"

An nodded.

"Sure. Let's have a look."

The hair on the back of his neck pawed the chain as he bent to remove it.

I held it up to see.

Some blue liquid, a fairly large air bubble and a glob of black-speckled jelly in a transparent globe, the size of an eyeball; it was set in two rings, one within the other, pivoted so the globe turned in all directions. Mounted on the outside ring was a curved tongue of metal at the top of which was a small tube with a pin-sized lens. The tube was threaded into a bushing, and I guess you used it to look at what was going on in the sphere.

"Self-contained," explained An. "The only thing needed to keep the whole thing going is light. Just about any frequency will do, except way up on the blue end. And the shell cuts that out."

I looked through the brass eyepiece.

I'd swear there were over a hundred life forms with five to fifty stages each: spores, zygotes, seeds, eggs, growing and developing through larvae, pupae, buds, reproducing through sex, syzygy, fission. And the whole ecological cycle took about two minutes.

Spongy masses like red lotuses clung to the air bubble. Every few seconds one would expel a cloud of black things like wrinkled bits of carbon paper into the gas where they were attacked by tiny motes I could hardly see even with the lens. Black became silver. It fell back to the liquid like globules of mercury, and coursed toward the jelly that was emitting a froth of bubbles. Something in the froth made the silver beads reverse direction. They reddened, sent out threads and alveoli, until they reached the main bubble again as lotuses.

The reason the lotuses didn't crowd each other out was because every eight or nine seconds a swarm of green paramecia devoured most of them. I couldn't tell where they came from; I never saw one of them split or get eaten, but they must have had something to do with the thorn-balls — if only because there were either thorn-balls or paramecia floating in the liquid, but never both at once.

A black spore in the jelly wiggled, then burst the surface as a white worm. Exhausted, it laid a couple of eggs, rested until it developed fins and a tail, then swam to the bubble where it laid more eggs among the lotuses. Its fins grew larger, its tail shriveled, splotches of orange and blue appeared, till it took off like a weird butterfly to sail around the inside of the bubble. The motes that silvered the black offspring of the lotus must have eaten the parti-colored fan because it just grew thinner and frailer till it disappeared. The eggs by the lotus would hatch into bloated fish forms that swam back through the froth to vomit a glob of jelly on the mass at the bottom, then collapse. The first eggs didn't do much except turn into black spores when they were covered with enough jelly.

All this was going on amidst a kaleidoscope of frail, wilting flowers and blooming jeweled webs, vines and worms, warts and jellyfish, symbiotes and saprophytes, while rainbow herds of algae careened back and forth like glittering confetti. One rough-rinded galoot, so big you could see him without the eyepiece, squatted on the wall, feeding on jelly, batting his eye-spots while the tide surged through quivering tears of gills.

I blinked as I took it from my eye.

"That looks complicated." I handed it back to him.

"Not really." He slipped it around his neck. "Took me two weeks with a notebook to get the whole thing figured out. You saw the big fellow?"

"The one who winked?"

"Yes. Its reproductive cycle is about two hours, which trips you up at first. Everything else goes so fast. But once you see him mate with the thing that looks like a spider web with sequins—same creature, different sex—and watch the offspring aggregate into paramecia, then dissolve again, the whole thing falls into—"

"One creature!" I said. "The whole thing is a single creature!"

An nodded vigorously. "Has to be to stay self-contained." The grin on his face whipped away like a snapped windowshade. A very serious look was underneath. "Even after I saw the big fellow mate, it took me a week to understand it was all one."

"But if goofus and the fishnet have paramecia—" I began. It seemed logical when I made the guess.

"You've seen one before."

I shook my head. "Not like that one, anyway. I once saw something similar, but it was much bigger, about six feet across."

An's seriousness was replaced by horror. I mean he really started to shake. "How could you . . . ever even see all the . . . stuff inside, much less catalogue it? You say . . . this is complicated?"

"Hey, relax. Relax!" I said. He did. Like that. "It was much simpler," I explained and went on to describe the one our kids had made so many years ago as best I remembered.

"Oh," An said at last, his face set in its original impassivity. "It wasn't microorganisms. Simple. Yes." He looked at the pavement. "Very simple." When he looked up, another expression had scrambled his features. It took a moment to identify. "I don't see the point at all."

There was surprising physical surety in the boy's movement; his nervousness was a cat's, not a human's. But it was one of the psychological qualities of golden.

"Well," I said, "it showed the kids a picture of the way the cycles of life progress."

An rattled his chain. "That is why they gave us these things. But everything in the one you had was so primitive. It wasn't a very good picture."

"Don't knock it," I told him. "When I was a kid, all I had was an ant colony. I got my infantile *Weltanschauung* watching a bunch of bugs running around between two plates of glass. I think I would have better prepared by a couple of hungry rats on a treadmill. Or maybe a torus-shaped fish tank alternating sharks with schools of piranhas: get them all chasing around after each other real fast—"

"Ecology wouldn't balance," An said. "You'd need snails to get rid of the waste. Then a lot of plants to reoxygenate the water, and some sort of herbivore to keep down the plants because they'd tend to choke out everything since neither the sharks nor the piranhas would eat them." Kids and their damn literal minds. "If the herbivores had some way to keep the sharks off, then you might do it."

"What's wrong with the first one I described?"

The explanation worked around the muscles of his face. "The lizards, the segment worms, the plants, worts, all their cycles were completely circular. They were born, grew up, reproduced, maybe took care of the kids awhile, then died. Their only function was reproduction. That's a pretty awful picture." He made an unintelligible face.

There was something about this wise-alecky kid who was golden, younger than Alegra, older than Ratlit, I liked.

"There are stages in here," An tapped his globe with his pinky nail, "that don't get started on their most important functions till after they've reproduced and grown up through a couple more metamorphoses as well. Those little green worms are a sterile end stage of the blue feathery things. But they put out free phosphates that the algae live on. Everything else, just about, lives on the algae—except the thorn-balls. They eat the worms when they die. There're phagocytes in there that injest the dust-things when they get out of the bubble and start infecting the liquid." All at once he got very excited. "Each of us in the class got one of these! They made us figure them out! Then we had to prepare these recordings on whether the reproductive process was the primary function in life or an adjunctive one." Something white frothed the corners of his mouth. "I think grown-ups should just *leave* their kids the hell *alone*, go on and do something *else*, stop bothering us! That's what I said! That's what I *told* them!" He stopped, his tongue flicked the foam at the cusp of his lips; he seemed all right again.

"Sometimes," I said evenly, "if you leave them alone and forget about them, you end up with monsters who aren't kids any more. If you'd been left alone, you wouldn't have had a chance to put your two cents in in the first place and you wouldn't have that thing around your neck." And he was really trying to follow what I was saying. A moment past his rage, his face was as open and receptive as a two-year-old's. God, I want to stop thinking about Antoni!

"That's not what I mean." He wrapped his arms around his shoulders and bit on his forearm pensively.

"An—you're not stupid, kid-boy. You're cocky, but I don't think you're mean. You're golden." There was all my resentment, out now, Ratlit. There it is, Alegra. I didn't grow up with the word, so it meant something different to me. An looked up to ingest my meaning. The toothmarks were white on his skin, then red around that. "How long have you been one?"

He watched me, arms still folded. "They found out when I was seven."

"That long ago?"

"Yes." He turned and started walking again. "I was very precocious."

"Oh." I nodded. "Just about half your life then. How's it been, little brother, being a golden?"

An dropped his arms. "They take you away from your group a lot of times." He shrugged. "Special classes. Training programs. I'm psychotic."

"I never would have guessed." What would you call Ratlit? What would you call Alegra?

"I know it shows. But it gets us through the psychic pressures at the reality breakdown at twenty thousand light-years. It really does. For the past few years, though, they've been planting the psychosis artificially, pretty far down in the preconscious, so it doesn't affect our ordinary behavior as much as it does the older ones. They can use this process on anybody whose hormone system is even close to golden. They can get a lot more and a lot better quality golden that way than just waiting for us to pop up by accident."

As I laughed, something else struck me. "Just what do you need a job out here for, though? Why not hitch out with some cousin or get a job on one of the intergalactics as an apprentice?"

"I have a job in another galaxy. There'll be a ship stopping for me in two months to take me out. A whole lot of Star-pits have been established in galaxies halfway to Un-dok. I'll be going back and forth, managing roboi-equipment, doing managerial work. I thought it would be a good idea to get some practical experience out here before I left."

"Precocious," I nodded. "Look, even with roboi-equipment you have to know one hell of a lot about the inside of how many different kinds of keeler drives. You're not going to get that kind of experience in two months as a grease monkey. And roboi-equipment? I don't even have any in my place. Poloscki's got some, but I don't think you'll get your hands on it."

"I know a good deal already," An said with strained modesty.

"Yeah?" I asked him a not-too-difficult question and got an adequate answer. Made me feel better that he didn't come back with something really brilliant. I did know more than he did. "Where'd you learn?"

"They gave me the information the same way they implanted my psychosis."

"You're pretty good for your age." Dear old Luna Vocational! Well, maybe educational methods have improved. "Come to think of it, I was just as old as you when I started playing around with those keeler models. Dozens and dozens of helical inserts—"

"And those oily organum sensitives in all that graphite? Yes, brother! But I've never even had my hands in a waldo."

I frowned. "Hell, when I was younger than you, I could—" I stopped. "Of course, with roboi-equipment, you don't need them. But it's not a bad thing to know how they work, just in case."

"That's why I want a job." He hooked one finger on his chain. "Brother-in-law Sandy and I got to talking, so I asked him about working here. He said you might help me get in someplace."

"I'm glad he did. My place only handles big ships, and it's all waldo. Me and an assistant can do the whole thing. Poloscki's place is smaller, but handles both inter- and intra-galactic jobs, so you get more variety and a bigger crew. You find Poloscki, say I sent you, tell what you can do and why you're out here. Belt or no, you'll probably get something better than a monkey."

"Thanks, brother."

We turned off Calle-D. Poloscki's hangar was ahead. Dull thunder sounded over the roof as a ship departed.

"As soon as I despair of the younger generation," I told him, "one of you kids comes by and I start to think there's hope. Granted you're a psychopath, you're a lot better than some of your older, distant relations."

An looked up at me, apprehensive.

"You've never had a run-in with some of your cousins out here. But don't be surprised if you're dead tomorrow and your job's been inherited by some character who decided to split your head open to check on what's inside. I try to get used to you, behaving like something that isn't even savage. But, boy-kid, can your kind really mess up a guy's picture of the universe."

"And what the hell do you expect us to act like?" An shot back. Spittle glittered on his lips again. "What would *you* do if you were trapped like *us?*"

"Huh?" I said questioningly. *"You,* trapped?"

"Look." A spasm passed over his shoulders. "The psycho-technician who made sure I was properly psychotic *wasn't* a golden, *brother!* You *pay* us to bring back the weapons, dad! *We* don't fight your damn wars, *grampa! You're* the ones who take us away from our groups, say we're *too* valuable to submit to *your* laws, then deny us our heredity because we don't *breed* true, no-relative-of *mine!"*

"Now, wait a minute!"

An snatched the chain from around his neck and held it taut in front of him. His voice ground to a whisper, his eyes glittered. "I strangled one of my classmates with this chain, the one I've got in my hands now." One by one, his features blanked all expression. "They took it away from me for a week, as punishment for killing the little girl."

The whisper stopped decibels above silence, then went on evenly. "Out here, nobody will punish me. And my reflexes are faster than yours."

Fear lashed my anger as I followed the insanity flickering in his eyes.

"Now!" He made a quick motion with his hands; I ducked. "I give it to you!" He flung the chain toward me. Reflexively I caught it. An turned away instantly and stalked into Poloscki's.

When I burst through the rattling hangar door at my place, the lift was coming down. Sandy yelled through the mesh walls, "Did he get the job?"

"Probably," I yelled back, going toward the office.

I heard the cage settle on the silicon cushion. Sandy was at my side a moment later, grinning. "So how do you like my brother-in-law, Androcles?"

"Brother-in-law?" I remembered An using the phrase, but I'd thought it was part of the slang golden. Something about the way Sandy said it though. "He's your *real* brother-in-law?"

"He's Joey's kid brother. I didn't want to say anything until after you met him." Sandy came along with me toward the office door. "Joey wrote me again and said since An was coming out here he'd tell him to stop by and see me and maybe I could help him out."

"Now how the hell am I supposed to know who Joey is?" I pushed open the door. It banged the wall.

"He's one of my husbands, the one who wrote me that letter you told me you'd read."

"Oh, yeah. Him." I started stacking papers.

"I thought it was pretty nice of him after all that to tell An to look me up when he got out here. It means that there's still somebody left who doesn't think I'm a complete waste. So what do you think of Androcles?"

"He's quite a boy." I scooped up the mail that had come in after lunch, started to go through it but put it down to hunt for my coveralls.

"An used to come visit us when he got his one weekend a month off from his training program as golden," Sandy was going on. "Joey's and An's parents lived in the reeds near the estuary. But we lived back up the canyon by Chroma Falls. An and Joey were pretty close, even though Joey's my age and An was only eight or nine back then. I guess Joey was the only one who really knew what An was going through, since they were both golden."

Surprised and shocked, I turned back to the desk. "You were married with a golden?" One of the letters on the top of the pile was addressed to Alegra from Carlson's Labs. I had a carton of the kids' junk in the locker and had gotten the mail—there wasn't much—sent to the hangar, as though I were waiting for somebody to come for it.

"Yeah," Sandy said, surprised at my surprise. "Joey."

So I wouldn't stand there gaping, I picked up Alegra's letter.

"Since the traits that are golden are polychromazoic, it dies out if they only breed with each other. There's a big campaign back in galactic center to encourage them to join heterogeneous proke-groups."

"Like bluepoint Siamese cats, huh?" I ran my blackened thumbnail through the seal.

"That's right. But they're *not* animals, boss. I remember what they put that kid-boy through for psychotic reinforcement of the factors that were golden to make sure they stuck. It tore me up to hear him talk about it when he'd visit us."

I pulled a porta-pix out of Alegra's envelope. Carlson's tries to personalize its messages.

"I'm sure glad they can erase the conscious memory from the kids' minds when they have to do that sort of stuff."

"Small blessings and all that." I flipped the porta-pix on.

Personalized but mass produced: ". . . blessed addit . . ." the little speaker echoed me. Poloscki and I had used Carlson's a couple of times, I know. I guess every other mechanic up here had too. The porta-pix had started in the middle. Now it hummed back to the beginning.

"You know," Sandy went on, "Joey was different, yeah, sort of dense about some things . . ."

"Alegra," beamed the chic, grandmotherly type Carlson's always uses for messages of this sort, "we were so glad to receive the urine sample you sent us by Mr. Ratlit last Thursday . . ."

". . . even so, Joey was one of the sweetest men or women I've ever known. He was the easiest person in the group to live with. Maybe it was because he was away a lot . . ."

". . . and now, just a week later—remember, Carlson's gives results immediately and confirms them by personalized porta-pix in seven days —we are happy to tell you that there will be a blessed addition to your group. However . . ."

". . . All right, he was different, reacted funny to a lot of things. But nothing like this rank, destructive stupidity you find out here at the Star-pit . . ."

". . . the paternity is not Mr. Ratlit's. If you are interested, for your eugenic records, in further information, please send us other possible urine samples from the men in your group, and we will be glad to confirm paternity . . ."

". . . I can't understand the way people act out here, boss. And that's why I'm pushing on."

". . . Thank you so much for letting us give you this wonderful news. Remember, when in doubt, call Carlson's."

I said to Sandy, "You were married with—you loved a golden?"

Unbidden, the porta-pix began again. I flipped it off without looking.

"Sandy," I said, "you were hired because you were a fair mechanic and you kept off my back. Do what you're paid for. Get out of here."

"Oh. Sure, boss." He backed quickly from the office.

I sat down.

Maybe I'm old-fashioned, but when someone runs off and abandons a sick girl like that, it gets me. That was the trip to Carlson's, the one last little favor Ratlit never came back from. On-the-spot results, and formal confirmation in seven days. In her physical condition, pregnancy would have been as fatal as the withdrawal. And she was too ill for any abortive method I know of not to kill her. On-the-spot results. Ratlit must have known all that too when he got the results back, the results that Alegra was probably afraid of, the results she sent him to find. Ratlit knew Alegra was going to die anyway. And so he stole a golden belt. "Loving someone, I mean really loving someone—" Alegra had said. When someone runs off and leaves a sick girl like that, there's got to be a reason. It came together for me like two fissionables. The explosion cut some moorings in my head I thought were pretty solidly fixed.

I pulled out the books, plugged in the computer, unplugged it, put the books away and stared into the ecologarium in my fist.

Among the swimming, flying, crawling things, mating, giving birth, growing, changing, busy at whatever their business was, I picked out those dead-end, green worms. I hadn't noticed them before because they were at the very edge of things, bumping against the wall. After they released their free phosphates and got tired of butting at the shell, they turned on each other and tore themselves to pieces.

Fear and anger is a bad combination in me.

I came close to being killed by a golden once, through that meanness and stupidity.

The same meanness and stupidity that killed Alegra and Ratlit.

And now when this damn kid threatens to—I mean at first I had thought he was threatening to—

I reached Gerg's a few minutes after the daylights went out and the streetlamps came on. But I'd stopped in nearly a dozen places on the way. I remember trying to explain to a sailor from a star-shuttle who was just stopping over at the Star-pit for the first time and was all upset because one woman golden had just attacked another with a broken glass; I remember saying to the three-headed bulge of his shoulder, ". . . an ant colony! You know what it is, two pieces of glass with dirt between them, and you can see all the little ants make tunnels and hatch eggs and stuff. When I was a kid, I had an ant colony . . ." I started to shake my hand in his face. The chain from the ecologarium was tangled up in my fingers.

"Look." He caught my wrist and put it down on the counter. "It's all right now, pal. Just relax."

"You look," I said as he turned away. "When I was a kid, all I had was an *ant* colony!"

He turned back and leaned his rusty elbow on the bar. "Okay," he said affably. Then he made the most stupid and frustrating mistake he possibly could have just then. "What about your aunt?"

"My mother—"

"I thought you were telling me about your aunt?"

"Naw," I said. "My aunt, she drank too much. This is about my mother."

"All right. Your mother then."

"My mother, see, she always worried about me, getting sick and things. I got sick a lot when I was a little kid. She made me mad! Used to go down and watch the ships take off from the place they called the Brooklyn Navy Yards. They were ships that went to the stars."

The sailor's Oriental face grinned. "Yeah, me too. Used to watch 'em when I was a kid."

"But it was raining, and she wouldn't let me go."

"Aw, that's too bad. Little rain never hurt a kid. Why didn't she call up and have it turned off so you could go out? Too busy to pay attention to you, huh? One of my old men was like that."

"Both of mine were," I said. "But not my ma. She was all over me all the time when she was there. But she made me mad!"

He nodded with real concern. "Wouldn't turn off the rain."

"Naw, couldn't. You didn't grow up where I did, narrow-minded, dark-side world. No modern conveniences."

"Off the main trading routes, huh?"

"Way off. She wouldn't let me go out, and that made me mad."

He was still nodding.

"So I broke it!" My fist came down hard on the counter, and the plastic globe in its brass cage clacked on the wood. "Broke it! Sand, glass all over the rug, on the windowsill!"

"What'd you break?"

"Smashed it, stamped on it, threw sand whenever she tried to make me stop!"

"Sand? You lived on a beach? We had a beach when I was a kid. A beach is nice for kids. What'd you break?"

"Let all the damn bugs out. Bugs in everything for days. Let 'em all out."

"Didn't have no bugs on our beach. But you said you were off the main trading routes."

"Let 'em *out!*" I banged my fist again. "Let *every*body out, whether they like it or not! It's their problem whether they make it, not mine!

Don't care, I don't—" I was laughing now.

"She let you go out, and you didn't care?"

My hand came down on top of the metal cage, hard. I caught my breath at the pain. "On our beach," I said, turning my palm up to look. There were red marks across it. "There weren't any bugs on our beach." Then I started shaking.

"You mean you were just putting me on, before, about the bugs. Hey, are you all right?"

". . . broke it," I whispered. Then I smashed fist and globe and chain into the side of the counter. "Let 'em *out!*" I whirled away, clutching my bruised hand against my stomach.

"*Watch* it, kid-boy!"

"I'm not a kid-boy!" I shouted. "You think I'm some stupid, half-crazy kid!"

"So you're older than me. Okay?"

"I'm not a kid any more!"

"So you're ten years older than Sirius, all right? Quiet down, or they'll kick us out."

I bulled out of Gerg's. A couple of people came after me because I didn't watch where I was going. I don't know who won, but I remember somebody yelling, "Get out! Get out!" It may have been me.

I remember later, staggering under the mercury streetlamp, the world-wind slapping my face, stars swarming back and forth below me, gravel sliding under my boots, the toes inches over the Edge. The gravel clicked down the metal siding, the sound terribly clear as I reeled in the loud wind, shaking my arm against the night.

As I brought my hand back, the wind lashed the cold chain across my cheek and the bridge of my nose. I lurched back, trying to claw it away. But it stayed all tangled on my fingers while the globe swung, gleaming in the street light. The wind roared. Gravel chattered down the siding.

Later, I remember the hangar door ajar, stumbling into the darkness, so that in a moment I was held from plummeting into nothing only by my own footsteps as black swerved around me. I stopped when my hip hit a workbench. I pawed around under the lip of the table till I found a switch. In the dim orange light, racked along the back of the bench in their plastic shock-cases, were the row of master-gauntlets. I slipped one out and slid my hand into it.

"Who's over there?"

"Go 'way, Sandy." I turned from the bench, switched up the power on the wrist controls. Somewhere in the dark above, a fifteen-foot slave-hand hummed to life.

"Sorry, buster. This isn't Sandy. Put that down and get away from there."

I squinted as the figure approached in the orange light, hand extended. I saw the vibra-gun and didn't bother to look at the face.

Then the gun went down. "Vyme, baby? That you? What the hell are you doing here this hour of the night?"

"Poloscki?"

"Who'd you think it was?"

"Is this your—?" I looked around, shook my head. "But I thought it was my—" I shook my head again.

Poloscki sniffed. "Hey, have you been a naughty kid-boy tonight!"

I swung my hand, and the slave-hand overhead careened twenty feet.

The gun jumped. "Look, you mess up my waldo and I will kill you, don't care who you are! Take that thing off."

"Very funny." I brought the talon down where I could see its clawing shadow.

"Come on, Vyme. I'm serious. Turn it off and put it down. You're a mess now and you don't know what you're doing."

"That kid, the golden. Did you give him a job?"

"Sure. He said you sent him. Smart so-and-so. He rehulled a little yacht with the roboi-anamechaniakatasthy-sizer, just to show me what he could do. If I knew a few more people who could handle them that well, I'd go all roboi. He's not worth a damn with a waldo, but as long as he's got that little green light in front of him, he's fine."

I brought the talons down another ten feet so that the spider hung between us. "Well, I happen to be very handy with a waldo, Poloscki."

"Vyme, you're gonna get *hurrrt* . . ."

"Poloscki," I said, "will you stop coming on like an overprotective aunt? I don't need another one."

"You're very drunk, Vyme."

"Yeah. But I'm no clumsy kid-boy who is going to mess up your equipment."

"If you do, you'll be—"

"Shut up and watch." I pulled the chain out of my pouch and tossed it onto the concrete floor. In the orange light you couldn't tell whether the cage was brass or silver.

"What's that?"

The claws came down, and the fine-point tips, millimeters above the floor, closed on the ecologarium.

"Oh, hey! I haven't seen one of those since I was ten. What are you going to do with it? Those are five-hundred-to-one strength, you know. You're gonna break it."

"That's right. Break this one too."

"Aw, come on. Let me see it first."

I lifted the globe. "Could be an eggshell," I said. "Drunk or sober I can handle this damn equipment, Poloscki."

"I haven't seen one for years. Used to have one."

"You mean it wasn't spirited back from some distant galaxy by golden, from some technology beyond our limited ken?"

"Product of the home spiral. Been around since the fifties."

I raised it over Poloscki's extended hand.

"They're supposed to be very educational. What do you want to break it for?"

"I never saw one."

"You came from someplace off the routes. didn't you? They weren't that common. Don't break it."

"I want to."

"Why, Vyme?"

Something got wedged in my throat. "Because I want to get out, and if it's not that globe, it's gonna be somebody's head." Inside the gauntlet my hand began to quiver. The talons jerked. Poloscki caught the globe and jumped back.

"Vyme!"

"I'm hanging, here at the Edge." My voice kept getting caught on the things in my throat. "I'm useless, with a bunch of monsters and fools!" The talons swung, contracted, clashed on each other. "And then when the children . . . when the *children* get so bad you can't even reach them . . . ." The claw opened, reached for Poloscki who jumped back in the half-dark.

"Damn it, Vyme—"

". . . can't even reach the children any more." The talon stopped shaking, came slowly back, knotting. "I want to break something and get out. Very childishly, yes. Because nobody is paying any attention to *me.*" The claw jumped. "Even when I'm trying to help. I *don't* want to hurt anybody any *more.* I *swear* it, so help me, I swear—"

"Vyme, take off the glove and listen!"

I raised the slave-hand because it was about to scrape the cement.

"Vyme, I want to pay some attention to you." Slowly Poloscki walked back into the orange light. "You've been sending me kids for five years now, coming around and checking up on them, helping them out of the stupid scrapes they get in. They haven't all been Ratlits. I like kids too. That's why I take them on. I think what you do is pretty great. Part of me loves kids. Another part of me loves you."

"Aw, Poloscki . . ." I shook my head. Somewhere disgust began.

"It doesn't embarrass me. I love you a little and wouldn't mind loving you a lot. More than once I've thought about asking you to start a group."

"*Please*, Poloscki. I've had too many weird things happen to me this week. Not tonight, huh?" I then turned the power off in the glove.

"Love shouldn't frighten you, no matter when or how it comes, Vyme. Don't run from it. A marriage between us? Yeah, it would be a little hard for somebody like you, at first. But you'd get used to it before long. Then when kids came around, there'd be two—"

"I'll send Sandy over," I said. "He's the big-hearted, marrying kind. Maybe he's about ready to try again." I pulled off the glove.

"Vyme, don't go out like that. Stay for just a minute!"

"Poloscki," I said, "I'm just not that God damn drunk!" I threw the glove on the table.

"Please, Vyme."

"You're gonna use your gun to keep me here?"

"Don't be like—"

"I hope the kids I send over here appreciate you more than I do right now. I'm sorry I busted in here. Good night!"

I turned from the table.

Nine thousand miles away the Stellarplex turned too. Circles of silver dropped through the roof. Behind the metal cage of the relaxed slave-claw I saw Poloscki's large, injured eyes, circles of crushed turquoise, glistening now.

And nine feet away someone said, "Ma'am?"

Poloscki glanced over her shoulder. "An, you awake?"

An stepped into the silver light, rubbing his neck. "That office chair is pretty hard, sister."

"He's here?" I asked.

"Sure," Poloscki said. "He didn't have any place to stay so I let him sleep in the office while I finished up some work in the back. Vyme, I meant what I said. Leave if you want, but not like this. Untwist."

"Poloscki," I said, "you're very sweet, you're fun in bed, and a good mechanic too. But I've been there before. Asking me to join a group is like asking me to do something obscene. I know what I'm worth."

"I'm also a good businesswoman. Don't think that didn't enter my head when I thought about marrying you." An came and stood beside her. He was breathing hard, the way an animal does when you wake it all of a sudden.

"Poloscki, you said it, I didn't: I'm a mess. That's why I'm not with my own group now."

"You're not always like this. I've never seen you touch a drop before."

"For a while," I said, "it happened with disgusting frequency. Why do you think my group dropped me?"

"Must have been a while ago. I've known you a long time. So you've grown up since then. Now it only happens every half-dozen years or so. Congratulations. Come have some coffee. An, run into the office and plug in the pot. I showed you where it was." An turned like something blown by the world-wind and was gone in shadow. "Come on," Poloscki said. She took my arm, and I came with her. Before we left the light, I saw my reflection in the polished steel tool cabinet.

"Aw, no." I pulled away from her. "No, I better go home now."

"Why? An's making coffee."

"The kid. I don't want the kid to see me like this."

"He already has. Won't hurt him. Come on."

When I walked into Poloscki's office, I felt I didn't have a damn thing left. No. I had one. I decided to give it away.

When An turned to me with the cup, I put my hands on his shoulders. He jumped, but not enough to spill the coffee. "First and last bit of alcoholic advice for the evening, kid-boy. Even if you are crazy, don't go around telling people who are not golden how they've trapped you. That's like going to Earth and complimenting a nigger on how well he sings and dances and his great sense of rhythm. He may be able to tap seven with one hand against thirteen with the other while whistling a tone row. It still shows a remarkable naïvete about the way things are." That's one of the other things known throughout the galaxy about the world I come from. When I say primitive, I mean primitive.

An ducked from under my hands, put the coffee on the desk and turned back. "I didn't say you trapped us."

"You said we treated you lousy and exploited you, which we may, and that this trapped you—"

"I said you exploited us, which you do, *and* that we were trapped. I *didn't* say by what."

Poloscki sat down on the desk, picked up my coffee and sipped it.

I raised my head. "All right. Tell me how you're trapped."

"Oh, I'm sorry," Poloscki said. "I started drinking your coffee."

"Shut up. How are you trapped, An?"

He moved his shoulders around as though he was trying to get them comfortable. "It started in Tyber-44 cluster. Golden were coming back with really bad psychic shock."

"Yes. I heard about it. That was a few years back."

An's face started to twitch; the muscles around his eyes twisted below the skin. "*Something* out there . . ."

I put my hand on the back of his neck, my thumb in the soft spot behind his ear and began to stroke, the way you get a cat to calm down. "Take it easy. Just tell me."

"Thanks," An said and bent his head forward. "We found them first in Tyber-44, but then they turned up all *over*, on half the planets in every galaxy that could support any life, and a lot more that shouldn't have been able to at all." His breathing grew coarser. I kept rubbing, and it slowed again. "I guess we have such a funny psychology that working with them, studying them, even thinking about them too much . . . there was something about them that changes our sense of reality. The shock was bad."

"An," I said, "to be trapped, there has to be somewhere you can't go. For it to bug you, there has to be something else around that can."

He nodded under my hand, then straightened up. "I'm all right now. Just tired. You want to know where and what?"

Poloscki had put down the coffee now and was dangling the chain. An whirled to stare.

"Where?" he said. "Other universes."

"Galaxies farther out?" asked Poloscki.

"No. Completely different matrices of time and space." Staring at the swinging ball seemed to calm him even more. "No physical or temporal connection to this one at all."

"A sort of parallel—"

"Parallel? Hell!" It was almost a drawl. "There's nothing parallel about them. Out of the billions-to-the-billionth of them, most are hundreds of times the size of ours and empty. There are a few, though, whose entire spatial extent is even smaller than this galaxy. Some of them are completely dense to us, because even though there seems to be matter in them, distributed more or less as in this universe, there's no electromagnetic activity at all. No radio waves, no heat, no light." The globe swung; the voice was a whisper.

I closed my fist around the globe and took it from Poloscki. "How do you know about them? Who brings back the information? Who is it who can get out?"

Blinking, An looked back at me.

When he told me, I began to laugh. To accommodate the shifting reality tensions, the psychotic personality that is golden is totally labile. An laughed with me, not knowing why. He explained through his torrential hysteria how with the micro-micro surgical techniques from Tyber-44 they had read much of the information from a direct examination of the creature's nervous system, which covered its surface like velvet. It could take intense cold or heat, a range of pressure from vacuum to hundreds of pounds per square millimeter; but a fairly small amount of ultraviolet destroyed the neural synapses, and it died. They were small and deceptively organic because in an organic environment they appeared to breathe and eat. They had four sexes, two of which carried the young. They had clusters of retractable sense organs that first appeared to be eyes, but were sensitive to twelve distinct senses, stimulation for three of which didn't even exist in our continuum. They traveled around on four suction cups when using kinetic motion for ordinary traversal of space, were small and looked furry. The only way to make them jump universes was to scare the life out of them. At which point they just disappeared.

An kneaded his stomach under his belt to ease the pain from so much laughter. "Working with them at Tyber-44 just cracked up a whole bunch of golden." He leaned against the desk, panting and grinning. "They had to be sent home for therapy. We still can't think about them directly, but it's easier for us to control what we think about than for you; that's part of being golden. I even had one of them for a pet, up until yesterday. The damn creatures are either totally apathetic, or vicious. Mine was a baby, all white and soft." He held out his arms. "Yesterday it bit me and disappeared." On his wrist there was a bluish place centered on which was a crescent of pinpricks. "Lucky it was a baby. The bites infect easily."

Poloscki started drinking from my cup again as An and I started laughing all over.

As I walked back that night, black coffee slopped in my belly.

There are certain directions in which you cannot go. Choose one in which you can move as far as you want. Sandy said that? He did. And there was something about Sandy, very much like someone golden. It doesn't matter how, he's going on.

Under a streetlamp I stopped and lifted up the ecologarium. The reproductive function, was it primary or adjunctive? If, I thought with the whiskey lucidity always suspect at dawn, you consider the whole ecological balance a single organism, it's adjunctive, a vital reparative process along with sleeping and eating, to the primary process which is living, working, growing. I put the chain around my neck.

I was still half-soused, and it felt bad. But I howled. Androcles, is drunken laughter appropriate to mourn all my dead children? Perhaps not. But tell me, Ratlit; tell me Alegra: what better way to launch my live ones who are golden into night? I don't know. I know I laughed. Then I put my fists into my overall pouch and crunched homeward along the Edge while on my left the world-wind roared.

A. BERTRAM CHANDLER

# Giant Killer

*Science fiction is a difficult form for many capable writers because in addition to all the "normal" tasks of plotting, character development, mood-building, setting and attention to style, the SF author must often present nonhuman species, future "history" and civilizations, carefully extrapolated technological developments and many other wonders—in short, invent entire cosmos of the imagination.*

*That this is attempted frequently is attested to by the large amount of science fiction published each year. That it can be done well can be attested to by such stories as "Giant Killer," one of the most convincing depictions of an alien society ever written.*

Shrick should have died before his baby eyes had opened on his world. Shrick would have died, but Weena, his mother, was determined that he, alone of all her children, should live. Three previous times since her mating with Skreer had she borne, and on each occasion the old, gray Sterret, Judge of the Newborn, had condemned her young as Different Ones.

Weena had no objection to the law when it did not affect her or hers. She, as much as any other member of the tribe, keenly enjoyed the feasts of fresh, tasty meat following the ritual slaughter of the Different Ones. But when those sacrificed were the fruit of her own womb it wasn't the same.

It was quiet in the cave where Weena awaited the coming of her lord. Quiet, that is, save for the sound of her breathing and an occasional plaintive, mewling cry from the newborn child. And even these sounds were deadened by the soft spongy walls and ceiling.

She sensed the coming of Skreer long before his actual arrival. She anticipated his first question and, as he entered the cave, said quietly, "One. A male."

"A male?" Skreer radiated approval. Then she felt his mood change to one of questioning, of doubt. "Is it . . . he—?"

"Yes."

447

Skreer caught the tiny, warm being in his arms. There was no light, but he, like all his race, was accustomed to the dark. His fingers told him all that he needed to know. The child was hairless. The legs were too straight. And—this was worst of all—the head was a great, bulging dome.

"Skreer!" Weena's voice was anxious. "Do you—?"

"There is no doubt. Sterret will condemn it as a Different One."

"But—"

"There is no hope." Weena sensed that her mate shuddered, heard the faint, silken rustle of his fur as he did so. "His head! He is like the Giants!"

The mother sighed. It was hard, but she knew the law. And yet—this was her fourth childbearing, and she was never to know, perhaps, what it was to watch and wait with mingled pride and terror while her sons set out with the other young males to raid the Giants' territory, to bring back spoils from the great Cave-of-Food, the Place-of-Green-Growing-Things or, even, precious scraps of shiny metal from the Place-of-Life-That-Is-Not-Life.

She clutched at a faint hope.

"His head is like a Giant's? Can it be, do you think, that the Giants are Different Ones? I have heard it said."

"What if they are?"

"Only this. Perhaps he will grow to be a Giant. Perhaps he will fight the other Giants for us, his own people. Perhaps—"

"Perhaps Sterret will let him live, you mean." Skreer made the short, unpleasant sound that passed among his people for a laugh. "No, Weena. He must die. And it is long since we feasted—"

"But—"

"Enough. Or do *you* wish to provide meat for the tribe also? I may wish to find a mate who will bear me sturdy sons, not monsters!"

The Place-of-Meeting was almost deserted when Skreer and Weena, she with Shrick clutched tightly in her arms, entered. Two more couples were there, each with newborn. One of the mothers was holding two babies, each of whom appeared to be normal. The other had three, her mate holding one of them.

Weena recognized her as Teeza, and flashed her a little half-smile of sympathy when she saw that the child carried by Teeza's mate would certainly be condemned by Sterret when he choose to appear. For it was, perhaps, even more revolting than her own Different One, having two hands growing from the end of each arm.

Skreer approached one of the other males, he unburdened with a child.

"How long have you been waiting?" he asked.

"Many heartbeats. We—"

The guard stationed at the doorway through which light entered from Inside hissed a warning:

"Quiet! A Giant is coming!"

The mothers clutched their children to them yet more tightly, their fur standing on end with superstitious dread. They knew that if they remained silent there was no danger, that even if they should betray themselves by some slight noise there was no immediate peril. It was not size alone that made the Giants dreaded, it was the supernatural powers that they were known to possess. The food-that-kills had slain many an unwary member of the tribe, also their fiendishly cunning devices that crushed and mangled any of the People unwise enough to reach greedily for the savory morsels left exposed on a kind of little platform. Although there were those who averred that, in the latter case, the risk was well worth it, for the yellow grains from the many bags in the Cave-of-Food were as monotonous as they were nourishing.

"The Giant has passed!"

Before those in the Place-of-Meeting could resume their talk, Sterret drifted out from the entrance of his cave. He held in his right hand his wand of office, a straight staff of the hard, yet soft, stuff dividing the territory of the People from that of the Giants. It was tipped with a sharp point of metal.

He was old, was Sterret.

Those who were themselves grandparents had heard their grandparents speak of him. For generations he had survived attacks by young males jealous of his prerogatives as chief, and the more rare assaults by parents displeased by his rulings as Judge of the Newborn. In this latter case, however, he had had nothing to fear, for on those isolated occasions the tribe had risen as one and torn the offenders to pieces.

Behind Sterret came his personal guards and then, floating out from the many cave entrances, the bulk of the tribe. There had been no need to summon them; they *knew*.

The chief, deliberate and unhurried, took his position in the center of the Place-of-Meeting. Without orders, the crowd made way for the parents and their newborn. Weena winced as she saw their gloating eyes fixed on Shrick's revolting baldness, his misshapen skull. She knew what the verdict would be.

She hoped that the newborn of the others would be judged before her own, although that would merely delay the death of her own child by the space of a very few heartbeats. She hoped—

"Weena! Bring the child to me that I may see and pass judgment!"

The chief extended his skinny arms, took the child from the mother's reluctant hands. His little, deep-set eyes gleamed at the thought of the draught of rich, red blood that he was soon to enjoy. And yet he was reluctant to lose the savor of a single heartbeat of the mother's agony. Perhaps she could be provoked into an attack—

"You insult us," he said slowly, "by bringing forth *this!*" He held Shrick, who squalled feebly, at arm's length. "Look, oh People, at this *thing* the miserable Weena has brought for my judgment!"

"He has a Giant's head." Weena's timid voice was barely audible. "Perhaps—"

"—his father was a Giant!"

A tittering laugh rang through the Place-of-Meeting.

"No. But I have heard it said that perhaps the Giants, or their fathers and mothers, were Different Ones. And—"

"Who said that?"

"Strela."

"Yes, Strela the Wise. Who, in his wisdom, ate largely of the food-that-kills!"

Again the hateful laughter rippled through the assembly.

Sterret raised the hand that held the spear, shortening his grip on the haft. His face puckered as he tasted in anticipation the bright bubble of blood that would soon well from the throat of the Different One. Weena screamed. With one hand she snatched her child from the hateful grasp of the chief, with the other she seized his spear.

Sterret was old, and generations of authority had made him careless. Yet, old as he was, he evaded the vicious thrust aimed at him by the mother. He had no need to cry orders, from all sides the People converged upon the rebel.

Already horrified by her action, Weena knew that she could expect no mercy. And yet life, even as lived by the tribe, was sweet. Gaining a purchase from the gray, spongy floor of the Place-of-Meeting she jumped. The impetus of her leap carried her up to the doorway through which streamed the light from Inside. The guard there was unarmed, for of what avail would a puny spear be against the Giants? He fell back before the menace of Weena's bright blade and bared teeth. And then Weena was Inside.

She could, she knew, hold the doorway indefinitely against pursuit. But this was Giant country. In an agony of indecision she clung to the rim of the door with one hand, the other still holding the spear. A face appeared in the opening, and then vanished, streaming with blood. It was only later that she realized that it had been Skreer's.

She became acutely conscious of the fierce light beating around and about her, of the vast spaces on all sides of a body that was accustomed to the close quarters of the caves and tunnels. She felt naked and, in spite of her spear, utterly defenseless.

Then that which she dreaded came to pass.

Behind her, she sensed the approach of two of the Giants. Then she could hear their breathing, and the low, infinitely menacing rumble of their voices as they talked one with the other. They hadn't seen her—of that she was certain, but it was only a matter of heartbeats before they did so. The open doorway, with the certainty of death that lay beyond, seemed infinitely preferable to the terror of the unknown. Had it been only her life at stake she would have returned to face the righteous wrath of her chief, her mate and her tribe.

Fighting down her blind panic, she forced herself to a clarity of thought normally foreign to her nature. If she yielded to instinct, if she fled madly before the approaching Giants, she would be seen. Her only hope was to remain utterly still. Skreer, and others of the males who had been on forays Inside, had told her that the Giants, careless in their size and power, more often than not did not notice the People unless they made some betraying movement.

The Giants were very close.

Slowly, cautiously, she turned her head.

She could see them now, two enormous figures floating through the air with easy arrogance. They had not seen her, and she knew that they would not see her unless she made some sudden movement to attract their attention. Yet it was hard not to yield to the impulse to dive back into the doorway to the Place-of-Meeting, there to meet certain death at the hands of the outraged tribe. It was harder still to fight the urge to relinquish her hold on the rim of the doorway and flee—anywhere—in screaming panic.

But she held on.

The Giants passed.

The dull rumble of their voices died in the distance, their acrid, unpleasant odor, of which she had heard but never before experienced, diminished. Weena dared to raise her head once more.

In the confused, terrified welter of her thoughts one idea stood out with dreadful clarity. Her only hope of survival, pitifully slim though it was, lay in following the Giants. There was no time to lose, already she could hear the rising clamor of voices as those in the caves sensed that the Giants had passed. She relinquished her hold on the edge of the door and floated slowly up.

When Weena's head came into sudden contact with something hard she screamed. For long seconds she waited, eyes close shut in terror, for the doom that would surely descend upon her. But nothing happened. The pressure upon the top of her skull neither increased nor diminished.

Timidly, she opened her eyes.

As far as she could see, in two directions, stretched a long, straight shaft or rod. Its thickness was that of her own body, and it was made, or covered with, a material not altogether strange to the mother. It was like the ropes woven by the females with fibers from the Place-of-Green-Growing-Things—but incomparably finer. Stuff such as this was brought back sometimes by the males from their expeditions. It had been believed, once, that it was the fur of the Giants, but now it was assumed that it was made by them for their own purposes.

On three sides of the shaft was the glaring emptiness so terrifying to the people of the caves. On the fourth side was a flat, shiny surface. Weena found that she could insinuate herself into the space between the two without discomfort. She discovered, also, that with comforting solidity at her back and belly she could make reasonably fast progress along the shaft. It was only when she looked to either side that she felt a return of her vertigo. She soon learned not to look.

It is hard to estimate the time taken by her journey in a world where time was meaningless. Twice she had to stop and feed Shrick—fearful lest his hungry wailings betray their presence either to Giants or any of the People who might—although this was highly improbable—have followed her. Once she felt the shaft vibrating, and froze to its matt surface in utter and abject terror. A Giant passed, pulling himself rapidly along with his two hands. Had either of those hands fallen upon Weena it would have been the finish. For many heartbeats after his passing she clung there limp and helpless, scarcely daring to breathe.

It seemed that she passed through places of which she had heard the males talk. This may have been so—but she had no means of knowing. For the world of the People, with its caves and tunnels, was familiar territory, while that of the Giants was known only in relation to the doorways through which a daring explorer could enter.

Weena was sick and faint with hunger and thirst when, at last, the long shaft led her into a place where she could smell the tantalizing aroma of food. She stopped, looked in all directions. But here, as everywhere in this alien country, the light was too dazzling for her untrained eyes. She could see, dimly, vast shapes beyond her limited understanding. She could see no Giants, nor anything that moved.

Cautiously, keeping a tight hold on the rough surface of the shaft, she edged out to the side away from the polished, flat surface along which she had been traveling. Back and forth her head swung, her sensitive nostrils dilated. The bright light confused her, so she shut her eyes. Once again her nose sought the source of the savory smell, swinging ever more slowly as the position was determined with reasonable accuracy.

She was loath to abandon the security of her shaft, but hunger overruled all other considerations. Orienting her body, she jumped. With a thud she brought up against another flat surface. Her free hand found a projection, to which she clung. This she almost relinquished as it turned. Then a crack appeared, with disconcerting suddenness, before her eyes, widening rapidly. Behind this opening was black, welcome darkness. Weena slipped inside, grateful for relief from the glaring light of the Inside. It wasn't until later that she realized that this was a door such as was made by her own people in the Barrier, but a door of truly gigantic proportions. But all that mattered at first was the cool, refreshing shade.

Then she took stock of her surroundings.

Enough light came in through the barely open doorway for her to see that she was in a cave. It was the wrong shape for a cave, it is true, having flat, perfectly regular walls and floor and ceiling. At the far end, each in its own little compartment, were enormous, dully shining globes. From them came a smell that almost drove the famishing mother frantic.

Yet she held back. She knew that smell. It was that of fragments of food that had been brought into the caves, won by stealth and guile from the killing platforms of the Giants. Was this a killing platform? She wracked her brains to recall the poor description of these devices given by the males, decided that this, after all, must be a Cave-of-Food. Relinquishing her hold of Shrick and Sterret's spear she made for the nearest globe.

At first she tried to pull it from its compartment, but it appeared to be held. But it didn't matter. Bringing her face against the surface of the sphere she buried her teeth in its thin skin. There was flesh beneath the skin, and blood—a thin, sweet, faintly acid juice. Skreer had, at times, promised her a share of this food when next he won some from a killing platform, but that promise had never been kept. And now Weena had a whole cave of this same food all to herself.

Gorged to repletion, she started back to pick up the now loudly complaining Shrick. He had been playing with the spear and had cut himself on the sharp point. But it was the spear that Weena snatched, swinging swiftly to defend herself and her child. For a voice said, understandable, but with an oddly slurred intonation, "Who are you? What are you doing in our country?"

It was one of the People, a male. He was unarmed, otherwise it is certain that he would never have asked questions. Even so, Weena knew that the slightest relaxation of vigilance on her part would bring a savage, tooth-and-nail attack.

She tightened her grasp on the spear, swung it so that its point was directed at the stranger.

"I am Weena," she said, "of the Tribe of Sterret."

"Of the Tribe of Sterret? But the Tribe of Sessa holds the ways between our countries."

"I came Inside. But who are you?"

"Tekka. I am one of Skarro's people. You are a spy."

"So I brought my child with me."

Tekka was looking at Shrick.

"I see," he said at last. "A Different One. But how did you get through Sessa's country?"

"I didn't. I came Inside."

It was obvious that Tekka refused to believe her story.

"You must come with me," he said, "to Skarro. He will judge."

"And if I come?"

"For the Different One, death. For you, I do not know. But we have too many females in our tribe already."

"This says that I will not come." Weena brandished her spear.

She would not have defied a male of her own tribe thus—but this Tekka was not of her people. And she had always been brought up to believe that even a female of the Tribe of Sterrett was superior to a male—even a chief —of any alien community.

"The Giants will find you here." Tekka's voice showed an elaborate unconcern. Then— "That is a fine spear."

"Yes. It belonged to Sterret. With it I wounded my mate. Perhaps he is dead."

The male looked at her with a new respect. If her story were true— this was a female to be handled with caution. Besides—

"Would you give it to me?"

"Yes." Weena laughed nastily. There was no mistaking her meaning.

"Not that way. Listen. Not long ago, in our tribe, many mothers, two whole hands of mothers with Different Ones, defied the Judge of the Newborn. They fled along the tunnels, and live outside the Place-of-Little-Lights. Skarro has not yet led a war party against them. Why, I do not know, but there is always a Giant in that place. It may be that Skarro fears that a fight behind the Barrier would warn the Giants of our presence—"

"And you will lead me there?"

"Yes. In return for the spear."

Weena was silent for the space of several heartbeats. As long as Tekka preceded her she would be safe. It never occurred to her that she could let the other fulfill his part of the bargain, and then refuse him his payment. Her people were a very primitive race.

"I will come with you," she said.

"It is well."

Tekka's eyes dwelt long and lovingly upon the fine spear. Skarro would not be chief much longer.

"First," he said, "we must pull what you have left of the good-to-eat-ball into our tunnel. Then I must shut the door lest a Giant should come—"

Together they hacked and tore the sphere to pieces. There was a doorway at the rear of one of the little compartments, now empty. Through this they pushed and pulled their fragrant burden. First Weena went into the tunnel, carrying Shrick and the spear, then Tekka. He pushed the round door into place, where it fitted with no sign that the Barrier had been broken. He pushed home two crude locking bars.

"Follow me," he ordered the mother.

The long journey through the caves and tunnels was heaven after the Inside. Here there was no light—or, at worst, only a feeble glimmer from small holes and cracks in the Barrier. It seemed that Tekka was leading her along the least frequented ways and tunnels of Skarro's country, for they met none of his people. Nevertheless, Weena's perceptions told her that she was in densely populated territory. From all around her beat the warm, comforting waves of the routine, humdrum life of the People. She knew that in snug caves males, females and children were living in cozy intimacy. Briefly, she regretted having thrown away all this for the ugly, hairless bundle in her arms. But she could never return to her own tribe, and should she wish to throw in her lot with this alien community the alternatives would be death or slavery.

"Careful!" hissed Tekka. "We are approaching Their country."

"You will—?"

"Not me. They will kill me. Just keep straight along this tunnel and you will find Them. Now, give me the spear."

"But—"

"*You* are safe. There is your pass." He lightly patted the uneasy, squirming Shrick. "Give me the spear, and I will go."

Reluctantly, Weena handed over the weapon. Without a word Tekka took it. Then he was gone. Briefly the mother saw him in the dim light that, in this part of the tunnel, filtered through the Barrier—a dim, gray figure rapidly losing itself in the dim grayness. She felt very lost and lonely and frightened. But the die was cast. Slowly, cautiously, she began to creep along the tunnel.

When They found her she screamed. For many heartbeats she had sensed their hateful presence, had felt that beings even more alien than the Giants were closing in on her. Once or twice she called, crying that she came in peace, that she was the mother of a Different One. But not even echo answered her, for the soft, spongy tunnel walls deadened the shrill sound of her voice. And the silence that was not silence was, if that were possible, more menacing than before.

Without warning the stealthy terror struck. Weena fought with the courage of desperation, but she was overcome by sheer weight of numbers. Shrick, protesting feebly, was torn from her frantic grasp. Hands—and surely there were far too many hands for the number of her assailants— pinned her arms to her sides, held her ankles in a viselike grip. No longer able to struggle, she looked at her captors. Then she screamed again. Mercifully, the dim light spared her the full horror of their appearance, but what she saw would have been enough to haunt her dreams to her dying day had she escaped.

Softly, almost caressingly, the hateful hands ran over her body with disgusting intimacy.

Then— "She is a Different One."

She allowed herself to hope.

"And the child?"

"Two-Tails has newborn. She can nurse him."

And as the sharp blade found her throat Weena had time to regret most bitterly ever having left her snug, familiar world. It was not so much the forfeit of her own life—that she had sacrificed when she defied Sterret —it was the knowledge that Shrick, instead of meeting a clean death at the hands of his own people, would live out his life among these unclean monstrosities.

Then there was a sharp pain and a feeling of utter helplessness as the tide of her life swiftly ebbed—and the darkness that Weena had loved so well closed about her for evermore.

No-Fur—who, at his birth, had been named Shrick—fidgeted impatiently at his post midway along what was known to his people as Skarro's Tunnel. It was time that Long-Nose came to relieve him. Many heartbeats had passed since he had heard the sounds on the other side of the Barrier proclaiming that the Giant in the Place-of-Little-Lights had been replaced by another of his kind. It was a mystery what the Giants did there —but the New People had come to recognize a strange regularity in the actions of the monstrous beings, and to regulate their time accordingly.

No-Fur tightened his grip on his spear—of Barrier material it was, roughly sharpened at one end—as he sensed the approach of somebody along the tunnel, coming from the direction of Tekka's country. It could be a Different One bearing a child who would become one of the New People, it could be attack. But, somehow, the confused impressions that his mind received did not bear out either of these assumptions.

No-Fur shrank against the wall of the tunnel, his body sinking deep into the spongy material. Now he could dimly see the intruder—a solitary form flitting furtively through the shadows. His sense of smell told him that it was a female. Yet he was certain that she had no child with her. He tensed himself to attack as soon as the stranger should pass his hiding place.

Surprisingly, she stopped.

"I come in peace," she said. "I am one of you. I am," here she paused a little, "one of the New People."

Shrick made no reply, no betraying movement. It was barely possible, he knew, that this female might be possessed of abnormally keen eyesight. It was even more likely that she had smelled him out. But then—how was it that she had known the name by which the New People called themselves? To the outside world they were Different Ones—and had the stranger called herself such she would at once have proclaimed herself an alien whose life was forfeit.

"You do not know," the voice came again, "how it is that I called myself by the proper name. In my own tribe I am called a Different One—"

"Then how is it," No-Fur's voice was triumphant, "that you were allowed to live?"

"Come to me! No, leave your spear. Now come!"

No-Fur stuck his weapon into the soft cavern wall. Slowly, almost fearfully, he advanced to where the female was waiting. He could see her better now—and she seemed no different from those fugitive mothers of Different Ones—at whose slaughter he had so often assisted. The body was well-proportioned and covered with fine, silky fur. The head was well-shaped. Physically she was so normal as to seem repugnant to the New People.

And yet—No-Fur found himself comparing her with the females of his own tribe, to the disadvantage of the latter. Emotion rather than reason told him that the hatred inspired by the sight of an ordinary body was the result of a deep-rooted feeling of inferiority rather than anything else. And he wanted this stranger.

"No," she said slowly, "it is not my body that is different. It is in my head. I didn't know myself until a little while—about two hands of feeding—ago. But I can tell, now, what is going on inside your head, or the head of any of the People—"

"But," asked the male, "how did they—"

"I was ripe for mating. I was mated to Trillo, the son of Tekka, the chief. And in our cave I told Trillo things of which he only knew. I thought that I should please him, I thought that he would like to have a mate with magical powers that he could put to good use. With my aid he could have made himself chief. But he was angry—and very frightened. He ran to Tekka, who judged me as a Different One. I was to have been killed, but I was able to escape. They dare not follow me too far into this country—"

Then— "You want me."

It was a statement rather than a question.

"Yes. But—"

"No-Tail? She can die. If I fight her and win, I become your mate."

Briefly, half regretfully, No-Fur thought of his female. She had been patient, she had been loyal. But he saw that, with this stranger for a mate, there were no limits to his advancement. It was not that he was more enlightened than Trillo had been, it was that as one of the New People he regarded abnormality as the norm.

"Then you will take me." Once again there was no hint of questioning. Then— "My name is Wesel."

The arrival of No-Fur, with Wesel in tow, at the Place-of-Meeting could not have been better timed. There was a trial in progress, a young male named Big-Ears having been caught red-handed in the act of stealing a coveted piece of metal from the cave of one Four-Arms. Long-Nose, who should have relieved No-Fur, had found the spectacle of a trial with the prospect of a feast to follow far more engrossing than the relief of the lonely sentry.

It was he who first noticed the newcomers.

"Oh, Big-Tusk," he called, "No-Fur has deserted his post!"

The chief was disposed to be lenient.

"He has a prisoner," he said. "A Different One. We shall feast well."

*"He is afraid of you,"* hissed Wesel. *"Defy him!"*

"It is no prisoner." No-Fur's voice was arrogant. "It is my new mate. And you, Long-Nose, go at once to the tunnel."

"Go, Long-Nose. My country must not remain unguarded. No-Fur, hand the strange female over to the guards that she may be slaughtered."

No-Fur felt his resolution wavering under the stern glare of the chief. As two of Big-Tusk's bullies approached he slackened his grip on Wesel's arm. She turned to him, pleading and desperation in her eyes.

"No, no. He is afraid of you, I say. Don't give in to him. Together we can—"

Ironically, it was No-Tail's intervention that turned the scales. She confronted her mate, scorn written large on her unbeautiful face, the shrewish tongue dreaded by all the New People, even the chief himself, fast getting under way.

"So," she said, "you prefer this drab, common female to me. Hand her over, so that she may, at least, fill our bellies. As for you, my bucko, you will pay for this insult!"

No-Fur looked at the grotesque, distorted form of No-Tail, and then at the slim, sleek Wesel. Almost without volition he spoke.

"Wesel is my mate," he said. "She is one of the New People!"

Big-Tusk lacked the vocabulary to pour adequate scorn upon the insolent rebel. He struggled for words, but could find none to cover the situation. His little eyes gleamed redly, and his hideous tusks were bared in a vicious snarl.

"*Now!*" prompted the stranger. "His head is confused. He will be rash. His desire to tear and maul will cloud his judgment. Attack!"

No-Fur went into the fight coldly, knowing that if he kept his head he must win. He raised his spear to stem the first rush of the infuriated chief. Just in time Big-Tusk saw the rough point and, using his tail as a rudder, swerved. He wasn't fast enough, although his action barely saved him from immediate death. The spear caught him in the shoulder and broke off short, leaving the end in the wound. Mad with rage and pain the chief was now a most dangerous enemy—and yet, at the same time, easy meat for an adversary who kept his head.

No-Fur was, at first, such a one. But his self-control was cracking fast. Try as he would he could not fight down the rising tides of hysterical fear, of sheer, animal blood lust. As the enemies circled, thrust and parried, he with his almost useless weapon, Big-Tusk with a fine, metal-tipped spear, it took all his willpower to keep himself from taking refuge in flight or closing to grapple with his more powerful antagonist. His reason told him that both courses of action would be disastrous—the first would end in his being hunted down and slaughtered by the tribe, the second would bring him within range of the huge, murderous teeth that had given Big-Tusk his name.

So he thrust and parried, thrust and parried, until the keen edge of the chief's blade nicked his arm. The stinging pain made him all animal, and with a shrill scream of fury he launched himself at the other.

But if nature had provided Big-Tusk with a fine armory she had not been niggardly with the rebel's defensive equipment. True, he had nothing outstanding in the way of teeth or claws, had not the extra limbs possessed by so many of his fellow New People. His brain may have been a little more nimble—but at this stage of the fight that counted for nothing. What saved his life was his hairless skin.

Time after time the chief sought to pull him within striking distance, time after time he pulled away. His slippery hide was crisscrossed with a score of scratches, many of them deep but none immediately serious. And all the time he himself was scratching and pummeling with both hands and feet, biting and gouging.

It seemed that Big-Tusk was tiring, but he was tiring too. And the other had learned that it was useless to try to grab a handful of fur, that he must try to take his enemy in an unbreakable embrace. Once he succeeded. No-Fur was pulled closer and closer to the slavering fangs, felt the foul breath of the other in his face, knew that it was a matter of heartbeats before his throat was torn out. He screamed, threw up his legs and lunged viciously at Big-Tusk's belly. He felt his feet sink into the soft flesh, but the chief grunted and did not relax his pressure. Worse—the failure of his desperate counterattack had brought No-Fur even closer to death.

With one arm, his right, he pushed desperately against the other's chest. He tried to bring his knees up in a crippling blow, but they were held in a viselike grip by Big-Tusk's heavily muscled legs. With his free, left arm he flailed viciously and desperately, but he might have been beating against the Barrier itself.

The People, now that the issue of the battle was decided, were yelling encouragement to the victor. No-Fur heard among the cheers the voice of his mate, No-Tail. The little, cold corner of his brain in which reason was still enthroned told him that he couldn't blame her. If she were vociferous in *his* support, she could expect only death at the hands of the triumphant chief. But he forgot that he had offered her insult and humiliation, remembered only that she was his mate. And the bitterness of it kept him fighting when others would have relinquished their hold on a life already forfeit.

The edge of his hand came down hard just where Big-Tusk's thick neck joined his shoulder. He was barely conscious that the other winced, that a little whimper of pain followed the blow. Then, high and shrill, he heard Wesel.

"Again! Again! That is his weak spot!"

Blindly groping, he searched for the same place. And Big-Tusk was afraid, of that there was no doubt. His head twisted, trying to cover his vulnerability. Again he whimpered, and No-Fur knew that the battle was his. His thin, strong fingers with their sharp nails dug and gouged. There was no fur here, and the flesh was soft. He felt the warm blood welling beneath his hand as the chief screamed dreadfully. Then the iron grip was abruptly relaxed. Before Big-Tusk could use hands or feet to cast his enemy from him No-Fur had twisted and, each hand clutching skin and fur, had buried his teeth in the other's neck. They found the jugular. Almost at once the chief's last, desperate struggles ceased.

No-Fur drank long and satisfyingly.

Then, the blood still clinging to his muzzle, he wearily surveyed the People.

"I am chief," he said.

"You are the chief!" came back the answering chorus.

"And Wesel is my mate."

This time there was hesitation on the part of the People. The new chief heard mutters of *"The feast . . . Big-Tusk is old and tough . . . are we to be cheated—?"*

"Wesel is my mate," he repeated. Then— "There is your feast—"

At the height of his power he was to remember No-Tail's stricken eyes, the dreadful feeling that by his words he had put himself outside all custom, all law.

*"Above* the law," whispered Wesel.

He steeled his heart.

"There is your feast," he said again.

It was Big-Ears who, snatching a spear from one of the guards, with one swift blow dispatched the cringing No-Tail.

"I am your mate," said Wesel.

No-Fur took her in his arms. They rubbed noses. It wasn't the old chief's blood that made her shudder ever so slightly. It was the feel of the disgusting, hairless body against her own.

Already the People were carving and dividing the two corpses and wrangling over an even division of the succulent spoils.

There was one among the New People who, had her differences from the racial stock been only psychological, would have been slaughtered long since. Her three eyes notwithstanding, the imprudent exercise of her gift would have brought certain doom. But, like her sisters in more highly civilized communities, she was careful to tell those who came to her only that which they desired to hear. Even then, she exercised restraint. Experience had taught her that foreknowledge of coming events on the part of the participants often resulted in entirely unforeseen results. This annoyed her. Better misfortune on the main stream of time than well-being on one of its branches.

To this Three-Eyes came No-Fur and Wesel.

Before the chief could ask his questions the seeress raised one emaciated hand.

"You are Shrick," she said. "So your mother called you. Shrick, the Giant Killer."

"But—"

"Wait. You came to ask me about your war against Tekka's people. Continue with your plans. You will win. You will then fight the Tribe of Sterret the Old. Again you will win. You will be Lord of the Outside. And then—"

"And then?"

"The Giants will know of the People. Many, but not all, of the People will die. You will fight the Giants. And the last of the Giants you will kill, but he will plunge the world into—Oh, if I could make you see! But we have no words."

"What—?"

"No, you cannot know. You will never know till the end is upon you. But this I can tell you. The People are doomed. Nothing you or they can do will save them. But you will kill those who will kill us, and that is good."

Again No-Fur pleaded for enlightenment. Abruptly, his pleas became threats. He was fast lashing himself into one of his dreaded fits of blind fury. But Three-Eyes was oblivious of his presence. Her two outer eyes were tight shut and that strange, dreaded inner one was staring at *something*, something outside the limits of the cave, outside the framework of things as they are.

Deep in his throat the chief growled.

He raised the fine spear that was the symbol of his office and buried it deep in the old female's body. The inner eye shut and the two outer ones flickered open for the last time.

"I am spared the End—" she said.

Outside the little cavern the faithful Big-Ears was waiting.

"Three-Eyes is dead," said his master. "Take what you want, and give the rest to the People—"

For a little there was silence.

Then— "I am glad you killed her," said Wesel. "She frightened me. I got inside her head—and I was lost!" Her voice had a hysterical edge. "I was lost! It was mad, mad. *What Was* was a *place*, a *PLACE*, and *Now*, and *What Will Be*. And l saw the End."

"What did you see?"

"A great light, far brighter than the Giants' lights Inside. And heat, stronger than the heat of the floors of the Far Outside caves and tunnels. And the People gasping and dying and the great light bursting into our world and eating them up—"

"But the Giants?"

"I did not see. I was lost. All I saw was the End."

No-Fur was silent. His active, nimble mind was scurrying down the vistas opened up by the dead prophetess. Giant Killer, *Giant Killer*. Even in his most grandiose dreams he had never seen himself thus. And what was that name? Shrick? He repeated it to himself—Shrick the Giant Killer. It had a fine swing to it. As for the rest, the End, if he could kill the Giants then, surely, he could stave off the doom that they would mete out to the People. Shrick, the Giant Killer—

"It is a name that I like better than No-Fur," said Wesel.

"Shrick, Lord of the Outside. Shrick, Lord of the World. Shrick, the Giant Killer—"

"Yes," he said, slowly. "But the End—"

"You will go through that door when you come to it."

The campaign against Tekka's people had opened.

Along the caves and tunnels poured the nightmare hordes of Shrick. The dim light but half-revealed their misshapen bodies, limbs where no limbs should be, heads like something from a half-forgotten bad dream.

All were armed. Every male and female carried a spear, and that in itself was a startling innovation in the wars of the People. For sharp metal, with which the weapons were tipped, was hard to come by. True, a staff of Barrier material could be sharpened, but it was a liability rather than an asset in a pitched battle. With the first thrust the point would break off, leaving the fighter with a weapon far inferior to his natural armory of teeth and claws.

Fire was new to the People—and it was Shrick who had brought them fire. For long periods he had spied upon the Giants in the Place-of-Little-Lights, had seen them bring from the pouches in their fur little glittering devices from which when a projection was pressed, issued a tiny, naked light. And he had seen them bring this light to the end of strange, white sticks that they seemed to be sucking. And the end of the stick would glow, and there would be a cloud like the cloud that issued from the mouths of the People in some of the Far Outside caverns where it was very cold. But this cloud was fragrant, and seemed to be strangely soothing.

And one of the Giants had lost his little hot light. He had put it to one to the white sticks, had made to return it to his pouch, and his hand had missed the opening. The Giant did not notice. He was doing something which took all his attention—and strain his eyes and his imagination as he might Shrick could not see what it was. There were strange glittering machines through which he peered intently at the glittering Little Lights beyond their transparent Barrier. Or were they on the inside of the Barrier? Nobody had ever been able to decide. There was something alive that wasn't alive that clicked. There were sheets of fine, white skin on which the Giant was making black marks with a pointed stick.

But Shrick soon lost interest in these strange rites that he could never hope to comprehend. All his attention was focused on the glittering prize that was drifting ever so slowly toward him on the wings of some vagrant eddy.

When it seemed that it would surely fall right into the doorway where Shrick crouched waiting, it swerved. And, much as he dreaded the pseudo-life that hummed and clicked, Shrick came out. The Giant, busy with his sorcery, did not notice him. One swift leap carried him to the drifting trophy. And then he had it, tight clasped to his breast. It was bigger than he had thought, it having appeared so tiny only in relationship to its previous owner. But it wasn't too big to go through the door in the Barrier. In triumph Shrick bore it to his cave.

Many were the experiments that he, eager but fumbling, performed. For a while both he and Wesel nursed painful burns. Many were the experiments that he intended to perform in the future. But he had stumbled on one use for the hot light that was to be of paramount importance in his wars.

Aping the Giants, he had stuck a long splinter of Barrier material in his mouth. The end he had brought to the little light. There was, as he had half expected, a cloud. But it was neither fragrant nor soothing. Blinded and coughing, Wesel snatched at the glowing stick, beat out its strange life with her hands.

Then—"It is hard," she said. "It is almost as hard as metal—"

And so Shrick became the first mass producer of armaments that his world had known. The first few sharpened staves he treated himself. The rest he left to Wesel and the faithful Big-Ears. He dare not trust his wonderful new power to any who were not among his intimates.

Shrick's other innovation was a direct violation of all the rules of war. He had pressed the females into the fighting line. Those who were old and infirm, together with the old and infirm males, brought up the rear with bundles of the mass-produced spears. The New People had been wondering for some little time why their chief had refused to let them slaughter those of their number who had outlived their usefulness. Now they knew.

The caves of the New People were deserted save for those few females with newborn.

And through the tunnels poured the hordes of Shrick.

There was little finesse in the campaign against Tekka's people. The outposts were slaughtered out of hand, but not before they had had time to warn the Tribe of the attack.

Tekka threw a body of picked spearmen into his van, confident that he, with better access to those parts of Inside where metal could be obtained, would be able to swamp the motley horde of the enemy with superior arms and numbers.

When Tekka saw, in the dim light, only a few betraying gleams of metal scattered among Shrick's massed spears, he laughed.

"This No-Fur is mad," he said. "And I shall kill him with this." He brandished his own weapon. "His mother gave it to me many, many feedings ago."

"Is Wesel—?"

"Perhaps, my son. You shall eat her heart, I promise you."

And then Shrick struck.

His screaming mob rushed along the wide tunnel. Confident the Tekkan spearmen waited, knowing that the enemy's weapons were good for only one thrust, and that almost certainly not lethal.

Tekka scowled as he estimated the numbers of the attackers. There couldn't be that many males among the New People. There couldn't—· and then the wave struck.

In the twinkling of an eye the tunnel was tightly packed with struggling bodies. Here was no dignified, orderly series of single combats such as had always, in the past, graced the wars of the People. And with growing terror Tekka realized that the enemy spears were standing up to the strain of battle at least as well as his own few metal-tipped weapons.

Slowly, but with ever mounting momentum, the attackers pressed on, gaining impetus from the many bodies that now lay behind them. Gasping for air in the affluvium of sweat and newly shed blood Tekka and the last of his guards were pressed back and ever back.

When one of the New People was disarmed he fell to the rear of his own front line. As though by magic a fresh fighter would appear to replace him.

Then—"He's using females!" cried Trillo. "He's—"

But Tekka did not answer. He was fighting for his life with a four-armed monster. Every hand held a spear—and every spear was bright with blood. For long heartbeats he parried the other's thrusts, then his nerve broke. Screaming, he turned his back on the enemy. It was the last thing he did.

And so the remnant of the fighting strength of the Tribe of Tekka was at last penned up against one wall of their Place-of-Meeting. Surrounding them was a solid hemisphere of the New People. Snarl was answered by snarl. Trillo and his scant half-dozen guards knew that there was no surrender. All they could do was to sell their lives as dearly as possible.

And so they waited for the inevitable, gathering the last reserves of their strength in this lull of the battle, gasping the last sweet mouthfuls of air that they would ever taste. From beyond the wall of their assailants they could hear the cries and screams as the females and children, who had hidden in their caves, were hunted out and slaughtered. They were not to know that the magnanimous Shrick was sparing most of the females. They, he hoped, would produce for him more New People.

And then Shrick came, elbowing his way to the forefront of his forces. His smooth, naked body was unmarked, save by the old scars of his battle with Big-Tusk. And with him was Wesel, not a hair of her sleek fur out of place. And Big-Ears—but he, obviously, had been in the fight. With them came more fighters, fresh and eager.

"Finish them!" ordered Shrick.

"Wait!" Wesel's voice was imperative. "I want Trillo."

Him she pointed out to the picked fighters, who raised their spears—weapons curiously slender and light, too fragile for hand-to-hand combat. A faint hope stirred in the breasts of the last defenders.

"Now!"

Trillo and his guards braced themselves to meet the last rush. It never came. Instead, thrown with unerring aim, came those sharp, flimsy spears, pinning them horribly against the gray, spongy wall of the Place-of-Meeting.

Spared in this final slaughter, Trillo looked about him with wide, fear-crazed eyes. He started to scream, then launched himself at the laughing Wesel. But she slipped back through the packed masses of the New People. Blind to all else but that hateful figure, Trillo tried to follow. And the New People crowded about him, binding his arms and legs with their strong cords, snatching his spear from him before its blade drank blood.

Then again the captive saw she who had been his mate.

Shamelessly, she was caressing Shrick.

"My hairless one," she said. "I was once mated to *this*. You shall have his fur to cover your smooth body." And then—"Big-Ears! You know what to do!"

Grinning, Big-Ears found the sharp blade of a spear that had become detached from its haft. Grinning, he went to work. Trillo started to whimper, then to scream. Shrick felt a little sick. "Stop!" he said. "He is not dead. You must—"

"What does it matter?" Wesel's eyes were avid, and her little, pink tongue came out to lick her thin lips. Big-Ears had hesitated in his work but, at her sign, continued.

"What does it matter?" she said again.

As had fared the Tribe of Tekka so fared the Tribe of Sterret, and a hand or more of smaller communities owing a loose allegiance to these two.

But it was in his war with Sterret that Shrick almost met disaster. To the cunning oldster had come survivors from the massacre of Tekka's army. Most of these had been slaughtered out of hand by the frontier guards, but one or two had succeeded in convincing their captors that they bore tidings of great importance.

Sterret heard them out.

He ordered that they be fed and treated as his own people, for he knew that he would need every ounce of fighting strength that he could muster.

Long and deeply he pondered upon their words, and then sent foray after foray of his young males to the Place-of-Life-That-Is-Not-Life. Careless he was of detection by the Giants. They might or might not act against him—but he had long been convinced that, for all their size, they were comparatively stupid and harmless. Certainly, at this juncture, they were not such a menace as Shrick, already self-styled Lord of the Outside.

And so his store of sharp fragments of metal grew, while his armorers worked without cessation binding these to hafts of Barrier stuff. And he, too, could innovate. Some of the fragments were useless as spearheads, being blunt, rough and irregular. But, bound like a spearhead to a shaft, they could deliver a crushing blow. Of this Sterret was sure after a few experiments on old and unwanted members of his tribe.

Most important, perhaps, his mind, rich in experience but not without a certain youthful zest, busied itself with problems of strategy. In the main tunnel from what had been Tekka's country his females hacked and tore at the spongy wall, the material being packed tightly and solidly into another small tunnel that was but rarely used.

At last his scouts brought the word that Shrick's forces were on the move. Careless in the crushing weight of his military power, Shrick disdained anything but a direct frontal attack. Perhaps he should have been warned by the fact that all orifices admitting light from the Inside had been closed, that the main tunnel along which he was advancing was in total darkness.

This, however, hampered him but little. The body of picked spearmen opposing him fought in the conventional way, and these, leaving their dead and wounded, were forced slowly but surely back. Each side relied upon smell, and hearing, and a certain perception possessed by most, if not all, of the People. At such close quarters these were ample.

Shrick himself was not in the van—that honor was reserved for Big-Ears, his fighting general. Had the decision rested with him alone he would have been in the forefront of the battle—but Wesel averred that the leader was of far greater importance than a mere spear-bearer, should be shielded from needless risk. Not altogether unwillingly, Shrick acquiesced.

Surrounded by his guard, with Wesel at his side, the leader followed the noise of the fighting. He was rather surprised at the reports back to him concerning the apparent numbers of the enemy, but assumed that this was a mere delaying action and that Sterret would make his last stand in the Place-of-Meeting. It never occurred to him in his arrogance that others could innovate.

Abruptly, Wesel clutched his arm.

"Shrick! Danger—from the side!"

"From the side? But—"

There was a shrill cry, and a huge section of the tunnel wall fell inward. The spongy stuff was in thin sheets, and drifted among the guard, hampering their every movement. Then, led by Sterret in person, the defenders came out. Like mountaineers they were roped together, for in this battle in the darkness their best hope lay in keeping in one, compact body. Separated, they would fall easy prey to the superior numbers of the hordes of Shrick.

With spear and mace they lay about them lustily. The first heartbeat of the engagement would have seen the end of Shrick, and it was only the uncured hide of Trillo, stiff and stinking, that saved his life. Even so, the blade of Sterret penetrated the crude armor, and, sorely wounded, Shrick reeled out of the battle.

Ahead, Big-Ears was no longer having things all his own way. Reinforcements had poured along the tunnel and he dare not return to the succor of his chief. And Sterret's maces were having their effect. Stabbing and slashing the People could understand—but a crushing blow was, to them, something infinitely horrible.

It was Wesel who saved the day. With her she had brought the little, hot light. It had been her intention to try its effect on such few prisoners as might be taken in this campaign—she was too shrewd to experiment on any of the New People, even those who had incurred the displeasure of herself or her mate.

Scarce knowing what she did she pressed the stud.

With dazzling suddenness the scene of carnage swam into full view. From all sides came cries of fear.

"Back!" cried Wesel. "Back! Clear a space!"

In two directions the New People retreated.

Blinking but dogged, Sterret's phalanx tried to follow, tried to turn what was a more or less orderly withdrawal into a rout. But the cords that had, at first, served them so well now proved their undoing. Some tried to pursue those making for the Place-of-Meeting, others those of the New People retiring to their own territory. Snarling viciously, blood streaming from a dozen minor wounds, Sterret at last cuffed and bullied his forces into a semblance of order. He attempted to lead a charge to where Wesel, the little, hot light still in her hand, was retreating among her personal, amazon guards.

But again the cunning—too cunning—ropes defeated his purpose. Not a few corpses were there to hamper fast movement, and almost none of his fighters had the intelligence to cut them free.

And the spear throwers of Shrick came to the fore, and, one by one, the people of Sterret were pinned by the slim deadly shafts to the tunnel walls. Not all were killed outright, a few unfortunates squirmed and whimpered, plucking at the spears with ineffectual hands.

Among these was Sterret.

Shrick came forward, spear in hand, to administer the *coup de grâce*. The old chief stared wildly, then—"Weena's hairless one!" he cried.

Ironically it was his own spear—the weapon that, in turn, had belonged to Weena and to Tekka—that slit his throat.

Now that he was Lord of the Outside Shrick had time in which to think and to dream. More and more his mind harked back to Three-Eyes and her prophecy. It never occurred to him to doubt that he was to be the Giant Killer—although the vision of the End he dismissed from his mind as the vaporings of a half-crazed old female.

And so he sent his spies to the Inside to watch the Giants in their mysterious comings and goings, tried hard to find some pattern for their incomprehensible behavior. He himself often accompanied these spies— and it was with avid greed that he saw the vast wealth of beautiful, shining things to which the Giants were heir. More than anything he desired another little hot light, for his own had ceased to function, and all the clumsy, ignorant tinkerings of himself and Wesel could not produce more than a feeble, almost heatless spark from its baffling intricacies.

It seemed, too, that the Giants were now aware of the swarming, fecund life surrounding them. Certain it was that their snares increased in number and ingenuity. And the food-that-kills appeared in new and terrifying guise. Not only did those who had eaten of it die, but their mates and—indeed all who had come into contact with them.

It smacked of sorcery, but Shrick had learned to associate cause and effect. He made the afflicted ones carry those already dead into a small tunnel. One or two of them rebelled—but the spear throwers surrounded them, their slim, deadly weapons at the ready. And those who attempted to break through the cordon of guards were run through repeatedly before ever they laid their defiling hands on any of the unafflicted People.

Big-Ears was among the sufferers. He made no attempt to quarrel with his fate. Before he entered the yawning tunnel that was to be his tomb he turned and looked at his chief. Shrick made to call him to his side— even though he knew that his friend's life could not be saved, and that by associating with him he would almost certainly lose his own.

But Wesel was at his side.

She motioned to the spear throwers, and a full two hands of darts transfixed the ailing Big-Ears.

"It was kinder this way," she lied.

But, somehow, the last look that his most loyal supporter had given him reminded him of No-Tail. With a heavy heart he ordered his people to seal the tunnel. Great strips of the spongy stuff were brought and stuffed into the entrance. The cries of those inside grew fainter and ever fainter. Then there was silence. Shrick ordered guards posted at all points where, conceivably, the doomed prisoners might break out. He returned to his own cave. Wesel, when one without her gift would have intruded, let him go in his loneliness. Soon he would want her again.

It had long been Wesel's belief that, given the opportunity, she could get inside the minds of the Giants just as she could those of the People. And if she could—who knew what prizes might be hers? Shrick, still inaccessible and grieving for his friend, she missed more than she cared to admit. The last of the prisoners from the last campaign had been killed, ingeniously, many feedings ago. Though she had no way of measuring time, it hung heavily on her hands.

And so, accompanied by two of her personal attendants, she roamed those corridors and tunnels running just inside the Barrier. Through spyhole after spyhole she peered, gazing in wonderment that long use could not stale at the rich and varied life of the Inside.

At last she found that for which she was searching—a Giant, alone and sleeping. Experience among the People had taught her that from a sleeping mind she could read the most secret thoughts.

For a heartbeat she hesitated. Then—"Four-Arms, Little-Head, wait here for me. Wait and watch."

Little-Head grunted an affirmative, but Four-Arms was dubious. "Lady Wesel," she said, "what if the Giant should wake? What—?"

"What if you should return to the Lord of the Outside without me? Then he would, without doubt, have your hides. The one he is wearing now is old, and the fur is coming out. But do as I say."

There was a door in the Barrier here, a door but rarely used. This was opened, and Wesel slipped through. With the ease that all the People were acquiring with their more frequent ventures to the Inside she floated up to the sleeping Giant. Bonds held him in a sort of framework, and Wesel wondered if, for some offense, he had been made prisoner by his own kind. She would soon know.

And then a glittering object caught her eye. It was one of the little hot lights, its polished metal case seeming to Wesel's covetous eyes the most beautiful thing in the world. Swiftly she made her decision. She could take the shining prize now, deliver it to her two attendants, and then return to carry out her original intentions.

In her eagerness she did not see that it was suspended in the middle of an interlacing of slender metal bars—or she did not care. And as her hands grabbed the bait something not far away began a shrill, not unmusical metallic beating. The Giant stirred and awoke. What Wesel had taken for bonds fell away from his body. In blind panic she turned to flee back to her own world. But, somehow, more of the metal bars had fallen into place and she was a prisoner.

She started to scream.

Surprisingly, Four-Arms and Little-Head came to her aid. It would be nice to be able to place on record that they were actuated by devotion to their mistress—but Four-Arms knew that her life was forfeit. And she had seen those who displeased either Shrick or Wesel flayed alive. Little-Head blindly followed the other's leadership. Hers not to reason why—

Slashing with their spears they assailed the Giant. He laughed—or so Wesel interpreted the deep, rumbling sound that came from his throat. Four-Arms he seized first. With one hand he grasped her body, with the other her head. He twisted. And that was the end of Four-Arms.

Anybody else but Little-Head would have turned and fled. But her dim mind refused to register that which she had seen. Perhaps a full feeding or so after the event the horror of it all would have stunned her with its impact—perhaps not. Be that as it may, she continued her attack. Blindly, instinctively, she went for the Giant's throat. Wesel sensed that he was badly frightened. But after a short struggle one of his hands caught the frenzied, squealing Little-Head. Violently, he flung her from him. She heard the thud as her attendant's body struck something hard and unyielding. And the impressions that her mind had been receiving from that of the other abruptly ceased.

Even in her panic fear she noticed that the Giant had not come out of the unequal combat entirely unscathed. One of his hands had been scratched, and was bleeding freely. And there were deep scratches on the hideous, repulsively naked face. The Giants, then, were vulnerable. There might have been some grain of truth after all in Three-Eye's insane babbling.

And then Wesel forgot her unavailing struggle against the bars of her cage. With sick horror she watched what the Giant was doing. He had taken the limp body of Four-Arms, had secured it to a flat surface. From somewhere he had produced an array of glittering instruments. One of these he took, and drew it down the body from throat to crotch. On either side of the keen blade the skin fell away, leaving the flesh exposed.

And the worst part of it was that it was not being done in hate or anger, neither was the unfortunate Four-Arms being divided up that she might be eaten. There was an impersonal quality about the whole business that sickened Wesel—for, by this time, she had gained a certain limited access to the mind of the other.

The Giant paused in his work. Another of his kind had come, and for many heartbeats the two talked together. They examined the mutilated carcass of Four-Arms, the crushed body of Little-Head. Together, they peered into the cage where Wesel snarled impotently.

But, in spite of her hysterical fear, part of her mind was deadly cold, was receiving and storing impressions that threw the uninhibited, animal part of her into still greater panic. While the Giants talked the impressions were clear—and while their great, ungainly heads hung over her cage, scant handbreadths away, they were almost overpowering in their strength. She knew who she and the People were, what their world was. She had not the ability to put it into words—but she *knew*. And she saw the doom that the Giants were preparing for the People.

With a few parting words to his fellow the second Giant left. The first one resumed his work of dismembering Four-Arms. At last he was finished. What was left of the body was put into transparent containers.

The Giant picked up Little-Head. For many heartbeats he examined her, turning her over and over in his great hands. Wesel thought that he would bind the body to the flat surface, do with it as he had done with that of Four-Arms. But, at last he put the body to one side. Over his hands he pulled something that looked like a thick, additional skin. Suddenly, the metal bars at one end of the cage fell away, and one of those enormous hands came groping for Wesel.

After the death of Big-Ears, Shrick slept a little. It was the only way in which he could be rid of the sense of loss, of the feeling that he had betrayed his most loyal follower. His dreams were troubled, haunted by ghosts from his past. Big-Ears was in them, and Big-Tusk, and a stranger female with whom he felt a sense of oneness, whom he knew to be Weena, his mother.

And then all these phantasms were gone, leaving only the image of

Wesel. It wasn't the Wesel he had always known, cool, self-assured, ambitious. This was a terrified Wesel—Wesel descending into a black abyss of pain and torture even worse than that which she had, so often, meted out to others. And she wanted him.

Shrick awoke, frightened by his dreams. But he knew that ghosts had never hurt anybody, could not hurt him, Lord of the Outside. He shook himself, whimpering a little, and then tried to compose himself for further sleep.

But the image of Wesel persisted. At last Shrick abandoned his attempts to seek oblivion and, rubbing his eyes, emerged from his cave.

In the dim, half-light of the Place-of-Meeting little knots of the People hung about, talking in low voices. Shrick called to the guards. There was a sullen silence. He called again. At last one answered.

"Where is Wesel?"

"I do not know . . . lord." The last word came out grudgingly.

Then one of the others volunteered the information that she had been seen, in company with Four-Arms and Little-Head, proceeding along the tunnels that led to that part of the Outside in the way of the Place-of-Green-Growing-Things.

Shrick hesitated.

He rarely ventured abroad without his personal guards, but then, Big-Ears was always one of them. And Big-Ears was gone.

He looked around him, decided that he could trust none of those at present in the Place-of-Meeting. The People had been shocked and horrified by his necessary actions in the case of those who had eaten of the food-that-kills and regarded him, he knew, as a monster even worse than the Giants. Their memories were short—but until they forgot he would have to walk with caution.

"Wesel is my mate. I will go alone," he said.

At his words he sensed a change of mood, was tempted to demand an escort. But the instinct that—as much as any mental superiority—maintained him in authority warned him against throwing away his advantage.

"I go alone," he said.

One Short-Tail, bolder than his fellows, spoke up.

"And if you do not return, Lord of the Outside? Who is to be—?"

"I shall return," said Shrick firmly, his voice displaying a confidence he did not feel.

In the more populous regions the distinctive scent of Wesel was overlaid by that of many others. In tunnels but rarely frequented it was strong and compelling—but now he had no need to use his olfactory powers. For the terrified little voice in his brain—from outside his brain—was saying *hurry, HURRY*—and some power beyond his ken was guiding him unerringly to where his mate was in such desperate need of him.

From the door in the Barrier through which Wesel had entered the Inside—it had been left open—streamed a shaft of light. And now Shrick's natural caution reasserted itself. The voice inside his brain was no less urgent, but the instinct of self-preservation was strong. Almost timorously, he peered through the doorway.

He smelled death. At first he feared that he was too late, then identified the personal odors of Four-Arms and Little-Head. That of Wesel was there too—intermingled with the acrid scent of terror and agony. But she was still alive.

Caution forgotten, he launched himself from the doorway with all the power of his leg muscles. And he found Wesel, stretched supine on a flat surface that was slippery with blood. Most of it was Four-Arms', but some of it was hers.

"Shrick!" she screamed. "The Giant!"

He looked away from his mate and saw hanging over him, pale and enormous, the face of the Giant. He screamed, but there was more of fury than terror in the sound. He saw, not far from where he clung to Wesel, a huge blade of shining metal. He could see that its edge was keen. The handle had been fashioned for a hand far larger than his, nevertheless he was just able to grasp it. It seemed to be secured. Feet braced against Wesel's body for purchase, he tugged desperately.

Just as the Giant's hand, fingers outstretched to seize him, came down the blade pulled free. As Shrick's legs suddenly and involuntarily straightened he was propelled away from Wesel. The Giant grabbed at the flying form, and howled in agony as Shrick swept the blade around and lopped off a finger.

He heard Wesel's voice: "You are the Giant Killer!"

Now he was level with the Giant's head. He swerved, and with his feet caught a fold of the artificial skin covering the huge body. And he hung there, swinging his weapon with both hands, cutting and slashing. Great hands swung wildly and he was bruised and buffeted. But not once did they succeed in finding a grip. Then there was a great and horrid spurting of blood and a wild threshing of mighty limbs. This ceased, but it was only the voice of Wesel that called him from the fury of his slaughter lust.

So he found her again, still stretched out for sacrifice to the Giants' dark gods, still bound to that surface that was wet with her blood and that of her attendant. But she smiled up at him, and in her eyes was respect that bordered on awe.

"Are you hurt?" he demanded, a keen edge of anxiety to his voice.

"Only a little. But Four-Arms was cut in pieces . . . I should have been had you not come. And," her voice was a hymn of praise, "you killed the Giant!"

"It was foretold. Besides," for once he was honest, "it could not have been done without the Giant's weapon."

With its edge he was cutting Wesel's bonds. Slowly she floated away from the place of sacrifice. Then: "I can't move my legs!" Her voice was terror-stricken. "I can't move!"

Shrick guessed what was wrong. He knew a little of anatomy—his knowledge was that of the warrior who may be obliged to immobilize his enemy prior to his slaughter—and he could see that the Giant's keen blade had wrought this damage. Fury boiled up in him against these cruel, monstrous beings. And there was more than fury. There was the feeling, rare among his people, of overwhelming pity for his crippled mate.

"The blade . . . it is very sharp . . . I shall feel nothing."

But Shrick could not bring himself to do it.

Now they were floating up against the huge bulk of the dead Giant. With one hand he grasped Wesel's shoulder—the other still clutched his fine, new weapon—and kicked off against the gigantic carcass. Then he was pushing Wesel through the doorway in the Barrier, and sensed her relief as she found herself once more in familiar territory. He followed her, then carefully shut and barred the door.

For a few heartbeats Wesel busied herself smoothing her bedraggled fur. He couldn't help noticing that she dare not let her hands stray to the lower part of her body where were the wounds, small but deadly, that had robbed her of the power of her limbs. Dimly, he felt that something might be done for one so injured, but knew that it was beyond his powers. And fury—not helpless now—against the Giants returned again, threatening to choke him with its intensity.

"Shrick!" Wesel's voice was grave. "We must return at once to the People. We must warn the People. The Giants are making a sorcery to bring the End."

"The great, hot light?"

"No. But wait! First I must tell you of what I learned. Otherwise, you would not believe. I have learned what we are, what the world is. And it is strange and wonderful beyond all our beliefs.

"What is Outside?" She did not wait for his answer, read it in his mind before his lips could frame the words. "The world is but a bubble of emptiness in the midst of a vast piece of metal, greater than the mind can imagine. But it is not so! Outside the metal that lies outside the Outside there is nothing. *Nothing!* There is no air."

"But there must be air, at least."

"No, I tell you. There is *nothing.*

"And the world—how can I find words? Their name for the world is —*ship,* and it seems to mean something big going from one place to another place. And all of us—Giants and People—are inside the ship. The Giants made the ship."

"Then it is not alive?"

"I cannot say. *They* seem to think that it is a female. It must have some kind of life that is not life. And it is going from one world to another world."

"And these other worlds?"

"I caught glimpses of them. They are dreadful, dreadful. *We* find the open spaces of the Inside frightening—but these other worlds are *all* open space except for one side."

"But what are we?" In spite of himself, Shrick at least half believed Wesel's fantastic story. Perhaps she possessed, to some slight degree, the power of projecting her own thoughts into the mind of another with whom she was intimate. "What are we?"

She was silent for the space of many heartbeats. Then: *"Their* name for us is—*mutants.* The picture was . . . not clear at all. It means that we —the People—have changed. And yet their picture of the People before the change was like the Different Ones before we slew them all.

"Long and long ago—many hands of feedings—the first People, our parents' parents' parents, came into the world. They came from that greater world—the world of dreadful, open spaces. They came with the food in the great Cave-of-Food—and that is being carried to another world.

"Now, in the horrid, empty space outside the Outside there is—light that is not light. And this light—changes persons. No, not the grown person or the child, but the child before the birth. Like the dead and gone chiefs of the People, the Giants fear change in themselves. So they have kept the light that is not light from the Inside.

"And this is how. Between the Barrier and the Far Outside they filled the space with the stuff in which we have made our caves and tunnels. The first People left the great Cave-of-Food, they tunneled through the Barrier and into the stuff Outside. It was their nature. And some of them mated in the Far Outside caves. Their children were—*different.*"

"That is true," said Shrick slowly. "It has always been thought that children born in the Far Outside were never like their parents, and that those born close to the Barrier were—"

"Yes.

"Now, the Giants always knew that the People were here, but they did not fear them. They did not know our numbers, and they regarded us as beings much lower than themselves. They were content to keep us down with their traps and the food-that-kills. Somehow, they found that we had changed. Like the dead chiefs they feared us then—and like the dead chiefs they will try to kill us all before we conquer them."

"And the End?"

"Yes, the End." She was silent again, her big eyes looking past Shrick at something infinitely terrible. "Yes," she said again, "the End. *They* will make it, and *They* will escape it. *They* will put on artificial skins that will cover *Their* whole bodies, even *Their* heads, and *They* will open huge doors in the . . . skin of the ship, and all the air will rush out into the terrible empty space outside the Outside. And all the the People will die."

"I must go," said Shrick. "I must kill the Giants before this comes to pass."

"No! There was one hand of Giants—now that you have killed Fat-Belly there are four of them left. And they know, now, that they can be killed. They will be watching for you.

"Do you remember when we buried the People with the sickness? That is what we must do to all the People. And then when the Giants fill the world with air again from their store we can come out."

Shrick was silent awhile. He had to admit that she was right. One unsuspecting Giant had fallen to his blade—but four of them, aroused, angry and watchful, he could not handle. In any case there was no way of knowing when the Giants would let the air from the world. The People must be warned—and fast.

Together, in the Place-of-Meeting, Shrick and Wesel faced the People. They had told their stories, only to be met with blank incredulity. True, there were some who, seeing the fine, shining blade that Shrick had brought from the Inside, were inclined to believe. But they were shouted down by the majority. It was when he tried to get them to immure themselves against the End that he met with serious opposition. The fact that he had so treated those suffering from the sickness still bulked big in the mob memory.

It was Short-Tail who precipitated the crisis.

"He wants the world to himself!" he shouted. "He has killed Big-Tusk and No-Tail, he has killed all the Different Ones, and Big-Ears he slew because he would have been chief. He and his ugly, barren mate want the world to themselves!"

Shrick tried to argue, but Big-Ears's following shouted him down. He squealed with rage and, raising his blade with both hands, rushed upon the rebel. Short-Tail scurried back out of reach. Shrick found himself alone in a suddenly cleared space. From somewhere a long way off he heard Wesel screaming his name. Dazedly, he shook his head, and then the red mist cleared from in front of his eyes.

All around him were the spear throwers, their slender weapons poised. He had trained them himself, had brought their specialized art of war into being. And now—

"Shrick!" Wesel was saying, "don't fight! They will kill you, and I shall be alone. I shall have the world to myself. Let them do as they will with us, and *we* shall live through the End."

At her words a tittering laugh rippled through the mob.

"*They* will live through the End! They will die as Big-Ears and his friends died!"

"I want your blade," said Short-Tail.

"Give it to him," cried Wesel. "You will get it back after the End!"

Shrick hesitated. The other made a sign. One of the throwing spears buried itself in the fleshy part of his arm. Had it not been for Wesel's voice, pleading, insistent, he would have charged his tormenters and met his end in less than a single heartbeat. Reluctantly, he released his hold upon the weapon. Slowly—as though loath to leave its true owner—it floated away from him. And then the People were all around him, almost suffocating him with the pressure of their bodies.

The cave into which Shrick and Wesel were forced was their own dwelling place. They were in pitiable state when the mob retreated to the entrance—Wesel's wounds had reopened and Shrick's arm was bleeding freely. Somebody had wrenched out the spear—but the head had broken off.

Outside, Short-Tail was laying about him with the keen blade he had taken from his chief. Under its strokes great masses of the spongy stuff of the Outside were coming free, and many willing hands were stuffing this tight into the cave entrance.

"We will let you out after the End!" called somebody. There was a hoot of derision. Then: "I wonder which will eat the other first?"

"Never mind," said Wesel softly. "We shall laugh last."

"Perhaps. But . . . the People. *My* People. And you are barren. The Giants have won—"

Wesel was silent. Then he heard her voice again. She was whimpering to herself in the darkness. Shrick could guess her thoughts. All their grandiose dreams of world dominion had come to this—a tiny cramped space in which there was barely room for either of them to stir a finger.

And now they could no longer hear the voices of the People outside their prison. Shrick wondered if the Giants had already struck, then reassured himself with the memory of how the voices of those suffering from the sickness had grown fainter and fainter and then, at the finish, ceased altogether. And he wondered how he and Wesel would know when the End had come, and how they would know when it was safe to dig themselves out. It would be a long, slow task with only their teeth and claws with which to work.

But he had a tool.

The fingers of the hand of his uninjured arm went to the spearhead still buried in the other. He knew that by far the best way of extracting it would be one, quick pull—but he couldn't bring himself to do it. Slowly, painfully, he worked away at the sharp fragment of metal.

"Let me do it for you."

"No." His voice was rough. "Besides, there is no haste."

Slowly, patiently, he worried at the wound. He was groaning a little, although he was not conscious of doing so. And then, suddenly, Wesel screamed. The sound was so unexpected, so dreadful in that confined space, that Shrick started violently. His hand jerked away from his upper arm, bringing with it the spearhead.

His first thought was that Wesel, telepath as she was, had chosen this way to help him. But he felt no gratitude, only a dull resentment.

"What did you do that for?" he demanded angrily.

She didn't answer his question. She was oblivious of his presence.

"The People . . ." she whispered. "The People . . . I can feel their thoughts . . . I can feel what they are feeling. And they are gasping for air . . . they are gasping and dying . . . and the cave of Long-Fur the spearmaker . . . but they are dying, and the blood is coming out of their mouths and noses and ears . . . I can't bear it . . . I can't—"

And then a terrifying thing happened. The sides of the cave pressed in upon them. Throughout the world, throughout the ship, the air cells in the spongy insulation were expanding as the air pressure dropped to zero. It was this alone that saved Shrick and Wesel, although they never knew it. The rough plug sealing their cave that, otherwise, would have blown out swelled to meet the expanding walls of the entrance, making a near perfect air-tight joint.

But the prisoners were in no state to appreciate this, even had they been in possession of the necessary knowledge. Panic seized them both. Claustrophobia was unknown among the People—but walls that closed upon them were outside their experience.

Perhaps Wesel was the more levelheaded of the pair. It was she who tried to restrain her mate as he clawed and bit savagely, madly, at the distended, bulging walls. He no longer knew what lay outside the cave, had he known it would have made no difference. His one desire was to get out.

At first he made little headway, then he bethought himself of the little blade still grasped in his hand. With it he attacked the pulpy mass. The walls of the cells were stretched thin, almost to bursting, and under his onslaught they put up no more resistance than so many soap bubbles. A space was cleared, and Shrick was able to work with even greater vigor.

"Stop! Stop, I tell you! There is only the choking death outside the cave. And you will kill us both!"

But Shrick paid no heed, went on stabbing and hacking. It was only slowly, now, that he was able to enlarge upon the original impression he had made. As the swollen surfaces burst and withered beneath his blade, so they bulged and bellied in fresh places.

"Stop!" cried Wesel again.

With her arms, her useless legs trailing behind her, she pulled herself toward her mate. And she grappled with him, desperation lending her strength. So for many heartbeats they fought—silent, savage, forgetful of all that each owed to the other. And yet, perhaps, Wesel never quite forgot. For all her blind, frantic will to survive her telepathic powers were at no time entirely in abeyance. In spite of herself she, as always, shared the other's mind. And this psychological factor gave her an advantage that offset the paralysis of the lower half of her body—and at the same time inhibited her from pressing that advantage home to its logical conclusion.

But it did not save her when her fingers, inadvertently, dug into the wound in Shrick's arm. His ear-splitting scream was compounded of pain and fury, and he drew upon reserves of strength that the other never even guessed that he possessed. And the hand gripping the blade came round with irresistible force.

For Wesel there was a heartbeat of pain, of sorrow for herself and Shrick, of blind anger against the Giants who, indirectly, had brought this thing to pass.

And then the beating of her heart was stilled forever.

With the death of Wesel Shrick's frenzy left him.

There, in the darkness, he ran his sensitive fingers over the lifeless form, hopelessly hoping for the faintest sign of life. He called her name, he shook her roughly. But at last the knowledge that she was dead crept into his brain—and stayed there. In his short life he had known many times this sense of loss, but never with such poignancy.

And worst of all was the knowledge that *he* had killed her.

He tried to shift the burden of blame. He told himself that she would have died, in any case, of the wounds received at the hands of the Giants. He tried to convince himself that, wounds or no wounds, the Giants were directly responsible for her death. And he knew that he was Wesel's murderer, just as he knew that all that remained for him in life was to bring the slayers of his people to a reckoning.

This made him cautious.

For many heartbeats he lay there in the thick darkness, not daring to renew his assault on the walls of his prison. He told himself that, somehow, he would know when the Giants let the air back into the world. How he would know he could not say, but the conviction persisted.

And when at last, with returning pressure, the insulation resumed its normal consistency, Shrick took this as a sign that it was safe for him to get out. He started to hack at the spongy material, then stopped. He went back to the body of Wesel. Just once he whispered her name, and ran his hands over the stiff, silent form in a last caress.

He did not return.

And when, at last, the dim light of the Place-of-Meeting broke through she was buried deep in the debris that he had thrown behind him as he worked.

The air tasted good after the many times breathed atmosphere of the cave. For a few heartbeats Shrick was dizzy with the abrupt increase of pressure, for much of the air in his prison had escaped before the plug expanded to seal the entrance. It is probable that had it not been for the air liberated from the burst cells of the insulation he would long since have asphyxiated.

But this he was not to know—and if he had known it would not have worried him overmuch. He was alive, and Wesel and all the People were dead. When the mist cleared from in front of his eyes he could see them, their bodies twisted in the tortuous attitudes of their last agony, mute evidence of the awful powers of the Giants.

And now that he saw them he did not feel the overwhelming sorrow that he knew he should have done. He felt instead a kind of anger. By their refusal to heed his warning they had robbed him of his kingdom. None now could dispute his mastery of the Outside—but with no subjects, willing or unwilling, the vast territory under his sway was worthless.

With Wesel alive it would have been different.

What was it that she had said—? . . . *and the cave of Long-Fur the spearmaker . . .*

He could hear her voice as she said it . . . *and the cave of Long-Fur the spearmaker.*

Perhaps—But there was only one way to make sure.

He found the cave, saw that its entrance had been walled up. He felt a wild upsurge of hope. Frantically, with tooth and claw, he tore at the insulation. The fine blade that he had won from the Inside gleamed dully not a dozen handbreadths from where he was working, but such was his blind, unreasoning haste that he ignored the tool that would have made his task immeasurably shorter. At last the entrance was cleared. A feeble cry greeted the influx of air and light. For a while Shrick could not see who was within, and then could have screamed in his disappointment.

For here were no tough fighting males, no sturdy, fertile females, but two hands or so of weakly squirming infants. Their mothers must have realized, barely in time, that he and Wesel had been right, that there was only one way to ward off the choking death. Themselves they had not been able to save.

*But they will grow up,* Shrick told himself. *It won't be long before they are able to carry a spear for the Lord of the Outside, before the females are able to bear his children.*

Conquering his repugnance, he dragged them out. There was a hand of female infants, all living, and a hand of males. Three of these were dead.

But here, he knew, was the nucleus of the army with which he would reestablish his rule over the world, Inside as well as Outside.

But first, they had to be fed.

He saw, now, his fine blade, and seizing it he began to cut up the three lifeless male children. The scent of their blood made him realize that he was hungry. But it was not until the children, now quieted, were all munching happily that he cut a portion for himself.

When he had finished it he felt much better.

It was some time before Shrick resumed his visits to the Inside. He had the pitiful remnant of his people to nurse to maturity and, besides, there was no need to make raids upon the Giants' stocks of food. They themselves had provided him with sustenance beyond his powers of reckoning. He knew, too, that it would be unwise to let his enemies know that there had been any survivors from the cataclysm that they had launched. The fact that he had survived the choking death did not mean that it was the only weapon that the Giants had at their disposal.

But as time went on he felt an intense longing to watch once more the strange life beyond the Barrier. Now that he had killed a Giant he felt a strange sense of kinship with the monstrous beings. He thought of the Thin-One, Loud-Voice, Bare-Head and the Little Giant almost as old friends. At times he even caught himself regretting that he must kill them all. But he knew that in this lay the only hope for the survival of himself and his People.

And then, at last, he was satisfied that he could leave the children to fend for themselves. Even should he fail to return from the Inside they would manage. No-Toes, the eldest of the female children, had already proved to be a capable nurse.

And so he roamed once more the maze of caves and tunnels just outside the Barrier. Through his doorways and peepholes he spied upon the bright, fascinating life of the Inner World. From the Cave-of-Thunders —though how it had come by its name none of the People has ever known —to the Place-of-Little-Lights he ranged. Many feedings passed, but he was not obliged to return to his own food store. For the corpses of the People were everywhere. True, they were beginning to stink a little, but like all his race Shrick was never a fastidious eater.

And he watched the Giants going about the strange, ordered routine of their lives. Often he was tempted to show himself, to shout defiance. But this action had to remain in the realm of wish-fulfillment dreams—

he knew full well that it would bring sure and speedy calamity.

And then, at last, came the opportunity for which he had been waiting. He had been in the Place-of-Little-Lights, watching the Little Giant going about his mysterious, absorbing business. He had wished that he could understand its purport, that he could ask the Little Giant in his own tongue what it was that he was doing. For, since the death of Wesel, there had been none with whom a communion of mind was possible. He sighed, so loudly that the Giant must have heard.

He started uneasily and looked up from his work. Hastily Shrick withdrew into his tunnel. For many heartbeats he remained there, occasionally peeping out. But the other was still alert, must have known in some way that he was not alone. And so, eventually, Shrick had retired rather than risk incurring the potent wrath of the Giants once more.

His random retreat brought him to a doorway but rarely used. On the other side of it was a huge cavern in which there was nothing of real interest or value. In it, as a rule, at least one of the Giants would be sleeping, and others would be engaged in one of their incomprehensible pastimes.

This time there was no deep rumble of conversation, no movement whatsoever. Shrick's keen ears could distinguish the breathing of three different sleepers. The Thin-One was there, his respiration, like himself, had a meager quality. Loud-Voice was loud even in sleep. And Bare-Head, the chief of the Giants, breathed with a quiet authority.

And the Little Giant who, alone of all his people, was alert and awake was in the Place-of-Little-Lights.

Shrick knew that it was now or never. Any attempt to deal with the Giants singly must surely bring the great, hot light foretold by Three-Eyes. Now, with any luck at all, he could deal with the three sleepers and then lay in wait for the Little Giant. Unsuspecting, unprepared, he could be dealt with as easily as had Fat-Belly.

And yet—he did not want to do it.

It wasn't fear; it was that indefinable sense of kinship, the knowledge that, in spite of gross physical disparities, the Giants and the People were as one. For the history of man, although Shrick was not to know this, is but the history of the fire-making, tool-using animal.

Then he forced himself to remember Wesel, and Big-Ears, and the mass slaughter of almost all his race. He remembered Three-Eyes' words —*but this I can tell you, the People are doomed. Nothing you or they can do will save them. But you will kill those who will kill us, and that is good.*

*But you will kill those who will like us—*

But if I kill all the Giants before they kill us, he thought, then the world, all the world, will belong to the People . . .

And he still hung back.

It was not until the Thin-One, who must have been in the throes of a bad dream, murmured and stirred in his sleep that Shrick came out of his doorway. The keen blade with which he had slain Fat-Belly was grasped in both his hands. He launched himself toward the uneasy sleeper. His weapon sliced down once only—how often had he rehearsed this in his imagination!—and for the Thin-One the dream was over.

The smell of fresh blood, as always, excited him. It took him all of his willpower to restrain himself from hacking and slashing at the dead Giant. But he promised himself that this would come later. And he jumped from the body of the Thin-One to where Loud-Voice was snoring noisily.

The abrupt cessation of that all too familiar sound must have awakened Bare-Head. Shrick saw him shift and stir, saw his hands go out to loosen the bonds that held him to his sleeping place. And when the Giant Killer, his feet scrabbling for a hold, landed on his chest he was ready. And he was shouting in a great voice, so that Shrick knew that it was only a matter of heartbeats before the Little Giant came to his assistance.

Fat-Belly had been taken off guard, the Thin-One and Loud-Voice had been killed in their sleep. But here was no easy victory for the Giant Killer.

For a time it looked as though the chief of the Giants would win. After a little he ceased his shouting and fought with grim, silent desperation. Once one of his great hands caught Shrick in a bone-crushing grip, and it seemed as though the battle was over. Shrick could feel the blood pounding in his head, his eyeballs almost popping out of their sockets. It took him every ounce of resolution he possessed to keep from dropping his blade and scratching frenziedly at the other's wrist with ineffectual hands.

Something gave—it was his ribs—and in the fleeting instant of relaxed pressure he was able to twist, to turn and slash at the monstrous, hairy wrist. The warm blood spurted and the Giant cried aloud. Again and again Shrick plied his blade, until it became plain that the Giant would not be able to use that hand again.

He was single-handed now against an opponent as yet—insofar as his limbs were concerned—uncrippled. True, every movement of the upper part of his body brought spears of pain lancing through Shrick's chest. But he could move, and smite—and slay.

For Bare-Head weakened as the blood flowed from his wounds. No longer was he able to ward off the attacks on his face and neck. Yet he fought, as his race had always fought, to his dying breath. His enemy would have given no quarter—this much was obvious—but he could have sought refuge with the Little Giant in the Place-of-Little-Lights.

Toward the end he started shouting again.

And as he died, the Little Giant came into the cave.

It was sheer, blind luck that saved the Giant Killer from speedy death at the intruder's hands. Had the Little Giant known of the pitifully small forces arrayed against him it would have gone hard with Shrick. But No-Toes, left with her charges, had grown bored with the Place-of-Meeting. She had heard Shrick talk of the wonders of the Inside; and now, she thought, was her chance to see them for herself.

Followed by her charges she wandered aimlessly along the tunnels just outside the Barrier. She did not know the location of the doors to the Inside, and the view through the occasional peepholes was very circumscribed.

Then she came upon the doorway which Shrick had left open when he made his attack on the sleeping Giants. Bright light streamed through the aperture—light brighter than any No-Toes had seen before in her short life. Like a beacon it lured her on.

She did not hesitate when she came to the opening. Unlike her parents, she had not been brought up to regard the Giants with superstitious awe. Shrick was the only adult she could remember having known—and he, although he had talked of the Giants, had boasted of having slain one in single combat. He had said, also, that he would, at some time or other, kill all the Giants.

In spite of her lack of age and experience, No-Toes was no fool. Womanlike, already she had evaluated Shrick. Much of his talk she discounted as idle bragging, but she had never seen any reason to disbelieve his stories of the deaths of Big-Tusk, Sterret, Tekka, Fat-Belly—and all the myriads of the People who had perished with them.

So it was that—foolhardy in her ignorance—she sailed through the doorway. Behind her came the other children, squealing in their excitement. Even if the Little Giant had not at first seen them he could not have failed to hear the shrill tumult of their irruption.

There was only one interpretation that he could put upon the evidence of his eyes. The plan to suffocate the People had failed. They had sallied

out from their caves and tunnels to the massacre of his fellow Giants—
and now fresh reinforcements were arriving to deal with him.

He turned and fled.

Shrick rallied his strength, made a flying leap from the monstrous
carcass of Bare-Head. But in mid-flight a hard, polished surface interposed
itself between him and the fleeing Giant. Stunned, he hung against it for
many heartbeats before he realized that it was a huge door which had shut
in his face.

He knew that the Little Giant was not merely seeking refuge in flight
—for where in the world could he hope to escape the wrath of the People?
He had gone, perhaps, for arms of some kind. Or—and at the thought
Shrick's blood congealed—he had gone to loose the final doom foretold
by Three-Eyes. Now that his plans had begun to miscarry he remembered
the prophecy in its entirety, was no longer able to ignore those parts that,
in his arrogance, he had found displeasing.

And then No-Toes, her flight clumsy and inexpert in these—to her—
strange, vast spaces was at his side.

"Are you hurt?" she gasped. "They are so big—and you fought them."

As she spoke, the world was filled with a deep humming sound. Shrick
ignored the excited female. That noise could mean only one thing. The
Little Giant was back in the Place-of-Little-Lights, was setting in motion
vast, incomprehensible forces that would bring to pass the utter and
irrevocable destruction of the People.

With his feet against the huge door he kicked off, sped rapidly down
to the open doorway in the Barrier. He put out his hand to break the shock
of his landing, screamed aloud as his impact sent a sickening wave of pain
through his chest. He started to cough—and when he saw the bright
blood that was welling from his mouth he was very frightened.

No-Toes was with him again. "You are hurt, you are bleeding. Can
I—?"

"No!" He turned a snarling mask to her. "No! Leave me alone!"

"But where are you going?"

Shrick paused. Then: "I am going to save the world," he said slowly.
He savored the effect of his words. They made him feel better, they made
him bulk big in his own mind, bigger, perhaps, than the Giants. "I am
going to save you all."

"But how—?"

This was too much for the Giant Killer. He screamed again, but this time with anger. With the back of his hand he struck the young female across the face.

"Stay here!" he ordered.

And then he was gone along the tunnel.

The gyroscopes were still singing their quiet song of power when Shrick reached the Control Room. Strapped in his chair, the navigator was busy over his plotting machine. Outside the ports the stars wheeled by in orderly succession.

And Shrick was frightened.

He had never quite believed Wesel's garbled version of the nature of the world until now. But he could see, at last, that the ship was moving. The fantastic wonder of it all held him spellbound until a thin edge of intolerable radiance crept into view from behind the rim of one of the ports. The navigator touched something and, suddenly, screens of dark blue glass mitigated the glare. But it was still bright, too bright, and the edge became a rapidly widening oval and then, at last, a disk.

The humming of the gyroscope stopped.

Before the silence had time to register a fresh sound assailed Shrick's ears. It was the roar of the main drive.

A terrifying force seized him and slammed him down upon the deck. He felt his bones crack under the acceleration. True child of free fall as he was, all this held for him the terror of the supernatural. For a while he lay there, weakly squirming, whimpering a little. The navigator looked down at him and laughed. It was this sound more than anything else that stung Shrick to his last, supreme effort. He didn't want to move. He just wanted to lie there on the deck slowly coughing his life away. But the Little Giant's derision tapped unsuspected reserves of strength, both moral and physical.

The navigator went back to his calculations, handling his instruments for the last time with a kind of desperate elation. He knew that the ship would never arrive at her destination, neither would her cargo of seed grain. But she would not—and this outweighed all other considerations —drift forever among the stars carrying within her hull the seeds of the destruction of man and all his works.

He knew that—had he not taken this way out—he must have slept at last, and then death at the hands of the mutants would inevitably have been his portion. And with mutants in full charge anything might happen.

The road he had taken was the best.

Unnoticed, inch by inch Shrick edged his way along the deck. Now, he could stretch his free hand and touch the Giant's foot. In the other he still held his blade, to which he had clung as the one thing sure and certain in this suddenly crazy world.

Then he had a grip on the artificial skin covering the Giant's leg. He started to climb, although every movement was unadulterated agony. He did not see the other raise his hand to his mouth, swallow the little pellet that he held therein.

So it was that when, at long last, he reached the soft, smooth throat of the Giant, the Giant was dead.

It was a very fast poison.

For a while he clung there. He should have felt elation at the death of the last of his enemies but—instead—he felt cheated. There was so much that he wanted to know, so much that only the Giants could have told him. Besides—it was his blade that should have won the final victory. He knew that, somewhere, the Little Giant was still laughing at him.

Through the blue-screened ports blazed the sun. Even at this distance, even with the intervening filters, its power and heat were all too evident. And aft the motors still roared, and would roar until the last ounce of fuel had been fed into hungry main drive.

Shrick clung to the dead man's neck, looked long and longingly at the glittering instruments, the shining switches and levers, whose purpose he would never understand, whose inertia would have defeated any attempt of his fast ebbing strength to move them. He looked at the flaming doom ahead, and knew that this was what had been foretold.

Had the metaphor existed in his language, he would have told himself that he and the few surviving People were caught like rats in a trap.

But even the Giants would not have used that phrase in its metaphorical sense.

For that is all that the People were—rats in a trap.

# A Case of Conscience

*Science fiction has occasionally been used as a vehicle to convey religious messages, particularly in the work of C.S. Lewis. The transcendental possibilities, inherent in fiction, about the nature of the universe have provided the basis for some of the most popular and important works in science fiction. Most of these books approached the subject of religion obliquely, but in "A Case of Conscience," the late James Blish engaged in a direct examination of the role of reason in religious questions and produced one of the most memorable works in the history of the field.*

I

The stone door slammed. It was Cleaver's trademark: there had never been a door too heavy, complex or cleverly tracked to prevent him from closing it with a sound like a clap of doom. And no planet in the universe could possess an air sufficiently thick and curtained with damp to muffle that sound. Not even Lithia.

Ruiz-Sanchez continued to read. It would take Cleaver's impatient fingers quite a while to free him from his jungle suit, and in the meantime the problem remained. It was a century-old problem, first propounded in 1939, but the Church had never cracked it. And it was diabolically complex (that adverb was official, precisely chosen and literally intended). Even the novel which proposed the case was on the Index, and Father Ramon Ruiz-Sanchez, S.J., had access to it only by virtue of his Order.

He turned the page, scarcely hearing the stamping and muttering in the hall. On and on the text ran, becoming more tangled, more evil, more insoluble with every word:

"... and Magravius knows from spies that Anita has formerly committed double sacrilege with Michael, *vulgo* Cerularius, a perpetual curate, who wishes to seduce Eugenius. Magravius threatens to have Anita molested by Sulla, an orthodox savage (and leader of a band of twelve mercenaries, the Sullivani), who desires to procure Felicia for Gregorius, Leo, Viteilius and Macdugalius, four excavators, if she will not yield to him and also deceive Honuphrius by rendering conjugal duty when demanded. Anita, who claims to have discovered incestuous temptations from Jeremias and Eugenius—"

There now, he was lost again. He backtracked resignedly. Jeremias and Eugenius were—? Oh, yes, the "brotherly lovers" at the beginning of the case, consanguineous to the lowest degree with both Felicia and Honuphrius—the latter the apparent prime villain and the husband of Anita. It was Magravius, who seemed to admire Honuphrius, who had been urged by the slave Mauritius to solicit Anita, seemingly under the urging of Honuphrius himself. This, however, had come to Anita through her tirewoman Fortissa, who was or at one time had been the common-law wife of Mauritius himself and had borne him children—so that the whole story had to be weighed with the utmost caution. And that entire initial confession of Honuphrius had come out under torture—voluntarily consented to, to be sure, but still torture. The Fortissa-Mauritius relationship was even more dubious, really only a supposition of Father Ware's, though certainly a plausible one considering the public repentance of Sulla after the death of Canicula, who was—yes, that was correct, Mauritius's second wife. No, his first wife; he had never been legally married to Fortissa. It was Magravius's desire for Felicia after the death of Gillia that had confused him there.

"Ramon, give me a hand, will you?" Cleaver shouted suddenly. "I'm stuck and—and I don't feel well."

The Jesuit biologist arose in alarm. Such an admission from Cleaver was unprecedented.

The physicist was sitting on a pouf of woven rushes, stuffed with a sphagnumlike moss, which was bulging at the equator under his weight. He was halfway out of his glass-fiber jungle suit, and his face was white and beaded with sweat, although his helmet was already off. His uncertain fingers tore at a jammed zipper.

"Paul! Why didn't you say you were ill in the first place? Here, let go of that; you're only making things worse. What happened?"

"Don't know exactly," Cleaver said, breathing heavily but relinquishing the zipper. Ruiz-Sanchez knelt beside him and began to work it carefully back onto its tracks. "Went a ways into the jungle to see if I could spot more pegmatite lies; it's been in the back of my mind that a pilot-plant for turning out tritium might locate here eventually—ought to be able to produce on a prodigious scale."

"God forbid," Ruiz-Sanchez said under his breath.

"Hm? Anyhow, I didn't see anything. Few lizards, hoppers, the usual thing. Then I ran up against a plant that looked a little like a pineapple, and one of the spines jabbed right through my suit and nicked me. Didn't seem serious, but—"

"But we don't have the suits for nothing. Let's look at it. Here, put up your feet and we'll haul those boots off. Where did you get—oh. Well, it's angry-looking, I'll give it that. Any other symptoms?"

"My mouth feels raw," Cleaver complained.

"Open up," the Jesuit commanded. When Cleaver complied, it became evident that his complaint had been the understatement of the year. The mucosa inside his mouth was nearly covered with ugly and undoubtedly painful ulcers, their edges as sharply defined as if cut with a cookie-punch.

Ruiz-Sanchez made no comment, however, and deliberately changed his expression to one of carefully calculated dismissal. If the physicist needed to minimize his ailments, it was all right with Ruiz-Sanchez. An alien planet is not a good place to strip a man of his inner defenses. "Come into the lab," he said. "You've got some inflammation in there."

Cleaver arose, a little unsteadily, and followed the Jesuit into the laboratory. There Ruiz-Sanchez took smears from several of the ulcers onto microscope slides and Gram-stained them. He filled the time consumed by the staining process with the ritual of aiming the microscope's substage mirror out the window at a brilliant white cloud. When the timer's alarm went off, he rinsed and flame-dried the first slide and slipped it under the clips.

As he had half-feared, he saw few of the mixed bacilli and spirochaetes which would have indicated a case of ordinary, Earthly, Vincent's angina —which the clinical picture certainly suggested. Cleaver's oral flora were normal, though on the increase because of all the exposed tissue.

"I'm going to give you a shot," Ruiz-Sanchez said gently. "And then I think you'd better go to bed."

"The hell with that," Cleaver said. "I've got nine times as much work to do as I can hope to clean up, without any additional handicaps."

"Illness is never convenient," Ruiz-Sanchez agreed. "But why worry about losing a day or so, since you're in over your head anyhow?"

"What have I got?" Cleaver asked suspiciously.

"You haven't *got* anything," Ruiz-Sanchez said, almost regretfully. "That is, you aren't infected. But your 'pineapple' did you a bad turn. Most plants of that family on Lithia bear thorns or leaves coated with polysaccharides that are poisonous to us. The particular glucoside you got today was evidently squill, or something closely related to it. It produces symptoms like those of trench-mouth, but a lot harder to clear up."

"How long will that take?" Cleaver said. He was still balking, but he was on the defensive now.

"Several days at least—until you've built up an immunity. The shot I'm going to give you is a gamma globulin specific against squill, and it ought to moderate the symptoms until you've developed a high antibody titer of your own. But in the process you're going to run quite a fever, Paul; and I'll have to keep you well-stuffed with antipyretics, because even a little fever is dangerous in this climate."

"I know it," Cleaver said, mollified. "The more I learn about this place, the less disposed I am to vote 'aye' when the time comes. Well, bring on your shot—and your aspiring. I suppose I ought to be glad it isn't a bacterial infection, or the Snakes would be jabbing me full of antibiotics."

"Small chance of that," Ruiz-Sanchez said. "I don't doubt that the Lithians have at least a hundred different antibiotics we'll be able to use eventually, but—there, that's all there is to it; you can relax now—but we'll have to study their pharmacology from the ground up, first. All right, Paul, hit the hammock. In about ten minutes you're going to wish you were born dead, that I promise you."

Cleaver grinned. His sweaty face under its thatch of dirty blonde hair was craggy and powerful even in illness. He stood up and deliberately rolled down his sleeve. "Not much doubt about how you'll vote, either," he said. "You like this planet, don't you, Ramon? It's a biologist's paradise, as far as I can see."

"I do like it," the priest said, smiling back. He followed Cleaver into the small room which served them both as sleeping quarters. Except for the window, it strongly resembled the inside of a jug. The walls were curving and continuous, and were made of some ceramic material which never beaded or felt wet, but never seemed to be quite dry, either. The hammocks were slung from hooks which projected smoothly from the walls. "But don't forget that Lithia's my first extrasolar planet. I think I'd find any new habitable world fascinating. The infinite mutability of life forms, and the cunning inherent in each of them . . . it's all amazing and very delightful."

Cleaver sprawled heavily in his hammock. After a decent interval, Ruiz-Sanchez took the liberty of heaving up after him the foot he seemed to have forgotten. Cleaver didn't notice. The reaction was setting in.

"Read me no tracts, father," Cleaver said. Then: "I didn't mean that. I'm sorry . . . but for a physicist, this place is hell. . . . You'd better get me that aspirin. I'm cold."

"Surely." Ruiz-Sanchez went quickly back into the lab, made up a salicylate-barbiturate paste in one of the Lithians' superb mortars, and pressed it into a set of pills. He wished he could stamp each pill "Bayer" before it dried—if Cleaver's personal cure-all was aspirin, it would be just as well to let him think he was taking aspirin—but he had no dies for the purpose. He took two of the pills back to Cleaver with a mug and a carafe of Berkefeld-filtered water.

The big man was already asleep; Ruiz-Sanchez woke him. Cleaver would sleep longer and awake farther along the road to recovery if he were done that small unkindness now. As it was, he hardly noticed when the pills were put down him, and soon resumed his heavy, troubled breathing.

That done, Ruiz-Sanchez returned to the front room of the house, sat down and began to inspect the jungle suit. The tear which the plant spine had made was not difficult to find, and would be easy to repair. It would be much harder to repair Cleaver's notion that their defenses were invulnerable, and that plants could be blundered against with impunity. Ruiz-Sanchez wondered if one or both of the other members of the commission still shared that notion.

Cleaver had called the thing which had brought him low a "pineapple." Any biologist could have told Cleaver that even on Earth the pineapple is a prolific and dangerous weed, edible only by a happy and irrelevant accident. In Hawaii, as Ruiz-Sanchez remembered, the tropical forest was quite impassable to anyone not wearing heavy boots and tough trousers. The close-packed, irrepressible pineapples outside of the plantations could tear unprotected legs to ribbons.

The Jesuit turned the suit over. The zipper that Cleaver had jammed was made of a plastic into the molecule of which had been incorporated radicals from various terrestrial anti-fungal substances, chiefly thiolutin. The fungi of Lithia respected these, all right, but the elaborate molecule of the plastic itself had a tendency, under Lithian humidities and heats, to undergo polymerization more or less spontaneously. That was what had happened here. One of the teeth of the zipper had changed into something resembling a piece of popcorn.

It grew slowly dark as Ruiz-Sanchez worked. There was a muted puff of sound, and the room was illuminated with small, soft yellow flames from recesses in every wall. The burning substance was natural gas, of which Lithia had an inexhaustible and constantly renewed supply. The flames were lit by adsorption against a catalyst, as soon as the gas came on. A lime mantle, which worked on a rack and pinion of heatproof glass, could be moved into the flame to provide a brighter light; but the priest liked the yellow light the Lithians themselves preferred, and used the limelight only in the laboratory.

For some things, of course, the Earthmen had to have electricity, for which they had been forced to supply their own generators. The Lithians had a far more advanced science of electrostatics than Earth had, but of electrodynamics they knew comparatively little. They had discovered magnetism only a few years before, since natural magnets were unknown on the planet. They had first observed the phenomenon, not in iron, of which they had next to none, but in liquid oxygen—a difficult substance from which to make generator coil cores!

The results in terms of Lithian civilization were peculiar to an Earthman. The tall, reptilian people had built several huge electrostatic generators and scores of little ones, but had nothing even vaguely resembling telephones. They knew a great deal on the practical level about electrolysis, but carrying a current over a long distance—say one kilometer—was regarded by them as impossible. They had no electric motors as an Earthman would understand the term, but made fast intercontinental flights in jet airdraft powered by *static* electricity. Cleaver said he understood this feat, but Ruiz-Sanchez certainly did not.

They had a completely marvelous radio network, which among other things provided a "live" navigational grid for the whole planet, zeroed on (and here perhaps was the epitome of the Lithian genius for paradox) a tree. Yet they had never produced a commercial vacuum tube and their atomic theory was not much more sophisticated than Democritus's had been!

These paradoxes, of course, could be explained in part by the things that Lithia lacked. Like any large rotating mass, Lithia had a magnetic field of its own, but a planet which almost entirely lacks iron provides its people with no easy way to discover magnetism. Radioactivity, at least until the Earthmen had arrived, had been entirely unknown on the surface of Lithia, which explained the hazy atomic theory. Like the Greeks, the Lithians had discovered that friction between silk and glass produces one kind of charge, and between silk and amber another. They had gone on from there to Widmanstetten generators, electrochemistry and the static jet—but without suitable metals they were unable to make batteries or do more than begin to study electricity in motion.

In the fields where they had been given fair clues, they had made enormous progress. Despite the constant cloudiness and endemic drizzle, their descriptive astronomy was excellent, thanks to the fortunate presence of a small moon which had drawn their attention outward early. This in turn made for basic advances in optics. Their chemistry took full advantage of both the seas and the jungles. From the one they took such vital and diversified products as agar, iodine, salt, trace metals and foods of many kinds. The other provided nearly everything else that they needed: resins, rubbers, woods of all degrees of hardness, edible and essential oils, vegetable "butters," rope and other fibers, fruits and nuts, tannins, dyes, drugs, cork, paper. Indeed, the sole forest product which they did *not* take was game, and the reason for this oversight was hard to find it. It seemed to the Jesuit to be religious—yet the Lithians had no religion, and they certainly ate many of the creatures of the sea without qualms of conscience.

He dropped the jungle suit into his lap with a sigh, though the pop-corned tooth still was not completely trimmed back into shape. Outside, in the humid darkness, Lithia was in full concert. It was a vital somehow fresh, new-sounding drone, covering most of the sound spectrum audible to an Earthman. It came from the myriad insects of Lithia. Many of these had wiry, ululating songs, almost like birds, in addition to the scrapes and chirrups and wing-buzzes of the insects of Earth.

Had Eden sounded like that, before evil had come into the world? Ruiz-Sanchez wondered. Certainly his native Peru sang no such song. Qualms of conscience—these were, in the long run, his essential business, rather than the taxonomical jungles of biology, which had already become tangled into near-hopelessness on Earth before spaceflight had come along to add whole new volumes of puzzles. It was only interesting that the Lithians were bipedal reptiles with marsupial-like pouches and pteropsid circulatory systems. But it was vital that they had qualms of conscience —if they did.

He and the other three men were on Lithia to decide whether or not Lithia would be suitable as a port of call for Earth, without risk of damage to either Earthmen or Lithians. The other three men were primarily scientists, but Ruiz-Sanchez's own recommendation would in the long run depend upon conscience, not upon taxonomy.

He looked down at the still-imperfect suit with a troubled face until he heard Cleaver moan. Then he arose and left the room to the softly hissing flames.

## II

From the oval front window of the house to which Cleaver and Ruiz-Sanchez had been assigned, the land slanted away with insidious gentleness toward the ill-defined south edge of Lower Bay, a part of the Gulf of Sfath. Most of the area was salt marsh, as was the seaside nearly everywhere on Lithia. When the tide was in, the flats were covered to a depth of a meter or so almost half the way to the house. When it was out, as it was tonight, the jungle symphony was augmented by the agonized barking of a score of species of lungfish. Occasionally, when the small moon was unoccluded and the light from the city was unusually bright, one could see the leaping shadow of some amphibian, or the sinuously advancing sigmoid track of the Lithian crocodile, in pursuit of some prey faster than itself but which it would nonetheless capture in its own geological good time.

Still farther—and usually invisible even in daytime because of the pervasive mists—was the opposite shore of Lower Bay, beginning with tidal flats again, and then more jungle, which ran unbroken thereafter for hundreds of kilometers to the equatorial sea.

Behind the house, visible from the sleeping room, was the rest of the city, Xoredeshch Sfath, capital of the great southern continent. Like all the cities the Lithians built, its most striking characteristic to an Earthman was that it hardly seemed to be there at all. The Lithian houses were low, and made of the earth which had been dug from their foundations, so that they tended to fade into the soil even to a trained observer.

Most of the older buildings were rectangular, put together without mortar, of rammed-earth blocks. Over the course of decades the blocks continued to pack and settle themselves until it became easier to abandon an unwanted building than to tear it down. One of the first setbacks the Earthmen had suffered on Lithia had come through an ill-advised offer to raze one such structure with TDX, a gravity-polarized explosive unknown to the Lithians. The warehouse in question was large, thick-walled and three Lithian centuries old. The explosive created an uproar which greatly distressed the Lithians, but when it was over, the storehouse still stood, unshaken.

Newer structures were more conspicuous when the sun was out, for just during the past half-century the Lithians had begun to apply their enormous knowledge of ceramics to house construction. The new houses assumed thousands of fantastic, quasi-biological shapes, not quite amorphous but not quite resembling any form in experience either. Each one was unique and to the choice of its owner, yet all markedly shared the character of the community and the earth from which it sprang. These houses, too, would have blended well with the background of soil and jungle, except that most of them were glazed and so shone blindingly for brief moments on sunny days when the light and the angle of the observer was just right. These shifting coruscations, seen from the air, had been the Earthmen's first intimation that there was intelligent life in the ubiquitous Lithian jungle.

Ruiz-Sanchez looked out the sleeping-room window at the city for at least the ten thousandth time on his way to Cleaver's hammock. Xoredeshch Sfath was alive to him; it never looked the same twice. He found it singularly beautiful.

He checked Cleaver's pulse and respiration. Both were fast, even for Lithia, where a high carbon dioxide partial pressure raised the pH of the blood of Earthmen to an abnormal level and stimulated the breathing reflex. The priest judged, however, that Cleaver was in little danger as long as his actual oxygen utilization was not increased. At the moment he was certainly sleeping deeply—if not very restfully—and it would do no harm to leave him alone for a little while.

Of course, if a wild allosaur should blunder into the city . . . but that was about as likely as the blundering of an untended elephant into the heart of New Delhi. It could happen, but almost never did. And no other dangerous Lithian animal could break into the house if it were sealed.

Ruiz-Sanchez checked the carafe of fresh water in the niche beside the hammock, went into the hall, and donned boots, macintosh and waterproof hat. The night sounds of Lithia burst in upon him as he opened the stone door, along with a gust of sea air and the characteristic halogen odor most people call "salty." There was a thin drizzle falling, making haloes around the lights of Xoredeshch Sfath. Far out, on the water, another light moved. That was probably the coastal side wheeler to Yllith, the enormous island which stood athwart the Upper Bay, barring the Gulf of Sfath as a whole from the equatorial sea.

Outside, Ruiz-Sanchez turned the wheel which extended bolts on every margin of the door. Drawing from his macintosh a piece of soft chalk, he marked on the sheltered tablet designed for such uses the Lithian symbols which meant "Illness is here." That would be sufficient. Anybody who chose to could open the door simply by turning the wheel, but the Lithians were overridingly social beings, who respected their own conventions as they would respect natural law.

That done, Ruiz-Sanchez set out for the center of the city and the Message Tree. The asphalt streets shone in the yellow lights cast from windows, and in the white light of the mantled, wide-spaced street lanterns. Occasionally he passed the eight-foot, kangaroolike shape of a Lithian, and the two exchanged glances of frank curiosity, but there were not many Lithians abroad now. They kept to their houses at night, doing Ruiz-Sanchez knew not what. He could see them frequently, alone or by twos or threes, moving behind the oval windows of the houses he passed. Sometimes they seemed to be talking.

What about?

It was a nice question. The Lithians had no crime, no newspapers, no household communications systems, no arts that could be differentiated clearly from their crafts, no political parties, no public amusements, no nations, no games, no religions, no sports, no celebrations. Surely they didn't spend every waking minute of their lives exchanging knowledge, discussing philosophy or history? Or did they? Perhaps, Ruiz-Sanchez thought suddenly, they simply went inert once they were inside their jugs, like so many pickles! But even as the thought came, the priest passed another house, and saw their silhouettes moving to and fro . . .

A puff of wind scattered cool droplets in his face. Automatically, he quickened his step. If the night were to turn out especially windy, there would doubtless be many voices coming and going in the Message Tree. It loomed ahead of him now, a sequoialike giant, standing at the mouth of the valley of the River Sfath—the valley which led in great serpentine folds into the heart of the continent, where Gleshchetk Sfath, or Blood Lake in English, poured out its massive torrents.

As the winds came and went along the valley, the tree nodded and swayed. With every movement, the tree's root system, which underlay the entire city, tugged and distorted the buried crystalline cliff upon which the city had been founded as long ago in Lithian prehistory as was the founding of Rome on Earth. At every such pressure, the buried cliff responded with a vast heart-pulse of radio waves—a pulse detectable not only all over Lithia, but far out in space as well.

These bursts, of course, were sheer noise. How the Lithians modified them to carry information—not only messages, but the amazing navigational grid, the planetwide time-signal system, and much more—was something Ruiz-Sanchez never expected to learn, although Cleaver said it was all perfectly simple once you understood it. It had something to do with semi-conduction and solid-state physics, which—again according to

Cleaver—the Lithians understood better than any Earthman.

Almost all knowledge, Ruiz-Sanchez reflected with amusement, fell into that category. It was either perfectly simple once you understood it, or else it fell apart into fiction. As a Jesuit—even here, forty light-years from Rome—Ruiz-Sanchez knew something about knowledge that Cleaver would never learn: that all knowledge goes through *both* stages, the annunciation out of noise into fact and the disintegration back into noise again. The process involved was the making of increasingly finer distinctions. The outcome was an endless series of theoretical catastrophes. The residuum was faith.

The high, sharply vaulted chamber, like an egg stood on its large end, which had been burned out in the base of the Message Tree, was droning with life as Ruiz-Sanchez entered it. It would have been difficult to imagine anything less like an Earthly telegraph office or other message center, however.

Around the circumference of the lower end of the egg there was a continual whirling of tall figures, Lithians entering and leaving through the many doorless entrances and changing places in the swirl of movement like so many electrons passing from orbit to orbit. Despite their numbers, their voices were pitched so low that Ruiz-Sanchez could hear blended in with their murmuring the soughing of the wind through the enormous branches far aloft.

The inner side of this band of moving figures was bounded by a high railing of black, polished wood, evidently cut from the phloëm of the tree itself. On the other side of this Encke's Division a thin circlet of Lithians took and passed out messages steadily and without a moment's break, handling the total load faultlessly—if one were to judge by the way the outer band was kept in motion—and without apparent effort by memory alone. Occasionally one of these specialists would leave the circlet and go to one of the desks which were scattered over most of the rest of the sloping floor, increasingly thinly, like a Crêpe Ring, to confer there with the desk's occupant. Then he went back to the black rail, or, sometimes, he took the desk and its previous occupant went to the rail.

The bowl deepened, the desks thinned, and at the very center stood a single, aged Lithian, his hands clapped to the ear-whorls behind his heavy jaws, his eyes covered by their nictitating membrane, only his nasal fossae and heat-receptive postnasal pits uncovered. He spoke to no one, and no one consulted him—but the absolute stasis in which he stood was obviously the reason, the sole reason, for the torrents and countertorrents of people which poured along the outermost ring.

Ruiz-Sanchez stopped, astonished. He had never himself been to the Message Tree before—communicating with the other two Earthmen on Lithia had been, until now, one of Cleaver's tasks—and the priest found that he had no idea what to do. The scene before him was more suggestive of a bourse than of a message center in any ordinary sense. It seemed unlikely that so many Lithians could have urgent personal messages to send each time the winds were active; yet it seemed equally uncharacteristic that the Lithians, with their stable, abundance-based economy, should have any equivalent of stock or commodity brokerage.

There seemed to be no choice, however, but to plunge in, try to reach the polished black rail, and ask one of those who stood on the other side to try and raise Agronski or Michelis again. At worst, he supposed, he could only be refused, or fail to get a hearing at all. He took a deep breath.

Simultaneously, his left elbow was caught in a firm four-fingered grip. Letting the stored breath out again in a snort of surprise, the priest looked around and up at the solicitously bent head of a Lithian. Under the long, traplike mouth, the being's wattles were a delicate, curious aquamarine, in contrast to its vestigial comb, which was a permanent and silvery sapphire, shot through with veins of fuchsia.

"You are Ruiz-Sanchez," the Lithian said in his own language. The priest's name, unlike that of most of the other Earthmen, fell easily in that tongue. "I know you by your robe."

This was pure chance; any Earthman out in the rain in a macintosh would have been identified as Ruiz-Sanchez, because he was the only Earthman who seemed to the Lithians to wear the same garment indoors. "I am Chtexa, the metallist, who consulted with you earlier on medicine and on your mission and other matters. We have not seen you here before. Do you wish to talk with the Tree?"

"I do," Ruiz-Sanchez said gratefully. "It is so that I am new here. Can you explain to me what to do?"

"Yes, but not to any profit," Chtexa said, tilting his head so that his completely inky pupils shone down into Ruiz-Sanchez's eyes. "One must have observed the ritual, which is very complex, until it is habit. We have grown up with it, but you I think lack the coordination to follow it on the first attempt. If I may hear your message instead . . ."

"I would be most indebted. It is for our colleagues Agronski and Michelis. They are at Xoredeshch Gton on the northeast continent, at about thirty-two degrees east, thirty-two degrees north—"

"Yes, the second benchmark, at the outlet of the Lesser Lakes; the city of the potters. And you will say?"

"That they are to join us now, here, at Xoredeshch Sfath. And that our time on Lithia is almost up."

"That me regards. But I will bear it."

Chtexa lept into the whirling crowd, and Ruiz-Sanchez was left behind, considering again his thankfulness at the pains he had taken to learn the Lithian language. Several members of the terrestrial commission had shown a regrettable lack of interest in that tongue: "Let 'em learn English," had been Cleaver's classic formulation. Ruiz-Sanchez was all the less likely to view this idea sympathetically considering that his own native language was Spanish and his preferred foreign language German.

Agronski had taken a slightly more sophisticated stand: it was not, he said, that Lithian was too difficult to pronounce—certainly it wasn't any harder than Arabic or Russian on the soft palate—but, after all, "it's hopeless to attempt to grasp the concepts that lie behind a really alien language in the time we have to spend here, isn't it?"

To both views, Michelis had said nothing; he had simply set out to learn to read the language first, and if he found his way from there into speaking it, he would not be surprised, and neither would his confreres. That was Michelis's way of doing things, thorough and untheoretical at the same time. As for the other two approaches, Ruiz-Sanchez thought privately that it was close to criminal to allow any contact-man for a new planet ever to leave Earth with such parochial notions. Of Cleaver's tendency to refer to the Lithians themselves as "the Snakes," Ruiz-Sanchez's opinion was such as to be admissible only to his remote confessor.

And in view of what lay before him now in this egg-shaped hollow, what was Ruiz-Sanchez to think of Cleaver's conduct as communications officer for the group? Surely he could never have transmitted or received a single message through the Tree, as he had claimed to have done. Probably he had never been nearer to the Tree than the priest had been.

Of course, it went without saying that he had been in contact with Agronski and Michelis by *some* method, but that method evidently had been a private transmitter concealed in his luggage. . . . Yet, physicist though he most definitely was not, Ruiz-Sanchez rejected that solution on the spot; he had some idea of the practical difficulties of ham radio on a world like Lithia, swamped as it was on all wavelengths by the tremendous pulses which the Tree wrung from the buried crystalline cliff. The problem was beginning to make him feel decidedly uncomfortable.

Then Chtexa was back, recognizable not so much by any physical detail —for his wattles were now the same ambiguous royal purple as those of most of the other Lithians in the crowd—as by the fact that he was obviously bearing down upon the Earthman.

"I have sent your message," he said at once. "It is recorded at Xoredeshch Gton. But the other Earthmen are not there. They have not been in the city for some days."

That was impossible. Cleaver had said he had spoken to Agronski only a day ago. "Are you sure?" Ruiz-Sanchez said cautiously.

"It admits of no uncertainty. The house which we gave them stands empty. The many things which they had with them are gone." The tall shape raised its small hands in a gesture which might have been solicitous. "I think this is an ill word. I dislike to bring it you. The words which you brought me when we first met were full of good."

"Thank you. Don't worry," Ruiz-Sanchez said distractedly. "No man could hold the bearer responsible for the word, surely."

"Whom else would he hold responsible for it? At least that is our custom," Chtexa said. "And under it, you have lost by our exchange. Your words on iron have been shown to contain great good. I would take pleasure in showing you how we have used them, especially so since I have brought you in return an ill message. If you would share my house tonight, without prejudice to your work . . ."

Sternly Ruiz-Sanchez stifled his sudden excitement. Here was the first chance, at long last, to see something of the private life of Lithia! And through that, perhaps, gain some inkling of the moral life, the role in which God had cast the Lithians in the ancient drama of good and evil in the past and in the times to come. Until that was known, the Lithians in their Eden were only spuriously good: all reason, all organic thinking machines, ULTIMACs with tails and without souls.

But there was the hard fact that he had left behind a sick man. There was not much chance that Cleaver would awaken before morning; he had been given nearly fifteen milligrams of sedative per kilogram of body weight. But if his burly frame should somehow throw it off, driven perhaps by some anaphylactic crisis impossible to rule out this early, he would need prompt attention. At the very least, he would want badly for the sound of a human voice on this planet which he hated and which had struck him down.

Still, the danger to Cleaver was not great. He most certainly did not require a minute-by-minute vigil. There was, after all, such a thing as an excess of devotion, a form of pride among the pious which the Church had long found peculiarly difficult to stifle. At its worst, it produced a St. Simon Stylites, who though undoubtedly acceptable to God had for centuries been very bad public relations for the Church. And had Cleaver really earned the kind of devotion Ruiz-Sanchez had been proposing, up to now, to tender him as a creature of God? And with a whole planet at stake, a whole people—

A lifetime of meditation over just such problems of conscience had made Ruiz-Sanchez, like any other gifted member of his Order, quick to find his way through all but the most complex ethical labyrinths to a decision. An unsympathetic observer might almost have called him "agile."

"Thank you," he said, a little shakily. "I will share your house very gladly."

## III

"Cleaver! Cleaver! Wake up, you big slob. Where the hell have you been?"

Cleaver groaned and tried to turn over. At his first motion, the world began to rock gently, sickeningly. His mouth was filled with burning pitch.

"Cleaver, turn out. It's me—Agronski. Where's the father? What's wrong? Why didn't we hear from you? *Look out*, you'll—"

The warning came too late and Cleaver could not have understood it anyhow; he had been profoundly asleep and had no notion of his situation in space or time. At his convulsive twist away from the nagging voice, the hammock rotated on its hooks and dumped him.

He struck the floor stunningly, taking the main blow across his right shoulder, though he hardly felt it as yet. His feet, not yet part of him at all, still remained afloat far aloft, twisted in the hammock webbing.

"Good Lord!" There was a brief chain of footsteps, like chestnuts dropping on a roof, and then an overstated crash. "Cleaver, are you sick? Here, lie still a minute and let me get your feet free. Mike—Mike, can't you turn the gas up in this jug? Something's wrong back here."

After a moment, yellow light began to pour from the glistening walls. Cleaver dragged an arm across his eyes, but it did him no good; it tired too quickly. Agronski's mild face, plump and anxious, floated directly above him like a captive balloon. He could not see Michelis anywhere, and at the moment he was just as glad. Agronski's presence was hard enough to understand.

"How . . . the hell . . ." he said. At the words, his lips split painfully at both corners. He realized for the first time that they had become gummed together, somehow, while he was asleep. He had no idea how long he had been out of the picture.

Agronski seemed to understand the aborted question. "We came in from the lakes in the 'copter," he said. "We didn't like the silence down here and we figured that we'd better come in under our own power, instead of registering in on the regular jet-liner and tipping the Lithians off—just in case there'd been any dirty work afloat."

"Stop jawing him," Michelis said, appearing suddenly, magically in the doorway. "He's got a bug, that's obvious. I don't like to feel pleased about misery, but I'm glad it's that instead of the Lithians."

The rangy, long-jawed chemist helped Agronski lift Cleaver to his feet. Tentatively, despite the pain, Cleaver got his mouth open again. Nothing came out but a hoarse croak.

"Shut up," Michelis said, not unkindly. "Let's get him back into the hammock. Where's the father? He's the only one capable of dealing with sickness here."

"I'll bet he's dead," Agronski burst out suddenly, his face glistening with alarm. "He'd be here if he could. It must be catching, Mike."

"I didn't bring my mitt," Michelis said dryly. "Cleaver, lie still or I'll have to clobber you. Agronski, you seem to have dumped his water carafe; better go get him some more, he needs it. And see if the father left anything in the lab that looks like medicine."

Agronski went out, and, maddeningly, so did Michelis—at least out of Cleaver's field of vision. Setting his every muscle against the pain, Cleaver pulled his lips apart once more.

"Mike."

Instantly, Michelis was there. He had a pad of cotton between two fingers, wet with some solution, with which he gently cleaned Cleaver's lips and chin.

"Easy. Agronski's getting you a drink. We'll let you talk in a little while, Paul. Don't rush it."

Cleaver relaxed a little. He could trust Michelis. Nevertheless, the vivid and absurd insult of having to be swabbed like a baby was more than he could bear; he felt tears of helpless rage swelling on either side of his nose.

With two deft, noncommittal swipes, Michelis removed them.

Agronski came back, holding out one hand tentatively, palm up. "I found these," he said. "There's more in the lab, and the father's pillpress is still out. So's his mortar and pestle, though they've been cleaned."

"All right, let's have 'em," Michelis said. "Anything else?"

"No. There's a syringe cooking in the sterilizer, if that means anything."

Michelis swore briefly and to the point. "It means that there's a pertinent antitoxin in the shop someplace," he added. "But unless Ramon left notes, we'll not have a prayer of figuring out which one it is."

As he spoke, he lifted Cleaver's head and tipped the pills into his mouth. The water which followed was cold at the first contact, but a split second later it was liquid fire. Cleaver chocked, and at that precise moment Michelis pinched his nostrils shut. The pills went down.

"There's no sign of the father?" Michelis said.

"Not a one, Mike. Everything's in good order, and his gear's still here. Both jungle suits are in the locker."

"Maybe he went visiting," Michelis said thoughtfully. "He must have gotten to know quite a few of the Lithians by now."

"With a sick man on his hands? That's not like him, Mike. Not unless there was some kind of emergency. Or maybe he went on a routine errand, expected to be back in just a few moments, and—"

"And was set upon by trolls for forgetting to stamp his foot three times before crossing the bridge."

"All right, laugh."

"I'm not laughing, believe me."

"*Mike . . .*"

Michelis took a step back and looked down at Cleaver, his face floating as if detached through a haze of tears. He said: "All right, Paul. Tell us what it is. We're listening."

But it was too late. The doubled barbiturate dose had gotten to Cleaver first. He could only shake his head, and with the motion Michelis seemed to go reeling away into a whirlpool of fuzzy rainbows.

Curiously, he did not quite go to sleep. He had had nearly a normal night's sleep, and he had started out the enormously long day a powerful and healthy man. The conversation of the two Earthmen and an obsessive consciousness of his need to speak to them before Ruiz-Sanchez returned helped to keep him, if not totally awake, at least not far below a state of light trance—and the presence in his system of thirty grains of acetylsalicylic acid had seriously raised his oxygen consumption, bringing with it not only dizziness but a precarious, emotionally untethered alertness. That the fuel which was being burned to maintain it was largely the protein substrate of his own cells he did not know, and it could not have alarmed him had he known it.

The voices continued to reach him, and to convey a little meaning. With them were mixed fleeting, fragmentary dreams, so slightly removed from the surface of his waking life as to seem peculiarly real, yet at the same time peculiarly pointless and depressing. In the semi-conscious intervals there came plans, a whole succession of them, all simple and grandiose at once, for taking command of the expedition, for communicating with the authorities on Earth, for bringing forward secret papers proving that Lithia was uninhabitable, for digging a tunnel under Mexico to Peru, for detonating Lithia in one single mighty fusion of all its lightweight atoms into an atom of cleaverium, the element whose cardinal number was aleph-null . . .

AGRONSKI: Mike, come here and look at this; you read Lithian. There's a mark on the front door, on the message tablet.

(Footsteps.)

MICHELIS: It says "Sickness inside." The strokes aren't casual or deft enough to be the work of the natives. Ideographs are hard to write rapidly. Ramon must have written it there.

AGRONSKI: I wish I knew where he went afterwards.

(Footsteps. Door shutting, not loudly. Footsteps. Hassock creaking.)

AGRONSKI: Well, we'd better be thinking about getting up a report. Unless this damn twenty-hour day has me thrown completely off, our time's just about up. Are you still set on opening up the planet?

MICHELIS: Yes. I've seen nothing to convince me that there's anything on Lithia that's dangerous to us. Except maybe Cleaver in there, and I'm not prepared to say that the father would have left him if he were in any serious danger. And I do not see how Earthmen could harm this society: it's too stable emotionally, economically, in every other way.

(*Danger, danger,* said somebody in Cleaver's dream. *It will explode. It's all a popish plot.* Then he was marginally awake again and conscious of how his mouth hurt.)

AGRONSKI: Why do you suppose these two jokers never called us after we went north?

MICHELIS: I don't have any answer. I won't even guess until I talk to Ramon. Or until Paul's able to sit up and take notice.

AGRONSKI: I don't like it, Mike. It smells bad to me. This town's right at the heart of the communications system of the planet. And yet—no messages, Cleaver sick, the father not here . . . there's a hell of a lot we don't know about Lithia.

MICHELIS: There's a hell of a lot we don't know about central Brazil.

AGRONSKI: Nothing essential, Mike. What we know about the periphery gives us all the clues we need about the interior—even to those fish that eat people, the what-are-they, the piranhas. That's not true on Lithia. We don't know whether our peripheral clues about Lithia are germane or just incidental. Something enormous could be hidden under the surface without our being able to detect it.

MICHELIS: Agronski, stop sounding like a Sunday supplement. You underestimate your own intelligence. What kind of enormous secret could that be? That the Lithians eat people? That they're cattle for unknown gods that live in the jungle? That they're actually mind-wrenching, soul-twisting, heart-stopping, bowel-moving intelligences in disguise? The moment you see any such proposition, you'll deflate it yourself. I would not even need to take the trouble of examining it, or discussing how we might meet it if it were true.

AGRONSKI: All right, all right. I'll reserve judgment for the time being, anyhow. If everything turns out to be all right here, with the father and Cleaver I mean, I'll probably go along with you. I don't have any reason I could defend for voting against the planet, I admit.

MICHELIS: Good for you. I'm sure Ramon is for opening it up, so that should make it unanimous. I can't see why Cleaver would object.

(Cleaver was testifying before a packed court convened in the UN General Assembly chambers in New York, with one finger pointed dramatically, but less in triumph than in sorrow, at Ramon Ruiz-Sanchez, S.J. At the sound of his name the dream collapsed and he realized that the room had grown a little lighter. Dawn—or the dripping, wool-gray travesty of it which prevailed on Lithia—was on its way. He wondered what he had just said to the court. It had been conclusive, damning, good enough to be used when he awoke; but he could not remember a word of it. All that remained of it was a sensation, almost the taste of the words, but with nothing of their substance.)

AGRONSKI: It's getting light. I suppose we'd better knock off.

MICHELIS: Did you stake down the 'copter? The winds here are higher than they are up north, I seem to remember.

AGRONSKI: Yes. And covered it with the tarp. Nothing left to do but sling our hammocks—

MICHELIS: *Shh.* What's that?

Footsteps. Faint ones, but Cleaver knew them. He forced his eyes to open a little, but there was nothing to see but the ceiling. Its even color, and its smooth, ever-changing slope into a dome of nothingness, drew him almost immediately upward into the mists of trance once more.)

AGRONSKI: Somebody's coming. It's the father, Mike—look out here. He seems to be all right. Dragging his feet a bit, but who wouldn't after being out helling all night?

MICHELIS: Maybe you'd better meet him at the door. It'd probably be better than our springing out at him after he gets inside. After all he doesn't expect us. I'll get to unpacking the hammocks.

AGRONSKI: Sure, Mike.

Footsteps going away from Cleaver. A grating sound of stone on stone: the door-wheel being turned).

AGRONSKI: Welcome home, father! We got in just a little while ago and —what's wrong? Are you ill? Is there something that—Mike! *Mike!*

Somebody was running. Cleaver willed his neck muscles to turn his head, but they refused to obey. Instead, the back of his head seemed to force itself deeper into the stiff pillow of the hammock. After a momentary and endless agony he cried out.)

CLEAVER: Mike!

AGRONSKI: Mike!

With a gasp, Cleaver lost the long battle at last. He was asleep.)


IV


As the door of Chtexa's house closed behind him, Ruiz-Sanchez looked about the gently glowing foyer with a feeling of almost unbearable anticipation, although he could hardly have said what it was that he hoped to see. Actually, it looked exactly like his own quarters, which was all he could in justice have expected—all the furniture at "home" was Lithian except the lab equipment.

"We have cut up several of the metal meteors from our museums, and hammered them as you suggested," Chtexa said behind him, while he struggled out of his raincoat and boots. "They show very definite, very strong magnetism, just as you predicted. We now have the whole planet alerted to pick up meteorites and send them to our electrical laboratory here, regardless of where found. The staff of the observatory is attempting to predict possible falls. Unhappily, meteors are rare here. Our astronomers say that we have never had a 'shower' such as you described as frequent on your native planet."

"No; I should have thought of that," Ruiz-Sanchez said, following the Lithian into the front room. This, too, was quite ordinary, and empty except for the two of them. "In our system we have a sort of giant grinding-wheel—a whole ring of little planets, many thousands of them, distributed around an orbit where we had expected to find only one normal-sized world. Collisions between these bodies are incessant, and our plague of meteors is the result. Here I suppose you have only the usual few strays from comets."

"It is hard to understand how so unstable an arrangement could have come about," Chtexa said, sitting down and pointing out another hassock to his guest. "Have you an explanation?"

"Not a good one," Ruiz-Sanchez said. "Some of us think that there was a respectable planet in that orbit ages ago, which exploded somehow. A similar accident happened to a satellite in our system—at least one of our planets has a similar ring. Others think that at the formation of our solar system the raw materials of what might have been a planet just never succeeded in coalescing. Both ideas have many flaws, but each satisfies certain objections to the other, so perhaps there is some truth in both."

Chtexa's eyes filmed with the mildly disquieting "inner blink" characteristic of Lithians at their most thoughtful. "There would seem to be no way to test either answer," he said at length. "By our logic, lack of such tests makes the original question meaningless."

"That rule of logic has many adherents on Earth. My colleague Dr. Cleaver would certainly agree with it." Ruiz-Sanchez smiled suddenly. He had labored long and hard to master the Lithian language, and to have understood and recognized so completely abstract a point as the one just made by Chtexa was a bigger victory than any quantitative gains in vocabulary alone could ever have been. "But I can see that we are going to have difficulties in collecting these meteorites. Have you offered incentives?"

"Oh, certainly. Everyone understands the importance of the program. We are all eager to advance it."

This was not quite what the priest had meant by his question. He searched his memory for some Lithian equivalent of *reward,* but found nothing but the word he had already used, *incentive.* He realized that he knew no word for *greed,* either. Evidently offering Lithians a hundred dollars a meteorite would simply baffle them. Instead he said, "Since the potential meteor-fall is so small, you're not likely to get anything like the supply of metal that you need for a real study, no matter how thoroughly you cooperate on it. You need a supplementary iron-finding program: some way of concentrating the traces of the metal you have on the planet. Our smelting methods would be useless to you, since you have no ore-beds. Hmm. What about the iron-fixing bacteria?"

"Are there such?" Chtexa said, cocking his head dubiously.

"I don't know. Ask your bacteriologists. If you have any bacteria here that belong to the genus we call *Leptothrix,* one of them should be an iron-fixing species. In all the millions of years that this planet has had life on it, that mutation must have occurred, and probably very early."

"But why have we never seen it before? We have done perhaps more research in bacteriology than we have in any other field."

"Because," Ruiz-Sanchez said earnestly, "you didn't know what to look for, and because such a species would be as rare as iron itself. On Earth, because we have iron in abundance, our *Leptothrix ochracea* has found plenty of opportunity to grow. We find their fossil sheaths by uncountable millions in our great ore-beds. It used to be thought, as a matter of fact, that the bacteria *produced* the ore-beds, but I've never believed that. While they do obtain their energy by oxidizing ferrous iron, such salts in solution change spontaneously to ferric salts if the oxidation-reduction potential and the pH of the water are right—and those are conditions that are affected by ordinary decay bacteria. On our planet the bacteria grew in the ore-beds because the iron was there, not the other way around. In your case, you just don't have the iron to make them numerous, but I'm sure there must be a few."

"We will start a soil-sampling program at once," Chtexa said, his wattles flaring a subdued orchid. "Our antibiotics research centers screen soil samples by the thousands every month, in search of new microflora of therapeutic importance. If these iron-fixing bacteria exist, we are certain to find them eventually."

"They must exist," Ruiz-Sanchez repeated. "Do you have a bacterium that is a sulphur-concentrating obligate anaerobe?"

"Yes—yes, certainly!"

"There you are," the Jesuit said, leaning back contentedly and clasping his hands across one knee. "You have plenty of sulphur and so you have the bacterium. Please let me know when you find the iron-fixing species. I'd like to make a sub culture and take it home with me when I leave. There are two Earthmen whose noses I'd like to rub in it."

The Lithian stiffened and thrust his head forward a little, as if baffled. Ruiz-Sanchez said hastily, "Pardon me. I was translating literally an aggressive idiom of my own tongue. It was not meant to describe an actual plan of action."

"I think I understand," Chtexa said. Ruiz-Sanchez wondered if he did. In the rich storehouse of the Lithian language he had yet to discover any metaphors, either living or dead. Neither did the Lithians have any poetry or other creative arts. "You are of course welcome to any of the results of this program which you would honor us by accepting. One problem in the social sciences which has long puzzled us is just how one may adequately honor the innovator. When we consider how new ideas change our lives, we despair of giving in kind, and it is helpful when the innovator himself has wishes which society can gratify."

Ruiz-Sanchez was at first not quite sure he had understood the proposition. After he had gone over it once more in his mind, he was not sure that he could bring himself to like it, although it was admirable enough. From an Earthman it would have sounded intolerably pompous, but it was evident that Chtexa meant it.

It was probably just as well that the commission's report on Lithia was about to fall due. Ruiz-Sanchez had begun to think that he could absorb only a little more of this kind of calm sanity. And all of it—a disquieting thought from somewhere near his heart reminded him—all of it derived from reason, none from precept, none from faith. The Lithians did not know God. They did things rightly, and thought righteously, because it was reasonable and efficient and natural to do and to think that way. They seemed to need nothing else.

Or could it be that they thought and acted as they did because, not being born of man, and never in effect having left the Garden in which they lived, they did not share the terrible burden of original sin? The fact that Lithia had never once had a glacial epoch, that its climate had been left unchanged for seven hundred million years, was a geological fact that an alert geologist could scarcely afford to ignore. Could it be that, free from the burden, they were also free from the curse of Adam?

And if they were—could men bear to live among them?

"I have some questions to ask you, Chtexa," the priest said after a moment. "You owe me no debt whatsoever, but we four Earthmen have a hard decision to make shortly. You know what it is. And I don't believe that we know enough yet about your planet to make that decision properly."

"Then of course you must ask questions," Chtexa said immediately. "I will answer, wherever I can."

"Well, then—do your people die? I see you have the word, but perhaps it isn't the same as our word in meaning."

"It means to stop changing and to go back to existing," Chtexa said. "A machine exists, but only a living thing, like a tree, progresses along a line of changing equilibriums. When that progress stops, the entity is dead."

"And that happens to you?"

"It always happens. Even the great trees, like the Message Tree, die sooner or later. Is that not true on Earth?"

"Yes," Ruiz-Sanchez said, "yes, it is. For reasons it would take me a long time to explain, it occurred to me that you might have escaped this evil."

"It is not evil as we look at it," Chtexa said. "Lithia lives because of death. The death of leaves supplies our oil and gas. The death of some creatures is always necessary for the life of others. Bacteria must die, and viruses be prevented from living, if illness is to be cured. We ourselves must die simply to make room for others, at least until we can slow the rate at which our people arrive in the world—a thing impossible to us at present."

"But desirable, in your eyes?"

"Surely desirable," Chtexa said. "Our world is rich, but not inexhaustible. And other planets, you have taught us, have peoples of their own. Thus we cannot hope to spread to other planets when we have overpopulated this one."

"No real thing is ever inexhaustible," Ruiz-Sanchez said abruptly, frowning at the iridescent floor. "That we have found to be true over many thousands of years of our history."

"But inexhaustible in what way?" said Chtexa. "I grant you that any small object, any stone, any drop of water, any bit of soil can be explored without end. The amount of information which can be gotten from it is quite literally infinite. But a given soil can be exhausted of nitrates. It is difficult, but with bad cultivation it can be done. Or take iron, about which we have already been talking. Our planet's supply of iron has limits which we already know, at least approximately. To allow our economy to develop a demand for iron which exceeds the total known supply of Lithia —and exceeds it beyond any possibility of supplementation by meteors or by import—would be folly. This is not a question of information. It is a question of whether or not the information can be used. If it cannot, then limitless information is of no help."

"You could certainly get along without more iron if you had to," Ruiz-Sanchez admitted. "Your wooden machinery is precise enough to satisfy any engineer. Most of them, I think, don't remember that we used to have something similar: I've a sample in my own home. It's a kind of timer called a cuckoo clock, nearly two of our centuries old, made entirely of wood, and still nearly 100 percent accurate. For that matter, long after we began to build seagoing vessels of metal, we continued to use lignum vitae for ships' bearings."

"Wood is an excellent material for most uses," Chtexa agreed. "Its only deficiency, compared to ceramic materials or perhaps metal, is that it is variable. One must know it well to be able to assess its qualities from one tree to the next. And of course complicated parts can always be grown inside suitable ceramic molds; the growth pressure inside the mold rises so high that the resulting part is very dense. Larger parts can be ground direct from the plank with soft sandstone and polished with slate. It is a gratifying material to work, we find."

Ruiz-Sanchez felt, for some reason, a little ashamed. It was a magnified version of the same shame he had always felt at home toward that old Black Forest cuckoo clock. The electric clocks elsewhere in his villa back home all should have been capable of performing silently, accurately and in less space—but the considerations which had gone into the making of them had been commercial as well as purely technical. As a result, most of them operated with a thin, asthmatic whir, or groaned softly but dismally at irregular hours. All of them were "streamlined," over-sized and ugly. None of them kept good time, and several of them, since they were powered by constant-speed motors operating very simple gearboxes, could not be adjusted, but had been sent out from the factory with built-in, ineluctable inaccuracies.

The wooden cuckoo clock, meanwhile, ticked evenly away. A quail emerged from one of two wooden doors every quarter of an hour and let you know about it, and on the hour first the quail came out, then the cuckoo, and there was a soft bell that rang just ahead of the cuckoo's call. It was accurate to a minute a week, all for the price of running up the three weights which drove it, each night before bedtime.

The maker had been dead before Ruiz-Sanchez had been born. In contrast, the priest would probably buy and jettison at least a dozen cheap electric clocks in the course of one lifetime, as their makers had intended he should.

"I'm sure it is," he said humbly. "I have one more question, if I may. It is really part of the same question: I have asked if you die; now I should like to ask how you are born. I see many adults on your streets and sometimes in your houses—though I gather you yourself are alone—but never any children. Can you explain this to me? Or if the subject is not allowed to be discussed . . ."

"But why should it not be? There can never be any closed subjects," Chtexa said. "You know, of course, that our mates have abdominal pouches where the eggs are carried. It was a lucky mutation for us, for there are a number of nest-robbing species on this planet."

"Yes, we have a few animals with a somewhat similar arrangement on Earth, although they are live-bearers."

"Our eggs are laid into these pouches once a year," Chtexa said. "It is then that the women leave their own houses and seek out the male of their choice to fertilize the eggs. I am alone because, thus far, I am no woman's first choice this season. In contrast you may see men's houses at this time of year which shelter three or four women who favor him."

"I see," Ruiz-Sanchez said carefully. "And how is the choice determined? Is it by emotion, or by reason alone?"

"The two are in the long run the same," Chtexa said. "Our ancestors did not leave our genetic needs to chance. Emotion with us no longer runs counter to our eugenic knowledge. It cannot, since it was itself modified to follow that knowledge by selective breeding for such behavior.

"At the end of the season, then, comes Migration Day. At that time all the eggs are fertilized, and ready to hatch. On that day—you will not be here to see it, I am afraid, for your announced date of departure precedes it by a short time—our whole nation goes to the seashores. There, with the men to protect them from predators, the women wade out to swimming depth, and the children are born."

"In the sea?" Ruiz-Sanchez said faintly.

"Yes, in the sea. Then we all return, and resume our other affairs until the next mating season."

"But—but what happens to the children?"

"Why, they take care of themselves, if they can. Of course many perish, particularly to our voracious brother the great fish-lizard, whom for that reason we kill when we can. But a majority return when the time comes."

"Return? Chtexa, I don't understand. Why don't they drown when they are born? And if they return, why have we never seen one?"

"But you have," Chtexa said. "And you have heard them often. Here, come with me." He arose and led the way out into the foyer. Ruiz-Sanchez followed, his head whirling with conjecture.

Chtexa opened the door. The night, the priest saw with a subdued shock, was on the wane; there was the faintest of pearly glimmers on the cloudy sky to the east. The multifarious humming and singing of the jungle continued unabated. There was a high, hissing whistle, and the shadow of a pterodon drifted over the city toward the sea. From the mudflats came a hoarse barking.

"There," Chtexa said softly. "Did you hear it?"

The stranded creature, or another of his kind—it was impossible to tell which—croaked protestingly again.

"It is hard for them at first," Chtexa said. "But actually the worst of their dangers are over. They have come ashore."

"Chtexa," Ruiz-Sanchez said. "Your children—*the lungfish?*"

"Yes," Chtexa said. "Those are our children."


V


In the last analysis it was the incessant barking of the lungfish which caused Ruiz-Sanchez to faint when Agronski opened the door for him. The late hour, and the dual strains of Cleaver's illness and the subsequent discovery of Cleaver's direct lying, contributed. So did the increasing sense of guilt toward Cleaver which the priest had felt while walking home under the gradually brightening, weeping sky; and so, of course, did the shock of discovering that Agronski and Michelis had arrived sometime during the night while he had been neglecting his charge.

But primarily it was the diminishing, gasping clamor of the children of Lithia, battering at his every mental citadel, all the way from Chtexa's house to his own.

The sudden fugue only lasted a few moments. He fought his way back to consciousness to find that Agronski and Michelis had propped him up on a stool in the lab and were trying to remove his macintosh without unbalancing him or awakening him—as difficult a problem in topology as removing a man's vest without taking off his jacket. Wearily, the priest pulled his own arm out of a macintosh sleeve and looked up at Michelis.

"Good morning, Mike. Please excuse my bad manners."

"Don't be an idiot," Michelis said evenly. "You don't have to talk now, anyhow. I've already spent much of tonight trying to keep Cleaver quiet until he's better. Don't put me through it again, Ramon, please."

"I won't. I'm not ill; I'm just very tired and a little overwrought."

"What's the matter with Cleaver?" Agronski demanded. Michelis made as if to shoo him off.

"No, no, Mike. I'm all right, I assure you. As for Paul, he got a dose of glucoside poisoning when a plant-spine stabbed him this afternoon. No, it's yesterday afternoon now. How has he been since you arrived?"

"He's sick," Michelis said. "Since you weren't here, we did not know what to do. We settled for two of the pills you'd left out."

"You did?" Ruiz-Sanchez slid his feet heavily to the floor and tried to stand up. "As you say, you couldn't have known what else to do, but I think I'd better look in on him—"

"Sit down, please, Ramon." Michelis spoke gently, but his tone showed that he meant the request to be honored. Obscurely glad to be forced to yield to the big man's well-meant implacability, the priest let himself be propped back on the stool. His boots fell off his feet to the floor.

"Mike, who's the father here?" he said tiredly. "Still, I'm sure you've done a good job. He's in no apparent danger?"

"Well, he seems very sick. But he had energy enough to keep himself half-awake most of the night. He only passed out a short while ago."

"Good. Let him stay out. Tomorrow we'll probably have to begin intravenous feeding, though. In this atmosphere one doesn't give a salicylate overdose without penalties." He sighed. "Can we put off further questions?"

"If there's nothing else wrong here, of course we can."

"Oh," Ruiz-Sanchez said, "there's a great deal wrong, I'm afraid."

"I knew it," Agronski said. "I knew damn well there was. I told you so, Mike, didn't I?"

"Is it urgent?"

"No, Mike—there's no danger to us, of that I'm positive. It's nothing that won't keep until we have all had a rest. You two look as though you need one as badly as I."

"We're tired," Michelis agreed.

"But why didn't you ever call us?" Agronski burst in aggrievedly. "You had us scared half to death, father. If there's really something wrong here, you should have—"

"There's no immediate danger," Ruiz-Sanchez repeated patiently. "As for why we didn't call you, I don't understand that any more than you do. Up to tonight, I thought we were in regular contact with you both. That was Paul's job and he seemed to be carrying it out. I didn't discover that he wasn't doing it until after he became ill."

"Then obviously we'll have to wait," Michelis said. "Let's hit the hammock, in God's name. Flying that 'copter through twenty-five hundred miles of fog-bank wasn't exactly restful, either; I'll be glad to turn in. . . . But, Ramon—"

"Yes, Mike?"

"I have to say that I don't like this any better than Agronski does. Tomorrow we've got to clear it up, and get our commission business done. We've only a day or so to make our decision before the ship comes and takes us off for good, and by that time we *must* know everything there is to know, and just what we're going to tell the Earth about it."

"Yes," Ruiz-Sanchez said. "Just as you say, Mike—in God's name."

The Peruvian priest-biologist awoke before the others: actually, he had undergone far less purely physical strain than had the other three. It was just beginning to be cloudy dusk when he rolled out of his hammock and padded over to look at Cleaver.

The physicist was in a coma. His face was dirty gray and looked oddly shrunken. It was high time that the neglect and inadvertent abuse to which he had been subjected was rectified. Happily, his pulse and respiration were close to normal now.

Ruiz-Sanchez went quietly into the lab and made up a fructose IV feeding. At the same time he reconstituted a can of powdered egg into a sort of soufflé, setting it in a covered crucible to bake at the back of the little oven; that was for the rest of them.

In the sleeping-chamber, the priest set up his IV stand. Cleaver did not stir when the needle entered the big vein just above the inside of his elbow. Ruiz-Sanchez taped the tubing in place, checked the drip from the inverted bottle and went back into the lab.

There he sat, on the stool before the microscope, in a sort of suspension of feeling while the new night drew on. He was still poisoned-tired, but at least now he could stay awake without constantly fighting himself. The slowly rising soufflé in the oven went *plup-plup, plup-plup,* and after a while a thin tendril of aroma suggested that it was beginning to brown on top, or at least thinking about it.

Outside, it abruptly rained buckets. Just as abruptly, it stopped.

"Is that breakfast I smell, Ramon?"

"Yes, Mike, in the oven. In a few minutes now."

"Right."

Michelis went away again. On the back of the workbench, Ruiz-Sanchez saw the dark blue book with the gold stamping which he had brought with him all the way from Earth. Almost automatically he pulled it to him and opened it to page 573. It would at least give him something to think about with which he was not personally involved.

He had quitted the text last with Anita, who "would yield to the lewdness of Honuphrius to appease the savagery of Sulla and the mercenariness of the twelve Sullivani, and (as Gilbert first suggested), to save the virginity of Felicia for Magravius"—now hold on a moment, how could Felicia be considered still a virgin at this point? Ah: ". . . when converted by Michael after the death of Gillia"; that covered it, since Felicia had been guilty only of simple infidelities in the first place. ". . . but she fears that, by allowing his marital rights, she may cause reprehensible conduct between Eugenius and Jeremias. Michael, who has formerly debauched Anita, dispenses her from yielding to Honuphrius"—yes, that figured, since Michael also had had designs on Eugenius. "Anita is disturbed, but Michael comminates that he will reserve her case tomorrow for the ordinary Guglielmus even if she should practice a pious fraud during affriction which, from experience, she knows (according to Wadding) to be leading to nullity."

Well. This was all very well. It even seemed to be shaping up, for the first time. Still, Ruiz-Sanchez reflected, he would not like to have known the family hidden behind the conventional Latin aliases, or to have been the confessor to any one of them. Now then:

"Fortissa, however, is encouraged by Gregorius, Leo, Viteilius and Macdugalius, reunitedly, to warn Anita by describing the strong chastisements of Honuphrius and the depravities *(turpissimas)* of Canicula, the deceased wife of Mauritius, with Sulla, the simoniac, who is abnegand and repents."

Yes, it added up, when one tried to view it without outrage either at the persons involved—and there was every assurance that these were fictitious—or at the author, who for all his mighty intellect, the greatest perhaps of the preceding century among novelists, had still to be pitied as much as the meanest victim of the Evil One. To view it, as it were, in a sort of gray twilight of emotion, wherein everything, even the barnaclelike commentaries which the text had accumulated, could be seen in the same light.

"Is it done, father?"

"Smells like it, Agronski. Take it out and help yourself, why don't you?"

"Thanks. Can I bring Cleaver—"

"No, he's getting a IV."

Unless his impression that he understood the problem at last was once more going to turn out to be an illusion, he was now ready for the basic question, the stumper that had deeply disturbed both the Order and the Church for so many years now. He reread it carefully. It asked:

"Has he hegemony and shall she submit?"

To his astonishment, he saw as if for the first time that it was two questions, despite the omission of a comma between the two. And so it demanded two answers. Did Honuphrius have hegemony? Yes, he did, for Michael, the only member of the whole complex who had been gifted from the beginning with the power of grace, had been egregiously compromised. Therefore, Honuphrius regardless of whether his sins were all to be laid at his door or were real only in rumor could not be divested of his privileges by anyone. But should Anita submit? No, she should not. Michael had forfeited his right to dispense or to reserve her in any way, and so she could not be guided by the curate or by anyone else in the long run but her own conscience—which in view of the grave accusations against Honuphrius could lead her to no recourse but to deny him. As for Sulla's repentance, and Felicia's conversion, they meant nothing, since the defection of Michael had deprived both of them, and everyone else, of spiritual guidance.

The answer, then, had been obvious all the time. It was: yes, and no.

He closed the book and looked up across the bench, feeling neither more nor less dazed than he had before, but with a small stirring of elation deep inside him which he could not suppress. As he looked out of the window into the dripping darkness, a familiar, sculpturesque head and shoulders moved into the truncated tetrahedron of yellow light being cast out through the fine glass into the rain.

It was Chtexa, moving away from the house.

Suddenly Ruiz-Sanchez realized that nobody had bothered to rub away the sickness ideograms on the door tablet. If Chtexa had come here on some errand, he had been turned back unnecessarily. The priest leaned forward, snatched up an empty slidebox and rapped with a corner of it against the inside of the window.

Chtexa turned and looked in through the steaming curtains of rain, his eyes completely filmed. Ruiz-Sanchez beckoned to him, and got stiffly off the stool to open the door. In the oven his share of breakfast dried slowly and began to burn.

The rapping had summoned forth Agronski and Michelis as well. Chtexa looked down at the three of them with easy gravity, while drops of water ran like oil down the minute, prismatic scales of his supple skin.

"I did not know that there was sickness here," the Lithian said. "I called because your brother Ruiz-Sanchez left my house this morning without the gift I had hoped to give him. I will leave if I am invading your privacy in any way."

"You are not," Ruiz-Sanchez assured him. "And the sickness is only a poisoning, not communicable and we think not likely to end badly for our colleague. These are my friends from the north, Agronski and Michelis."

"I am happy to see them. The message was not in vain, then?"

"What message is this?" Michelis said, in his pure but hesitant Lithian.

"I sent a message, as your colleague Ruiz-Sanchez asked me to do, last night. I was told by Xoredeshch Gton that you had already departed."

"As we had," Michelis said. "Ramon, what's this? I thought you told us that sending messages was Paul's job. And you certainly implied that you didn't know how to do it after Paul took sick."

"I didn't. I don't. I asked Chtexa to send it for me."

Michelis looked up at the Lithian. "What did the message say?" he asked.

"That you were to join them now, here, in Xoredeshch Sfath. And that your time on our world was almost up."

"What does that mean?" Agronski said. He had been trying to follow the conversation, but he was not much of a linguist, and evidently the few words he had been able to pick up had served only to inflame his ready fears. "Mike, translate, please."

Michelis did so, briefly. Then he said: "Ramon, was that really all you had to say to us, especially after what you had found out? We knew that departure time was coming, too, after all. We can keep a calendar as well as you, I hope."

"I know that, Mike. But I had no idea what previous messages you'd received, if indeed you'd received any. For all I knew, Cleaver might have been in touch with you some other way, privately. I thought at first of a transmitter in his personal luggage, but later it occurred to me that he might have been sending dispatches over the regular jet-liners. Or he might have told you that we were going to stay on beyond the official time. He might have told you I was dead. He might have told you anything. I had to be sure you'd arrive here *regardless* of what he had or had not said.

"And when I got to the local message center, I had to revise my message again, because I found that I couldn't communicate with you directly, or send anything at all detailed. Everything that goes out from Xoredeshch Sfath by radio goes out through the Tree, and until you have seen it you haven't any idea what an Earthman is up against there in sending even the simplest message."

"Is that true?" Michelis asked Chtexa.

"True?" Chtexa repeated. "It is accurate, yes."

"Well, then," Ruiz-Sanchez said, a little nettled, "you can see why, when Chtexa appeared providentially, recognized me and offered to act as an intermediary, I had to give him only the gist of what I had to say. I couldn't hope to explain all the details to him, and I couldn't hope that any of those details would get to you undistorted after passing through at least two Lithian intermediaries. All I could do was yell at the top of my voice for you two to get down here on the proper date—and hope that you heard me."

"This is a time of trouble, which is like a sickness in the house," Chtexa said. "I must not remain. I will wish to be left alone when I am troubled, and I cannot ask that, if I now force my presence on others who are troubled. I will bring my gift at a better time."

He ducked out through the door, without any formal gesture of farewell, but nevertheless leaving behind an overwhelming impression of graciousness. Ruiz-Sanchez watched him go helplessly, and a little forlornly. The Lithians always seemed to understand the essences of situations; they were never, like even the most cocksure of Earthmen, beset by the least apparent doubt.

And why should they be? They were backed—if Ruiz-Sanchez was right—by the second-best Authority in the universe, and backed directly, without intermediaries or conflicting interpretations. The very fact that they were never tormented by indecision identified them as creatures of that Authority. Only the children of God had been given free choice, and hence were often doubtful.

Nevertheless, Ruiz-Sanchez would have delayed Chtexa's departure had he been able. In a short-term argument it is helpful to have pure reason on your side—even though such an ally could be depended upon to stab you to the heart if you depended upon him too long.

"Let's go inside and thrash this thing out," Michelis said, shutting the door and turning back toward the front room. "It's a good thing we got some sleep, but we have so little time left now that it's going to be touch and go to have a formal decision ready when the ship comes."

"We can't go ahead yet," Agronski objected, although, along with Ruiz-Sanchez, he followed Michelis obediently enough. "How can we do anything sensible without having heard what Cleaver has to say? Every man's voice counts on a job of this sort."

"That's very true," Michelis said. "And I don't like the present situation any better than you do—I've already said that. But I don't see that we have any choice. What do you think, Ramon?"

"I'd like to hold out for waiting," Ruiz-Sanchez said frankly. "Anything I may say now is, to put it realistically, somewhat compromised with you two. And don't tell me that you have every confidence in my integrity, because we had every confidence in Cleaver's, too. Right now, trying to maintain both confidences just cancels out both."

"You have a nasty way, Ramon, of saying aloud what everybody else is thinking," Michelis said, grinning bleakly. "What alternatives do you see, then?"

"None," Ruiz-Sanchez admitted. "Time is against us, as you said. We'll just have to go ahead without Cleaver."

"No, you won't." The voice, from the doorway to the sleeping chamber, was at once both uncertain and much harshened by weakness.

The others sprang up. Cleaver, clad only in his shorts, stood in the doorway, clinging to both sides of it. On one forearm Ruiz-Sanchez could see the marks where the adhesive tape which had held the IV tubing had been ripped off.

## VI

"Paul, you must be crazy," Michelis said, almost angrily. "Get back into your hammock before you make things twice as bad for yourself. You're a sick man, can't you realize that?"

"Not as sick as I look," Cleaver said, with a ghastly grin. Actually I feel pretty fair. My mouth is almost all cleared up and I don't think I've got any fever. And I'll be damned if this commission is going to proceed an inch without me. It isn't empowered to do it, and I'll appeal against any decision—*any* decision, I hope you guys are listening—that it makes without me."

The other two turned helplessly to Ruiz-Sanchez.

"How about it, Ramon?" Michelis said, frowning. "Is it safe for him to be up like this?"

Ruiz-Sanchez was already at the physicist's side, peering into his mouth. The ulcers were indeed almost gone, with granulation tissue forming nicely over the few that still remained. Cleaver's eyes were still slightly suffused, indicating that the toxemia was not completely defeated, but except for these two signs the effect of the accidental squill inoculation was no longer visible. It was true that Cleaver looked awful, but that was inevitable in a man recently quite sick, and in one who had been burning his own body proteins for fuel to boot.

"If he wants to kill himself, I guess he's got a right to do so, at least by indirection," Ruiz-Sanchez said. "Paul, the first thing you'll have to do is get off your feet, and get into a robe, and get a blanket around your legs. Then you'll have to eat something; I'll fix it for you. You have staged a wonderful recovery, but you're a sitting duck for a real infection if you abuse yourself during convalescence."

"I'll compromise," Cleaver said immediately. "I don't want to be a hero, I just want to be heard. Give me a hand over to that hassock. I still don't walk very straight."

It took the better part of half an hour to get Cleaver settled to Ruiz-Sanchez's satisfaction. The physicist seemed in a wry way to be enjoying every minute of it. At last he had a mug of *gchteka*, the local equivalent of tea, in his hand, and Michelis said:

"All right, Paul, you've gone out of your way to put yourself on the spot. Evidently that's where you want to be. So let's have the answer: why didn't you communicate with us?"

"I didn't want to."

"Now wait a minute," Agronski said. "Paul, don't break your neck to say the first damn thing that comes into your head. Your judgment may not be well yet, even if your talking apparatus is. Wasn't your silence just a matter of your being unable to work the local message system—the Tree or whatever it is?"

"No, it wasn't," Cleaver insisted. "Thanks, Agronski, but I don't need to be shepherded down the safe and easy road, or have any alibis set up for me. I know exactly what I did that was ticklish, and I know that it's going to be impossible to set up consistent alibis for it now. My chances for keeping anything under my hat depended on my staying in complete control of everything I did. Naturally those chances went out the window when I got stuck by that damned pineapple. I realized that last night, when I fought like a demon to get through to you before the father could get back, and found that I couldn't make it."

"You seem to take it calmly enough now," Michelis observed.

"Well, I'm feeling a little washed out. But I'm a realist. And I also know, Mike, that I had damned good reasons for what I did. I'm counting on the chance that you'll agree with me wholeheartedly when I tell you why I did it."

"All right," Michelis said, "begin."

Cleaver sat back, folding his hands quietly in the lap of his robe. He was obviously still enjoying the situation. He said:

"First of all, I didn't call you because I didn't want to, as I said. I could have mastered the problem of the Tree easily enough by doing what the father did—that is by getting a Snake to ferry my messages. Of course I don't speak Snake, but the father does, so all I had to do was to take him into my confidence. Barring that, I could have mastered the Tree itself. I already know all the technical principles involved. Mike, you should see that Tree, it's the biggest single junction transistor anywhere in this galaxy, and I'll bet that it's the biggest one anywhere.

But I wanted a gap to spring up between our party and yours. I wanted both of you to be completely in the dark about what was going on, down here on this continent. I wanted you to imagine the worst, and blame it on the Snakes, too, if that could be managed. After you got here—if you did—I was going to be able to show you that I hadn't sent any messages because the Snakes wouldn't let me. I've got more plants to that effect squirrelled away around here than I'll bother to list now; there'd be no point in it; since it's all come to nothing. But I'm sure it would have looked conclusive, regardless of anything the father would have been able to offer to the contrary.

"It was just a damned shame, from my point of view, that I had to run up against a pineapple at the last minute. It gave the father a chance to find out something about what was up. I'll swear that if that hadn't happened, he wouldn't have smelled anything until you actually got here —and then it would have been too late."

"I probably wouldn't have, that's true," Ruiz-Sanchez said, watching

Cleaver steadily. "But your running up against that 'pineapple' was no accident. If you'd been observing Lithia as you were sent here to do, instead of spending all your time building up a fictitious Lithia for purposes of your own, you'd have known enough about the planet to have been more careful about 'pineapples.' You'd also have spoken at least as much Lithian as Agronski by this time."

"That," Cleaver said, "is probably true, and again it doesn't make any difference to me. I observed the one fact about Lithia that overrides all other facts, and that is going to turn out to be sufficient. Unlike you, father, I have no respect for petty niceties in extreme situations, and I'm not the kind of man who thinks anyone learns anything from analysis after the fact."

"Let's not get to bickering," Michelis said. "You've told us your story without any visible decoration, and it's evident that you have a reason for confessing. You expect us to excuse you, or at least not to blame you too heavily, when you tell us what that reason is. Let's hear it."

"It's this," Cleaver said, and for the first time he seemed to become a little more animated. He leaned forward, the glowing gaslight bringing the bones of his face into sharp contrast with the sagging hollows of his cheeks, and pointed a not-quite-steady finger at Michelis.

"Do you know, Mike, what it is that we're sitting on here. Do you know, just to begin with, how much rutile there is here?"

"Of course I know. If we decide to vote for opening the planet up, our titanium problem will be solved for a century, maybe even longer. I'm saying as much in my personal report. But we figured that that would be true even before we first landed here, as soon as we got accurate figures on the mass of the planet."

"And what about the pegmatite?" Cleaver demanded softly.

"What about it?" Michelis said, looking puzzled. "I suppose it's abundant; I really didn't bother to look. Titanium's important to us, but I don't quite see why lithium should be; the days when the metal was used as a rocket fuel are fifty years behind us."

"And yet the stuff's still worth about twenty thousand dollars an English ton back home, Mike, and that's exactly the same price it was drawing in the 1960's, allowing for currency changes since then. Doesn't that mean anything to you?"

"I'm more interested in what it means to you," Michelis said. "None of us can make a nickel out of this trip, even if we find the planet solid platinum inside—which is hardly likely. And if price is the only consideration, surely the fact that lithium is common here will break the market for it? What's it good for, after all, on a large scale?"

"It's good for bombs," Cleaver said. "Fusion bombs. And, of course, controlled fusion power, if we ever lick that problem."

Ruiz-Sanchez suddenly felt sick and tired all over again. It was exactly what he had feared had been on Cleaver's mind, and he had not wanted to find himself right.

"Cleaver," he said, "I've changed my mind. I would have sought you out, even if you had never blundered against your 'pineapple.' That same day you mentioned to me that you were checking for pegmatite when you had your accident, and that you thought Lithia might be a good place for tritium production on large scale. Evidently you thought that I wouldn't know what you were talking about. If you hadn't hit the 'pineapple,' you would have given yourself away to me before now by talk like that; your estimate of me was based on as little observation as is your estimate of Lithia."

"It's easy," Cleaver observed indulgently, "to say 'I knew it all the time.'"

"Of course it's easy, when the other man is helping you," Ruiz-Sanchez said. "But I think that your view of Lithia as a cornucopia of potential hydrogen bombs is only the beginning of what you have in mind. I don't believe that it's even your real objective. What you would like most is to see Lithia removed from the universe as far as you're concerned. You hate the place, it's injured you, you'd like to think that it really doesn't exist. Hence the emphasis on Lithia as a source of tritium, to the exclusion of every other fact about the planet; for if that emphasis wins out, Lithia will be placed under security seal. Isn't that right?"

"Of course it's right, except for the phony mind-reading," Cleaver said contemptuously. "When even a priest can see it, it's got to be obvious. Mike, this is the most tremendous opportunity that man's ever had. This planet is made to order to be converted, root and branch, into a thermonuclear laboratory and production center. It has indefinitely large supplies of the most important raw materials. What's even more important, it has no nuclear knowledge of its own for us to worry about. All the clue materials, the radioactive elements and so on which you need to work out real knowledge of the atom, we'll have to import; the Snakes don't know a thing about them. Furthermore, the instruments involved, the counters and particle-accelerators and so on, all depend on materials like iron that the Snakes don't have, and on principles they do not know, like magnetism to begin with, and quantum theory. We'll be able to stock our plant here with an immense reservoir of cheap labor which doesn't know and —if we take proper precautions—never will have a prayer of learning enough to snitch classified techniques.

"All we need to do is to turn in a triple-E Unfavorable on the planet to shut off for a whole century any use of Lithia as a way-station or any other kind of general base. At the same time, we can report separately to the UN Review Committee exactly what we do have in Lithia: a triple-A arsenal for the whole of Earth, for the whole commonwealth of planets we control!"

"Against whom?" Ruiz-Sanchez said.

"What do you mean?"

"Against whom are you stocking this arsenal? Why do we need a whole planet devoted to making tritium bombs?"

"The UN itself can use weapons," Cleaver said dryly. "The time isn't very far gone since there were still a few restive nations on Earth, and it could come around again. Don't forget also that thermonuclear weapons only last a few years—they can't be stockpiled indefinitely, like fission bombs. The half-life of tritium is very short. I suppose you wouldn't know anything about that. But take my word for it, the UN's police would be glad to know that they could have access to a virtually inexhaustible stock of tritium bombs, and to hell with the shelf-life problem!

"Besides, if you've thought about it at all, you know as well as I do that this endless consolidation of peaceful planets can't go on forever. Sooner or later—well, what happens if the next planet we touch on is a place like Earth? If it is, its inhabitants may fight, and fight like a planetful of madmen, to stay out of our frame of influence. Or what happens if the next planet we hit is an outpost for a whole federation, maybe bigger than ours? When that day comes—and it will, it's in the cards—we'll be damned glad if we're able to plaster the enemy from pole to pole with fusion bombs, and clean up the matter with as little loss of life as possible."

"On our side," Ruiz-Sanchez added.

"Is there any other side?"

"By golly, it makes sense to me," Agronski said. "Mike, what do you think?"

"I'm not sure yet," Michelis said. "Paul, I still don't understand why you thought it necessary to go through all the cloak-and-dagger maneuvers. You tell your story fairly enough now, and it has its merits, but you also admit you were going to trick the three of us into going along with you, if you could. Why? Could not you trust the force of your argument alone?"

"No," Cleaver said bluntly. "I've never been on a commission like this before, where there was no single, definite chairman, where there was deliberately an even number of members so that a split opinion couldn't be settled if it occurred—and where the voice of a man whose head is full of pecksniffian, irrelevant moral distinctions and two-thousand-year-old metaphysics carries exactly the same weight as the voice of a scientist."

"That's mighty loaded language," Michelis said.

"I know it. If it comes to that, I'll say here or anywhere that I think the father is a hell of a fine biologist, and that that makes him a scientist like the rest of us—insofar as biology's science.

"But I remember once visiting the labs at Notre Dame, where they have a complete little world of germ-free animals and plants and have pulled I don't know how many physiological miracles out of the hat. I wondered then how one goes about being as good a scientist as that, and a churchman at the same time. I wondered in which compartment in their brains they filed their religion, and in which their science. I'm still wondering.

"I didn't propose to take chances on the compartments getting interconnected on Lithia. I had every intention of cutting the father down to a point where his voice would be nearly ignored by the rest of you. That's why I undertook the cloak-and-dagger stuff. Maybe it was stupid of me —I suppose that it takes training to be a successful *agent provocateur* and that I should have realized it. But I'm not sorry I tried. *I'm only sorry I failed.*"


## VII

There was a short, painful silence.

"Is that it, then?" Michelis said.

"That's it, Mike. Oh—one more thing. My vote, if anybody is in doubt about it, is to keep the planet closed. Take it from there."

"Ramon," Michelis said, "do you want to speak next? You're certainly entitled to it—the air's a mite murky at the moment."

"No, Mike; let's hear from you."

"I'm not ready to speak yet either, unles the majority wants me to. Agronski, how about you?"

"Sure," Agronski said. "Speaking as a geologist and also as an ordinary slob that doesn't follow rarefied reasoning very well, I'm on Cleaver's side. I don't see anything either for or against the planet on any other grounds but Cleaver's. It's a fair planet as planets go, very quiet, not very rich in anything else we need, not subject to any kind of trouble that I've been able to detect. It'd make a good way-station, but so would lots of other worlds hereabouts. It'd also make a good arsenal, the way Cleaver defined the term. In every other category it's as dull as ditch-water, and it's got plenty of that. The only other thing it can have to offer is titanium, which isn't quite as scarce back home these days as Mike seems to think, and gem-stones, particularly the semi-precious ones, which we can make at home without traveling forty light-years. I'd say, either set up a way-station here and forget about the planet otherwise, or else handle the place as Cleaver suggested."

"But which?" Ruiz-Sanchez asked.

"Well, which is more important, father? Aren't way stations a dime a dozen? Planets that can be used as thermonuclear labs, on the other hand, are rare—Lithia, is the *first* one that can be used that way, at least in my experience. Why use a planet for a routine purpose if it can be used for a unique purpose? Why not apply Occam's Razor—the law of parsimony? It works in all other scientific problems. It's my bet that it's the best tool to use on this one."

"You vote to close the planet, then," Michelis said.

"Sure. That's what I was saying, wasn't it?"

"I wanted to be certain," Michelis said. "Ramon, I guess it's up to us. Shall I speak first?"

"Of course, Mike."

"Then," Michelis said evenly, and without changing in the slightest his accustomed tone of grave impartiality, "I'll say that I think both of these gentlemen are fools, and calamitous fools at that because they're supposed to be scientists. Paul, your maneuvers to set up a phony situation are perfectly beneath contempt, and I shan't mention them again. I shan't even bother to record them, so you needn't feel that you have to mend any fences as far as I'm concerned. I'm looking solely at the purpose those maneuvers were supposed to serve, just as you asked me to do."

Cleaver's obvious self-satisfaction began to dim a little around the edges. He said, "Go ahead," and wound the blanket a little bit tighter around his legs.

"Lithia is not even the beginning of an arsenal," Michelis said. "Every piece of evidence you offered to prove that it might be is either a half-truth or the purest trash. Cheap labor, for instance: with what will you pay the Lithians? They have no money, and they can't be rewarded with goods. They have everything they need, and they like the way they're living right now—God knows they're not even slightly jealous of the achievements we think make Earth great." He looked around the gently rounded room, shining softly in the gaslight. "I don't seem to see any place in here where a vacuum cleaner would find much use. How will you pay the Lithians to work in your thermonuclear plants?"

"With knowledge," Cleaver said gruffly. "There's a lot they'd like to know."

"But what knowledge? The things they'd like to know are specifically the things you can't tell them if they're to be valuable to you as a labor force. Are you going to teach them quantum theory? You can't; that would be dangerous. Are you going to teach them electrodynamics? Again, that would enable them to learn other things you think dangerous. Are you going to teach them how to get titanium from ore, or how to accumulate enough iron to enable them to leave their present Stone Age? Of course you aren't. As a matter of fact, we haven't a thing to offer them in that sense. They just won't work for us under those terms."

"Offer them other terms," Cleaver said shortly. "If necessary, tell them what they're going to do, like it or lump it. It'd be easy enough to introduce a money system on this planet: you give a Snake a piece of paper that says it's worth a dollar, and if he asks you just what makes it worth a dollar—well, the answer is, We say it is."

"And we put a machine-pistol to his belly to emphasize the point," Ruiz-Sanchez interjected.

"Do we make machine-pistols for nothing? I never figured out what else they were good for. Either you point them at someone or you throw them away."

"Item: slavery," Michelis said. "That disposes, I think, of the argument for cheap labor. I won't vote for slavery. Ramon won't. Agronski?"

"No," Agronski said uneasily. "But it's a minor point."

"The hell it is. It's the reason that we're here. We're supposed to think of the welfare of the Lithians as well as of ourselves—otherwise this commission procedure would be a waste of time, of thought, of money. If we want cheap labor, we can enslave any planet."

Agronski was silent.

"Speak up," Michelis said stonily. "Is that true, or isn't it?"

Argronski said, "I guess it is."

"Cleaver?"

"Slavery's a swear word," Cleaver said sullenly. "You're deliberately clouding the issue."

*"Say that again."*

"Oh, hell. All right, Mike, I know you wouldn't. But you're wrong."

"I'll admit that the instant that you can demonstrate it to me," Michelis said. He got up abruptly from his hassock, walked over to the sloping window-sill and sat down again, looking out into the rain-stippled darkness. He seemed to be more deeply troubled than Ruiz-Sanchez had ever before thought possible for him.

"In the meantime," he resumed, "I'll go on with my own demonstration. Now what's to be said about this theory of automatic security that you've propounded, Paul? You think that the Lithians can't learn the techniques they would need to be able to understand secret information and pass it on, and so they won't have to be screened. There again, you're wrong, as you'd have known if you'd bothered to study the Lithians even perfunctorily. The Lithians are highly intelligent, and they already have many of the clues they need. I've given them a hand toward pinning down magnetism, and they absorbed the material like magic and put it to work with enormous ingenuity."

"So did I," Ruiz-Sanchez said. "And I've suggested to them a technique for accumulating iron that should prove to be pretty powerful. I had only to suggest it, and they were already halfway down to the bottom of it and traveling fast. They can make the most of the smallest of clues."

"If I were the UN I'd regard both actions as the plainest kind of treason," Cleaver said harshly. "Since that may be exactly the way Earth will regard them, I think it'd be just as well if you told the folks at home that the Snakes found out both items by themselves."

"I don't plan to do any falsifying of the report," Michelis said, "but thanks anyhow—I appreciate the intent behind what you say, if not the ethics. I'm not through, however. So far as the actual, practical objective that you want to achieve is concerned, Paul, I think it's just as useless as it is impossible. The fact that you have here a planet that's especially rich in lithium doesn't mean that you're sitting on a bonanza, no matter what price per ton the metal is commanding back home. The fact of the matter is that you can't ship lithium home.

"Its density is so low that you couldn't send away more than a ton of it per shipload; by the time you got it to Earth the shipping charges on it would more than outweight the price you'd get for it on arrival. As you ought to know, there's lots of lithium on Earth's own moon, too, and it isn't economical to fly it back to Earth even over that short distance. No more would it be economical to ship from Earth to Lithia all the heavy equipment that would be needed to make use of lithium here. By the time you got your cyclotron and the rest of your needs to Lithia, you'd have cost the UN so much money that no amount of locally available pegmatite could compensate for it."

"Just extracting the metal would cost a fair sum," Agronski said, frowning slightly. "Lithium would burn like gasoline in this atmosphere."

Michelis looked from Agronski to Cleaver and back again. "Of course it would," he said. "The whole plan's just a chimera. It seems to me, also, that we have a lot to learn from the Lithians, as well as they from us. Their social system works like the most perfect of our physical mechanisms, and it does so without any apparent repression of the individual. It's a thoroughly liberal society, that nevertheless never even begins to tip over toward the other side, toward the kind of Gandhiism that keeps a people tied to the momma-and-poppa-farm and the roving-brigand economy. It's in balance, and not precarious balance, either, but perfect chemical equilibrium.

"The notion of using Lithia as a tritium bomb plant is easily the strangest anachronism I've ever encountered—it's as crude as proposing to equip a spaceship with canvas sails. Right here on Lithia is the real secret, the secret that's going to make bombs of all kinds, and all the rest of the antisocial armamentarium, as useless, unnecessary, obsolete as the Iron Boot!

"And on top of all that—no, please, I'm not quite finished, Paul—on top of all that, the Lithians are centuries ahead of us in some purely technical matters, just as we're ahead of them in others. You should see what they can do with ceramics, with semi-conductors, with static electricity, with mixed disciplines like histochemistry, immunochemistry, biophysics, teratology, electrogenetics, limnology and half a hundred more. If you'd been looking, you *would* have seen.

"We have much more to do, it seems to me, than just vote to open the planet. That's a passive move. We have to realize that being able to use Lithia is only the beginning. The fact of the matter is that we actively *need* Lithia. We should say so in our recommendation."

He unfolded himself from the window-sill and stood up, looking down on them all, but most especially at Ruiz-Sanchez. The priest smiled at him, but as much in anguish as in admiration, and then had to look back at his shoes.

"Well, Agronski?" Cleaver said, spitting the words out like bullets on which he had been clenching his teeth during an amputation without anesthetics. "What do you say now? Do you like the pretty picture?"

"Sure, I like it," Agronski said, slowly but forthrightly. It was a virtue in him, as well as it was often a source of exasperation, that he always said exactly what he was thinking, the moment he was asked to do so. "Mike makes sense; I wouldn't expect him not to, if you see what I mean. Also he's got another advantage: he told us what he thought *without* trying first to trick us into his way of thinking."

"Oh, don't be a thumphead!" Cleaver exclaimed. "Are we scientists or Boy Rangers? Any rational man up against a majority of do-gooders would have taken the same precautions that I did."

"Maybe," Agronski said. "I don't know. They still smell to me like a confession of weakness somewhere in the argument. I don't like to be finessed. And I don't much like to be called a thumphead, either. But before you call me any more names, I'm going to say that I think you're more right than Mike is. I don't like your methods, but your aim seems sensible to me. Mike's shot some of your major arguments full of holes, that I'll admit; but as far as I'm concerned, you're still leading—by a nose."

He paused, breathing heavily and glaring at the physicist. Then he said: "But *don't push*, Paul. I don't like being pushed."

Michelis remained standing for a moment longer. Then he shrugged, walked back to his hassock and sat down, locking his hands between his knees.

"I did my best, Ramon," he said. "But so far it looks like a draw. See what you can do."

Ruiz-Sanchez took a deep breath. What he was about to do would without any doubt hurt him for the rest of his life, regardless of the goodness of his reasons, or the way time had of turning any knife. The decision had already cost him many hours of concentrated, agonized doubt. But he believed that it had to be done.

"I disagree with all of you," he said. "I believe that Lithia should be reported triple-E unfavorable, as Cleaver does. But I think it should also be given a special classification: X-1."

"X-1—but that's a quarantine label," Michelis said. "As a matter of fact—"

"Yes, Mike. I vote to seal Lithia off from *all* contact with the human race. Not only now, or for the next century, but forever."


## VIII


The words did not produce the consternation that he had been dreading—or, perhaps, had been hoping for, somewhere in the back of his mind. Evidently they were all too tired for that. They took his announcement with a kind of stunned emptiness, as though it were so far out of the expected order of events as to be quite meaningless. It was hard to say whether Cleaver or Michelis had been hit the harder. All that could be seen for certain was that Agronski recovered first, and was now ostentatiously cleaning his ears, as if he were ready to listen again when Ruiz-Sanchez changed his mind.

"Well," Cleaver began. And then again, shaking his head amazedly, like an old man: "Well. . . ."

"Tell us why, Ramon," Michelis said, clenching and unclenching his fists. His voice was quite flat, but Ruiz-Sanchez thought he could feel the pain under it.

"Of course. But I warn you, I'm going to be very roundabout. What I have to say seems to me to be of the utmost importance, and I don't want to see it rejected out of hand as just the product of my peculiar training and prejudices—interesting perhaps as a study in aberration, but not germane to the problem. The evidence for my view of Lithia is overwhelming. It overwhelmed me quite against my natural hopes and inclinations. I want you to hear that evidence."

"He wants us also to understand," Cleaver said, recovering a little of his natural impatience, "that his reasons are religious and won't hold water if he states them right out."

"Hush," Michelis said. "Listen."

"Thank you, Mike. All right, here we go. This planet is what I think is called in English a 'setup.' Let me describe it for you briefly as I see it, or rather as I've come to see it.

"Lithia is a paradise. It resembles most closely the Earth in its pre-Adamic period just before the coming of the great glaciers. The resemblance ends just there, because on Lithia the glaciers never came, and life continued to be spent in the paradise, as it was not allowed to do on Earth. We find a completely mixed forest, with plants which fall from one end of the creative spectrum to the other living side by side in perfect amity. To a great extent that's also true of the animals. The lion doesn't lie down with the lamb here because Lithia has neither animal, but as an analogy the phrase is apt. Parasitism occurs far less often on Lithia than it does on Earth, and there are very few carnivores of any sort. Almost all the surviving land animals eat plants only, and by a neat arrangement which is typically Lithian, the plants are admirably set up to attack animals rather than each other.

"It's an unusual ecology, and one of the strangest things about it is its rationality, its extreme, almost single-minded insistence on one-for-one relationships. In one respect it looks almost as though someone had arranged the whole planet to demonstrate the theory of sets.

"In this paradise we have a dominant creature, the Lithian, the man of Lithia. This creature is rational. It conforms as if naturally and without constraint or guidance to the highest ethical code we have evolved on Earth. It needs no laws to enforce this code; somehow, everyone obeys it as a matter of course, although it has never even been written down. There are no criminals, no deviants, no aberrations of any kind. The people are not standardized—our own very bad and partial answer to the ethical dilemma—but instead are highly individual. Yet somehow no antisocial act of any kind is ever committed.

"Mike, let me stop here and ask: what does this suggest to you?"

"Why, just what I've said before that it suggested," Michelis said. "An enormously superior social science, evidently founded in a precise psychological science."

"Very well, I'll go on. I felt as you did at first. Then I came to ask myself: how does it happen that the Lithians not only have no deviants —think of that, *no* deviants—but it just happens, by the uttermost of all coincidences, that the code by which they live so perfectly is point for point the code we strive to obey. Consider, please, the imponderables involved in such a coincidence. Even on Earth we never have found a society which evolved independently *exactly* the same precepts as the Christian precepts. Oh, there were some duplications, enough to encourage the twentieth century's partiality toward synthetic religions like Theosophism and Hollywood Vedanta, but no ethical system on Earth that grew up independently of Christianity agreed with it point for point.

"And yet here, forty light-years from Earth, what do we find? A Christian people, lacking nothing but the specific proper names and the symbolic appurtenances of Christianity. I don't know how you three react to this, but I found it extraordinary and indeed completely impossible—mathematically impossible—under any assumption but one. I'll get to that assumption in a moment."

"You can't get there too soon for me," Cleaver said morosely. "How a man can stand forty light-years from home in deep space and talk such parochial nonsense is beyond my comprehension."

"Parochial?" Ruiz-Sanchez said, more angrily than he had intended. "Do you mean that what we think true on Earth is automatically made suspect just by the fact of its removal into deep space? I beg to remind you, Cleaver, that quantum mechanics seems to hold good on Lithia, and that you see nothing parochial about behaving as if it did. If I believe in Peru that God created the universe, I see nothing parochial about believing it on Lithia.

"A while back I thought I had been provided an escape hatch, incidentally. Chtexa told me that the Lithians would like to modify the growth of their population, and he implied that they would welcome some form of birth control. But, as it turned out, birth control in the sense that my Church interdicts it is impossible to Lithia, and what Chtexa had in mind was obviously some form of conception control, a proposition to which my Church has already given its qualified assent. So there I was, even on this small point, forced again to realize that we had found on Lithia the most colossal rebuke to our aspirations that we had ever encountered: a people that seemed to live with ease the kind of life which we associate with saints alone.

"Bear in mind that a Muslim who visited Lithia would find no such thing. Neither would a Taoist. Neither would a Zoroastrian, presuming that there were still such, or a classical Greek. But for the four of us—and I include you, Cleaver, for despite your tricks and your agnosticism you still subscribe to the Christian ethical doctrines enough to be put on the defensive when you flout them—what we have here on Lithia is a coincidence which beggars description. It is more than an astronomical coincidence—that tired old phrase for numbers that do not seem very large any more—it is a transfinite coincidence. It would take Cantor himself to do justice to the odds against it."

"Wait a minute," Agronski said. "Holy smoke. Mike, I don't know any anthropology, I'm lost here. I was with the father up to the part about the mixed forest, but I don't have any standards to judge the rest. Is it so, what he says?"

"Yes, I think it's so," Michelis said slowly. "But there could be differences of opinion as to what it means, if anything. Ramon, go on."

"I've scarcely begun. I'm still describing the planet, and more particularly the Lithians. The Lithians take a lot of explaining; what I've said about them thus far states only the most obvious fact. I could go on to point out many more equally obvious facts that they have no nations and no national rivalries (and if you'll look at the map of Lithia you'll see every reason why they should have developed such rivalries), that they have emotions and passions but are never moved by them to irrational acts, that they have only one language, that they exist in complete harmony with everything, large and small, that they find in their world. In short, they are a people that couldn't exist, and yet do.

"Mike, I'd go beyond your view to say that the Lithians are the most perfect example of how human beings *ought* to behave than we're ever likely to find, for the very simple reason that they behave now the way human beings once did before a series of things happened of which we have record. I'd go even farther beyond it, far enough to say that as an example the Lithians are useless to us, because until the coming of the Kingdom of God no substantial number of human beings will ever be able to imitate Lithian conduct. Human beings seem to have built-in imperfections that the Lithians lack, so that after thousands of years of trying we are farther away than ever from our original emblems of conduct, while the Lithians have never departed from theirs.

"And don't allow yourselves to forget for an instant that these emblems of conduct are the same on both planets. That couldn't ever have happened, either. But it did.

"I'm now going to describe another interesting fact about Lithian civilization. It is a fact, whatever you may think of its merits as evidence. It is this: that your Lithian is a creature of logic. Unlike Earthmen of all stripes, he has no gods, no myths, no legends. He has no belief in the supernatural, or, as we're calling it in our barbarous jargon these days, the 'paranormal.' He has no traditions. He has no tabus. He has no faiths, blind or otherwise. He is as rational as a machine. Indeed, the only way in which we can distinguish the Lithian from an organic computer is his possession and use of a moral code.

"And that, I beg you to observe, is completely irrational. It is based upon a set of axioms, of propositions which were 'given' from the beginning—though your Lithian will not allow that there was ever any Giver. The Lithian, for instance Chtexa, believes in the sanctity of the individual. Why? Not by reason, surely, for there is no way to reason to that proposition. It is an axiom. Chtexa believes in juridical defence, in the equality of all before the code. Why? It's possible to behave reasonably *from* the proposition but not to reason one's way *to* it.

"If you assume that the responsibility to the code varies with age, or with the nature of one's work, or with what family you happen to belong to, logical behavior can follow from one of those assumptions, but there again one can't arrive at the principle by reason alone. One begins with belief: 'I think that all people ought to be equal before the law.' That is a statement of faith. Nothing more. Yet Lithian civilization is so set up as to suggest that one can arrive at such basic axioms of Christianity, and of Western civilization on Earth as a whole, by reason alone, in the plain face of the fact that one cannot."

"Those are axioms," Cleaver growled. "You don't arrive at them by faith, either. You don't arrive at them at all. They're self-evident."

"Like the axiom that only one parallel can be drawn to a given line? Go on, Cleaver, you are a physicist; kick a stone for me and tell me it's self-evident that the thing is solid."

"It's peculiar," Michelis said in a low voice, "that Lithian culture should be so axiom-ridden without the Lithians being aware of it. I hadn't formulated it in quite this way before, Ramon, but I've been disturbed myself at the bottomless assumptions that lie behind Lithian reasoning. Look at what they've done in solid-state physics, for instance. It's a structure of the purest kind of reason, and yet when you get down to its fundamental assumptions you discover the axiom that matter is real. How can they know that? How did logic lead them to it? If I say that the atom is just a hole-inside-a-hole-through-a-hole, where can reason intervene?"

"But it works," Cleaver said.

"So does our solid-state physics—but we work on opposite axioms," Michelis said. "That's not the issue. I don't myself see how this immense structure of reason which the Lithians have evolved can stand for an instant. It does not seem to rest on anything."

"I'm going to tell you," Ruiz-Sanchez said. "You won't believe me, but I'm going to tell you anyhow, because I have to. *It stands because it's being propped up.* That's the simple answer and the whole answer. But first I want to add one more fact about the Lithians.

"They have complete physical recapitulation outside the body."

"What does that mean?" Agronski said.

"Do you know how a human child grows inside its mother's body? It is a one-cell animal to begin with, and then a simple metazoan resembling the freshwater hydra or the simplest jellyfish. Then, very rapidly, it goes through many other animal forms, including the fish, the amphibian, the reptile, the lower mammal, and finally becomes enough like a man to be born. This process biologists call recapitulation.

"They assume that the embryo is passing through the various stages of evolution which brought life from the single-celled organism to man, on a contracted time scale. There is a point, for instance, in the development of the fetus when it has gills. It has a tail almost to the very end of its time in the womb, and sometimes still has it when it is born. Its circulatory system at one point is reptilian, and if it fails to pass successfully through that stage, it is born as a 'blue baby' with patent ductus arteriosus, the tetralogy of Fallot or a similar heart defect. And so on."

"I see," Agronski said. "I've encountered the idea before, of course, but I didn't recognize the term."

"Well, the Lithians, too, go through this series of metamorphoses as they grow up, but they go through it *outside* the bodies of their mothers. This whole planet is one huge womb. The Lithian female lays her eggs in her abdominal pouch, and then goes to the sea to give birth to her children. What she bears is not a reptile, but a fish. The fish lives in the sea a while, and then develops rudimentary lungs and comes ashore. Stranded by the tides on the flats, the lungfish develops rudimentary legs and squirms in the mud, becoming an amphibian and learning to endure the rigors of living away from the sea. Gradually their limbs become stronger, and better set on their bodies, and they become the big froglike things we sometimes see leaping in the moonlight, trying to get away from the crocodiles.

"Many of them do get away. They carry their habit of leaping with them into the jungle, and there they change once again to became the small, kangaroolike reptiles we've all seen, at one time or another, fleeing from us among the trees. Eventually, they emerge, fully grown, from the jungles and take their places among the folk of the cities as young Lithians, ready for education. But they have already learned every trick of every environment that their world has to offer except those of their own civilization."

Michelis locked his hands together again and looked up at Ruiz-Sanchez. "But that's a discovery beyond price!" he said with quiet excitement. "Ramon, that alone is worth our trip to Lithia. I can't imagine why it would lead you to ask that the planet be closed! Surely your Church can't object to it in any way—after all, your theorists did accept recapitulation in the human embryo, and also the geological record that showed the same process in action over longer spans of time."

"Not," Ruiz-Sanchez said, "in the way that you think we did. The Church accepted the facts, as it always accepts facts. But—as you yourself suggested not ten minutes ago—facts have a way of pointing in several different directions at once. The Church is as hostile to the doctrine of evolution—particularly in respect to man—as it ever was, and with good reason."

"Or with obdurate stupidity," Cleaver said.

"All right, Paul, look at it very simply with the original premises of the Bible in mind. If we assume just for the sake of argument that God created man, did he create him perfect? I should suppose that he did. Is a man perfect without a navel? I don't know, but I'd be inclined to say that he isn't. Yet the first man—Adam, again for the sake of argument—wasn't born of woman, and so didn't really *need* to have a navel. Nevertheless he would have been imperfect without it, and I'll bet that he had one."

"What does that prove?"

"That the geological record, and recapitulation too, do not prove the doctrine of evolution. Given *my* initial axiom, which is that God created everything from scratch, it's perfectly logical that he should have given Adam a navel, Earth a geological record and the embryo the process of recapitulation. None of these indicate a real past; all are there because the creations involved would have been imperfect otherwise."

"Wow," Cleaver said. "And I used to think that Milne relativity was abstruse."

"Oh, any coherent system of thought becomes abstruse if it's examined long enough. I don't see why my belief in a God you can't accept is any more rarefied than Mike's vision of the atom as a hole-inside-a-hole-through-a-hole. I expect that in the long run, when we get right down to the fundamental particles of the universe, we'll find that there's nothing there at all—just nothings moving no-place through no-time. On the day that that happens, I'll have God and you will not—otherwise there'll be no difference between us.

"But in the meantime, what we have here on Lithia is very clear indeed. We have—and now I'm prepared to be blunt—a planet and a people propped up by the Ultimate Enemy. It is a gigantic trap prepared for all of us. We can do nothing with it but reject it, nothing but say to it, *Retro me, Sathanas.* If we compromise with it in any way, we are damned."

"Why, father?" Michelis said quietly.

"Look at the premises, Mike. One: reason is always a sufficient guide. Two: the self-evident is always the real. Three: good works are an end in themselves. Four: faith is irrelevant to right action. Five: right action can exist without love. Six: peace need not pass understanding. Seven: ethics can exist without evil alternatives. Eight: morals can exist without conscience. Nine—but do I really need to go on? We have heard all these propositions before, and we know who proposes them.

"And we have seen these demonstrations before—the demonstration, for instance, in the rocks which was supposed to show how the horse evolved from Eohippus, but which somehow never managed to convince the whole of mankind. Then the discovery of intra-uterine recapitulation, which was to have clinched the case for the so-called descent of man— and yet, somehow, failed again to produce general agreement. These were both very subtle arguments, but the Church is not easily swayed; it is founded on a rock.

"Now we have, on Lithia, a new demonstration, both the subtlest and at the same time the crudest of all. It will sway many people who could have been swayed in no other way, and who lack the intelligence or the background to understand that it is a rigged demonstration. It seems to show us evolution in action on an inarguable scale. It is supposed to settle the question once and for all, to rule God out of the picture, to snap the chains that have held Peter's rock together all these many centuries. Henceforth there is to be no more question; there is to be no more God, but only phenomenology—and, of course, behind the scenes, within the hole that's inside the hole that's through a hole, the Great Nothing itself, the thing that has never learned any word but *no:* it has many other names, but we know the name that counts. That's left us.

"Paul, Mike, Agronski, I have nothing more to say than this: we are all of us standing on the brink of hell. By the grace of God, we may still turn back. We must turn back—for I at least think that this is our last chance."

## IX

The vote was cast, and that was that. The commission was tied, and the question would be thrown open again in higher echelons on Earth, which would mean tying Lithia up for years to come. The planet was now, in effect, on the Index.

The ship arrived the next day. The crew was not much surprised to find that the two opposing factions of the commission were hardly speaking to each other. It often happened that way.

The four commission members cleaned up the house the Lithians had given them in almost complete silence. Ruiz-Sanchez packed the blue book with the gold stamping without being able to look at it except out of the corner of his eye, but even obliquely he could not help seeing its title:

FINNEGANS WAKE
*James Joyce*

He felt as though he himself had been collated, bound and stamped, a tortured human text for future generations of Jesuits to explicate and argue.

He had rendered the verdict he had found it necessary for him to render. But he knew that it was not a final verdict, even for himself, and certainly not for the UN, let alone the Church. Instead, the verdict itself would be the knotty question for members of his Order yet unborn:

*Did Father Ruiz-Sanchez correctly interpret the divine case, and did his ruling, if so, follow from it?*

"Let's go, father. It'll be take-off time in a few minutes."

"All ready, Mike."

It was only a short journey to the clearing, where the mighty spindle of the ship stood ready to weave its way back through the geodesics of deep space to the sun that shone on Peru. The baggage went on board smoothly and without fuss. So did the specimens, the films, the special reports, the recordings, the sample cases, the vivariums, the aquariums, the type-cultures, the pressed plants, the tubes of soil, the chunks of ore, the Lithian manuscripts in their atmosphere of neon; everything was lifted decorously by the cranes and swung inside.

Agronski went up the cleats to the airlock first, with Michelis following him. Cleaver was stowing some last-minute bit of gear, something that seemed to require delicate, almost reverent care before the cranes could be allowed to take it in their indifferent grip. Ruiz-Sanchez took advantage of the slight delay to look around once more at the near margins of the forest.

At once, he saw Chtexa. The Lithian was standing at the entrance to the path the Earthmen themselves had taken away from the city to reach the ship. He was carrying something.

Cleaver swore under his breath and undid something he had just done to do it in another way. Ruiz-Sanchez raised his hand. Immediately Chtexa walked toward the ship.

"I wish you a good journey," the Lithian said, "wherever you may go. I wish also that your road may lead back to this world at some future time. I have brought you the gift that I sought before to give you, if the moment is appropriate."

Cleaver had straightened up and was now glaring suspiciously at the Lithian. Since he did not understand the language, he was unable to find anything to which he could object; he simply stood and radiated unwelcomeness.

"Thank you," Ruiz-Sanchez said. This creature of Satan made him miserable, made him feel intolerably in the wrong. How could Chtexa know—?

The Lithian was holding out to him a small vase, sealed at the top and provided with two gently looping handles. The gleaming porcelain of which it had been made still carried inside it, under the glaze, the fire which had formed it; it was iridescent, alive with long quivering festoons and plumes of rainbows, and the form as a whole would have made any potter of Greece abandon his trade in shame. It was so beautiful that one could imagine no use for it at all. Certainly one could not fill it with left-over beets and put it in the refrigerator. Besides, it would take up too much space.

"This is my gift," Chtexa said. "It is the finest container yet to come from Xoredeshch Gton; the material of which it is made contains traces of every element to be found on Lithia, even including iron, and thus, as you see, it shows the colors of every shade of emotion and of thought. On Earth, it will tell Earthmen much of Lithia."

"We will be unable to analyze it," Ruiz-Sanchez said. "It is too perfect to destroy, too perfect even to open."

"Ah, but we wish you to open it," Chtexa said. "For it contains our other gift."

"Another gift?"

"Yes, a more important one. A fertilized, living egg of our species. Take it with you. By the time you reach Earth, it will be ready to hatch, and to grow up with you in your strange and marvelous world. The container is the gift of all of us; but the child inside is my gift, for it is my child."

Ruiz-Sanchez took the vase in trembling hands, as though he expected it to explode. It shook with subdued flame in his grip.

"Goodbye," Chtexa said. He turned and walked away, back toward the entrance to the path. Cleaver watched him go, shading his eyes.

"Now what was that all about?" the physicist said. "The Snake couldn't have made a bigger thing of it if he'd been handing you his own head on a platter. And all the time it was only a pot!"

Ruiz-Sanchez did not answer. He could not have spoken even to himself. He turned away and began to ascend the cleats, cradling the vase carefully under one elbow. While he was still climbing, a shadow passed rapidly over the hull—Cleaver's last crate, being borne aloft into the hold by a crane.

Then he was in the airlock, with the rising whine of the ship's generators around him. A long shaft of light outside was cast ahead of him, picking out his shadow on the deck. After a moment, a second shadow overlaid his own: Cleaver's. Then the light dimmed and went out.

The airlock door slammed.

# Dio

*Cosmetic surgery, an obsession with diets and the desire to look youthful characterize an important value for millions of people in the Western world, who yearly spend billions of dollars in an attempt to slow the aging process. But what if one were perpetually young? This is the question addressed by Damon Knight in this powerful and moving story of immortality and the dignity of death.*

It is noon. Overhead the sky like a great silver bowl shimmers with heat; the yellow sand hurls it back; the distant ocean is dancing with white fire. Emerging from underground, Dio the Planner stands blinking a moment in the strong salt light; he feels the heat like a cap on his head, and his beard curls crisply, iridescent in the sun.

A few yards away are five men and women, their limbs glinting pink against the sand. The rest of the seascape is utterly bare; the sand seems to stretch empty and hot for miles. There is not even a gull in the air. Three of the figures are men; they are running and throwing a beach ball at one another, with far-off shouts. The two women are half reclining, watching the men. All five are superbly muscled, with great arched chests, ponderous as Percherons. Their skins are smooth; their eyes sparkle. Dio looks at his own forearm: is there a trace of darkness? is the skin coarsening?

He drops his single garment and walks toward the group. The sand's caress is briefly painful to his feet; then his skin adapts, and he no longer feels it. The five incuriously turn to watch him approach. They are all players, not students, and there are two he does not even know. He feels uncomfortable, and wishes he had not come. It isn't good for students and players to meet informally; each side is too much aware of the other's good-natured contempt. Dio tries to imagine himself a player, exerting himself to be polite to a student, and as always, he fails. The gulf is too wide. It takes both kinds to make a world, students to remember and make, players to consume and enjoy; but the classes should not mix.

Even without their clothing, these are players; the wide, innocent eyes that flash with enthusiasm, or flicker with easy boredom; the soft mouths that can be gay or sulky by turns. Now he deliberately looks at the blonde woman, Claire, and in her face he sees the same unmistakable signs. But, against all reason and usage, the soft curve of her lips is beauty; the poise of her dark blonde head on the strong neck wrings his heart. It is illogical, almost unheard-of, perhaps abnormal; but he loves her.

Her gray eyes are glowing up at him like sea-agates; the quick pleasure of her smile warms and soothes him. "I'm so glad to *see* you." She takes his hand. "You know Katha of course, and Piet. And this is Tanno, and that's Mark. Sit here and talk to me, I can't move, it's so hot."

The ball throwers go cheerfully back to their game. The brunette, Katha, begins talking immediately about the choirs at Bethany: has Dio heard them? No? But he must; the voices are stupendous, the choir-master is brilliant; nothing like it has been heard for centuries.

The word *centuries* falls carelessly. How old is Katha—eight hundred, a thousand? Recently, in a three-hundred-year-old journal, Dio has been surprised to find a reference to Katha. There are so many people; it's impossible to remember. That's why the students keep journals; and why the players don't. He might even have met Claire before, and forgotten. . . . "No," he says, smiling politely, "I've been rather busy with a project."

"Dio is an Architectural Planner," says Claire, mocking him with the exaggerated syllables; and yet there's a curious, inverted pride in her voice. "I told you, Kat, he's a student among students. He rebuilds this whole sector, every year."

"Oh," says Katha, wide-eyed, "I think that's absolutely fascinating." A moment later, without pausing, she has changed the subject to the new sky circus in Littlam—perfectly vulgar, but hilarious. The sky clowns! The tumblers! The delicious mock animals!

Claire's smooth face is close to his, haloed by the sun, gilded from below by the reflection of the hot sand. Her half-closed eyelids are delicate and soft, bruised by heat; her pupils are contracted, and the wide gray irises are intricately patterned. A fragment floats to the top of his mind, something he has read about the structure of the iris: raylike dilating muscles interlaced with a circular contractile set, pigmented with a little melanin. For some reason, the thought is distasteful, and he pushes it aside. He feels a little light-headed; he has been working too hard.

"Tired?" she asks, her voice gentle.

He relaxes a little. The brunette, Katha, is still talking; she is one of those who talk and never care if anyone listens. He answers, "This is our busiest time. All the designs are coming back for a final check before they go into the master integrator. It's our last chance to find any mistakes."

"Dio, I'm sorry," she says contritely. "I know I shouldn't have asked you." Her brows go up; she looks at him anxiously under her lashes. "You should rest, though."

"Yes," says Dio.

She lays her soft palm on the nape of his neck. "Rest, then. Rest."

"Ah," says Dio wearily, letting his head drop into the crook of his arm. Under the sand where he lies are seventeen inhabited levels of which three are his immediate concern, over a sector that reaches from Alban to Detroy. He has been working almost without sleep for two weeks. Next season there is talk of beginning an eighteenth level; it will mean raising the surface again, and all the force-planes will have to be shifted. The details swim past, thousands of them; behind his closed eyes, he sees architectural tracings, blueprints, code sheets, specifications.

"Darling," says her caressing voice in his ear, "you know I'm happy you came, anyhow, even if you didn't want to. *Because* you didn't want to. Do you understand that?"

He peers at her with one half-open eye. "A feeling of power?" he suggests ironically.

"*No.* Reassurance is more like it. Did you know I was jealous of your work? . . . I am, very much. I told myself: if he'll just leave his project, now, today—"

He rolls over, smiling crookedly up at her. "And yet you don't know one day from the next."

Her answering smile is quick and shy. "I know, isn't it awful of me: but *you* do."

As they look at each other in silence, he is aware again of the gulf between them. *They need us*, he thinks, *to make their world over every year —keep it bright and fresh, cover up the past—but they dislike us because they know that whatever they forget, we keep and remember.*

His hand finds hers. A deep, unreasoning sadness wells up in him; he asks silently, *Why should I love you?*

He has not spoken, but he sees her face contract into a rueful, pained smile; and her fingers grip hard.

Above them, the shouts of the ball throwers have changed to noisy protests. Dio looks up. Piet, the cotton-headed man, laughing, is afloat over the heads of the other two. He comes down slowly and throws the ball; the game goes on. But a moment later Piet is in the air again: the others shout angrily, and Tanno leaps up to wrestle with him. The ball drops, bounds away: the two striving figures turn and roll in midair. At length the cotton-headed man forces the other down to the sand. They both leap up and run over, laughing.

"Someone's got to tame this wild man," says the loser, panting. "I can't do it, he's too slippery. How about you, Dio?"

"He's resting," Claire protests, but the others chorus, "Oh, yes!" "Just a fall or two," says Piet, with a wide grin, rubbing his hands together. "There's lots of time before the tide comes in—unless you'd rather not?"

Dio gets reluctantly to his feet. Grinning, Piet floats up off the sand. Dio follows, feeling the taut surge of back and chest muscles, and the curious sensation of pressure on the spine. The two men circle, rising slowly. Piet whips his body over, head downward, arms slashing for Dio's legs. Dio overleaps him, and, turning, tries for a leg-and-arm; but Piet squirms away like an eel and catches him in a waist lock. Dio strains against the taut chest, all his muscles knotting; the two men hang unbalanced for a moment. Then, suddenly, something gives way in the force that buoys Dio up. They go over together, hard and awkwardly into the sand. There is a surprised babble of voices.

Dio picks himself up. Piet is kneeling nearby, whitefaced, holding his forearm. "Bent?" asks Mark, bending to touch it gently.

"Came down with all my weight," says Piet. "Wasn't expecting—" He nods at Dio. "That's a new one."

"Well, let's hurry and fix it," says the other, "or you'll miss the spout." Piet lays the damaged forearm across his own thighs. "Ready?" Mark plants his bare foot on the arm, leans forward and presses sharply down. Piet winces, then smiles; the arm is straight.

"Sit down and let it knit," says the other. He turns to Dio. "What's this?"

Dio is just becoming aware of a sharp pain in one finger, and dark blood welling. "Just turned back the nail a little," says Mark. "Press it down, it'll close in a second."

Katha suggests a word game, and in a moment they are all sitting in a circle, shouting letters at each other. Dio does poorly; he cannot forget the dark blood falling from his fingertip. The silver sky seems oppressively distant; he is tired of the heat that pours down on his head, of the breathless air and the sand like hot metal under his body. He has a sense of helpless fear, as if something terrible had already happened; as if it were too late.

Someone says, "It's time," and they all stand up, whisking sand from their bodies. "Come on," says Claire over her shoulder. "Have you ever been up the spout? It's fun."

"No, I must get back, I'll call you later," says Dio. Her fingers lie softly on his chest as he kisses her briefly, then he steps away. "Good-by," he calls to the others, "good-by," and turning, trudges away over the sand.

The rest, relieved to be free of him, are halfway to the rocks above the water's edge. A white feather of spray dances from a fissure as the sea rushes into the cavern below. The water slides back, leaving mirror-wet sand that dries in a breath. It gathers itself; far out a comber lifts its green head, and rushes onward. "Not this one, but the next," calls Tanno.

"Claire," says Katha, approaching her, "it was so peculiar about your friend. Did you notice? When he left, his finger was still bleeding."

The white plume leaps higher, provoking a gust of nervous laughter. Piet dances up after it, waving his legs in a burlesque entrechat. "What?" says Claire. "You must be wrong. It couldn't have been."

"Now, come on, everybody. Hang close!"

"All the same," says Katha, "it was bleeding." No one hears her; she is used to that.

Far out, the comber lifts its head menacingly high; it comes onward, white-crowned, hard as bottle glass below, rising, faster, and as it roars with a shuddering of earth into the cavern, the Immortals are dashed high on the white torrent, screaming their joy.

Dio is in his empty rooms alone, pacing the resilient floor, smothered in silence. He pauses, sweeps a mirror into being on the bare wall: leans forward to peer at his own gray face, then wipes the mirror out again. All around him the universe presses down, enormous, inexorable.

The time stripe on the wall has turned almost black: the day is over. He has been here alone all afternoon. His door and phone circuits are set to reject callers, even Claire—his only instinct has been to hide.

A scrap of yellow cloth is tied around the hurt finger. Blood has saturated the cloth and dried, and now it is stuck tight. The blood has stopped, but the hurt nail has still not reattached itself. There is something wrong with him; how could there be anything wrong with him?

He has felt it coming for days, drawing closer, invisibly. Now it is here.

It has been eight hours . . . his finger has still not healed itself.

He remembers that moment in the air, when the support dropped away under him. Could that happen again? He plants his feet firmly now, thinks, *Up*, and feels the familiar straining of his back and chest. But nothing happens. Incredulously, he tries again. Nothing!

His heart is thundering in his chest; he feels dizzy and cold. He sways, almost falls. It isn't possible that this should be happening to him. . . . Help; he must have help. Under his trembling fingers the phone index lights; he finds Claire's name, presses the selector. She may have gone out by now, but sector registry will find her. The screen pulses grayly. He waits. The darkness is a little farther away. Claire will help him, will think of something.

The screen lights, but it is only the neutral gray face of an autosec. "One moment please."

The screen flickers; at last, Claire's face!

"—is a recording, Dio. When you didn't call, and I couldn't reach you, I was very hurt. I know you're busy, but—Well, Piet has asked me to go over to Toria to play skeet polo, and I'm going. I may stay a few weeks for the flower festival, or go on to Rome. I'm sorry, Dio, we started out so nicely. Maybe the classes really don't mix. Good-by."

The screen darkens. Dio is down on his knees before it. "Don't go," he says breathlessly. "Don't go." His last courage is broken; the hot, salt, shameful tears drop from his eyes.

The room is bright and bare, but in the corners the darkness is gathering, curling high, black as obsidian, waiting to rush.

## II

The crowds on the lower level are a river of color, deep electric blue, scarlet, opaque yellow, all clean, crisp and bright. Flower scents puff from the folds of loose garments; the air is filled with good-natured voices and laughter. Back from five months' wandering in Africa, Pacifica and Europe, Claire is delightfully lost among the moving ways of Sector Twenty. Where the main concourse used to be, there is a maze of narrow adventure streets, full of gay banners and musky with perfume. The excursion cars are elegant little baskets of silver filigree, hung with airy grace. She gets into one and soars up the canyon of windows on a long, sweeping curve, past terraces and balconies, glimpse after intimate glimpse of people she need never see again: here a woman feeding a big blue macaw, there a couple of children staring at her from a garden, solemn-eyed, both with ragged yellow hair like dandelions. How long it has been since she last saw a child! . . . She tries to imagine what it must be like, to be a child now in this huge world full of grown people, but she can't. Her memories of her own childhood are so far away, quaint and small, like figures in the wrong side of an opera glass. Now here is a man with a bushy black beard, balancing a bottle on his nose for a group of laughing people . . . off it goes! Here are two couples obliviously kissing. . . . Her heart beats a little faster; she feels the color coming into her cheeks. Piet was so tiresome, after a while; she wants to forget him now. She has already forgotten him; she hums in her sweet, clear contralto, "Dio, Dio, Dio . . ."

On the next level she dismounts and takes a robocab. She punches Dio's name; the little green-eyed driver "hunts" for a moment, flickering; then the cab swings around purposefully and gathers speed.

The building is unrecognizable; the white street has been done over in baroque facades of vermilion and green. The shape of the lobby is familiar, though, and here is Dio's name on the directory.

She hesitates, looking up the uninformative blank shaft of the elevator well. Is he there, behind that silent bulk of marble? After a moment she turns with a shrug and takes the nearest of a row of fragile silver chairs. She presses "three"; the chair whisks her up, decants her.

She is in the vestibule of Dio's apartment. The walls are faced with cool blue-veined marble. On one side, the spacious oval of the shaft opening; on the other, the wide, arched doorway, closed. A mobile turns slowly under the lofty ceiling. She steps on the annunciator plate.

"Yes?" A pleasant male voice, but not a familiar one. The screen does not light.

She gives her name. "I want to see Dio—is he in?"

A curious pause. "Yes, he's *in*. . . . Who sent you?"

"No one *sent* me." She has the frustrating sense that they are at cross purposes, talking about different things. "Who are you?"

"That doesn't matter. Well, you can come in, though I don't know when you'll get time today." The doors slide open.

Bewildered and more than half-angry, Claire crosses the threshold. The first room is a cool gray cavern: overhead are fixed-circuit screens showing views of the sector streets. They make a bright frieze around the walls, but shed little light.

The next room is a huge disorderly space full of machinery carelessly set down; Claire wrinkles her nose in distaste. Down at the far end, a few men are bending over one of the machines, their backs turned. She moves on.

The third room is a cool green space, terrazzo-floored, with a fountain playing in the middle. Her sandals click pleasantly on the hard surface. Fifteen or twenty people are sitting on the low curving benches around the walls, using the service machines, readers and so on: it's for all the world like the waiting room of a fashionable healer. Has Dio taken up mind-fixing?

Suddenly unsure of herself, she takes an isolated seat and looks around her. No, her first impression was wrong, these are not clients waiting to see a healer, because, in the first place, they are all students—every one.

She looks them over more carefully. Two are playing chess in an alcove; two more are strolling up and down separately; five or six are grouped around a little table on which some papers are spread; one of these is talking rapidly while the rest listen. The distance is too great; Claire cannot catch any words.

Farther down on the other side of the room, two men and a woman are sitting at a hooded screen, watching it intently, although at this distance it appears dark.

Water tinkles steadily in the fountain. After a long time the inner doors open and a man emerges; he leans over and speaks to another man sitting nearby. The second man gets up and goes through the inner doors; the first moves out of sight in the opposite direction. Neither reappears. Claire waits, but nothing more happens.

No one has taken her name, or put her on a list; no one seems to be paying her any attention. She rises and walks slowly down the room, past the group at the table. Two of the men are talking vehemently, interrupting each other. She listens as she passes, but it is all student gibberish: "the delta curve clearly shows . . . a stochastic assumption . . ." She moves on to the three who sit at the screen.

The screen still seems dark to Claire, but faint glints of color move on its glossy surface, and there is a whisper of sound.

There are two vacant seats. She hesitates, then takes one of them and leans forward under the hood.

Now the screen is alight, and there is a murmur of talk in her ears. She is looking into a room dominated by a huge oblong slab of gray marble, three times the height of a man. Though solid, its appears to be descending with a steady and hypnotic motion, like a waterfall.

Under this falling curtain of stone sit two men. One of them is a stranger. The other—

She leans forward, peering. The other is in shadow; she cannot see his features. Still, there is something familiar about the outlines of his head and body. . . .

She is almost sure it is Dio, but when he speaks she hesitates again. It is a strange, low, hoarse voice, unlike anything she has ever heard before: the sound is so strange that she forgets to listen for the words.

Now the other man is speaking: "—these notions. It's just an ordinary procedure—one more injection."

"No," says the dark man with repressed fury, and abruptly stands up. The lights in that pictured room flicker as he moves, and the shadow swerves to follow him.

"Pardon me," says an unexpected voice at her ear. The man next to her is leaning over, looking inquisitive. "I don't think you're authorized to watch this session, are you?"

Claire makes an impatient gesture at him, turning back fascinated to the screen. In the pictured room, both men are standing now; the dark man is saying something hoarsely while the other moves as if to take his arm.

"Please," says the voice at her ear, "*are* you authorized to watch this session?"

The dark man's voice has risen to a hysterical shout—hoarse and thin, like no human voice in the world. In the screen, he whirls and makes as if to run back into the room.

"Catch him!" says the other, lunging after the running form.

The dark man doubles back suddenly, past the other who reaches for him. Then two other men run past the screen; then the room is vacant: only the moving slab drops steadily, smoothly, into the floor.

The three beside Claire are standing. Across the room, heads turn. "What is it?" someone calls.

One of the men calls back, "He's having some kind of a fit!" In a lower voice, to the woman, he adds, "It's the discomfort, I suppose. . . ."

Claire is watching, uncomprehendingly, when a sudden yell from the far side of the room makes her turn.

The doors have swung back, and in the opening a shouting man is wrestling helplessly with two others. They have his arms pinned and he cannot move any farther, but that horrible, hoarse voice goes on shouting, and shouting. . . .

There are no more shadows: she can see his face.

"Dio!" she calls, getting to her feet.

Through his own din, he hears her and his head turns. His face gapes blindly at her, swollen and red, the eyes glaring. Then with a violent motion he turns away. One arm comes free, and jerks up to shield his head. He is hurrying away; the others follow. The doors close. The room is full of standing figures, and a murmur of voices.

Claire stands where she is, stunned, until a slender figure separates itself from the crowd. That other face seems to hang in the air, obscuring his —red and distorted, mouth agape.

The man takes her by the elbow, urges her toward the outer door. "What are you to Dio? Did you know him before?"

"Before what?" she asks faintly. They are crossing the room of machines, empty and echoing.

"Hm. I remember you now—I let you in, didn't I? Sorry you came?" His tone is light and negligent; she has the feeling that his attention is not really on what he is saying. A faint irritation at this is the first thing she feels through her numbness. She stirs as they walk, disengaging her arm from his grasp. She says, "What was wrong with him?"

"A very rare complaint," answers the other without pausing. They are in the outer room now, in the gloom under the bright frieze, moving toward the doors. "Didn't you know?" he asks in the same careless tone.

"I've been away." She stops, turns to face him. "Can't you tell me? What *is* wrong with Dio?"

She sees now that he has a thin face, nose and lips keen, eyes bright and narrow. "Nothing you want to know about," he says curtly. He waves at the door control, and the doors slide noiselessly apart. "Good-by."

She does not move, and after a moment the doors close again. *"What's wrong with him?"* she says.

He sighs, looking down at her modish robe with its delicate clasps of gold. "How can I tell you? Does the verb *to die* mean anything to you?"

She is puzzled and apprehensive. "I don't know . . . isn't it something that happens to the lower animals?"

He gives her a quick mock bow. "Very good."

"But I don't know what it is. Is it—a kind of fit, like—" She nods toward the inner rooms.

He is staring at her with an expression half-compassionate, half-wildly exasperated. "Do you really want to know?" He turns abruptly and runs his fingers down a suddenly glowing index stripe on the wall. "Let's see . . . don't know what there is in this damned reservoir. Hm. Animals, terminus." At his finger's touch, a cabinet opens and tips out a shallow oblong box into his palm. He offers it.

In her hands, the box lights up; she is looking into a cage in which a small animal crouches—a white rat. Its fur is dull and rough-looking; something is caked around its muzzle. It moves unsteadily, noses a cup of water, then turns away. Its legs seem to fail; it drops and lies motionless except for the slow rise and fall of its tiny chest.

Watching, Claire tries to control her nausea. Students' cabinets are full of nastinesses like this; they expect you not to show any distaste. "Something's the matter with it," is all she can find to say.

"Yes. It's dying. That means to cease living: to stop. Not to be any more. Understand?"

"No," she breathes. In the box, the small body has stopped moving. The mouth is stiffly open, the lip drawn back from the yellow teeth. The eye does not move, but glares up sightless.

"That's all," says her companion, taking the box back. "No more rat. Finished. After a while it begins to decompose and make a bad smell, and a while after that, there's nothing left but bones. And that has happened to every rat that was ever born."

"I don't *believe* you," she says. "It isn't like that; I never heard of such a thing."

"Didn't you ever have a pet?" he demands. "A parakeet, a cat, a tank of fish?"

"Yes," she says defensively, "I've had cats, and birds. What of it?"

"What happened to them?"

"Well—*I* don't know, I suppose I lost them. You know how you lose things."

"One day they're there, the next, not," says the thin man. "Correct?"

"Yes, that's right. But why?"

"We have such a tidy world," he says wearily. "Dead bodies would clutter it up; that's why the house circuits are programmed to remove them when nobody is in the room. Every one: it's part of the basic design. Of course, if you stayed in the room, and didn't turn your back, the machine would have to embarrass you by cleaning up the corpse in front of your eyes. But that never happens. Whenever you saw there was something wrong with any pet of yours, you turned around and went away, isn't that right?"

"Well, I really can't remember—"

"And when you came back, how odd, the beast was gone. It wasn't 'lost,' it was dead. They die. They all die."

She looks at him, shivering. "But that doesn't happen to *people.*"

"No?" His lips are tight. After a moment he adds, "Why do you think he looked that way? You see he knows; he's known for five months."

She catches her breath suddenly. "That day at the beach!"

"Oh, were you there?" He nods several times, and opens the door again. "Very interesting for you. You can tell people you saw it happen." He pushes her gently out into the vestibule.

"But I want—" she says desperately.

"What? To love him again, as if he were normal? Or do you want to help him? Is that what you mean?" His thin face is drawn tight, arrow-shaped between the brows. "Do you think you could stand it? If so—" He stands aside, as if to let her enter again.

She takes a step forward, hesitantly.

"Remember the rat," he says sharply.

She stops.

"It's up to you. Do you really want to help him? He could use some help, if it wouldn't make you sick. Or else—Where were you all this time?"

"Various places," she says stiffly. "Littlam, Paris, New Hol."

He nods. "Or you can go back and see them all again. Which?"

She does not move. Behind her eyes, now, the two images are intermingled: she sees Dio's gorged face staring through the stiff jaw of the rat.

The thin man nods briskly. He steps back, holding her gaze. There is a long suspended moment; then the doors close.

## III

The years fall away like pages from an old notebook. Claire is in Stambul, Winthur, Kumoto, BahiBlanc . . . other places, too many to remember. There are the intercontinental games, held every century on the baroque wheel-shaped ground in Campan: Claire is one of the spectators who hover in clouds, following their favorites. There is a love affair, brief but intense; it lasts four or five years; the man's name is Nord, he has gone off now with another woman to Deya, and for nearly a month Claire has been inconsolable. But now comes the opera season in Milan, and in Tusca, afterwards, she meets some charming people who are going to spend a year in Papeete. . . .

Life is good. Each morning she awakes refreshed; her lungs fill with the clean air; the blood tingles in her fingertips.

On a spring morning, she is basking in a bubble of green glass, three-quarters submerged in an emerald green ocean. The water sways and breaks, frothily, around the bright disk of sunlight at the top. Down below where she lies, the cool green depths are like mint to the fire white bite of the sun. Tiny flat golden fishes swarm up to the bubble, turn, glinting like tarnished coins, and flow away again. The memory unit near the floor of the bubble is muttering out a muted tempest of Wagner: half-listening, she hears the familiar music mixed with a gabble of foreign syllables. Her companion, with his massive bronze head almost touching the speakers, is listening attentively. Claire feels a little annoyed; she prods him with a bare foot: "Ross, turn that horrible thing off, won't you please?"

He looks up, his blunt face aggrieved. "It's *The Rhinegold.*"

"Yes, I know, but I can't understand a word. It sounds as if they're clearing their throats. . . . Thank you."

He has waved a dismissing hand at the speakers, and the guttural chorus subsides. "Billions of people spoke that language once," he says portentously. Ross is an artist, which makes him almost a player, really, but he has the student's compulsive habit of bringing out these little kernels of information to lay in your lap.

"And I can't even stand four of them," she says lazily. "I only listen to opera for the music, anyhow, the stories are always so foolish; I wonder why?"

She can almost see the learned reply rising to his lips; but he represses it politely—he knows she doesn't really want an answer—and busies himself with the visor. It lights under his fingers to show a green chasm, slowly flickering with the last dim ripples of the sunlight.

"Going down now?" she asks.

"Yes, I want to get those corals." Ross is a sculptor, not a very good one, fortunately, or a very devoted one, or he would be impossible company. He has a studio on the bottom of the Mediterranean, in ten fathoms, and spends part of his time concocting menacing tangles of stylized undersea creatures. Finished with the visor, he touches the controls and the bubble drifts downward. The waters meet overhead with a white splash of spray; then the circle of light dims to yellow, to lime color, to deep green.

Beneath them now is the coral reef—acre upon acre of bare skeletal fingers, branched and splayed. A few small fish move brilliantly among the pale branches. Ross touches the controls again; the bubble drifts to a stop. He stares down through the glass for a moment, then gets up to open the inner lock door. Breathing deeply, with a distant expression, he steps in and closes the transparent door behind him. Claire sees the water spurt around his ankles. It surges up quickly to fill the airlock; when it is chest high, Ross opens the outer door and plunges out in a cloud of air bubbles.

He is a yellow kicking shape in the green water; after a few moments he is half-obscured by clouds of sediment. Claire watches, vaguely troubled; the largest corals are like bleached bone.

She fingers the memory unit for the Sea Pieces from *Peter Grimes*, without knowing why; it's cold, northern ocean music, not appropriate. The cold, far calling of the gulls makes her shiver with sadness, but she goes on listening.

Ross grows dimmer and more distant in the clouding water. At length he is only a flash, a flicker of movement down in the dusky green valley. After a long time she sees him coming back, with two or three pink corals in his hand.

Absorbed in the music, she has allowed the bubble to drift until the entrance is almost blocked by corals. Ross forces himself between them, levering himself against a tall outcropping of stone, but in a moment he seems to be in difficulty. Claire turns to the controls and backs the bubble off a few feet. The way is clear now, but Ross does not follow.

Through the glass she sees him bend over, dropping his specimens. He places both hands firmly and strains, all the great muscles of his limbs and back bulging. After a moment he straightens again, shaking his head. He is caught, she realizes; one foot is jammed into a crevice of the stone. He grins at her painfully and puts one hand to his throat. He has been out a long time.

Perhaps she can help, in the few seconds that are left. She darts into the airlock, closes and floods it. But just before the water rises over her head, she sees the man's body stiffen.

Now, with her eyes open under water, in that curious blurred light, she sees his gorged face break into lines of pain. Instantly, his face becomes another's—Dio's—vividly seen through the ghost of a dead rat's grin. The vision comes without warning, and passes.

Outside the bubble, Ross's stiff jaw wrenches open, then hangs slack. She sees the pale jelly come bulging slowly up out of his mouth; now he floats easily, eyes turned up, limbs relaxed.

Shaken, she empties the lock again, goes back inside and calls Antibe Control for a rescue cutter. She sits down and waits, careful not to look at the still body outside.

She is astonished and appalled at her own emotion. It has nothing to do with Ross, she knows: he is perfectly safe. When he breathed water, his body reacted automatically: his lungs exuded the protective jelly, consciousness ended, his heartbeat stopped. Antibe Control will be here in twenty minutes or less, but Ross could stay like that for years, if he had to. As soon as he gets out of the water, his lungs will begin to reabsorb the jelly; when they are clear, heartbeat and breathing will start again.

It's as if Ross were only acting out a part, every movement stylized and meaningful. In the moment of his pain, a barrier in her mind has gone down, and now a doorway stands open.

She makes an impatient gesture, she is not used to being tyrannized in this way. But her arm drops in defeat; the perverse attraction of that doorway is too strong. *Dio*, her mind silently calls. *Dio*.

The designer of Sector Twenty, in the time she has been away, has changed the plan of the streets "to bring the surface down." The roof of every level is a screen faithfully repeating the view from the surface, and with lighting and other ingenious tricks the weather up there is parodied down below. Just now it is a gray cold November day, a day of slanting gray rain: looking up, one sees it endlessly falling out of the leaden sky: and down here, although the air is as always pleasantly warm, the great bare slabs of the building fronts have turned bluish gray to match, and silvery insubstantial streamers are twisting endlessly down, to disappear before they strike the pavement.

Claire does not like it; it does not feel like Dio's work. The crowds have a nervous air, curious, half-protesting; they look up and laugh, but uneasily, and the refreshment bays are full of people crammed together under bright yellow light. Claire pulls her metallic cloak closer around her throat; she is thinking with melancholy of the turn of the year, and the earth turning cold and hard as iron, the trees brittle and black against the unfriendly sky. This is a time for blue skies underground, for flushed skins and honest laughter, not for this echoed grayness.

In her rooms, at least, there is cheerful warmth. She is tired and perspiring from the trip; she does not want to see anyone just yet. Some American gowns have been ordered; while she waits for them, she turns on the fire-bath in the bedroom alcove. The yellow spiky flames jet up with a black-capped *whoom*, then settle to a high murmuring curtain of yellow white. Claire binds her head in an insulating scarf, and without bothering to undress, steps into the fire.

The flame blooms up around her body, cool and caressing; the fragile gown flares and is gone in a whisper of sparks. She turns, arms outspread against the flow. Depilated, refreshed, she steps out again. Her body tingles, invigorated by the flame. Delicately, she brushes away some clinging wisps of burnt skin; the new flesh is glossy pink, slowly paling to rose and ivory.

In the wall mirror, her eyes sparkle; her lips are liquidly red, as tender and dark as the red wax that spills from the edge of a candle.

She feels a somber recklessness; she is running with the tide. Responsive to her mood, the silvered ceiling begins to run with swift bloody streaks, swirling and leaping, striking flares of light from the bronze dado and the carved crystal lacework of the furniture. With a sudden exultant laugh, Claire tumbles into the great yellow down bed: she rolls there, half-smothered, the luxuriant silky fibers cool as cream to her skin; then the mood is gone, the ceiling dims to grayness; and she sits up with an impatient murmur.

What can be wrong with her? Sobered, already regretting the summery warmth of the Mediterranean, she walks to the table where Dio's card lies. It is his reply to the formal message she sent en route; it says simply:

THE PLANNER DIO
WILL BE AT HOME.

There is a discreet chime from the delivery chute, and fabrics tumble in in billows of canary yellow, crimson, midnight blue. Claire chooses the blue, anything else would be out of key with the day; it is gauzy but long-sleeved. With it she wears no rings or necklaces, only a tiara of dark aquamarines twined in her hair.

She scarcely notices the new exterior of the building; the ascensor shaft is dark and padded now, with an endless chain of cushioned seats that slowly rise, occupied or not, like a disjointed flight of stairs. The vestibule above slowly comes into view, and she feels a curious shock of recognition.

It is the same: the same blue-veined marble, the same mobile idly turning, the same arched doorway.

Claire hesitates, alarmed and displeased. She tries to believe that she is mistaken: no scheme of decoration is ever left unchanged for as much as a year. But here it is, untouched, as if time had queerly stopped here in this room when she left it: as if she had returned, not only to the same choice, but to the same instant.

She crosses the floor reluctantly. The dark door screen looks back at her like a baited trap.

Suppose she had never gone away—what then? Whatever Dio's secret is, it has had ten years to grow, here behind this unchanged door. There it is, a darkness, waiting for her.

With a shudder of almost physical repulsion, she steps onto the annunciator plate.

The screen lights. After a moment a face comes into view. She sees without surprise that it is the thin man, the one who. . . .

He is watching her keenly. She cannot rid herself of the vision of the rat, and of the dark struggling figure in the doorway. She says, "Is Dio—" She stops, not knowing what she meant to say.

"At home?" the thin man finishes. "Yes, of course. Come in."

The doors slide open. About to step forward, she hesitates again, once more shocked to realize that the first room is also unchanged. The frieze of screens now displays a row of gray-lit streets; that is the only difference; it is as if she were looking into some far-distant world where time still had meaning, from this still, secret place where it has none.

The thin man appears in the doorway, black-robed. "My name is Benarra," he says, smiling. "Please come in; don't mind all this, you'll get used to it."

"Where is Dio?"

"Not far. . . . But we make a rule," the thin man says, "that only students are admitted to see Dio. Would you mind?"

She looks at him with indignation. "Is this a joke? Dio sent me a note . . ." She hesitates; the note was noncommittal enough, to be sure.

"You can become a student quite easily," Benarra says. "At least, you can begin, and that would be enough for today." He stands waiting, with a pleasant expression; he seems perfectly serious.

She is balanced between bewilderment and surrender. "I don't—what do you want me to do?"

"Come and see." He crosses the room, opens a narrow door. After a moment she follows.

He leads her down an inclined passage, narrow and dark. "I'm living on the floor below now," he remarks over his shoulder, "to keep out of Dio's way." The passage ends in a bright central hall from which he leads her through a doorway into dimness.

"Here your education begins," he says. On both sides, islands of light glow up slowly: in the nearest, and brightest, stands a curious group of beings, not ape, not man: black skins with a bluish sheen, tiny eyes peering upward under shelving brows, hair a dusty black. The limbs are knot-jointed like twigs; the ribs show; the bellies are soft and big. The head of the tallest comes to Claire's waist. Behind them is a brilliant glimpse of tropical sunshine, a conical mass of what looks like dried vegetable matter, trees and horned animals in the background.

"Human beings," says Benarra.

She turns a disbelieving, almost offended gaze on him. "Oh, no!"

"Yes, certainly. Extinct several thousand years. Here, another kind."

In the next island the figures are also black-skinned, but taller—shoulder high. The woman's breasts are limp leathery bags that hang to her waist. Claire grimaces. "Is something wrong with her?"

"A different standard of beauty. They did that to themselves, deliberately. Woman creating herself. See what you think of the next."

She loses count. There are coppery-skinned ones, white ones, yellowish ones, some half-naked, others elaborately trussed in metal and fabric. Moving among them, Claire feels herself suddenly grown titanic, like a mother animal among her brood: she has a flash of absurd, degrading tenderness. Yet, as she looks at these wrinkled gnomish faces, they seem to hold an ancient and stubborn wisdom that glares out at her, silently saying, *Upstart!*

"What happened to them all?"

"They died," says Benarra. "Every one."

Ignoring her troubled look, he leads her out of the hall. Behind them, the lights fall and dim.

The next room is small and cool, unobtrusively lit, unfurnished except for a desk and chair, and visitor's seat to which Benarra waves her. The domed ceiling is pierced just above their heads with round transparencies, each glowing in a different pattern of simple blue and red shapes against a colorless ground.

"They are hard to take in, I know," says Benarra. "Possibly you think they're fakes."

"No." No one could have imagined those fierce, wizened faces; somewhere, sometime, they must have existed.

A new thought strikes her. "What about *our* ancestors—what were they like?"

Benarra's gaze is cool and thoughtful. "Claire, you'll find this hard to believe. Those were our ancestors."

She is incredulous again. "Those—absurdities in there?"

"Yes. All of them."

She is stubbornly silent a moment. "But you said, they *died.*"

"They did; they died. Claire—did you think our race was always immortal?"

"Why—" She falls silent, confused and angry.

"No, impossible. Because if we were, where are all the old ones? No one in the world is older than, perhaps, two thousand years. That's not very long. . . . What are you thinking?"

She looks up, frowning with concentration. "You're saying it happened. But how?"

"It didn't happen. We did it, we created ourselves." Leaning back, he gestures at the glowing transparencies overhead. "Do you know what those are?"

"No. I've never seen any designs quite like them. They'd make lovely fabric patterns."

He smiles. "Yes, they are pretty, I suppose, but that's not what they're for. These are enlarged photographs of very small living things—too small to see. They used to get into people's bloodstreams and make them die. That's bubonic plague—" blue and purple dots alternating with larger pink disks—"that's tetanus—" blue rods and red dots—"that's leprosy—" dark-spotted blue lozenges with a cross-hatching of red behind them. "That thing that looks something like a peacock's tail is a parasitic fungus called *streptothrix actinomyces.* That one—" a particularly dainty design of pale blue with darker accents—"is from a malignant oedema with gas gangrene."

The words are meaningless to her, but they call up vague images that are all the more horrible for having no definite outlines. She thinks again of the rat, and of a human face somehow assuming that stillness, that stiffness . . . frozen into a bright pattern, like the colored dots on the wall. . . .

She is resolved not to show her revulsion. "What happened to them?" she asks in a voice that does not quite tremble.

"Nothing. The Planners left them alone, but changed us. Most of the records have been lost in two thousand years, and of course we have no real science of biology as they knew it. I'm no biologist, only a historian and collector." He rises. "But one thing we know they did was to make our bodies chemically immune to infection. Those things—" he nods to the transparencies above—"are simply irrelevant now, they can't harm us. They still exist—I've seen cultures taken from living animals. But they're only a curiosity. Various other things were done, to make the body's chemistry, to put it crudely, more stable. Things that would have killed our ancestors by toxic reactions—poisoned them—don't harm us. Then there are the protective mechanisms, and the paraphysical powers that *homo sapiens* had only in potential. Levitation, regeneration of lost organs. Finally, in general we might say that the body was very much more homeostatized than formerly, that is, there's a cycle of functions which always tends to return to the norm. The cumulative processes that used to impair function don't happen—the 'matrix' doesn't thicken, progressive dehydration never gets started and so on. But you see all these are just delaying actions, things to prevent you and me from dying prematurely. The main thing—" he fingers an index stripe, and a linear design springs out on the wall—"was this. Have you ever read a chart, Claire?"

She shakes her head dumbly. The chart is merely an unaesthetic curve drawn on a reticulated background: it means nothing to her. "This is a schematic way of representing the growth of an organism," says Benarra. "You see here, this up-and-down scale is numbered in one-hundredths of mature weight—from zero here at the bottom, to one hundred percent here at the top. Understand?"

"Yes," she says doubtfully. "But what good is that?"

"You'll see. Now this other scale, along the bottom, is numbered according to the age of the organism. Now: this sharply rising curve here represents all other highly developed species except man. You see, the organism is born, grows very rapidly until it reaches almost its full size, then the curve rounds itself off, becomes almost level. Here it declines. And here it stops: the animal dies."

He pauses to look at her. The world hangs in the air; she says nothing, but meets his gaze.

"Now this," says Benarra, "this long shallow curve represents man as he was. You notice it starts far to the left of the animal curve. The Planners had this much to work with: man was already unique, in that he

had this very long juvenile period before sexual maturity. Here: see what
they did."

With a gesture, he superimposes another chart on the first.

"It looks almost the same," says Claire.

"Yes. Almost. What they did was quite a simple thing, in principle.
They lengthened that juvenile period still further, they made the curve
rise still more slowly . . . and never quite reach the top. The curve now
becomes asymptotic, that is, it approaches sexual maturity by smaller and
smaller amounts, and never gets there, no matter how long it goes on."

Gravely, he returns her stare.

"Are you saying," she asks, "that we're *not* sexually mature? Not anybody?"

"Correct," he says. "Maturity in every other complex organism is the
first stage of death. We never mature, Claire, and that's why we don't die.
We're the eternal adolescents of the universe. That's the price we paid."

"The price . . ." she echoes. "But I still don't see." She laughs. "Not
*mature*—" Unconsciously she holds herself straighter, shoulders back.

Benarra leans casually against the desk, looking down at her. "Have you
ever thought to wonder why there are so few children? In the old days,
loving without any precautions, a grown woman would have a child a year.
Now it happens perhaps once in a hundred billion meetings. It's an
anomaly, freak of nature, and even then the woman can't carry the child
to term herself. Oh, we *look* mature; that's the joke—they gave us the
shape of their own dreams of adult power." He fingers his glossy beard,
thumps his chest. "It isn't real. We're all pretending to be grown-up, but
not one of us knows what it's really like."

A silence falls.

"Except Dio?" says Claire, looking down at her hands.

"He's on the way to find out. Yes."

"And you can't stop it . . . you don't know why."

Benarra shrugs. "He was under strain, physical and mental. Some link
of the chain broke, we may never know which one. He's already gone a
long way up that slope—I think he's near the crest now. There isn't a hope
that we can pull him back again."

Her fists clench impotently. "Then what good is it all?"

Benarra's eyes are hooded; he is playing with a memocube on the desk.
"We learn," he says. "We can do something now and then, to alleviate,
to make things easier. We don't give up."

She hesitates. "How long?"

"Actually, we don't know. We can guess what the maximum is; we know that from analogy with other mammals. But with Dio, too many other things might happen." He glances up at the transparencies.

"Surely you don't mean—" The bright ugly shapes glow down at her, motionless, inscrutable.

"Yes. Yes. He had one of them already, the last time you saw him— a virus infection. We were able to control it; it was what our ancestors used to call 'the common cold'; they thought it was mild. But it nearly destroyed Dio—I mean, not the disease itself, but the moral effect. The symptoms were unpleasant. He wasn't prepared for it."

She is trembling. "Please."

"You have to know all this," says Benarra mercilessly, "or it's no use your seeing Dio at all. If you're going to be shocked, do it now. If you can't stand it, then go away now, not later." He pauses, and speaks more gently. "You can see him today, of course; I promised that. Don't try to make up your mind now, if it's hard. Talk to him, be with him this afternoon; see what it's like."

Claire does not understand herself. She has never been so foolish about a man before: love is all very well; love never lasts very long and you don't expect that it should, but while it lasts, it's pleasantness. Love is joy, not this wrenching pain.

Time flows like a strong, clean torrent, if only you let things go. She could give Dio up now and be unhappy, perhaps, a year or five years, or fifty, but then it would be over, and life would go on just the same.

She sees Dio's face, vivid in memory—not the stranger, the dark shouting man, but Dio himself, framed against the silver sky: sunlight curved on the strong brow, the eyes gleaming in shadow.

"We've got him full of antibiotics," says Benarra compassionately. "We don't think he'll get any of the bad ones. . . . But aging itself is the worst of them all. . . . What do you say?"

IV

Under the curtain of falling stone, Dio sits at his workbench. The room is the same as before, the only visible change is the statue which now juts from one wall overhead, in the corner above the stone curtain: it is the figure of a man reclining, weight on one elbow, calf crossed over thigh, head turned pensively down toward the shoulder. The figure is powerful, but there is a subtle feeling of decay about it: the bulging muscles seem about to sag; the face, even in shadow, has a deformed, damaged look. Forty feet long, sprawling immensely across the corner of the room, the statue has a raw, compulsive power: it is supremely ugly, but she can hardly look away.

A motion attracts her eye. Dio is standing beside the bench, waiting for her. She advances hesitantly: the statue's face is in shadow, but Dio's is not, and already she is afraid of what she may see there.

He takes her hand between his two palms; his touch is warm and dry, but something like an electric shock seems to pass between them, making her start.

"Claire—it's good to see you. Here, sit down, let me look." His voice is resonant, confident, even a trifle assertive; his eyes are alert and preternaturally bright. He talks, moves, holds himself with an air of suppressed excitement. She is relieved and yet paradoxically alarmed: there is nothing really different in his face; the skin glows clear and healthy, his lips are firm. And yet every line, every feature, seems to be hiding some unpleasant surprise; it is like looking at a mask which may suddenly be whipped aside.

In her excitement, she laughs, murmurs a few words without in the least knowing what she is saying. He sits facing her across the corner of the desk, commandingly intent.

"I've just been sketching some plans for the next year. I have some ideas . . . it won't be like anything people expect." He laughs, glancing down; the bench is covered with little gauzy boxes full of shadowy line and color. His tools lie in disorder, solidopens, squirts, calipers. "What do you think of this, by the way?" He points up, behind him at the heroic statue.

"It's very unusual. . . . Yours?"

"A copy, from stereographs—the original was by Michelangelo, something called 'Evening.' But I did the copy myself."

She raises her eyebrows, not understanding.

"I mean I didn't do it by machine. I carved the stone myself—with mallet and chisel, in these hands, Claire." He holds them out, strong, calloused. It was those flat pads of thickened skin, she realizes, that felt so warm and strange against her hand.

He laughs again. "It was an experience. I found out about texture, for one thing. You know, when a machine melts or molds a statue, there's no texture, because to a machine granite is just like cheese. But when you carve, the stone fights back. Stone has character, Claire, it can be stubborn or evasive—it can throw chips in your face, or make your chisel slip aside. Stone fights." His hand clenches, and again he laughs that strange, exultant laugh.

In her apartment late that evening, Claire feels herself confused and overwhelmed by conflicting emotions. Her day with Dio has been like nothing she ever expected. Not once has he aroused her pity: he is like a man in whom a flame burns. Walking with her in the streets, he has made her see the sector as he imagines it: an archaic vision of buildings made for permanence rather than for change; of masonry set by hand, woods hand-carved and hand-polished. It is a terrifying vision, and yet she does not know why. People endure; things should pass away. . . .

In the wide cool rooms an air whispers softly. The border lights burn low around the bed, inviting sleep. Claire moves aimlessly in the outer rooms, letting her robe fall, pondering a languorous stiffness in her limbs. Her mouth is bruised with kisses. Her flesh remembers the touch of his strange hands. She is full of a delicious tiredness; she is at the floating, bodiless zenith of love, neither demanding nor regretting.

Yet she wanders restively through the rooms, once idly evoking a gust of color and music from the wall; it fades into an echoing silence. She pauses at the door of the playroom, and looks down into the deep darkness of the diving well. To fall is a luxury like bathing in water or flame. There is a sweetness of danger in it, although the danger is unreal. Smiling, she breathes deep, stands poised and steps out into emptiness. The gray walls hurtle upward around her: with an effort of will she withholds the pulse of strength that would support her in midair. The floor rushes nearer, the effort mounts intolerably. At the last minute she releases it; the surge buoys her up in a brief paroxysmal joy. She comes to rest, inches away from the hard stone. With her eyes dreamily closed, she rises slowly again to the top. She stretches: now she will sleep.

## V

First come the good days. Dio is a man transformed, a demon of energy. He overflows with ideas and projects; he works unremittingly, accomplishes prodigies. Sector Twenty is the talk of the continent, of the world. Dio builds for permanence, but, dissatisfied, he tears down what he has built and builds again. For a season all his streets are soaring, incredibly beautiful laceworks of stone; then all the ornament vanishes and his buildings shine with classical purity: the streets are full of white light that shines from the stone. Claire waits for the cycle to turn again, but Dio's work becomes ever more massive and crude; his stone darkens. Now the streets are narrow and full of shadows; the walls frown down with heavy magnificence. He builds no more ascensor shafts; to climb in Dio's buildings, you walk up ramps or even stairs, or ride in closed elevator cars. The people murmur, but he is still a novelty; they come from all over the planet to protest, to marvel, to complain; but they still come.

Dio's figure grows heavier, more commanding: his cheeks and chin, all his features thicken; his voice becomes hearty and resonant. When he enters a public room, all heads turn: he dominates any company; where his laugh booms out, the table is in a roar.

Women hang on him by droves; drunken and triumphant, he sometimes staggers off with one while Claire watches. But only she knows the defeat, the broken words and the tears, in the sleepless watches of the night.

There is a timeless interval when they seem to drift, without anxiety and without purpose, as if they had reached the crest of the wave. Then Dio begins to change again, swiftly and more swiftly. They are like passengers on two moving ways that have run side by side for a little distance, but now begin to separate.

She clings to him with desperation, with a sense of vertigo. She is terrified by the massive, inexorable movement that is carrying her off: like him, she feels drawn to an unknown destination.

Suddenly the bad days are upon them. Dio is changing under her eyes. His skin grows slack and dull; his nose arches more strongly. He trains vigorously, under Benarra's instruction; when streaks of gray appear in his hair, he conceals them with pigments. But the lines are cutting themselves deeper around his mouth and at the corners of the eyes. All his bones grow knobby and thick. She cannot bear to look at his hands, they are thick-fingered, clumsy; they hold what they touch, and yet they seem to fumble.

Claire sometimes surprises herself by fits of passionate weeping. She is thin; she sleeps badly and her appetite is poor. She spends most of her time in the library, pursuing the alien thoughts that alone make it possible for her to stay in contact with Dio. One day, taking the air, she passes Katha on the street, and Katha does not recognize her.

She halts as if struck, standing by the balustrade of the little stone bridge. The building fronts are shut faces, weeping with the leaden light that falls from the ceiling. Below her, down the long straight perspective of stair, Katha's little dark head bobs among the crowd and is lost.

The crowds are thinning; not half as many people are here this season as before. Those who come are silent and unhappy; they do not stay long. Only a few miles away, in Sector Nineteen, the air is full of streamers and pulsing with music: the light glitters, people are hurrying and laughing. Here, all colors are gray. Every surface is amorphously rounded, as if mumbled by the sea; here a baluster is missing, here a brick has fallen; here, from a ragged alcove in the wall, a deformed statue leans out to peer at her with its malevolent terra-cotta face. She shudders, averting her eyes, and moves on.

A melancholy sound surges into the street, filling it brimful. The silence throbs; then the sound comes again. It is the tolling of the great bell in Dio's latest folly, the building he calls a "cathedral." It is a vast enclosure, without beauty and without a function. No one uses it, not even Dio himself. It is an emptiness waiting to be filled. At one end, on a platform, a few candles burn. The tile floor is always gleaming, as if freshly damp; shadows are piled high along the walls. Visitors hear their footsteps echo sharply as they enter; they turn uneasily and leave again. At intervals, for no good reason, the great bell tolls.

Suddenly Claire is thinking of the Bay of Napol, and the white gulls wheeling in the sky: the freshness, the tang of ozone and the burning clear light.

As she turns away, on the landing below she sees two slender figures, hand in hand: a boy and a girl, both with shocks of yellow hair. They stand isolated; the slowly moving crowd surrounds them with a changing ring of faces. A memory stirs: Claire recalls the other afternoon, the street, so different then, and the two small yellow-haired children. Now they are almost grown; in a few more years they will look like anyone else.

A pang strikes at Claire's heart. She thinks, *If we could have a child. . . .*

She looks upward in a kind of incredulous wonder that there should be so much sorrow in the world. Where has it all come from? How could she have lived for so many decades without knowing of it?

The leaden light flickers slowly and ceaselessly along the blank stone ceiling overhead.

Tiny as an ant in the distance, Dio swings beside the shoulder of the gigantic, half-carved figure. The echo of his hammer drifts down to Claire and Benarra at the doorway.

The figure is female, seated; that is all they can distinguish as yet. The blind head broods, turned downward; there is something malign in the shapeless hunch of the back and the thick, half-defined arms. A cloud of stone dust drifts free around the tiny shape of Dio; the bitter smell of it is in the air; the white dust coats everything.

"Dio," says Claire into the annunciator. The chatter of the distant hammer goes on. "Dio."

After a moment the hammer stops. The screen flicks on and Dio's white-masked face looks out at them. Only the dark eyes have life; they are hot and impatient. Hair, brows and beard are whitened; even the skin glitters white, as if the sculptor had turned to stone.

"Yes, what is it?"

"Dio—let's go away for a few weeks. I have such a longing to see Napol again. You know, it's been years."

"You go," says the face. In the distance, they see the small black figure hanging with its back turned to them, unmoving beside the gigantic shoulder. "I have too much to do."

"The rest would be good for you," Benarra puts in. "I advise it, Dio."

"I have too much to do," the face repeats curtly. The image blinks out; the chatter of the distant hammer begins again. The black figure blurs in dust again.

Benarra shakes his head. "No use." They turn and walk out across the balcony, overlooking the dark reception hall. Benarra says, "I didn't want to tell you this just yet. The Planners are going to ask Dio to resign his post this year."

"I've been afraid of it," says Claire after a moment. "Have you told them how it will make him feel?"

"They say the sector will become an Avoided Place. They're right; people already are beginning to have a feeling about it. In another few seasons they would stop coming at all."

Her hands are clasping each other restlessly. "Couldn't they give it to him, for a project, or a museum, perhaps—?" She stops; Benarra is shaking his head.

"He's got this to go through," he says. "I've seen it coming."

"I know." Her voice is flat, defeated. "I'll help him . . . all I can."

"That's just what I don't want you to do," Benarra says.

She turns, startled; he is standing erect and somber against the balcony rail, with the gloomy gulf of the hall below. He says, "Claire, you're holding him back. He dyes his hair for you, but he has only to look at himself when he comes down to the studio, to realize what he actually looks like. He despises himself . . . he'll end hating you. You've got to go away now, and let him do what he has to."

For a moment she cannot speak; her throat aches. "What does he have to do?" she whispers.

"He has to grow old, very fast. He's put it off as long as he can." Benarra turns, looking out over the deserted hall. In a corner, the old cloth drapes trail on the floor. "Go to Napol, or to Timbuk. Don't call, don't write. You can't help him now. He has to do this all by himself."

In Djuba she acquires a little ring made of iron, very old, shaped like a serpent that bites its own tail. It is a curiosity, a student's thing; no one would wear it, and besides it is too small. But the cold touch of the little thing in her palm makes her shiver, to think how old it must be. Never before has she been so aware of the funnel-shaped maw of the past. It feels precarious, to be standing over such gulfs of time.

In Winthur she takes the waters, makes a few friends. There is a lodge on the crest of Mont Blanc, new since she was last here, from which one looks across the valley of the Doire. In the clear Alpine air, the tops of the mountains are like ships, afloat in a sea of cloud. The sunlight is pure and thin, with an aching sweetness; the cries of the skiers echo up remotely.

In Cair she meets a collector who has a curious library, full of scraps and oddments that are not to be found in the common supply. He has a baroque fancy for antiquities; some of his books are actually made of paper and bound in synthetic leather, exact copies of the originals.

" 'Again, the Alfurs of Poso, in Central Celebes'," she reads aloud, " 'tell how the first men were supplied with their requirements direct from heaven, the Creator passing down his gifts of them by means of a rope. He first tied a stone to the rope and let it down from the sky. But the men would have none of it, and asked somewhat peevishly of what use to them was a stone. The Good God then let down a banana, which, of course, they gladly accepted and ate with relish. This was their undoing. 'Because you have chosen the banana,' said the deity, 'you shall propagate and perish like the banana, and your offspring shall step into your place. . . .' " She closes the book. "What was a banana, Alf?"

"A phallic symbol, my dear," he says, stroking his beard, with a pleasant smile.

In Prah, she is caught up briefly in a laughing horde of athletes, playing follow-my-leader; they have volplaned from Omsk to the Baltic, tobogganed down the Rose Club chute from Danz to Warsz, cycled from there to Bucur, ballooned, rocketed, leaped from precipices, run afoot all night. She accompanies them to the mountains; they stay the night in a hostel, singing, and in the morning they are away again, like a flock of swallows. Claire stands grave and still; the horde rushes past her, shining faces, arrows of color, laughs, shouts. "Claire, aren't you coming?" . . . "Claire, what's the matter?" . . . "Claire, come with us, we're swimming to Linz!" But she does not answer; the bright throng passes into silence.

Over the roof of the world, the long cloud-packs are moving swiftly, white against the deep blue. Northward is their destination; the sharp wind blows among the pines, breathing of icy fiords.

Claire steps back into the empty forum of the hostel. Her movements are slow; she is weary of escaping. For half a decade she has never been in the same spot more than a few weeks. Never once has she looked into a news unit, or tried to call anyone she knows in Sector Twenty. She has even deliberately failed to register her whereabouts: to be registered is to expect a call, and expecting one is halfway to making one.

But what is the use? Wherever she goes, she carries the same darkness with her.

The phone index glows at her touch. Slowly, with unaccustomed fingers, she selects the sector, group and name: Dio.

The screen pulses; there is a long wait. Then the gray face of an autosec says politely, "The registrant has removed, and left no forwarding information."

Claire's throat is dry. "How long ago did his registry stop?"

"One moment please." The blank face falls silent. "He was last registered three years ago, in the index of November thirty."

"Try central registry," says Claire.

"No forwarding information has been registered."

"I know. Try central, anyway. Try everywhere."

"There will be a delay for checking." The blank face is silent a long time. Claire turns away, staring without interest at the living frieze of color which flows along the borders of the room. "Your attention please."

She turns. "Yes?"

"The registrant does not appear in any sector registry."

For a moment she is numb and speechless. Then, with a gesture, she abolishes the autosec, fingers the index again: the same sector, same group; the name: Benarra.

The screen lights: his remembered face looks out at her. "Claire! Where are you?"

"In Cheky. Ben, I tried to call Dio, and it said there was no registry. Is he—?"

"No. He's still alive, Claire; he's retreated. I want you to come here as soon as you can. Get a special; my club will pay the overs, if you're short."

"No, I have a surplus. All right, I'll come."

"This was made the season after you left," says Benarra. The wall screen glows; it is a stereo view of the main plaza in Level Three, the hub section: dark, unornamented buildings, like a cliff-dweller's canyon. The streets are deserted; no face shows at the windows.

"Changing Day," says Benarra. "Dio had formally resigned, but he still had a day to go. Watch."

In the screen one of the tall building fronts suddenly swells and crumbles at the top. Dingy smoke spurts. Like a stack of counters, the building leans down into the street, separating as it goes into individual bricks and stones. The roar comes dimly to them as the next building erupts, and then the next.

"He did it himself," says Benarra. "He laid all the explosive charges, didn't tell anybody. The council was horrified. The integrators weren't designed to handle all that rubble—it had to be amorphized and piped away in the end. They begged Dio to stop, and finally he did. He made a bargain with them, for Level One."

"The whole level?"

"Yes. They gave it to him; he pointed out that it would not be for long. All the game areas and so on up there were due to be changed, anyhow; Dio's successor merely canceled them out of the integrator."

She still does not understand. "Leaving nothing but the bare earth?"

"He wanted it bare. He got some seeds from collectors, and planted them. I've been up frequently. He actually grows cereal grain up there, and grinds it into bread."

In the screen, the canyon of the street has become a lake of dust. Benarra touches the controls; the scene shifts.

The sky is a deep luminous blue; the level land is bare. A single small building stands up blocky and stiff; behind it there are a few trees, and the evening light glimmers on fields scored in parallel rows. A dark figure is standing motionless beside the house; at first Claire does not recognize it as human. Then it moves, turns its head. She whispers, "Is that Dio?"

"Yes."

She cannot repress a moan of sorrow. The figure is too small for any details of face or body to be seen, but something in the proportions of it makes her think of one of Dio's grotesque statues, all stony bone, hunched, shrunken. The figure turns, moving stiffly, and walks to the hut. It enters and disappears.

She says to Benarra, "Why didn't you tell me?"

"You didn't leave any word; I couldn't reach you."

"I know, but you should have told me. I didn't know . . ."

"Claire, what do you feel for him now? Love?"

"I don't know. A great pity, I think. But maybe there is love mixed up in it too. I pity him because I once loved him. But I think that much pity is love, isn't it, Ben?"

"Not the kind of love you and I used to know anything about," says Benarra, with his eyes on the screen.

He was waiting for her when she emerged from the kiosk.

He had a face like nothing human. It was like a turtle's face, or a lizard's: horny and earth-colored, with bright eyes peering under the shelf of brow. His cheeks sank in; his nose jutted, and the bony shape of the teeth bulged behind the lips. His hair was white and fine, like thistle-down in the sun.

They were like strangers together, or like visitors from different planets. He showed her his grain fields, his kitchen garden, his stand of young fruit trees. In the branches, birds were fluttering and chirping. Dio was dressed in a robe of coarse weave that hung awkwardly from his bony shoulders. He had made it himself, he told her; he had also made the pottery jug from which he poured her a clear tart wine, pressed from his own grapes. The interior of the hut was clean and bare. "Of course, I get food supplements from Ben, and a few things like needles, thread. Can't do everything, but on the whole, I haven't done too badly." His voice was abstracted; he seemed only half-aware of her presence.

They sat side by side on the wooden bench outside the hut. The afternoon sunlight lay pleasantly on the flagstones; a little animation came to his withered face, and for the first time she was able to see the shape of Dio's features there.

"I don't say I'm not bitter. You remember what I was, and you see what I am now." His eyes stared broodingly; his lips worked. "I sometimes think, why did it have to be me? The rest of you are going on, like children at a party, and I'll be gone. But, Claire, I've discovered something. I don't quite know if I can tell you about it."

He paused, looking out across the fields. "There's an attraction in it, a beauty. That sounds impossible, but it's true. Beauty in the ugliness. It's symmetrical, it has its rhythm. The sun rises, the sun sets. Living up here, you feel that a little more. Perhaps that's why we went below."

He turned to look at her. "No, I can't make you understand. I don't want you to think, either, that I've surrendered to it. I feel it coming sometimes, Claire, in the middle of the night. Something coming up over the horizon. Something—" He gestured. "A feeling. Something very huge, and cold. Very cold. And I sit up in my bed, shouting, 'I'm not ready yet!' No. I don't want to go. Perhaps if I had grown up getting used to the idea, it would be easier now. It's a big change to make in your thinking. I tried—all this—and the sculpture, you remember—but I can't quite do it. And yet—now, this is the curious thing. I wouldn't go back, if I could. That sounds funny. Here I am, going to die, and I wouldn't go back. You see, I want to be myself; yes, I want to go on being myself. Those other men were not me, only someone on the way to be me."

They walked back together to the kiosk. At the doorway, she turned for a last glimpse. He was standing, bent and sturdy, white-haired in his rags, against a long sweep of violet sky. The late light glistened grayly on the fields; far behind, in the grove of trees the birds' voices were stilled. There was a single star in the east.

To leave him, she realized suddenly, would be intolerable. She stepped out, embraced him: his body was shockingly thin and fragile in her arms. "Dio, we mustn't be apart now. Let me come and stay in your hut; let's be together."

Gently he disengaged her arms and stepped away. His eyes gleamed in the twilight. "No, no," he said. "It wouldn't do, Claire. Dear, I love you for it, but you see . . . you see, you're a goddess. An immortal goddess—and I'm a man."

She saw his lips work, as if he were about to speak again, and she waited, but he only turned, without a word or gesture, and began walking away across the empty earth: a dark spindling figure, garments flapping gently in the breeze that spilled across the earth. The last light glowed dimly in his white hair. Now he was only a dot in the middle distance. Claire stepped back into the kiosk, and the door closed.

## VI

For a long time she cannot persuade herself that he is gone.

She has seen the body, stretched in a box like someone turned to painted wax: it is not Dio, Dio is somewhere else.

She catches herself thinking, *When Dio comes back . . .* as if he had only gone away, around to the other side of the world. But she knows there is a mound of earth over Sector Twenty, with a tall polished stone over the spot where Dio's body lies in the ground. She can repeat by rote the words carved there:

> Weak and narrow are the powers implanted in the limbs of men; many the woes that fall on them and blunt the edges of thought; short is the measure of the life in death through which they toil. Then are they borne away; like smoke they vanish into air; and what they dream they know is but the little that each hath stumbled upon in wandering about the world. Yet boast they all that they have learned the whole. Vain fools! For what that is, no eye hath seen, no ear hath heard, nor can it be conceived by the mind of man.
> —Empedocles
> (Fifth century B.C.)

One day she closes up the apartment; let the Planner, Dio's successor, make of it whatever he likes. She leaves behind all her notes, her student's equipment, useless now. She goes to a public inn, and that afternoon the new fashions are brought to her: robes in flame silk and in cold metallic mesh; new perfumes, new jewelry. There is new music in the memory units, and she dances to it tentatively, head cocked to listen, living into the rhythm. Already it is like a long-delayed spring; dark withered things are drifting away into the past, and the present is fresh and lovely.

She tries to call a few old friends. Katha is in Centram, Ebert in the South; Piet and Tanno are not registered at all. It doesn't matter; in the plaza of the inn, before the day is out, she makes a dozen new friends. The group, pleased with itself, grows by accretion; the resulting party wanders from the plaza to the Vermilion Club gardens, to one member's rooms and then another's, and finally back to Claire's own apartment.

Leaving the circle toward midnight, she roams the apartment alone, eased by comradeship, content to hear the singing blur and fade behind her. In the playroom, she stands idly looking down into the deep darkness of the diving well. How luxurious, she thinks, to fall and fall, and never reach the bottom. . . .

But the bottom is always there, of course, or it would not be a diving well. A paradox: the well must be a shaft closed at the bottom; it's the sense of danger, the imagined smashing impact, that gives it its thrill. And yet there is no danger of injury: levitation and the survival instinct will always prevent it.

*"We have such a tidy world. . . ."*

Things pass away; people endure.

Then where is Piet, the cottony-haired man, with his laughter and his wild jokes? Hiding, somewhere around the other side of the world, perhaps; forgetting to register. It often happens; no one thinks about it. But then, her own mind asks coldly, where is the woman named Marla, who used to hold you on her knee when you were small? Where is Hendry, your own father, whom you last saw . . . when? Five hundred, six hundred years ago, that time in Rio. Where do people go when they disappear . . . the people no one talks about?

The singing drifts up to her along the dark hallway. Claire is staring transfixed down into the shadows of the well. She thinks of Dio, looking out at the gathering darkness: "I feel it coming sometimes, up over the horizon. Something very huge, and cold."

The darkness shapes itself in her imagination into a gray face, beautiful and terrible. The smiling lips whisper, for her ears alone, *Some day.*

# Houston, Houston, Do You Read?

*When science fiction consisted mainly of magazine stories, some sub-jects were tabu, or could only be handled in certain restricted ways; among them were sexuality, religion and the role of women. When women ap-peared at all in the magazines, they were likely to be either the scientist's daughter or the proverbial damsel in distress (although there were a few notable exceptions). This situation has changed dramatically since the early 1960's, and now SF stands near the center of intelligent writing about the role of women and the sexual revolution.*

*The award-winning "Houston, Houston, Do You Read?" is a perfect example of this transformation.*

Lorimer gazes around the crowded cabin, trying to listen to the voices, trying to ignore the twitch in his insides that means he is about to remember something bad. No help; he lives it again, that long-ago mo-ment. Himself running blindly—or was he pushed?—into the strange toilet at Evanston Junior High. His fly open, his dick in his hand, he can still see the gray zipper edge of his jeans around his pale exposed pecker. The hush. The sickening wrongness of shapes, faces turning. The first blaring giggle. *Girls.* He was in the *girls' can.*

He flinches now wryly, so many years later, not looking at the women's faces. The big cabin surrounds him with their alien things, curved around over his head: the beading rack, the twins' loom, Andy's leather work, the damned kudzu vine wriggling everywhere, the chickens. So cozy. . . . Trapped, he is. Irretrievably trapped for life in everything he does not enjoy. Structurelessness. Personal trivia, unmeaning intimacies. The claims he can somehow never meet. Ginny: *you never talk to me . . .* Ginny, love, he thinks involuntarily. The hurt doesn't come.

Bud Geirr's loud chuckle breaks in on him. Bud is joking with some of them, out of sight around a bulkhead. Dave is visible, though. Major

Norman Davis on the far side of the cabin, his bearded profile bent toward a small dark woman Lorimer can't quite focus on. But Dave's head seems oddly tiny and sharp, in fact the whole cabin looks unreal. A cackle bursts out from the "ceiling"—the bantam hen in her basket.

At this moment Lorimer becomes sure he has been drugged.

Curiously, the idea does not anger him. He leans or rather tips back, perching cross-legged in the zero gee, letting his gaze go to the face of the woman he has been talking with. Connie. Constantia Morelos. A tall moonfaced woman in capacious green pajamas. He has never really cared for talking to women. Ironic.

"I suppose," he says aloud, "it's possible that in some sense we are not here."

That doesn't sound too clear, but she nods interestedly. She's watching my reactions, Lorimer tells himself. Women are natural poisoners. Has he said that aloud too? Her expression doesn't change. His vision is taking on a pleasing local clarity. Connie's skin strikes him as quite fine, healthy-looking. Olive tan even after two years in space. She was a farmer, he recalls. Big pores, but without the caked look he associates with women her age.

"You probably never wore make-up," he says. She looks puzzled. "Face paint, powder. None of you have."

"Oh!" Her smile shows a chipped front tooth. "Oh yes, I think Andy has."

"Andy?"

"For plays. Historical plays, Andy's good at that."

"Of course. Historical plays."

Lorimer's brain seems to be expanding, letting in light. He is understanding actively now, the myriad bits and pieces linking into patterns. Deadly patterns, he perceives; but the drug is shielding him in some way. Like an amphetamine high without the pressure. Maybe it's something they use socially? No, they're watching, too.

"Space bunnies, I still don't dig it," Bud Geirr laughs infectiously. He has a friendly buoyant voice people like; Lorimer still likes it after two years.

"You chicks have kids back home, what do your folks think about you flying around out here with old Andy, hmm?" Bud floats into view, his arm draped around a twin's shoulders. The one called Judy Paris, Lorimer decides; the twins are hard to tell. She drifts passively at an angle to Bud's big body: a jut-breasted plain girl in flowing yellow pajamas, her black hair raying out. Andy's red head swims up to them. He is holding a big green space-ball, looking about sixteen.

"Old Andy." Bud shakes his head, his grin flashing under his thick dark moustache. "When I was your age folks didn't let their women fly around with me."

Connie's lips quirk faintly. In Lorimer's head the pieces slide toward pattern. I know, he thinks. Do you know I know? His head is vast and crystalline, very nice really. Easier to think. Women. . . . No compact generalization forms in his mind, only a few speaking faces on a matrix of pervasive irrelevance. Human, of course. Biological necessity. Only so, so . . . diffuse? Pointless? . . . His sister Amy, *soprano con tremulo: of course women could contribute as much as men if you'd treat us as equals. You'll see!* And then marrying that idiot the second time. Well, now he can see.

"Kudzu vines," he says aloud. Connie smiles. How they all smile.

"How 'boot that?" Bud says happily, "Ever think we'd see chicks in zero gee, hey, Dave? Artits-stico. Woo-ee!" Across the cabin Dave's bearded head turns to him, not smiling.

"And ol' Andy's had it all to hisself. Stunt your growth, lad." He punches Andy genially on the arm, Andy catches himself on the bulkhead. Bud can't be drunk, Lorimer thinks; not on that fruit cider. But he doesn't usually sound so much like a stage Texan either. A drug.

"Hey, no offense," Bud is saying earnestly to the boy, "I mean that. You have to forgive one underprilly, underprivileged brother. These chicks are good people. Know what?" he tells the girl, "You could look stu-pen-dous if you fix yourself up a speck. Hey, I can show you, old Buddy's a expert. I hope you don't mind my saying that. As a matter of fact you look real stupendous to me right now."

He hugs her shoulders, flings out his arm and hugs Andy too. They float upwards in his grasp, Judy grinning excitedly, almost pretty.

"Let's get some more of that good stuff." Bud propels them both toward the serving rack which is decorated for the occasion with sprays of greens and small real daisies.

"Happy New Year! Hey, Happy New Year, y'all!"

Faces turn, more smiles. Genuine smiles, Lorimer thinks, maybe they really like their new years. He feels he has infinite time to examine every event, the implications evolving in crystal facets. I'm an echo chamber. Enjoyable, to be the observer. But others are observing too. They've started something here. Do they realize? So vulnerable, three of us, five of them in this fragile ship. They don't know. A dread unconnected to action lurks behind his mind.

"By God we made it," Bud laughs. "You space chickies, I have to give it to you. I commend you, by God I say it. We wouldn't be here, wherever we are. Know what, I jus' might decide to stay in the service after all. Think they have room for old Bud in your space program, sweetie?"

"Knock that off, Bud," Dave says quietly from the far wall. "I don't want to hear us use the name of the Creator like that." The full chestnut beard gives him a patriarchal gravity. Dave is forty-six, a decade older than Bud and Lorimer. Veteran of six successful missions.

"Oh my apologies, Major Dave old buddy." Bud chuckles intimately to the girl. "Our commanding ossifer. Stupendous guy. Hey, Doc!" he calls, "How's your attitude? You making out dinko?"

"Cheers," Lorimer hears his voice reply, the complex stratum of his feelings about Bud rising like a kraken in the moonlight of his mind. The submerged silent thing he has about them all, all the Buds and Daves and big, indomitable, cheerful, able, disciplined, slow-minded mesomorphs he has cast his life with. Meso-ectos, he corrected himself; astronauts aren't muscleheads. They like him, he has been careful about that. Liked him well enough to get him on *Sunbird,* to make him the official scientist on the first circumsolar mission. That little Doc Lorimer, he's cool, he's on the team. No shit from Lorimer, not like those other scientific assholes. He does the bit well with his small neat build and his dead-pan remarks. And the years of turning out for the bowling, the volleyball, the tennis, the skeet, the skiing that broke his ankle, the touch football that broke his collarbone. Watch that Doc, he's a sneaky one. And the big men banging him on the back, accepting him. Their token scientist. . . . The trouble is, he isn't any kind of scientist any more. Living off his postdoctoral plasma work, a lucky hit. He hasn't really been into the math for years, he isn't up to it now. Too many other interests, too much time spent explaining elementary stuff. I'm a half-jock, he thinks. A foot taller and a hundred pounds heavier and I'd be just like them. One of them. An alpha. They probably sense it underneath, the beta bile. Had the jokes worn a shade thin in *Sunbird,* all that year going out? A year of Bud and Dave playing gin. That damn exercycle, gearing it up too tough for me. They didn't mean it, though. We were a team.

The memory of gaping jeans flicks at him, the painful end part—the grinning faces waiting for him when he stumbled out. The howls, the dribble down his leg. Being cool, pretending to laugh too. You shit-heads, I'll show you. I am not a girl.

Bud's voice rings out, chanting "And a Hap-pee New Year to you-all down there!" Parody of the oily NASA tone. "Hey, why don't we shoot 'em a signal? Greetings to all you Earthlings, I mean, all you little Lunies. Hap-py New Year in the good year whatsis." He snuffles comically. "There is a Santy Claus, Houston, ye-ew nevah saw nothin' like this! Houston, wherever you are," he sings out. "Hey, Houston! Do you read?"

In the silence Lorimer sees Dave's face set into Major Norman Davis, commanding.

And without warning he is suddenly back there, back a year ago in the cramped, shook-up command module of *Sunbird*, coming out from behind the sun. It's the drug doing this, he thinks as memory closes around him, it's so real. Stop. He tries to hang onto reality, to the sense of trouble building underneath.

—But he can't, he is *there*, hovering behind Dave and Bud in the triple couches, as usual avoiding his official station in the middle, seeing beside them their reflections against blackness in the useless port window. The outer layer has been annealed, he can just make out a bright smear that has to be Spica floating through the image of Dave's head, making the bandage look like a kid's crown.

"Houston, Houston, *Sunbird,*" Dave repeats; *"Sunbird* calling Houston. Houston, do you read? Come in, Houston."

The minutes start by. They are giving it seven out, seven back; seventy-eight million miles, ample margin.

"The high gain's shot, that's what it is," Bud says cheerfully. He says it almost every day.

"No way." Dave's voice is patient, also as usual. "It checks out. Still too much crap from the sun, isn't that right, Doc?"

"The residual radiation from the flare is just about in line with us," Lorimer says. "They could have a hard time sorting us out." For the thousandth time he registers his own faint, ridiculous gratification at being consulted.

"Shit, we're outside Mercury." Bud shakes his head. "How we gonna find out who won the Series?"

He often says that too. A ritual, out here in eternal night. Lorimer watches the sparkle of Spica drift by the reflection of Bud's curly face-bush. His own whiskers are scant and scraggly, like a blond Fu Manchu.

In the aft corner of the window is a striped glare that must be the remains of their port energy accumulators, fried off in the solar explosion that hit them a month ago and fused the outer layers of their windows. That was when Dave cut his head open on the sexlogic panel. Lorimer had been banged in among the gravity wave experiment, he still doesn't trust the readings. Luckily the particle stream has missed one piece of the front window; they still have about twenty degrees of clear vision straight ahead. The brilliant web of the Pleiades shows there, running off into a blur of light.

Twelve minutes . . . thirteen. The speaker sighs and clicks emptily. Fourteen. Nothing.

"*Sunbird* to Houston, *Sunbird* to Houston. Come in, Houston. *Sunbird* out." Dave puts the mike back in its holder. "Give it another twenty-four."

They wait ritually. Tomorrow Packard will reply. Maybe.

"Be good to see old Earth again," Bud remarks.

"We're not using any more fuel on attitude," Dave reminds him. "I trust Doc's figures."

It's not my figures, it's the elementary facts of celestial mechanics, Lorimer thinks; in October there's only one place for Earth to be. He never says it. Not to a man who can fly two-body solutions by intuition once he knows where the bodies are. Bud is a good pilot and a better engineer; Dave is the best there is. He takes no pride in it. "The Lord helps us, Doc, if we let him."

"Going to be a bitch docking if the radar's screwed up," Bud says idly. They all think about that for the hundredth time. It will be a bitch. Dave will do it. That was why he is hoarding fuel.

The minutes tick off.

"That's it," Dave says—and a voice fills the cabin, shockingly.

"Judy?" It is high and clear. A girl's voice.

"Judy, I'm so glad we got you. What are you doing on this band?"

Bud blows out his breath; there is a frozen instant before Dave snatches up the mike.

"*Sunbird,* we read you. This is Mission *Sunbird* calling Houston, ah, *Sunbird One* calling Houston Ground Control. Identify, who are you? Can you relay our signal? Over."

"Some skip," Bud says. "Some incredible ham."

"Are you in trouble, Judy?" the girl's voice asks. "I can't hear, you sound terrible. Wait a minute."

"This is United States Space Mission *Sunbird One,*" Dave repeats. "Mission *Sunbird* calling Houston Space Center. You are dee-exxing our channel. Identify, repeat identify yourself and say if you can relay to Houston. Over."

"Dinko, Judy, try it again," the girl says.

Lorimer abruptly pushes himself up to the Lurp, the Long-Range Particle Density Cumulator experiment, and activates its shaft motor. The shaft whines, jars; lucky it was retracted during the flare, lucky it hasn't fused shut. He sets the probe pulse on max and begins a rough manual scan.

"You are intercepting official traffic from the United States space mission to Houston Control," Dave is saying forcefully. "If you cannot relay to Houston get off the air, you are committing a federal offense. Say again, can you relay our signal to Houston Space Center? Over."

"You still sound terrible," the girl says. "What's Houston? Who's talking, anyway? You know we don't have much time." Her voice is sweet but very nasal.

"Jesus, that's close," Bud says. "That is close."

"Hold it." Dave twists around to Lorimer's improvised radarscope.

"There." Lorimer points out a tiny stable peak at the extreme edge of the read-out slot, in the transcoronal scatter. Bud cranes too.

"A bogey!"

"Somebody else out here."

"Hello, hello? We have you now," the girl says. "Why are you so far out? Are you dinko, did you catch the flare?"

"Hold it," warns Dave. "What's the status, Doc?"

"Over three hundred thousand kilometers, guesstimated. Possibly headed away from us, going around the sun. Could be cosmonauts, a Soviet mission?"

"Out to beat us. They missed."

"With a *girl?*" Bud objects.

"They've done that. You taping this, Bud?"

"Roger-r-r." He grins. "That sure didn't sound like a Russky chick. Who the hell's Judy?"

Dave thinks for a second, clicks on the mike. "This is Major Norman Davis commanding United States spacecraft *Sunbird One.* We have you on scope. Request you identify yourself. Repeat, who are you? Over."

"Judy, stop joking," the voice complains. "We'll lose you in a minute, don't you realize we worried about you?"

"*Sunbird* to unidentified craft. This is not Judy. I say again, this is not Judy. Who are you? Over."

"What—" the girl says, and is cut off by someone saying, "Wait a minute, Ann." The speaker squeals. Then a different woman says, "This is Lorna Bethune in *Escondita*. What is going on here?"

"This is Major Davis commanding United States Mission *Sunbird* on course for Earth. We do not recognize any spacecraft *Escondita*. Will you identify yourself? Over."

"I just did." She sounds older with the same nasal drawl. "There is no spaceship *Sunbird* and you're not on course for Earth. If this is an andy joke it isn't any good."

"This is no joke, madam!" Dave explodes. "This is the American circumsolar mission and we are American astronauts. We do not appreciate your interference. Out."

The woman starts to speak and is drowned in a jibber of static. Two voices come through briefly. Lorimer thinks he hears the words "*Sunbird* program" and something else. Bud works the squelcher; the interference subsides to a drone.

"Ah, Major Davis?" The voice is fainter. "Did I hear you say you are on course for Earth?"

Dave frowns at the speaker and then says curtly, "Affirmative."

"Well, we don't understand your orbit. You must have very unusual flight characteristics, our readings show you won't node with anything on your present course. We'll lose the signal in a minute or two. Ah, would you tell us where you see Earth now? Never mind the coordinates, just tell us the constellation."

Dave hesitates and then holds up the mike. "Doc."

"Earth's apparent position is in Pisces," Lorimer says to the voice. "Approximately three degrees from P. Gamma."

"It is not," the woman says. "Can't you see it's in Virgo? Can't you see out at all?"

Lorimer's eyes go to the bright smear in the port window. "We sustained some damage—"

"Hold it," snaps Dave.

"—to one window during a disturbance we ran into at perihelion. Naturally we know the relative direction of Earth on this date, October 19."

"October? It's March, March 15. You must—" Her voice is lost in a shriek.

"E-M front," Bud says, tuning. They are all leaning at the speaker from different angles, Lorimer is head-down. Space-noise wails and crashes like surf, the strange ship is too close to the coronal horizon. "—Behind you," they hear. More howls. "Band, try . . . ship . . . if you can, your signal—" Nothing more comes through.

Lorimer pushes back, staring at the spark in the window. It has to be Spica. But is it elongated, as if a second point-source is beside it? Impossible. An excitement is trying to flare out inside him, the women's voices resonate in his head.

"Playback," Dave says. "Houston will really like to hear this."

They listen again to the girl calling Judy, the woman saying she is Lorna Bethune. Bud holds up a finger. "Man's voice in there." Lorimer listens hard for the words he thought he heard. The tape ends.

"Wait till Packard gets this one." Dave rubs his arms. "Remember what they pulled on Howie? Claiming they rescued him."

"Seems like they want us on their frequency." Bud grins. "They must think we're fa-a-ar gone. Hey, looks like this other capsule's going to show up, getting crowded out here."

"If it shows up," Dave says. "Leave it on voice alert, Bud. The batteries will do that."

Lorimer watches the spark of Spica, or Spica-plus-something, wondering if he will ever understand. The casual acceptance of some trick or ploy out here in this incredible loneliness. Well, if these strangers are from the same mold, maybe that is it. Aloud he says, *Escondita* is an odd name for a Soviet mission. I believe it means 'hidden' in Spanish."

"Yeah," says Bud. "Hey, I know what that accent is, it's Australian. We had some Aussie bunnies at Hickam. Or-stryle-ya, woo-ee! You s'pose Woomara is sending up some kind of com-bined do?"

Dave shakes his head. "They have no capability whatsoever."

"We ran into some fairly strange phenomena back there, Dave," Lorimer says thoughtfully. "I'm beginning to wish we could take a visual check."

"Did you goof, Doc?"

"No. Earth is where I said, if it's October. Virgo is where it would appear in March."

"Then that's it," Dave grins, pushing out of the couch. "You been asleep five months, Rip van Winkle? Time for a hand before we do the roadwork."

"What I'd like to know is what that chick looks like," says Bud, closing down the transceiver. "Can I help you into your space suit, miss? Hey, miss, pull that in, psst-psst-psst! You going to listen, Doc?"

"Right." Lorimer is getting out his charts. The others go aft through the tunnel to the small day-room, making no further comment on the presence of the strange ship or ships out here. Lorimer himself is more shaken than he likes; it was that damn phrase.

The tedious exercise period comes and goes. Lunchtime: they give the containers a minimum warm to conserve the batteries. Chicken à la king again; Bud puts ketchup on his and breaks their usual silence with a funny anecdote about an Australian girl, laboriously censoring himself to conform to *Sunbird's* unwritten code on talk. After lunch Dave goes forward to the command module. Bud and Lorimer continue their current task of checking out the suits and packs for a damage-assessment EVA to take place as soon as the radiation count drops.

They are just clearing away when Dave calls them. Lorimer comes through the tunnel to hear a girl's voice blare, "—dinko trip. What did Lorna say? *Gloria* over!"

He starts up the Lurp and begins scanning. No results this time. "They're either in line behind us or in the sunward quadrant," he reports finally. "I can't isolate them."

Presently the speaker holds another thin thread of sound.

"That could be their ground control," says Dave. "How's the horizon, Doc?"

"Five hours; Northwest Siberia, Japan, Australia."

"I told you the high gain is fucked up." Bud gingerly feeds power to his antenna motor. "Easy, eas-ee. The frame is twisted, that's what it is."

"Don't snap it," Dave says, knowing Bud will not.

The squeaking fades, pulses back. "Hey, we can really use this," Bud says. "We can calibrate on them."

A hard soprano says suddenly "—should be outside your orbit. Try around Beta Aries."

"Another chick. We have a fix," Bud says happily. "We have a fix now. I do believe our troubles are over. That monkey was torqued one hundred forty-nine degrees. Woo-ee!"

The first girl comes back. "We see them, Margo! But they're so small, how can they live in there? Maybe they're tiny aliens! Over."

"That's Judy," Bud chuckles. "Dave, this is screwy, it's all in English. It has to be some UN thingie."

Dave massages his elbows, flexes his fists; thinking. They wait. Lorimer considers a hundred and forty-nine degrees from Gamma Piscium.

In thirteen minutes the voice from Earth says, "Judy, call the others, will you? We're going to play you the conversation, we think you should all hear. Two minutes. Oh, while we're waiting, Zebra wants to tell Connie the baby is fine. And we have a new cow."

"Code," says Dave.

The recording comes on. The three men listen once more to Dave calling Houston in a rattle of solar noise. The transmission clears up rapidly and cuts off with the woman saying that another ship, the *Gloria*, is behind them, closer to the sun.

"We looked up history," the Earth voice resumes. "There was a Major Norman Davis on the first *Sunbird* flight. Major was a military title. Did you hear them say 'Doc'? There was a scientific doctor on board, Dr. Orren Lorimer. The third member was Captain—that's another title—Bernhard Geirr. Just the three of them, all males of course. We think they had an early reaction engine and not too much fuel. The point is, the first *Sunbird* mission was lost in space. They never came out from behind the sun. That was about when the big flares started. Jan thinks they must have been close to one, you heard them say they were damaged."

Dave grunts. Lorimer is fighting excitement like a brush discharge sparking in his gut.

"Either they are who they say they are or they're ghosts; or they're aliens pretending to be people. Jan says maybe the disruption in those super-flares could collapse the local time dimension. Pluggo. What did you observe there, I mean the highlights?"

*Time dimension . . . never came back . . .* Lorimer's mind narrows onto the reality of the two unmoving bearded heads before him, refuses to admit the words he thought he heard: *before the year 2000.* The language, he thinks. The language would have to have changed. He feels better.

A deep baritone voice says, "Margo?" In *Sunbird* eyes come alert.

"—like the big one fifty years ago." The man has the accent too. "We were really lucky being right there when it popped. The most interesting part is that we confirmed the gravity turbulence. Periodic but not waves. It's violent, we got pushed around some. Space is under monster stress in those things. We think France's theory that our system is passing through a micro-black-hole cluster looks right as long as one doesn't plonk us."

"France?" Bud mutters. Dave looks at him speculatively.

"It's hard to imagine anything being kicked out in time. But they're here, whatever they are, they're over eight hundred kays outside us scooting out toward Aldebaran. As Lorna said, if they're trying to reach Earth they're in trouble unless they have a lot of spare gees. Should we try to talk to them? Over. Oh, great about the cow. Over again."

"Black holes," Bud whistles softly. "That's one for you, Doc. Was we in a black hole?"

"Not in one or we wouldn't be here." If we are here, Lorimer adds to himself. A micro-black-hole cluster . . . what happens when fragments of totally collapsed matter approach each other, or collide, say in the photosphere of a star? Time disruption? Stop it. Aloud he says, "They could be telling us something, Dave."

Dave says nothing. The minutes pass.

Finally the Earth voice comes back, saying that it will try to contact the strangers on their original frequency. Bud glances at Dave, tunes the selector.

"Calling *Sunbird One?*" the girl says slowly through her nose. "This is Luna Central calling Major Norman Davis of *Sunbird One*. We have picked up your conversation with our ship *Escondita*. We are very puzzled as to who you are and how you got here. If you really are *Sunbird One* we think you must have been jumped forward in time when you passed the solar flare." She pronounces it Cockney-style, "toime."

"Our ship *Gloria* is near you, they see you on their radar. We think you may have a serious course problem because you told Lorna you were headed for Earth and you think it is now October with Earth in Pisces. It is not October, it is March 15. I repeat, the Earth date—" she says "dyte" "—is March 15, time twenty hundred hours. You should be able to see Earth very close to Spica in Virgo. You said your window is damaged. Can't you go out and look? We think you have to make a big course correction. Do you have enough fuel? Do you have a computer? Do you have enough air and water and food? Can we help you? We're listening on this frequency. Luna to *Sunbird One*, come in."

On *Sunbird* nobody stirs. Lorimer struggles against internal eruptions. *Never came back. Jumped forward in time.* The cyst of memories he has schooled himself to suppress bulges up in the lengthening silence. "Aren't you going to answer?"

"Don't be stupid," Dave says.

"Dave. A hundred and forty-nine degrees is the difference between Gamma Piscium and Spica. That transmission is coming from where they say Earth is."

"You goofed."

"I did not goof. It has to be March."

Dave blinks as if a fly is bothering him.

In fifteen minutes the Luna voice runs through the whole thing again, ending "Please, come in."

"Not a tape." Bud unwraps a stick of gum, adding the plastic to the neat wad back of the gyro leads. Lorimer's skin crawls, watching the ambiguous dazzle of Spica. Spica-plus-Earth? Unbelief grips him, rocks him with a complex pang compounded of faces, voices, the sizzle of bacon frying, the creak of his father's wheelchair, chalk on a sunlit blackboard, Ginny's bare legs on the flowered couch, Jenny and Penny running dangerously close to the lawnmower. The girls will be taller now, Jenny is already as tall as her mother. His father is living with Amy in Denver, determined to last till his son gets home. *When I get home.* This has to be insanity, Dave's right; it's a trick, some crazy trick. The language.

Fifteen minutes more; the flat, earnest female voice comes back and repeats it all, putting in more stresses. Dave wears a remote frown, like a man listening to a lousy sports program. Lorimer has the notion he might switch off and propose a hand of gin; wills him to do so. The voice says it will now change frequencies.

Bud tunes back, chewing calmly. This time the voice stumbles on a couple of phrases. It sounds tired.

Another wait; an hour, now. Lorimer's mind holds only the bright point of Spica digging at him. Bud hums a bar of *Yellow Ribbons*, falls silent again.

"Dave," Lorimer says finally, "our antenna is pointed straight at Spica. I don't care if you think I goofed, if Earth is over there we have to change course soon. Look, you can see it could be a double light source. We have to check this out."

Dave says nothing. Bud says nothing but his eyes rove to the port window, back to his instrument panel, to the window again. In the corner of the panel is a polaroid snap of his wife. Patty: a tall, giggling, rump-switching redhead; Lorimer has occasional fantasies about her. Little-girl voice, though. And so tall. . . . Some short men chase tall women; it strikes Lorimer as undignified. Ginny is an inch shorter than he. Their girls will be taller. And Ginny insisted on starting a pregnancy before he left, even though he'll be out of commo. Maybe, maybe a boy, a son—*stop it.* Think about anything. Bud. . . . Does Bud love Patty? Who knows? He loves Ginny. At seventy million miles. . . .

"Judy?" Luna Central or whoever it is says. "They don't answer. You want to try? But listen, we've been thinking. If these people really are from the past this must be very traumatic for them. They could be just realizing they'll never see their world again. Myda says these males had children and women they stayed with, they'll miss them terribly. This is exciting for us but it may seem awful to them. They could be too shocked to answer. They could be frightened, maybe they think we're aliens or hallucinations even. See?"

Five seconds later the nearby girl says, "Da, Margo, we were into that too. Dinko. Ah, *Sunbird?* Major Davis of *Sunbird*, are you there? This is Judy Paris in the ship *Gloria*, we're only about a million kay from you, we see you on our screen." She sounds young and excited. "Luna Central has been trying to reach you, we think you're in trouble and we want to help. Please don't be frightened, we're people just like you. We think you're way off course if you want to reach Earth. Are you in trouble? Can we help? If your radio is out can you make any sort of signal? Do you know Old Morse? You'll be off our screen soon, we're truly worried about you. Please reply somehow if you possibly can, *Sunbird*, come in!"

Dave sits impassive. Bud glances at him, at the port window, gazes stolidly at the speaker, his face blank. Lorimer has exhausted surprise, he wants only to reply to the voices. He can manage a rough signal by heterodyning the probe beam. But what then, with them both against him?

The girl's voice tries again determinedly. Finally she says, "Margo, they won't peep. Maybe they're dead? I think they're aliens."

Are we not?, Lorimer thinks. The Luna station comes back with a different, older voice.

"Judy, Myda here, I've had another thought. These people had a very rigid authority code. You remember your history, they peck-ordered everything. You notice Major Davis repeated about being commanding. That's called dominance-submission structure, one of them gave orders and the others did whatever they were told, we don't know quite why. Perhaps they were frightened. The point is that if the dominant one is in shock or panicked maybe the others can't reply unless this Davis lets them."

Jesus Christ, Lorimer thinks. Jesus H. Christ in colors. It is his father's expression for the inexpressible. Dave and Bud sit unstirring.

"How weird," the Judy voice says. "But don't they know they're on a bad course? I mean, could the dominant one make the others fly right out of the system? Truly?"

"It's happened, Lorimer thinks; it has happened. I have to stop this.

I have to act now, before they lose us. Desperate visions of himself defying Dave and Bud loom before him. Try persuasion first.

Just as he opens his mouth he sees Bud stir slightly, and with immeasurable gratitude hears him say, "Dave-o, what say we take an eyeball look? One little old burp won't hurt us."

Dave's head turns a degree or two.

"Or should I go out and see, like the chick said?" Bud's voice is mild.

After a long minute Dave says neutrally, "All right. . . . Attitude change." His arm moves up as though heavy; he starts methodically setting in the values for the vector that will bring Spica in line with their functional window.

Now why couldn't I have done that, Lorimer asks himself for the thousandth time, following the familiar check sequence. Don't answer. . . . And for the thousandth time he is obscurely moved by the rightness of them. The authentic ones, the alphas. Their bond. The awe he had felt first for the absurd jocks of his school ball team.

"That's go, Dave, assuming nothing got creamed."

Dave throws the ignition safety, puts the computer on real time. The hull shudders. Everything in the cabin drifts sidewise while the bright point of Spica swims the other way, appears on the front window as the retros cut in. When the star creeps out onto clear glass Lorimer can clearly see its companion. The double light steadies there; a beautiful job. He hands Bud the telescope.

"The one on the left."

Bud looks. "There she is, all right. Hey, Dave, look at that!"

He puts the scope in Dave's hand. Slowly, Dave raises it and looks. Lorimer can hear him breathe. Suddenly Dave pulls up the mike.

"Houston!" he says harshly. *"Sunbird* to Houston, *Sunbird* calling Houston. Houston, come in!"

Into the silence the speaker squeals, "They fired their engines—wait, she's calling!" And shuts up.

In *Sunbird*'s cabin nobody speaks. Lorimer stares at the twin stars ahead, impossible realities shifting around him as the minutes congeal. Bud's reflected face looks downwards, grin gone. Dave's beard moves silently; praying, Lorimer realizes. Alone of the crew Dave is deeply religious; at Sunday meals he gives a short, dignified grace. A shocking pity for Dave rises in Lorimer; Dave is so deeply involved with his family, his four sons, always thinking about their training, taking them hunting, fishing, camping. And Doris his wife so incredibly active and sweet, going on their trips, cooking and doing things for the community. Driving Penny and Jenny to classes while Ginny was sick that time. Good people, the backbone. . . . This can't be, he thinks; Packard's voice is going to come through in a minute, the antenna's beamed right now. Six minutes now. This will all go away. *Before the year 2000*—stop it, the language would have changed. Think of Doris. . . . She has that glow, feeding her five men; women with sons are different. But Ginny, but his dear woman, his *wife*, his *daughters*—grandmothers now? All dead and dust? *Quit that.* Dave is still praying. . . . Who knows what goes on inside those heads? Dave's cry. . . . Twelve minutes, it has to be all right. The second sweep is stuck, no, it's moving. Thirteen. It's all insane, a dream. Thirteen plus . . . fourteen. The speaker hissing and clicking vacantly. Fifteen now. A dream. . . . Or are those women staying off, letting us see? Sixteen. . . .

At twenty Dave's hand moves, stops again. The seconds jitter by, space crackles. Thirty minutes coming up.

"Calling Major Davis in *Sunbird?*" It is the older woman, a gentle voice. "This is Luna Central. We are the service and communication facility for spaceflight now. We're sorry to have to tell you that there is no space center at Houston any more. Houston itself was abandoned when the shuttle base moved to White Sands, over two centuries ago."

A cool dust-colored light enfolds Lorimer's brain, isolating it. He will remain so a long time.

The woman is explaining it all again, offering help, asking if they were hurt. A nice dignified speech. Dave still sits immobile, gazing at Earth. Bud puts the mike in his hand.

"Tell them, Dave-o."

Dave looks at it, takes a deep breath, presses the send button.

"*Sunbird* to Luna Control," he says quite normally. (It's "Central," Lorimer thinks.) "We copy. Ah, negative on life support, we have no problems. We copy the course change suggestion and are proceeding to recompute. Your offer of computer assistance is appreciated. We suggest you transmit position data so we can get squared away. Ah, we are economizing on transmission until we see how our accumulators have held up. *Sunbird* out."

And so it had begun.

Lorimer's mind floats back to himself now floating in *Gloria*, nearly a year, or three hundred years, later; watching and being watched by them. He still feels light, contented; the dread underneath has come no nearer.

But it is so silent. He seems to have heard no voices for a long time. Or was it a long time? Maybe the drug is working on his time sense, maybe it was only a minute or two.

"I've been remembering," he says to the woman Connie, wanting her to speak.

She nods. "You have so much to remember. Oh, I'm sorry—that wasn't good to say." Her eyes speak sympathy.

"Never mind." It is all dreamlike now, his lost world and this other which he is just now seeing plain. "We must seem like very strange beasts to you."

"We're trying to understand," she says. "It's history, you learn the events but you don't really feel what the people were like, how it was for them. We hope you'll tell us."

The drug, Lorimer thinks, that's what they're trying. Tell them . . . how can he? Could a dinosaur tell how it was? A montage flows through his mind, dominated by random shots of Operations' north parking lot and Ginny's yellow kitchen telephone with the sickly ivy vines. . . . Women and vines. . . .

A burst of laughter distracts him. It's coming from the chamber they call the gym, Bud and the others must be playing ball in there. Bright idea, really, he muses: using muscle power, sustained mild exercise. That's why they are all so fit. The gym is a glorified squirrel-wheel, when you climb or pedal up the walls it revolves and winds a gear train, which among other things rotates the sleeping drum. A real Woolagong. . . . Bud and Dave usually take their shifts together, scrambling the spinning gym like big pale apes. Lorimer prefers the easy rhythm of the women, and the cycle here fits him nicely. He usually puts in his shift with Connie, who doesn't talk much, and one of the Judys, who do.

No one is talking now, though. Remotely uneasy he looks around the big cylinder of the cabin, sees Dave and Lady Blue by the forward window. Judy Dakar is behind them, silent for once. They must be looking at Earth; it has been a beautiful expanding disk for some weeks now. Dave's beard is moving, he is praying again. He has taken to doing that, not ostentatiously, but so obviously sincere that Lorimer, a life atheist, can only sympathize.

The Judys have asked Dave what he whispers, of course. When Dave understood that they had no concept of prayer and had never seen a Christian Bible there had been a heavy silence.

"So you have lost all faith," he said finally.

"We have faith," Judy Paris protested.

"May I ask in what?"

"We have faith in ourselves, of course," she told him.

"Young lady, if you were my daughter I'd tan your britches," Dave said, not joking. The subject was not raised again.

But he came back so well after that first dreadful shock, Lorimer thinks. A personal god, a father-model, man needs that. Dave draws strength from it and we lean on him. Maybe leaders have to believe. Dave was so great; cheerful, unflappable, patiently working out alternatives, making his decisions on the inevitable discrepancies in the position readings in a way Lorimer couldn't do. A bitch. . . .

Memory takes him again; he is once again back in *Sunbird*, gritty-eyed, listening to the women's chatter, Dave's terse replies. God, how they chattered. But their computer works checks out. Lorimer is suffering also from a quirk of Dave's, his reluctance to transmit their exact thrust and fuel reserve. He keeps holding out a margin and making Lorimer compute it back in.

But the margins don't help; it is soon clear that they are in big trouble. Earth will pass too far ahead of them on her next orbit, they don't have the acceleration to catch up with her before they cross her path. They can carry out an ullage maneuver, they can kill enough velocity to let Earth catch them on the second go-by; but that would take an extra year and their life-support would be long gone. The grim question of whether they have enough to enable a single man to wait it out pushes into Lorimer's mind. He pushes it back; that one is for Dave.

There is a final possibility: Venus will approach their trajectory three months hence and they may be able to gain velocity by swinging by it. They go to work on that.

Meanwhile Earth is steadily drawing away from them and so is *Gloria*, closer toward the sun. They pick her out of the solar interference and then lose her again. They know her crew now: the man is Andy Kay, the senior woman is Lady Blue Parks; they appear to do the navigating. Then there is a Connie Morelos and the two twins, Judy Paris and Judy Dakar, who run the communications. The chief Luna voices are women too, Margo and Azella. The men can hear them talking to the *Escondita* which is now swinging in toward the far side of the sun. Dave insists on monitoring and taping everything that comes through. It proves to be largely replays of their exchanges with Luna and *Gloria*, mixed with a variety of highly personal messages. As references to cows, chickens and other livestock multiply Dave reluctantly gives up his idea that they are code. Bud counts a total of five male voices.

"Big deal," he says. "There were more chick drivers on the road when we left. Means space is safe now, the girlies have taken over. Let them sweat their little asses off." He chuckles. "When we get this bird down, the stars ain't gonna study old Buddy no more, no ma'am. A nice beach and about a zillion steaks and ale and all those sweet things. Hey, we'll be living history, we can charge admission."

Dave's face takes on the expression that means an inappropriate topic has been breached. Much to Lorimer's impatience, Dave discourages all speculation as to what may await them on this future Earth. He confines their transmissions strictly to the problem in hand; when Lorimer tries to get him at least to mention the unchanged-language puzzle Dave only says firmly, "Later." Lorimer fumes; inconceivable that he is three centuries in the future, unable to learn a thing.

They do glean a few facts from the women's talk. There have been nine successful *Sunbird* missions after theirs and one other casualty. And the *Gloria* and her sister ship are on a long-planned fly-by of the two inner planets.

"We always go along in pairs," Judy says. "But those planets are no good. Still, it was worth seeing."

"For Pete's sake Dave, ask them how many planets have been visited," Lorimer pleads.

"Later."

But about the fifth meal-break Luna suddenly volunteers.

"Earth is making up a history for you, *Sunbird,*" the Margo voice says. "We know you don't want to waste power asking so we thought we'd send you a few main points right now." She laughs. "It's much harder than we thought, nobody here does history."

Lorimer nods to himself; he has been wondering what he could tell a man from 1690 who would want to know what happened to Cromwell —was Cromwell then?—and who had never heard of electricity, atoms or the USA.

"Let's see, probably the most important is that there aren't as many people as you had, we're just over two million. There was a world epidemic not long after your time. It didn't kill people but it reduced the population. I mean there weren't any babies in most of the world. Ah, sterility. The country called Australia was affected least." Bud holds up a finger.

"And North Canada wasn't too bad. So the survivors all got together in the south part of the American states where they could grow food and the best communications and factories were. Nobody lives in the rest of the world but we travel there sometimes. Ah, we have five main activities, was industries the word? Food, that's farming and fishing. Communications, transport and space—that's us. And the factories they need. We live a lot simpler than you did, I think. We see your things all over, we're very grateful to you. Oh, you'll be interested to know we use zeppelins just like you did, we have six big ones. And our fifth thing is the children. Babies. Does that help? I'm using a children's book we have here."

The men have frozen during this recital; Lorimer is holding a cooling bag of hash. Bud starts chewing again and chokes.

"Two million people and a space capability?" He coughs. "That's incredible."

Dave gazes reflectively at the speaker. "There's a lot they're not telling us."

"I gotta ask them," Bud says. "Okay?"

Dave nods. "Watch it."

"Thanks for the history, Luna," Bud says. "We really appreciate it. But we can't figure out how you maintain a space program with only a couple of million people. Can you tell us a little more on that?"

In the pause Lorimer tries to grasp the staggering figures. From eight billion to two million . . . Europe, Asia, Africa, South America, America itself—wiped out. *There weren't any more babies.* World sterility, from what? The Black Death, the famines of Asia—those had been decimations. This is magnitudes worse. No, it is all the same: beyond comprehension. An empty world, littered with junk.

"*Sunbird?*" says Margo, "Da, I should have thought you'd want to know about space. Well, we have only the four real spaceships and one building. You know the two here. Then there's *Indira* and *Pech*, they're on the Mars run now. Maybe the Mars dome was since your day. You had the satellite stations though, didn't you? And the old Luna dome, of course—I remember now, it was during the epidemic. They tried to set up colonies to, ah, breed children, but the epidemic got there too. They struggled terribly hard. We owe a lot to you really, you men I mean. The history has it all, how you worked out a minimal viable program and trained everybody and saved it from the crazies. It was a glorious achievement. Oh, the marker here has one of your names on it. Lorimer. We love to keep it all going and growing, we all love traveling. Man is a rover, that's one of our mottoes."

"Are you hearing what I'm hearing?" Bud asks, blinking comically.

Dave is still staring at the speaker. "Not one word about their government," he says slowly. "Not a word about economic conditions. We're talking to a bunch of monkeys."

"Should I ask them?"

"Wait a minute . . . Roger, ask the name of their chief of state and the head of the space program. And—no, that's all."

"President?" Margo echoes Bud's query. "You mean like queens and kings? Wait, here's Myda. She's been talking about you with Earth."

The older woman they hear occasionally says *"Sunbird?* Da, we realize you had a very complex activity, your governments. With so few people we don't have that type of formal structure at all. People from the different activities meet periodically and our communications are good, everyone is kept informed. The people in each activity are in charge of doing it while they're there. We rotate, you see. Mostly in five-year hitches, for example Margo here was on the zeppelins and I've been on several factories and farms and of course the, well, the education, we all do that. I believe that's one big difference from you. And of course we all work. And things are basically far more stable now, I gather. We change slowly. Does that answer you? Of course you can always ask Registry, they keep track of us all. But we can't, ah, take you to our leader, if that's what you mean." She laughs, a genuine, jolly sound. "That's one of our old jokes. I must say," she goes on seriously, "it's been a joy to us that we can understand you so well. We make a big effort not to let the language drift, it would be tragic to lose touch with the past."

Dave takes the mike. "Thank you, Luna. You've given us something to think about. *Sunbird* out."

"How much of that is for real, Doc?" Bud rubs his curly head. "They're giving us one of your science fiction stories."

"The real story will come later," says Dave. "Our job is to get there."

"That's a point that doesn't look too good."

By the end of the session it looks worse. No Venus trajectory is any good. Lorimer reruns all the computations; same result.

"There doesn't seem to be any solution to this one, Dave," he says at last. "The parameters are just too tough. I think we've had it."

Dave massages his knuckles thoughtfully. Then he nods. "Roger. We'll fire the optimum sequence on the Earth heading."

"Tell them to wave if they see us go by," says Bud.

They are silent, contemplating the prospect of a slow death in space eighteen months hence. Lorimer wonders if he can raise the other question, the bad one. He is pretty sure what Dave will say. What will he himself decide, what will he have the guts to do?

"Hello, *Sunbird?*" the voice of *Gloria* breaks in. "Listen, we've been figuring. We think if you use all your fuel you could come back in close enough to our orbit so we could swing out and pick you up. You'd be using solar gravity that way. We have plenty of maneuver but much less acceleration than you do. You have suits and some kind of propellants, don't you? I mean, you could fly across a few kays?"

The three men look at each other; Lorimer guesses he had not been the only one to speculate on that.

"That's a good thought, *Gloria,*" Dave says. "Let's hear what Luna says."

"Why?" asks Judy. "It's our business, we wouldn't endanger the ship. We'd only miss another look at Venus, who cares. We have plenty of water and food and if the air gets a little smelly we can stand it."

"Hey, the chicks are all right," Bud says. They wait.

The voice of Luna comes on. "We've been looking at that too, Judy. We're not sure you understand the risk. Ah, *Sunbird,* excuse me. Judy, if you manage to pick them up you'll have to spend nearly a year in the ship with these three male persons from a *very different culture.* Myda says you should remember history and it's a risk no matter what Connie says. *Sunbird,* I hate to be so rude. Over."

Bud is grinning broadly, they all are. "Cave men," he chuckles. "All the chicks land preggers."

"Margo, they're human beings," the Judy voice protests. "This isn't just Connie, we're all agreed. Andy and Lady Blue say it would be very interesting. If it works, that is. We can't let them go without trying."

"We feel that way too, of course," Luna replies. "But there's another problem. They could be carrying diseases. *Sunbird,* I know you've been isolated for fourteen months, but Murti says people in your day were immune to organisms that aren't around now. Maybe some of ours could harm you, too. You could all get mortally sick and lose the ship."

"We thought of that, Margo," Judy says impatiently. "Look, if you have contact with them at all somebody has to test, true? So we're ideal. By the time we get home you'll know. And how could we get sick so fast we couldn't put *Gloria* in a stable orbit where you could get her later on?"

They wait. "Hey, what about that epidemic?" Bud pats his hair elaborately. "I don't know if I want a career in gay lib."

"You rather stay out here?" Dave asks.

"Crazies," says a different voice from Luna. *"Sunbird,* I'm Murti, the health person here. I think what we have to fear most is the meningitis-influenza complex, they mutate so readily. Does your Dr. Lorimer have any suggestions?"

"Roger, I'll put him on," says Dave. "But as to your first point, madam, I want to inform you that at time of takeoff the incidence of rape in the United States space cadre was zero point zero. I guarantee the conduct of my crew provided you can control yours. Here is Dr. Lorimer."

But Lorimer cannot of course tell them anything useful. They discuss the men's polio shots, which luckily have used killed virus, and various childhood diseases which still seem to be around. He does not mention their epidemic.

"Luna, we're going to try it," Judy declares. "We couldn't live with ourselves. Now let's get the course figured before they get any farther away."

From there on there is no rest on *Sunbird* while they set up and refigure and rerun the computations for the envelope of possible intersecting trajectories. The *Gloria's* drive, they learn, is indeed low-thrust, although capable of sustained operation. *Sunbird* will have to get most of the way to the rendezvous on her own if they can cancel their outward velocity.

The tension breaks once during the long session, when Luna calls *Gloria* to warn Connie to be sure the female crew members wear conceal-ing garments at all times if the men came aboard.

"Not·suit-liners, Connie, they're much too tight." It is the older woman, Myda. Bud chuckles.

"Your light sleepers, I think. And when the men unsuit, your Andy is the only one who should help them. You others stay away. The same for all body functions and sleeping. This is very important, Connie, you'll have to watch it the whole way home. There are a great many complicated tabus. I'm putting an instruction list on the bleeper, is your receiver working?"

"Da, we used it for France's black-hole paper."

"Good. Tell Judy to stand by. Now listen, Connie, listen carefully. Tell Andy he has to read it all. I repeat, *he* has to read every word. Did you hear that?"

"Ah, dinko," Connie answers. "I understand, Myda. He will."

"I think we just lost the ball game, fellas," Bud laments. "Old mother Myda took it all away."

Even Dave laughs. But later when the modulated squeal that is a whole text comes through the speaker, he frowns again. "There goes the good stuff."

The last factors are cranked in; the revised program spins, and Luna confirms them. "We have a pay-out, Dave," Lorimer reports. "It's tight but there are at least two viable options. Provided the main jets are fully functional."

"We're going EVA to check."

That is exhausting; they find a warp in the deflector housing of the port engines and spend four sweating hours trying to wrestle it back. It is only Lorimer's third sight of open space but he is soon too tired to care.

"Best we can do," Dave pants finally. 'We'll have to compensate in the psychic mode."

"You can do it, Dave-o," says Bud. "Hey, I gotta change those suit radios, don't let me forget."

In the psychic mode . . . Lorimer surfaces back to his real self, cocooned in *Gloria*'s big cluttered cabin, seeing Connie's living face. It must be hours, how long has he been dreaming?"

"About two minutes," Connie smiles.

"I was thinking of the first time I saw you."

"Oh yes. We'll never forget that, ever."

Nor will he . . . He lets it unroll again in his head. The interminable hours after the first long burn, which has sent *Sunbird* yawing so they all have to gulp nausea pills. Judy's breathless voice reading down their approach: "Oh, very good, four hundred thousand. . . . Oh great, *Sunbird,* you're almost three, you're going to break a hundred for sure—" Dave has done it, the big one.

Lorimer's probe is useless in the yaw, it isn't until they stabilize enough for the final burst that they can see the strange blip bloom and vanish in the slot. Converging, hopefully, on a theoretical near-intersection point.

"Here goes everything."

The final burn changes the yaw into a sickening tumble with the starfield looping past the glass. The pills are no more use and the fuel feed to the attitude jets goes sour. They are all vomiting before they manage to hand-pump the last of the fuel and slow the tumble.

"That's it, *Gloria.* Come and get us. Lights on, Bud. Let's get those suits up."

Fighting nausea they go through the laborious routine in the fouled cabin. Suddenly Judy's voice sings out, "We see you, *Sunbird!* We see your light! Can't you see us?"

"No time," Dave says. But Bud, half-suited, points at the window. "Fellas, oh, hey, look at that."

Lorimer stares, thinks he sees a faint spark between the whirling stars before he has to retch.

"Father, we thank you," says Dave quietly. "All right, move it on, Doc. Packs."

The effort of getting themselves plus the propulsion units and a couple of cargo nets out of the rolling ship drives everything else out of mind. It isn't until they are floating linked together and stabilized by Dave's hand jet that Lorimer has time to look.

The sun blanks out their left. A few meters below them *Sunbird* tumbles empty, looking absurdly small. Ahead of them, infinitely far away, is a point too blurred and yellow to be a star. It creeps: *Gloria,* on her approach tangent.

"Can you start, *Sunbird?*" says Judy in their helmets. "We don't want to brake any more on account of our exhaust. We estimate fifty kay in an hour, we're coming out on a line."

"Roger. Give me your jet, Doc."

"Goodbye, *Sunbird,*" says Bud. "Plenty of lead, Dave-o."

Lorimer finds it restful in a chidish way, being towed across the abyss tied to the two big men. He has total confidence in Dave, he never considers the possibility that they will miss, sail by and be lost. Does Dave feel contempt? Lorimer wonders; that banked-up silence, is it partly contempt for those who can manipulate only symbols, who have no mastery of matter? . . . He concentrates on mastering his stomach.

It is a long, dark trip. *Sunbird* shrinks to a twinkling light, slowly accelerating on the spiral course that will end her ultimately in the sun with their precious records that are three hundred years obsolete. With, also, the packet of photos and letters that Lorimer has twice put in his suit-pouch and twice taken out. Now and then he catches sight of *Gloria,* growing from a blur to an incomprehensible tangle of lighted crescents.

"Woo-ee, it's big," Bud says. "No wonder they can't accelerate, that thing is a flying trailer park. It'd break up."

"It's a spaceship. Got those nets tight, Doc?"

Judy's voice suddenly fills their helmets. "I see your lights! Can you see me? Will you have enough left to brake at all?"

"Affirmative to both, *Gloria,*" says Dave.

At that moment Lorimer is turned slowly forward again and he sees will see it forever: the alien ship in the starfield and on its dark side the tiny lights that are women in the stars, waiting for them. Three—no, four; one suit-light is way out, moving. If that is a tether it must be over a kilometer.

"Hello, I'm Judy Dakar!" The voice is close. "Oh, mother, you're big! Are you all right? How's your air?"

"No problem."

They are in fact stale and steaming wet; too much adrenalin. Dave uses the jets again and suddenly she is growing, is coming right at them, a silvery spider on a trailing thread. Her suit looks trim and flexible; it is mirror-bright, and the pack is quite small. Marvels of the future, Lorimer thinks; Paragraph One.

"You made it, you made it! Here, tie in. Brake!"

"There ought to be some historic words," Bud murmurs. "If she gives us a chance."

"Hello, Judy," says Dave calmly. "Thanks for coming."

"Contact!" She blasts their ears. "Haul us in, Andy! Brake, brake—the exhaust is back there!"

And they are grabbed hard, deflected into a great arc toward the ship. Dave uses up the last jet. The line loops.

"Don't jerk it," Judy cries. "Oh, I'm *sorry.*" She is clinging on them like a gibbon, Lorimer can see her eyes, her excited mouth. Incredible. "Watch out, it's slack."

"Teach me, honey," says Andy's baritone. Lorimer twists and sees him far back at the end of a heavy tether, hauling them smoothly in. Bud offers to help, is refused. "Just hang loose, please," a matronly voice tells them. It is obvious Andy has done this before. They come in spinning slowly, like space fish. Lorimer finds he can no longer pick out the twinkle that is *Sunbird.* When he is swung back, *Gloria* has changed to a disorderly cluster of bulbs and spokes around a big central cylinder. He can see pods and miscellaneous equipment stowed all over her. Not like science fiction.

Andy is paying the line into a floating coil. Another figure floats beside him. They are both quite short, Lorimer realizes as they near.

"Catch the cable," Andy tells them. There is a busy moment of shifting inertial drag.

"Welcome to *Gloria*, Major Davis, Captain Geirr, Dr. Lorimer. I'm Lady Blue Parks. I think you'll like to get inside as soon as possible. If you feel like climbing go right ahead, we'll pull all this in later."

"We appreciate it, ma'am."

They start hand-over-hand along the catenary of the main tether. It has a good rough grip. Judy coasts up to peer at them, smiling broadly, towing the coil. A taller figure waits by the ship's open airlock.

"Hello, I'm Connie. I think we can cycle in two at a time. Will you come with me, Major Davis?"

It is like an emergency on a plane, Lorimer thinks as Dave follows her in. Being ordered about by supernaturally polite little girls.

"Space-going stews," Bud nudges him. "How 'bout that?" His face is sprouting sweat. Lorimer tells him to go next, his own LSP has less load.

Bud goes in with Andy. The woman named Lady Blue waits beside Lorimer while Judy scrambles on the hull securing their cargo nets. She doesn't seem to have magnetic soles; perhaps ferrous metals aren't used in space now. When she begins hauling in the main tether on a simple hand winch Lady Blue looks at it critically.

"I used to make those," she says to Lorimer. What he can see of her features looks compressed, her dark eyes twinkle. He has the impression she is part black.

"I ought to get over and clean that aft antenna." Judy floats up. "Later," says Lady Blue. They both smile at Lorimer. Then the hatch opens and he and Lady Blue go in. When the toggles seat there comes a rising scream of air and Lorimer's suit collapses.

"Can I help you?" She has opened her faceplate, the voice is rich and live. Eagerly Lorimer catches the latches in his clumsy gloves and lets her lift the helmet off. His first breath surprises him, it takes an instant to identify the gas as fresh air. Then the inner hatch opens, letting in greenish light. She waves him through. He swims into a short tunnel. Voices are coming from around the corner ahead. His hand finds a grip and he stops, feeling his heart shudder in his chest.

When he turns that corner the world he knows will be dead. Gone, rolled up, blown away forever with *Sunbird.* He will be irrevocably in the future. A man from the past, a time traveler. In the future. . . .

He pulls himself around the bend.

The future is a vast bright cylinder, its whole inner surface festooned with unidentifiable objects, fronds of green. In front of him floats an odd tableau: Bud and Dave, helmets off, looking enormous in their bulky white suits and packs. A few meters away hang two bare-headed figures in shiny suits and a dark-haired girl in flowing pink pajamas.

They are all simply staring at the two men, their eyes and mouths open in identical expressions of pleased wonder. The face that has to be Andy's is grinning open-mouthed like a kid at the zoo. He is a surprisingly young boy, Lorimer sees, in spite of his deep voice; blonde, downy-cheeked, compactly muscular. Lorimer finds he can scarcely bear to look at the pink woman, can't tell if she really is surpassingly beautiful or plain. The taller suited woman has a shiny, ordinary face.

From overhead bursts an extraordinary sound which he finally recognizes as a chicken cackling. Lady Blue pushes past him.

"All right, Andy, Connie, stop staring and help them get their suits off. Judy, Luna is just as eager to hear about this as we are."

The tableau jumps to life. Afterwards Lorimer can recall mostly eyes, bright curious eyes tugging his boots, smiling eyes upside-down over his pack—and always that light, ready laughter. Andy is left alone to help them peel down, blinking at the fittings which Lorimer still finds embarrassing. He seems easy and nimble in his own half-open suit. Lorimer struggles out of the last lacings, thinking, a boy! A boy and four women orbiting the sun, flying their big junky ships to Mars. Should he feel humiliated? He only feels grateful, accepting a short robe and a bulb of tea somebody—Connie?—gives him.

The suited Judy comes in with their nets. The men follow Andy along another passage, Bud and Dave clutching at the small robes. Andy stops by a hatch.

"This greenhouse is for you, it's your toilet. Three's a lot but you have full sun."

Inside is a brilliant jungle, foliage everywhere, glittering water droplets, rustling leaves. Something whirs away—a grasshopper.

"You crank that handle." Andy points to a seat on a large cross-duct. "The piston rams the gravel and waste into a compost process and it ends up in the soil core. That vetch is a heavy nitrogen user and a great oxidator. We pump $CO_2$ in and oxy out. It's a real Woolagong."

He watches critically while Bud tries out the facility.

"What's a Woolagong?" asks Lorimer dazedly.

"Oh, she's one of our inventors. Some of her stuff is weird. When we have a pluggy-looking thing that works we call it a Woolagong." He grins. "The chickens eat the seeds and the hoppers, see, and the hoppers and iguanas eat the leaves. When a greenhnouse is going darkside we turn them in to harvest. With this much light I think we could keep a goat, don't you? You didn't have any life at all on your ship, true?"

"No," Lorimer says, "not a single iguana."

"They promised us a Shetland pony for Christmas," says Bud, rattling gravel. Andy joins perplexedly in the laugh.

Lorimer's head is foggy; it isn't only fatigue, the year in *Sunbird* has atrophied his ability to take in novelty. Numbly he uses the Woolagong and they go back out and forward to *Gloria's* big control room, where Dave makes a neat short speech to Luna and is answered graciously.

"We have to finish changing course now," Lady Blue says. Lorimer's impression has been right, she is a small light part-Negro in late middle age. Connie is part something exotic too, he sees; the others are European types.

"I'll get you something to eat," Connie smiles warmly. "Then you probably want to rest. We saved all the cubbies for you." She says "syved"; their accents are all identical.

As they leave the control room Lorimer sees the withdrawn look in Dave's eyes and knows he must be feeling the reality of being a passenger in an alien ship; not in command, not deciding the course, the communications going on unheard.

That is Lorimer's last coherent observation, that and the taste of the strange, good food. And then being led aft through what he now knows is the gym, to the shaft of the sleeping drum. There are six irised ports like dog-doors; he pushes through his assigned port and finds himself facing a roomy mattress. Shelves and a desk are in the wall.

"For your excretions." Connie's arm comes through the iris, pointing at bags. "If you have a problem stick your head out and call. There's water."

Lorimer simply drifts toward the mattress, too sweated out to reply. His drifting ends in a curious heavy settling and his final astonishment: the drum is smoothly, silently starting to revolve. He sinks gratefully onto the pad, growing "heavier" as the minutes pass. About a tenth gee, maybe more, he thinks, it's still accelerating. And falls into the most restful sleep he has known in the long weary year.

It isn't till next day that he understands that Connie and two others have been on the rungs of the giant chamber, sending it around hour after hour without pause or effort and chatting as they went.

How they talk, he thinks again floating back to real present time. The bubbling irritant pours through his memory, the voices of Ginny and Jenny and Penny on the kitchen telephone, before that his mother's voice, his sister Amy's. Interminable. What do they always have to talk, talk, talk of?

"Why, everything," says the real voice of Connie beside him now, "it's natural to share."

"Natural. . . ." Like ants, he thinks. They twiddle their antennae together every time they meet. Where did you go, what did you do? Twiddle-twiddle. How do you *feel?* Oh, I feel this, I feel that, blah blah twiddle-twiddle. Total coordination of the hive. Women have no self-respect. Say anything, no sense of the strategy of words, the dark danger of naming. Can't hold in.

"Ants, bee hives," Connie laughs, showing the bad tooth. "You truly see us as insects, don't you? Because they're females?"

"Was I talking aloud? I'm sorry." He blinks away dreams.

"Oh, please don't be. It's so sad to hear about your sister and your children and your, your wife. They must have been wonderful people. We think you're very brave."

But he has only thought of Ginny and them all for an instant—what has he been babbling? What is the drug doing to him?

"What are you doing to us?" he demands, lanced by real alarm now, almost angry.

"It's all right, truly." Her hand touches his, warm and somehow shy. "We all use it when we need to explore something. Usually it's pleasant. It's a laevonoramine compound, a disinhibitor, it doesn't dull you like alcohol. We'll be home so soon, you see. We have the responsibility to understand and you're so locked in." Her eyes melt at him. "You don't feel sick, do you? We have the antidote."

"No. . . ." His alarm has already flowed away somewhere. Her explanation strikes him as reasonable enough. "We're not locked in," he says or tries to say. "We talk . . ." He gropes for a word to convey the judiciousness, the adult restraint. Objectivity, maybe? "We talk when we have something to say." Irrelevantly he thinks of a mission coordinator named Forrest, famous for his blue jokes. "Otherwise it would all break down," he tells her. "You'd fly right out of the system." That isn't quite what he means; let it pass.

The voices of Dave and Bud ring out suddenly from opposite ends of the cabin, awakening the foreboding of evil in his mind. They don't know us, he thinks. They should look out, stop this. But he is feeling too serene, he wants to think about his own new understanding, the pattern of them all he is seeing at last.

"I feel lucid," he manages to say, "I want to think."

She looks pleased. "We call that the ataraxia effect. It's so nice when it goes that way."

Ataraxia, philosophical calm. Yes. But there are monsters in the deep, he thinks or says. The night side. The night side of Orren Lorimer, a self hotly dark and complex, waiting in leash. They're so vulnerable. They don't know we can take them. Images rush up: a Judy spread-eagled on the gym rungs, pink pajamas gone, open to him. Flash sequence of the three of them taking over the ship, the women tied up, helpless, shrieking, raped and used. The team—get the satellite station, get a shuttle down to Earth. Hostages. Make them do anything, no defense whatever. . . . Has Bud actually said that? But Bud doesn't know, he remembers. Dave knows they're hiding something, but he thinks it's socialism or sin. When they find out. . . .

How has he himself found out? Simply listening, really, all these months. He listens to their talk much more than the others; "fraternizing," Dave calls it. . . . They all listened at first, of course. Listened and looked and reacted helplessly to the female bodies, the tender bulges so close under the thin, tantalizing clothes, the magnetic mouths and eyes, the smell of them, their electric touch. Watching them touch each other, touch Andy, laughing, vanishing quietly into shared bunks. *What goes on? Can I? My need, my need—*

The power of them, the fierce resentment. . . . Bud muttered and groaned meaningfully despite Dave's warnings. He kept needling Andy until Dave banned all questions. Dave himself was noticeably tense and read his Bible a great deal. Lorimer found his own body pointing after them like a famished hound, hoping to Christ the cubicles are as they appeared to be, unwired.

All they learn is that Myda's instructions must have been ferocious. The atmosphere has been implacably antiseptic, the discretion impenetrable. Andy politely ignored every probe. No word or act has told them what, if anything, goes on; Lorimer was irresistibly reminded of the weekend he spent at Jenny's scout camp. The men's training came presently to their rescue, and they resigned themselves to finishing their mission on a super-*Sunbird*, weirdly attended by a troop of Boy and Girl Scouts.

In every other way their reception couldn't be more courteous. They have been given the run of the ship and their own dayroom in a cleaned-out gravel storage pod. They visit the control room as they wish. Lady Blue and Andy give them specs and manuals and show them every circuit and device of *Gloria*, inside and out. Luna has bleeped up a stream of science texts and the data on all their satellites and shuttles and the Mars and Luna dome colonies.

Dave and Bud plunged into an orgy of engineering. *Gloria* is, as they suspected, powered by a fission plant that uses a range of Lunar minerals. Her ion drive is only slightly advanced over the experimental models of their own day. The marvels of the future seem so far to consist mainly of ingenious modifications.

"It's primitive," Bud tells him. "What they've done is sacrifice everything to keep it simple and easy to maintain. Believe it, they can hand-feed fuel. And the back-ups, brother! They have redundant redundancy."

But Lorimer's technical interest soon flags. What he really wants is to be alone a while. He makes a desultory attempt to survey the apparently few new developments in his field, and finds he can't concentrate. What the hell, he tells himself, I stopped being a physicist three hundred years ago. Such a relief to be out of the cell of *Sunbird;* he has given himself up to drifting solitary through the warren of the ship, using their excellent four hundred millimeter telescope, noting the odd life of the crew.

. When he finds that Lady Blue likes chess they form a routine of biweekly games. Her personality intrigues him; she has reserve and an aura of authority. But she quickly stops Bud when he calls her "captain."

"No one here commands in your sense. I'm just the oldest." Bud goes back to "ma'am."

She plays a solid positional game, somewhat more erratic than a man but with occasional elegant traps. Lorimer is astonished to find that there is only one new chess opening, an interesting queen-side gambit called the Dagmar. One new opening in three centuries? He mentions it to the others when they come back from helping Andy and Judy Paris overhaul a standby converter.

"They haven't done much anywhere," Dave says. "Most of your new stuff dates from the epidemic, Andy, if you'll pardon me. The program seems to be stagnating. You've been gearing up this Titan project for eighty years."

"We'll get there." Andy grins.

"C'mon Dave," says Bud. "Judy and me are taking on you two for the next chicken dinner, we'll get a bridge team here yet. Woo-ee, I can taste that chicken! Losers get the iguana."

The food is so good. Lorimer finds himself lingering around the kitchen end, helping whoever is cooking, munching on their various seeds and chewy roots as he listens to them talk. He even likes the iguana. He begins to put on weight, in fact they all do. Dave decrees double exercise shifts.

"You going to make us *climb* home, Dave-o?" Bud groans. But Lorimer enjoys it, pedaling or swinging easily along the rungs while the women chat and listen to tapes. Familiar music: he identifies a strange spectrum from Handel, Brahms, Sibelius, through Strauss to ballad tunes and intricate light jazz-rock. No lyrics. But plenty of informative texts doubtless selected for his benefit.

From the promised short history he finds out more about the epidemic. It seems to have been an airborne quasi-virus escaped from Franco-Arab military labs, possibly potentiated by pollutants.

"It apparently damaged only the reproductive cells," he tells Dave and Bud. "There was little actual mortality, but almost universal sterility. Probably a molecular substitution in the gene code in the gametes. And the main effect seems to have been on the men. They mention a shortage of male births afterwards, which suggests that the damage was on the Y-chromosome where it would be selectively lethal to the male fetus."

"Is it still dangerous, Doc?" Dave asks. "What happens to us when we get back home?"

"They can't say. The birthrate is normal now, about 2 percent and rising. But the present population may be resistant. They never achieved a vaccine."

"Only one way to tell," Bud says gravely. "I volunteer."

Dave merely glances at him. Extraordinary how he still commands, Lorimer thinks. Not submission, for Pete's sake. A team.

The history also mentions the riots and fighting which swept the world when humanity found itself sterile. Cities bombed, and burned, massacres, panics, mass rapes and kidnapping of women, marauding armies of biologically desperate men, bloody cults. The crazies. But it is all so briefly told, so long ago. Lists of honored names. "We must always be grateful to the brave people who held the Denver Medical Laboratories —" And then on to the drama of building up the helium supply for the dirigibles.

In three centuries it's all dust, he thinks. What do I know of the hideous Thirty Years War that was three centuries back for me? *Fighting devastated Europe for two generations.* Not even names.

The description of their political and economic structure is even briefer. They seem to be, as Myda had said, almost ungoverned.

"It's a form of loose social credit system run by consensus," he says to Dave. "Somewhat like a permanent frontier period. They're building up slowly. Of course they don't need an army or airforce. I'm not sure if they even use cash money or recognize private ownership of land. I did notice one favorable reference to early Chinese communalism," he adds to see

Dave's mouth set. "But they aren't tied to a community. They travel about. When I asked Lady Blue about their police and legal system she told me to wait and talk with real historians. This Registry seems to be just that, it's not a policy organ."

"We've run into a situation here, Lorimer," Dave says soberly. "Stay away from it. They're not telling the story."

"You notice they never talk about their husbands?" Bud laughs. "I asked a couple of them what their husbands did and I swear they had to think. And they all have kids. Believe me, it's a swinging scene down there, even if old Andy acts like he hasn't found out what it's for."

"I don't want any prying into their personal family lives while we're on this ship, Geirr. None whatsoever. That's an order."

"Maybe they don't have families. You ever hear 'em mention anybody getting married? That has to be the one thing on a chick's mind. Mark my words, there's been some changes made."

"The social mores are bound to have changed to some extent," Lorimer says. "Obviously you have women doing more work outside the home, for one thing. But they have family bonds; for instance Lady Blue has a sister in an aluminum mill and another in health. Andy's mother is on Mars and his sister works in Registry. Connie has a brother or brothers on the fishing fleet near Biloxi, and her sister is coming out to replace her here next trip, she's making yeast now."

"That's the top of the iceberg."

"I doubt the rest of the iceberg is very sinister, Dave."

But somewhere along the line the blandness begins to bother Lorimer too. So much is missing. Marriage, love affairs, children's troubles, jealousy squabbles, status, possessions, money problems, sicknesses, funerals even —all the daily minutiae that occupied Ginny and her friends seems to have been edited out of these women's talk. *Edited.* . . . Can Dave be right, is some big, significant aspect being deliberately kept from them?

"I'm still surprised your language hasn't changed more," he says one day to Connie during their exertions in the gym.

"Oh, we're very careful about that." She climbs at an angle beside him, not using her hands. "It would be a dreadful loss if we couldn't understand the books. All the children are taught from the same original tapes, you see. Oh, there's faddy words we use for a while, but our communicators have to learn the old texts by heart, that keeps us together."

Judy Paris grunts from the pedicycle. "You, my dear children, will never know the oppression we suffered," she declaims mockingly.

"Judys talk too much," says Connie.

"We do, for a fact." They both laugh.

"So you still read our so-called great books, our fiction and poetry?" asks Lorimer. "Who do you read, H.G. Wells? Shakespeare? Dickens, ah, Balzac, Kipling, Brian?" He gropes; Brian had been a bestseller Ginny liked. When had he last looked at Shakespeare or the others?

"Oh, the historicals," Judy says. "It's interesting, I guess. Grim. They're not very realistic. I'm sure it was to you," she adds generously.

And they turn to discussing whether the laying hens are getting too much light, leaving Lorimer to wonder how what he supposes are the eternal verities of human nature can have faded from a world's reality. Love, conflict, heroism, tragedy—all "unrealistic"? Well, flight crews are never great readers; still, women read more. . . . Something *has* changed, he can sense it. Something basic enough to affect human nature. A physical development perhaps; a mutation? What is really under those floating clothes?

It is the Judys who give him part of it.

He is exercising alone with both of them, listening to them gossip about some legendary figure named Dagmar.

"The Dagmar who invented the chess opening?" he asks.

"Yes. She does anything, when she's good she's great."

"Was she bad sometimes?"

A Judy laughs. "The Dagmar problem, you can say. She has this tendency to organize everything. It's fine when it works but every so often it runs wild, she thinks she's queen or what. Then they have to get out the butterfly nets."

All in present tense—but Lady Blue has told him the Dagmar gambit is over a century old.

*Longevity*, he thinks; by God, that's what they're hiding. Say they've achieved a doubled or tripled life span, that would certainly change human psychology, affect their outlook on everything. Delayed maturity, perhaps? We were working on endocrine cell juvenescence when I left. How old are these girls, for instance?

He is framing a question when Judy Dakar says, "I was in the crèche when she went pluggo. But she's good, I loved her later on."

Lorimer thinks she has said "crash" and then realizes she means a communal nursery. "Is that the same Dagmar?" he asks. "She must be very old."

"Oh no, her sister."

"A sister a hundred years apart?"

"I mean, her daughter. Her, her *grand*daughter." She starts pedaling fast.

"Judys," says her twin, behind them.

Sister again. Everybody he learns of seems to have an extraordinary number of sisters, Lorimer reflects. He hears Judy Paris saying to her twin, "I think I remember Dagmar at the crèche. She started uniforms for everybody. Colors and numbers."

"You couldn't have, you weren't born," Judy Dakar retorts.

There is a silence in the drum.

Lorimer turns on the rungs to look at them. Two flushed cheerful faces stare back warily, make identical head-dipping gestures to swing the black hair out of their eyes. Identical. . . . But isn't the Dakar girl on the cycle a shade more mature, her face more weathered?

"I thought you were supposed to be twins."

"Ah, Judys talk a lot," they say together—and grin guiltily.

"You aren't sisters," he tells them. "You're what we called clones."

Another silence.

"Well, yes," says Judy Dakar. "We call it sisters. Oh, mother! We weren't supposed to tell you, Myda said you would be frightfully upset. It was illegal in your day, true?"

"Yes. We considered it immoral and unethical, experimenting with human life. But it doesn't upset me personally."

"Oh, that's beautiful, that's great," they say together. "We think of you as different," Judy Paris blurts, "you're more hu—more like us. Please, you don't have to tell the others, do you? Oh, *please* don't."

"It was an accident there were two of us here," says Judy Dakar. "Myda *warned* us. Can't you wait a little while?" Two identical pairs of dark eyes beg him.

"Very well," he says slowly. "I won't tell my friends for the time being. But if I keep your secret you have to answer some questions. For instance, how many of your people are created artificially this way?"

He begins to realize he *is* somewhat upset. Dave is right, damn it, they are hiding things. Is this brave new world populated by subhuman slaves, run by master brains? Decorticate zombies, workers without stomachs or sex, human cortexes wired into machines, monstrous experiments rush through his mind. He had been naïve again. These normal-looking women can be fronting for a hideous world.

"How many?"

"There's only about eleven thousand of us," Judy Dakar says. The two Judys look at each other, transparently confirming something. They're unschooled in deception, Lorimer thinks; is that good? And is diverted by Judy Paris exclaiming, "What we can't figure out is why did you think it was wrong?"

Lorimer tries to tell them, to convey the horror of manipulating human identity, creating abnormal life. The threat to individuality, the fearful power it would put in a dictator's hand.

"Dictator?" one of them echoes blankly. He looks at their faces and can only say, "Doing things to people without their consent. I think it's sad."

"But that's just what we think about you," the younger Judy bursts out. "How do you know who you *are?* Or who anybody is? All alone, no sisters to share with! You don't know what you can do, or what would be interesting to try. All you poor singletons, you—why, you just have to blunder along and die, all for nothing!"

Her voice trembles. Amazed, Lorimer sees both of them are misty-eyed.

"We better get this m-moving," the other Judy says.

They swing back into the rhythm and in bits and pieces Lorimer finds out how it is. Not bottled embryos, they tell him indignantly. Human mothers like everybody else, young mothers, the best kind. A somatic cell nucleus is inserted in an enucleated ovum and reimplanted in the womb. They have each borne two "sister" babies in their late teens and nursed them a while before moving on. The crèches always have plenty of mothers.

His longevity notion is laughed at; nothing but some rules of healthy living have as yet been achieved. "We should make ninety in good shape," they assure him. "A hundred and eight, that was Judy Eagle, she's our record. But she was pretty blah at the end."

The clone-strains themselves are old, they date from the epidemic. They were part of the first effort to save the race when the babies stopped and they've continued ever since.

"It's so perfect," they tell him. "We each have a book, it's really a library. All the recorded messages. The Book of Judy Shapiro, that's us. Dakar and Paris are our personal names, we're doing cities now." They laugh, trying not to talk at once about how each Judy adds her individual memoir, her adventures and problems and discoveries in the genotype they all share.

"If you make a mistake it's useful for the others. Of course you try not to—or at least make a *new* one."

"Some of the old ones aren't so realistic," her other self puts in. "Things were so different, I guess. We make excerpts of the parts we like best. And practical things, like Judys should watch out for skin cancer."

"But we have to read the whole thing every ten years," says the Judy called Dakar. "It's inspiring. As you get older you understand some of the ones you didn't before."

Bemused, Lorimer tries to think how it would be, hearing the voices of three hundred years of Orren Lorimers. Lorimers who were mathematicians or plumbers or artists or bums or criminals, maybe. The continuing exploration and completion of self. And a dozen living doubles; aged Lorimers, infant Lorimers. And other Lorimers' women and children . . . would he enjoy it or resent it? He doesn't know.

"Have you made your records yet?"

"Oh, we're too young. Just notes in case of accident."

"Will we be in them?"

"You can say!" They laugh merrily, then sober. "Truly you won't tell?" Judy Paris asks. "Lady Blue, we have to let her know what we did. Oof. But *truly* you won't tell your friends?"

He hadn't told on them, he thinks now, emerging back into his living self. Connie beside him is drinking cider from a bulb. He has a drink in his hand too, he finds. But he hasn't told.

"Judys will talk." Connie shakes her head, smiling. Lorimer realizes he must have gabbled out the whole thing.

"It doesn't matter," he tells her. "I would have guessed soon anyhow. There were too many clues . . . Woolagongs invent, Mydas worry, Jans are brains, Billy Dees work so hard. I picked up six different stories of hydroelectric stations that were built or improved or are being run by one Lala Singh. Your whole way of life. I'm more interested in this sort of thing than a respectable physicist should be," he says wryly. "You're all clones, aren't you? Every one of you. What do Connies do?"

"You really do know." She gazes at him like a mother whose child has done something troublesome and bright. "Whew! Oh, well, Connies farm like mad, we grow things. Most of our names are plants. I'm Veronica, by the way. And of course the crèches, that's our weakness. The runt mania. We tend to focus on anything smaller or weak."

Her warm eyes focus on Lorimer, who draws back involuntarily.

"We control it." She gives a hearty chuckle. "We aren't all that way. There's been engineering Connies, and we have two young sisters who love metallurgy. It's fascinating what the genotype can do if you try. The

original Constantia Morelos was a chemist, she weighed ninety pounds
and never saw a farm in her life." Connie looks down at her own muscular
arms. "She was killed by the crazies, she fought with weapons. It's so hard
to understand . . . And I had a sister Timothy who made dynamite and
dug two canals and she wasn't even an andy."

"*An* andy," he says.

"Oh, dear."

"I guessed that too. Early androgen treatments."

She nods hesitantly. "Yes. We need the muscle-power for some jobs.
A few. Kays are quite strong anyway. Whew!" She suddenly stretches her
back, wriggles as if she'd been cramped. "Oh, I'm glad you know. It's been
such a strain. We couldn't even sing."

"Why not?"

"Myda was sure we'd make mistakes, all the words we'd have had to
change. We sing a lot." She softly hums a bar or two.

"What kinds of songs do you sing?"

"Oh, every kind. Adventure songs, work songs, mothering songs, roaming songs, mood songs, trouble songs, joke songs—everything."

"What about love songs?" he ventures. "Do you still have, well, love?"

"Of course, how could people not love?" But she looks at him doubtfully. "The love stories I've heard from your time are so, I don't know,
so weird. Grim and pluggy. It doesn't seem like love. . . . Oh, yes, we have
famous love songs. Some of them are partly sad too. Like Tamil and
Alcmene O, they're fated together. Connies are fated too, a little," she
grins bashfully. "We love to be with Ingrid Anders. It's more one-sided.
I hope there'll be an Ingrid on my next hitch. She's so exciting, she's like
a little diamond."

Implications are exploding all about him, sparkling with questions. But
Lorimer wants to complete the darker pattern beyond.

"Eleven thousand genotypes, two million people: that averages two
hundred of each of you alive now." She nods. "I suppose it varies? There's
more of some?"

"Yes, some types aren't as viable. But we haven't lost any since early
days. They tried to preserve all the genes they could, we have people from
all the major races and a lot of small strains. Like me, I'm the Carib Blend.
Of course we'll never know what was lost. But eleven thousand is a lot,
really. We all try to know everyone, it's a life hobby."

A chill penetrates his ataraxi. Eleven thousand, period. That is the true
population of Earth now. He thinks of two hundred tall olive-skinned

women named after plants, excited by two hundred little bright Ingrids; two hundred talkative Judys, two hundred self-possessed Lady Blues, two hundred Margos and Mydas and the rest. He shivers. The heirs, the happy pall-bearers of the human race.

"So evolution ends," he says somberly.

"No, why? It's just slowed down. We do everything much slower than you did, I think. We like to experience things *fully*. We have time." She stretches again, smiling. "There's all the time."

"But you have no new genotypes. It is the end."

"Oh but there are, now. Last century they worked out the way to make haploid nuclei combine. We can make a stripped egg-cell function like pollen," she says proudly. "I mean sperm. It's tricky, some don't come out too well. But now we're finding both X's viable we have over a hundred new types started. Of course it's hard for them, with no sisters. The donors try to help."

Over a hundred, he thinks. Well. Maybe. . . . But "both X's viable," what does that mean? She must be referring to the epidemic. But he had figured it primarily affected the men. His mind goes happily to work on the new puzzle, ignoring a sound from somewhere that is trying to pierce his calm.

"It was a gene or genes on the X-chromosome that was injured," he guesses aloud. "Not the Y. And the lethal trait had to be recessive, right? Thus there would have been no births at all for a time, until some men recovered or were isolated long enough to manufacture undamaged X-bearing gametes. But women carry their lifetime supply of ova, they could never regenerate reproductively. When they mated with the recovered males only female babies would be produced, since the female carries two X's and the mother's defective gene would be compensated by a normal X from the father. But the male is XY, he receives only the mother's defective X. Thus the lethal defect would be expressed, the male fetus would be finished. . . . A planet of girls and dying men. The few odd viables died off."

"You truly do understand," she says admiringly.

The sound is becoming urgent; he refuses to hear it, there is significance here.

"So we'll be perfectly all right on Earth. No problem. In theory we can marry again and have families, daughters anyway."

"Yes," she says. "In theory."

The sound suddenly broaches his defenses, becomes the loud voice of

Bud Geirr raised in song. He sounds plain drunk now. It seems to be coming from the main garden pod, the one they use to grow vegetables, not sanitation. Lorimer feels the dread alive again, rising closer. Dave ought to keep an eye on him. But Dave seems to have vanished too, he recalls seeing him go towards Control with Lady Blue.

"OH, THE SUN SHINES BRIGHT ON PRET-TY RED WI-I-ING," carols Bud.

Something should be done, Lorimer decides painfully. He stirs; it is an effort.

"Don't worry," Connie says. "Andy's with them."

"You don't know, you don't know what you've started." He pushes off toward the garden hatchway.

"—AS SHE LAY SLE-EEPING, A COWBOY CREE-E-EEPING—" General laughter from the hatchway. Lorimer coasts through into the green dazzle. Beyond the radial fence of snap-beans he sees Bud sailing in an exaggerated crouch after Judy Paris. Andy hangs by the iguana cages, laughing.

Bud catches one of Judy's ankles and stops them both with a flourish, making her yellow pajamas swirl. She giggles at him upside-down, making no effort to free herself.

"I don't like this," Lorimer whispers.

"Please don't interfere." Connie has hold of his arm, anchoring them both to the tool rack. Lorimer's alarm seems to have ebbed; he will watch, let serenity return. The others have not noticed them.

"Oh, there once was an Indian maid." Bud sings more restrainedly, "Who never was a-fraid, that some buckaroo would slip it up her, ahem, ahem," he coughs ostentatiously, laughing. "Hey, Andy, I hear them calling you."

"What?" says Judy, "I don't hear anything."

"They're calling you, lad. Out there."

"Who?" asks Andy, listening.

"*They* are, for Crissake." He lets go of Judy and kicks over to Andy. "Listen, you're a great kid. Can't you see me and Judy have some business to discuss in private?" He turns Andy gently around and pushes him at the bean-stakes. "It's New Year's Eve, dummy."

Andy floats passively away through the fence of vines, raising a hand at Lorimer and Connie. Bud is back with Judy.

"Happy New Year, kitten," he smiles.

"Happy New Year. Did you do special things on New Year?" she asks curiously.

"What we did on New Year's." He chuckles, taking her shoulders in his hands. "On New Year's Eve, yes we did. Why don't I show you some of our primitive Earth customs, hmm?"

She nods, wide-eyed.

"Well, first we wish each other well, like this." He draws her to him and lightly kisses her cheek. "Kee-rist, what a dumb bitch," he says in a totally different voice. "You can tell you've been out too long when the geeks start looking good. Knockers, ahhh—" His hand plays with her blouse. The man is unaware, Lorimer realizes. He doesn't know he's drugged, he's speaking his thoughts. I must have done that. Oh, God. . . . He takes shelter behind his crystal lens, an observer in the protective light of eternity.

"And then we smooch a little." The friendly voice is back, Bud holds the girl closer, caressing her back. "Fat ass." He puts his mouth on hers; she doesn't resist. Lorimer watches Bud's arms tighten, his hands working on her buttocks, going under her clothes. Safe in the lens his own sex stirs. Judy's arms are waving aimlessly.

Bud breaks for breath, a hand at his zipper.

"Stop staring," he says hoarsely. "One fucking more word, you'll find out what that big mouth is for. Oh, man, a flagpole. Like steel. . . . Bitch, this is your lucky day." He is baring her breasts now, big breasts. Fondling them. "Two fucking years in the ass end of noplace," he mutters, "shit on me will you? Can't wait, watch it—titty-titty-titties—"

He kisses her again quickly and smiles down at her. "Good?" he asks in his tender voice, and sinks his mouth on her nipples, his hand seeking in her thighs. She jerks and says something muffled. Lorimer's arteries are pounding with delight, with dread.

"I, I think this should stop," he makes himself say falsely, hoping he isn't saying more. Through the pulsing tension he hears Connie whisper back, it sounds like "Don't worry, Judy's very athletic." Terror stabs him, they don't know. But he can't help.

"Cunt," Bud grunts, "you have to have a cunt in there, is it froze up? You dumb cunt—" Judy's face appears briefly in her floating hair, a remote part of Lorimer's mind notes that she looks amused and uncomfortable. His being is riveted to the sight of Bud expertly controlling her body in midair, peeling down the yellow slacks. Oh god—her dark pubic mat, the thick white thighs—a perfectly normal woman, no mutation. Ohhh, God. . . . But there is suddenly a drifting shadow in the way: Andy again floating over them with something in his hands.

"You dinko, Jude?" the boy asks.

Bud's face comes up red and glaring. "Bug out, you!"

"Oh, I won't bother."

"Jee-sus Christ." Bud lunges up and grabs Andy's arm, his legs still hooked around Judy. "This is man's business, boy, do I have to spell it out?" He shifts his grip. "Shoo!"

In one swift motion he has jerked Andy close and back-handed his face hard, sending him sailing into the vines.

Bud gives a bark of laughter, bends back to Judy. Lorimer can see his erection poking through his fly. He wants to utter some warning, tell them their peril, but he can only ride the hot pleasure surging through him, melting his crystal shell. Go on, more—avidly he sees Bud mouth her breasts again and then suddenly flip her whole body over, holding her wrists behind her in one fist, his legs pinning hers. Her bare buttocks bulge up helplessly, enormous moons. "Ass-s-s," Bud groans. "Up you bitch, ahhh-hh—" he pulls her butt onto him.

Judy gives a cry, begins to struggle futilely. Lorimer's shell boils and bursts. Amid the turmoil ghosts outside are trying to rush in. And something *is* moving, a real ghost—to his dismay he sees it is Andy again, floating toward the joined bodies, holding a whirring thing. Oh, no—a camera. The fools.

"Get away!" he tries to call to the boy.

But Bud's head turns, he has seen. "You little pissass." His long arm shoots out and captures Andy's shirt, his legs still locked around Judy.

"I've had it with you." His fist slams into Andy's mouth, the camera goes spinning away. But this time Bud doesn't let him go, he is battering the boy, all of them rolling in a tangle in the air.

"Stop!" Lorimer hears himself shout, plunging at them through the beans. "Bud, stop it! You're hitting a woman."

The angry face comes around, squinting at him.

"Get lost Doc, you little fart. Get your own ass."

"Andy is a *woman*, Bud. You're hitting a girl. She's not a man."

"Huh?" Bud glances at Andy's bloody face. He shakes the shirt-front. "Where's the boobs?"

"She doesn't have breasts, but she's a woman. Her real name is Kay. They're all women. Let her go, Bud."

Bud stares at the androgyne, his legs still pinioning Judy, his penis poking the air. Andy put up his/her hands in a vaguely combative way.

"A dyke?" says Bud slowly. "A God damn little bull dyke? This I gotta see."

He feints casually, thrusts a hand into Andy's crotch.

"No balls!" he roars, "No balls at all!" Convulsing with laughter he lets himself tip over in the air, releasing Andy, his legs letting Judy slip free. "Na-ah," he interrupts himself to grab her hair and goes on guffawing. "A dyke! Hey, dykey!" He takes hold of his hard-on, waggles it at Andy. "Eat your heart out, little dyke." Then he pulls up Judy's head. She has been watching unresisting all along.

"Take a good look, girlie. See what old Buddy has for you? Tha-a-at's what you want, say it. How long since you saw a real man, hey, dog-face?"

Maniacal laughter bubbles up in Lorimer's gut, farce too strong for fear. "She never saw a man in her life before, none of them has. You imbecile, don't you get it? There aren't any other men, they've all been dead three hundred years."

Bud slowly stops chuckling, twists around to peer at Lorimer.

"What'd I hear you say, Doc?"

"The men are all gone. They died off in the epidemic. There's nothing but women left alive on Earth."

"You mean there's, there's two million women down there and no men?" His jaw gapes. "Only little bull dykes like Andy. . . . Wait a minute. Where do they get the kids?"

"They grow them artificially. They're all girls."

"Gawd. . . ." Bud's hand clasps his drooping penis, jiggles it absently. It stiffens. "Two million hot little cunts down there, waiting for old Buddy. Gawd. The last man on Earth. . . . You don't count, Doc. And old Dave, he's full of crap."

He begins to pump himself, still holding Judy by the hair. The motion sends them slowly backward. Lorimer sees that Andy—Kay—has the camera going again. There is a big star-shaped smear of blood on the boyish face; cut lip, probably. He himself feels globed in thick air, all action spent. Not lucid.

"Two million cunts," Bud repeats. "Nobody home, nothing but pussy everywhere. I can do anything I want, any time. No more shit." He pumps faster. "They'll be spread out for miles begging for it. Clawing each other for it. All for me, King Buddy. . . . I'll have strawberries and cunt for breakfast. Hot buttered boobies, man. 'N' head, there'll be a couple little twats licking whip cream off my cock all day long. . . . Hey, I'll have contests! Only the best for old Buddy now. Not you, cow." He jerks Judy's head. "Li'l teenies, tight li'l holes. I'll make the old broads hot 'em up while I watch." He frowns slightly, working on himself. In a clinical corner of his mind Lorimer guesses the drug is retarding ejaculation. He tells himself that he should be relieved by Bud's self-absorption, is instead obscurely terrified.

"King, I'll be their god," Bud is mumbling. "They'll make statues of me, my cock a mile high, all over. . . . His Majesty's sacred balls. They'll worship it. . . . Buddy Geirr, the last cock on Earth. Oh man, if old George could see that. When the boys hear that they'll really shit themselves, woo-ee!"

He frowns harder. "They can't all be gone." His eyes rove, find Lorimer. "Hey, Doc, there's some men left someplace, aren't there? Two or three, anyway?"

"No." Effortfully Lorimer shakes his head. "They're all dead, all of them."

"Balls." Bud twists around, peering at them. "There has to be some left. Say it." He pulls Judy's head up. *"Say it,* cunt."

"No, it's true," she says.

"No men," Andy/Kay echoes.

"You're lying." Bud scowls, frigs himself faster, thrusting his pelvis. "There has to be some men, sure there are. . . . They're hiding out in the hills, that's what it is. Hunting, living wild. . . . Old wild men, I knew it."

"Why do there have to be men?" Judy asks him, being jerked to and fro.

"Why, you stupid bitch." He doesn't look at her, thrusts furiously. "Because, dummy, otherwise nothing counts, that's why. . . . There's some men, some good old buckaroos—Buddy's a good old buckaroo—"

"Is he going to emit sperm now?" Connie whispers.

"Very likely," Lorimer says, or intends to say. The spectacle is of merely clinical interest, he tells himself, nothing to dread. One of Judy's hands clutches something: a small plastic bag. Her other hand is on her hair that Bud is yanking. It must be painful.

"Uhhh, ahh," Bud pants distressfully, "fuck away, fuck—" Suddenly he pushes Judy's head into his groin, Lorimer glimpses her nonplussed expression.

"You have a mouth, bitch, get working! . . . Take it for shit's sake, *take* it! Uh, uh—" A small oyster jets limply from him. Judy's arm goes after it with the bag as they roll over in the air.

*"Geirr!"*

Bewildered by the roar, Lorimer turns and sees Dave—Major Norman Davis—looming in the hatchway. His arms are out, holding back Lady Blue and the other Judy.

"Geirr! I said there would be no misconduct on this ship and I mean it. Get away from that woman!"

Bud's legs only move vaguely, he does not seem to have heard. Judy swims through them bagging the last drops.

"You, what the hell are you doing?"

In the silence Lorimer hears his own voice say, "Taking a sperm sample, I should think."

"Lorimer? Are you out of your perverted mind? Get Geirr to his quarters."

Bud slowly rotates upright. "Ah, the reverend Leroy," he says tonelessly.

"You're drunk, Geirr. Go to your quarters."

"I have news for you, Dave-o," Bud tells him in the same flat voice. "I bet you don't know we're the last men on Earth. Two million twats down there."

"I'm aware of that," Dave says furiously. "You're a drunken disgrace. Lorimer, get that man out of here."

But Lorimer feels no nerve of action stir. Dave's angry voice has pushed back the terror, created a strange hopeful stasis encapsulating them all.

"I don't have to take that any more . . . ." Bud's head moves back and forth, silently saying no, no, as he drifts toward Lorimer. "Nothing counts any more. All gone. What for, friends?" His forehead puckers. "Old Dave, he's a man. I'll let him have some. The dummies. . . . Poor old Doc, you're a creep but you're better'n nothing, you can have some too. . . . We'll have places, see, big spreads. Hey, we can run drags, there has to be a million good old cars down there. We can go hunting. And then we find the wild men."

Andy, or Kay, is floating toward him, wiping off blood.

"Ah, no you don't!" Bud snarls and lunges for her. As his arm stretches out Judy claps him on the triceps.

Bud gives a yell that dopplers off, his limbs thrash—and then he is floating limply, his face suddenly serene. He is breathing, Lorimer sees, releasing his own breath, watching them carefully straighten out the big body. Judy plucks her pants out of the vines, and they start towing him out through the fence. She has the camera and the specimen bag.

"I put this in the freezer, dinko?" she says to Connie as they come by. Lorimer has to look away.

Connie nods. "Kay, how's your face?"

"I felt it!" Andy/Kay says excitedly through puffed lips, "I felt physical anger, I wanted to hit him. Woo-ee!"

"Put that man in my wardroom," Dave orders as they pass. He has moved into the sunlight over the lettuce rows. Lady Blue and Judy Dakar are back by the wall, watching. Lorimer remembers what he wanted to ask.

"Dave, do you really know? Did you find out they're all women?"

Dave eyes him broodingly, floating erect with the sun on his chestnut beard and hair. The authentic features of man. Lorimer thinks of his own father, a small pale figure like himself. He feels better.

"I always knew they were trying to deceive us, Lorimer. Now that this woman has admitted the facts I understand the full extent of the tragedy."

It is his deep, mild Sunday voice. The women look at him interestedly.

"They are lost children. They have forgotten he who made them. For generations they have lived in darkness."

"They seem to be doing all right," Lorimer hears himself say. It sounds rather foolish.

"Women are not capable of running anything. You should know that, Lorimer. Look what they've done here, it's pathetic. Marking time, that's all. Poor souls." Dave sighs gravely. "It is not their fault. I recognize that. Nobody has given them any guidance for three hundred years. Like a chicken with its head off."

Lorimer recognizes his own thought; the structureless, chattering, trivial, two-million-celled protoplasmic lump.

"The head of the woman is the man," Dave says crisply. "Corinthians one eleven three. No discipline whatsoever." He stretches out his arm, holding up his crucifix as he drifts toward the wall of vines. "Mockery. Abominations." He touches the stakes and turns, framed in the green arbor.

"We were sent here, Lorimer. This is God's plan. *I* was sent here. Not you, you're as bad as they are. My middle name is Paul," he adds in a conversational tone. The sun gleams on the cross, on his uplifted face, a strong, pure, apostolic visage. Despite some intellectual reservations Lorimer feels a forgotten nerve respond.

"Oh Father, send me strength," Dave prays quietly, his eyes closed. "You have spared us from the void to bring your light to this suffering world. I shall lead thy erring daughters out of the darkness. I shall be a stern but merciful father to them in thy name. Help me to teach the children thy holy law and train them in the fear of thy righteous wrath. Let the women learn in silence and all subjection; Timothy two eleven. They shall have sons to rule over them and glorify thy name."

He could do it, Lorimer thinks, a man like that really could get life going again. Maybe there is some mystery, some plan. I was too ready to give up. No guts. . . . He becomes aware of women whispering.

"This tape is about through." It is Judy Dakar. "Isn't that enough? He's just repeating."

"Wait," murmurs Lady Blue.

"And she brought forth a man child to rule the nations with a rod of iron, Revelations twelve five," Dave says, louder. His eyes are open now, staring intently at the crucifix. *"For God so loved the world that he sent his only begotten son."*

Lady Blue nods; Judy pushes off toward Dave. Lorimer understands, protest rising in his throat. They mustn't do that to Dave, treating him like an animal for Christ's sake, a man—

"Dave! Look out, don't let her get near you!" he shouts.

"May I look, major? It's beautiful, what is it?" Judy is coasting close, her hand out toward the crucifix.

"She's got a hypo, watch it!"

But Dave has already wheeled round. "Do not profane, woman!"

He thrusts the cross at her like a weapon, so menacing that she recoils in mid air and shows the glinting needle in her hand.

"Serpent!" He kicks her shoulder away, sending himself upward. "Blasphemer. All right," he snaps in his ordinary voice, "there's going to be some order around here starting now. Get over by that wall, all of you."

Astounded, Lorimer sees that Dave actually has a weapon in his other hand, a small gray handgun. He must have had it since Houston. Hope and ataraxia shrivel away, he is shocked into desperate reality.

"Major Davis," Lady Blue is saying. She is floating right at him, they all are, right at the gun. Oh God, do they know what it is?

"Stop!" he shouts at them. "Do what he says, for God's sake. That's a ballistic weapon, it can kill you. It shoots metal slugs." He begins edging toward Dave along the vines.

"Stand back." Dave gestures with the gun. "I am taking command of this ship in the name of the United States of America under God."

"Dave, put that gun away. You don't want to shoot people."

Dave sees him, swings the gun around. "I warn you, Lorimer, get over there with them. Geirr's a man, when he sobers up." He looks at the women still drifting puzzledly toward him and understands. "All right, lesson one. Watch this."

He takes deliberate aim at the iguana cages and fires. There is a pinging crack. A lizard explodes bloodily, voices cry out. A loud mechanical warble starts up and overrides everything.

"A leak!" Two bodies go streaking toward the far end, everybody is moving. In the confusion Lorimer sees Dave calmly pulling himself back to the hatchway behind them, his gun ready. He pushes frantically across the tool rack to cut him off. A spray cannister comes loose in his grip, leaving him kicking in the air. The alarm warble dies.

"You will stay here until I decide to send for you," Dave announces. He has reached the hatch, is pulling the massive lock door around. It will seal off the pod, Lorimer realizes.

"Don't do it, Dave! Listen to me, you're going to kill us all." Lorimer's own internal alarms are shaking him, he knows now what all that damned volleyball has been for and he is scared to death. "Dave, listen to me!"

"Shut up." The gun swings toward him. The door is moving; Lorimer gets a foot on solidity.

"Duck! It's a bomb!" With all his strength he hurls the massive cannister at Dave's head and launches himself after it.

"Look out!" And he is sailing helplessly in slow motion, hearing the gun go off again, voices yelling. Dave must have missed him, overhead shots are tough—and then he is doubling downwards, grabbing hair. A hard blow strikes his gut, it is Dave's leg kicking past him but he has his arm under the beard, the big man bucking like a bull, throwing him around.

"Get the gun, get it!" People are bumping him, getting hit. Just as his hold slips a hand snakes by him onto Dave's shoulder and they are colliding into the hatch door in a tangle. Dave's body is suddenly no longer at war.

Lorimer pushes free, sees Dave's contorted face tip slowly backward looking at him.

"Judas—"

The eyes close. It is over.

Lorimer looks around. Lady Blue is holding the gun, sighting down the barrel.

"Put that down," he gasps, winded. She goes on examining it.

"Hey, thanks!" Andy—Kay—grins lopsidedly at him, rubbing her jaw. They are all smiling, speaking warmly to him, feeling themselves, their torn clothes. Judy Dakar has a black eye starting, Connie holds a shattered iguana by the tail.

Beside him Dave drifts breathing stertorously, his blind face pointing at the sun. *Judas* . . . Lorimer feels the last shield break inside him, desolation flooding in. *On the deck my captain lies.*

Andy-who-is-not-a-man comes over and matter-of-factly zips up Dave's jacket, takes hold of it and begins to tow him out. Judy Dakar stops them long enough to wrap the crucifix chain around his hand. Somebody laughs, not unkindly, as they go by.

For an instant Lorimer is back in that Evanston toilet. But they are gone, all the little giggling girls. All gone forever, gone with the big boys waiting outside to jeer at him. Bud is right, he thinks. Nothing counts any more. Grief and anger hammer at him. He knows now what he has been dreading: not their vulnerability, his.

"They were good men," he says bitterly. "They aren't bad men. You don't know what bad means. You did it to them, you broke them down. You made them do crazy things. Was it interesting? Did you learn enough?" His voice is trying to shake. "Everybody has aggressive fantasies. They didn't act on them. Never. Until you poisoned them."

They gaze at him in silence. "But nobody does," Connie says finally. "I mean, the fantasies."

"They were good men," Lorimer repeats elegaically. He knows he is speaking for it all, for Dave's Father, for Bud's manhood, for himself, for Cro-Magnon, for the dinosaurs too, maybe. "I'm a man. By God yes, I'm angry. I have a right. We gave you all this, we made it all. We built your precious civilization and your knowledge and comfort and medicines and your dreams. All of it. We protected you, we worked our balls off keeping you and your kids. It was hard. It was a fight, a bloody fight all the way. We're tough. We had to be, can't you understand? Can't you for Christ's sake understand that?"

Another silence.

"We're trying," Lady Blue sighs. "We are trying, Dr. Lorimer. Of course we enjoy your inventions and we do appreciate your evolutionary role. But you must see there's a problem. As I understand it, what you protected people from was largely other males, wasn't it? We've just had an extraordinary demonstration. You have brought history to life for us." Her wrinkled brown eyes smile at him; a small, tea-colored matron holding an obsolete artifact.

"But the fighting is long over. It ended when you did, I believe. We can hardly turn you loose on Earth, and we simply have no facilities for people with your emotional problems."

"Besides, we don't think you'd be very happy," Judy Dakar adds earnestly.

"We could clone them," says Connie. "I know there's people who would volunteer to mother. The young ones might be all right, we could try."

"We've been *over* all that." Judy Paris is drinking from the water tank. She rinses and spits into the soil bed, looking worriedly at Lorimer. "We ought to take care of that leak now, we can talk tomorrow. And tomorrow and tomorrow." She smiles at him, unself-consciously rubbing her crotch. "I'm sure a lot of people will want to meet you."

"Put us on an island," Lorimer says wearily. "On three islands." That look; he knows that look of preoccupied compassion. His mother and sister had looked just like that the time the diseased kitten came in the yard. They had comforted it and fed it and tenderly taken it to the vet to be gassed.

An acute, complex longing for the women he has known grips him. Ginny . . . dear God. His sister Amy. Poor Amy, she was good to him when they were kids. His mouth twists.

"Your problem is," he says, "if you take the risk of giving us equal rights, what could we possibly contribute?"

"Precisely," says Lady Blue. They all smile at him relievedly, not understanding that he isn't.

"I think I'll have that antidote now," he says.

Connie floats toward him, a big, warm-hearted, utterly alien woman. "I thought you'd like yours in a bulb." She smiles kindly.

"Thank you." He takes the small, pink bulb. "Just tell me," he says to Lady Blue, who is looking at the bullet gashes, "what do you call yourselves? Women's World? Liberation? Amazonia?"

"Why, we call ourselves human beings." Her eyes twinkle absently at him, go back to the bullet marks. "Humanity, mankind." She shrugs. "The human race."

The drink tastes cool going down, something like peace and freedom, he thinks. Or death.

# On the Storm Planet

*"On the Storm Planet" is about Henriada, a world of constant and never-ending storms, of creatures that are less and more than human, and about the nature of truth. In most of science fiction, its practitioners write about* other worlds. *In the best of science fiction, authors write of* other worlds, *as in this remarkable story by the equally remarkable Cordwainer Smith (pseudonym of Paul Myron Anthony Linebarger).*

"At two seventy-five in the morning," said the administrator to Casher O'Neill, "you will kill this girl with a knife. At two seventy-seven, a fast groundcar will pick you up and bring you back here. Then the power cruiser will be yours. Is that a deal?"

He held out his hand as if he wanted Casher O'Neill to shake it then and there, making some kind of an oath or bargain.

Casher did not slight the man, so he picked up his glass and said, "Let's drink to the deal first!"

The administrator's quick, restless, darting eyes looked Casher up and down very suspiciously. The warm sea-wet air blew through the room. The administrator seemed wary, suspicious, alert, but underneath his slight hostility there was another emotion, of which Casher could perceive just the edge. Fatigue with its roots in bottomless despair: despair set deep in irrecoverable fatigue?

That other emotion, which Casher could barely discern, was very strange indeed. On all his voyages back and forth through the inhabited worlds, Casher had met many odd types of men and women. He had never seen anything like this administrator before—brilliant, erratic, boastful. His title was "Mr. Commissioner" and he was an ex-Lord of the Instrumentality on this planet of Henriada, where the population had dropped from six hundred million persons down to some forty thousand. Indeed, local government had disappeared into limbo, and this odd man, with the title of administrator, was the only law and civil authority which the planet knew.

Nevertheless, he had a surplus power cruiser and Casher O'Neill was determined to get that cruiser as a part of his long plot to return to his home planet of Mizzer and to unseat the usurper, Colonel Wedder.

The administrator stared sharply, wearily at Casher and then he too lifted his glass. The green twilight colored his liquor and made it seem like some strange poison. It was only Earth byegarr, though a little on the strong side.

With a sip, only a sip, the older man relaxed a little. "You may be out to trick me, young man. You may think that I am an old fool running an abandoned planet. You may even be thinking that killing this girl is some kind of a crime. It is not a crime at all. I am the administrator of Henriada and I have ordered that girl killed every year for the last eighty years. She isn't even a girl, to start with. Just an underperson. Some kind of an animal turned into a domestic servant. I can even appoint you a deputy sheriff. Or chief of detectives. That might be better. I haven't had a chief of detectives for a hundred years and more. You are my chief of detectives. Go in tomorrow. The house is not hard to find. It's the biggest and best house left on this planet. Go in tomorrow morning. Ask for her master and be sure that you use the correct title: the Mister and Owner Murray Madigan. The robots will tell you to keep out. If you persist, she will come to the door. That's when you will stab her through the heart, right there in the doorway. My groundcar will race up one metric minute later. You jump in and come back here. We've been through this before. Why don't you agree? Don't you know who I am?"

"I know perfectly well"—Casher O'Neill smiled—"who you are, Mr. Commissioner and Administrator. You are the honorable Rankin Meiklejohn, once of Earth Two. After all, the Instrumentality itself gave me a permit to land on this planet on private business. They knew who *I* was too, and what I wanted. There's something funny about all this. Why should you give me a power cruiser—the best ship, you yourself say, in your whole fleet—just for killing one modified animal which looks and talks like a girl? Why me? Why the visitor? Why the man from off-world? Why should you care whether this particular underperson is killed or not? If you've given the order for her death eighty times in eighty years, why hasn't it been carried out long ago? Mind you, Mr. Administrator, I'm not saying no. I want that cruiser. I want it very much indeed. But what's the deal? What's the trick? Is it the house you want?"

"Beauregard? No, I don't want Beauregard. Old Madigan can rot in it for all that I care. It's between Ambiloxi and Mottile, on the Gulf of Esperanza. You can't miss it. The road is good. You could drive yourself there."

"What is it, then?" Casher's voice had an edge of persistence to it.

The administrator's response was singular indeed. He filled his huge inhaler glass with the potent byegarr. He stared over the full glass at Casher O'Neill as if he were an enemy. He drained the glass. Casher knew that that much liquor, taken suddenly, could kill the normal human being.

The administrator did not fall over dead.

He did not even become noticeably more drunk.

His face turned red and his eyes almost popped out, as the harsh one hundred sixty–proof liquor took effect, but he still did not say anything. He just stared at Casher. Casher, who had learned in his long exile to play many games, just stared back.

The administrator broke first.

He leaned forward and burst into a birdlike shriek of laughter. The laughter went on and on until it seemed that the man had hogged all the merriment in the galaxy. Casher snorted a little laugh along with the man, more out of nervous reflex than anything else, but he waited for the administrator to stop laughing.

The administrator finally got control of himself. With a broad grin and a wink at Casher, he poured himself four fingers more of the byegarr into his glass, drank it down as if he had had a sip of cream and then—only very slightly unsteady—stood up, came over and patted Casher on the shoulder.

"You're a smart boy, my lad. I'm cheating you. I don't care whether the power cruiser is there or not. I'm giving you something which has no value at all to me. Who's ever going to take a power cruiser off this planet? It's ruined. It's abandoned. And so am I. Go ahead. You can have the cruiser. For nothing. Just take it. Free. Unconditionally."

This time it was Casher who leaped to his feet and stared down into the face of the feverish, wanton little man.

"Thank you, Mr. Administrator!" he cried, trying to catch the hand of the administrator so as to seal the deal.

Rankin Meiklejohn looked awfully sober for a man with that much liquor in him. He held his right hand behind his back and would not shake.

"You can have the cruiser, all right. No terms. No conditions. No deal. It's yours. *But kill that girl first!* Just as a favor to me. I've been a good host. I like you. I want to do you a favor. Do me one. Kill that girl. At two seventy-five in the morning. Tomorrow."

"Why?" asked Casher, his voice loud and cold, trying to wring some sense out of the chattering man.

"Just—just—just because I say so . . ." stammered the administrator.

"Why?" asked Casher, cold and loud again.

The liquor suddenly took over inside the administrator. He groped back for the arm of his chair, sat down suddenly and then looked up at Casher. He was very drunk indeed. The strange emotion, the elusive fatigue-despair, had vanished from his face. He spoke straightforwardly. Only the excessive care of his articulation would have shown a passerby that he was drunk.

"Because, you fool," said Meiklejohn, "those people, more than eighty in eighty years, that I have sent to Beauregard with orders to kill the girl . . . those people—" he repeated, and stopped speaking, clamping his lips together.

"What happened to them?" asked Casher calmly and persuasively.

The administrator grinned again and seemed to be on the edge of one of his wild laughs.

"What happened?" shouted Casher at him.

"I don't know," said the administrator. "For the life of me, I don't know. Not one of them ever came back."

"What happened to them? Did she kill them?" cried Casher.

"How would I know?" said the drunken man, getting visibly more sleepy.

"Why didn't you report it?"

This seemed to rouse the administrator. "Report that one little girl had stopped me, the planetary administrator? Just one little girl, and not even a human being! They would have sent help, and laughed at me. By the bell, young man, I've been laughed at enough! I need no help from outside. You're going in there tomorrow morning. At two seventy-five, with a knife. And a groundcar waiting."

He stared fixedly at Casher and then suddenly fell asleep in his chair. Casher called to the robots to show him to his room; they tended to the master as well.

II

The next morning at two seventy-five sharp, nothing happened. Casher walked down the baroque corridor, looking into beautiful barren rooms. All the doors were open.

Through one door he heard a sick deep bubbling snore.

It was the administrator, sure enough. He lay twisted in his bed. A small nursing machine was beside him, her white-enameled body only slightly rusty. She held up a mechanical hand for silence and somehow managed to make the gesture seem light, delicate and pretty, even from a machine.

Casher walked lightly back to his own room, where he ordered hot-cakes, bacon and coffee. He studied a tornado through the armored glass of his window, while the robots prepared his food. The elastic trees clung to the earth with a fury which matched the fury of the wind. The trunk of the tornado reached like the nose of a mad elephant down into the gardens, but the flora fought back. A few animals whipped upward and out of sight. The tornado then came straight for the house, but did not damage it outside of making a lot of noise.

"We have two or three hundred of those a day," said a butler robot. "That is why we store all spacecraft underground and have no weather machines. It would cost more, the people said, to make this planet livable than the planet could possibly yield. The radio and news are in the library, sir. I do not think that the honorable Rankin Meiklejohn will wake until evening, say seven fifty or eight o'clock."

"Can I go out?"

"Why not, sir? You are a true man. You do what you wish."

"I mean is it safe for me to go out?"

"Oh, no, sir! The wind would tear you apart or carry you away."

"Don't people ever go out?"

"Yes, sir. With groundcars or with automatic body armor. I have been told that if it weighs fifty tons or better, the person inside is safe. I would not know, sir. As you see, I am a robot. I was made here, though my brain was formed on Earth Two, and I have never been outside this house."

Casher looked at the robot. This one seemed unusually talkative. He chanced the opportunity of getting some more information.

"Have you ever heard of Beauregard?"

"Yes, sir. It is the best house on this planet. I have heard people say that it is the most solid building on Henriada. It belongs to the Mister and Owner Murray Madigan. He is an Old North Australian, a renunciant who left his home planet and came here when Henriada was a busy world. He brought all his wealth with him. The underpeople and robots say that it is a wonderful place on the inside."

"Have you seen it?"

"Oh, no, sir. I have never left this building."

"Does the man Madigan ever come here?"

The robot seemed to be trying to laugh, but did not succeed. He answered, very unevenly, "Oh, no, sir. He never goes anywhere."

"Can you tell me anything about the female who lives with him?"

"No sir," said the robot.

"Do you know anything about her?"

"Sir, it is not that. I know a great deal about her."

"Why can't you talk about her, then?"

"I have been commanded not to, sir."

"I am," said Casher O'Neill, "a true human being. I herewith countermand those orders. Tell me about her."

The robot's voice became formal and cold. "The orders cannot be countermanded, sir."

"Why not?" snapped Casher. "Are they the administrator's?"

"No, sir."

"Whose, then?"

"Hers," said the robot softly, and left the room.

### III

Casher O'Neill spent the rest of the day trying to get information; he obtained very little.

The deputy administrator was a young man who hated his chief.

When Casher, who dined with him—the two of them having a poorly cooked state luncheon in a dining room which would have seated five hundred people—tried to come to the point by asking bluntly, "What do you know about Murray Madigan?" he got an answer which was blunt to the point of incivility.

"Nothing."

"You never heard of him?" cried Casher.

"Keep your troubles to yourself, mister visitor," said the deputy administrator. "I've got to stay on this planet long enough to get promoted off. You can leave. You shouldn't have come."

"I have," said Casher, "an all-world pass from the Instrumentality."

"All right," said the young man. "That shows that you are more important than I am. Let's not discuss the matter. Do you like your lunch?"

Casher had learned diplomacy in his childhood, when he was the heir apparent to the dictatorship of Mizzer. When his horrible uncle, Kuraf, lost the rulership, Casher had approved of the coup by the Colonels

Wedder and Gibna; but now Wedder was supreme and enforcing a period of terror and virtue. Casher thus knew courts and ceremony, big talk and small talk, and on this occasion he let the small talk do. The young deputy administrator had only one ambition, to get off the planet Henriada and never to see or hear of Rankin Meiklejohn again.

Casher could understand the point.

Only one curious thing happened during dinner.

Toward the end, Casher slipped in the question, very informally: "Can underpeople give orders to robots?"

"Of course," said the young man. "That's one of the reasons we use underpeople. They have more initiative. They amplify our orders to robots on many occasions."

Casher smiled. "I didn't mean it quite that way. Could an underperson give an order to a robot which a real human being could not then countermand?"

The young man started to answer, even though his mouth was full of food. He was not a very polished young man. Suddenly he stopped chewing and his eyes grew wide. Then, with his mouth half-full, he said, "You are trying to talk about this planet, I guess. You can't help it. You're on the track. Stay on the track, then. Maybe you will get out of it alive. I refuse to get mixed up with it, with you, with him and his hateful schemes. All I want to do is to leave when my time comes."

The young man resumed chewing, his eyes fixed steadfastly on his plate.

Before Casher could pass off the matter by making some casual remark, the butler robot stopped behind him and leaned over.

"Honorable sir, I heard your question. May I answer it?"

"Of course," said Casher softly.

"The answer, sir," said the butler robot, softly but clearly, "to your question is *no, no, never*. That is the general rule of the civilized worlds. But on this planet of Henriada, sir, the answer is *yes.*"

"Why?" asked Casher.

"It is my duty, sir," said the robot butler, "to recommend to you this dish of fresh artichokes. I am not authorized to deal with other matters."

"Thank you," said Casher, straining a little to keep himself looking imperturbable.

Nothing much happened that night, except that Meiklejohn got up long enough to get drunk all over again. Though he invited Casher to come and drink with him, he never seriously discussed the girl except for one outburst.

"Leave it till tomorrow. Fair and square. Open and aboveboard. Frank and honest. That's me. I'll take you around Beauregard myself. You'll see it's easy. A knife, eh? A traveled young man like you would know what to do with a knife. And a little girl too. Not very big. Easy job. Don't give it another thought. Would you like some apple juice in your byegarr?"

Casher had taken three contraintoxicant pills before going to drink with the ex-lord, but even at that he could not keep up with Meiklejohn. He accepted the dilution of apple juice gravely, gracefully and gratefully.

The little tornadoes stamped around the house. Meiklejohn, now launched into some drunken story of ancient injustices which had been done to him on other worlds, paid no attention to them. In the middle of the night, past nine fifty in the evening, Casher woke alone in his chair, very stiff and uncomfortable. The robots must have had standing instructions concerning the administrator, and had apparently taken him off to bed. Casher walked wearily to his own room, cursed the thundering ceiling and went to sleep again.

IV

The next day was very different indeed.

The administrator was as sober, brisk and charming as if he had never taken a drink in his life.

He had the robots call Casher to join him at breakfast and said, by way of greeting, "I'll wager you thought I was drunk last night."

"Well . . ." said Casher.

"Planet fever. That's what it was. Planet fever. A bit of alcohol keeps it from developing too far. Let's see. It's three sixty now. Could you be ready to leave by four?"

Casher frowned at his watch, which had the conventional twenty-four hours.

The administrator saw the glance and apologized. "Sorry! My fault, a thousand times. I'll get you a metric watch right away. Ten hours a day, a hundred minutes an hour. We're very progressive here on Henriada."

He clapped his hands and ordered that a watch be taken to Casher's room, along with the watch-repairing robot to adjust it to Casher's body rhythms.

"Four, then," he said, rising briskly from the table. "Dress for a trip by groundcar. The servants will show you how."

There was a man already waiting in Casher's room. He looked like a

plump, wise ancient Hindu, as shown in the archaeology books. He bowed
pleasantly and said, "My name is Gosigo. I am a forgetty, settled on this
planet, but for this day I am your guide and driver from this place to the
mansion of Beauregard."

Forgetties were barely above underpeople in status. They were persons
convicted of various major crimes, to whom the courts of the worlds, or
the Instrumentality, had allowed total amnesia instead of death or some
punishment worse than death, such as the planet Shayol.

Casher looked at him curiously. The man did not carry with him the
permanent air of bewilderment which Casher had noticed in many forgetties. Gosigo saw the glance and interpreted it.

"I'm well enough now, sir. And I am strong enough to break your back
if I had the orders to do it."

"You mean damage my spine? What a hostile, unpleasant thing to do!"
said Casher. "Anyhow, I rather think I could kill you first if you tried it.
Whatever gave you such an idea?"

"The administrator is always threatening people that he will have me
do it to them."

"Have you ever really broken anybody's back?" asked Casher, looking
Gosigo over very carefully and rejudging him. The man, though shorter
than Casher, was luxuriously muscled; like many plump men, he looked
pleasant on the outside but could be very formidable to an enemy.

Gosigo smiled briefly, almost happily. "Well, no, not exactly."

"Why, haven't you? Does the administrator always countermand his
own orders? I should think that he would sometimes be too drunk to
remember to do it."

"It's not that," said Gosigo.

"Why don't you, then?"

"I have other orders," said Gosigo, rather hesitantly. "Like the orders
I have today. One set from the administrator, one set from the deputy
administrator and a third set from an outside source."

"Who's the outside source?"

"She has told me not to explain just yet."

Casher stood stock still. "Do you mean who I think you mean?"

Gosigo nodded very slowly, pointing at the ventilator as though it might
have a microphone in it.

"Can you tell me what your orders are?"

"Oh, certainly. The administrator has told me to drive both himself and
you to Beauregard, to take you to the door, to watch you stab the undergirl

and to call the second groundcar to your rescue. The deputy administrator has told me to take you to Beauregard and to let you do as you please, bringing you back here by way of Ambiloxi if you happen to come out of Mr. Murray's house alive."

"And the other orders?"

"To close the door upon you when you enter and to think of you no more in this life, because you will be very happy."

"Are you crazy?" cried Casher.

"I am a forgetty," said Gosigo, with some dignity, "but I am not insane."

"Whose orders are you going to obey, then?"

Gosigo smiled a warmly human smile at him. "Doesn't that depend on you, sir, and not on me? Do I look like a man who is going to kill you soon?"

"No, you don't," said Casher.

"Do you know what you look like to me?" went on Gosigo, with a purr. "Do you really think that I would help you if I thought that you would kill a small girl?"

"You know it!" cried Casher, feeling his face go white.

"Who doesn't?" said Gosigo. "What else have we got to talk about, here on Henriada? Let me help you on with these clothes, so that you will at least survive the ride." With this he handed shoulder padding and padded helmet to Casher, who began to put on the garments, very clumsily.

Gosigo helped him.

When Casher was fully dressed, he thought that he had never dressed this elaborately for space itself. The world of Henriada must be a tumultuous place if people needed this kind of clothing to make a short trip.

Gosigo had put on the same kind of clothes.

He looked at Casher in a friendly manner, with an arch smile which came close to humor. "Look at me, honorable visitor. Do I remind you of anybody?"

Casher looked honestly and carefully, and then said, "No, you don't."

The man's face fell. "It's a game," he said. "I can't help trying to find out who I really am. Am I a Lord of the Instrumentality who has betrayed his trust? Am I a scientist who twisted knowledge into unimaginable wrong? Am I a dictator so foul that even the Instrumentality, which usually leaves things alone, had to step in and wipe me out? Here I am, healthy, wise, alert. I have the name Gosigo on this planet. Perhaps I am a mere native of this planet, who has committed a local crime. I am triggered. If anyone ever did tell me my true name or my actual past, I have been conditioned to shriek loud, fall unconscious and forget anything which might be said on such an occasion. People told me that I must have chosen this instead of death. Maybe. Death sometimes looks tidy to a forgetty."

"Have you ever screamed and fainted?"

"I don't even know *that,*" said Gosigo, "no more than you know where you are going this very day."

Casher was tied to the man's mystifications, so he did not let himself be provoked into a useless show of curiosity. Inquisitive about the forgetty himself, he asked:

"Does it hurt—does it hurt to be a forgetty?"

"No," said Gosigo, "it doesn't hurt, no more than you will."

Gosigo stared suddenly at Casher. His voice changed tone and became at least one octave higher. He clapped his hands to his face and panted through his hands as if he would never speak again.

"But—oh! The fear—the eerie, dreary fear of *being me!*"

He still stared at Casher.

Quieting down at last, he pulled his hands away from his face, as if by sheer force, and said in an almost normal voice, "Shall we get on with our trip?"

Gosigo led the way out into the bare bleak corridor. A perceptible wind was blowing through it, though there was no sign of an open window or door. They followed a majestic staircase; with steps so broad that Casher had to keep changing pace on them, all the way down to the bottom of the building. This must, at some time, have been a formal reception hall. Now it was full of cars.

Curious cars.

Land vehicles of a kind which Casher had never seen before. They looked a little bit like the ancient "fighting tanks" which he had seen in pictures. They also looked a little like submarines of a singularly short and ugly shape. They had high spiked wheels, but their most complicated feature was a set of giant corkscrews, four on each side, attached to the car by intricate yet operational apparatus. Since Casher had been landed right into the palace by planoform, he had never had occasion to go outside among the tornadoes of Henriada.

The administrator was waiting, wearing a coverall on which was stenciled his insignia of rank.

Casher gave him a polite bow. He glanced down at the handsome metric wristwatch which Gosigo had strapped on his wrist, outside the coverall. It read three ninety-five.

Casher bowed to Rankin Meiklejohn and said, "I'm ready, sir, if you are."

"Watch him!" whispered Gosigo, half a step behind Casher.

The administrator said, "Might as well be going." The man's voice trembled.

Casher stood polite, alert, immobile. Was this danger? Was this foolishness? Could the administrator already be drunk again?

Casher watched the administrator carefully but quietly, waiting for the older man to precede him into the nearest groundcar, which had its door standing open.

Nothing happened, except that the administrator began to turn pale.

There must have been six or eight people present. The others must have seen the same sort of thing before, because they showed no sign of curiosity or bewilderment. The administrator began to tremble. Casher could see it, even through the bulk of the travelwear. The man's hands shook.

The administrator said, in a high nervous voice, "Your knife. You have it with you?"

Casher nodded.

"Let me see it," said the administrator.

Casher reached down to his boot and brought out the beautiful, superbly balanced knife. Before he could stand erect, he felt the clamp of Gosigo's heavy fingers on his shoulder.

"Master," said Gosigo to Meiklejohn, "tell your visitor to put his weapon away. It is not allowed for any of us to show weapons in your presence."

Casher tried to squirm out of the heavy grip without losing his balance or his dignity. He found that Gosigo was knowledgeable about karate too. The forgetty held ground, even when the two men waged an immobile, invisible sort of wrestling match, the leverage of Casher's shoulder working its way hither and yon against the strong grip of Gosigo's powerful hand.

The administrator ended it. He said, "Put away your knife . . ." in that high funny voice of his.

The watch had almost reached four, but no one had yet got into the car.

Gosigo spoke again, and when he did there was a contemptuous laugh from the deputy administrator, who had stood by in ordinary indoor clothes.

"Master, isn't it time for 'one for the road'?"

"Of course, of course," chattered the administrator. He began breathing almost normally again.

"Join me," he said to Casher. "It's a local custom."

Casher had let his knife slip back into his bootsheath. When the knife dropped out of sight, Gosigo released his shoulder; he now stood facing the administrator and rubbed his bruised shoulder. He said nothing, but shook his head gently, showing that he did not want a drink.

One of the robots brought the administrator a glass, which appeared to contain at least a liter and a half of water. The administrator said, very politely, "Sure you won't share it?"

This close, Casher could smell the reek of it. It was pure byegarr, and at least one hundred sixty proof. He shook his head again, firmly but also politely.

The administrator lifted the glass.

Casher could see the muscles of the man's throat work as the liquid went down. He could hear the man breathing heavily between swallows. The white liquid went lower and lower in the gigantic glass.

At last it was all gone.

The administrator cocked his head sidewise and said to Casher in a parrotlike voice, "Well, toodle-oo!"

"What do you mean, sir?" asked Casher.

The administrator had a pleasant glow on his face. Casher was surprised that the man was not dead after that big and sudden a drink.

"I just mean g'by. I'm—not—feeling—well."

With that he fell straight forward, as stiff as a rock tower. One of the servants, perhaps another forgetty, caught him before he hit the ground.

"Does he always do this?" asked Casher of the miserable and contemptuous deputy administrator.

"Oh, no," said the deputy. "Only at times like these."

"What do you mean, 'like these'?"

"When he sends one more armed man against the girl at Beauregard. They never come back. You won't come back, either. You could have left earlier, but you can't now. Go along and try to kill the girl. I'll see you here about five twenty-five if you succeed. As a matter of fact, if you come back at all, I'll try to wake *him* up. But you won't come back. Good luck."

I suppose that's what you need. Good luck."

Casher shook hands with the man without removing his gloves. Gosigo had already climbed into the driver's seat of the machine and was testing the electric engines. The big corkscrews began to plunge down, but before they touched the floor, Gosigo had reversed them and thrown them back into the up position.

The people in the room ran for cover as Casher entered the machine, though there was no immediate danger in sight. Two of the human servants dragged the administrator up the stairs, the deputy administrator following them rapidly.

"Seat belt," said Gosigo.

Casher found it and snapped it closed.

"Head belt," said Gosigo.

Casher stared at him. He had never heard of a head belt.

"Pull it down from the roof, sir. Put the net under your chin."

Casher glanced up.

There was a net fitted snugly against the roof of the vehicle, just above his head. He started to pull it down, but it did not yield. Angrily, he pulled harder, and it moved slowly downward. *By the bell and bank, do they want to hang me in this!* he thought to himself as he dragged the net down. There was a strong fiber belt attached to each end of the net, while the net itself was only fifteen to twenty centimeters wide. He ended up in a foolish position, holding the head belt with both hands lest it snap back into the ceiling and not knowing what to do with it. Gosigo leaned over and, half-impatiently, helped him adjust the web under his chin. It pinched for a moment and Casher felt as though his head were being dragged by a heavy weight.

"Don't fight it," said Gosigo. "Relax."

Casher did. His head was lifted several centimeters into a foam pocket, which he had not previously noticed, in the back of the seat. After a second or two, he realized that the position was odd but comfortable.

Gosigo had adjusted his own head belt and had turned on the lights of the vehicle. They blazed so bright that Casher almost thought they might be a laser, capable of charring the inner doors of the big room.

The lights must have keyed the door.

# V

Two panels slid open and a wild uproar of wind and vegetation rushed in. It was rough and stormy but far below hurricane velocity.

The machine rolled forward clumsily and was out of the house and on the road very quickly.

The sky was brown, bright luminous brown, shot through with streaks of yellow. Casher had never seen a sky of that color on any other world he had visited, and in his long exile he had seen many planets.

Gosigo, staring straight ahead, was preoccupied with keeping the vehicle right in the middle of the black, soft, tarry road.

"Watch it!" said a voice speaking right into his head.

It was Gosigo, using an intercom which must have been built into the helmets.

Casher watched, though there was nothing to see except for the rush of mad wind. Suddenly the groundcar turned dark, spun upside down and was violently shaken. An oily, pungent stench of pure fetor immediately drenched the whole car.

Gosigo pulled out a panel with a console of buttons. Light and fire, intolerably bright, burned in on them through the windshield and the portholes on the side.

The battle was over before it began.

The groundcar lay in a sort of swamp. The road was visible thirty or thirty-five meters away.

There was a grinding sound inside the machine and the groundcar righted itself. A singular sucking noise followed, then the grinding sound stopped. Casher could glimpse the big corkscrews on the side of the car eating their way into the ground.

At last the machine was steady, pelted only by branches, leaves and what seemed like kelp.

A small tornado was passing over them.

Gosigo took time to twist his head sidewise and to talk to Casher.

"An air whale swallowed us and I had to burn our way out."

"A what?" cried Casher.

"An air whale," repeated Gosigo calmly on the intercom. "There are no indigenous forms of life on this planet, but the imported Earth forms have changed wildly since we brought them in. The tornadoes lifted the whales around enough so that some of them got adapted to flying. They were the meat-eating kind, so they like to crack our groundcars open and eat the goodies inside. We're safe enough from them for the time being, provided we can make it back to the road. There are a few wild men who live in the wind, but they would not become dangerous to us unless we found ourselves really helpless. Pretty soon I can unscrew us from the ground and try to get back on the road. It's not really too far from here to Ambiloxi."

The trip to the road was a long one, even though they could see the road itself all the time that they tried various approaches.

The first time, the groundcar tipped ominously forward. Red lights showed on the panel and buzzers buzzed. The great spiked wheels spun in vain as they chewed their way into a bottomless quagmire.

Gosigo, calling back to his passenger, cried, "Hold steady! We're going to have to shoot ourselves out of this one backward!"

Casher did not know how he could be any steadier, belted, hooded and strapped as he was, but he clutched the arms of his seat.

The world went red with fire as the front of the car spat flame in rocketlike quantities. The swamp ahead of them boiled into steam, so that they could see nothing. Gosigo changed the windshield over from visual to radar, and even with radar there was not much to be seen—nothing but a gray swirl of formless wraiths, and the weird lurching sensation as the machine fought its way back to solid ground. The console suddenly showed green and Gosigo cut the controls. They were back where they had been, with the repulsive burnt entrails of the air whale scattered among the coral trees.

"Try again," said Gosigo, as though Casher had something to do with the matter.

He fiddled with the controls and the groundcar rose several feet. The spikes on the wheels had been hydraulically extended until they were each at least one hundred fifty centimeters long. The car felt like a large enclosed bicycle as it teetered on its big wheels. The wind was strong and capricious but there was no tornado in sight.

"Here we go," said Gosigo redundantly. The groundcar pressed forward in a mad rush, hastening obliquely through the vegetation and making for the highway on Casher's right.

A bone-jarring crash told them that they had not made it. For a moment Casher was too dizzy to see where they were.

He was glad of his helmet and happy about the web brace which held his neck. That crash would have killed him if he had not had full protection.

Gosigo seemed to think the trip normal. His classic Hindu features relaxed in a wise smile as he said, "Hit a boulder. Fell on our side. Try again."

Casher managed to gasp, "Is the machine unbreakable?"

There was a laugh in Gosigo's voice when he answered, "Almost. We're the most vulnerable items in it."

Again fire spat at the ground, this time from the side of the groundcar. It balanced itself precariously on the four high wheels. Gosigo turned on the radar screen to look through the steam which their own jets had called up.

There the road was, plain and near.

"Try again!" he shouted, as the machine lunged forward and then performed a veritable ballet on the surface of the marsh. It rushed, slowed, turned around on a hummock, gave itself an assist with the jets and then scrambled through the water.

Casher saw the inverted cone of a tornado, half a kilometer or less away, veering toward them.

Gosigo sensed his unspoken thought, because he answered, "Problem: who gets to the road first, that or we?"

The machine bucked, lurched, twisted, spun.

Casher could see nothing anymore from the windshield in front, but it was obvious that Gosigo knew what he was doing.

There was the sickening, stomach-wrenching twist of a big drop and then a new sound was heard—a grinding as of knives.

Gosigo, unworried, took his head out of the headnet and looked over at Casher with a smile. "The twister will probably hit us in a minute or two, but it doesn't matter now. We're on the road and I've bolted us to the surface."

"Bolted?" gasped Casher.

"You know, those big screws on the outside of the car. They were made to go right into the road. All the roads here are neo-asphaltum and self-repairing. There will be traces of them here when the last known person on the last known planet is dead. These are *good* roads." He stopped for the sudden hush. "Storm's going over us—"

It began again before he could finish his sentence. Wild raving winds tore at the machine, which sat so solid that it seemed bedded in permastone.

Gosigo pushed two buttons and calibrated a dial. He squinted at his instruments, then pressed a button mounted on the edge of his navigator's seat. There was a sharp explosion, like a blasting of rock by chemical methods.

Casher started to speak but Gosigo held out a warning hand for silence.

He turned his dials quickly. The windshield faded out, radar came on and then went off, and at last a bright map—bright red in background with sharp gold lines—appeared across the whole width of the screen. There were a dozen or more bright points on the map. Gosigo watched these intently.

The map blurred, faded, dissolved into red chaos.

Gosigo pushed another button and then could see out of the front glass screen again.

"What was that?" asked Casher.

"Miniaturized radar rocket. I sent it up twelve kilometers for a look around. It transmitted a map of what it saw and I put it on our radar screen. The tornadoes are heavier than usual, but I think we can make it. Did you notice the top right of the map?"

"The top right?" asked Casher.

"Yes, the top right. Did you see what was there?"

"Why, nothing," said Casher. "Nothing was there."

"You're utterly right," said Gosigo. "What does that mean to you?"

"I don't understand you," said Casher. "I suppose it means that there is nothing there."

"Right again. But let me tell you something. There never is."

"Never is what?"

"Anything," said Gosigo. "There never is anything on the maps at that point. That's east of Ambiloxi. That's Beauregard. It never shows on the maps. Nothing happens there."

"No bad weather—ever?" asked Casher.

"Never," said Gosigo.

"Why not?" asked Casher.

"*She* will not permit it," said Gosigo firmly, as though his words made sense.

"You mean her weather machines work?" said Casher, grasping for the only rational explanation possible.

"Yes," said Gosigo.

"Why?"

"She pays for them."

"How can she?" exclaimed Casher. "Your whole world of Henriada is bankrupt!"

"Her part isn't."

"Stop mystifying me," said Casher. "Tell me who she is and what this is all about."

"Put your head in the net," said Gosigo. "I'm not making puzzles because I want to do so. I have been commanded not to talk."

"Because you are a forgetty?"

"What's that got to do with it? Don't talk to me that way. Remember, I am not an animal or an underperson. I may be your servant for a few hours, but I am a *man*. You'll find out, soon enough. *Hold tight!*"

The groundcar came to a panic stop, the spiked teeth eating into the resilient firm neo-asphaltum of the road. At the instant they stopped, the outside corkscrews began chewing their way into the ground. First Casher felt as though his eyes were popping out, because of the suddenness of the deceleration; now he felt like holding the arms of his seat as the tornado reached directly for their car, plucking at it again and again. The enormous outside screws held and he could feel the car straining to meet the gigantic suction of the storm.

"Don't worry," shouted Gosigo over the noise of the storm. "I always pin us down a little bit more by firing the quickrockets straight up. These cars don't often go off the road."

Casher tried to relax.

The funnel of the tornado, which seemed almost like a living being, plucked after them once or twice more and then was gone.

This time Casher had seen no sign of the air whales which rode the storms. He had seen nothing but rain and wind and desolation.

The tornado was gone in a moment. Ghostlike shapes trailed after it in enormous prancing leaps.

"Wind men," said Gosigo glancing at them incuriously. "Wild people who have learned to live on Henriada. They aren't much more than animals. We are close to the territory of the lady. They would not dare attack us here."

Casher O'Neill was too stunned to query the man or to challenge him.

Once more the car picked itself up and coursed along the smooth, narrow, winding neo-asphaltum road, almost as though the machine itself were glad to function and to function well.

## VI

Casher could never quite remember when they went from the howling wildness of Henriada into the stillness and beauty of the domains of Mr. Murray Madigan. He could recall the feeling but not the facts.

The town of Ambiloxi eluded him completely. It was so normal a town, so old-fashioned a little town that he could not think of it very much. Old people sat on the wooden boardwalk taking their afternoon look at the strangers who passed through. Horses were tethered in a row along the main street, between the parked machines. It looked like a peaceful picture from the ancient ages.

Of torandoes there was no sign, nor of the hurt and ruin which showed around the house of Rankin Meiklejohn. There were few underpeople or robots about, unless they were so cleverly contrived as to look almost exactly like real people. How can you remember something which is pleasant and nonmemorable? Even the buildings did not show signs of being fortified against the frightful storms which had brought the prosperous planet of Henriada to a condition of abandonment and ruin.

Gosigo, who had a remarkable talent for stating the obvious, said tonelessly, "The weather machines are working here. There is no need for special precaution."

But he did not stop in the town for rest, refreshments, conversation or fuel. He went through deftly and quietly, the gigantic armored groundcar looking out of place among the peaceful and defenseless vehicles. He went as though he had been on the same route many times before, and knew the routine well.

Once beyond Ambiloxi he speeded up, though at a moderate pace compared to the frantic elusive action he had taken against storms in the earlier part of the trip. The landscape was Earthlike, wet, and most of the ground was covered with vegetation.

Old radar countermissile towers stood along the road. Casher could not imagine their possible use, even though he was sure, from the looks of them, that they were long obsolete.

"What's the countermissile radar for?" he asked, speaking comfortably now that his head was out of the headnet.

Gosigo turned around and gave him a tortured glance in which pain and bewilderment were mixed. "Countermissile radar? Countermissile radar? I don't know that word, though it seems as though I should. . . ."

"Radar is what you were using to see with, back in the storm, when the ceiling and visibility were zero."

Gosigo turned back to his driving, narrowly missing a tree. "That? That's just artificial vision. Why did you use the term 'countermissile radar'? There isn't any of that stuff here except what we have on our machine, though the mistress may be watching us if her set is on."

"Those towers," said Casher. "They look like countermissile towers from the ancient times."

"Towers. There aren't any towers here," snapped Gosigo.

"Look," cried Casher. "Here are two more of them."

"No man made those. They aren't buildings. It's just air coral. Some of the coral which people brought from earth mutated and got so it could live in the air. People used to plant it for windbreaks, before they decided to give up Henriada and move out. They didn't do much good, but they are pretty to look at."

They rode along a few minutes without asking questions. Tall trees had Spanish moss trailing over them. They were close to a sea. Small marshes appeared to the right and left of the road; here, where the endless tornadoes were kept out, everything had a parklike effect. The domains of the estate of Beauregard were unlike anything else on Henriada—an area of peaceful wildness in a world which was rushing otherwise toward uninhabitability and ruin. Even Gosigo seemed more relaxed, more cheerful as he steered the groundcar along the pleasant elevated road.

Gosigo sighed, leaned forward, managed the controls and brought the car to a stop.

He turned around calmly and looked full face at Casher O'Neill.

"You have your knife?"

Casher automatically felt for it. It was there, safe enough in his boot-sheath. He simply nodded.

"You have your orders."

"You mean, killing the girl?"

"Yes," said Gosigo. "Killing the girl."

"I remember that. You didn't have to stop the car to tell me that."

"I'm telling you now," said Gosigo, his wise Hindu face showing neither humor nor outrage. "Do it."

"You mean kill her? Right at first sight?"

"Do it," said Gosigo. "You have your orders."

"I'm the judge of that," said Casher. "It will be on my conscience. Are you watching me for the administrator?"

"That drunken fool?" said Gosigo. "I don't care about him, except that I am a forgetty and I belong to him. We're in *her* territory now. You are going to do whatever she wants. You have orders to kill her. All right. Kill her."

"You mean—she wants to be murdered?"

"Of course not!" said Gosigo, with the irritation of an adult who has to explain too many things to an inquisitive child.

"Then how can I kill her without finding out what this is all about?"

"She knows. She knows herself. She knows her master. She knows this planet. She knows me and she knows something about you. Go ahead and kill her, since those are your orders. If she wants to die, that's not for you or me to decide. It's her business. If she does not want to die, you will not succeed."

"I'd like to see the person," said Casher, "who could stop me in a sudden knife attack. Have *you* told her that I am coming?"

"I've told her nothing, but she knows we are coming and she is pretty sure what you have been sent for. Don't think about it. Just do what you are told. Jump for her with the knife. She will take care of the matter."

"But—" cried Casher.

"Stop asking questions," said Gosigo. "Just follow orders and remember that she will take care of you. Even you." He started up the groundcar.

Within less than a kilometer they had crossed a low ridge of land and there before them lay Beauregard—the mansion at the edge of the waters, its white pillars shining, its pergolas glistening in the bright air, its yards and palmettos tidy.

Casher was a brave man, but he felt the palms of his hands go wet when he realized that in a minute or two he would have to commit a murder.

## VII

The groundcar swung up the drive. It stopped. Without a word, Gosigo activated the door. The air smelled calm, sea-wet, salt and yet coolly fresh.

Casher jumped out and ran to the door.

He was surprised to feel that his legs trembled as he ran.

He had killed before, real men in real quarrels. Why should a mere animal matter to him?

The door stopped him.

Without thinking, he tried to wrench it open.

The knob did not yield and there was no automatic control in sight. This was indeed a very antique sort of house. He struck the door with his hands. The thuds sounded around him. He could not tell whether they resounded in the house. No sound or echo came from beyond the door.

He began rehearsing the phrase "I want to see the Mister and Owner Madigan. . . ."

The door did open.

A little girl stood there.

He knew her. He had always known her. She was his sweetheart, come back out of his childhood. She was the sister he had never had. She was his own mother, when young. She was at the marvelous age, somewhere between ten and thirteen, where the child—as the phrase goes— "becomes an old child and not a raw grown-up." She was kind, calm, intelligent, expectant, quiet, inviting, unafraid. She felt like someone he had never left behind: yet, at the same moment, he knew he had never seen her before.

He heard his voice asking for the Mister and Owner Madigan while he wondered, at the back of his mind, who the girl might be. Madigan's daughter? Neither Rankin Meiklejohn nor the deputy had said anything about a human family.

The child looked at him levelly.

He must have finished braying his question at her.

"Mister and Owner Madigan," said the child, "sees no one this day, but you are seeing me." She looked at him levelly and calmly. There was an odd hint of humor, of fearlessness in her stance.

"Who are you?" he blurted out.

"I am the housekeeper of this house."

"You?" he cried, wild alarm beginning in his throat.

"My name," she said, "is T'ruth."

His knife was in his hand before he knew how it had got there. He remembered the advice of the administrator: *plunge, plunge, stab, stab, run!*

She saw the knife but her eyes did not waver from his face.

He looked at her uncertainly.

If this was an underperson, it was the most remarkable one he had ever seen. But even Gosigo had told him to do his duty, to stab, to kill the woman named T'ruth. Here she was. He could not do it.

He spun the knife in the air, caught it by its tip and held it out to her, handle first.

"I was sent to kill you," he said, "but I find I cannot do it. I have lost a cruiser."

"Kill me if you wish," she said, "because I have no fear of you."

Her calm words were so far outside his experience that he took the knife in his left hand and lifted his arm as if to stab toward her.

He dropped his arm.

"I cannot do it," he whined. "What have you done to me?"

"I have done nothing to you. You do not wish to kill a child and I look to you like a child. Besides, I think you love me. If this is so, it must be very uncomfortable for you."

Casher heard his knife clatter to the floor as he dropped it. He had never dropped it before.

"Who are you," he gasped, "that you should do this to me?"

"I am me," she said, her voice as tranquil and happy as that of any girl, provided that the girl was caught at a moment of great happiness and poise. "I am the housekeeper of this house." She smiled almost impishly and added, "It seems that I must almost be the ruler of this planet as well." Her voice turned serious. *"Man,"* she said, "can't you see it, man? I am an animal, a turtle. I am incapable of disobeying the word of man. When I was little I was trained and I was given orders. I shall carry out those orders as long as I live. When I look at you, I feel strange. You look as though you loved me already, but you do not know what to do. Wait a moment. I must let Gosigo go."

The shining knife on the floor of the doorway she saw; she stepped over it.

Gosigo had got out of the groundcar and was giving her a formal, low bow.

"Tell me," she cried, "what have you just seen!" There was friendliness in her call, as though the routine were an old game.

"I saw Casher O'Neill bound up the steps. You yourself opened the door. He thrust his dagger into your throat and the blood spat out in a big stream, rich and dark and red. You died in the doorway. For some reason Casher O'Neill went on into the house without saying anything to me. I became frightened and I fled."

He did not look frightened at all.

"If I am dead," she said, "how can I be talking to you?"

"Don't ask me," cried Gosigo. "I am just a forgetty. I always go back to the honorable Rankin Meiklejohn, each time that you are murdered, and I tell him the truth of what I saw. Then he gives me the medicine and I tell him something else. At that point he will get drunk and gloomy again, the way that he always does."

"It's a pity," said the child. "I wish I could help him, but I can't. He won't come to Beauregard."

"Him?" Gosigo laughed. "Oh, no, not him! Never! He just sends other people to kill you."

"And he's never satisfied," said the child sadly, "no matter how many times he kills me!"

"Never," said Gosigo cheerfully, climbing back into the groundcar. "'Bye now."

"Wait a moment," she called. "Wouldn't you like something to eat or drink before you drive back? There's a bad clutch of storms on the road."

"Not me," said Gosigo. "He might punish me and make me a forgetty all over again. Say, maybe that's already happened. Maybe I'm a forgetty who's been put through it several times, not just once." Hope surged into his voice. "T'ruth! T'ruth! Can *you* tell me?"

"Suppose I did tell you," said she. "What would happen?"

His face became sad, "I'd have a convulsion and forget what I told you. Well, good-by anyhow. I'll take a chance on the storms. If you ever see that Casher O'Neill again," called Gosigo, looking right through Casher O'Neill, "tell him I liked him but that we'll never meet again."

"I'll tell him," said the girl gently. She watched as the heavy brown man climbed nimbly into the car. The top crammed shut with no sound. The wheels turned and in a moment the car had disappeared behind the palmettos in the drive.

While she had talked to Gosigo in her clear warm high girlish voice, Casher had watched her. He could see the thin shape of her shoulders under the light blue shift that she wore. There was the suggestion of a pair of panties under the dress, so light was the material. Her hips had not begun to fill. When he glanced at her in one-quarter profile, he could see that her cheek was smooth, her hair well-combed, her little breasts just beginning to bud on her chest. Who was this child who acted like an empress?

She turned back to him and gave him a warm, apologetic smile.

"Gosigo and I always talk over the story together. Then he goes back and Meiklejohn does not believe it and spends unhappy months planning my murder all over again. I suppose, since I am just an animal, that I should not call it a murder when somebody tries to kill me, but I resist, of course. I do not care about me, but I have orders, strong orders, to keep my master and his house safe from harm."

"How old are you?" asked Casher. He added, "If you can tell the truth."

"I can tell nothing but the truth. I am conditioned. I am nine hundred and six Earth years old."

"Nine hundred?" he cried. "But you look like a child. . . ."

"I am a child," said the girl, "and not a child. I am an earth turtle, changed into human form by the convenience of man. My life expectancy was increased three hundred times when I was modified. They tell me that my normal life span should have been three hundred years. Now it is ninety thousand years, and sometimes I am afraid. You will be dead of happy old age, Casher O'Neill, while I am still opening the drapes in this house to let the sunlight in. But let's not stand in the door and talk. Come on in and get some refreshments. You're not going anywhere, you know."

Casher followed her into the house but he put his worry into words. "You mean I am your prisoner."

"Not my prisoner, Casher. Yours. How could you cross that ground which you traveled in the groundcar? You could get to the ends of my estate all right, but then the storms would pick you up and whirl you away to a death which nobody would even see."

She turned into a big old room, bright with light-colored wooden furniture.

Casher stood there awkwardly. He had returned his knife to its boot-sheath when they left the vestibule. Now he felt very odd, sitting with his victim on a sun porch.

T'ruth was untroubled. She rang a brass bell which stood on an old-fashioned round table. Feminine footsteps clattered in the hall. A female servant entered the room, dressed in a black dress with a white apron. Casher had seen such servants in the old drama cubes, but he had never expected to meet one in the flesh.

"We'll have high tea," said T'ruth. "Which do you prefer, tea or coffee, Casher? Or I have beer and wines. Even two bottles of whiskey brought all the way from Earth."

"Coffee would be fine for me," said Casher.

"And you know what I want, Eunice," said T'ruth to the servant.

"Yes, ma'am," said the maid, disappearing.

Casher leaned forward.

"That servant—is she human?"

"Certainly," said T'ruth.

"Then why is she working for an underperson like you? I mean—I don't mean to be unpleasant or anything—but I mean—that's against all laws."

"Not here, on Henriada, it isn't."

"And why not?" persisted Casher.

"Because, on Henriada, I am myself the law."

"But the government?"

"It's gone."

"The Instrumentality?"

T'ruth frowned. She looked like a wise, puzzled child. "Maybe you know that part better than I do. They leave an administrator here, probably because they do not have any other place to put him and because he needs some kind of work to keep him alive. Yet they do not give him enough real power to arrest my master or to kill me. They ignore me. It seems to me that if I do not challenge them, they leave me alone."

"But their rules?" insisted Casher.

"They don't enforce them, neither here in Beauregard nor over in the town of Ambiloxi. They leave it up to me to keep these places going. I do the best I can."

"That servant, then? Did they lease her to you?"

"Oh, no," laughed the girl-woman. "She came to kill me twenty years ago, but she was a forgetty and she had no place else to go, so I trained her as a maid. She has a contract with my master, and her wages are paid every month into the satellite above the planet. She can leave if she ever wants to. I don't think she will."

Casher sighed. "This is all too hard to believe. You are a child but you are almost a thousand years old. You're an underperson, but you command a whole planet—"

"Only when I need to!" she interrupted him.

"You are wiser than most of the people I have ever known and yet you look young. How old do you feel?"

"I feel like a child," she said, "a child one thousand years old. And I have had the education and the memory and the experience of a wise lady stamped right into my brain."

"Who was the lady?" asked Cahser.

"The Owner and Citizen Agatha Madigan. The wife of my master. As she was dying they transcribed her brain on mine. That's why I speak so well and know so much."

"But that's illegal!" cried Casher.

"I suppose it was," said T'ruth, "but my master had it done, anyhow."

Casher leaned forward in his chair. He looked earnestly at the person. One part of him still loved her for the wonderful little girl whom he had thought she was, but another part was in awe of a being more powerful than anyone he had seen before. She returned his gaze with that composed half-smile which was wholly feminine and completely self-possessed; she looked tenderly upon him as their faces were reflected by the yellow morning light of Henriada. "I begin to understand," he said, "that you are what you have to be. It is very strange, here in this forgotten world."

"Henriada is strange," she said, "and I suppose that I must seem strange to you. You are right, though, about each of us being what she has to be. Isn't that liberty itself? If we each one *must* be something, isn't liberty the business of finding it out and then doing it—that one job, that uttermost mission compatible with our natures? How terrible it would be, to be something and never know what!"

"Like who?" said Casher.

"Like Gosigo, perhaps. He was a great king and he was a good king, on some faraway world where they still need kings. But he committed an intolerable mistake and the Instrumentality made him into a forgetty and sent him here."

"So that's the mystery!" said Casher. "And what am I?"

She looked at him calmly and steadfastly before she answered. "You are a killer too. It must make your life very hard in many ways. You keep having to justify yourself."

This was so close to the truth—so close to Casher's long worries as to whether justice might not just be a cover name for revenge—that it was his turn to gasp and be silent.

"And I have work for you," added the amazing child.

"Work? Here?"

"Yes. Something much worse than killing. And you must do it, Casher, if you want to go away from here before I die, eighty-nine thousand years from now." She looked around. "Hush!" she added. "Eunice is coming and I do not want to frighten her by letting her know the terrible things that you are going to have to do."

"Here?" he whispered urgently. "Right here, in this house?"

"Right here in this house," she said in a normal voice, as Eunice entered the room bearing a huge tray covered with plates of food and two pots of beverage.

Casher stared at the human woman who worked so cheerfully for an animal; but neither Eunice, who was busy setting things out on the table, nor T'ruth, who, turtle and woman that she was, could not help rearranging the dishes with gentle peremptories, paid the least attention to him.

The words rang in his head. "In this house . . . something worse than killing." They made no sense. Neither did it make sense to have high tea before five hours, decimal time.

He sighed and they both glanced at him, Eunice with amused curiosity, T'ruth with affectionate concern.

"He's taking it better than most of them do, ma'am," said Eunice. "Most of them who come here to kill you are very upset when they find out that they cannot do it."

"He's a killer, Eunice, a real killer, so I think he wasn't too bothered."

Eunice turned to him very pleasantly and said, "A killer, sir. It's a pleasure to have you here. Most of them are terrible amateurs and then the lady has to heal them before we can find something for them to do."

Casher couldn't resist a spot inquiry. "Are all the other would-be killers still here?"

"Most of them, sir. The ones that nothing happened to. Like me. Where else would we go? Back to the administrator, Rankin Meiklejohn?" She said the last with heavy scorn indeed curtsied to him, bowed deeply to the woman-girl T'ruth and left the room.

T'ruth looked friendlily at Casher O'Neill. "I can tell that you will not digest your food if you sit here waiting for bad news. When I said you had to do something worse than killing, I suppose I was speaking from a woman's point of view. We have a homicidal maniac in the house. He is a house guest and he is covered by Old North Australian law. That means we cannot kill him or expel him, though he is almost as immortal as I am. I hope that you and I can frighten him away from molesting my master. I cannot cure him or love him. He is too crazy to be reached through his emotions. Pure, utter, awful fright might do it, and it takes a man for that job. If you do this, I will reward you richly."

"And if I don't?" said Casher.

Again she stared at him as though she were trying to see through his eyes all the way down to the bottom of his soul; again he felt for her that tremor of compassion, ever so slightly tinged with male desire, which he had experienced when he first met her in the doorway of Beauregard.

Their locked glances broke apart.

T'ruth looked at the floor. "I cannot lie," she said, as though it were a handicap. "If you do not help me I shall have to do the things which it is in my power to do. The chief thing is nothing. To let you live here, to let you sleep and eat in this house until you get bored and ask me for some kind of routine work around the estate. I could make you work," she went on, looking up at him and blushing all the way to the top of her bodice, "by having you fall in love with me, but that would not be kind. I will not do it that way. Either you make a deal with me or you do not. It's up to you. Anyhow, let's eat first. I've been up since dawn, expecting one more killer. I even wondered if you might be the one who would succeed. That would be terrible, to leave my master all alone!"

"But you—wouldn't you yourself mind being killed!"

"Me? When I've already lived a thousand years and have eighty-nine thousand more to go! It couldn't matter less to me. Have some coffee."

And she poured his coffee.

## VIII

Two or three times Casher tried to get the conversation back to the work at hand, but T'ruth diverted him with trivialities. She even made him walk to the enormous window, where they could see far across the marshes and the bay. The sky in the remote distance was dark and full of worms. Those were tornadoes, beyond the reach of her weather machines, which coursed around the rest of Henriada but stopped short at the boundaries of Ambiloxi and Beauregard. She made him admire the weird coral castles which had built themselves up from the bay bottom, hundreds of feet into the air. She tried to make him see a family of wild wind people who were slyly and gently stealing apples from her orchard, but either his eyes were not used to the landscape or T'ruth could see much farther than he could.

This was a world rich in water. If it had not been located within a series of bad pockets of space, the water itself could have become an export. Mankind had done the best it could, raising kelp to provide the iron and phosphorus so often lacking in off-world diets, controlling the weather at great expense. Finally the Instrumentality recommended that they give up. The exports of Henriada never quite balanced the imports. The subsidies had gone far beyond the usual times. The Earth life had adapted with a vigor which was much too great. Ordinary forms rapidly found new shapes, challenged by the winds, the rains, the novel chemistry and the odd radiation patterns of Henriada. Killer whales became airborne, coral took to the air, human babies lost in the wind sometimes survived to become subhuman and wild, jellyfish became sky sweepers. The former inhabitants of Henriada had chosen a planet at a reasonable price—not cheap, but reasonable—from the owner who had in turn bought it from a post-Soviet settling cooperative. They had leased the new planet, had worked out an ecology, had emigrated and were now doing well.

Henriada kept the wild weather, the lost hopes and the ruins.

And of these ruins, the greatest was Murray Madigan.

Once a prime landholder and host, a gentleman among gentlemen, the richest man on the whole world, Madigan had become old, senile, weak. He faced death or catalepsis. The death of his wife made him fear his own death and with his turtle-girl, T'ruth, he had chosen catalepsis. Most of the time he was frozen in a trance, his heartbeat imperceptible, his metabolism very slow. Then, for a few hours or days, he was normal. Sometimes the sleeps were for weeks, sometimes for years. The Instrumentality doctors had looked him over—more out of scientific curiosity than from any judicial right—and had decided that though this was an odd way to live, it was a legal one. They went away and left him alone. He had had the whole personality of his dying wife, Agatha Madigan, impressed on the turtle-child, though this was illegal; the doctor had, quite simply, been bribed.

All this was told by T'ruth to Casher as they ate and drank their way slowly through an immense repast.

An archaic wood fire roared in a real fireplace.

While she talked, Casher watched the gentle movement of her shoulder blades when she moved forward, the loose movement of her light dress as she moved, the childish face which was so tender, so appealing and yet so wise.

Knowing as little as he did about the planet of Henriada, Casher tried desperately to fit his own thinking together and to make sense out of the predicament in which he found himself. Even if the girl *was* attractive, this told him nothing of the real challenges which he still faced inside this very house. No longer was his preoccupation with getting the power cruiser his main job on Henriada; no evidence was at hand to show that the drunken, deranged administrator, Rankin Meiklejohn, would give him anything at all unless he, Casher, killed the girl.

Even that had become a forgotten mission. Despite the fact that he had come to the estate of Beauregard for the purpose of killing her, he was now on a journey without a destination. Years of sad experience had taught him that when a project went completely to pieces, he still had the mission of personal survival, if his life was to mean anything to his home planet, Mizzer, and if his return, in any way or any fashion, could bring real liberty back to the Twelve Niles.

So he looked at the girl with a new kind of unconcern. How could she help his plans? Or hinder them? The promises she made were too vague to be of any real use in the sad, complicated world of politics.

He just tried to enjoy her company and the strange place in which he found himself.

The Gulf of Esperanza lay just within his vision. At the far horizon he could see the helpless tornadoes trying to writhe their way past the weather machines which still functioned, at the expense of Beauregard, all along the coast from Ambiloxi to Mottile. He could see the shoreline choked with kelp, which had once been a cash crop and was now a nuisance. Ruined buildings in the distance were probably the left-overs of processing plants; the artificial-looking coral castles obscured his view of them.

And this house—how much sense did this house make?

An undergirl, eerily wise, who herself admitted that she had obtained an unlawful amount of conditioning; a master who was a living corpse; a threat which could not even be mentioned freely within the house; a household which seemed to have displaced the planetary government; a planetary government which the Instrumentality, for unfathomable reasons of its own, had let fall into ruin. Why? Why? And why again?

The turtle-girl was looking at him. If he had been an art student, he would have said that she was giving him the tender, feminine and irrecoverably remote smile of a madonna, but he did not know the motifs of the ancient pictures; he just knew that it was a smile characteristic of T'ruth herself.

"You are wondering . . . ?" she said.

He nodded, suddenly feeling miserable that mere words had come between them.

"You are wondering why the Instrumentality let you come here?"

He nodded again.

"I don't know either," she said, reaching out and taking his right hand. His hand felt and looked like the hairy paw of a giant as she held it with her two pretty, well-kept little-girl hands; but the strength of her eyes and the steadfastness of her voice showed that it was she who was giving the reassurance, not he.

The child was helping *him!*

The idea was outrageous, impossible, true.

It was enough to alarm him, to make him begin to pull back his hand. She clutched him with tender softness, with weak strength, and he could not resist her. Again he had the feeling, which had gripped him so strongly when he first met her at the door of Beauregard and failed to kill her, that he had always known her and had always loved her. (Was there not some planet on which eccentric people believed a weird cult, thinking that human beings were endlessly reborn with fragmentary recollections of their own previous human lives? It was almost like that. Here. Now. He did not know the girl but he had always known her. He did not love the girl and yet had loved her from the beginning of time.)

She said, so softly that it was almost a whisper, "Wait. . . . Wait. . . . Your death may come through that door pretty soon and I will tell you how to meet it. But before that, even, I have to show you the most beautiful thing in the world."

Despite her little hand lying tenderly and firmly on his, Casher spoke irritably: "I'm tired of talking riddles here on Henriada. The administrator gives me the mission of killing you and I fail in it. Then you promise me a battle and give me a good meal instead. Now you talk about the battle and start off with some other irrelevance. You're going to make me angry if you keep on and—and—and—" He stammered out at last: "I get pretty useless if I'm angry. If you want me to do a fight for you, let me know the fight and let me go do it now. I'm willing enough."

Her remote, kind half-smile did not waver. "Casher," she said, "what I am going to show you is your most important weapon in the fight."

With her free left hand she tugged at the fine chain of a thin gold necklace. A piece of jewelry came out of the top of her shift dress, under which she had kept it hidden. It was the image of two pieces of wood with a man nailed to them.

Casher stared and then he burst into hysterical laughter.

"Now you've done it, ma'am," he cried. "I'm no use to you or to anybody else. I know what that is, and up to now I've just suspected it. It's what the robot, rat and Copt agreed on when they went exploring back in Space Three. It's the Old Strong Religion. You've put it in my mind and now the next person who meets me will peep it and will wipe it out. Me too, probably, along with it. That's no weapon. That's a defeat.

You've done me in. I knew the Sign of the Fish a long time ago, but I had a chance of getting away with just that little bit."

"Casher!" she cried. "Casher! Get hold of yourself. You will know nothing about this before you leave Beauregard. You will forget. You will be safe."

He stood on his feet, not knowing whether to run away, to laugh out loud or to sit down and weep at the silly sad misfortune which had befallen him. To think that he himself had become brain-branded as a fanatic—forever denied travel between the stars—just because an undergirl had shown him an odd piece of jewelry!

"It's not as bad as you think," said the little girl, and stood up too. Her face peered lovingly at Casher's. "Do you think, Casher, that I am afraid?"

"No," he admitted.

"You will not remember this, Casher. Not when you leave. I am not just the turtle-girl T'ruth. I am also the imprint of the citizen Agatha. Have you ever heard of her?"

"Agatha Madigan?" He shook his head slowly. "No. I don't see how . . . no, I'm sure that I never heard of her."

"Didn't you ever hear the story of the Hechizera of Gonfalon?"

Casher looked surprised. "Sure I saw it. It's a play. A drama. It is said to be based on some legend out of immemorial time. The 'space witch' they called her, and she conjured fleets out of nothing by sheer hypnosis. It's an old story."

"Eleven hundred years isn't so long," said the girl. "Eleven hundred years, fourteen local months come next tonight."

"You weren't alive eleven hundred years ago," said Casher accusingly.

He stood up from the remains of their meal and wandered over toward the window. That terrible piece of religious jewelry made him uncomfortable. He knew that it was against all laws to ship religion from world to world. What would he do, what could he do, now that he had actually beheld an image of the God Nailed High? That was exactly the kind of contraband which the police and customs robots of hundreds of worlds were looking for.

The Instrumentality was easy about most things, but the transplanting of religion was one of its hostile obsessions. Religions leaked from world to world anyhow. It was said that sometimes even the underpeople and robots carried bits of religion through space, though this seemed improbable. The Instrumentality left religion alone when it had a settled place on a single planet, but the Lords of the Instrumentality themselves shunned other people's devotional lives and simply took good care that fanaticisms did not once more flare up between the stars, bringing wild hope and great death to all the mankinds again.

*And now,* thought Casher, *the Instrumentality has been good to me in its big impersonal collective way, but what will it do when my brain is on fire with forbidden knowledge?*

The girl's voice called him back to himself.

"I have the answer to your problem, Casher," said she, "if you would only listen to me. I *am* the Hechizera of Gonfalon, at least I am as much as any one person can be printed on another."

His jaw dropped as he turned back to her. "You mean that you, child, really are imprinted with this woman Agatha Madigan? Really imprinted?

"I have all her skills, Casher," said the girl quietly, "and a few more which I have learned on my own."

"But I thought it was just a story . . ." said Casher. "If you're that terrible woman from Gonfalon, you don't need me. I'm quitting. Now."

Casher walked toward the door. Disgusted, finished, through. She might be a child, she might be charming, she might need help, but if she came from that terrible old story, she did not need him.

"Oh, no, you don't," she said.

## IX

Unexpectedly, she took her place in the doorway, barring it.

In her hand was the image of the man on the two pieces of wood.

Ordinarily Casher would not have pushed a lady. Such was his haste that he did so this time. When he touched her, it was like welded steel; neither her gown nor her body yielded a thousandth of a millimeter to his strong hand and heavy push.

"And now what?" she asked gently.

Looking back, he saw that the real T'ruth, the smiling girl-woman, still stood soft and real in the window.

Deep within, he began to give up; he had heard of hypnotists who could project, but he had never met one as strong as this.

She was doing it. How was she doing it? Or was she doing it? The operation could be subvolitional. There might be some art carried over from her animal past which even her re-formed mind could not explain.

Operations too subtle, too primordial for analysis. Or skills which she used without understanding.

"I project," she said.

"I see you do," he replied glumly and flatly.

"I do kinesthetics," she said. His knife whipped out of his bootsheath and floated in the air in front of him.

He snatched it out of the air instinctively. It wormed a little in his grasp, but the force on the knife was nothing more than he had felt when passing big magnetic engines.

"I blind," she said. The room went totally dark for him.

"I hear," he said, and prowled at her like a beast, going by his memory of the room and by the very soft sound of her breathing. He had noticed by now that the simulacrum of herself which she had put in the doorway did not make any sound at all, not even that of breathing.

He knew that he was near her. His fingertips reached out for her shoulder or her throat. He did not mean to hurt her, merely to show her that two could play at tricks.

"I stun," she said, and her voice came at him from all directions. It echoed from the ceiling, came from all five walls of the old odd room, from the open windows, from both the doors. He felt as though he were being lifted into space and turned slowly in a condition of weightlessness. He tried to retain self-control, to listen for the one true sound among the many false sounds, to trap the girl by some outside chance.

"I make you remember," said her multiple echoing voice.

For an instant he did not see how this could be a weapon, even if the turtle-girl had learned all the ugly tricks of the Hechizera of Gonfalon.

But then he knew.

He saw his uncle, Kuraf, again. He saw his old apartments vividly around himself. Kuraf was there. The old man was pitiable, hateful, drunk, horrible; the girl on Kuraf's lap laughed at him, Casher O'Neill, and she laughed at Kuraf too. Casher had once had a teenager's passionate concern with sex and at the same time had had a teenager's dreadful fear of all the unstated, invisible implications of what the man-woman relationship, gone sour, gone wrong, gone bad, might be. The present-moment Casher remembered the long-ago Casher and as he spun in the web of T'ruth's hypnotic powers he found himself back with the ugliest memory he had.

The killings in the palace at Mizzer.

The colonels had taken Kaheer itself, and they ultimately let Kuraf run away to the pleasure planet of Ttiolle.

But Kuraf's companions, who had debauched the old republic of the Twelve Niles, those people! They did not go. The soldiers, stung to fury, had cut them down with knives. Casher thought of the blood, blood sticky on the floors, blood gushing purple into the carpets, blood bright red and leaping like a fountain when a white throat ended its last gurgle, blood turning brown where handprints, themselves bloody, had left it on marble tables. The warm palace, long ago, had got the sweet sick stench of blood all the way through it. The young Casher had never known that people had so much blood inside them, or that so much could pour out on the perfumed sheets, the tables still set with food and drink, or that blood could creep across the floor in growing pools as the bodies of the dead yielded up their last few nasty sounds and their terminal muscular spasms.

Before that day of butchery had ended, one thousand, three hundred and eleven human bodies, ranging in age from two months to eighty-nine years, had been carried out of the palaces once occupied by Kuraf. Kuraf, under sedation, was waiting for a starship to take him to perpetual exile and Casher—Casher himself O'Neill!—was shaking the hand of Colonel Wedder, whose orders had caused all the blood. The hand was washed and the nails pared and cleaned, but the cuff of the sleeve was still rimmed with the dry blood of some other human being. Colonel Wedder either did not notice his own cuff, or he did not care.

"Touch and yield!" said the girl-voice out of nowhere.

Casher found himself on all fours in the room, his sight suddenly back again, the room unchanged, and T'ruth smiling.

"I fought you," she said.

He nodded. He did not trust himself to speak.

He reached for his water glass, looking at it closely to see if there was any blood on it.

Of course not. Not here. Not this time, not this place.

He pulled himself to his feet.

The girl had sense enough not to help him.

She stood there in her thin modest shift, looking very much like a wise female child, while he stood up and drank thirstily. He refilled the glass and drank again.

Then, only then, did he turn to her and speak:

"Do you do all that?"

She nodded.

"Alone? Without drugs or machinery?"

She nodded again.

"Child," he cried out, "you're not a person! You're a whole weapons system all by yourself. What are you, really? *Who* are you?"

"I am the turtle-child T'ruth," she said, "and I am the loyal property and loving servant of my good master, the Mister and Owner Murray Madigan."

"Madam," said Casher, "you are almost a thousand years old. I am at your service. I do hope you will let me go free later on. And especially that you will take that religious picture out of my mind."

As Casher spoke, she picked a locket from the table. He had not noticed it. It was an ancient watch or a little round box, swinging on a thin gold chain.

"Watch this," said the child, "if you trust me, and repeat what I then say."

(Nothing at all happened: nothing—anywhere.)

Casher said to her, "You're making me dizzy, swinging that ornament. Put it back on. Isn't that the one you were wearing?"

"No, Casher, it isn't."

"What were we talking about?" demanded Casher.

"Something," said she. "Don't you remember?"

"No," said Casher brusquely. "Sorry, but I'm hungry again." He wolfed down a sweet roll encrusted with sugar and decorated with fruits. His mouth full, he washed the food down with water. At last he spoke to her. "Now what?"

She had watched with timeless grace.

"There's no hurry, Casher. Minutes or hours, they don't matter."

"Didn't you want me to fight somebody after Gosigo left me here?"

"That's right," she said, with terrible quiet.

"I seem to have had a fight right here in this room." He stared around stupidly.

She looked around the room, very cool. "It doesn't look as though anybody's been fighting here, does it?"

"There's no blood here, no blood at all. Everything is clean," he said.

"Pretty much so."

"Then why," said Casher, "should I think I had a fight?"

"This wild weather on Henriada sometimes upsets off-worlders until they get used to it," said T'ruth mildly.

"If I didn't have a fight in the past, am I going to get into one in the future?"

The old room with the golden-oak furniture swam around him. The world outside was strange, with the sunlit marshes and wide bayous trailing off to the forever-thundering storm, just over the horizon, which lay beyond the weather machines. Casher shrugged and shivered. He looked straight at the girl. She stood erect and looked at him with the even regard of a reigning empress. Her young budding breasts barely showed through the thinness of her shift; she wore golden flat-heeled shoes. Around her neck there was a thin gold chain, but the object on the chain hung down inside her dress. It excited him a little to think of her flat chest barely budding into womanhood. He had never been a man who had an improper taste for children, but there was something about this person which was not childlike at all.

"You are a girl and not a girl . . ." he said in bewilderment.

She nodded gravely.

"You are that woman in the story, the Hechizera of Gonfalon. You are reborn."

She shook her head, equally seriously. "No, I am not reborn. I am a turtle-child, an underperson with very long life, and I have been imprinted with the personality of the citizen Agatha. That is all."

"You stun," he said, "but I do not know how you do it."

"I stun," she said flatly, and around the edge of his mind there flickered up hot little torments of memory.

"Now I remember," he cried. "You have me here to kill somebody. You are sending me into a fight."

"You are going to a fight, Casher. I wish I could send somebody else, not you, but you are the only person here strong enough to do the job."

Impulsively he took her hand. The moment he touched her, she ceased to be a child or an underperson. She felt tender and exciting, like the most desirable and important person he had ever known. His sister? But he had no sister. He felt that he was himself terribly, unendurably important to her. He did not want to let her hand go, but she withdrew from his touch with an authority which no decent man could resist.

"You must fight to the death now, Casher," she said, looking at him as evenly as might a troop commander examining a special soldier selected for a risky mission.

He nodded. He was tired of having his mind confused. He knew something had happened to him after the forgetty, Gosigo, had left him at the front door, but he was not at all sure of what it was. They seemed to have had a sort of meal together in this room. He felt himself in love with the child. He knew that she was not even a human being. He remembered something about her living ninety thousand years and he remembered something else about her having gotten the name and the skills of the greatest battle hypnotist of all history, the Hechizera of Gonfalon. There was something strange, something frightening about that chain around her neck: there were things he hoped he would never have to know.

He strained at the thought and it broke like a bubble.

"I'm a fighter," he said. "Give me my fight and let me know."

*"He* can kill you. I hope not. You must not kill him. He is immortal and insane. But in the law of Old North Australia, from which my master, the Mister and Owner Murray Madigan, is an exile, we must not hurt a house guest, nor may we turn him away in a time of great need."

"What do I *do?*" snapped Casher impatiently.

"You fight him. You frighten him. You make his poor crazy mind fearful that he will meet you again."

"I'm supposed to do this."

"You can," she said very seriously. "I've already tested you. That's where you have the little spot of amnesia about this room."

"But *why?* Why bother? Why not get some of your human servants and have them tie him up or put him in a padded room?"

"They can't deal with him. He is too strong, too big, too clever, even though insane. Besides, they don't dare follow him."

"Where does he go?" said Casher sharply.

"Into the control room," replied T'ruth, as if it were the saddest phrase ever uttered.

"What's wrong with that? Even a place as fine as Beauregard can't have too much of a control room. Put locks on the control."

"It's not that kind of a control room."

Almost angry, he shouted, "What is it, then?"

"The control room," she answered, "is for a planoform ship. This house. These counties, all the way to Mottile on the one side and to Ambiloxi on the other. The sea itself, way out into the Gulf of Esperanza. All this is one ship."

Casher's professional interest took over. "If it's turned off, he can't do any harm."

"It's not turned off," she said. "My master leaves it on a very little bit.

That way, he can keep the weather machines going and make this edge of Henriada a very pleasant place."

"You mean," said Casher, "that you'd risk letting a lunatic fly all these estates off into space."

"He doesn't even fly," said T'ruth gloomily.

"What does he *do*, then?" yelled Casher.

"When he gets at the controls, he just hovers."

"He hovers? By the bell, girl, don't try to fool me. If you hover a place as big as this, you could wipe out the whole planet any moment. There have been only two or three pilots in the history of space who would be able to hover a machine like this one."

"He can, though," insisted the little girl.

"Who is he, anyhow?"

"I thought you knew. Or had heard somewhere about it. His name is John Joy Tree."

"Tree the go captain?" Casher shivered in the warm room. "He died a long time ago after he made that record flight."

"He did not die. He bought immortality and went mad. He came here and he lives under my master's protection."

"Oh," said Casher. There was nothing else he could say. John Joy Tree, the great Norstrilian who took the first of the Long Plunges outside the galaxy: he was like Magno Taliano of ages ago, who could fly space on his living brain alone.

But fight him? How could anybody fight him?

Pilots are for piloting; killers are for killing; women are for loving or forgetting. When you mix up the purposes, everything goes wrong.

Casher sat down abruptly. "Do you have any more of that coffee?"

"You don't need coffee," she said.

He looked up inquiringly.

"You're a fighter. You need a war. That's it," she said, pointing with her girlish hand to a small doorway which looked like the entrance to a closet. "Just go in there. He's in there now. Tinkering with the machines again. Making me wait for my master to get blown to bits at any minute! And I've put up with it for over a hundred years."

"Go yourself," he said.

"You've been in a ship's control room," she declared.

"Yes." He nodded.

"You know how people go all naked and frightened inside. You know how much training it takes to make a go captain. What do you think happens to me?" At last, long last, her voice was shrill, angry, excited, childish.

"What happens?" said Casher dully, not caring very much; he felt weary in every bone. Useless battles, murder he had to try, dead people arguing after their ballads had already grown out of fashion. Why didn't the Hechizera of Gonfalon do her own work?

Catching his thought, she screeched at him, "Because I *can't!*"

"All right," said Casher. "Why not?"

*"Because I turn into me."*

"You what?" said Casher, a little startled.

"I'm a turtle-child. My shape is human. My brain is big. But I'm a *turtle*. No matter how much my master needs me, I'm just a turtle."

"What's that got to do with it?"

"What do turtles do when they're faced with danger? Not underpeople-turtles, but real turtles, little animals. You must have heard of them somewhere."

"I've even seen them," said Casher, "on some world or other. They pull into their shells."

"That's what I do"—she wept—"when I should be defending my master. I can meet most things. I am not a coward. But in that control room, I forget, forget, forget!"

"Send a robot, then!"

She almost screamed at him. "A robot against John Joy Tree? Are you mad too?"

Casher admitted, in a mumble, that on second thought it wouldn't do much good to send a robot against the greatest go captain of them all. He concluded, lamely, "I'll go, if you want me to."

"Go now," she shouted, "go right in!"

She pulled at his arm, half-dragging and half-leading him to the little brightened door which looked so innocent.

"But—" he said.

"Keep going," she pleaded. "This is all we ask of you. Don't kill him, but frighten him, fight him, wound him if you must. You can do it. I can't." She sobbed as she tugged at him. "I'd just be *me.*"

Before he knew quite what had happened she had opened the door. The light beyond was clear and bright and tinged with blue, the way the skies of Manhome, Mother Earth, were shown in all the viewers.

He let her push him in.

He heard the door click behind him.

Before he even took in the details of the room or noticed the man in the go captain's chair, the flavor and meaning of the room struck him like a blow against his throat.

*This room,* he thought, is *hell.*

He wasn't even sure that he remembered where he had learned the word *hell.* It denoted all good turned to evil, all hope to anxiety, all wishes to greed.

Somehow, this room was it.

And then . . .

# X

And then the chief occupant of hell turned and looked squarely at him.

If this was John Joy Tree, he did not look insane.

He was a handsome, chubby man with a red complexion, bright eyes, dancing blue in color, and a mouth which was as mobile as the mouth of a temptress.

"Good day," said John Joy Tree.

"How do you do," said Casher inanely.

"I do not know your name," said the ruddy brisk man, speaking in a tone of voice which was not the least bit insane.

"I am Casher O'Neill, from the city of Kaheer on the planet Mizzer."

"Mizzer?" John Joy Tree laughed. I spent a night there, long, long ago. The entertainment was most unusual. But we have other things to talk about. You have come here to kill the undergirl T'ruth. You received your orders from the honorable Rankin Meiklejohn, may he soak in drink! The child has caught you and now she wants you to kill me, but she does not dare utter those words."

John Joy Tree, as he spoke, shifted the spaceship controls to standby, and got ready to get out of his captain's seat.

Casher protested, "She said nothing about killing you. She said you might kill me."

"I might, at that." The immortal pilot stood on the floor. He was a full head shorter than Casher but he was a strong and formidable man. The blue light of the room made him look clear, sharp, distinct.

The whole flavor of the situation tickled the fear nerves inside Casher's body. He suddenly felt that he wanted very much to go to a bathroom, but he felt—quite surely—that if he turned his back on this man, in this place, he would die like a felled ox in a stockyard. He *had* to face John Joy Tree.

"Go ahead," said the pilot. "Fight me."

"I didn't say that I would fight you," said Casher. "I am supposed to frighten you and I do not know how to do it."

"This isn't getting us anywhere," said John Joy Tree. "Shall we go into the outer room and let poor little T'ruth give us a drink? You can just tell her that you failed."

"I think," said Casher, "that I am more afraid of her than I am of you."

John Joy Tree flung himself into a comfortable passenger's chair. "All right, then. Do something. Do you want to box? Gloves? Bare fists? Or would you like swords? Or wirepoints? There are some over there in the closet. Or we can each take a pilot ship and have a ship duel out in space."

"That wouldn't make much sense," said Casher, "me fighting a ship against the greatest go captain of them all. . . ."

John Joy Tree greeted this with an ugly underlaugh, a barely audible sound which made Casher feel that the whole situation was ridiculous.

"But I do have one advantage," said Casher. "I know who you are and you do not know who I am."

"How could I tell," said John Joy Tree, "when people keep on getting born all over the place?"

He gave Casher a scornful, comfortable grin. There was charm in the man's poise. Keeping his eyes focused directly on Casher, he felt for a carafe and poured himself a drink.

He gave Casher an ironic toast and Casher took it, standing frightened and alone. More alone than he had ever been before in his life.

Suddenly John Joy Tree sprang lightly to his feet and stared with a complete change of expression past Casher. Casher did not dare look around. This was some old fight trick.

Tree spat out the words, *"You've* done it, then. This time you will violate all the laws and kill me. This fashionable oaf is not just one more trick."

A voice behind Casher called very softly, "I don't know." It was a man's voice, old, slow and tired.

Casher had heard no one come in.

Casher's years of training stood him in good stead. He skipped sidewise in four or five steps, never taking his eyes off John Joy Tree, until the other man had come into his field of vision.

The man who stood there was tall, thin, yellow-skinned and yellow-haired. His eyes were an old sick blue. He glanced at Casher and said, "I'm Madigan."

*Was this the master?* thought Casher. *Was this the being whom that lovely child had been imprinted to adore?*

He had no more time for thought.

Madigan whispered, as if to no one in particular, "You find me waking. You find him sane. Watch out."

Madigan lunged for the pilot's controls, but his tall, thin old body could not move very fast.

John Joy Tree jumped out of his chair and ran for the controls too.

Casher tripped him.

Tree fell, rolled over and got halfway up, one knee and one foot on the floor. In his hand there shimmered a knife very much like Casher's own.

Casher felt the flame of his body as some unknown force flung him against the wall. He stared, wild with fear.

Madigan had climbed into the pilot's seat and was fiddling with the controls as though he might blow Henriada out of space at any second. John Joy Tree glanced at his old host and then turned his attention to the man in front of him.

There was another man there.

Casher knew him.

He looked familiar.

It was himself, rising and leaping like a snake, left arm weaving the knife for the neck of John Joy Tree.

The image Casher hit Tree with a thud that resounded through the room.

Tree's bright blue eyes had turned crazy-mad. His knife caught the image Casher in the abdomen, thrust hard and deep, and left the young man gasping on the floor, trying to push the bleeding entrails back into his belly. The blood poured from the image Casher all over the rug.

Blood!

Casher suddenly knew what he had to do and how he could do it—all without anybody telling him.

He created a third Casher on the far side of the room and gave him iron gloves. There was himself, unheeded against the wall; there was the dying Casher on the floor; there was the third, stalking toward John Joy Tree.

"Death is here," screamed the third Casher, with a voice which Casher recognized as a fierce crazy simulacrum of his own.

Tree whirled around. "You're not real," he said.

The image Casher stepped around the console and hit Tree with an iron glove. The pilot jumped away, a hand reaching up to his bleeding face.

John Joy Tree screamed at Madigan, who was playing with the dials without even putting on the pinlighter helmet.

"You got her in here," he screamed, "you got her in here with this young man! Get her out!"

"Who?" said Madigan softly and absentmindedly.

"T'ruth. That witch of yours. I claim guest-right by all the ancient laws. *Get her out.*"

The real Casher, standing at the wall, did not know how he controlled the image Casher with the iron gloves, but control him he did. He made him speak, in a voice as frantic as Tree's own voice.

"John Joy Tree, I do not bring you death. I bring you blood. My iron hands will pulp your eyes. Blind sockets will stare in your face. My iron hands will split your teeth and break your jaw a thousand times, so that no doctor, no machine will ever fix you. My iron hands will crush your arms, turn your hands into living rags. My iron hands will break your legs. Look at the blood, John Joy Tree. . . . There will be a lot more blood. You have killed me once. See that young man on the floor."

They both glanced at the first image Casher, who had finally shuddered into death in the great rug. A pool of blood lay in front of the body of the youth.

John Joy Tree turned to image Casher and said to him, "You're the Hechizera of Gonfalon. You can't scare me. You're a turtle-girl and can't really hurt me."

"Look at me," said the real Casher.

John Joy Tree glanced back and forth between the duplicates.

Fright began to show.

Both the Cashers now shouted, in crazy voices which came from the depths of Casher's own mind:

"Blood you shall have! Blood and ruin. But we will not kill you. You will live in ruin, blind, emasculated, armless, legless. You will be fed through tubes. You cannot die and you will weep for death but no one will hear you."

"Why?" screamed Tree. "Why? What have I done to you?"

"You remind me," howled Casher, "of my home. You remind me of the blood poured by Colonel Wedder when the poor useless victims of ·

my uncle's lust paid with their blood for his revenge. You remind me of myself, John Joy Tree, and I am going to punish you as I myself might be punished."

Lost in the mists of lunacy, John Joy Tree was still a brave man.

He flung his knife unexpectedly at the real Casher. The image Casher, in a tremendous bound, leaped across the room and caught the knife on an iron glove. It clattered against the glove and then fell silent onto the rug.

Casher saw what he had to see.

He saw the palace of Kaheer, covered with death, with the intimate sticky silliness of sudden death—the dead men holding little packages they had tried to save, the girls, with their throats cut, lying in their own blood but with the lipstick still even and the eyebrow pencil still pretty on their dead faces. He saw a dead child, ripped open from groin upward to chest, holding a broken doll while the child itself, now dead, looked like a broken doll itself. He saw these things and he made John Joy Tree see them too.

"You're a bad man," said John Joy Tree.

"I am very bad," said Casher.

"Will you let me go if I never enter this room again?"

The image Casher snapped off, both the body on the floor and the fighter with the iron gloves. Casher did not know how T'ruth had taught him the lost art of fighter replication, but he had certainly done it well.

"The lady told me you could go."

"But who are you going to use," said John Joy Tree, calm, sad and logical, "for your dreams of blood if you don't use me?"

"I don't know," said Casher. "I follow my fate. Go now, if you do not want my iron gloves to crush you."

John Joy Tree trotted out of the room, beaten.

Only then did Casher, exhausted, grab a curtain to hold himself upright and look around the room freely.

The evil atmosphere had gone.

Madigan, old though he was, had locked all the controls on standby.

He walked over to Casher and spoke. "Thank you. She did not invent you. She found you and put you to my service."

Casher coughed out, "The girl. Yes."

"*My* girl," corrected Madigan.

"Your girl," said Casher, remembering the sight of that slight feminine body, those budding breasts, the sensitive lips, the tender eyes.

"She could not have thought you up. She is my dead wife over again. The citizeness Agatha might have done it. But not T'ruth."

Casher looked at the man as he talked. The host wore the bottoms of some very cheap yellow pajamas and a washable bathrobe which had once been stripes of purple, lavender and white. Now it was faded, like its wearer. Casher also saw the white clean plastic surgical implants on the man's arms, where the machines and tubes hooked in to keep him alive.

"I sleep a lot," said Murray Madigan, "but I am still the master of Beauregard. I am grateful to you."

The hand was frail, withered, dry, without strength.

The old voice whispered, "Tell her to reward you. You can have anything on my estate. Or you can have anything on Henriada. She manages it all for me." Then the old blue eyes opened wide and sharp and Murray Madigan was once again the man, just momentarily, that he had been hundreds of years ago—a Norstrilian trader, sharp, shrewd, wise and not unkind. He added sharply, "Enjoy her company. She is a good child. But do not take her. Do not try to take her."

"Why not?" said Casher, surprised at his own bluntness.

"Because if you do, she will die. She is *mine*. Imprinted to me. I had her made and she is mine. Without me she would die in a few days. Do not take her."

Casher saw the old man leave the room by a secret door. He left himself, the way he had come in. He did not see Madigan again for two days, and by that time the old man had gone far back into his cataleptic sleep.

## XI

Two days later T'ruth took Casher to visit the sleeping Madigan.

"You can't go in there," said Eunice in a shocked voice. "*Nobody* goes in there. That's the master's room."

"I'm taking him in," said T'ruth calmly.

She had pulled a cloth-of-gold curtain aside and she was spinning the combination locks on a massive steel door. It was set in Daimoni material.

The maid went on protesting. "But even you, little ma'am, can't take him in there!"

"Who says I can't?" said T'ruth calmly and challengingly.

The awfulness of the situation sank in on Eunice.

In a small voice she muttered, "If you're taking him in, you're taking him in. But it's never been done before."

"Of course it hasn't, Eunice, not in your time. But Casher O'Neill has already met the Mister and Owner. He has fought for the Mister and Owner. Do you think I would take a stray or random guest in to look at the master, just like that?"

"Oh, not at all, no," said Eunice.

"Then go away, woman," said the lady-child. "You don't want to see this door open, do you?"

"Oh, no," shrieked Eunice and fled, putting her hands over her ears as though that would shut out the sight of the door.

When the maid had disappeared, T'ruth pulled with her whole weight against the handle of the heavy door. Casher expected the mustiness of the tomb or the medicinality of a hospital; he was astonished when fresh air and warm sunlight poured out from that heavy, mysterious door. The actual opening was so narrow, so low, that Casher had to step sidewise as he followed T'ruth into the room.

The master's room was enormous. The windows were flooded with perpetual sunlight. The landscape outside must have been the way Henriada looked in its prime, when Mottile was a resort for the carefree millions of vacationers, and Ambiloxi a port feeding worlds halfway across the galaxy. There was no sign of the ugly snaky storms which worried and pestered Henriada in these later years. Everything was landscape, order, neatness, the triumph of man, as though Poussin had painted it.

The room itself, like the other great living rooms of the estate of Beauregard, was exuberant neo-baroque in which the architect, himself half-mad, had been given wild license to work out his fantasies in steel, plastic, plaster, wood and stone. The ceiling was not flat, but vaulted. Each of the four corners of the room was an alcove, cutting deep into each of the four sides, so that the room was, in effect, an octagon. The propriety and prettiness of the room had been a little diminished by the shoving of the furniture to one side, sofas, upholstered armchairs, marble tables and knickknack stands all in an indescribable mélange to the left; while the right-hand part of the room—facing the master window with the illusory landscape—was equipped like a surgery with an operating table, hydraulic lifts, bottles of clear and colored fluid hanging from chrome stands and two large devices which (Casher later surmised) must have been heart-lung and kidney machines. The alcoves, in their turn, were wilder. One was an archaic funeral parlor with an immense coffin, draped in black velvet, resting on a heavy teak stand. The next was a spaceship control cabin of the old kind, with the levers, switches and controls all in plain sight—the meters actually read the galactically stable location of this very place, and to do so they had to whirl mightily—as well as a pilot's chair with the usual choice of helmets and the straps and shock absorbers. The third alcove was a simple bedroom done in very old-fashioned taste, the walls a Wedgwood blue with deep wine-colored drapes, coverlets and pillowcases marking a sharp but tolerable contrast. The fourth alcove was the copy of a fortress: it might even have been a fortress: the door was heavy and the walls looked as though they might be Daimoni material, indestructible by any imaginable means. Cases of emergency food and water were stacked against the walls. Weapons which looked oiled and primed stood in their racks, together with three different calibers of wirepoint, each with its own fresh-looking battery.

The alcoves had no people in them.

The parlor was deserted.

The Mister and Owner Murray Madigan lay naked on the operating table. Two or three wires led to gauges attached to his body. Casher thought that he could see a faint motion of the chest, as the cataleptic man breathed at a rate one-tenth normal or less.

The girl-lady, T'ruth, was not the least embarrassed.

"I check him four or five times a day. I never let people in here. But you're special, Casher. He's talked with you and fought beside you and he knows that he owes you his life. You're the first human person ever to get into this room."

"I'll wager," said Casher, "that the administrator of Henriada, the honorable Rankin Meiklejohn, would give up some of his 'honorable' just to get in here and have one look around. He wonders what Madigan is doing when Madigan is doing nothing. . . ."

"He's not just doing nothing," said T'ruth sharply. "He's sleeping. It's not everybody who can sleep for forty or fifty or sixty thousand years and can wake up a few times a month, just to see how things are going."

Casher started to whistle and then stopped himself, as though he feared to waken the unconscious, naked old man on the table. "So that's why he chose *you.*"

T'ruth corrected him as she washed her hands vigorously in a washba-sin. "That's why he had me made. Turtle stock, three hundred years. Multiply that with intensive stroon treatments, three hundred times. Ninety thousand years. Then he had me printed to love him and adore him. He's not my master, you know. He's my god."

"Your what?"

"You heard me. Don't get upset. I'm not going to give you any illegal memories. I worship him. That's what I was printed for, when my little turtle eyes opened and they put me back in the tank to enlarge my brain and to make a woman out of me. That's why they printed every memory of the citizeness Agatha Madigan right into my brain. I'm what he wanted. Just what he wanted. I'm the most wanted being on any planet. No wife, no sweetheart, no mother has ever been wanted as much as he wants me now, when he wakes up and knows that I am still here. You're a smart man. Would you trust any machine—any machine at all—for ninety thousand years?"

"It would be hard," said Casher, "to get batteries of monitors long enough for them to repair each other over that long a time. But that means you have ninety thousand years of it. Four times, five times a day. I can't even multiply the numbers. Don't you ever get tired of it?"

"He's my love, he's my joy, he's my darling little boy," she caroled, as she lifted his eyelids and put colorless drops in each eye. Absentmindedly, she explained. "With his slow metabolism, there's always some danger that his eyelids will stick to his eyeballs. This is part of the checkup."

She tilted the sleeping man's head, looked earnestly into each eye. She then stepped a few paces aside and put her face close to the dial of a gently humming machine. There was the sound of a shot. Casher almost reached for his gun, which he did not have.

The child turned back to him with a free mischievous smile. "Sorry, I should have warned you. That's my noisemaker. I watch the encephalograph to make sure his brain keeps a little auditory intake. It showed up with the noise. He's asleep, very deeply asleep, but he's not drifting downward into death."

Back at the table she pushed Madigan's chin upward so that the head leaned far back on its neck. Deftly holding the forehead, she took a retractor, opened his mouth with her fingers, depressed the tongue and looked down into the throat.

"No accumulation there," she muttered, as if to herself.

She pushed the head back into a comfortable position. She seemed on the edge of another set of operations when it was obvious that an idea occurred to her. "Go wash your hands, thoroughly, over there, at the basin. Then push the timer down and be sure you hold your hands under the sterilizer until the timer goes off. You can help me turn him over. I don't have help here. You're the first visitor."

Casher obeyed and while he washed his hands, he saw the girl drench her hands with some flower-scented unguent. She began to massage the unconscious body with professional expertness, even with a degree of roughness. As he stood with his hands under the sterilizer-dryer, Casher marveled at the strength of those girlish arms and those little hands. Indefatigably they stroked, rubbed, pummeled, pulled, stretched and poked the old body. The sleeping man seemed to be utterly unaware of it, but Casher thought that he could see a better skin color and muscle tone appearing.

He walked back to the table and stood facing T'ruth.

A huge peacock walked across the imaginary lawn outside the window, his tail shimmering in a paroxysm of colors.

T'ruth saw the direction of Casher's glance.

"Oh, I program that too. He likes it when he wakes up. Don't you think he was clever, before he went into catalepsis—to have me made, to have me created to love him and to care for him? It helps that I'm a girl. I can't ever love anybody but him, and it's easy for me to remember that this is the man I love. And it's safer for him. Any man might get bored with these responsibilities. I don't."

"Yet—" said Casher.

"Shh," she said, "wait a bit. This takes care." Her strong little fingers were now plowing deep into the abdomen of the naked old man. She closed her eyes so that she could concentrate all her senses on the one act of tactile impression. She took her hands away and stood erect. "All clear," she said. "I've got to find out what's going on inside him. But I don't dare use X rays on him. Think of the radiation he'd build up in a hundred years or so. He defecates about twice a month while he's sleeping. I've got to be ready for that. I also have to prime his bladder every week or so. Otherwise he would poison himself just with his own body wastes. Here, now, you can help me turn him over. But watch the wires. Those are the monitor controls. They report his physiological processes, radio a message to me if anything goes wrong, and meanwhile supply the missing neurophysical impulses if any part of the automatic nervous system began to fade out or just simply went off."

"Has that ever happened?"

"Never," she said, "not yet. But I'm ready. Watch that wire. You're turning him too fast. There now, that's right. You can stand back while I massage him on the back."

She went back to her job of being a masseuse. Starting at the muscles joining the skull to the neck, she worked her way down the body, pouring ointment on her hands from time to time. When she got to his legs, she seemed to work particularly hard. She lifted the feet, bent the knees, slapped the calves.

Then she put on a rubber glove, dipped her hand into another jar— one which opened automatically as her hand approached—and came out with her hand greasy. She thrust her fingers into his rectum, probing, thrusting, groping, her brow furrowed.

Her face cleared as she dropped the rubber glove in a disposal can and wiped the sleeping man with a soft linen towel, which also went into a disposal can. "He's all right. He'll get along well for the next two hours. I'll have to give him a little sugar then. All he's getting now is normal saline."

She stood facing him. There was a faint glow in her cheeks from the violent exercise in which she had been indulging, but she still looked both the child and the lady—the child irrecoverably remote, hidden in her own wisdom from the muddled world of adults, and the lady, mistress in her own home, her own estates, her own planet, serving her master with almost immortal love and zeal.

"I was going to ask you, back there—" said Casher, and then stopped.

"You were going to ask me?"

He spoke heavily. "I was going to ask you, what happens to you when he dies? Either at the right time or possibly before his time. What happens to *you?*"

"I couldn't care less," her voice sang out. He could see by the open, honest smile on her face that she meant it. "I'm *his.* I belong to *him.* That's what I'm *for.* They may have programmed something into me, in case he dies. Or they may have forgotten. What matters is his life, not mine. He's going to get every possible hour of life that I can help him get. Don't you think I'm doing a good job?"

"A good job, yes," said Casher. "A strange one too."

"We can go now," she said.

"What are those alcoves for?"

"Oh, those—they're his make-believes. He picks one of them to go to sleep in—his coffin, his fort, his ship or his bedroom. It doesn't matter which. I always get him up with the hoist and put him back on his table, where the machines and I can take proper care of him. He doesn't really mind waking up on the table. He has usually forgotten which room he went to sleep in. We can go now."

They walked toward the door.

Suddenly she stopped. "I forgot something. I never forget things, but this is the first time I ever let anybody come in here with me. You were such a *good* friend to him. He'll talk about you for thousands of years. Long, long after you're dead," she added somewhat unnecessarily. Casher looked at her sharply to see if she might be mocking or deprecating him. There was nothing but the little-girl solemnity, the womanly devotion to an established domestic routine.

"Turn your back," she commanded peremptorily.

"Why?" he asked. "Why—when you have trusted me with all the other secrets."

"He wouldn't want you to see this."

"See what?"

"What I'm going to do. When I was the citizeness Agatha—or when I seemed to be her—I found that men are awfully fussy about some things. This is one of them."

Casher obeyed and stood facing the door.

A different odor filled the room—a strong wild scent, like a geranium pomade. He could hear T'ruth breathing heavily as she worked beside the sleeping man.

She called to him: "You can turn around now."

She was putting away a tube of ointment, standing high to get it into its exact position on a tile shelf.

Casher looked quickly at the body of Madigan. It was still asleep, still breathing very lightly and very slowly.

"What on earth did you *do?*"

T'ruth stopped in midstep. "You're going to get nosy."

Casher stammered mere sounds.

"You can't help it," she said. "People are inquisitive."

"I suppose they are," he said, flushing at the accusation.

"I gave him his bit of fun. He never remembers it when he wakes up, but the cardiograph sometimes shows increased activity. Nothing happened this time. That was my own idea. I read books and decided that it would be good for his body tone. Sometimes he sleeps through a whole Earth year, but usually he wakes up several times a month."

She passed Casher, almost pulled herself clear of the floor tugging on the inside levers of the main door.

She gestured him past. He stooped and stepped through.

"Turn away again," she said. "All I'm going to do is to spin the dials, but they're cued to give any viewer a bad headache so he will forget the combination. Even robots. I'm the only person tuned to these doors."

He heard the dials spinning but did not look around.

She murmured, almost under her breath, "I'm the only one. The only one."

"The only one for what?" asked Casher.

"To love my master, to care for him, to support his planet, to guard his weather. But isn't he beautiful? Isn't he wise? Doesn't his smile win your heart?"

Casher thought of the faded old wreck of a man with the yellow pajama bottoms. Tactfully, he said nothing.

T'ruth babbled on, quite cheerfully. "He is my father, my husband, my baby son, my master, my owner. Think of that, Casher, he owns me! Isn't he lucky—to have me? And aren't I lucky—to belong to him?"

"But what for?" asked Casher a little crossly, thinking that he was falling in and out of love with this remarkable girl himself.

"For life!" she cried, "In any form, in any way. I am made for ninety thousand years and he will sleep and wake and dream and sleep again, a large part of that."

"What's the use of it?" insisted Casher.

"The use," she said, "the use? What's the use of the little turtle egg they took and modified in its memory chains, right down to the molecular level? What's the use of turning me into an undergirl, so that even you have to love me off and on? What's the use of little me, meeting my master for the first time, when I had been manufactured to love him? I can tell you, man, what the use is. Love."

"What did you say?" said Casher.

"I said the use was love. Love is the only end of things. Love on the one side, and death on the other. If you are strong enough to use a real weapon, I can give you a weapon which will put all Mizzer at your mercy. Your cruiser and your laser would just be toys against the weapon of love. You can't fight love. You can't fight me."

They had proceeded down a corridor, forgotten pictures hanging on the walls, unremembered luxuries left untouched by centuries of neglect.

The bright yellow light of Henriada poured in through an open doorway on their right.

From the room came snatches of a man singing while playing a stringed instrument. Later, Casher found that this was a verse of the Henriada Song, the one which went:

*Don't put your ship in the Boom Lagoon,*
*Look up north for the raving wave.*
*Henriada's boiled away*
*But Ambiloxi's a saving grave.*

They entered the room.

A gentleman stood up to greet them.

It was the great go pilot, John Joy Tree. His ruddy face smiled, his bright blue eyes lit up, a little condescendingly, as he greeted his small hostess, but then his glance took in Casher O'Neill.

The effect was sudden, and evil.

John Joy Tree looked away from both of them. The phrase which he had started to use stuck in his throat.

He said, in a different voice, very "away" and deeply troubled, "There is blood all over this place. There is a man of blood right here. Excuse me. I am going to be sick."

He trotted past them and out the door which they had entered.

"You have passed a test," said T'ruth. "Your help to my master has solved the problem of the captain and honorable John Joy Tree. He will not go near that control room if he thinks that you are there."

"Do you have more tests for me? Still more? By now you ought to know me well enough not to need tests."

"I am not a person," she said, "but just a built-up copy of one. I am getting ready to give you your weapon. This is a communications room as well as a music room. Would you like something to eat or drink?"

"Just water," he said.

"At your hand," said T'ruth.

A rock crystal carafe had been standing on the table beside him, unnoticed. Or had she transported it into the room with one of the tricks of the Hechizera, the dreaded Agatha herself? It didn't matter. He drank. Trouble was coming.


## XII


T'ruth had swung open a polished cabinet panel. The communicator was the kind they mount in planoforming ships right beside the pilot. The rental on one of them was enough to make any planetary government reconsider its annual budget.

"That's *yours?*" cried Casher.

"Why not?" said the little-girl lady. "I have four or five of them."

"But you're *rich!*"

"I'm not. My master is. I belong to my master too."

"But things like this. . . . He can't handle them. How does he manage?"

"You mean money and things?" The girlish part of her came out. She looked pleased, happy and mischievous. "I manage them for him. He was the richest man on Henriada when I came here. He had credits of stroon. Now he is about forty times richer."

"He's a Rod McBan!" exclaimed Casher.

"Not even near. Mr. McBan had a lot more money than we. But he's rich. Where do you think all the people from Henriada went?"

"I don't know," said Casher.

"To four new planets. They belong to my master and he charges the new settlers a very small land rent."

"You bought them?" Casher asked.

"For him." T'ruth smiled. "Haven't you heard of planet brokers?"

"But that's a gambler's business!" said Casher.

"I gambled," she said, "and I won. Now keep quiet and watch me." She pressed a button. "Instant message."

"Instant message," repeated the machine. "What priority?"

"War news, double-A one, subspace penalty."

"Confirmed," said the machine.

"The planet Mizzer. Now. War and peace information. Will fighting end soon?"

The machine clucked to itself.

Casher, knowing the prices of this kind of communication, almost felt that he could see the arterial spurt of money go out of Henriada's budget as the machines reached across the galaxy, found Mizzer and came back with the answer.

"Skirmishing. Seventh Nile. Ends three local days."

"Close message," said T'ruth.

The machine went off.

T'ruth turned to him. "You're going home soon, Casher, if you can pass a few little tests."

He stared at her.

He blurted, "I need my weapons, my cruiser and my laser."

"You'll have weapons. Better ones than those. Right now I want you to go to the front door. When you have opened the door, you will not let anybody in. Close the door. Then please come back to me here, dear Casher, and if you are still alive, I will have some other things for you to do."

Casher turned in bewilderment. It did not occur to him to contradict her. He could end up a forgetty, like the maidservant Eunice or the administrator's brown man, Gosigo.

Down the halls he walked. He met no one except for a few shy cleaning robots, who bowed their heads politely as he passed.

He found the front door. It stopped him. It looked like wood on the outside, but it was actually a Daimoni door, made of near-indestructible material. There was no sign of a key or dials or controls. Acting like a man in a dream, he took a chance that the door might be keyed to himself. He put his right palm firmly against it, at the left or opening edge.

The door swung in.

Meiklejohn was there. Gosigo held the administrator upright. It must have been a rough trip. The administrator's face was bruised and blood trickled from the corner of his mouth. His eyes focused on Casher.

"You're alive. She caught you too?"

Quite formally Casher asked, "What do you want in this house?"

"I have come," said the administrator, "to see her."

"To see whom?" insisted Casher.

The administrator hung almost slack in Gosigo's arms. By his own standard and in his own way, he was a very brave man indeed. His eyes looked clear, even though his body was collapsing.

"To see T'ruth, if she will see me," said Rankin Meiklejohn.

"She cannot," said Casher, "see you now, Gosigo!"

The forgetty turned to Casher and gave him a bow.

"You will forget me. You have not seen me."

"I have not seen you, lord. Give my greetings to your lady. Anything else?"

"Yes. Take you master home, as safely and swiftly as you can."

"My lord!" cried Gosigo, though this was an improper title for Casher. Casher turned around.

"My lord, tell her to extend the weather machines for just a few more kilometers and I will have him home safe in ten minutes. At top speed."

"I can tell her," said Casher, "but I cannot promise she will do it."

"Of course," said Gosigo. He picked up the administrator and began putting him into the groundcar. Rankin Meiklejohn bawled once, like a man crying in pain. It sounded like a blurred version of the name *Murray*

*Madigan*. No one heard it but Gosigo and Casher; Gosigo busy closing the groundcar, Casher pushing on the big house door.

The door clicked.

There was silence.

The opening of the door was remembered only by the warm sweet salty stink of seaweed, which had disturbed the odor pattern of the changeless, musty old house.

Casher hurried back with the message about the weather machines.

T'ruth received the message gravely. Without looking at the console, she reached out and controlled it with her extended right hand, not taking her eyes off Casher for a moment. The machine clicked its agreement. T'ruth exhaled.

"Thank you, Casher. Now the Instrumentality and the forgetty are gone."

She stared at him, almost sadly and inquiringly. He wanted to pick her up, to crush her to his chest, to rain his kisses on her face. But he stood stock still. He did not move. This was not just the forever-loving turtle-child; this was the real mistress of Henriada. This was the Hechizera of Gonfalon, whom he had formerly thought about only in terms of a wild, melodic grand opera.

"I think you are seeing me, Casher. It is hard to see people, even when you look at them every day. I think I can see you too, Casher. It is almost time for us both to do the things which we have to do."

"Which *we* have to do?" He whispered, hoping she might say something else.

"For me, my work here on Henriada. For you, your fate on your homeland of Mizzer. That's what life is, isn't it? Doing what you have to do in the first place. We're lucky people if we find it out. You are ready, Casher. I am about to give you weapons which will make bombs and cruisers and lasers seem like nothing at all."

"By the bell, girl! Can't you tell me what those weapons are?"

T'ruth stood in her innocently revealing sheath, the yellow light of the old music room pouring like a halo around her.

"Yes," she said, "I can tell you now. Me."

"You?"

Casher felt a wild surge of erotic attraction for the innocently voluptuous child. He remembered his first insane impulse to crush her with kisses, to sweep her up with hugs, to exhaust her with all the excitement which his masculinity could bring to both of them.

He stared at her.

She stood there, calm.

That sort of idea did not ring right.

He was going to get her, but he was going to get something far from fun or folly—something, indeed, which he might not even like.

When at last he spoke, it was out of the deep bewilderment of his own thoughts, "What do you mean, you're going to give me yourself? It doesn't sound very romantic to me, nor the tone in which you said it."

The child stepped close to him, reaching up and patting his forehead.

"You're not going to get me for a night's romance, and if you did you would be sorry. I am the property of my master and of no other man. But I can do something with you which I have never done to anyone else. I can get myself imprinted on you. The technicians are already coming. You will be the turtle-child. You will be the citizeness Agatha Madigan, the Hechizera of Gonfalon herself. You will be many other people. And yourself. You will then win. Accidents may kill you, Casher, but no one will be able to kill you on purpose. Not when you're me. Poor man! Do you know what you will be giving up?"

"What?" he croaked, at the edge of a great fright. He had seen danger before, but never before had danger loomed up from within himself.

"You will not fear death, ever again, Casher. You will have to lead your life minute by minute, second by second, and you will not have the alibi that you are going to die anyhow. You will know that's not special."

He nodded, understanding her words and scrabbling around his mind for a meaning.

"I'm a girl, Casher. . . ."

He looked at her and his eyes widened. She was a girl—a beautiful, wonderful girl. But she was something more. She was the mistress of Henriada. She was the first of the underpeople really and truly to surpass humanity. To think that he had wanted to grab her poor little body. The body—ah, that was sweet!—but the power within it was the kind of thing that empires and religions are made of.

". . . and if you take the print of me, Casher, you will never lie with a woman without realizing that you know more about her than she does. You will be a seeing man among blind multitudes, a hearing person in the world of the deaf. I don't know how much fun romantic love is going to be to you after this."

Gloomily he said, "If I can free my home planet of Mizzer, it will be worth it. Whatever it is."

"You're not going to turn into a woman!" She laughed. "Nothing that easy. But you are going to get wisdom. And I will tell you the whole story of the Sign of the Fish before you leave here."

"Not that, please," he begged. "That's a religion and the Instrumentality would never let me travel again."

"I'm going to have you scrambled, Casher, so that nobody can read you for a year or two. And the Instrumentality is not going to send you back. *I am.* Through Space Three."

"It'll cost you a fine, big ship to do it."

"My master will approve when I tell him, Casher. Now give me that kiss you have been wanting to give me. Perhaps you will remember something of it when you come out of scramble."

She stood there. He did nothing.

"Kiss me!" she commanded.

He put his arm around her. She felt like a big little girl. She lifted her face. She thrust her lips up toward his. She stood on tiptoe.

He kissed her the way a man might kiss a picture or a religious object. The heat and fierceness had gone out of his hopes. He had not kissed a girl, but power—tremendous power and wisdom put into a single slight form.

"Is that the way your master kisses you?"

She gave him a quick smile. "How clever of you! Yes, sometimes. Come along now. We have to shoot some children before the technicians are ready. It will give you a good last chance of seeing what you can do, when you have become what I am. Come along. The guns are in the hall."

## XIII

They went down an enormous light oak staircase to a floor which Casher had never seen before. It must have been the entertainment and hospitality center of Beauregard long ago, when the Mister and Owner Murray Madigan was himself young.

The robots did a good job of keeping away the dust and the mildew. Casher saw inconspicuous little air-dryers placed at strategic places, so that the rich tooled leather on the walls would not spoil, so that the velvet bar stools would not become slimy with mold, so that the pool tables would not warp nor the golf clubs go out of shape with age and damp. *By the bell*, he thought, *that man Madigan could have entertained a thousand people at one time in a place this size.*

The gun cabinet, now, that was functional. The glass shone. The velvet of oil showed on the steel and walnut of the guns. They were old Earth models, very rare and very special. For actual fighting, people used the cheap artillery of the present time or wirepoints for close work. Only the richest and rarest of connoisseurs had the old Earth weapons or could use them.

T'ruth touched the guard robot and waked him. The robot saluted, looked at her face and without further inquiry opened the cabinet.

"Do you know guns?" said T'ruth to Casher.

"Wirepoints," he said. "Never touched a gun in my life."

"Do you mind using a learning helmet, then? I could teach you hypnotically with the special rules of the Hechizera, but they might give you a headache or upset you emotionally. The helmet is neuroelectric and it has filters."

Casher nodded and saw his reflection nodding in the polished glass doors of the gun cabinet. He was surprised to see how helpless and lugubrious he looked.

But it was true. Never before in his life had he felt that a situation swept over him, washed him along like a great wave, left him with no choice and no responsibility. Things were her choice now, not his, and yet he felt that her power was benign, self-limited, restricted by factors at which he could no more than guess. He had come for one weapon—the cruiser which he had hoped to get from the administrator Rankin Meiklejohn. She was offering him something else—psychological weapons in which he had neither experience nor confidence.

She watched him attentively for a long moment and then turned to the gun-watching robot.

"You're little Harry Hadrian, aren't you? The gun-watcher."

"Yes, ma'am," said the silver robot brightly, "and I'm owl-brained too. That makes me very bright."

"Watch this," she said, extending her arms the width of the gun cabinet and then dropping them after a queer flutter of her hands. "Do you know what that means?"

"Yes, ma'am," said the little robot quickly, the emotion showing in his toneless voice by the speed with which he spoke, not by the intonation. "It-means-you-have-taken-over-and-I-am-off-duty! Can-I-go-sit-in-the-garden-and-look-at-the-live-things?"

"Not quite yet, little Harry Hadrian. There are some wind people out there now and they might hurt you. I have another errand for you first. Do you remember where the teaching helmets are?"

"Silver hats on the third floor in an open closet with a wire running to each hat. Yes."

"Bring one of those as fast as you can. Pull it loose very carefully from its electrical connection."

The little robot disappeared in a sudden fast, gentle clatter up the stairs.

T'ruth turned back to Casher. "I have decided what to do with you. I am helping you. You don't have to look so gloomy about it."

"I'm not gloomy. The administrator sent me here on a crazy errand, killing an unknown underperson. I find out that the person is really a little girl. Then I find out that she is not an underperson, but a frightening old dead woman, still walking around alive. My life gets turned upside down. All my plans are set aside. You propose to send me hope to fulfill my life's work on Mizzer. I've struggled for this, so many years! Now you're making it all come through, even though you are going to cook me through Space Three to do it, and throw in a lot of illegal religion and hypnotic tricks that I'm not sure I can handle. You tell me now to come along—to shoot children with guns. I've never done anything like that in my life and yet I find myself obeying you. I'm tired out, girl, tired out. If you have put me in your power, I don't even know it, I don't even want to know it."

"Here you are, Casher, on the ruined wet world of Henriada. In less than a week you will be recovering among the military casualties of Colonel Wedder's army. You will be under the clear sky of Mizzer, and the Seventh Nile will be near you, and you will be ready at long last to do what you have to do. You will have bits and pieces of memories of me —not enough to make you find your way back here or to tell people all the secrets of Beauregard, but enough for you to remember that you have been loved. You may even"—and she smiled very gently, with a tender wry humor on her face—"marry some Mizzer girl because her body or her face or her manner reminds you of me."

"In a week?" he gasped.

"Less than that."

"Who are you," he cried out, "that you, an underperson, should run real people and should manipulate their lives?"

"I didn't look for power, Casher. Power doesn't usually work if you look for it. I have eighty-nine thousand years to live, Casher, and as long as my master lives I shall love him and take care of him. Isn't he handsome? Isn't he wise? Isn't he the most perfect master you ever saw?"

Casher thought of the old ruined-looking body with the plastic knobs set into it; he thought of the faded pajama bottoms; he said nothing.

"You don't have to agree," said T'ruth. "I know I have a special way of looking at him. But they took my turtle brain and raised the IQ to above normal human level. They took me when I was a happy little girl, enchanted by the voice and the glance and the touch of my master—they took me to where this real woman lay dying and they put me into a machine and they put her into one too. When they were through, they picked me up. I had on a pink dress with pastel blue socks and pink shoes. They carried me out into the corridor, on a rug. They had finished with me. They knew that I wouldn't die. I was healthy. Can't you see it, Casher? I cried myself to sleep, nine hundred years ago."

Casher could not really answer. He nodded sympathetically.

"I was a girl, Casher. Maybe I was a turtle once, but I don't remember that, any more than you remember your mother's womb or your laboratory bottle. In that one hour I was never to be a girl again. I did not need to go to school. I had *her* education, and it was a good one. She spoke twenty or more languages. She was a psychologist and a hypnotist and a strategist. She was also the tyrannical mistress of this house. I cried because my childhood was finished, because I knew what I would have to do. I cried because I knew that I could do it. I *loved* my master so, but I was no longer to be the pretty little servant who brought him his tablets or his sweetmeats or his beer. Now I saw the truth—as she died I had myself become Henriada. The planet was mine to care for, to manage—to protect my master. If I come along and I protect and help you, is that so much for a woman who will just be growing up when your grandchildren will all be dead of old age?"

"No, no," stammered Casher O'Neill. "But your own life? A family, perhaps?"

Anger lashed across her pretty face. Her features were the features of the delicious girl-child T'ruth, but her expression was that of the citizeness Agatha Madigan, perhaps, a worldly woman reborn to the endless worldliness of her own wisdom.

"Should I order a husband from the turtle bank, perhaps? Should I hire out a piece of my master's estate, to be sold to somebody because I'm an underperson, or perhaps put to work somewhere in an industrial ship? I'm *me*, I may be an animal, but I have more civilization in me than all the wind people on this planet. Poor things! What kind of people are they, if they are only happy when they catch a big mutated duck and tear it to pieces, eating it raw? I'm not going to lose, Casher. I'm going to win. My master will live longer than any person has ever lived before. He gave me that mission when he was strong and wise and well in the prime of his life. I'm going to do what I was made for, Casher, and you're going to go back to Mizzer and make it free, whether you like it or not!"

They both heard a happy scurrying on the staircase.

The small silver robot, little Harry Hadrian, burst upon them; he carried a teaching helmet.

T'ruth said, "Resume your post. You are a good boy, little Harry, and you can have time to sit in the garden later on, when it is safe."

"Can I sit in a tree?" the little robot asked.

"Yes, if it is safe."

Little Harry Hadrian resumed his post by the gun cabinet. He kept the key in his hand. It was a very strange key, sharp at the end and as long as an awl. Casher supposed that it must be one of the straight magnetic keys, cued to its lock by a series of magnetized patterns.

"Sit on the floor for a minute," said T'ruth to Casher; "you're too tall for me." She slipped the helmet on his head, adjusted the levers on each side so that the helmet sat tight and true upon his skull.

With a touching gesture of intimacy, for which she gave him a sympathetic apologetic little smile, she moistened the two small electrodes with her own spit, touching her finger to her tongue and then to the electrode. These went to his temples.

She adjusted the verniered dials on the helmet itself, lifted the rear wire and applied it to her forehead.

Casher heard the click of a switch.

"That did it," he heard T'ruth's voice saying, very far away.

He was too busy looking into the gun cabinet. He knew them all and loved some of them. He knew the feel of their stocks on his shoulder, the glimpse of their barrels in front of his eyes, the dance of the target on their various sights, the welcome heavy weight of the gun on his supporting arm, the rewarding thrust of the stock against his shoulder when he fired. He knew all this, and did not know how he knew it.

"The Hechizera, Agatha herself, was a very accomplished sportswoman," murmured T'ruth to him. "I thought her knowledge would take a second printing when I passed it along to you. Let's take these."

She gestured to little Harry Hadrian, who unlocked the cabinet and took out two enormous guns, which looked like the long muskets mankind had had on earth even before the age of space began.

"If you're going to shoot children," said Casher with his new-found expertness, "these won't do. They'll tear the bodies completely to pieces."

T'ruth reached into the little bag which hung from her belt. She took out three shotgun shells. "I have three more," she said. "Six children is all we need."

Casher looked at the slug projecting slightly from the shotgun casing. It did not look like any shell he had ever seen before. The workmanship was unbelievably fine and precise.

"What are they? I never saw these before."

"Proximity stunners," she said. "Shoot ten centimeters above the head of any living thing and the stunner knocks it out."

"You want the children alive?"

"Alive, of course. And unconscious. They are a part of your final test."

Two hours later, after an exciting hike to the edge of the weather controls, they had the six children stretched out on the floor of the great hall. Four were little boys, two girls; they were fine-boned, soft-haired people, very thin, but they did not look too far from Earth normal.

T'ruth called up a doctor underman from among her servants. There must have been a crowd of fifty or sixty undermen and robots standing around. Far up the staircase, John Joy Tree stood hidden, half in shadow. Casher suspected that he was as inquisitive as the others but afraid of himself, Casher, "the man of blood."

T'ruth spoke quietly but firmly to the doctor, "Can you give them a strong euphoric before you waken them? We don't want to have to pluck them out of all the curtains in the house, if they go wild when they wake up."

"Nothing simpler," said the doctor underman. He seemed to be of dog origin, but Casher could not tell.

He took a glass tube and touched it to the nape of each little neck. The necks were all streaked with dirt. These children had never been washed in their lives, except by the rain.

"Wake them," said T'ruth.

The doctor stepped back to a rolling table. It gleamed with equipment. He must have preset his devices, because all he did was to press a button and the children stirred into life.

The first reaction was wildness. They got ready to bolt. The biggest of the boys, who by Earth standards would have been about ten, got three steps before he stopped and began laughing.

T'ruth spoke the Old Common Tongue to them, very slowly and with long spaces between the words:

"Wind—children—do—you—know—where—you—are?"

The biggest girl twittered back to her so fast that Casher could not understand it.

T'ruth turned to Casher and said, "The girl said that she is in the Dead Place, where the air never moves and where the Old Dead Ones move around on their own business. She means us." To the wind children she spoke again.

"What—would—you—like—most?"

The biggest girl went from child to child. They nodded agreement vigorously. They formed a circle and began a little chant. By the second repetition around, Casher could make it out.

> Shig—shag—shuggery,
> shuck shuck shuck!
> What all of us need is
> an all-around duck.
> Shig—shag—shuggery,
> shuck shuck shuck!

At the fourth or fifth repetition they all stopped and looked at T'ruth, who was so plainly the mistress of the house.

She in turn spoke to Casher O'Neill. "They think that they want a tribal feast of raw duck. What they are going to get is inoculations against the worst diseases of this planet, several duck meals and their freedom again. But they need something else beyond all measure. *You know what that is, Casher, if you can only find it."*

The whole crowd turned its eyes on Casher, the human eyes of the people and underpeople, the milky lenses of the robots.

Casher stood aghast.

"Is this a test?" he asked softly.

"You could call it that,' said T'ruth, looking away from him.

Casher thought furiously and rapidly. It wouldn't do any good to make them into forgetties. The household had enough of them. T'ruth had announced a plan to let them loose again. The Mister and Owner Murray Madigan must have told her, sometime or other, to "do something" about the wind people. She was trying to do it. The whole crowd watched him. What might T'ruth expect?

The answer came to him in a flash.

If she were asking *him*, it must be something to do with himself, something which he—uniquely among these people, underpeople and robots—had brought to the storm-sieged mansion of Beauregard.

Suddenly he saw it.

"Use me, my lady Ruth," said he, deliberately giving her the wrong title, "to print on them nothing from my intellectual knowledge, but everything from my emotional makeup. It wouldn't do them any good to know about Mizzer, where the Twelve Niles work their way down across the Intervening Sands. Nor about Pontoppidan, the Gem Planet, nor about Olympia, where the blind brokers promenade under numbered clouds. Knowing things would not help these children. But *wanting*—"

Wanting things was different.

He was unique. He had wanted to return to Mizzer. He had wanted return beyond all dreams of blood and revenge. He had wanted things fiercely, wildly, so that even if he could not get them, he zigzagged the galaxy in search of them.

T'ruth was speaking to him again, urgently and softly, but not in so low a voice that the others in the room could not hear.

"And what, Casher O'Neill, should I give them from you?"

"My emotional structure. My determination. My desire. Nothing else. Give them that and throw them back into the winds. Perhaps if they want something fiercely enough, they will grow up to find out what it is."

There was a soft murmur of approval around the room.

T'ruth hesitated a moment and then nodded. "You answered, Casher. You answered quickly and perceptively. Bring seven helmets, Eunice. Stay here, doctor."

Eunice, the forgetty, left, taking two robots with her.

"A chair," said T'ruth to no one in particular. "For him."

A large, powerful underman pushed his way through the crowd and dragged a chair to the end of the room.

T'ruth gestured that Casher should sit in it.

She stood in front of him. *Strange*, thought Casher, *that she should be a great lady and still a little girl.* How would he ever find a girl like her? He was not even afraid of the mystery of the Fish, or the image of the man on two pieces of wood. He no longer dreaded Space Three, where so many travelers had gone in and so few had come out. He felt safe, comforted by her wisdom and authority. He felt that he would never see the likes of this again—a child running a planet and doing it well; a half-dead man surviving through the endless devotion of his maidservant; a fierce woman hypnotist living on with all the anxieties and angers of humanity gone, but with the skill and obstinacy of turtle genes to sustain her in her reimprinted form.

"I can guess what you are thinking," said T'ruth, "but we have already said the things that we had to say. I've peeped your mind a dozen times and I know that you want to go back to Mizzer so bad that Space Three will spit you out right at the ruined fort where the big turn of the Seventh Nile begins. In my own way I love you, Casher, but I could not keep you here without turning you into a forgetty and making you a servant to my master. You know what always comes first with me, and always will."

"Madigan."

"Madigan," she answered, and with her voice the name itself was a prayer.

Eunice came back with the helmets.

"When we are through with these, Casher, I'll have them take you to the conditioning room. Good-by, my might-have-been!"

In front of everyone, she kissed him full on the lips.

He sat in the chair, full of patience and contentment. Even as his vision blacked out, he could see the thin light sheath of a smock on the girlish figure, he could remember the tender laughter lurking in her smile.

In the last instant of his consciousness, he saw that another figure had joined the crowd—the tall old man with the worn bathrobe, the faded blue eyes, the thin yellow hair. Murray Madigan had risen from his private life-in-death and had come to see the last of Casher O'Neill. He did not look weak, or foolish. He looked like a great man, wise and strange in ways beyond Casher's understanding.

There was the touch of T'ruth's little hand on his arm and everything became a velvety cluttered dark quiet inside his own mind.

## XIV

When he awoke, he lay naked and sunburned under the hot sky of Mizzer. Two soldiers with medical patches were rolling him onto a canvas litter.

"Mizzer!" he cried to himself. His throat was too dry to make a sound. "I'm home."

Suddenly the memories came to him and he scrabbled and snatched at them, seeing them dissolve within his mind before he could get paper to write them down.

Memory: there was the front hall, himself getting ready to sleep in the chair, with the old giant of Murray Madigan at the edge of the crowd and the tender light touch of T'ruth—his girl, his girl, now uncountable light-years away—putting her hand on his arm.

Memory: there was another room, with stained-glass pictures and incense, and the weepworthy scenes of a great life shown in frescoes around the wall. There were the two pieces of wood and the man in pain nailed to them. But Casher knew that scattered and coded through his mind there was the ultimate and undefeatable wisdom of the Sign of the Fish. He knew he could never fear fear again.

Memory: there was a gaming table in a bright room, with the wealth of a thousand worlds being raked toward him. He was a woman, strong, big-busted, bejeweled and proud. He was Agatha Madigan, winning at the games. *(That must have come,* he thought, *when they printed me with T'ruth.)* And in that mind of the Hechizera, which was now his own mind too, there was clear sure knowledge of how he could win men and women, officers and soldiers, even underpeople and robots, to his cause without a drop of blood or a word of anger.

The men, lifting him on the litter, made red waves of heat and pain roll over him.

He heard one of them say, "Bad case of burn. Wonder how he lost his clothes."

The words were matter-of-fact; the comment was nothing special; but the cadence, that special cadence, was the true speech of Mizzer.

As they carried him away, he remembered the face of Rankin Meiklejohn, enormous eyes staring with inward despair over the brim of a big glass. That was the administrator. On Henriada. That was the man who sent me past Ambiloxi to Beauregard at two seventy-five in the morning. The litter jolted a little.

He thought of the wet marshes of Henriada and knew that soon he would never remember them again. The worms of the tornadoes creeping up to the edge of the estate. The mad wise face of John Joy Tree.

Space Three? Space Three? Already, even now, he could not remember how they had put him into Space Three.

And Space Three itself—

All the nightmares which mankind has ever had pushed into Casher's mind. He twisted once in agony, just as the litter reached a medical military cart. He saw a girl's face—what *was* her name?—and then he slept.

## XV

Fourteen Mizzer days later, the first test came.

A doctor colonel and an intelligence colonel, both in the workaday uniform of Colonel Wedder's Special Forces, stood by his bed.

"Your name is Casher O'Neill and we do not know how your body fell among the skirmishers," the doctor was saying, roughly and emphatically. Casher O'Neill turned his head on the pillow and looked at the man.

"Say something more!" he whispered to the doctor.

The doctor said, "You are a political intruder and we do not know how you got mixed up among our troops. We do not even know how you got back among the people of this planet. We found you on the Seventh Nile."

The intelligence colonel standing beside him nodded agreement.

"Do you think the same thing, colonel?" whispered Casher O'Neill to the intelligence colonel.

"I ask questions. I don't answer them," said the man gruffly.

Casher felt himself reaching for their minds with a kind of fingertip which he did not know he had. It was hard to put into ordinary words, but it felt as though someone had said to him, Casher: "That one is vulnerable at the left forefront area of his consciousness, but the other one is well-armored and must be reached through the midbrain." Casher was not afraid of revealing anything by his expression. He was too badly burned and in too much pain to show nuances of meaning on his face. (Somewhere he had heard of the wild story of the Hechizera of Gonfalon! Somewhere endless storms boiled across ruined marshes under a cloudy yellow sky! But where, when, what was that? . . . He could not take time off for memory. He had to fight for his life.)

"Peace be with you," he whispered to both of them.

"Peace be with you," they responded in unison, with some surprise.

"Lean over me, please," said Casher, "so that I do not have to shout." They stood stock straight.

Somewhere in the resources of his own memory and intelligence, Casher found the right note of pleading which could ride his voice like a carrier wave and make them do as he wished.

"This is Mizzer," he whispered.

"Of course this is Mizzer," snapped the intelligence colonel, "and you are Casher O'Neill. What are you doing here?"

"Lean over, gentlemen," he said softly, lowering his voice so that they could barely hear him.

This time they did lean over.

His burned hands reached for their hands. The officers noticed it, but since he was sick and unarmed, they let him touch them.

Suddenly he felt their minds glowing in his as brightly as if he had swallowed their gleaming, thinking brains at a single gulp.

He spoke no longer.

He *thought* at them—torrential, irresistible thought.

*I am not Casher O'Neill. You will find his body in a room four doors down. I am the civilian Bindaoud.*

The two colonels stared, breathing heavily.

Neither said a word.

Casher went on: *Our fingerprints and records have gotten mixed. Give me the fingerprints and papers of the dead Casher O'Neill. Bury him then, quickly, but with honor. Once he loved your leader and there is no point in stirring up wild rumors about returns from out of space. I am Bindaoud. You will find my records in your front office. I am not a soldier. I am a civilian technician doing studies on the salt in blood chemistry under field conditions. You have heard me, gentlemen. You hear me now. You will hear me always. But you will not remember this, gentlemen, when you awaken. I am sick. You can give me water and a sedative.*

They still stood, enraptured by the touch of his tight burned hands.

Casher O'Neill said, "Awaken."

Casher O'Neill let go their hands.

The medical colonel blinked and said amiably, "You'll be better, Mister and Doctor Bindaoud. I'll have the orderly bring you water and a sedative."

To the other officer he said, "I have an interesting corpse four doors down. I think you had better see it."

Casher O'Neill tried to think of the recent past, but the blue light of Mizzer was all around him, the sand smell, the sound of horses galloping. For a moment, he thought of a big child's blue dress and he did not know why he almost wept.

# The Miracle Workers

*Modern man thinks that he has a pretty good idea of the difference between magic and science. But the distinction is really one of perspective, and perspective-giving is one of the great strengths of modern science fiction, as Jack Vance shows us in this richly romantic vision of a world where science and magic appear to coexist, and where men struggle to maintain order in the face of chaos.*

## I

The war party from Faide Keep moved eastward across the downs: a column of a hundred armored knights, five hundred foot soldiers, a train of wagons. In the lead rode Lord Faide, a tall man in his early maturity, spare and catlike, with a sallow dyspeptic face. He sat in the ancestral car of the Faides, a boat-shaped vehicle floating two feet above the moss, and carried, in addition to his sword and dagger, his ancestral side weapons.

An hour before sunset a pair of scouts came racing back to the column, their club-headed horses loping like dogs. Lord Faide braked the motion of his car. Behind him the Faide kinsmen, the lesser knights, and the leather-capped foot soldiers halted; to the rear the baggage train and the high-wheeled wagons of the jinxmen creaked to a stop.

The scouts approached at breakneck speed, at the last instant flinging their horses sidewise. Long shaggy legs kicked out, padlike hooves plowed through the moss. The scouts jumped to the ground, ran forward. "The way to Ballant Keep is blocked!"

Lord Faide rose in his seat, stood staring eastward over the gray green downs. "How many knights? How many men?"

"No knights, no men, Lord Faide. The First Folk have planted a forest between North and South Wildwood."

Lord Faide stood a moment in reflection, then seated himself and pushed the control knob. The car wheezed, jerked, moved forward. The knights touched up their horses; the foot soldiers resumed their slouching gait. At the rear the baggage train creaked into motion, together with the six wagons of the jinxmen.

The sun, large, pale and faintly pink, sank in the west. North Wildwood loomed down from the left, separated from South Wildwood by an area of stony ground, only sparsely patched with moss. As the sun passed behind the horizon, the new planting became visible: a frail new growth connecting the tracts of woodland like a canal between two seas.

Lord Faide halted his car, stepped down to the moss. He appraised the landscape, then gave the signal to make camp. The wagons were ranged in a circle, the gear unloaded. Lord Faide watched the activity for a moment, eyes sharp and critical, then turned and walked out across the downs through the lavender and green twilight. Fifteen miles to the east his last enemy awaited him: Lord Ballant of Ballant Keep. Contemplating the next day's battle, Lord Faide felt reasonably confident of the outcome. His troops had been tempered by a dozen campaigns; his kinsmen were loyal and singlehearted. Head jinxman to Faide Keep was Hein Huss, and associated with him were three of the most powerful jinxmen of Pangborn: Isak Comandore, Adam McAdam and the remarkable Enterlin, together with their separate troupes of cabalmen, spellbinders and apprentices. Altogether, an impressive assemblage. Certainly there were obstacles to be overcome: Ballant Keep was strong; Lord Ballant would fight obstinately; Anderson Grimes, the Ballant head jinxman, was efficient and highly respected. There was also this nuisance of the First Folk and the new planting which closed the gap between North and South Wildwood. The First Folk were a pale and feeble race, no match for human beings in single combat, but they guarded their forests with traps and deadfalls. Lord Faide cursed softly under his breath. To circle either North or South Wildwood meant a delay of three days, which could not be tolerated.

Lord Faide returned to the camp. Fires were alight, pots bubbled, orderly rows of sleep holes had been dug into the moss. The knights groomed their horses within the corral of wagons; Lord Faide's own tent had been erected on a hummock, beside the ancient car.

Lord Faide made a quick round of inspection, noting every detail, speaking no word. The jinxmen were encamped a little distance apart from the troops. The apprentices and lesser spellbinders prepared food, while the jinxmen and cabalmen worked inside their tents, arranging cabinets and cases, correcting whatever disorder had been caused by the jolting of the wagons.

Lord Faide entered the tent of his head jinxman. Hein Huss was an enormous man, with arms and legs heavy as tree trunks, a torso like a barrel. His face was pink and placid, his eyes were water-clear; a stiff gray brush rose from his head, which was innocent of the cap jinxmen customarily wore against the loss of hair. Hein Huss disdained such precautions; it was his habit, showing his teeth in a face-splitting grin, to rumble, "Why should any hoodoo me, old Hein Huss? I am so inoffensive. Whoever tried would surely die, of shame and remorse."

Lord Faide found Huss busy at his cabinet. The doors stood wide, revealing hundreds of mannikins, each tied with a lock of hair, a bit of cloth, a fingernail clipping, daubed with grease, sputum, excrement, blood. Lord Faide knew well that one of these mannikins represented himself. He also knew that should he request it Hein Huss would deliver it without hesitation. Part of Huss's *mana* derived from his enormous confidence, the effortless ease of his power. He glanced at Lord Faide and read the question in his mind. "Lord Ballant did not know of the new planting. Anderson Grimes has now informed him, and Lord Ballant expects that you will be delayed. Grimes has communicated with Gisborne Keep and Castle Cloud. Three hundred men march tonight to reinforce Ballant Keep. They will arrive in two days. Lord Ballant is much elated."

Lord Faide paced back and forth across the tent. "Can we cross this planting?"

Hein Huss made a heavy sound of disapproval. "There are many futures. In certain of these futures you pass. In others you do not pass. I cannot ordain these futures."

Lord Faide had long learned to control his impatience at what sometimes seemed to be pedantic obfuscation. He grumbled, "They are either very stupid or very bold planting across the downs in this fashion. I cannot imagine what they intend."

Hein Huss considered, then grudgingly volunteered an idea. "What if they plant west from North Wildwood to Sarrow Copse? What if they plant west from South Wildwood to Old Forest?"

"Then Faide Keep is almost ringed by forest."

"And what if they join Sarrow Copse to Old Forest?"

Lord Faide stood stock-still, his eyes narrow and thoughtful. "Faide Keep would be surrounded by forest. We would be imprisoned. . . . These plantings, do they proceed?"

"They proceed, so I have been told."

"What do they hope to gain?"

"I do not know. Perhaps they hope to isolate the keeps, to rid the planet of men. Perhaps they merely want secure avenues between the forests."

Lord Faide considered. Huss's final suggestion was reasonable enough. During the first centuries of human settlement, sportive young men had hunted the First Folk with clubs and lances, eventually had driven them from their native downs into the forests. "Evidently they are more clever than we realize. Adam McAdam asserts that they do not think, but it seems that he is mistaken."

Hein Huss shrugged. "Adam McAdam equates thought to the human cerebral process. He cannot telepathize with the First Folk, hence he deduces that they do not 'think.' But I have watched them at Forest Market, and they trade intelligently enough." He raised his head, appeared to listen, then reached into his cabinet and delicately tightened a noose around the neck of one of the mannikins. From outside the tent came a sudden cough and a whooping gasp for air. Huss grinned, twitched open the noose. "That is Isak Comandore's apprentice. He hopes to complete a Hein Huss mannikin. I must say he works diligently, going so far as to touch its feet into my footprints whenever possible."

Lord Faide went to the flap of the tent. "We break camp early. Be alert, I may require your help." He departed the tent.

Hein Huss continued the ordering of his cabinet. Presently he sensed the approach of his rival, Jinxman Isak Comandore, who coveted the office of head jinxman with all-consuming passion. Huss closed the cabinet and hoisted himself to his feet.

Comandore entered the tent, a man tall, crooked and spindly. His wedge-shaped head was covered with coarse russet ringlets; hot red brown eyes peered from under his red eyebrows. "I offer my complete rights to Keyril, and will include the masks, the headdress, the amulets. Of all the demons ever contrived he has won the widest public acceptance. To utter the name Keyril is to complete half the work of a possession. Keyril is a valuable property. I can give no more."

But Huss shook his head. Comandore's desire was the full simulacrum of Tharon Faide, Lord Faide's oldest son, complete with clothes, hair, skin, eyelashes, tears, excrement, sweat and sputum—the only one in existence, for Lord Faide guarded his son much more jealously than he did himself. "You offer convincingly," said Huss, "but my own demons suffice. The name Dant conveys fully as much terror as Keyril."

"I will add five hairs from the head of Jinxman Clarence Sears; they are the last, for he is now stark bald."

"Let us drop the matter; I will keep the simulacrum."

"As you please," said Comandore with asperity. He glanced out the flap of the tent. "That blundering apprentice. He puts the feet of the mannikin backwards into your prints."

Huss opened his cabinet, thumped a mannikin with his finger. From outside the tent came a grunt of surprise. Huss grinned. "He is young and earnest, and perhaps he is clever, who knows?" He went to the flap of the tent, called outside. "Hey, Sam Salazar, what do you do? Come inside."

Apprentice Sam Salazar came blinking into the tent, a thickset youth with a round florid face, overhung with a rather untidy mass of straw-colored hair. In one hand he carried a crude pot-bellied mannikin, evidently intended to represent Hein Huss.

"You puzzle both your master and myself," said Huss. "There must be method in your folly, but we fail to perceive it. For instance, this moment you place my simulacrum backwards into my track. I feel a tug on my foot, and you pay for your clumsiness."

Sam Salazar showed small evidence of abashment. "Jinxman Comandore has warned that we must expect to suffer for our ambitions."

"If your ambition is jinxmanship," Comandore declared sharply, "you had best mend your ways."

"The lad is craftier than you know," said Hein Huss. "Look now." He took the mannikin from the youth, spit into its mouth, plucked a hair from his head, thrust it into a convenient crevice. "He has a Hein Huss mannikin, achieved at very small cost. Now, Apprentice Salazar, how will you hoodoo me?"

"Naturally, I would never dare. I merely want to fill the bare spaces in my cabinet."

Hein Huss nodded his approval. "As good a reason as any. Of course you own a simulacrum of Isak Comandore?"

Sam Salazar glanced uneasily at Isak Comandore. "He leaves none of his traces. If there is so much as an open bottle in the room, he breathes behind his hand."

"Ridiculous!" exclaimed Hein Huss. "Comandore, what do you fear?"

"I am conservative," said Comandore, dryly. "You make a fine gesture, but some day an enemy may own that simulacrum; then you will regret your bravado."

"Bah. My enemies are all dead, save one or two who dare not reveal themselves." He clapped Sam Salazar a great buffet on the shoulder. "Tomorrow, Apprentice Salazar, great things are in store for you."

"What manner of great things?"

"Honor, noble self-sacrifice. Lord Faide must beg permission from the First Folk to pass Wildwood, which galls him. But beg he must. Tomorrow, Sam Salazar, I will elect you to lead the way to the parley, to deflect deadfalls, scythes and nettletraps from the more important person who follows."

Sam Salazar shook his head and drew back. "There must be others more worthy; I prefer to ride in the rear with the wagons."

Comandore waved him from the tent. "You will do as ordered. Leave us; we have had enough apprentice talk."

Sam Salazar departed. Comandore turned back to Hein Huss. "In connection with tomorrow's battle, Anderson Grimes is especially adept with demons. As I recall, he has developed and successfully publicized Pont, who spreads sleep; Everid, a being of wrath; Deigne, a force of fear. We must take care that in countering these effects we do not neutralize each other."

"True," rumbled Huss. "I have long maintained to Lord Faide that a single jinxman—the head jinxman in fact—is more effective than a group at cross-purposes. But he is consumed by ambition and does not listen."

"Perhaps he wants to be sure that should advancing years overtake the head jinxman other equally effective jinxmen are at hand."

"The future has many paths," agreed Hein Huss. "Lord Faide is well-advised to seek early for my successor, so that I may train him over the years. I plan to access all the subsidiary jinxmen, and select the most promising. Tomorrow I relegate to you the demons of Anderson Grimes."

Isak Comandore nodded politely. "You are wise to give over responsibility. When I feel the weight of my years I hope I may act with similar forethought. Good night, Hein Huss. I go to arrange my demon masks. Tomorrow Keyril must walk like a giant."

"Good night, Isak Comandore."

Comandore swept from the tent, and Huss settled himself on his stool. Sam Salazar scratched at the flap. "Well, lad?" growled Huss. "Why do you loiter?"

Sam Salazar placed the Hein Huss mannikin on the table. "I have no wish to keep this doll."

"Throw it in a ditch, then." Hein Huss spoke gruffly. "You must stop annoying me with stupid tricks. You efficiently obtrude yourself upon my attention, but you cannot transfer from Comandore's troupe without his express consent."

"If I gain his consent?"

"You will incur his enmity; he will open his cabinet against you. Unlike myself, you are vulnerable to a hoodoo. I advise you to be content. Isak Comandore is highly skilled and can teach you much."

Sam Salazar still hesitated. "Jinxman Comandore, though skilled, is intolerant of new thoughts."

Hein Huss shifted ponderously on his stool, examined Sam Salazar with his water-clear eyes. "What new thoughts are these? Your own?"

"The thoughts are new to me, and for all I know new to Isak Comandore. But he will say neither yes nor no."

Hein Huss sighed, settled his monumental bulk more comfortably. "Speak then, describe these thoughts, and I will assess their novelty."

"First, I have wondered about trees. They are sensitive to light, to moisture, to wind, to pressure. Sensitivity implies sensation. Might a man feel into the soul of a tree for these sensations? If a tree were capable of awareness, this faculty might prove useful. A man might select trees as sentinels in strategic sites, and enter into them as he chose."

Hein Huss was skeptical. "An amusing notion, but practically not feasible. The reading of minds, the act of possession, televoyance, all similar interplay, require psychic congruence as a basic condition. The minds must be able to become identities at some particular stratum. Unless there is sympathy, there is no linkage. A tree is at opposite poles from a man; the images of tree and man are incommensurable. Hence, anything more than the most trifling flicker of comprehension must be a true miracle of jinxmanship."

Sam Salazar nodded mournfully. "I realized this, and at one time hoped to equip myself with the necessary identification."

"To do this you must become a vegetable. Certainly the tree will never become a man."

"So I reasoned," said Sam Salazar. "I went alone into a grove of trees, where I chose a tall conifer. I buried my feet in the mold, I stood silent and naked—in the sunlight, in the rain; at dawn, noon, dusk, midnight. I closed my mind to manthoughts, I closed my eyes to vision, my ears to sound. I took no nourishment except from rain and sun. I sent roots forth from my feet and branches from my torso. Thirty hours I stood, and two days later another thirty hours, and after two days another thirty hours.

I made myself a tree, as nearly as possible to one of flesh and blood."

Hein Huss gave the great inward gurgle that signalized his amusement. "And you achieved sympathy?"

"Nothing useful," Sam Salazar admitted. "I felt something of the tree's sensations—the activity of light, the peace of dark, the coolness of rain. But visual and auditory experience—nothing. However, I do not regret the trial. It was a useful discipline."

"An interesting effort, even if inconclusive. The idea is by no means of startling originality, but the empiricism—to use an archaic word—of your method is bold, and no doubt antagonized Isak Comandore, who has no patience with the superstitions of our ancestors. I suspect that he harangued you against frivolity, metaphysics and inspirationalism."

"True," said Sam Salazar. "He spoke at length."

"You should take the lesson to heart. Isak Comandore is sometimes unable to make the most obvious truth seem credible. However, I cite you the example of Lord Faide who considers himself an enlightened man, free from superstition. Still, he rides in his feeble car, he carries a pistol sixteen hundred years old, he relies on Hellmouth to protect Faide Keep."

"Perhaps—unconsciously—he longs for the old magical times," suggested Sam Salazar thoughtfully.

"Perhaps," agreed Hein Huss. "And you do likewise?"

Sam Salazar hesitated. "There is an aura of romance, a kind of wild grandeur to the old days—but of course," he added quickly, "mysticism is no substitute for orthodox logic."

"Naturally not," agreed Hein Huss. "Now go; I must consider the events of tomorrow."

Sam Salazar departed, and Hein Huss, rumbling and groaning, hoisted himself to his feet. He went to the flap of his tent, surveyed the camp. All now was quiet. The fires were embers, the warriors lay in the pits they had cut into the moss. To the north and south spread the woodlands. Among the trees and out on the downs were faint flickering luminosities, where the First Folk gathered spore-pods from the moss.

Hein Huss became aware of a nearby personality. He turned his head and saw approaching the shrouded form of Jinxman Enterlin, who concealed his face, who spoke only in whispers, who disguised his natural gait with a stiff stiltlike motion. By this means he hoped to reduce his vulnerability to hostile jinxmanship. The admission carelessly let fall of failing eyesight, of stiff joints, forgetfulness, melancholy, nausea might be of critical significance in controversy by hoodoo. Jinxmen therefore maintained the pose of absolute health and virility, even though they must grope blindly or limp doubled up from cramps.

Hein Huss called out to Enterlin, lifted back the flap to the tent. Enterlin entered; Huss went to the cabinet, brought forth a flask, poured liquor into a pair of stone cups. "A cordial only, free of overt significance."

"Good," whispered Enterlin, selecting the cup farthest from him. "After all, we jinxmen must relax into the guise of men from time to time." Turning his back on Huss, he introduced the cup through the folds of his hood, drank. "Refreshing," he whispered. "We need refreshment; tomorrow we must work."

Huss issued his reverberating chuckle. "Tomorrow Isak Comandore matches demons with Anderson Grimes. We others perform only subsidiary duties."

Enterlin seemed to make a quizzical inspection of Hein Huss through the black gauze before his eyes. "Comandore will relish this opportunity. His vehemence oppresses me, and his is a power which feeds on success. He is a man of fire, you are a man of ice."

"Ice quenches fire."

"Fire sometimes melts ice."

Hein Huss shrugged. "No matter. I grow weary. Time has passed all of us by. Only a moment ago a young apprentice showed me to myself."

"As a powerful jinxman, as head jinxman to the Faides, you have cause for pride."

Hein Huss drained the stone cup, set it aside. "No. I see myself at the top of my profession, with nowhere else to go. Only Sam Salazar the apprentice thinks to search for more universal lore; he comes to me for counsel, and I do not know what to tell him."

"Strange talk, strange talk!" whispered Enterlin. He moved to the flap of the tent. "I go now," he whispered. "I go to walk on the downs. Perhaps I will see the future."

"There are many futures."

Enterlin rustled away and was lost in the dark. Hein Huss groaned and grumbled, then took himself to his couch, where he instantly fell asleep.

## II

The night passed. The sun, flickering with films of pink and green, lifted over the horizon. The new planting of the First Folk was silhouetted, a sparse stubble of saplings, against the green and lavender sky. The troops broke camp with practiced efficiency. Lord Faide marched to his car, leaped within; the machine sagged under his weight. He pushed a button, the car drifted forward, heavy as a waterlogged timber.

A mile from the new planting he halted, sent a messenger back to the wagons of the jinxmen. Hein Huss walked ponderously forward, followed by Isak Comandore, Adam McAdam and Enterlin. Lord Faide spoke to Hein Huss. "Send someone to speak to the First Folk. Inform them we wish to pass, offering them no harm, but that we will react savagely to any hostility."

"I will go myself," said Hein Huss. He turned to Comandore, "Lend me, if you will, your brash young apprentice. I can put him to good use."

"If he unmasks a nettle trap by blundering into it, his first useful deed will be done," said Comandore. He signaled to Sam Salazar, who came reluctantly forward. "Walk in front of Head Jinxman Hein Huss that he may encounter no traps or scythes. Take a staff to probe the moss."

Without enthusiasm Sam Salazar borrowed a lance from one of the foot soldiers. He and Huss set forth, along the low rise that previously had separated North from South Wildwood. Occasionally outcroppings of stone penetrated the cover of moss; here and there grew bayberry trees, clumps of tarplant, ginger-tea and rosewort.

A half-mile from the planting Huss halted. "Now take care, for here the traps will begin. Walk clear of hummocks, these often conceal swing-scythes; avoid moss which shows a pale blue; it is dying or sickly and may cover a deadfall or a nettle trap."

"Why cannot you locate the traps by clairvoyance?" asked Sam Salazar in a rather sullen voice. "It appears an excellent occasion for the use of these faculties."

"The question is natural," said Hein Huss with composure. "However you must know that when a jinxman's own profit or security is at stake his emotions play tricks on him. I would see traps everywhere and would never know whether clairvoyance or fear prompted me. In this case, that lance is a more reliable instrument than my mind."

Sam Salazar made a salute of understanding and set forth, with Hein Huss stumping behind him. At first he prodded with care, uncovering two traps, then advanced more jauntily; so swiftly indeed that Huss called out in exasperation, "Caution, unless you court death!"

Sam Salazar obligingly slowed his pace. "There are traps all around us, but I detect the pattern, or so I believe."

"Ah, ha, you do? Reveal it to me, if you will. I am only head jinxman, and ignorant."

"Notice. If we walk where the spore-pods have recently been harvested, then we are secure."

Hein Huss grunted. "Forward then. Why do you dally? We must do battle at Ballant Keep today."

Two hundred yards farther, Sam Salazar stopped short. "Go on, boy, go on!" grumbled Hein Huss.

"The savages threaten us. You can see them just inside the planting. They hold tubes which they point toward us."

Hein Huss peered, then raised his head and called out in the sibilant language of the First Folk.

A moment or two passed, then one of the creatures came forth, a naked humanoid figure, ugly as a demonmask. Foam-sacs bulged under its arms, orange-lipped foam-vents pointed forward. Its back was wrinkled and loose, the skin serving as a bellows to blow air through the foam-sacs. The fingers of the enormous hands ended in chisel-shaped blades, the head was sheathed in chitin. Billion-faceted eyes swelled from either side of the head, glowing like black opals, merging without definite limit into the chitin. This was a representative of the original inhabitants of the planet, who until the coming of man had inhabited the downs, burrowing in the moss, protecting themselves behind masses of foam exuded from the underarm sacs.

The creature wandered close, halted. "I speak for Lord Faide of Faide Keep," said Huss. "Your planting bars his way. He wishes that you guide him through, so that his men do not damage the trees, or spring the traps you have set against your enemies."

"Men are our enemies," responded the autochthon. "You may spring as many traps as you care to; that is their purpose." It backed away.

"One moment," said Hein Huss sternly. "Lord Faide must pass. He goes to battle Lord Ballant. He does not wish to battle the First Folk. Therefore it is wise to guide him across the planting without hindrance."

The creature considered a second or two. "I will guide him." He stalked across the moss toward the war party.

Behind followed Hein Huss and Sam Salazar. The autochthon, legs articulated more flexibly than a man's, seemed to weave and wander, occasionally pausing to study the ground ahead.

"I am puzzled," Sam Salazar told Hein Huss. "I cannot understand the creature's actions."

"Small wonder," grunted Hein Huss. "He is one of the First Folk, you are human. There is no basis for understanding."

"I disagree," said Sam Salazar seriously.

"Eh?" Hein Huss inspected the apprentice with vast disapproval. "You engage in contention with me, Head Jinxman Hein Huss?"

"Only in a limited sense," said Sam Salazar. "I see a basis for understanding with the First Folk in our common ambition to survive."

"A truism," grumbled Hein Huss. "Granting this community of interests with the First Folk, what is your perplexity?"

"The fact that it first refused, then agreed to conduct us across the planting."

Hein Huss nodded. "Evidently the information which intervened, that we go to fight at Ballant Keep, occasioned the change."

"This is clear," said Sam Salazar. "But think—"

"You exhort me to think?" roared Hein Huss.

"—here is one of the First Folk, apparently without distinction, who makes an important decision instantly. Is he one of their leaders? Do they live in anarchy?"

"It is easy to put questions," Hein Huss said gruffly. "It is not as easy to answer them."

"In short—"

"In short, I do not know. In any event, they are pleased to see us killing one another."

## III

The passage through the planting was made without incident. A mile to the east the autochthon stepped aside and without formality returned to the forest. The war party, which had been marching in single file, regrouped into its usual formation. Lord Faide called Hein Huss and made the unusual gesture of inviting him up into the seat beside him. The ancient car dipped and sagged; the power-mechanism whined and chattered. Lord Faide, in high good spirits, ignored the noise. "I feared that we might be forced into a time-consuming wrangle. What of Lord Ballant? Can you read his thoughts?"

Hein Huss cast his mind forth. "Not clearly. He knows of our passage. He is disturbed."

Lord Faide laughed sardonically. "For excellent reason! Listen now, I will explain the plan of battle so that all may coordinate their efforts."

"Very well."

"We approach in a wide line. Ballant's great weapon is of course Volcano. A decoy must wear my armor and ride in the lead. The yellow-haired apprentice is perhaps the most expendable member of the party. In this way we will learn the potentialities of Volcano. Like our own Hellmouth, it was built to repel vessels from space and cannot command the ground immediately under the keep. Therefore we will advance in dispersed formation, to regroup two hundred yards from the keep. At this point the jinxmen will impel Lord Ballant forth from the keep. You no doubt have made plans to this end."

Hein Huss gruffly admitted that such was the case. Like other jinxmen, he enjoyed the pose that his power suffered for extemporaneous control of any situation.

Lord Faide was in no mood for niceties and pressed for further information. Grudging each word, Hein Huss disclosed his arrangements. "I have prepared certain influences to discomfit the Ballant defenders and drive them forth. Jinxman Enterlin will sit at his cabinet, ready to retaliate if Lord Ballant orders a spell against you. Anderson Grimes undoubtedly will cast a demon—probably Everid—into the Ballant warriors; in return, Jinxman Comandore will possess an equal or a greater number of Faide warriors with the demon Keyril, who is even more ghastly and horrifying."

"Good. What more?"

"There is need for no more, if your men fight well."

"Can you see the future? How does today end?"

"There are many futures. Certain jinxmen—Enterlin for instance—profess to see the thread which leads through the maze; they are seldom correct."

"Call Enterlin here."

Hein Huss rumbled his disapproval. "Unwise, if you desire victory over Ballant Keep."

Lord Faide inspected the massive jinxman from under his black saturnine brows. "Why do you say this?"

"If Enterlin foretells defeat, you will be dispirited and fight poorly. If he predicts victory, you become overconfident and likewise fight poorly."

Lord Faide made a petulant gesture. "The jinxmen are loud in their boasts until the test is made. Then they always find reasons to retract, to qualify."

"Ha, ha!" barked Hein Huss. "You expect miracles, not honest jinxmanship. I spit—" he spat. "I predict that the spittle will strike the moss. The probabilities are high. But an insect might fly in the way. One of the First Folk might raise through the moss. The chances are slight. In the next instant there is only one future. A minute hence there are four futures. Five minutes hence, twenty futures. A billion futures could not express all the possibilities of tomorrow. Of these billion, certain are more probable than others. It is true that these probable futures sometimes send a delicate influence into the jinxman's brain. But unless he is completely impersonal and disinterested, his own desires overwhelm this influence. Enterlin is a strange man. He hides himself, he has no appetites. Occasionally his auguries are exact. Nevertheless, I advise against consulting him. You do better to rely on the practical and real uses of jinxmanship."

Lord Faide said nothing. The column had been marching along the bottom of a low swale; the car had been sliding easily downslope. Now they came to a rise, and the power-mechanism complained so vigorously that Lord Faide was compelled to stop the car. He considered. "Once over the crest we will be in view of Ballant Keep. Now we must disperse. Send the least valuable man in your troupe forward—the apprentice who tested out the moss. He must wear my helmet and corselet and ride in the car."

Hein Huss alighted, returned to the wagons, and presently Sam Salazar came forward. Lord Faide eyed the round, florid face with distaste. "Come close," he said crisply. Sam Salazar obeyed. "You will now ride in my place," said Lord Faide. "Notice carefully. This rod impels a forward motion. This arm steers—to right, to left. To stop, return the rod to its first position."

Sam Salazar pointed to some of the other arms, toggles, switches and buttons. "What of these?"

"They are never used."

"And these dials, what is their meaning?"

Lord Faide curled his lip, on the brink of one of his quick furies. "Since their use is unimportant to me, it is twenty times unimportant to you. Now. Put this cap on your head, and this helmet. See to it that you do not sweat."

Sam Salazar gingerly settled the magnificent black and green crest of Faide on his head, with a cloth cap underneath.

"Now this corselet."

The corselet was constructed of green and black metal sequins, with a pair of scarlet dragon-heads at either side of the breast.

"Now the cloak." Lord Faide flung the black cloak over Sam Salazar's shoulders. "Do not venture too close to Ballant Keep. Your purpose is to attract the fire of Volcano. Maintain a lateral motion around the keep, outside of dart range. If you are killed by a dart, the whole purpose of the deception is thwarted."

"You prefer me to be killed by Volcano?" inquired Sam Salazar.

"No. I wish to preserve the car and the crest. These are relics of great value. Evade destruction by all means possible. The ruse probably will deceive no one; but if it does, and if it draws the fire of Volcano, I must sacrifice the Faide car. Now—sit in my place."

Sam Salazar climbed into the car, settled himself on the seat.

"Sit straight," roared Lord Faide. "Hold your head up! You are simulating Lord Faide! You must not appear to slink!"

Sam Salazar heaved himself erect in the seat. "To simulate Lord Faide most effectively, I should walk among the warriors, with someone else riding in the car."

Lord Faide glared, then grinned sourly. "No matter. Do as I have commanded."

# IV

Sixteen hundred years before, with war raging through space, a group of space captains, their home bases destroyed, had taken refuge on Pangborn. To protect themselves against vengeful enemies, they built great forts armed with weapons from the dismantled spaceships.

The wars receded, Pangborn was forgotten. The newcomers drove the First Folk into the forests, planted and harvested the river valleys. Ballant Keep, like Faide Keep, Castle Cloud, Boghoten and the rest, overlooked one of these valleys. Four squat towers of a dense black substance supported an enormous parasol roof, and were joined by walls two-thirds as high as the towers. At the peak of the roof a cupola housed Volcano, the weapon corresponding to Faide's Hellmouth.

The Faide war party advancing over the rise found the great gates already secure, the parapets between the towers thronged with bowmen. According to Lord Faide's strategy, the war party advanced on a broad front. At the center rode Sam Salazar, resplendent in Lord Faide's armor. He made, however, small effort to simulate Lord Faide. Rather than sitting proudly erect, he crouched at the side of the seat, the crest canted at an angle. Lord Faide watched with disgust. Apprentice Salazar's reluctance to be demolished was understandable; if his impersonation failed to convince Lord Ballant, at least the Faide ancestral car might be spared. For a certainty Volcano was being manned; the Ballant weapon-tender could be seen in the cupola, and the snout protruded at a menacing angle.

Apparently the tactic of dispersal, offering no single tempting target, was effective. The Faide war party advanced quickly to a point two hundred yards from the keep, below Volcano's effective field, without drawing fire; first the knights, then the foot soldiers, then the rumbling wagons of the magicians. The slow-moving Faide car was far outdistanced; any doubt as to the nature of the ruse must now be extinguished.

Apprentice Salazar, disliking the isolation, and hoping to increase the speed of the car, twisted one of the other switches, then another. From under the floor came a thin screeching sound; the car quivered and began to rise. Sam Salazar peered over the side, threw out a leg to jump. Lord Faide ran forward, gesturing and shouting. Sam Salazar hastily drew back his leg, returned the switches to their previous condition. The car dropped like a rock. He snapped the switches up again, cushioning the fall.

"Get out of that car!" roared Lord Faide. He snatched away the helmet, dealt Sam Salazar a buffet which toppled him head over heels. "Out of the armor; back to your duties!"

Sam Salazar hurried to the jinxmen's wagons where he helped erect Isak Comandore's black tent. Inside the tent a black carpet with red and yellow patterns was laid; Comandore's cabinet, his chair and his chest were carried in, and incense set burning in a censer. Directly in front of the main gate Hein Huss superintended the assembly of a rolling stage, forty feet tall and sixty feet long, the surface concealed from Ballant Keep by a tarpaulin.

Meanwhile, Lord Faide had dispatched an emissary, enjoining Lord Ballant to surrender. Lord Ballant delayed his response, hoping to delay the attack as long as possible. If he could maintain himself a day and a half, reinforcements from Gisborne Keep and Castle Cloud might force Lord Faide to retreat.

Lord Faide waited only until the jinxmen had completed their preparations, then sent another messenger, offering two more minutes in which to surrender.

One minute passed, two minutes. The envoys turned on their heels, marched back to the camp.

Lord Faide spoke to Hein Huss. "You are prepared?"

"I am prepared," rumbled Hein Huss.

"Drive them forth."

Huss raised his arm; the tarpaulin dropped from the face of his great display, to reveal a painted representation of Ballant Keep.

Huss retired to his tent, and pulled the flaps together. Braziers burnt fiercely, illuminating the faces of Adam McAdam, eight cabalmen and six of the most advanced spellbinders. Each worked at a bench supporting several dozen dolls and a small glowing brazier. The cabalmen and spellbinders worked with dolls representing Ballant men-at-arms; Huss and Adam McAdam employed simulacra of the Ballant knights. Lord Ballant would not be hoodooed unless he ordered a jinx against Lord Faide—a courtesy the keep-lords extended each other.

Huss called out: "Sebastian!"

Sebastian, one of Huss's spellbinders, waiting at the flap to the tent, replied, "Ready, sir."

"Begin the display."

Sebastian ran to the stage, struck fire to a fuse. Watchers inside Ballant Keep saw the depicted keep take fire. Flame erupted from the windows, the roof glowed and crumbled. Inside the tent the two jinxmen, the cabalmen and the spellbinders methodically took dolls, dipped them into the heat of the braziers, concentrating, reaching out for the mind of the man whose doll they burnt. Within the keep men became uneasy. Many began to imagine burning sensations, which became more severe as their minds grew more sensitive to the idea of fire. Lord Ballant noted the uneasiness. He signaled to his chief jinxman Anderson Grimes. "Begin the counterspell."

Down the front of the keep unrolled a display even larger than Hein Huss's, depicting a hideous beast. It stood on four legs and was shown picking up two men in a pair of hands, biting off their heads. Grimes's cabalmen meanwhile took up dolls representing the Faide warriors, inserted them into models of the depicted beast, and closed the hinged jaws, all the while projecting ideas of fear and disgust. And the Faide warriors, staring at the depicted monster, felt a sense of horror and weakness.

Inside Huss's tent the braziers reeked and dolls smoked. Eyes stared, brows glistened. From time to time one of the workers gasped—signaling the entry of his projection into an enemy mind. Within the keep warriors began to mutter, to slap at burning skin, to eye each other fearfully, noting each other's symptoms. Finally one cried out, and tore at his armor. "I burn! The cursed witches burn me!" His pain aggravated the discomfort of the others; there was a growing sound throughout the keep.

Lord Ballant's oldest son, his mind penetrated by Hein Huss himself, struck his shield with his mailed fist. "They burn me! They burn us all! Better to fight than burn!"

"Fight! Fight!" came the voices of the tormented men.

Lord Ballant looked around at the twisted faces, some displaying blisters, scaldmarks. "Our own spell terrifies them; wait yet a moment!" he pleaded.

His brother called hoarsely, "It is not your belly that Hein Huss toasts in the flames, it is mine! We cannot win a battle of hoodoos; we must win a battle of arms!"

Lord Ballant cried desperately, "Wait, our own effects are working! They will flee in terror; wait, wait!"

His cousin tore off his corselet. "It's Hein Huss! I feel him! My leg's in the fire, the devil laughs at me. Next my head, he says. Fight, or I go forth to fight alone!"

"Very well," said Lord Ballant in a fateful voice. "We go forth to fight. First—the beast goes forth. Then we follow and smite them in their terror."

The gates to the keep swung suddenly wide. Out sprang what appeared to be the depicted monster: legs moving, arms waving, eyes rolling, issuing evil sounds. Normally the Faide warriors would have seen the monster for what it was: a model carried on the backs of three horses. But their minds had been influenced; they had been infected with horror; they drew back with arms hanging flaccid. From behind the monster the Ballant knights galloped, followed by the Ballant foot soldiers. The charge gathered momentum, tore into the Faide center. Lord Faide bellowed orders; discipline asserted itself. The Faide knights disengaged, divided into three platoons and engulfed the Ballant charge, while the foot soldiers poured darts into the advancing ranks.

There was the clatter and surge of battle; Lord Ballant, seeing that his sally had failed to overwhelm the Faide forces, and thinking to conserve his own forces, ordered a retreat. In good order the Ballant warriors began to back up toward the keep. The Faide knights held close contact, hoping to win to the courtyard. Close behind came a heavily loaded wagon pushed by armored horses, to be wedged against the gate.

Lord Faide called an order; a reserve platoon of ten knights charged from the side, thrust behind the main body of Ballant horsemen, rode through the foot soldiers, fought into the keep, cut down the gate-tenders.

Lord Ballant bellowed to Anderson Grimes, "They have won inside; quick with your cursed demon! If he can help us, let him do so now!"

"Demon possession is not a matter of an instant," muttered the jinx-man. "I need time."

"You have no time! Ten minutes and we're all dead!"

"I will do my best. Everid, Everid, come swift!"

He hastened into his workroom, donned his demonmask, tossed handful after handful of incense into the brazier. Against one wall stood a great form: black, slit-eyed, noseless. Great white fangs hung from its upper palate; it stood on heavy bent legs, arms reached forward to grasp. Anderson Grimes swallowed a cup of syrup, paced slowly back and forth. A moment passed.

"Grimes!" came Ballant's call from outside. "Grimes!"

A voice spoke. "Enter without fear."

Lord Ballant, carrying his ancestral side arm, entered. He drew back with an involuntary sound. "Grimes!" he whispered.

"Grimes is not here," said the voice. "I am here. Enter."

Lord Ballant came forward stiff-legged. The room was dark except for the feeble glimmer of the brazier. Anderson Grimes crouched in a corner, head bowed under his demonmask. The shadows twisted and pulsed with shapes and faces, forms struggling to become solid. The black image seemed to vibrate with life.

"Bring in your warriors," said the voice. "Bring them in five at a time, bid them look only at the floor until commanded to raise their eyes."

Lord Ballant retreated; there was no sound in the room.

A moment passed; then five limp and exhausted warriors filed into the room, eyes low.

"Look slowly up," said the voice. "Look at the orange fire. Breathe deeply. Then look at me. I am Everid, Demon of Hate. Look at me. Who am I?"

"You are Everid, Demon of Hate," quavered the warriors.

"I stand all around you, in a dozen forms. . . . I come closer. Where am I?"

"You are close."

"Now I am you. We are together."

There was a sudden quiver of motion. The warriors stood straighter, their faces distorted.

"Go forth," said the voice. "Go quietly into the court. In a few minutes we march forth to slay."

The five stalked forth. Five more entered.

Outside the wall the Ballant knights had retreated as far as the gate; within, seven Faide knights still survived, and with their backs to the wall held the Ballant warriors away from the gate mechanism.

In the Faide camp Huss called to Comandore, "Everid is walking. Bring forth Keyril."

"Send the men," came Comandore's voice, low and harsh. "Send the men to me. I am Keyril."

Within the keep twenty warriors came marching into the courtyard. Their steps were cautious, tentative, slow. Their faces had lost individuality, they were twisted and distorted, curiously alike.

"Bewitched!" whispered the Ballant soldiers, drawing back. The seven Faide knights watched with sudden fright. But the twenty warriors, paying them no heed, marched out the gate. The Ballant knights parted; for an instant there was a lull in the fighting. The twenty sprang like tigers. Their swords glistened, twinkling in water-bright arcs. They crouched, jerked, jumped; Faide arms, legs, heads were hewed off. The twenty were cut and battered, but the blows seemed to have no effect.

The Faide attack faltered, collapsed. The knights, whose armor was no protection against the demoniac swords, retreated. The twenty possessed warriors raced out into the open toward the foot soldiers, running with great strides, slashing and rending. The Faide foot soldiers fought for a moment, then they too gave way and turned to flee.

From behind Comandore's tent appeared thirty Faide warriors, marching stiffly, slowly. Like the Ballant twenty their faces were alike—but between the Everid-possessed and the Keyril-possessed was the difference between the face of Everid and the face of Keyril.

Keyril and Everid fought, using the men as weapons, without fear, retreat or mercy. Hack, chop, cut. Arms, legs, sundered torsos. Bodies fought headless for moments before collapsing. Only when a body was minced, hacked to bits, did the demoniac vitality depart. Presently there were no more men of Everid, and only fifteen men of Keyril. These hopped and limped and tumbled toward the keep where Faide knights still held the gate. The Ballant knights met them in despair, knowing that now was the decisive moment. Leaping, leering from chopped faces, slashing from tireless arms, the warriors cut a hole into the iron. The Faide knights, roaring victory cries, plunged after. Into the courtyard surged the battle, and now there was no longer doubt of the outcome. Ballant Keep was taken.

Back in his tent Isak Comandore took a deep breath, shuddered, flung down his demonmask. In the courtyard the twelve remaining warriors dropped in their tracks, twitched, gasped, gushed blood and died.

Lord Ballant, in the last gallant act of a gallant life, marched forth brandishing his ancestral side arm. He aimed across the bloody field at Lord Faide, pulled the trigger. The weapon spewed a brief gout of light; Lord Faide's skin prickled and hair rose from his head. The weapon crackled, turned cherry-red and melted. Lord Ballant threw down the weapon, drew his sword, marched forth to challenge Lord Faide.

Lord Faide, disinclined to unnecessary combat, signaled to his soldiers. A flight of darts ended Lord Ballant's life, saving him the discomfort of formal execution.

There was no further resistance. The Ballant defenders threw down their arms and marched grimly out to kneel before Lord Faide, while inside the keep the Ballant women gave themselves to mourning and grief.


# V


Lord Faide had no wish to linger at Ballant Keep, for he took no relish in his victories. Inevitably, a thousand decisions had to be made. Six of the closest Ballant kinsmen were summarily stabbed and the title declared defunct. Others of the clan were offered a choice: an oath of lifelong fealty together with a moderate ransom, or death. Only two, eyes blazing hate, chose death and were instantly stabbed.

Lord Faide had now achieved his ambition. For over a thousand years the keep-lords had struggled for power; now one, now another gaining ascendancy. None before had ever extended his authority across the entire continent—which meant control of the planet, since all other land was either sun-parched rock or eternal ice. Ballant Keep had long thwarted Lord Faide's drive to power; now—success, total and absolute. It still remained to chastise the lords of Castle Cloud and Gisborne, both of whom, seeing opportunity to overwhelm Lord Faide, had ranged themselves behind Lord Ballant. But these were matters that might well be assigned to Hein Huss.

Lord Faide, for the first time in his life, felt a trace of uncertainty. Now what? No real adversaries remained. The First Folk must be whipped back, but here was no great problem; they were numerous, but no more than savages. He knew that dissatisfaction and controversy would ultimately arise among his kinsmen and allies. Inaction and boredom would breed irritability; idle minds would calculate the pros and cons of mischief. Even the most loyal would remember the campaigns with nostalgia and long for the excitement, the release, the license, of warfare. Somehow he must find means to absorb the energy of so many active and keyed-up men. How and where, this was the problem. The construction of roads? New farmland claimed from the downs? Yearly tournaments-at-arms? Lord Faide frowned at the inadequacy of his solutions, but his imagination was impoverished by the lack of tradition. The original settlers of Pangborn had been warriors, and had brought with them a certain amount of practical rule-of-thumb knowledge, but little else. The tales they passed down the generations described the great spaceships which moved with magic speed and certainty, the miraculous weapons, the wars in the void, but told nothing of human history or civilized achievement. And so Lord Faide, full of power and success, but with no goal toward which to turn his strength, felt more morose and saturnine than ever.

He gloomily inspected the spoils from Ballant Keep. They were of no great interest to him. Ballant's ancestral car was no longer used, but displayed behind a glass case. He inspected the weapon Volcano, but this could not be moved. In any event it was useless, its magic lost forever. Lord Faide now knew that Lord Ballant had ordered it turned against the Faide car, but that it had refused to spew its vaunted fire. Lord Faide saw with disdainful amusement that Volcano had been sadly neglected. Corrosion had pitted the metal, careless cleaning had twisted the exterior tubing, undoubtedly diminishing the potency of the magic. No such neglect at Faide Keep! Jambart the weapon-tender cherished Hellmouth with absolute devotion. Elsewhere were other ancient devices, interesting but useless—the same sort of curios that cluttered shelves and cases at Faide Keep. (Peculiar, these ancient men! thought Lord Faide: at once so clever, yet so primitive and impractical. Conditions had changed; there had been enormous advances since the dark ages sixteen hundred years ago. For instance, the ancients had used intricate fetishes of metal and glass to communicate with each other. Lord Faide need merely voice his needs; Hein Huss could project his mind a hundred miles to see, to hear, to relay Lord Faide's words.) The ancients had contrived dozens of such objects, but the old magic had worn away and they never seemed to function. Lord Ballant's side arm had melted, after merely stinging Lord Faide. Imagine a troop armed thus trying to cope with a platoon of demonpossessed warriors! Slaughter of the innocents!

Among the Ballant trove Lord Faide noted a dozen old books and several reels of microfilm. The books were worthless, page after page of incomprehensible jargon; the microfilm was equally undecipherable. Again Lord Faide wondered skeptically about the ancients. Clever of course, but to look at the hard facts, they were little more advanced than the First Folk: neither had facility with telepathy or voyance or demon-command. And the magic of the ancients: might there not be a great deal of exaggeration in the legends? Volcano, for instance. A joke. Lord Faide wondered about his own Hellmouth. But no—surely Hellmouth was more trustworthy; Jambart cleaned and polished the weapon daily and washed the entire cupola with vintage wine every month. If human care could induce faithfulness, then Hellmouth was ready to defend Faide Keep!

Now there was no longer need for defense. Faide was supreme. Considering the future, Lord Faide made a decision. There should no longer be keep-lords on Pangborn; he would abolish the appellation. Habitancy of the keeps would gradually be transferred to trusted bailiffs on a yearly basis. The former lords would be moved to comfortable but indefensible manor houses, with the maintenance of private troops forbidden. Naturally they must be allowed jinxmen, but these would be made accountable to himself—perhaps through some sort of licensing provision. He must discuss the matter with Hein Huss. A matter for the future, however. Now he merely wished to settle affairs and return to Faide Keep.

There was little more to be done. The surviving Ballant kinsmen he sent to their homes after Hein Huss had impregnated fresh dolls with their essences. Should they default on their ransoms, a twinge of fire, a few stomach cramps would more than set them right. Ballant Keep itself Lord Faide would have liked to burn—but the material of the ancients was proof to fire. But in order to discourage any new pretenders to the Ballant heritage Lord Faide ordered all the heirlooms and relics brought forth into the courtyard, and then, one at a time, in order of rank, he bade his men choose. Thus the Ballant wealth was distributed. Even the jinxmen were invited to choose, but they despised the ancient trinkets as works of witless superstition. The lesser spellbinders and apprentices rummaged through the leavings, occasionally finding an overlooked bauble or some anomalous implement. Isak Comandore was irritated to find Sam Salazar staggering under a load of the ancient books. "And what is your purpose with these?" he barked. "Why do you burden yourself with rubbish?"

Sam Salazar hung his head. "I have no definite purpose. Undoubtedly there was wisdom—or at least knowledge—among the ancients; perhaps I can use these symbols of knowledge to sharpen my own understanding."

Comandore threw up his hands in disgust. He turned to Hein Huss who stood nearby. "First he fancies himself a tree and stands in the mud; now he thinks to learn jinxmanship through a study of ancient symbols."

Huss shrugged. "They were men like ourselves, and, though limited, they were not entirely obtuse. A certain simian cleverness is required to fabricate these objects."

"Simian cleverness is no substitute for sound jinxmanship," retorted Isak Comandore. "This is a point hard to overemphasize; I have drummed it into Salazar's head a hundred times. And now, look at him."

Huss grunted noncommittally. "I fail to understand what he hopes to achieve."

Sam Salazar tried to explain, fumbling for words to express an idea that did not exist. "I thought perhaps to decipher the writing, if only to understand what the ancients thought, and perhaps to learn how to perform one or two of their tricks."

Comandore rolled up his eyes. "What enemy bewitched me when I consented to take you as apprentice? I can cast twenty hoodoos in an hour, more than any of the ancients could achieve in a lifetime."

"Nevertheless," said Sam Salazar, "I notice that Lord Faide rides in his ancestral car, and that Lord Ballant sought to kill us all with Volcano."

"I notice," said Comandore with feral softness, "that my demon Keyril conquered Lord Ballant's Volcano, and that riding on my wagon I can outdistance Lord Faide in his car."

Sam Salazar thought better of arguing further. "True, Jinxman Comandore, very true. I stand corrected."

"Then discard that rubbish and make yourself useful. We return to Faide Keep in the morning."

"As you wish, Jinxman Comandore." Sam Salazar threw the books back into the trash.

## VI

The Ballant clan had been dispersed, Ballant Keep was despoiled. Lord Faide and his men banqueted somberly in the great hall, tended by silent Ballant servitors.

Ballant Keep had been built on the same splendid scale as Faide Keep. The great hall was a hundred feet long, fifty feet wide, fifty feet high, paneled in planks sawn from pale native hardwood, rubbed and waxed to a rich honey color. Enormous black beams supported the ceiling; from these hung candelabra, intricate contrivances of green, purple and blue glass, knotted with ancient but still bright light-motes. On the far wall hung portraits of all the lords of Ballant Keep—one hundred five grave faces in a variety of costumes. Below, a genealogical chart ten feet high detailed the descent of the Ballants and their connections with the other noble clans. Now there was a desolate air to the hall, and the one hundred five dead faces were meaningless and empty.

Lord Faide dined without joy, and cast dour side glances at those of his kinsmen who reveled too gladly. Lord Ballant, he thought, had conducted himself only as he himself might have done under the same circumstances; coarse exultation seemed in poor taste, almost as if it were disrespect for Lord Faide himself. His followers were quick to catch his mood, and the banquet proceeded with greater decorum.

The jinxmen sat apart in a smaller room to the side. Anderson Grimes, erstwhile Ballant head jinxman, sat beside Hein Huss, trying to put a good face on his defeat. After all, he had performed creditably against four powerful adversaries, and there was no cause to feel a diminution of *mana*. The five jinxmen discussed the battle, while the cabalmen and spellbinders listened respectfully. The conduct of the demonpossessed troops occasioned the most discussion. Anderson Grimes readily admitted that his conception of Everid was a force absolutely brutal and blunt, terrifying in its indomitable vigor. The other jinxmen agreed that he undoubtedly succeeded in projecting these qualities; Hein Huss however pointed out that Isak Comandore's Keyril, as cruel and vigorous as Everid, also combined a measure of crafty malice, which tended to make the possessed soldier a more effective weapon.

Anderson Grimes allowed that this might well be the case, and that in fact he had been considering such an augmentation of Everid's characteristics.

"To my mind," said Huss, "the most effective demon should be swift enough to avoid the strokes of the brute demons, such as Keyril and Everid. I cite my own Dant as example. A Dant-possessed warrior can easily destroy a Keyril or an Everid, simply through his agility. In an encounter of this sort the Keyrils and Everids presently lose their capacity to terrify, and thus half the effect is lost."

Isak Comandore pierced Huss with a hot russet glance. "You state a presumption as if it were fact. I have formulated Keyril with sufficient craft to counter any such displays of speed. I firmly believe Keyril to be the most fearsome of all demons."

"It may well be," rumbled Hein Huss thoughtfully. He beckoned to a steward, gave instructions. The steward reduced the light a trifle. "Behold," said Hein Huss. "There is Dant. He comes to join the banquet." To the side of the room loomed the tiger-striped Dant, a creature constructed of resilient metal, with four terrible arms, and a squat black head which seemed all gaping jaw.

"Look," came the husky voice of Isak Comandore. "There is Keyril." Keyril was rather more humanoid and armed with a cutlass. Dant spied Keyril. The jaws gaped wider, it sprang to the attack.

The battle was a thing of horror; the two demons rolled, twisted, bit, frothed, uttered soundless shrieks, tore each other apart. Suddenly Dant sprang away, circled Keyril with dizzying speed, faster, faster; became a blur, a wild coruscation of colors that seemed to give off a high-pitched wailing sound, rising higher and higher in pitch. Keyril hacked brutally with his cutlass, then seemed to grow feeble and wan. The light that once had been Dant blazed white, exploded in a mental shriek; Keyril was gone and Isak Comandore lay moaning.

Hein Huss drew a deep breath, wiped his face, looked about him with a complacent grin. The entire company sat rigid as stones, staring, all except the apprentice Sam Salazar, who met Hein Huss's glance with a cheerful smile.

"So," growled Huss, panting from his exertion, "you consider yourself superior to the illusion; you sit and smirk at one of Hein Huss's best efforts."

"No, no," cried Sam Salazar, "I mean no disrespect! I want to learn, so I watched you rather than the demons. What could they teach me? Nothing!"

"Ah," said Huss, mollified. "And what did you learn?"

"Likewise, nothing," said Sam Salazar, "but at least I do not sit like a fish."

Comandore's voice came soft but crackling with wrath. "You see in me the resemblance to a fish?"

"I except you, Jinxman Comandore, naturally," Sam Salazar explained.

"Please go to my cabinet, Apprentice Salazar, and fetch me the doll that is your likeness. The steward will bring a basin of water, and we shall have some sport. With your knowledge of fish you perhaps can breathe under water. If not—you may suffocate."

"I prefer not, Jinxman Comandore," said Sam Salazar. "In fact, with your permission, I now resign your service."

Comandore motioned to one of his cabalmen. "Fetch me the Salazar doll. Since he is no longer my apprentice, it is likely indeed that he will suffocate."

"Come now, Comandore," said Hein Huss gruffly. "Do not torment the lad. He is innocent and a trifle addled. Let this be an occasion of placidity and ease."

"Certainly, Hein Huss," said Comandore. "Why not? There is ample time in which to discipline this upstart."

"Jinxman Huss," said Sam Salazar, "since I am now relieved of my duties to Jinxman Comandore, perhaps you will accept me into your service."

Hein Huss made a noise of vast distaste. "You are not my responsibility."

"There are many futures, Hein Huss," said Sam Salazar. "You have said as much yourself."

Hein Huss looked at Sam Salazar with his water-clear eyes. "Yes, there are many futures. And I think that tonight sees the full amplitude of jinxmanship. . . . I think that never again will such power and skill gather at the same table. We shall die one by one and there shall be none to fill our shoes. . . . Yes, Sam Salazar. I will take you as apprentice. Isak Comandore, do you hear? This youth is now of my company."

"I must be compensated," growled Comandore.

"You have coveted my doll of Tharon Faide, the only one in existence. It is yours."

"Ah, ha!" cried Isak Comandore leaping to his feet. "Hein Huss, I salute you! You are generous indeed! I thank you and accept!"

Hein Huss motioned to Sam Salazar. "Move your effects to my wagon. Do not show your face again tonight."

Sam Salazar bowed with dignity and departed the hall.

The banquet continued, but now something of melancholy filled the room. Presently a messenger from Lord Faide came to warn all to bed, for the party returned to Faide Keep at dawn.

## VII

The victorious Faide troops gathered on the heath before Ballant Keep. As a parting gesture Lord Faide ordered the great gate torn off the hinges, so that ingress could never again be denied him. But even after sixteen hundred years the hinges were proof to all the force the horses could muster, and the gates remained in place.

Lord Faide accepted the fact with good grace and bade farewell to his cousin Renfroy, whom he had appointed bailiff. He climbed into his car, settled himself, snapped the switch. The car groaned and moved forward. Behind came the knights and the foot soldiers, then the baggage train, laden with booty, and finally the wagons of the jinxmen.

Three hours the column marched across the mossy downs. Ballant Keep dwindled behind; ahead appeared North and South Wildwood, darkening all the sweep of the western horizon. Where once the break had existed, the First Folk's new planting showed a smudge lower and less intense than the old woodlands.

Two miles from the woodlands Lord Faide called a halt and signaled up his knights. Hein Huss laboriously dismounted from his wagon, came forward.

"In the event of resistance," Lord Faide told the knights, "do not be tempted into the forest. Stay with the column and at all times be on your guard against traps."

Hein Huss spoke. "You wish me to parley with the First Folk once more?"

"No," said Lord Faide. "It is ridiculous that I must ask permission of savages to ride over my own land. We return as we came; if they interfere, so much the worse for them."

"You are rash," said Huss with simple candor.

Lord Faide glanced down at him with black eyebrows raised. "What damage can they do if we avoid their traps? Blow foam at us?"

"It is not my place to advise or to warn," said Hein Huss. "However, I point out that they exhibit a confidence which does not come from conscious weakness; also, that they carried tubes, apparently hollow grass-wood shoots, which imply missiles."

Lord Faide nodded. "No doubt. However, the knights wear armor, the soldiers carry bucklers. It is not fit that I, Lord Faide of Faide Keep, choose my path to suit the whims of the First Folk. This must be made clear, even if the exercise involves a dozen or so First Folk corpses."

"Since I am not a fighting man," remarked Hein Huss, "I will keep well to the rear, and pass only when the way is secure."

"As you wish." Lord Faide pulled down the visor of his helmet. "Forward."

The column moved toward the forest, along the previous track, which showed plain across the moss. Lord Faide rode in the lead, flanked by his brother, Gethwin Faide, and his cousin, Mauve Dermont-Faide.

A half-mile passed, and another. The forest was only a mile distant. Overhead the great sun rode at zenith; brightness and heat poured down; the air carried the oily scent of thorn and tarbush. The column moved on, more slowly; the only sound the clanking of armor, the muffled thud of hooves in the moss, the squeal of wagon wheels.

Lord Faide rose up in his car, watching for any sign of hostile preparation. A half-mile from the planting the forms of the First Folk, waiting in the shade along the forest's verge, became visible. Lord Faide ignored them, held a steady pace along the track they had traveled before.

The half-mile became a quarter-mile. Lord Faide turned to order the troops into single file and was just in time to see a hole suddenly open into the moss and his brother, Gethwin Faide, drop from sight. There was a rattle, a thud, the howling of the impaled horse; Gethwin's wild calls as the horse kicked and crushed him into the stakes. Mauve Dermont-Faide, riding beside Gethwin, could not control his own horse, which leaped aside from the pit and blundered upon a trigger. Up from the moss burst a tree trunk studded with foot-long thorns. It snapped, quick as a scorpion's tail; the thorns punctured Mauve Dermont-Faide's armor, his chest, and whisked him from his horse to carry him suspended, writhing and screaming. The tip of the scythe pounded into Lord Faide's car, splintered against the hull. The car swung groaning through the air. Lord Faide clutched at the windscreen to prevent himself from falling.

The column halted; several men ran to the pit, but Gethwin Faide lay twenty feet below, crushed under his horse. Others took Mauve Dermont-Faide down from the swaying scythe, but he, too, was dead.

Lord Faide's skin tingled with a gooseflesh of hate and rage. He looked toward the forest. The First Folk stood motionless. He beckoned to Bernard, sergeant of the foot soldiers. "Two men with lances to try out the ground ahead. All others ready with darts. At my signal spit the devils."

Two men came forward, and marching before Lord Faide's car, probed at the ground. Lord Faide settled in his seat. "Forward."

The column moved slowly toward the forest, every man tense and ready. The lances of the two men in the vanguard presently broke through the moss, to disclose a nettle trap—a pit lined with nettles, each frond ripe with globes of acid. Carefully they probed out a path to the side, and the column filed around, each man walking in the other's tracks.

At Lord Faide's side now rode his two nephews, Scolford and Edwin. "Notice," said Lord Faide in a voice harsh and tight. "These traps were laid since our last passage; an act of malice."

"But why did they guide us through before?"

Lord Faide smiled bitterly. "They were willing that we should die at Ballant Keep. But we have disappointed them."

"Notice, they carry tubes," said Scolford.

"Blowguns possibly," suggested Edwin.

Scolford disagreed. "They cannot blow through their foam-vents."

"No doubt we shall soon learn," said Lord Faide. He rose in his seat, called to the rear. "Ready with the darts!"

The soldiers raised their crossbows. The column advanced slowly, now only a hundred yards from the planting. The white shapes of the First Folk moved uneasily at the forest's edges. Several of them raised their tubes, seemed to sight along the length. They twitched their great hands.

One of the tubes was pointed toward Lord Faide. He saw a small black object leave the opening, flit forward, gathering speed. He heard a hum, waxing to a rasping, clicking flutter. He ducked behind the windscreen; the projectile swooped in pursuit, struck the windscreen like a thrown stone. It fell crippled upon the forward deck of the car—a heavy black insect like a wasp, its broken proboscis oozing ocher liquid, horny wings beating feebly, eyes like dumbbells fixed on Lord Faide. With his mailed fist, he crushed the creature.

Behind him other wasps struck knights and men; Corex Faide-Battaro took the prong through his visor into the eye, but the armor of the other knights defeated the wasps. The foot soldiers, however, lacked protection; the wasps half-buried themselves in flesh. The soldiers called out in pain, clawed away the wasps, squeezed the wounds. Corex Faide-Battaro toppled from his horse, ran blindly out over the heath, and after fifty feet fell into a trap. The stricken soldiers began to twitch, then fell on the moss, thrashed, leaped up to run with flapping arms, threw themselves in wild somersaults, forward, backward, foaming and thrashing.

In the forest, the First Folk raised their tubes again. Lord Faide bellowed, "Spit the creatures! Bowmen, launch your darts!"

There came the twang of crossbows, darts snapped at the quiet white shapes. A few staggered and wandered aimlessly away; most, however, plucked out the darts or ignored them. They took capsules from small sacks, put them to the end of their tubes.

"Beware the wasps!" cried Lord Faide. "Strike with your bucklers! Kill the cursed things in flight!"

The rasp of horny wings came again; certain of the soldiers found courage enough to follow Lord Faide's orders, and battered down the wasps. Others struck home as before; behind came another flight. The column became a tangle of struggling, crouching men.

"Footmen, retreat!" called Lord Faide furiously. "Footmen back! Knights to me!"

The soldiers fled back along the track, taking refuge behind the baggage wagons. Thirty of their number lay dying, or dead, on the moss.

Lord Faide cried out to his knights in a voice like a bugle. "Dismount, follow slow after me! Turn your helmets, keep the wasps from your eyes! One step at a time, behind the car! Edwin, into the car beside me, test the footing with your lance. Once in the forest there are no traps! Then attack!"

The knights formed themselves into a line behind the car. Lord Faide drove slowly forward, his kinsman Edwin prodding the ground ahead. The First Folk sent out a dozen more wasps, which dashed themselves vainly against the armor. Then there was silence . . . cessation of sound, activity. The First Folk watched impassively as the knights approached, step by step.

Edwin's lance found a trap, the column moved to the side. Another trap —and the column was diverted from the planting toward the forest. Step by step, yard by yard—another trap, another detour, and now the column was only a hundred feet from the forest. A trap to the left, a trap to the right: the safe path led directly toward an enormous heavy-branched tree. Seventy feet, fifty feet, then Lord Faide drew his sword.

"Prepare to charge, kill till your arms tire!"

From the forest came a crackling sound. The branches of the great tree trembled and swayed. The knights stared, for a moment frozen into place. The tree toppled forward, the knights madly tried to flee—to the rear, to the sides. Traps opened; the knights dropped upon sharp stakes. The tree fell; boughs cracked armored bodies like nuts; there was the hoarse yelling of pinned men, screams from the traps, the crackling subsidence of breaking branches. Lord Faide had been battered down into the car, and the car had been pressed groaning into the moss. His first instinctive act was to press the switch to rest position; then he staggered erect, clambered up through the boughs. A pale unhuman face peered at him; he swung his fist, crushed the faceted eye-bulge, and roaring with rage scrambled through the branches. Others of his knights were working themselves free, although almost a third were either crushed or impaled.

The First Folk came scrambling forward, armed with enormous thorns, long as swords. But now Lord Faide could reach them at close quarters. Hissing with vindictive joy he sprang into their midst, swinging his sword with both hands, as if demon-possessed. The surviving knights joined him and the ground became littered with dismembered First Folk. They drew back slowly, without excitement. Lord Faide reluctantly called back his knights. "We must succor those still pinned, as many as still are alive."

As well as possible branches were cut away, injured knights drawn forth. In some cases the soft moss had cushioned the impact of the tree. Six knights were dead, another four crushed beyond hope of recovery. To these Lord Faide himself gave the *coup de grâce*. Ten minutes further hacking and chopping freed Lord Faide's car, while the First Folk watched incuriously from the forest. The knights wished to charge once more, but Lord Faide ordered retreat. Without interference they returned the way they had come, back to the baggage train.

Lord Faide ordered a muster. Of the original war party, less than two-thirds remained. Lord Faide shook his head bitterly. Galling to think how easily he had been led into a trap! He swung on his heel, strode to the rear of the column, to the wagons of the magicians. The jinxmen sat around a small fire, drinking tea. "Which of you will hoodoo these white forest vermin? I want them dead—stricken with sickness, cramps, blindness, the most painful afflictions you can contrive!"

There was general silence. The jinxmen sipped their tea.

"Well?" demanded Lord Faide. "Have you no answer? Do I not make myself plain?"

Hein Huss cleared his throat, spat into the blaze. "Your wishes are plain. Unfortunately we cannot hoodoo the First Folk."

"And why?"

"There are technical reasons."

Lord Faide knew the futility of argument. "Must we slink home around the forest? If you cannot hoodoo the First Folk, then bring out your demons! I will march on the forest and chop out a path with my sword!"

"It is not for me to suggest tactics," grumbled Hein Huss.

"Go on, speak! I will listen."

"A suggestion has been put to me, which I will pass to you. Neither I nor the other jinxmen associate ourselves with it, since it recommends the crudest of physical principles."

"I await the suggestion," said Lord Faide.

"It is merely this. One of my apprentices tampered with your car, as you may remember."

"Yes, and I will see he gets the hiding he deserves."

"By some freak he caused the car to rise high into the air. The suggestion is this: that we load the car with as much oil as the baggage train affords, that we send the car aloft and let it drift over the planting. At a suitable moment, the occupant of the car will pour the oil over the trees, then hurl down a torch. The forest will burn. The First Folk will be at least discomfited; at best a large number will be destroyed."

Lord Faide slapped his hands together. "Excellent! Quickly, to work!" He called a dozen soldiers, gave them orders; four kegs of cooking oil, three buckets of pitch, six demijohns of spirit were brought and lifted into the car. The engines grated and protested, and the car sagged almost to the moss.

Lord Faide shook his head sadly. "A rude use of the relic, but all in good purpose. Now, where is that apprentice? He must indicate which switches and which buttons he turned."

"I suggest," said Hein Huss, "that Sam Salazar be sent up with the car."

Lord Faide looked sidewise at Sam Salazar's round, bland countenance. "An efficient hand is needed, a seasoned judgment. I wonder if he can be trusted?"

"I would think so," said Hein Huss, "inasmuch as it was Sam Salazar who evolved the scheme in the first place."

"Very well. In with you, apprentice! Treat my car with reverence! The wind blows away from us; fire this edge of the forest, in as long a strip as you can manage. The torch, where is the torch?"

The torch was brought and secured to the side of the car.

"One more matter," said Sam Salazar. "I would like to borrow the armor of some obliging knight, to protect myself from the wasps. Otherwise—"

"Armor!" bawled Lord Faide. "Bring armor!"

At last, fully accoutered and with visor down, Sam Salazar climbed into the car. He seated himself, peered intently at the buttons and switches.

In truth he was not precisely certain as to which he had manipulated before. . . . He considered, reached forward, pushed, turned. The motors roared and screamed; the car shuddered, sluggishly rose into the air. Higher, higher, twenty feet, forty feet, sixty feet—a hundred, two hundred. The wind eased the car toward the forest; in the shade the First Folk watched. Several of them raised tubes, opened the shutters. The onlookers saw the wasps dart through the air to dash against Sam Salazar's armor.

The car drifted over the trees; Sam Salazar began ladling out the oil. Below, the First Folk stirred uneasily. The wind carried the car too far over the forest; Sam Salazar worked the controls, succeeded in guiding himself back. One keg was empty, and another; he tossed them out, presently emptied the remaining two, and the buckets of pitch. He soaked a rag in spirit, ignited it, threw it over the side, poured the spirit after.

The flaming rag fell into leaves. A crackle, fire blazed and sprang. The car now floated at a height of five hundred feet. Salazar poured over the remaining spirits, dropped the demijohns, guided the car back over the heath, and fumbling nervously with the controls dropped the car in a series of swoops back to the moss.

Lord Faide sprang forward, clapped him on the shoulder. "Excellently done! The forest blazes like tinder!"

The men of Faide Keep stood back, rejoicing to see the flames soar and lick. The First Folk scurried back from the heat, waving their arms; foam of a peculiar purple color issued from their vents as they ran, small useless puffs discharged as if by accident or through excitement. The flames ate through first the forest, then spread into the new planting, leaping through the leaves.

"Prepare to march!" called Lord Faide. "We pass directly behind the flames, before the First Folk return."

Off in the forest the First Folk perched in the trees, blowing out foam in great puffs and billows, building a wall of insulation. The flames had eaten half across the new planting, leaving behind smoldering saplings.

"Forward! Briskly!"

The column moved ahead. Coughing in the smoke, eyes smarting, they passed under still blazing trees and came out on the western downs.

Slowly the column moved forward, led by a pair of soldiers prodding the moss with lances. Behind followed Lord Faide with the knights, then came the foot soldiers, then the rumbling baggage train and finally the six wagons of the jinxmen.

A thump, a creak, a snap. A scythe had broken up from the moss; the soldiers in the lead dropped flat; the scythe whipped past, a foot from Lord Faide's face. At the same time a plaintive cry came from the rear guard. "They pursue! The First Folk come!"

Lord Faide turned to inspect the new threat. A clot of First Folk, two hundred or more, came across the moss, moving without haste of urgency. Some carried wasp tubes, others thorn-rapiers.

Lord Faide looked ahead. Another hundred yards should bring the army out upon safe ground; then he could deploy and maneuver. "Forward!"

The column proceeded, the baggage train and the jinxmen's wagons pressing close up against the soldiers. Behind and to the side came the First Folk, moving casually and easily.

At last Lord Faide judged they had reached secure ground. "Forward, now! Bring the wagons out, hurry now!"

The troops needed no urging; they trotted out over the heath, the wagons trundling after. Lord Faide ordered the wagons into a close double line, stationed the soldiers between, with the horses behind and protected from the wasps. The knights, now dismounted, waited in front.

The First Folk came listlessly, formlessly forward. Blank white faces stared; huge hands grasped tubes and thorns; traces of the purplish foam showed at the lips of their underarm orifices.

Lord Faide walked along the line of knights. "Swords ready. Allow them as close as they care to come. Then a quick charge." He motioned to the foot soldiers. "Choose a target . . . !" A volley of darts whistled overhead, to plunge into white bodies. With chisel-bladed fingers the First Folk plucked them out, discarded them with no evidence of vexation. One or two staggered, wandered confusedly across the line of approach. Others raised their tubes, withdrew the shutter. Out flew the insects, horny wings rasping, prongs thrust forward. Across the moss they flickered, to crush themselves against the armor of the knights, to drop to the ground, to be stamped upon. The soldiers cranked their crossbows back into tension, discharged another flight of darts, caused several more First Folk casualties.

The First Folk spread into a long line, surrounding the Faide troops. Lord Faide shifted half his knights to the other side of the wagons.

The First Folk wandered closer. Lord Faide called for a charge. The knights stepped smartly forward, swords swinging. The First Folk advanced a few more steps, then stopped short. The flaps of skin at their backs swelled, pulsed; white foam gushed through their vents; clouds and billows rose up around them. The knights halted uncertainly, prodding and slashing into the foam but finding nothing. The foam piled higher, rolling in and forward, pushing the knights back toward the wagons. They looked questioningly toward Lord Faide.

Lord Faide waved his sword. "Cut through to the other side! Forward!" Slashing two-handed with his sword, he sprang into the foam. He struck something solid, hacked blindly at it, pushed forward. Then his legs were seized; he was upended and fell with a spine-rattling jar. Now he felt the grate of a thorn searching his armor. It found a crevice under his corselet and pierced him. Cursing he raised on his hands and knees, and plunged blindly forward. Enormous hard hands grasped him, heavy forms fell on his shoulders. He tried to breathe, but the foam clogged his visor; he began to smother. Staggering to his feet he half-ran, half-fell out into the open air, carrying two of the First Folk with him. He had lost his sword, but managed to draw his dagger. The First Folk released him and stepped back into the foam. Lord Faide sprang to his feet. Inside the foam came the sounds of combat; some of his knights burst into the open; others called for help. Lord Faide motioned to the knights. "Back within; the devils slaughter our kinsmen! In and on to the center!"

He took a deep breath. Seizing his dagger he thrust himself back into the foam. A flurry of shapes came at him: he pounded with his fists, cut with his dagger, stumbled over a mass of living tissue. He kicked the softness, and stepped on metal. Bending, he grasped a leg but found it limp and dead. First Folk were on his back, another thorn found its mark; he groaned and thrust himself forward, and once again fell out into the open air.

A scant fifty of his knights had won back into the central clearing. Lord Faide cried out, "To the center; mount your horses!" Abandoning his car, he himself vaulted into a saddle. The foam boiled and billowed closer. Lord Faide waved his arm. "Forward, all; at a gallop! After us the wagons —out into the open!"

They charged, thrusting the frightened horses into the foam. There was white blindness, the feel of forms underneath, then the open air once again. Behind came the wagons, and the foot soldiers, running along the channel cut by the wagons. All won free—all but the knights who had fallen under the foam.

Two hundred yards from the great white clot of foam, Lord Faide halted, turned, looked back. He raised his fist, shook it in a passion. "My knights, my car, my honor! I'll burn your forests, I'll drive you into the sea, there'll be no peace till all are dead!" He swung around. "Come," he called bitterly to the remnants of his war party. "We have been defeated. We retreat to Faide Keep."

## VIII

Faide Keep, like Ballant Keep, was constructed of a black, glossy sub-stance, half-metal, half-stone, impervious to heat, force and radiation. A parasol roof, designed to ward off hostile energy, rested on five squat outer towers, connected by walls almost as high as the lip of the overhanging roof.

The homecoming banquet was quiet and morose. The soldiers and knights ate lightly and drank much, but instead of becoming merry, lapsed into gloom. Lord Faide, overcome by emotion, jumped to his feet. "Every-one sits silent, aching with rage. I feel no differently. We shall take revenge. We shall put the forests to the torch. The cursed white savages will smother and burn. Drink now with good cheer; not a moment will be wasted. But we must be ready. It is no more than idiocy to attack as before. Tonight I take council with the jinxmen, and we will start a program of affliction."

The soldiers and knights rose to their feet, raised their cups and drank a somber toast. Lord Faide bowed and left the hall.

He went to his private trophy room. On the walls hung escutcheons, memorials, deathmasks, clusters of swords like many-petaled flowers; a rack of side arms, energy pistols, electric stilettos; a portrait of the original Faide, in ancient spacefarer's uniform and a treasured, almost unique, photograph of the great ship that had brought the first Faide to Pangborn.

Lord Faide studied the ancient face for several moments, then summoned a servant. "Ask the head jinxman to attend me."

Hein Huss presently stumped into the room. Lord Faide turned away from the portrait, seated himself, motioned to Hein Huss to do likewise. "What of the keep-lords?" he asked. "How do they regard the setback at the hands of the First Folk?"

"There are various reactions," said Hein Huss. "At Boghoten, Candel-wade and Havve there is distress and anger."

Lord Faide nodded. "These are my kinsmen."

"At Gisborne, Graymar, Castle Cloud and Alder there is satisfaction, veiled calculation."

"To be expected," muttered Lord Faide. "These lords must be humbled; in spite of oaths and undertakings, they still think rebellion."

"At Star Home, Julian-Douray and Oak Hall I read surprise at the abilities of the First Folk, but in the main disinterest."

Lord Faide nodded sourly. "Well enough. There is no actual rebellion in prospect; we are free to concentrate on the First Folk. I will tell you what is in my mind. You report that new plantings are in progress between Wildwood, Old Forest, Sarrow Copse and elsewhere—possibly with the intent of surrounding Faide Keep." He looked inquiringly at Hein Huss, but no comment was forthcoming. Lord Faide continued. "Possibly we have underestimated the cunning of the savages. They seem capable of forming plans and acting with almost human persistence. Or, I should say, more than human persistence, for it appears that after sixteen hundred years they still consider us invaders and hope to exterminate us."

"That is my own conclusion," said Hein Huss.

"We must take steps to strike first. I consider this a matter for the jinxmen. We gain no honor dodging wasps, falling into traps or groping through foam. It is a needless waste of lives. Therefore, I want you to assemble your jinxmen, cabalmen and spellbinders; I want you to formulate your most potent hoodoos—"

"Impossible."

Lord Faide's black eyebrows rose high. " 'Impossible'?"

Hein Huss seemed vaguely uncomfortable. "I read the wonder in your mind. You suspect me of disinterest, irresponsibility. Not true. If the First Folk defeat you, we suffer likewise."

"Exactly," said Lord Faide dryly. "You will starve."

"Nevertheless, the jinxmen cannot help you." He hoisted himself to his feet, started for the door.

"Sit," said Lord Faide. "It is necessary to pursue this matter."

Hein Huss looked around with his bland, water-clear eyes. Lord Faide met his gaze. Hein Huss sighed deeply. "I see I must ignore the precepts of my trade, break the habits of a lifetime. I must explain." He took his bulk to the wall, fingered the side arms in the rack, studied the portrait of the ancestral Faide. "These miracle workers of the old times—unfortunately we cannot use their magic! Notice the bulk of the spaceship! As heavy as Faide Keep." He turned his gaze on the table, teleported a candelabra two or three inches. "With considerably less effort they gave that spaceship enormous velocity, using ideas and forces they knew to be imaginary and irrational. We have advanced since then, of course. We no longer employ mysteries, arcane constructions, wild nonhuman forces. We are rational and practical—but we cannot achieve the effects of the ancient magicians."

Lord Faide watched Hein Huss with saturnine eyes. Hein Huss gave his deep rumbling laugh. "You think that I wish to distract you with talk? No, this is not the case. I am preparing to enlighten you." He returned to his seat, lowered his bulk with a groan. "Now I must talk at length, to which I am not accustomed. But you must be given to understand what we jinxmen can do and what we cannot do.

"First, unlike the ancient magicians, we are practical men. Naturally there is difference in our abilities. The best jinxman combines great telepathic facility, implacable personal force and intimate knowledge of his fellow humans. He knows their acts, motives, desires and fears; he understands the symbols that most vigorously represent these qualities. Jinxmanship in the main is drudgery—dangerous, difficult and unromantic—with no mystery except that which we employ to confuse our enemies." Hein Huss glanced at Lord Faide to encounter the same saturnine gaze. "Ha! I still have told you nothing; I still have spent many words talking around my inability to confound the First Folk. Patience."

"Speak on," said Lord Faide.

"Listen then. What happens when I hoodoo a man? First I must enter into his mind telepathically. There are three operational levels: the conscious, the unconscious, the cellular. The most effective jinxing is done if all three levels are influenced. I feel into my victim, I learn as much as possible, supplementing my previous knowledge of him, which is part of my stock in trade. I take up his doll, which carries his traces. The doll is highly useful but not indispensable. It serves as a focus for my attention; it acts as a pattern, or a guide, as I fix upon the mind of the victim, and he is bound by his own telepathic capacity to the doll which bears his traces.

"So! Now! Man and doll are identified in my mind, and at one or more levels in the victim's mind. Whatever happens to the doll the victim feels to be happening to himself. There is no more to simple hoodooing than that, from the standpoint of the jinxman. But naturally the victims differ greatly. Susceptibility is the key idea here. Some men are more susceptible than others. Fear and conviction breed susceptibility. As a jinxman succeeds he becomes ever more feared, and consequently the more efficacious he becomes. The process is self-generative.

"Demon possession is a similar technique. Susceptibility is again essential; again conviction creates susceptibility. It is easiest and most dramatic when the characteristics of the demon are well-known, as in the case of Comandore's Keyril. For this reason, demons can be exchanged or traded among jinxmen. The commodity actually traded is public acceptance and familiarity with the demon."

"Demons then do not actually exist?" inquired Lord Faide half-incredulously.

Hein Huss grinned vastly, showing enormous yellow teeth. "Telepathy works through a superstratum. Who knows what is created in this superstratum? Maybe the demons live on after they have been conceived; maybe they now are real. This of course is speculation, which we jinxmen shun.

"So much for demons, so much for the lesser techniques of jinxmanship. I have explained sufficient to serve as background to the present situation."

"Excellent," said Lord Faide. "Continue."

"The question, then, is: how does one cast a hoodoo into a creature of an alien race?" He looked inquiringly at Lord Faide. "Can you tell me?"

"I?" asked Lord Faide surprised. "No."

"The method is basically the same as in the hoodooing of men. It is necessary to make the creature believe, in every cell of his being, that he suffers or dies. This is where the problems begin to arise. Does the creature think—that is to say, does he arrange the processes of his life in the same manner as men? This is a very important distinction. Certain creatures of the universe use methods other than the human nerve-node system to control their environments. We call the human system *intelligence*—a word which properly should be restricted to human activity. Other creatures use different agencies, different systems, arriving sometimes at similar ends. To bring home these generalities, I cannot hope to merge my mind with the corresponding capacity in the First Folk. The key will not fit the lock. At least, not altogether. Once or twice when I watched the First Folk trading with men at Forest Market, I felt occasional weak significances. This implies that the First Folk mentality creates something similar to human telepathic impulses. Nevertheless, there is no real sympathy between the two races.

"This is the first and the least difficulty. If I were able to make complete telepathic contact—what then? The creatures are different from us. They have no words for *fear, hate, rage, pain, bravery, cowardice*. One may deduce that they do not feel these emotions. Undoubtedly they know other sensations, possibly as meaningful. Whatever these may be, they are unknown to me, and therefore I cannot either form or project symbols for these sensations."

Lord Faide stirred impatiently. "In short, you tell me that you cannot efficiently enter these creatures' minds; and that if you could, you do not know what influences you could plant there to do them harm."

"Succinct," agreed Hein Huss. "Substantially accurate."

Lord Faide rose to his feet. "In that case you must repair these deficiencies. You must learn to telepathize with the First Folk; you must find what influences will harm them. As quickly as possible."

Hein Huss stared reproachfully at Lord Faide. "But I have gone to great lengths to explain the difficulties involved! To hoodoo the First Folk is a monumental task! It would be necessary to enter Wildwood, to live with the First Folk, to become one of them, as my apprentice thought to become a tree. Even then an effective hoodoo is improbable! The First Folk must be susceptible to conviction! Otherwise there would be no bite to the hoodoo! I could guarantee no success. I would predict failure. No other jinxman would dare tell you this, no other would risk his *mana*. I dare because I am Hein Huss, with life behind me."

"Nevertheless we must attempt every weapon at hand," said Lord Faide in a dry voice. "I cannot risk my knights, my kinsmen, my soldiers against these pallid half-creatures. What a waste of good flesh and blood to be stuck by a poison insect! You must go to Wildwood; you must learn how to hoodoo the First Folk."

Hein Huss heaved himself erect. His great round face was stony; his eyes were like bits of water-worn glass. "It is likewise a waste to go on a fool's errand. I am no fool, and I will not undertake a hoodoo which is futile from the beginning."

"In that case," said Lord Faide, "I will find someone else." He went to the door, summoned a servant. "Bring Isak Comandore here."

Hein Huss lowered his bulk into the chair. "I will remain during the interview, with your permission."

"As you wish."

Isak Comandore appeared in the doorway, tall, loosely articulated, head hanging forward. He darted a glance of swift appraisal at Lord Faide, at Hein Huss, then stepped into the room.

Lord Faide crisply explained his desires. "Hein Huss refuses to undertake the mission. Therefore I call on you."

Isak Comandore calculated. The pattern of his thinking was clear: he possibly could gain much *mana;* there was small risk of diminution, for had not Hein Huss already dodged away from the project? Comandore nodded. "Hein Huss has made clear the difficulties; only a very clever and very lucky jinxman can hope to succeed. But I accept the challenge, I will go."

"Good," said Hein Huss. "I will go, too." Isak Comandore darted him a sudden hot glance. "I wish only to observe. To Isak Comandore goes the responsibility and whatever credit may ensue."

"Very well," said Comandore presently. "I welcome your company. Tomorrow morning we leave. I go to order our wagon."

Late in the evening Apprentice Sam Salazar came to Hein Huss where he sat brooding in his workroom. "What do you wish?" growled Huss.

"I have a request to make of you, Head Jinxman Huss."

"Head jinxman in name only," grumbled Hein Huss. "Isak Comandore is about to assume my position."

Sam Salazar blinked, laughed uncertainly. Hein Huss fixed wintry-pale eyes on him. "What do you wish?"

"I have heard that you go on an expedition to Wildwood, to study the First Folk."

"True, true. What then?"

"Surely they will now attack all men?"

Hein Huss shrugged. "At Forest Market they trade with men. At Forest Market men have always entered the forest. Perhaps there will be change, perhaps not."

"I would go with you, if I may," said Sam Salazar.

"This is no mission for apprentices."

"An apprentice must take every opportunity to learn," said Sam Salazar. "Also you will need extra hands to set up tents, to load and unload cabinets, to cook, to fetch water and other such matters."

"Your argument is convincing," said Hein Huss. "We depart at dawn; be on hand."


## IX


As the sun lifted over the heath the jinxmen departed Faide Keep. The high-wheeled wagon creaked north over the moss, Hein Huss and Isak Comandore riding the front seat, Sam Salazar with his legs hanging over the tail. The wagon rose and fell with the dips and mounds of the moss, wheels wobbling, and presently passed out of sight behind Skywatcher's Hill.

Five days later, an hour before sunset, the wagon reappeared. As before, Hein Huss and Isak Comandore rode the front seat, with Sam Salazar perched behind. They approached the keep, and without giving so much as a sign or a nod, drove through the gate into the courtyard.

Isak Comandore unfolded his long legs, stepped to the ground like a spider; Hein Huss lowered himself with a grunt. Both went to their quarters, while Sam Salazar led the wagon to the jinxmen's warehouse.

Somewhat later Isak Comandore presented himself to Lord Faide, who had been waiting in his trophy room, forced to a show of indifference through considerations of position, dignity and protocol. Isak Comandore stood in the doorway, grinning like a fox. Lord Faide eyed him with sour dislike, waiting for Comandore to speak. Hein Huss might have stationed himself an entire day, eyes placidly fixed on Lord Faide, awaiting the first word; Isak Comandore lacked the absolute serenity. He came a step forward, "I have returned from Wildwood."

"With what results?"

"I believe that it is possible to hoodoo the First Folk."

Hein Huss spoke from behind Comandore. "I believe that such an undertaking, if feasible, would be useless, irresponsible and possibly dangerous." He lumbered forward.

Isak Comandore's eyes glowed hot red brown; he turned back to Lord Faide. "You ordered me forth on a mission; I will render a report."

"Seat yourselves. I will listen."

Isak Comandore, nominal head of the expedition, spoke. "We rode along the river bank to Forest Market. Here was no sign of disorder or of hostility. A hundred First Folk traded timber, planks, posts and poles for knife blades, iron wire and copper pots. When they returned to their barge we followed them aboard, wagon, horses and all. They showed no surprise—"

"Surprise," said Hein Huss heavily, "is an emotion of which they have no knowledge."

Isak Comandore glared briefly. "We spoke to the bargetenders, explaining that we wished to visit the interior of Wildwood. We asked if the First Folk would try to kill us to prevent us from entering the forest. They professed indifference as to either our well-being or our destruction. This was by no means a guarantee of safe conduct; however, we accepted it as such, and remained aboard the barge." He spoke on with occasional emendations from Hein Huss.

They had proceeded up the river, into the forest, the First Folk poling against the slow current. Presently they put away the poles; nevertheless the barge moved as before. The mystified jinxmen discussed the possibility of teleportation, or symboligical force, and wondered if the First Folk had developed jinxing techniques unknown to men. Sam Salazar, however, noticed that four enormous water beetles, each twelve feet long with oil black carapaces and blunt heads, had risen from the river bed and pushed the barge from behind—apparently without direction or command. The First Folk stood at the bow, turning the nose of the barge this way or that to follow the winding of the river. They ignored the jinxmen and Sam Salazar as if they did not exist.

The beetles swam tirelessly; the barge moved for four hours as fast as a man could walk. Occasionally, First Folk peered from the forest shadows, but none showed interest or concern in the barge's unusual cargo. By midafternoon the river widened, broke into many channels and became a marsh; a few minutes later the barge floated out into the open water of a small lake. Along the shore, behind the first line of trees appeared a large settlement. The jinxmen were interested and surprised. It had always been assumed that the First Folk wandered at random through the forest, as they had originally lived in the moss of the downs.

The barge grounded; the First Folk walked ashore, the men followed with the horses and wagon. Their immediate impressions were of swarming numbers, of slow but incessant activity, and they were attacked by an overpoweringly evil smell.

Ignoring the stench, the men brought the wagon in from the shore, paused to take stock of what they saw. The settlement appeared to be a center of many diverse activities. The trees had been stripped of lower branches, and supported blocks of hardened foam three hundred feet long, fifty feet high, twenty feet thick, with a space of a man's height intervening between the underside of the foam and the ground. There were a dozen of these blocks, apparently of cellular construction. Certain of the cells had broken open and seethed with small white fishlike creatures—the First Folk young.

Below the blocks masses of First Folk engaged in various occupations, in the main unfamiliar to the jinxmen. Leaving the wagon in the care of Sam Salazar, Hein Huss and Isak Comandore moved forward among the

First Folk, repelled by the stench and the pressure of alien flesh, but drawn by curiosity. They were neither heeded nor halted; they wandered everywhere about the settlement. One area seemed to be an enormous zoo, divided into a number of sections. The purpose of one of these sections—a kind of range two hundred feet long—was all too clear. At one end a human corpse hung on a rope—a Faide casualty from the battle at the new planting. Certain of the wasps flew straight at the corpse; just before contact they were netted and removed. Others flew up and away or veered toward the First Folk who stood along the side of the range. These latter also were netted and killed at once.

The purpose of the business was clear enough. Examining some of the other activity in this new light, the jinxmen were able to interpret much that had hitherto puzzled them.

They saw beetles tall as dogs with heavy saw-toothed pincers attacking objects resembling horses; pens of insects even larger, long, narrow, segmented, with dozens of heavy legs and nightmare heads. All these creatures—wasps, beetles, centipedes—in smaller and less formidable form were indigenous to the forest; it was plain that the First Folk had been practicing selective breeding for many years, perhaps centuries.

Not all the activity was warlike. Moths were trained to gather nuts, worms to gnaw straight holes through timber; in another section caterpillars chewed a yellow mash, molded it into identical spheres. Much of the evil odor emanated from the zoo; the jinxmen departed without reluctance, and returned to the wagon. Sam Salazar pitched the tent and built a fire, while Hein Huss and Isak Comandore discussed the settlement.

Night came; the blocks of foam glowed with imprisoned light; the activity underneath proceeded without cessation. The jinxmen retired to the tent and slept, while Sam Salazar stood guard.

The following day Hein Huss was able to engage one of the First Folk in conversation; it was the first attention of any sort given to them.

The conversation was long; Hein Huss reported only the gist of it to Lord Faide. (Isak Comandore turned away, ostentatiously disassociating himself from the matter.)

Hein Huss first of all had inquired as to the purpose of the sinister preparations: the wasps, beetles, centipedes and the like.

"We intend to kill men," the creature had reported ingenuously. "We intend to return to the moss. This has been our purpose ever since men appeared on the planet."

Huss had stated that such an ambition was shortsighted, that there was ample room for both men and First Folk on Pangborn. "The First Folk," said Hein Huss, "should remove their traps and cease their efforts to surround the keeps with forest."

"No," came the response, "men are intruders. They mar the beautiful moss. All will be killed."

Isak Comandore returned to the conversation. "I noticed here a significant fact. All the First Folk within sight had ceased their work; all looked toward us, as if they, too, participated in the discussion. I reached the highly important conclusion that the First Folk are not complete individuals but components of a larger unity, joined to a greater or less extent by a telepathic phase not unlike our own."

Hein Huss continued placidly, "I remarked that if we were attacked, many of the First Folk would perish. The creature showed no concern, and in fact implied much of what Jinxman Comandore had already induced: 'There are always more in the cells to replace the elements which die. But if the community becomes sick, all suffer. We have been forced into the forests, into a strange existence. We must arm ourselves and drive away the men, and to this end we have developed the methods of men to our own purposes!' "

Isak Comandore spoke. "Needless to say, the creature referred to the ancient men, not ourselves."

"In any event," said Lord Faide, "they leave no doubt as to their intentions. We should be fools not to attack them at once, with every weapon at our disposal."

Hein Huss continued imperturbably. "The creature went on at some length. 'We have learned the value of irrationality.' 'Irrationality' of course was not his word or even his meaning. He said something like 'a series of vaguely motivated trials'—as close as I can translate. He said, 'We have learned to change our environment. We use insects and trees and plants and waterslugs. It is an enormous effort for us who would prefer a placid life in the moss. But you men have forced this life on us, and now you must suffer the consequences.' I pointed out once more that men were not helpless, that many First Folk would die. The creature seemed unworried. 'The community persists.' I asked a delicate question, 'If your purpose is to kill men, why do you allow us here?' He said, 'The entire community of men will be destroyed.' Apparently they believe the human society to be similar to their own, and therefore regard the killing of three wayfaring individuals as pointless effort."

Lord Faide laughed grimly. "To destroy us they must first win past Hellmouth, then penetrate Faide Keep. This they are unable to do."

Isak Comandore resumed his report. "At this time I was already convinced that the problem was one of hoodooing not an individual but an entire race. In theory this should be no more difficult than hoodooing one. It requires no more effort to speak to twenty than to one. With this end in view I ordered the apprentice to collect substances associated with the creatures. Skinflakes, foam, droppings, all other exudations obtainable. While he did so, I tried to put myself in rapport with the creatures. It is difficult, for their telepathy works across a different stratum from ours. Nevertheless, to a certain extent I have succeeded."

"Then you can hoodoo the First Folk?" asked Lord Faide.

"I vouchsafe nothing until I try. Certain preparations must be made."

"Go then; make your preparations."

Comandore rose to his feet and with a sly side glance for Hein Huss left the room. Huss waited, pinching his chin with heavy fingers. Lord Faide looked at him coldly. "You have something to add?"

Huss grunted, hoisted himself to his feet. "I wish that I did. But my thoughts are confused. Of the many futures, all seem troubled and angry. Perhaps our best is not good enough."

Lord Faide looked at Hein Huss with surprise; the massive head jinxman had never before spoken in terms so pessimistic and melancholy. "Speak then; I will listen."

Hein Huss said gruffly, "If I knew any certainties I would speak gladly. But I am merely beset by doubts. I fear that we can no longer depend on logic and careful jinxmanship. Our ancestors were miracle workers, magicians. They drove the First Folk into the forest. To put us to flight in our turn the First Folk have adopted the ancient methods: random trial and purposeless empiricism. I am dubious. Perhaps we must turn our backs on sanity and likewise return to the mysticism of our ancestors."

Lord Faide shrugged. "If Isak Comandore can hoodoo the First Folk, such a retreat may be unnecessary."

"The world changes," said Hein Huss. "Of so much I feel sure: the old days of craft and careful knowledge are gone. The future is for men of cleverness, of imagination untroubled by discipline; the unorthodox Sam Salazar may become more effective than I. The world changes."

Lord Faide smiled his sour dyspeptic smile. "When that day comes I will appoint Sam Salazar head jinxman and also name him Lord Faide, and you and I will retire together to a hut on the downs."

Hein Huss made a heavy fateful gesture and departed.

## X

Two days later Lord Faide, coming upon Isak Comandore, inquired as to his progress. Comandore took refuge in generalities. After another two days Lord Faide inquired again and this time insisted on particulars. Comandore grudgingly led the way to his workroom, where a dozen cabalmen, spellbinders and apprentices worked around a large table, building a model of the First Folk settlement in Wildwood.

"Along the lakeshore," said Comandore, "I will range a great number of dolls, daubed with First Folk essences. When this is complete I will work up a hoodoo and blight the creatures."

"Good. Perform well." Lord Faide departed the workroom, mounted to the topmost pinnacle of the keep, to the cupola where the ancestral weapon Hellmouth was housed. "Jambart! Where are you?"

Weapon-tender Jambart, short, blue-jowled, red-nosed and big-bellied, appeared. "My lord?"

"I come to inspect Hellmouth. Is it prepared for instant use?"

"Prepared, my lord, and ready. Oiled, greased, polished, scraped, burnished, tended—every part smooth as an egg."

Lord Faide made a scowling examination of Hellmouth—a heavy cylinder six feet in diameter, twelve feet long, studded with half-domes interconnected with tubes of polished copper. Jambart undoubtedly had been diligent. No trace of dirt or rust or corrosion showed; all was gleaming metal. The snout was covered with a heavy plate of metal and tarred canvas; the ring upon which the weapon swiveled was well-greased.

Lord Faide surveyed the four horizons. To the south was fertile Faide Valley; to the west open downs; to north and east the menacing loom of Wildwood.

He turned back to Hellmouth and pretended to find a smear of grease. Jambart boiled with expostulations and protestations; Lord Faide uttered a grim warning, enjoining less laxity, then descended to the workroom of Hein Huss. He found the head jinxman reclining on a couch, staring at the ceiling. At a bench stood Sam Salazar surrounded by bottles, flasks and dishes.

Lord Faide stared balefully at the confusion. "What are you doing?" he asked the apprentice.

Sam Salazar looked up guiltily. "Nothing in particular, my lord."

"If you are idle, go then and assist Isak Comandore."

"I am not idle, Lord Faide."

"Then what do you do?"

Sam Salazar gazed sulkily at the bench. "I don't know."

"Then you are idle!"

"No, I am occupied. I pour various liquids on this foam. It is First Folk foam. I wonder what will happen. Water does not dissolve it, or spirits. Heat chars and slowly burns it, emitting a foul smoke."

Lord Faide turned away with a sneer. "You amuse yourself as a child might. Go to Isak Comandore; he can find use for you. How do you expect to become a jinxman, dabbling and prattling like a baby among pretty rocks?"

Hein Huss gave a deep sound: a mingling of sigh, snort, grunt and clearing of the throat. "He does no harm, and Isak Comandore has hands enough. Salazar will never become a jinxman; that has been clear a long time."

Lord Faide shrugged. "He is your apprentice, and your responsibility. Well, then. What news from the keeps?"

Hein Huss, groaning and wheezing, swung his legs over the edge of the couch. "The lords share your concern, to greater or less extent. Your close allies will readily place troops at your disposal; the others likewise if pressure is brought to bear."

Lord Faide nodded in dour satisfaction. "For the moment there is no urgency. The First Folk hold to their forests. Faide Keep of course is impregnable, although they might ravage the valley . . ." he paused thoughtfully. "Let Isak Comandore cast his hoodoo. Then we will see."

From the direction of the bench came a hiss, a small explosion, a whiff of acrid gas. Sam Salazar turned guiltily to look at them, his eyebrows singed. Lord Faide gave a snort of disgust and strode from the room.

"What did you do?" Hein Huss inquired in a colorless voice.

"I don't know."

Now Hein Huss likewise snorted in disgust. "Ridiculous. If you wish to work miracles, you must remember your procedures. Miracle working is not jinxmanship, with established rules and guides. In matters so complex it is well that you take notes, so that the miracles may be repeated."

Sam Salazar nodded in agreement and turned back to the bench.

## XI

Late during the day, news of new First Folk truculence reached Faide Keep. On Honeymoss Hill, not far west of Forest Market, a camp of shepherds had been visited by a wandering group of First Folk, who began to kill the sheep with thorn-swords. When the shepherds protested they, too, were attacked, and many were killed. The remainder of the sheep were massacred.

The following day came other news: four children swimming in Brastock River at Gilbert Ferry had been seized by enormous water-beetles and cut into pieces. On the other side of Wildwood, in the foothills immediately below Castle Cloud, peasants had cleared several hillsides and planted them to vines. Early in the morning they had discovered a horde of black disklike flukes devouring the vines—leaves, branches, trunks and roots. They set about killing the flukes with spades and at once were stung to death by wasps.

Adam McAdam reported the incidents to Lord Faide, who went to Isak Comandore in a fury. "How soon before you are prepared?"

"I am prepared now. But I must rest and fortify myself. Tomorrow morning I work the hoodoo."

"The sooner the better! The creatures have left their forest; they are out killing men!"

Isak Comandore pulled his long chin. "That was to be expected; they told us as much."

Lord Faide ignored the remark. "Show me your tableau."

Isak Comandore took him into his workroom. The model was now complete, with the masses of simulated First Folk properly daubed and sensitized, each tied with a small wad of foam. Isak Comandore pointed to a pot of dark liquid. "I will explain the basis of the hoodoo. When I visited the camp I watched everywhere for powerful symbols. Undoubtedly there were many at hand, but I could not discern them. However, I remembered a circumstance from the battle at the planting: when the creatures were attacked, threatened with fire and about to die, they spewed foam of dull purple color. Evidently this purple foam is associated with death. My hoodoo will be based upon this symbol."

"Rest well, then, so that you may hoodoo to your best capacity."

The following morning Isak Comandore dressed in long robes of black, and set a mask of the demon Nard on his head to fortify himself. He entered his workroom, closed the door.

An hour passed, two hours. Lord Faide sat at breakfast with his kin, stubbornly maintaining a pose of cynical unconcern. At last he could contain himself no longer and went out into the courtyard where Comandore's underlings stood fidgeting and uneasy. "Where is Hein Huss?" demanded Lord Faide. "Summon him here."

Hein Huss came stumping out of his quarters. Lord Faide motioned to Comandore's workshop. "What is happening? Is he succeeding?"

Hein Huss looked toward the workshop. "He is casting a powerful hoodoo. I feel confusion, anger—"

"In Comandore, or in the First Folk?"

"I am not in rapport. I think he has conveyed a message to their minds. A very difficult task, as I explained to you. In this preliminary aspect he has succeeded."

" 'Preliminary'? What else remains?"

"The two most important elements of the hoodoo: the susceptibility of the victim and the appropriateness of the symbol."

Lord Faide frowned. "You do not seem optimistic."

"I am uncertain. Isak Comandore may be right in his assumption. If so, and if the First Folk are highly susceptible, today marks a great victory, and Comandore will achieve tremendous *mana*!"

Lord Faide stared at the door to the workshop. "What now?"

Hein Huss's eyes went blank with concentration. "Isak Comandore is near death. He can hoodoo no more today."

Lord Faide turned, waved his arm to the cabalmen. "Enter the workroom! Assist your master!"

The cabalmen raced to the door, flung it open. Presently they emerged supporting the limp form of Isak Comandore, his black robe spattered with purple foam. Lord Faide pressed close. "What did you achieve? Speak!"

Isak Comandore's eyes were half-closed, his mouth hung loose and wet. "I spoke to the First Folk, to the whole race. I sent the symbol into their minds—" His head fell limply sidewise.

Lord Faide moved back. "Take him to his quarters. Put him on his couch." He turned away, stood indecisively, chewing at his drooping lower lip. "Still we do not know the measure of his success."

"Ah," said Hein Huss, "but we do!"

Lord Faide jerked around. "What is this? What do you say?"

"I saw into Comandore's mind. He used the symbol of purple foam; with tremendous effort he drove it into their minds. Then he learned that purple foam means not death—purple foam means fear for the safety of the community, purple foam means desperate rage."

"In any event," said Lord Faide after a moment, "there is no harm done. The First Folk can hardly become more hostile."

Three hours later a scout rode furiously into the courtyard, threw himself off his horse, ran to Lord Faide. "The First Folk have left the forest! A tremendous number! Thousands! They are advancing on Faide Keep!"

"Let them advance!" said Lord Faide. "The more the better! Jambart, where are you?"

"Here, sir."

"Prepare Hellmouth! Hold all in readiness!"

"Hellmouth is always ready, sir!"

Lord Faide struck him across the shoulders. "Off with you! Bernard!"

The sergeant of the Faide troops came forward. "Ready, Lord Faide."

"The First Folk attack. Armor your men against wasps, feed them well. We will need all our strength."

Lord Faide turned to Hein Huss. "Send to the keeps, to the manor houses, order our kinsmen to join us, with all their troops and all their armor. Send to Bellgard Hall, to Boghoten, Camber and Candelwade. Haste, haste, it is only hours from Wildwood."

Huss held up his hand. "I have already done so. The keeps are warned. They know your need."

"And the First Folk—can you feel their minds?"

"No."

Lord Faide walked away. Hein Huss lumbered out the main gate, walked around the keep, casting appraising glances up the black walls of the squat towers, windowless and proof even against the ancient miracle weapons. High on top the great parasol roof Jambart the weapon-tender worked in the cupola, polishing that which already glistened, greasing surfaces already heavy with grease.

Hein Huss returned within. Lord Faide approached him, mouth hard, eyes bright. "What have you seen?"

"Only the keep, the walls, the towers, the roof and Hellmouth."

"And what do you think?"

"I think many things."

"You are noncommittal; you know more than you say. It is best that you speak, because if Faide Keep falls to the savages you die with the rest of us."

Hein Huss's water-clear eyes met the brilliant black gaze of Lord Faide. "I know only what you know. The First Folk attack. They have proved they are not stupid. They intend to kill us. They are not jinxmen; they cannot afflict us or force us out. They cannot break in the walls. To burrow under, they must dig through solid rock. What are their plans? I do not know. Will they succeed? Again, I do not know. But the day of the jinxman and his orderly array of knowledge is past. I think that we must grope for miracles, blindly and foolishly, like Salazar pouring liquids on foam."

A troop of armored horsemen rode in through the gates: warriors from nearby Bellgard Hall. And as the hours passed contingents from other keeps came to Faide Keep, until the courtyard was dense with troops and horses.

Two hours before sunset the First Folk were sighted across the downs. They seemed a very large company, moving in an undisciplined clot with a number of stragglers, forerunners and wanderers out on the flanks.

The hotbloods from outside keeps came clamoring to Lord Faide, urging a charge to cut down the First Folk; they found no seconding voices among the veterans of the battle at the planting. Lord Faide, however, was pleased to see the dense mass of First Folk. "Let them approach only a mile more—and Hellmouth will take them! Jambart!"

"At your call, Lord Faide."

"Come, Hellmouth speaks!" He strode away with Jambart after. Up to the cupola they climbed.

"Roll forth Hellmouth, direct it against the savages!"

Jambart leaped to the glistening array of wheels and levers. He hesitated in perplexity, then tentatively twisted a wheel. Hellmouth responded by twisting slowly around on its radial track, to the groan and chatter of long-frozen bearings. Lord Faide's brows lowered into a menacing line. "I hear evidence of neglect."

"Neglect, my lord, never! Find one spot of rust, a shadow of grime, you may have me whipped!"

"What of the sound?"

"That is internal and invisible—none of my responsibility."

Lord Faide said nothing. Hellmouth now pointed toward the great pale tide from Wildwood. Jambart twisted a second wheel and Hellmouth thrust forth its heavy snout. Lord Faide, in a voice harsh with anger, cried, "The cover, fool!"

"An oversight, my lord, easily repaired." Jambart crawled out along the top of Hellmouth, clinging to the protuberances for dear life, with below only the long smooth sweep of roof. With considerable difficulty he tore the covering loose, then grunting and cursing, inched himself back, jerking with his knees, rearing his buttocks.

The First Folk had slowed their pace a trifle, the main body only a half-mile distant.

"Now," said Lord Faide in high excitement, "before they disperse, we exterminate them!" He sighted through a telescopic tube, squinting through the dimness of internal films and incrustations, signaled to Jambart for the final adjustments. "Now! Fire!"

Jambart pulled the firing lever. Within the great metal barrel came a sputter of clicking sounds. Hellmouth whined, roared. Its snout glowed red, orange, white, and out poured a sudden gout of blazing purple radiation—which almost instantly died. Hellmouth's barrel quivered with heat, fumed, seethed, hissed. From within came a faint pop. Then there was silence.

A hundred yards in front of the First Folk a patch of moss burnt black where the bolt had struck. The aiming device was inaccurate. Hellmouth's bolt had killed perhaps twenty of the First Folk vanguard.

Lord Faide made feverish signals. "Quick! Raise the barrel. Now! Fire again!"

Jambart pulled the firing arm, to no avail. He tried again, with the same lack of success. "Hellmouth evidently is tired."

"Hellmouth is dead," cried Lord Faide. "You have failed me. Hellmouth is extinct."

"No, no," protested Jambart. "Hellmouth rests! I nurse it as my own child! It is polished like glass! Whenever a section wears off or breaks loose, I neatly remove the fracture, and every trace of cracked glass."

Lord Faide threw up his arms, shouted in vast, inarticulate grief, ran below. "Huss! Hein Huss!"

Hein Huss presented himself. "What is your will?"

"Hellmouth has given up its fire. Conjure me more fire for Hellmouth, and quickly!"

"Impossible."

"Impossible!" cried Lord Faide. "That is all I hear from you! Impossible, useless, impractical! You have lost your ability. I will consult Isak Comandore."

"Isak Comandore can put no more fire into Hellmouth than can I."

"What sophistry is this? He puts demons into men, surely he can put fire into Hellmouth!"

"Come, Lord Faide, you are overwrought. You know the difference between jinxmanship and miracle working."

Lord Faide motioned to a servant. "Bring Isak Comandore here to me!"

Isak Comandore, face haggard, skin waxy, limped into the courtyard. Lord Faide waved preemptorily. "I need your skill. You must restore fire to Hellmouth."

Comandore darted a quick glance at Hein Huss, who stood solid and cold. Comandore decided against dramatic promises that could not be fulfilled. "I cannot do this, my lord."

"What! You tell me this, too?"

"Remark the difference, Lord Faide, between man and metal. A man's normal state is something near madness; he is at all times balanced on a knife-edge between hysteria and apathy. His senses tell him far less of the world than he thinks they do. It is a simple trick to deceive a man, to possess him with a demon, to drive him out of his mind, to kill him. But metal is insensible; metal reacts only as its shape and condition dictates, or by the working of miracles."

"Then you must work miracles!"

"Impossible."

Lord Faide drew a deep breath, collected himself. He walked swiftly across the court. "My armor, my horse. We attack."

The column formed, Lord Faide at the head. He led the knights through the portals, with armored footmen behind.

"Beware the foam!" called Lord Faide. "Attack, strike, cut, draw back. Keep your visors drawn against the wasps! Each man must kill a hundred! Attack!"

The troop rode forth against the horde of First Folk, knights in the lead. The hooves of the horses pounded softly over the thick moss; in the west the large pale sun hung close to the horizon.

Two hundred yards from the First Folk the knights touched the club-headed horses into a lope. They raised their swords, and shouting, plunged forward, each man seeking to be first. The clotted mass of First Folk separated: black beetles darted forth and after them long segmented centipede creatures. They dashed among the horses, mandibles clicking, snouts slashing. Horses screamed, reared, fell over backwards; beetles cut open armored knights as a dog cracks a bone. Lord Faide's horse threw him and ran away; he picked himself up, hacked at a nearby beetle, lopped off its front leg. It darted forward, he lopped off the leg opposite; the heavy head dipped, tore up the moss. Lord Faide cut off the remaining legs, and it lay helpless.

"Retreat," he bellowed. "Retreat!"

The knights moved back, slashing and hacking at beetles and centipedes, killing or disabling all which attacked.

"Form into a double line, knights and men. Advance slowly, supporting each other!"

The men advanced. The First Folk dispersed to meet them, armed with their thorn-swords and carrying pouches. Ten yards from the men they reached into the pouches, brought dark balls which they threw at the men. The balls broke and spattered on the armor.

"Charge!" bawled Lord Faide. The men sprang forward into the mass of First Folk, cutting, slashing, killing. "Kill!" called Lord Faide in exultation. "Leave not one alive!"

A pang struck him, a sting inside his armor, followed by another and another. Small things crawled inside the metal, stinging, biting, crawling. He looked about: on all sides were harassed expressions, faces working in anguish. Sword arms fell limp as hands beat on the metal, futilely trying to scratch, rub. Two men suddenly began to tear off their armor.

"Retreat," cried Lord Faide. "Back to the keep!"

The retreat was a rout, the soldiers shedding articles of armor as they ran. After them came a flight of wasps—a dozen or more, and half as many men cried out as the poison prongs struck into their backs.

Inside the keep stormed the disorganized company, casting aside the last of their armor, slapping their skin, scratching, rubbing, crushing the ferocious red mites that infested them.

"Close the gates," roared Lord Faide.

The gates slid shut. Faide Keep was besieged.

## XII

During the night the First Folk surrounded the keep, forming a ring fifty yards from the walls. All night there was motion, ghostly shapes coming and going in the starlight.

Lord Faide watched from a parapet until midnight, with Hein Huss at his side. Repeatedly, he asked, "What of the other keeps? Do they send further reinforcements?" to which Hein Huss each time gave the same reply: "There is confusion and doubt. The keep-lords are anxious to help but do not care to throw themselves away. At this moment they consider and take stock of the situation."

Lord Faide at last left the parapet, signaling Hein Huss to follow. He went to his trophy room, threw himself into a chair, motioned Hein Huss to be seated. For a moment he fixed the jinxman with a cool, calculating stare. Hein Huss bore the appraisal without discomfort.

"You are head jinxman," said Lord Faide finally. "For twenty years you have worked spells, cast hoodoos, performed auguries—more effectively than any other jinxman of Pangborn. But now I find you inept and listless. Why is this?"

"I am neither inept nor listless. I am unable to achieve beyond my abilities. I do not know how to work miracles. For this you must consult my apprentice Sam Salazar, who does not know either, but who earnestly tries every possibility and many impossibilities."

"You believe in this nonsense yourself! Before my very eyes you become a mystic!"

Hein Huss shrugged. "There are limitations to my knowledge. Miracles occur—that we know. The relics of our ancestors lie everywhere. Their methods were supernatural, repellent to our own mental processes—but think! Using these same methods the First Folk threaten to destroy us. In the place of metal they use living flesh—but the result is similar. The men of Pangborn, if they assemble and accept casualties, can drive the First Folk back to Wildwood—but for how long? A year? Ten years? The First Folk plant new trees, dig more traps—and presently come forth again, with more terrible weapons: flying beetles, large as a horse; wasps strong enough to pierce armor, lizards to scale the walls of Faide Keep."

Lord Faide pulled at his chin. "And the jinxmen are helpless?"

"You saw for yourself. Isak Comandore intruded enough into their consciousness to anger them, no more."

"So then—what must we do?"

Hein Huss held out his hands. "I do not know. I am Hein Huss, jinxman. I watch Sam Salazar with fascination. He learns nothing, but he is either too stupid or too intelligent to be discouraged. If this is the way to work miracles, he will work them."

Lord Faide rose to his feet. "I am deathly tired. I cannot think, I must sleep. Tomorrow we will know more."

Hein Huss left the trophy room, returned to the parapet. The ring of First Folk seemed closer to the walls, almost within dart-range. Behind them and across the moors stretched a long pale column of marching First Folk. A little back from the keep a pile of white material began to grow, larger and larger as the night proceeded.

Hours passed, the sky lightened; the sun rose in the east. The First Folk tramped the downs like ants, bringing long bars of hardened foam down from the north, dropping them into piles around the keep, returning into the north once more.

Lord Faide came up on the parapet, haggard and unshaven. "What is this? What do they do?"

Bernard the sergeant responded. "They puzzle us all, my lord."

"Hein Huss! What of the other keeps?"

"They have armed and mounted; they approach cautiously."

"Can you communicate our urgency?"

"I can, and I have done so. I have only accentuated their caution."

"Bah!" cried Lord Faide in disgust. "Warriors they call themselves! Loyal and faithful allies!"

"They know of your bitter experience," said Hein Huss. "They ask themselves, reasonably enough, what they can accomplish which you who are already here cannot do first."

Lord Faide laughed sourly. "I have no answer for them. In the meantime we must protect ourselves against the wasps. Armor is useless; they drive us mad with mites. . . . Bernard!"

"Yes, Lord Faide."

"Have each of your men construct a frame two-feet square, fixed with a short handle. To these frames should be sewed a net of heavy mesh. When these frames are built we will sally forth, two soldiers to guard one half-armored knight on foot."

"In the meantime," said Hein Huss, "the First Folk proceed with their plans."

Lord Faide turned to watch. The First Folk came close up under the walls carrying rods of hardened foam. "Bernard! Put your archers to work! Aim for the heads!"

Along the walls bowmen cocked their weapons. Darts spun down into the First Folk. A few were affected, turned and staggered away; others plucked away the bolts without concern. Another flight of bolts, a few more First Folk were disabled. The others planted the rods in the moss, exuded foam in great gushes, their back-flaps vigorously pumping air. Other First Folk brought more rods, pushed them into the foam. Entirely around the keep, close under the walls, extended the mound of foam. The ring of First Folk now came close and all gushed foam; it bulked up swiftly. More rods were brought, thrust into the foam, reinforcing and stiffening the mass.

"More darts!" barked Lord Faide. "Aim for the heads! Bernard—your men, have they prepared the wasp nets?"

"Not yet, Lord Faide. The project requires some little time."

Lord Faide became silent. The foam, now ten feet high, rapidly piled higher. Lord Faide turned to Hein Huss. "What do they hope to achieve?"

Hein Huss shook his head. "For the moment I am uncertain."

The first layer of foam had hardened; on top of this the First Folk spewed another layer, reinforcing again with the rods, crisscrossing, horizontal and vertical. Fifteen minutes later, when the second layer was hard the First Folk emplaced and mounted rude ladders to raise a third layer. Surrounding the keep now was a ring of foam thirty feet high and forty feet thick at the base.

"Look," said Hein Huss. He pointed up. The parasol roof overhanging the walls ended only thirty feet above the foam. "A few more layers and they will reach the roof."

"So then?" asked Lord Faide. "The roof is as strong as the walls."

"And we will be sealed within."

Lord Faide studied the foam in the light of this new thought. Already the First Folk, climbing laboriously up ladders along the outside face of their wall of foam, were preparing to lay on a fourth layer. First—rods, stiff and dry, then great gushes of white. Only twenty feet remained between roof and foam.

Lord Faide turned to the sergeant. "Prepare the men to sally forth."

"What of the wasp nets, sir?"

"Are they almost finished?"

"Another ten minutes, sir."

"Another ten minutes will see us smothering. We must force a passage through the foam."

Ten minutes passed, and fifteen. The First Folk created ramps behind their wall: first, dozens of the rods, then foam, and on top, to distribute the weight, reed mats.

Bernard the sergeant reported to Lord Faide. "We are ready."

"Good." Lord Faide descended into the courtyard. He faced the men, gave them their orders. "Move quickly, but stay together; we must not lose ourselves in the foam. As we proceed, slash ahead and to the sides. The First Folk see through the foam; they have the advantage of us. When we break through, we use the wasp nets. Two foot soldiers must guard each knight. Remember, quickly through the foam, that we do not smother. Open the gates."

The gates slid back, the troops marched forth. They faced an unbroken blank wall of foam. No enemy could be seen.

Lord Faide waved his sword. "Into the foam." He strode forward, pushed into the white mass, now crisp and brittle and harder than he had bargained for. It resisted him; he cut and hacked. His troops joined him, carving a way into the foam. First Folk appeared above them, crawling carefully on the mats. Their back flaps puffed, pumped; foam issued from their vents, falling in a cascade over the troops.

Hein Huss sighed. He spoke to Apprentice Sam Salazar. "Now they must retreat, otherwise they smother. If they fail to win through, we all smother."

Even as he spoke the foam, piling up swiftly, in places reached the roof. Below, bellowing and cursing, Lord Faide backed out from under, wiped his face clear. Once again, in desperation, he charged forward, trying at a new spot.

The foam was friable and cut easily, but the chunks detached still blocked the opening. And again down tumbled a cascade of foam, covering the soldiers.

Lord Faide retreated, waved his men back into the keep. At the same moment First Folk crawling on mats on the same level as the parapet over the gate laid rods up from the foam to rest against the projecting edge of the roof. They gushed foam; the view of the sky was slowly blocked from the view of Hein Huss and Sam Salazar.

"In an hour, perhaps two, we will die," said Hein Huss. "They have now sealed us in. There are many men here in the keep, and all will now breathe deeply."

Sam Salazar said nervously, "There is a possibility we might be able to survive—or at least not smother."

"Ah?" inquired Hein Huss with heavy sarcasm. "You plan to work a miracle?"

"If a miracle, the most trivial sort. I observed that water has no effect on the foam, nor a number of other liquids: milk, spirits, wine or caustic. Vinegar, however, instantly dissolves the foam."

"Aha," said Hein Huss. "We must inform Lord Faide."

"Better that you do so," said Sam Salazar. "He will pay me no heed."

## XIII

Half an hour passed. Light filtered into Faide Keep only as a dim gray gloom. Air tasted flat, damp and heavy. Out from the gates sallied the troops. Each carried a crock, a jug, a skin or a pan containing strong vinegar.

"Quickly now," called Lord Faide, "but careful! Spare the vinegar, don't throw it wildly. In close formation now—forward."

The soldiers approached the wall, threw ladles of vinegar ahead. The foam crackled, melted.

"Waste no vinegar," shouted Lord Faide. "Forward, quickly now; bring forward the vinegar!"

Minutes later they burst out upon the downs. The First Folk stared at them, blinking.

"Charge," croaked Lord Faide, his throat thick with fumes. "Mind now, wasp nets! Two soldiers to each knight! Charge, double-quick. Kill the white beasts."

The men dashed ahead. Wasp tubes were leveled. "Halt!" yelled Lord Faide. "Wasps!"

The wasps came, wings rasping. Nets rose up; wasps struck with a thud. Down went the nets; hard feet crushed the insects. The beetles and the lizard-centipedes appeared, not so many as of the last evening, for a great number had been killed. They darted forward, and a score of men died, but the insects were soon hacked into chunks of reeking brown flesh. Wasps flew, and some struck home; the agonies of the dying men were unnerving. Presently the wasps likewise decreased in number, and soon there were no more.

The men faced the First Folk, armed only with thorn-swords and their foam, which now came purple with rage.

Lord Faide waved his sword; the men advanced and began to kill the First Folk, by dozens, by hundreds.

Hein Huss came forth and approoched Lord Faide. "Call a halt."

"A halt? Why? Now we kill these bestial things."

"Far better not. Neither need kill the other. Now is the time to show great wisdom."

"They have besieged us, caught us in their traps, stung us with their wasps! And you say halt?"

"They nourish a grudge sixteen hundred years old. Best not to add another one."

Lord Faide stared at Hein Huss. "What do you propose?"

"Peace between the two races, peace and cooperation."

"Very well. No more traps, no more plantings, no more breeding of deadly insects."

"Call back your men. I will try."

Lord Faide cried out, "Men, fall back, Disengage."

Reluctantly the troops drew back. Hein Huss approached the huddled mass of purple-foaming First Folk. He waited a moment. They watched him intently. He spoke in their language.

"You have attacked Faide Keep; you have been defeated. You planned well, but we have proved stronger. At this moment we can kill you. Then we can go on to fire the forest, starting a hundred blazes. Some of the fires you can control. Others not. We can destroy Wildwood. Some First Folk may survive, to hide in the thickets and breed new plans to kill men. This we do not want. Lord Faide has agreed to peace, if you likewise agree. This means no more death traps. Men will freely approach and pass through the forests. In your turn you may freely come out on the moss. Neither race shall molest the other. Which do you choose? Extinction—or peace?"

The purple foam no longer dribbled from the vents of the First Folk. "We choose peace."

"There must be no more wasps, beetles. The death traps must be disarmed and never replaced."

"We agree. In our turn we must be allowed freedom of the moss."

"Agreed. Remove your dead and wounded, haul away the foam rods."

Hein Huss returned to Lord Faide. "They have chosen peace."

Lord Faide nodded. "Very well. It is for the best." He called to his men. "Sheathe your weapons. We have won a great victory." He ruefully surveyed Faide Keep, swathed in foam and invisible except for the parasol roof. "A hundred barrels of vinegar will not be enough."

Hein Huss looked off into the sky. "Your allies approach quickly. Their jinxmen have told them of your victory."

Lord Faide laughed his sour laugh. "To my allies will fall the task of removing the foam from Faide Keep."

## XIV

In the hall of Faide Keep, during the victory banquet, Lord Faide called jovially across to Hein Huss. "Now, head jinxman, we must deal with your apprentice, the idler and the waster Sam Salazar."

"He is here, Lord Faide. Rise, Sam Salazar, take cognizance of the honor being done you."

Sam Salazar rose to his feet, bowed.

Lord Faide proffered him a cup. "Drink, Sam Salazar, enjoy yourself. I freely admit that your idiotic tinkerings saved the lives of us all. Sam Salazar, we salute you, and thank you. Now, I trust that you will put frivolity aside, apply yourself to your work and learn honest jinxmanship. When the time comes, I promise that you shall find a lifetime of employment at Faide Keep."

"Thank you," said Sam Salazar modestly. "However, I doubt if I will become a jinxman."

"No? You have other plans?"

Sam Salazar stuttered, grew faintly pink in the face, then straightened himself, and spoke as clearly and distinctly as he could. "I prefer to continue what you call my frivolity. I hope I can persuade others to join me."

"Frivolity is always attractive," said Lord Faide. "No doubt you can find other idlers and wasters, runaway farm boys, and the like."

Sam Salazar said staunchly, "This frivolity might become serious. Undoubtedly the ancients were barbarians. They used symbols to control entities they were unable to understand. We are methodical and rational; why can't we systematize and comprehend the ancient miracles?"

"Well, why can't we?" asked Lord Faide. "Does anyone have an answer?"

No one responded, although Isak Comandore hissed between his teeth and shook his head.

"I personally may never be able to work miracles; I suspect it is more complicated than it seems," said Sam Salazar. "However, I hope that you will arrange for a workshop where I and others who might share my views can make a beginning. In this matter I have the encouragement and the support of Head Jinxman Hein Huss."

Lord Faide lifted his goblet. "Very well, Apprentice Sam Salazar. Tonight I can refuse you nothing. You shall have exactly what you wish, and good luck to you. Perhaps you will produce a miracle during my lifetime."

Isak Comandore said huskily to Hein Huss, "This is a sad event! It signalizes intellectual anarchy, the degradation of jinxmanship, the prostitution of logic. Novelty has a way of attracting youth; already I see apprentices and spellbinders whispering in excitement. The jinxmen of the future will be sorry affairs. How will they go about demon-possession? With a cog, a gear and a push-button. How will they cast a hoodoo? They will find it easier to strike their victim with an axe."

"Times change,". said Hein Huss. "There is now the one rule of Faide on Pangborn, and the keeps no longer need to employ us. Perhaps I will join Sam Salazar in his workshop."

"You depict a depressing future," said Isak Comandore with a sniff of disgust.

"There are many futures, some of which are undoubtedly depressing."

Lord Faide raised his glass. "To the best of your many futures, Hein Huss. Who knows? Sam Salazar may conjure a spaceship to lead us back to home planet."

"Who knows?" said Hein Huss. He raised his goblet. "To the best of the futures!"